By the
Dawn's
Early Light

VOLUME 9

By the
Dawn's
Early Light

A NOVEL BY
RON CARTER

BOOKCRAFT

SALT LAKE CITY

PRELUDE TO GLORY

Volume 1: Our Sacred Honor
Volume 2: The Times That Try Men's Souls
Volume 3: To Decide Our Destiny
Volume 4: The Hand of Providence
Volume 5: A Cold, Bleak Hill
Volume 6: The World Turned Upside Down
Volume 7: The Impending Storm
Volume 8: A More Perfect Union
Volume 9: By the Dawn's Early Light

Library of Congress Cataloging-in-Publication Data

Carter, Ron, 1932-
    By the dawn's early light / Ron Carter.
      p.   cm. — (Prelude to glory ; v. 9)
    Includes bibliographical references.
    ISBN 1-59038-438-5 (alk. paper)
    1. United States—History—War of 1812—Fiction.   I. Title.   II. Series.
    PS3553.A7833B9   2005
    813'.54—dc22   2005017329

Printed in the United States of America
Sheridan Books Inc., Ann Arbor, MI

10   9   8   7   6   5   4   3   2   1

This series is dedicated to the
common people of long ago who paid the price

This volume is dedicated to the
freedom and liberty so dearly bought

Washington, June 1, 1812

To the Senate and House of Representatives of the United States:

I communicate to Congress certain documents, being a continuation of those heretofore laid before them on the subject of our affairs with Great Britain.

British cruisers have been in the continued practice of violating the American flag on the great highway of nations, and of seizing and carrying off persons sailing under it, not in the exercises of a belligerent right founded on the law of nations against an enemy, but of a municipal prerogative o'er British Subjects.

Whether the United States shall continue passive under these progressive usurpations and these accumulating wrongs, or, opposing force to force in defense of their natural rights, shall commit a just cause into the hands of the Almighty Dispoiser of Events . . . is a solemn question . . . .

James Madison
President, United States

The mad ambition, the lust for power, and commercial avarice of Great Britain, have left to neutral nations an alternative only between the base surrender of their rights and a manly vindication of them. I plead most vigorously an immediate appeal to arms.

John C. Calhoun
Chair, Foreign Relations Committee
House of Representatives

June 18, 1812, the United States declared war on Great Britain for the second time.

PROLOGUE

By June of 1807, the United States had been a free and independent nation for forty years, and it had been governing itself under the Constitution for just under thirty years. The American people were proud of these achievements, which no previous nation on earth could match. But these were hard-won victories, none of them guaranteed or foreordained. And there always was the possibility that things won even with such labor and pain could be lost, or taken away.

The Constitution went into effect on March 4, 1789, but the new House of Representatives did not achieve a quorum for doing business until 1 April, and the new Senate only amassed a quorum on 6 April. The new government thus had a slow and worrisome start, but it soon acquired momentum. Within a year it had established and set into motion the presidency, executive departments, and courts. Within two years it had proposed, and the states had ratified, amendments to the Constitution popularly known as the Bill of Rights. And its officials were hard at work, dealing with the major problem facing the United States—its staggering burden of debt from the Revolution.

Americans assured one another and the rest of the world that they had devised a new science of politics—but they could not agree on how it was to work or on what kind of nation it was to foster. As a result, Americans who had taken the same side against Great Britain now viewed one another with suspicion and distrust. Those who favored the brash, energetic treasury secretary Alexander Hamilton's fiscal plans for restoring the nation's public credit confronted those who joined Secretary of State Thomas Jefferson's and Representative James Madison's opposition to those plans. Would the United States be a nation of sturdy yeoman farmers, as Jefferson and Madison hoped, tilling the soil and refusing to risk the corruption and decadence of the Old World? Or would the United States encourage commerce and manufacturing, as Hamilton urged, rivaling the great powers of Britain and France and becoming a wealthy, powerful, and respected nation? Would the government authorized by the Constitution be strictly limited in its powers to those clearly authorized by the text, as Jefferson and Madison urged? Or would there be a bold and innovative government, claiming whatever powers were not specifically denied by the Constitution, as Hamilton maintained it should be? The divisions between these brilliant, confident, and stubborn men both shaped and reflected divisions emerging among the people as a whole.

Domestic issues seemed to promise trouble enough for the new nation. But then, in 1789, the French Revolution burst on the world. Some Americans agreed with Jefferson, embracing the French Revolution as the French people's bid to learn from the American Revolution, sweeping away centuries of corruption and oppression. Others agreed with Hamilton and John Adams that the French Revolution promised nothing but disaster. The matter worsened in 1793, when the French executed King Louis XVI and Queen Marie Antoinette and then plunged into war with the rest of Europe. Should the United States honor its 1778 treaty of alliance and friendship with France, or should it remain neutral, or should it take sides with the old monarchies of Europe against the dangerous French Republic?

President George Washington struggled to hold the nation on a steady course, as he struggled also to hold his cabinet together. The United States indeed stayed neutral in 1793 and thereafter, but the controversy further widened the splits among the people of the United States. By the mid-1790s, two loose partisan alliances competed for power and votes—the Federalists, led by Hamilton and Adams, and the Republicans, led by Jefferson and Madison. At first President Washington refused to take sides, trying to set an impartial standard for his countrymen. But, as partisan strife worsened and the pressures of age and politics wore him down, he sided more and more with Hamilton and the Federalists.

In September 1796, Washington announced his decision to retire from the presidency after two terms of office. In the election that fall, the electoral votes made Vice President John Adams the narrow but clear victor; but his rival, Thomas Jefferson, amassed the second-highest number of votes and became Adams's vice president. At his inauguration, Adams imagined that Washington was saying to him, "Aye, you are fairly in and I am fairly out. We will see which one of us is happiest." Awed by Washington, Adams kept Washington's cabinet as his own, even though its members looked down on him and repeatedly sought advice and leadership behind Adams's back from Alexander Hamilton, now a lawyer in private practice in New York City.

Adams's presidency was turbulent and unhappy. Attempting to smooth over the difficult relations between France and the United States, he sent a three-man diplomatic team to open negotiations—but French stubbornness, and the strong hint from three French officials (whom the Americans in their report to Adams called X, Y, and Z) that a bribe would be the only way to grease the wheel of diplomacy, enraged Charles C. Pinckney, John Marshall, and Elbridge Gerry. When news of the impasse broke, the American people reacted with fury against France. Congress proposed a package of laws designed to protect national security against enemy aliens and those who dared to criticize the president or other leaders of the government. The government's prosecutors used these laws against newspaper editors who dared to criticize Adams's war policies, one of the editors a member of the United States House of Representatives. Although the two nations never declared war on each other, the United States Navy fought a series of engagements with French vessels, and Adams called George Washington out of retirement to command a newly assembled American army, guarding against the possibility of a French invasion. To Adams's dismay, Washington insisted that Hamilton be named his second-in-command.

As time passed, however, Adams became more and more convinced that such an invasion never would happen, and he brooded over the possibility that Hamilton would use the army to make himself a dictator. Washington's death in December 1799 solidified Adams's decision not to continue with the war. He decided to send a new diplomatic mission to France, overruling his outraged cabinet members. Then Adams discovered that his chief advisors had been taking their marching orders from Hamilton. In a towering rage, he demanded the resignation of Secretary of War James McHenry and fired Secretary of State Timothy Pickering. Hamilton, equally outraged after a shouting match with the president, stalked off and penned a vitriolic pamphlet attacking Adams's character and conduct. He hoped to circulate this pamphlet privately among key Federalist leaders, but somehow the pamphlet got into the newspapers, embarrassing Adams and Hamilton alike and advertising to the world that the Federalists were splitting down the middle. Not even the success of Adams's emissaries to France could stop the Federalist free-fall in public opinion.

Meanwhile, the Republicans were united behind Vice President Jefferson and his chosen running-mate, former Senator Aaron Burr of New York. In the voting that fall, it became clear that the Republicans would take both houses of Congress and capture the presidency as well—but an unexpected development threw the nation into confusion. Jefferson and Burr tied with 73 electoral votes each. Burr was ready to defer to Jefferson, but the vehement demands of Jefferson's backers that Burr deny that he was worthy to be considered for president as opposed to Jefferson angered the proud New Yorker. In turn, the Jeffersonians became convinced that Burr was going to do a deal behind their backs with the defeated Federalists to grab the Presidency for himself. At the same time, an aghast Alexander Hamilton, who had distrusted and feared Burr since 1789, wrote a series of letters to leading Federalist politicians begging them not to deal with Burr, whose ambition was for himself and without any restraint of principle.

In cases where no candidate received a clear majority of electoral votes, the House of Representatives had to resolve the deadlock. In February 1801, the old House—the new House would not convene until that December—met and voted in ballot after ballot. Not until the thirty-sixth ballot did the House finally agree on Jefferson as the victor.

Early on the morning of March 4, 1801, John Adams boarded a coach to take him home to Quincy, Massachusetts. He was not only hurt by his defeat by his former friend and ally, Jefferson; he was mourning the death of his son Charles, who either had drowned by accident or committed suicide after having lost a large sum of money entrusted to him by his oldest brother, John Quincy Adams. Later that morning, Jefferson arose in his boarding house, dressed carefully, and walked down Pennsylvania Avenue in the city newly renamed Washington to the site of the Capitol of the United States. Only one wing had been completed, and it was there, before the assembled senators and representatives and other onlookers, that he took the oath of office from Chief Justice John Marshall. It was the first successful transfer of power from one political party to another, and Jefferson realized the importance of the event. He termed his victory in the election of 1800 a revolution as important as that of 1776.

Jefferson's first term in office was a great success. His efficient and capable treasury secretary, the Swiss-born Albert Gallatin, did great work in paring down the national debt and regularizing American finances—though Gallatin concluded that Hamilton's system was so well established and so well devised that it could not and should not be cast aside. Jefferson and his closest advisor, Secretary of State James Madison, sought to chart a careful course for the United States through the troubled waters of great-power politics. In particular, when the diplomatic team he sent to France to negotiate with First Consul Napoleon Bonaparte for the purchase of New Orleans reported instead that they had been offered a deal for the entire Louisiana Territory, Jefferson seized the opportunity—though wondering whether it was constitutional to do so. At the same time, he planned a major military, scientific, and diplomatic exploration of the vast Louisiana Territory, to be led by his secretary and distant relative Captain Meriwether Lewis and Lewis's chosen colleague, Captain William Clark. His major disappointment was that he and his allies in Congress could not use the impeachment power to clear the federal bench of Federalist judges committed, as he feared, to blocking his administration's measures and distorting the Constitution's meaning.

Jefferson triumphantly won re-election in 1804, but his second term was nowhere near as successful as his first. Whereas in his first term he had taken the lead in defining American policies and shaping events, in his second term events over which he had little control dominated what he tried to do. Former Vice President Aaron Burr, dropped from the Republican ticket in early 1804, had killed Alexander Hamilton in a controversial duel in New Jersey. Burr then had helped to frustrate the impeachment campaign by presiding over the Senate's impeachment trial of Justice Samuel Chase, Burr's last act as vice president. In early 1805, Burr headed west, engaging in mysterious discussions and murky plans with western politicians and sparking a host of rumors about his plans. Convinced that Burr intended to detach the western states and territories from the United States and establish himself as an emperor, Jefferson ordered Burr's seizure and arrest and hoped that he would be tried for and convicted of treason.

The most worrisome thing for Jefferson, however, was world affairs. His first term had seen a temporary cooling of hostilities between Napoleonic France, which had conquered most of Europe, and the alliance of Britain, Austria, Prussia, and Russia. Now the European continent was at war again, and each side was determined to cripple its adversary's trade. The United States had profited from trading with the several warring powers, but now its ships were fair prey under the generally accepted laws of war. Nobody knew what the new nation would do if its honor and its flag were insulted on the high seas . . .

Richard B. Bernstein

PART ONE

CHAPTER I

★ ★ ★

*T*he shout, too high, too strained, came cracking down from the crow's nest, seventy feet up the mainmast of the American Navy man-of-war USS *Chesapeake*.

"Sail! Nor'east, stern, portside. About three miles."

Every sun- and wind-burned face on the main deck of the small frigate jerked upward, squinting into the blinding light of the midday sun in a cloudless late June sky, to see the outthrust arm of the barefooted, bearded seaman, wearing the uniform of the fledgling United States Navy, pointing over the stern toward a sail those on deck could not yet see. For one breathless second the only sounds were the warm northeast wind in the rigging, the creaking of the two masts and six yardarms, and the quiet hiss of the sixteen-foot curl the little ship was cutting in the green-black waters of the Atlantic. Then the main-deck crew moved as one man to the stern of the ship, feet spread slightly against the gentle roll of the deck, hands shading their narrowed eyes as they carefully swept the straight line where the sky met the sea. There was no sail—nothing but the flat horizon.

Captain James Barron, United States Navy, tall, angular, long face, jutting chin, feet and hands too big, stood at his place on the quarterdeck next to the wheel, facing the stern, one huge hand shading his squinted eyes as he peered northeast. Beside him stood his first officer, Lieutenant George Budd, shorter, strongly built, both hands shading his slitted eyes as he studied the skyline, searching for the tell-tale fleck that would become a ship. His lined, aging, leathery face bore a prominent scar across the meat of his left cheek where a British musket ball had ripped a four-inch channel in the wild, desperate fight on Chesapeake Bay in August of 1781, when the French and British navies had collided head-on to determine whether British general Charles Cornwallis and his six thousand red-coated regulars, landlocked and surrounded by thirteen thousand American regulars and French infantry at the tiny tobacco-trading village of Yorktown, where the York River empties into the Bay, would remain British soldiers, or become American prisoners of war.

Captain Barron turned his face upward and bellowed to his seaman in the crow's nest, "Mister Yates, what flag?"

Every man stared upward, waiting for the answer that could well determine their fate and that of the USS *Chesapeake.*

Yates spread his feet to steady himself and raised his extended telescope to his eye. For ten seconds he remained silent, hunched forward, straining to define the flag popping in the wind at the top of the mainmast of the incoming ship.

"Can't tell yet, sir."

"Can you read her name?"

"No, sir."

Barron licked dry lips. "Man-o'-war or merchantman?"

"Too far. Can't be certain."

"Keep a sharp eye. Call out when you know!"

"Aye, sir."

They waited with tension building into a thing almost alive. Seamen came up from the second deck where the cannon were tied down behind closed gun ports, and from the third deck where their provisions and medicines and blankets were stored, along with a Holstein cow, half a dozen three-hundred-pound pigs, twenty chickens, and ten geese, for fresh meat and milk and eggs. The sailors came quietly and stood braced, straining to see the shape and build of the pursuing ship and the colors of her flag.

The tiny speck had broken the skyline just as Yates's voice blasted from the crow's nest.

"British! Union Jack. She's British. And she's a man-o'-war. Two decks of guns."

Every man on deck sucked in air, and Captain Barron shouted, "Are her gunports open? Can you count them?"

"No, sir. They're closed. Can't count yet."

"Her course?"

"Sou' by sou'west, sir."

"Her canvas?"

"All out. Full. Comin' hard, sir."

"Her name?"

"Can't tell yet."

Barron spoke quietly to Budd. "On that course, and with that speed, she means to close with us."

Budd bobbed his head but said nothing, waiting.

Barron stared downward as he muttered, "Do we outrun her, or stand?" The question was for himself, not his first officer. Barron raised his head and turned to the wheelman. "Steady as she goes." He shouted to his crew, gathered at the stern of the frigate. "Back to your duty posts. Follow the orders of the day. You men assigned to the gun crews, get your budge barrels open and both the solid shot and the grape ready for loading, and be prepared to roll your cannon into firing position, but do not open your gun ports until you get the order." He cupped his hand to his mouth to shout up to the crow's nest. "Keep us informed."

"Aye, sir."

Budd asked, "More canvas? The spankers? We can outrun her."

Barron shook his head and a look of defiance crept into his eyes. "We are in a state of peace with the British. We will not run, and we will not be intimidated."

Budd grunted and deep anger was in his voice. "A state of peace? You remember the incident last year? The British gunboat *Leander?* She followed an American merchantman into New York harbor and fired on her. Killed one American seaman. There were riots in the streets against the British. President Jefferson closed all American ports to the *Leander*. How many hundred of our merchantmen have the British stopped on the high seas and searched? How many embargoes against us at every port in the world? Some say we're at war with England right now, only neither side has declared it."

"I've forgotten none of it, Mister Budd," Barron growled, "but I repeat, we will not run, and we will not be intimidated. You see to it that our gun crews are ready."

A light came on in Budd's gray eyes, and a faint smile appeared and passed. "Aye, sir."

The crew took their orders and returned to their duties of the day, scrubbing decks on hands and knees, checking hawsers, opening the budge barrels mounted by each of the thirty-eight cannon to feel the black gunpowder for moisture, setting the stacked pyramids of 24-pound cannonballs and the wooden buckets of grapeshot—one inch lead balls—next to the heavy, shining black barrels of the cannon mounted on their carriages with the heavy wooden wheels, loosening the locks on the gun ports to open them instantly on command. Their heads were constantly turning to peer northeast, silent, waiting, while the wind moved their tied-back hair and their beards.

Every man flinched when the shout boomed down from the crow's nest.

"Her name is the *Leopard*. About forty-five or fifty guns and the gun crews are ready. Holding steady sou' by sou'west and moving hard. She means to come alongside."

The man at the wheel glanced at Captain Barron, waiting for any change in his orders, and there was none. He held his course, nearly due south while twelve miles to the west the capes of Virginia were steadily slipping past as the small frigate plowed on. The shiny little frigate had been refitted through the winter months of 1806 into 1807 and returned to duty as a a United States Navy warship only days before Captain Barron and his crew of seasoned American sailors were assigned to take her to sea on her shake-down voyage. They had brought her out of the Chesapeake into the great ocean thirty-six hours earlier, and turned her south toward the Carolinas, silently watching for tell-tale moisture on the inner hull, aware of how sensitive the small vessel was to the wheel, how she felt as she rose and fell with the swells of the ocean, how her masts creaked in the nor'east wind coming in from behind. They watched through the night, and with the morning sun half risen, they knew. She was a tight ship, responsive, balanced, masts set solid in the keel, and she answered the wheel as though she were a thing alive. In the way of men of the sea they said little, but there were faint smiles, and an occasional snatch of a sea shanty as a sailor broke into discordant song. By midmorning the small craft had become theirs. No longer "it." "She."

With each passing minute the oncoming British warship was closing. At one mile there was no mistaking the red, white, and blue cross of the Union Jack. At one thousand yards, the gun ports remained closed, but the count was clear. The *Leopard* carried fifty heavy cannon, divided evenly, port and starboard. The *Chesapeake,* smaller, carried thirty-eight guns, evenly divided, port and starboard sides. The American ship was out-gunned.

With the British man-of-war a scant four hundred yards off the port stern, the crew of the *Chesapeake* were at their duty posts, but they were glancing to their own quarter-deck, silently asking Captain Barron his intentions. All too well they understood the sneering arrogance of the British and the price the American navy and American merchantmen were paying every day because President Thomas Jefferson refused to rupture the fragile peace that existed between the two countries. Terms of peace written on a parchment scroll meant very little to them when the brutal reality included search and seizure on the high seas by British warships with cannon-muzzles less than ten feet away, ready and anxious to blast a ship and crew into shreds.

Barron understood the need of his crew to know what was going to happen in the next five minutes and called out, "Steady as she goes, lads. Steady as she goes. We'll know soon enough."

At one hundred yards the larger ship held her course and Budd moved his feet, preparing for the collision if neither ship yielded. At fifty yards the American crew was staring across the narrowing neck of water that separated the two vessels into the expressionless faces of British seamen standing at their guns. At thirty yards the captain of the British ship corrected course to run parallel to the smaller American ship. He raised his horn and his voice came loud.

"Ahoy the *Chesapeake!* I am Captain Salusbury Humphreys of the Royal Navy and commander of His Majesty's, the *Leopard.* Furl your sails and drop anchor. I hold orders from Admiral Sir George C. Berkeley of the Royal Navy, directing me to search your vessel for deserters from His Majesty's Navy."

Barron looked at Budd, dumbstruck, then raised his horn to shout back, "Admiral Berkeley ordered you to find this ship and send a boarding party?"

"Orders issued June 1, 1807. I have them in my hand. I will board your ship."

"To search for what?"

"British deserters who have been impressed into service in your navy."

Budd blurted, "We haven't got a British seaman in our entire crew! We're all Americans."

Barron raised his horn. "We have no British seamen aboard. Permission to board is denied."

The railings between the two ships were less than thirty feet apart. Seamen on both ships were staring at each other, and each knew the other was preparing to open their gun ports and ram their cannon forward. Sailors on both sides were picking the place they would place their first shot.

Humphreys' answer came back from the larger vessel. "For the last time, pursuant to my orders, I demand you stand down and permit a boarding party to search the *Chesapeake* for British deserters. I will not repeat the demand again."

Barron bellowed back his defiant answer. "Permission to board is denied!"

Instantly the gun ports on the British man-of-war yawed open and the muzzles of the big guns were driven forward. In that moment Budd screamed, "Open the gun ports and fire!" The American gun ports were half-opened when the deafening blast of twenty-five heavy British cannon thundered. The narrow strip of water separating the two ships was filled with billowing white smoke as the concussion wave rolled over the smaller ship. Solid shot smashed into the American gun ports, and grapeshot shattered railings and knocked American gun crews backwards, bloodied, stumbling, falling.

Both Barron and Budd immediately understood that the British had come broadside to them with the British crew already prepared to deliver the deadly broadside on a silent signal, and that signal had been the second time Barron refused the British demand for boarding. The British captain had never given the vocal order to fire, and the trickery gave the British gun crews a two-second advantage that had all but destroyed the American guns before they could fire. There was not one American gun on the port side of the *Chesapeake* left in operation. Barron's shouted orders were lost in the pandemonium of his bloodied crew trying to recover while British seamen prepared to cast grappling hooks and reload their guns, and then, unbelievably, they fired a second broadside into the smaller ship. Shattered timbers and railings flew, and more Americans staggered back as the British gunners loaded and fired a third broadside. The main deck of the *Chesapeake* was littered with smashed timbers and railings, and the lower sections of the rigging were shredded where grapeshot had come ripping. Hawsers dangled from the rigging, useless, blowing in the wind. Barron's face was covered with blood from two splinters of wood that had embedded in his chin and forehead, and he was desperately wiping with his sleeve to clear the gore from his eyes.

The British captain shouted orders, and the *Leopard* veered hard to starboard, and the two vessels slammed together. Twenty grappling hooks came arcing to catch on broken hatches or splintered wreckage, and within seconds the two moving ships were tied together. With muskets and swords in hand, British seamen leaped to the deck of the *Chesapeake*, shouting, driving the stunned American crew back into a circle where they held them at bayonet point amidst the jumbled litter and wounded, groaning men on the main deck of a crippled ship. The ship's surgeon, short, stout, perspiring, was moving feverishly among the wounded with his black bag, jaw muscles tight, face set, as he surveyed the torn flesh and broken bones.

With drawn sword the British captain came forward to face the bleeding Barron.

"Sir, I am going to find any British sailors you have impressed on this vessel."

Barron was nearly beyond control in his outrage. "A demand to board a ship of the American navy on the high seas! The United States is neutral! We are at peace with England! How dare you? How *dare* you!"

The British officer calmly raised a paper. "I have my orders."

"Does the name *Chesapeake* appear in those orders?"

"It does."

"You were ordered to board this ship, specifically? By name?"

"Specifically, by name. We watched her while she was being built and commissioned and launched. It was clear we had need to determine if the United States intended manning her with British sailors."

Blood was streaming from Barron's face, but he paid no heed. His voice was high, near hysteria. "You've committed half a dozen acts in breach of the treaty between the United States and England! You've broken every rule of civilized nations. Three unprovoked point-blank broadsides without warning! Worse than pirates! Scum! There will be a reckoning, sir."

A look of irritation crossed the face of the British captain. "As you wish." He turned to his first officer. "Search the ship."

"Aye, sir." The first officer gave a hand signal, and ten men who had been picked hours earlier stepped forward. There was a stir among the American seamen circled by the bayonets, and instantly twenty British muskets came onto full cock. Captain Barron raised a hand, and his men settled. With the first officer leading, the ten British seamen with muskets disappeared below decks, while those remaining stood their ground with their muskets at the ready, silently facing the furious Americans while the ship's surgeon continued his work among the wounded. The only sounds were of the wind in the rigging and the creaking of two ships tied together and the wrenching groans of men in pain.

In less than ten minutes the British search party came up the narrow passage into the sunlight on the main deck, with the first officer prodding four seamen with the flat of his sword. His squad of ten herded the grim Americans before the British captain, and the first officer reported.

"Sir, these men were among the gun crews on the second deck. I believe they are British seamen."

The British captain moved, stopping before each of them in turn while he studied their faces, their long hair, their beards, their uniforms. His forehead wrinkled in thought, his mouth puckered for a moment before he spoke.

"They are British seamen. We will take them."

Budd spun to face Captain Barron, arm raised, pointing. "Sir, three of those men are native-born Americans. Connecticut and Massachusetts. I've shipped with them before!"

Budd turned to face the British captain. "You know these men are not British. You aren't here to search for missing seamen. You're here to insult the United States Navy!" Budd was beyond any semblance of established international naval protocol toward officers of a foreign navy, and he didn't care. His finger was thrust nearly into the face of the British captain, voice shrill, echoing out across the water. "You expect us to take this infamy from you just because you're British? We beat you once, and by the Almighty, we'll do it again if we have to! Mark my words, Captain. Carry them back to your Admiral Berkeley. Tell him. We beat him once. We'll do it again if you drive us to it! Do you hear me?"

Budd turned back to Barron. "On your orders, sir, we will retake our ship! Say the words."

For one brief second every American who was still on his feet turned to Captain Barron, and he saw the hot defiance in their eyes. British redcoats glanced at their captain, suddenly nervous, apprehensive. No matter the cost, the Americans were ready to reclaim their ship. Barron made his decision and spoke to Budd.

"No. We will give no excuse. We will remain blameless. These men have committed an act of war, and I want the record to show that we gave no provocation. Not before they opened fire, and not after they boarded. They alone will bear the blame for what has happened here." He paused for a moment before he faced the British captain squarely and concluded. "But I will say that under other circumstances, my orders would be otherwise! And I repeat, there will be a reckoning!"

Every man on deck flinched at the shout from the British crow's nest. "Sail ho! Due south. About two miles."

The British captain called, "How many?"

"Only one so far."

"Course?"

"Due north, sir. Straight at us. She's seen us."

"What flag?"

There was a pause as the sailor peered through his telescope. "Not yet certain but I think American."

"Man-o'-war or merchantman?"

"Riding deep. Built broad. Heavy. Tacking into the wind, and she's a bit slow, sir. I'd say merchantman, loaded, sir."

"Her name?"

"Can't make it out yet, sir."

"Keep us advised."

"Aye, sir."

Barron thrust his face forward, eyes blazing. "You intend boarding that merchantman?"

The British captain shook his head. "Our orders are limited to the *Chesapeake*. We have what we came for." He turned to his first officer. "Take the four men back to the *Leopard* and get them below decks. Put them in chains if you have to. I'll follow with the remainder of our men and we'll be on our way."

"Aye, sir."

The four American sailors were forced onto the deck of the British gunship at bayonet point, glancing at Captain Barron and then the crew of the American ship, white-faced with rage. They disappeared below decks, and within minutes the first officer emerged back into the sunlight.

"All secure here, sir."

Minutes later the last of the hawsers lashing the two ships were loosened, the grappling hooks released, and immediately a swath of foaming Atlantic sea-water widened between them. On command, the British man-of-war turned hard to port and began the slow, tricky procedure of tacking back and into the wind, making her way north from whence she had come.

Captain Barron turned to Budd. "Start clearing away the wreckage and making repairs. Get a report damage immediately. Watch that incoming ship. Keep me advised on her whereabouts."

"Aye, sir."

Barron called to the ship's surgeon, "Doctor Samuels, I need a casualty count as soon as possible."

Samuels nodded, but remained silent as he continued working with a tourniquet and bandages to stop the flow of blood pulsing from the wrist of a pasty-faced seaman whose left hand was gone. He spoke without looking at Barron.

"Sir, I'll tend your wounds in a moment."

Barron replied, "See to the crew. My wounds are not serious."

Samuels rose and walked among the dead and wounded, counting, appraising, ordering others to carry them below decks out of the blazing sun, while Budd walked the portside of the frigate, eyes constantly moving, then disappeared below decks for three minutes. When he reappeared he approached Barron, Samuels by his side. The captain was still standing on the quarterdeck wiping at the blood on his tunic, trying to stanch the bleeding from his forehead. Barron leaned forward to address the doctor.

"Casualties?"

There was a cutting edge in the surgeon's voice. "Three dead. Eighteen wounded. Some serious. We may lose one or two more." Samuels watched the muscles in Barron's jaw flex and then release. Barron turned to Budd.

"Damage?"

"Hulled twice. High. We are not taking on water. Eight of the guns on the port side are out of commission—carriages destroyed. The other two are being repaired. All guns on the starboard side are operable. Some loss of sail and hawsers and damage to the mainmast, but not serious. We're seaworthy."

Barron turned his face upward toward the crow's nest. "Mister Yates! The incoming ship?"

"American," came the call. "Merchantman. She'll be alongside within ten minutes."

Barron peered at the broad sails for a moment, studying the ship as it came on, tacking into the wind, then spoke to the two men before him. "Carry on. We'll deal with whoever that is when they reach us." He turned to the wheelman. "Hard to starboard and bring her about to due north. We're returning to Norfolk."

The sturdy little frigate answered the wheel, and her two masts leaned left as she turned hard right while the sailors nimbly climbed the ropes to the spars to begin the intricate shifting of the sails to tack a course due north, into the wind.

They were on course when the call came from the crow's nest. "The ship behind us is the *Camille*. Merchantman out of Boston harbor. I recognize her. She means to come alongside."

Captain Barron cupped his hands to call to his men in the rigging. "Reduce sail. Let her come alongside!"

The crews of both ships watched in silence as the little warship slowed, and the larger merchantman labored up to within fifty yards of her portside with the crew of the *Camille* studying the shattered railing and torn canvas on the lower sails, flapping in the wind. The captain took his horn in hand and made the call.

"Ahoy, *Chesapeake*. I am Captain Adam Dunson of the *Camille*. Merchantman out of Boston. We heard cannon. We saw the British man-o'-war withdraw. Are you sound?"

Barron answered. "We're sound."

"We see the damage. Do you have dead or wounded?"

"We do."

"Seek permission to board. We have a ship's surgeon and medicine. Seamen if you need them."

Barron looked at Samuels, who nodded, and Barron answered through his horn. "Permission to board granted."

Carefully the two ships maneuvered until they touched, and men on both sides lashed them together. Captain Adam Dunson led his boarding party onto the splintered deck of the *Chesapeake,* stepping over and around the wreckage that still remained, and he read the tell-tale signs as though they were a written page. Dunson was middle-aged, just under six feet in height, solidly built, with dark, intense eyes, square jaw, regular features. He fronted Captain Barron and bowed slightly from the hip.

"I am Captain Adam Dunson. May we be of service, sir?"

"I am Captain James Barron. Your home port, sir?"

"Boston. Dunson and Weems."

Barron reflected for a moment. "*Matthew* Dunson?"

"Yes. My older brother. He and Billy Weems own the company."

"I know of your company. Would you permit us the services of your ship's surgeon?"

Dunson turned and gave a hand signal, and a sparse, gray-haired man stepped forward. In his face one could see forty years on the sea and countless sea battles in which he had treated unknown numbers of injured sailors. He took two steps toward Samuels and said, "Where should I start, sir?" He followed the blood-spattered doctor to a hatch, and they disappeared into the hold of the ship.

Dunson spoke to Barron. "May I inquire what was the occasion that caused the damage?"

"The British ship was a man-o'-war named the *Leopard.* She demanded to board to search for British deserters. We had none on board. When I refused the demand, she opened fire without provocation or warning. Three broadsides."

Barron saw the anger rise in Dunson as he inquired. "Dead? Wounded?"

"Three dead so far. Near twenty wounded. They took four of my crew. Three native-born Americans. I do not know about the fourth man."

"You are short seven of your crew and have others disabled? I have seasoned sailors who we can spare. Would that be of help?"

Budd looked at his captain, and the need was clear in his eyes.

Barron nodded. "It would. We could use up to ten men if you can spare them."

Dunson turned to his first officer. "Can you see to it?"

"Aye, sir." The man spun on his heel and quickly returned to the deck of his own ship to begin pointing at men who nodded.

Dunson continued. "What port do you intend making?"

"Norfolk. The nearest one with a hospital. The wounded need a hospital."

Dunson nodded. "Two days from here, if this nor'east wind holds. May we accompany you? I can get my crew back when you're docked."

"It will cost you three days."

Dunson raised a hand as though to brush off the concern. "No matter."

Barron replied, "Your help would be appreciated."

Dunson glanced about. "Would some of your crew care to take mess with us this evening?"

"How many?"

"All, if necessary."

"Could you prepare strong broth for the wounded?"

"We can, sir. Is there anything else?"

Barron's eyes narrowed, and his words came measured, clipped. "Yes, Captain Dunson, there is. Could you have one of your officers inspect this ship for all damage? All of it. Get the names of the dead and wounded and the names of the four men the British took. When your inspection is complete, have that man write what he has seen. Have it witnessed by yourself and your first officer. I want that document as evidence of this incident. It is my intention to call the British to account for taking my men, and for the murder and the unprovoked attack on the high seas on a ship of a neutral nation with which the British were not at war. If you could provide that to me, I would be most grateful."

Dunson turned, gave a hand signal, and a younger man stepped to his side, waiting. He was slightly taller and more slender than Adam Dunson, but with the same intensity in his dark eyes. His face tended to be heart-shaped, features regular and strong.

Dunson gestured. "This is our navigator. John Matthew Dunson. My nephew. Does well with writing. I will have your document ready for you when we leave you in Norfolk."

"Thank you."

Dunson looked about at the shattered, splintered timbers and the litter on the bloodied deck, and took a deep breath. "Captain Barron, if there is nothing else pressing at this moment, there is much for both of our crews to do. Shall we be about it?"

Notes

On June 22, 1807, off the Virginia capes, the captain of the British man-of-war HMS *Leopard,* Salusbury Humphreys, ordered the American warship USS *Chesapeake* to stop while the British boarded her to search for British seamen reportedly being held by the *Chesapeake.* The British captain was acting on written orders of Admiral George C. Berkeley. The *Chesapeake* was a newly built frigate and was on her maiden voyage, out through Chesapeake Bay into the Atlantic. The American captain, James Barron, refused to obey the order. The British ship carried fifty cannon, the American ship, thirty-eight. At that time America and England were officially at peace, and the American ship was neutral; thus, the order by the British admiral and the British captain was illegal and unprecedented. Nonetheless, upon Barron's refusal, and without warning, the British gunboat delivered three broadsides at point-blank range and badly damaged the ship, killing three American seamen and injuring eighteen others, including Captain Barron. Then the British forcibly boarded the crippled American ship and removed four seamen. Three were Americans. The incident infuriated the United States and later became one of the pivotal reasons for America's declaration of war against the British on June 19, 1812.

The historical accounts of this incident are not all consistent, with some differences in the details; however, the essence of the matter is as above set forth and as presented in this chapter.

Bernstein, *Thomas Jefferson,* pp. 166–7; Malcomson, *Lords of the Lake,* pp. 12–13; Whitehorne, *The Battle for Baltimore, 1814,* pp. 5–6.

For the detail of the incident wherein the British gunboat *Leander* pursued an American merchantman into New York harbor and fired at her, killing at least one American seaman and wounding others, which resulted in President Jefferson's banning the HMS *Leander* from all American ports, see Whitehorne, *The Battle for Baltimore, 1814,* p. 5.

The merchantman *Camille* and the parts played by Adam Dunson and John Dunson are fictional.

CHAPTER II

*I*n the still warmth of a bright, rare October morning, Matthew Dunson, tall, slender, striking, dark eyes, dark hair showing prominent gray at the temples, stood still and silent at the rail of the Dunson & Weems schooner *Ohio,* staring west in disbelief at Washington, D.C., as the crew lowered the gangplank to the newly constructed dock of the United States navy yards on the Anacostia River on the eastern border of the city. His face showed the burn of wind and weather that marked men who had spent much of their lives on ships at sea.

He had come here expecting to see a proud city rising from the wilderness between Maryland and Virginia—a city worthy of a new nation that had challenged England, the greatest military power on earth, and won a six-year war, fought on the insane notion that common people could govern themselves. And the upstart Americans had won! More unthinkable, fifty-five of them had created a document they called their Constitution in which they had gambled everything on the common man; they had vested the ultimate power of government in the vote of the people! Think of it! The uneducated man mixing the mortar to bind the bricks into the walls that would become the Executive Mansion for the president, would have his say in who came to live there! The notion had rocked the world. This city was intended to become the gem that would represent this infant, impudent, upstart nation, and take its place among the great capitals of the world, grand and elegant. Paris. London. Petersburg. Moscow. Amsterdam.

But on this day, from the docks of the navy yard, Matthew stared in shock at a muddled, disconnected chaos of trash dumps, meandering dirt roads, and the rudimentary beginnings of buildings that suggested no sense of organization, scheme, or design. The dock was nearly deserted. In the distance, a few men moved back and forth, carrying planks from a wagon to a nearby stack. The only sounds were the seabirds, the high-pitched hum of mosquitoes, and the lap of water against the huge pilings that had been driven forty feet into the mud of the river to support the fourteen-inch square, rough-hewn timbers of the wharf.

Matthew grasped the handle of his sea bag and walked down the gangplank onto the dock, unaware of the slight roll to his gait, common to men who had spent much of their lives on the undulating decks of ships at sea. He picked his way through the piles of junk and rubble that had been randomly tossed aside, toward the six men working on the lumber stack. He was ten feet away when the nearest one turned to face him, and they all stopped and gathered.

Matthew nodded. "Good morning. I'm Matthew Dunson. I have need for transportation to the city. I expected there would be hacks for hire here at the navy yard, but apparently I was wrong."

One of the men eyed him for a moment. "Not many hacks for hire anywhere around here. No need. The city, you say? You have business there?"

"Yes. With the secretary of state. James Madison."

The man scratched at stubble under his chin. "Don't have an idea where to find him, but when we get this lumber unloaded, we got to go back into town—such as it is—for another load. You don't mind riding a lumber wagon, we can get you there. You'll have to ask someone there how to find the secretary of state, whoever he is. We won't be too long. Want to wait?"

"I'll wait. Can I help?"

A wry smile crossed the man's face. "Don't look to me like you're much dressed for it. You got to see someone in the gov'ment, you best let us do this. Why don't you sit a spell out of the sun?"

Matthew nodded and carried his sea bag to where nine kegs of nails were lined against the wall of a tool shed and sat down on the nearest keg, his sea bag at his feet. For several minutes he watched the six men work in teams of two, moving the twelve-foot planks from the wagon to the stack. He glanced about, then stood and walked to the center of the clearing that was called the navy yard, and studied the land to the west for a time before he returned to sit down once again while his thoughts reached back, and he let them go. A smile came and went at the remembrance of the convoluted history of how the city of Washington, D.C., came to be.

Article I, Section 8, Clause 17 of the United States Constitution authorized the seat of the government to be established on a parcel of land " . . . not exceeding ten miles square . . . ," but failed to designate *where* the land was to be. In the battle for ratification of the Constitution that spilled over from 1787 to 1788, Alexander Hamilton, slender, sharp-faced, self-confident to the point of occasional cockiness, had joined with James Madison and John Jay to write a series of political essays under the title *The Federalist Papers,* which were published in several leading newspapers. Hamilton found himself rising on the national scene with new celebrity, and President George Washington appointed him secretary of the treasury, an office refused by the financial wizard, Robert Morris of Pennsylvania. On January 14, 1790, Hamilton made his first *Report on Public Credit* to Congress, wherein he proposed consolidating state and national debt and issuing securities to retire both, and at the same time promote economic growth. An incidental to the plan was Hamilton's suggestion of where the ten-mile-square plot of ground was to be.

Congress deadlocked on the proposal, with James Madison of Virginia, his colleague in creating *The Federalist Papers,* leading the contingent violently opposed to the Hamilton plan. Hamilton was driven to near distraction by the deadlock, and in a chance meeting with tall, lanky Secretary of State Thomas Jefferson in the street fronting the home of the president, walked him up and down the cobblestones while he harangued him with his terrible fear that failure of his proposal would threaten the nation's credit at home, and worse, with nations abroad. Indeed, he argued, it could lead to dissolution of the Union! And it would leave unresolved the issue of where the seat of government was to find its ten-square-miles of land.

Bright in Jefferson's mind was the painful remembrance of his own crippling problems with the national debt while he was in the diplomatic service of the fledgling country. More critical to Jefferson was his deep conviction that the seat of government ought to be in a rural area, among common farming people who were close to the earth. Was it not absolutely clear that those who worked with Mother Earth stood infinitely closer to The Almighty than those who flocked to cities for wealth and power? The opposition was equally clear that the seat of the government ought to be in a great city that was a crossroads of world commerce, driven by the pulse of international affairs.

Thoughtfully, Jefferson tugged at his chin, and then made a proposal that was a stroke of genius, but loaded with the possibility of fireworks, not to mention high hilarity. He, Jefferson, would host a dinner to which he would invite both Hamilton and Madison. In the course of the evening, they would see to it that Hamilton and Madison engaged in a discussion of their battle over Hamilton's plan. With some of the country's prominent celebrities seated at the table, neither Hamilton nor Madison would dare turn the discussion into a shouting match, and with some clever guidance provided by Jefferson and others, it was possible the one-time colleagues would find a solution, renew their fractured friendship, and resolve their differences.

The dinner was held, and with a modicum of sour expressions and disgruntled concessions from both sides, their suffering friendship was restored sufficiently to support their agreement on Hamilton's plan, which included terms providing that the ten-mile square would be on the Potomac River. Further, it would include a piece of Maryland joined with a piece of Virginia, so dear to the hearts of the Virginians, Washington, Madison, and Jefferson. Finally, to allow time to survey the

ten-mile square, obtain land titles from Maryland and Virginia, lay out
the new city, and build enough of it to house the new government, the
seat of the government would remain in Philadelphia until the year
1800, and then take up its new residence.

Thus, Washington, District of Columbia, was born! President
George Washington named the French-born Major Pierre Charles
L'Enfant to plan the new city, and Vice President Jefferson called on
Benjamin Banneker, a self-educated former slave, to assist. One could not
fail to notice that the design of the city, with the Capitol on the highest
hill and the great boulevards laid out like spokes of a gigantic wheel, was
decidedly French.

Surveying these early and humble beginnings of the capital's lofty
design, Matthew impatiently waited for the wagonload of lumber to be
stacked. Restless and anxious to be about his business, he reached to
touch the letter in the inside breast pocket of his black coat. It was this
letter from James Madison that had brought him from Boston to the
navy yard docks. The letter requested that Matthew find time to visit
with Secretary of State Madison in his office in Washington, D.C., " . . .
at your earliest convenience . . . to discuss critically important matters of
state." Matthew had made the voyage on the Dunson & Weems schooner
Ohio, loaded with New England stoves, kettles, and plows for delivery to
Norfolk, Virginia, where she had taken on two hundred tons of Virginia
rice for delivery back in Boston before turning north on Chesapeake Bay,
then sailing northwest up the Potomac River to the site of the new capital city to wait one day at the navy yard docks while Matthew met with
James Madison. Now, sitting on a keg of nails at the nearly deserted navy
yards, Matthew's mind reached back to the strange path that had led him
to James Madison those many years before.

In the six years following the surrender of the British at Yorktown
in 1781, thinking men throughout the new nation had watched the
North-South factionalism, epidemic bankruptcies, and burgeoning distrust pull the thirteen states to pieces and threaten the destruction of all
they had won in eight bloody, hard-fought years. Fear that America was
on the brink of war between the states rode heavily in the minds of

Washington, Franklin, Madison, Jefferson, Mason, and too many others. Sick at heart, in the winter of 1786–1787, Matthew sought out Thomas Jefferson and laid bare his worst fears. Jefferson, soon to leave for Europe on political assignment, directed Matthew to James Madison. When Matthew learned of the last-ditch effort by Madison to save it all by gathering representatives from all thirteen states to one last convention on May 14, 1787, in Philadelphia, he made the journey to meet Madison. Too well he recalled his surprise at first seeing the little man. Madison, scarcely over five feet tall, heart-shaped face, regular features, piercing blue eyes, soft voice, educated, brilliant, the astute politician, arrived at the convention with a plan that became known as "The Virginia Plan," which eventually shaped the new Constitution; but no one doubted by whose genius it had been created. Matthew, a Harvard College-educated Boston navigator, who had been caught up in the shooting war at the age of twenty-one and who had survived some of the deadliest and bloodiest sea battles in the Revolutionary War, came to meet him. Madison the politician, Matthew the warrior. Madison the theorist, Matthew the realist. Madison and Matthew each saw the strength of the other and sensed that both would be vastly broadened in their grasp of the affairs of their new, infant country if they would share their gifts. A bond quickly formed between them.

The convention wore on in the sealed east room of the Pennsylvania Statehouse, through the unbearable heat and humidity of the Philadelphia summer, before the exhausted delegates emerged on September 17, 1787, with a new Constitution. In the time following, the two men had exchanged letters. Madison rose ever higher in the new government while the Dunson & Weems shipping company grew to become one of the largest on the eastern seaboard.

During that same time, across the Atlantic, Napoleon had risen to dominance in France, filled with lust for world conquest. The result was war with England and Russia, and within weeks those major powers were engaged in a do-or-die battle for supremacy at sea. They declared endless embargoes against each other and against all ships of all countries, which closed most major ports to foreign shipping, and the warring nations issued policies claiming the right to stop and search commercial ships of any origin, wherever they found them, with the power to confiscate their cargoes if they were destined for delivery to an enemy. Instantly, the international shipping trade of the civilized world was plunged into chaos, and the impact on American foreign trade was catastrophic. Dunson & Weems, and all other American shipping companies who depended on open and free seas and open foreign ports to stay alive, found themselves crippled, desperate, dying.

In those dark years, Madison had sent word to Matthew nine times: *I need your advice—come to my office*—and nine times Matthew had made the journey from Boston, first to Philadelphia, then to New York, when the seat of government was transferred. In the privacy of Madison's office they had exchanged the brutal facts, neither holding back, and they gave and received the best that was in them.

In the clean, cool October air, Matthew stood once more, and judged it would take the six men ten more minutes to have the lumber wagon empty and ready to go northwest, into the city, if such there was. He drew out the letter and for a moment studied the even, scrolled handwriting. "Mister Matthew Dunson, Esq." He slipped it back into his pocket and sat back down with the thought clear in his mind.

I know why Madison wants to see me. The Chesapeake. *He has John's report—wants to know if that unprovoked attack by the British man-o'-war* Leopard *is justification to declare war on England. Three American seamen dead—four taken—twenty-two injured—the* Chesapeake *shot half to pieces—justification for war? It was war. It's coming—sooner or later we'll fight it out with England again—I can feel it.*

War! The ugly evils of war! Memories came flashing in his mind and for a few moments he bowed his head while a deep sense of sadness welled up inside, and scenes came flashing in his mind.

October 11, 1776—Lake Champlain—seventeen tiny, flat-bottomed American boats built in three months of green lumber—twenty-four British gunboats—the desperate battle to save George Washington and the American Continental Army—lost every American boat and half the crews, but they stopped the British.

He reached to touch the three-inch scar on his cheek that was his constant reminder of how close he had come to being dead in that fight, and his memories continued.

September 23, 1779—dusk—twelve miles off Flamborough Head—western coast of England—John Paul Jones—the Bon Homme Richard—*attacked the far-superior British man-o'-war* Serapis—*rammed her—lashed the railings of the two ships together—under pale moonlight the big guns roared and the din deafened both crews as they fought face-to-face, hand-to-hand—the shout from the* Serapis *to strike colors—Jones's defiant answer—"I have not yet begun to fight"—Tom Sievers up in the rigging—the grenade—thrown down the open hatch of the* Serapis—*the horrendous blast when it ignited a dozen barrels of gunpowder—second deck—blew all the guns and crews to oblivion—the British surrender—recalling the sickening thud of the British musket ball in Tom's chest as his old, dear friend descended from the rigging—then holding Tom in his arms as he died.*

Matthew swallowed hard as he felt once more the heart-wrenching emptiness that had seized him as he cradled the old man to his chest, stroking his hair, and feeling life leave him. He brushed his hand across his eyes as though to push out the scene, while his thoughts ran on.

September 5, 1781—Yorktown—the French ships filing out of the York River in their run to the open water of Chesapeake Bay to meet the waiting British fleet—the great men-of-war of both sides squaring with each other—the world filled with the roar and the white smoke of the big guns—the British retreat out into the Atlantic and down to the South Carolina capes—British General Cornwallis and his army of six thousand regulars landlocked in the tiny village of Yorktown—the American army and the French infantry putting the red-coated army under relentless cannon siege—battering them into submission.

For a time Matthew pondered. How many lesser sea battles had he survived? He could not count them. How many men had he seen killed and maimed? There was no way to know. How many men had he killed? He shuddered at the thought. In his mind he saw Kathleen and their children, and Margaret and Dorothy Weems, and then he saw the tens of thousands of faceless mothers and wives on both sides who had waited and counted days, and then months, and then years, for husbands and fathers and sons who would never return. And the single unanswered question that had haunted him since the shooting began at Lexington on April 19, 1775, came surging once again.

Why war? What's wrong with the human race that it can't avoid the insane evil of war? The answer is so simple! So simple! Charity! So simple.

Matthew started from his thoughts at the sound of the workman's voice calling from the wagon.

"Finished. You want to get up in the driver's seat? We're ready to go for the next load."

Matthew stood, nodded his understanding, picked up his sea bag, and walked rapidly to the heavy lumber wagon, while one man climbed to the driver's seat and the other five clambered into the empty bed. Matthew passed his bag to them and climbed up the big wheel to take his place beside the driver. The man unwound the long leather lines from the brake pole, sorted them out, threaded three between the fingers of each hand, and called to the six horses as he slapped the reins on the rumps of the leaders. The horses, which had been standing hipshot, dozing with their heads down, jerked alive and leaned into their horse-collars. Their caulked shoes bit into the heavy timbers as the wagon lurched forward and rumbled hollowly on the dock while the horses came into their pulling stride.

They moved steadily west with Matthew gaping, dumbstruck at what he was seeing on all sides. They passed hollow-eyed men with filthy beards and ragged clothing who were standing idly or rooting with hogs through the garbage and trash and discard for something to eat, or wear, or sell. Some stopped to stare at the passing wagon, and in their faces Matthew saw heart-wrenching black despair and hopelessness. In a few of them he saw envy and hatred of his black suit and top hat, and his black, square-toed shoes with the silver buckles. They were the forgotten vagabonds and riff-raff of the world, who had gravitated to a place where they believed they would find food and housing and purpose. Surely the seat of power of this new, young, vibrant nation with the dream of the common man would provide for its neglected needy. Instead, they found closed doors, starvation, and people who refused to look at them. The hope in their hearts and the light in their eyes died,

and their lives went on unchanged, with them digging with pigs in rotting, stinking garbage heaps to stay alive.

The wagon rumbled west on dirt trails that meandered around
marshes and bogs. There were no markers naming streets or locations.
Windowless shacks nailed together from discarded scraps of lumber were
everywhere. They passed the putrefying carcass of a dead horse left to
rot where the animal had broken a leg and been unhitched from its har-
ness and shot. Snakes slithered from the dirt road into the swamps of
green, stagnant water, where mosquitoes and dragonflies and flies
swarmed. Matthew was suddenly struck with the realization that there
was no pedestrian traffic to be seen; no one was moving about, conduct-
ing the business of government, or any other business he could identify.

Matthew turned to peer intently at the highest of the rolling hills to
the northwest, seeking the rounded dome of the capitol building that
was intended to dominate the entire city. It was not there. Rather, two
square, half-finished, white-stoned, widely separated buildings stood on
the dusty, barren hilltop, connected by a long wooden walkway that had
a roof overhead, but no walls. It took Matthew a full minute to understand he was looking at the twin buildings that would house the Senate
 and the House of Representatives. He recalled the sadly comic article
that had appeared on the front page of a Boston newspaper four years
earlier, announcing to the world that shoddy workmanship had resulted
in a section of the roof of the Senate wing collapsing. The collapse was
bad enough, the article trumpeted, but the falling roof very nearly struck
the seat occupied by the vice president of the United States. That the
debris had missed him was either fortunate or unfortunate, depending
on your political views. With plaster and dust still falling, the terrified
vice president had called an immediate adjournment, which was quite
unnecessary, since every senator was already madly scrambling for the
doors. Nor was the roof of the House of Representatives wing to be
spared. It was constructed of glass, and when it rained, it leaked so badly
that puddles and pools of water formed on the floor of the House, and
soaked the representatives, their chairs and desks, and the documents left
in the open.

Matthew turned to the driver. "How far to the Executive Mansion? Someone there should be able to tell me where to find Mister Madison."

The man pointed with his chin. "Right on up this road, just a little way."

Matthew craned his neck. *What road? There is no road! No markers, no signs, no directions. Just a dirt trail winding through tree stumps and discarded gravel piles and trash dumps and garbage heaps, among a hundred other dirt trails, leading only heaven knows where!*

They plowed through stagnant water that had accumulated in a shallow gravel pit, and crested a rise, and there, two hundred yards ahead of them were the incomplete walls of what was called the Executive Mansion. There was no road leading to either door, no fence, no yard, no signs directing traffic to the front door, the servants' entrance, delivery entrance, or any other entrance. Matthew sat aghast at the huge piles of rubbish and cast-off building materials thrown and scattered about the treeless, barren grounds. A few workers paused to stare at the passing wagon, but there was not one person at the Executive Mansion to pay respects or to conduct business with the president of the United States.

The driver of the lumber wagon hauled back on the reins, and the heavy draft horses came back on their hind quarters to bring it to a stop in a cloud of dust that reached the large double doors in front.

"There she is," he said.

Matthew spoke. "Thank you. What do I owe you?"

"Nothin'," the driver said. "Compliments of the United States of America. They're payin' our wages."

Matthew climbed down from the wagon, and the men in the bed of the wagon passed his sea bag to him. He nodded his thanks, turned, and walked to the great double doors set in the stark, white walls. There was no doorman, and Matthew lifted the heavy brass knocker and let it fall three times. It was a full minute before a man in work clothes opened the door and peered into Matthew's face. Behind him, Matthew could see enough of the huge, vacuous reception room to realize that the great circular staircase connecting the first floor to the second floor had not yet been constructed. From the front door, it appeared that the two floors were not yet connected.

The man asked, "Something I can do for you?"

Matthew removed his hat. "I'm Matthew Dunson. I need direction to find Mister James Madison. Secretary of state. He sent for me. I thought someone here might direct me."

A quizzical expression crossed the man's face. "He told you to come here?"

Matthew repeated himself. "Not here. He requested I visit him here in Washington, D.C. I have a letter. I don't know the location of his office. Is there someone who can direct me?"

The man stepped back. "Yes, I expect I can do that. Mister Jefferson isn't here right now. Left this morning early to see someone in the Senate. Excuse us for not having the usual doorman here, but we got an emergency. Some of the roof fell in on the big audience chamber up the hall, and we're doin' all we can to get it back up. It irritated Mister Jefferson considerable. The room had a lot of wet wash hung to dry when the roof came down."

The man paused for a moment to collect his thoughts. "All right. You're looking for Mister Madison. Secretary of state. I think he's likely at his office right about now. On up the street. They haven't finished the capitol building yet, or any of the other government buildings. Follow me. I'll show you how to get there."

Matthew followed the man out into the dust of the clearing in the front of the building, and the man pointed northwest.

"Right on up this street about five minutes. Right side. Still under construction. Nobody taken up residence yet, so some of our government people got their offices there. I think you'll find Mister Madison there."

Matthew tried to mask his uncertainty. "This street? What's the name of this street?"

The man snorted. "Pennsylvania. It'll be a street someday. Right now you just follow that path. You'll know the building when you come to it. On the right side of the road."

Matthew nodded and settled his hat back on his head. "Thank you, sir."

"Good luck."

There was no street, nor anything resembling a street. There was only a dirt trail, tromped by countless feet, that twisted and turned and meandered around bogs and marshes and piles of cast-off trash. Five minutes became ten before a building was suddenly there, thirty yards from the trail, partially hidden behind aspen trees with leaves that had been touched by October frost. Matthew picked his way to the front door, which was closed and had a hole bored through for the handle. He looked for the knocker, could find none, and rapped with his knuckles. He waited, and was raising his hand to rap again when he heard rapid footsteps inside. The door swung open and an elderly man with a trimmed beard and faded gray eyes, and dressed in a suit, faced him.

"Yes, sir. Is there something I can do for you?"

"I am Matthew Dunson. I received a letter from Mister Madison requesting that I visit him. Have I found his office?"

"Oh, yes, temporarily. Come in. I'll fetch his assistant."

Matthew removed his hat and stepped inside as the man turned on his heel and disappeared down a hall with lumber stacked against one wall. The walls of the large reception room were plastered but not painted. A thin, white dust covered the hardwood floor. Within one minute the little man hurried back to motion to Matthew.

"Will you follow me? Mister Madison's assistant will see you."

Matthew followed the man down the hall, glancing through the open doors of rooms on both sides, startled to see that most of their walls had not yet been plastered. None had finished floors or finished woodwork. Fireplaces were half built, with stacks of brick and stones lying in heaps. They stopped at a large, stained oak door and knocked. A voice called, "Enter," and the man pushed the door open.

"Mister Dunson is here to see Mister Madison."

The walls were plastered and partially covered with dark oak. None of the windows had draperies. The hardwood flooring showed dust, and Matthew's heels clicked as he approached the large desk facing him, with the well-dressed man seated behind, silhouetted by the great window in the far wall. At Matthew's approach, the man raised his head. He was solidly built with a heavy brow and a square chin, and at the moment of recognition a smile came, cordial, warm, and he rose from his desk, hand extended.

"Mister Dunson! How nice to see you again. I presume you received Mister Madison's letter?"

Matthew nodded, and as the two men shook hands, Matthew replied, "Mister Keeler, it's good to be here. I came as soon as I could. I understand Mister Madison is here?"

"He is." Keeler gestured and smiled. "We're here temporarily. Our quarters in the Capitol building are not finished." He chuckled. "Finished? They aren't even begun. Give me a minute. I'll tell Mister Madison you're here." As he strode to the large, heavy oaken door to his right, he asked, "How is your health? Your family?"

"Both fine."

"Good. Excellent."

Keeler rapped, then opened the door and disappeared inside for a few moments, And then the door swung wide, and James Madison strode into the room. He was dressed as usual in a quality black suit with white stockings to his knees, and white lace at his cuffs and his throat. A light came into his eyes the moment he saw Matthew, and as they shook hands he exclaimed, "You don't know how grateful I am to see you. How are you? How are things at home?"

Matthew grinned. "I'm fine. Things at home are excellent. It's good to see you. How are you? How is this business of being secretary of state?"

"I'm fine. Being secretary of state is punishment inflicted on me by the Almighty for sins in my past! We're forced to make do with just about everything, including this office."

All three men chuckled, and Madison turned to Keeler. "I'm unavailable to anyone except the president."

Keeler nodded. "I understand, sir."

Madison held the door while Matthew entered his private office,

then closed it, and the two men took leather-upholstered seats on opposite sides of a beautifully crafted round table that stood before a massive
window. A great desk was to their right, covered with papers in orderly
stacks, and two hand-painted China lamps. One wall was shelved in oak,
with books of every description and content, all set in order. All other
walls were plastered but unpainted. The hardwood floor was polished but
uncarpeted. On the round table was a bound document that Matthew
recognized instantly. Madison spoke.

"I take it you received my letter."

Matthew drew it from his pocket and set it on the table. "I did."

Madison gestured to the bound document on the table between
them. "That's the report written by your son John on the *Chespeake* affair."

Matthew replied, "I recognize it."

"Have you read it?"

"Several times."

"Three unprovoked broadsides on an American naval vessel on the
high seas. Justification for war?"

Matthew drew and released a great breath. "I dislike it, but
the answer is yes. Are you considering it? Has the president made a
decision?"

"Not yet. But we are drafting a complaint to the British admiralty,
demanding a public apology and restitution, and the return of the
American sailors they kidnapped. Lacking their compliance, we are
including a threat of war."

Matthew's expression did not change as he spoke. "Are we prepared
for war if they refuse?"

Madison shook his head sadly. "I agree with you. I deplore it. I cannot yet speak for the president. Answer me this. Do the British hold us in
such contempt they think they can get away with such a thing?"

Matthew's answer came slowly. "Yes. They still see us as their rebel
colonies. Nothing but contempt. Arrogance."

"What will we have to do to wake them up?"

"File your complaint. Fight it out. If they refuse the apology and restitution, declare war. If it comes to war, be certain you have enough naval power."

Madison's face clouded. "That's one of the problems. We don't. Let me continue. If we do have a hearing on our complaint, will your son John be available to substantiate his report by appearing as a witness if it becomes necessary?"

"Any time, any place."

Suddenly Madison leaned forward, small, soft hands on his knees, eyes pinpoints of intensity. His next question caught Matthew by surprise.

"If the United States were to take Canada away from the British, would the loss of the commercial items now being produced by the Canadians for the British cripple the British enough to bring them to the bargaining table?"

Matthew leaned back to let the impact of that suggestion settle in. "You mean the timber?"

"Among other things. England has to have lumber from somewhere to support their navy. They can get it from Canada. If we held Canada, England would have to look elsewhere, and right now they couldn't get it from France or Russia because those three powers are at each other's throats. Nor could they get it from any other reliable source. What do you think? Would it cripple them?"

For a time Matthew lowered his head and labored with his thoughts. Then he raised his eyes. "I doubt it. I doubt the United States could shut down the trade. We might take Canada, but one way or another, the Canadians would find a way to get the timber to England, if there was a profit in it. And there would be a profit. Probably a big one. Some Americans up there might even help them do it."

Matthew saw the disappointment in Madison's eyes and asked, "Why? Are you thinking of recommending to the president that we take Canada?"

Madison puckered for a moment before he spoke. "It had crossed my mind."

Matthew shook his head. "Be careful. Be careful."

Madison studied Matthew's eyes for a moment, then abruptly changed the subject again. "I need to know the truth about what's happening to American commercial shipping on the high seas and in foreign ports. I get reports, but I'm nervous about their authenticity. Has Dunson & Weems suffered?"

Matthew took a deep breath. "I've lost track of the embargoes and the tariffs and the policies of the British and the French and now the Russians. It's past arrogance. Past contempt. So far as they're concerned, we're nothing more than a nuisance. They stop our ships at will, confiscate our cargoes, sometimes they take our ships as prizes at sea, and we never see them again. They've seized our crews and forced them into British naval service at bayonet point. And they've closed ports all over Europe to our ships, and if we protest they use cannon."

Matthew's eyes were alive, his face showing color. "We've never been without insurance on our cargoes until lately, but it can't be bought now because the insurance companies nearly went bankrupt paying for confiscated cargoes before they realized what was going on and quit issuing insurance at any price. We've begun mounting cannon on our commercial ships with orders to our captains to defend themselves if they have to. We're using small frigates for most of our loads. They can't carry as much, so profits are down on every load, but at least they can outrun the big men-o'-war."

Matthew stopped for a moment, then finished. "We're already in an undeclared war! Either we find a way to stop all this, or the United States will go down in bankruptcy. Can you imagine what would happen if a British gunboat attacked one of my commercial ships on the high seas, and my ship decided to fight back with the two cannon they carry and by some stroke of luck sank the British man-o'-war? Within one day of the British admiralty's finding out about it, they would declare war on the United States. Bankruptcy or war. Those appear to be our choices."

For a time Madison digested Matthew's statement, dissected it, and filed the pieces away, each in its proper place in his orderly mind. "That bad?"

"Worse. If you need witnesses to all this, I can provide at least twenty captains from my fleet who will give first-hand accounts of breach by both British and French ships of just about every rule of the sea."

"I'll keep that in mind." Madison paused to clear his throat and changed course again. "Do you recall that individual who was taken by the Indians when he was small and raised Iroquois? He was close to your associate, Billy Weems. You knew him well. The one who never learned to salute General Washington?"

Matthew smiled at the remembrance. "Eli Stroud? My son John married his daughter, Laura, not long ago. They have an infant son, James."

Madison straightened in surprise. "Your son married Mister Stroud's daughter? I was unaware! And they named their firstborn James? Am I to feel honored?"

"Yes. You now have a godson."

"I am without words! I will find an occasion to meet them, and I insist they have my godson available."

Matthew grinned. "I'll see to it whenever you say."

Madison continued. "Regarding Mister Stroud—wasn't he living in the wilderness in Vermont? Or was it New Hampshire?"

"Vermont. About eight years ago he realized his daughter, Laura, would not receive an education if she stayed there. Civilization was catching up with them out there in the wilderness, and if she was to be ready for it she needed to learn the ways of life in a city. He brought her to Boston, and Billy Weems took her in. You may remember that Billy is married to my sister Brigitte—and Laura has been there since. An educated, beautiful young lady—a lot like her mother, Mary."

"Where's Mister Stroud? He surely didn't stay in the city!"

Matthew laughed. "No, he didn't. He went back to Vermont, but he became restless with new people coming in and villages and towns taking shape. He moved on west, to the Ohio Valley. He's become a force for good over there. Remarkable man. Remarkable."

"How old?"

Matthew shrugged. "Perhaps fifty-five. Why do you ask about Eli?"

Madison took time to order his thoughts. "We have serious problems taking shape to the west—with the Indians. There are two Shawnee—a chief named Tecumseh and his brother who is called 'The Prophet'—who are friendly to the British and are organizing the tribes to resist the western migration of our people. There is reason to think the British are trading with them—the Shawnee, Ojibwa, Ottawa, Miami, Delaware, Wea, Piankashaw, Kaskaskia—all of them. We learned that last year the British met at Fort Amherstburg at the west end of Lake Erie with two thousand of those Indians and armed them. They apparently intend using them against Americans who come into what the Shawnee feel to be their territory."

Matthew's brow furrowed. "The British are preparing to use the Indians against us?"

"It is likely."

Matthew continued. "Those two you mentioned—The Prophet and his brother. Haven't I heard of them?"

"You have. The Prophet's Shawnee name is Tenskwatawa. He has acquired a reputation for seeing visions. As I say, his brother's name is Tecumseh. He's the practical one. He's moving up and down the entire country to the west, as far south as the Carolinas, persuading all the tribes to band together to push us back to the Atlantic. If he succeeds, this country will be in trouble."

"You see Eli as someone to help with that?"

"What do you think?"

"I hadn't thought of it. Eli speaks their language. Knows their customs. Habits. Religion. He's accepted by all the tribes I know. He has stature among the Indians."

Madison leaned forward, eager. "Could you find him? Ask him to track down both The Prophet and Tecumseh, and carry a message from the president of the United States? We want peace. We will parley with them. We will protect them. But we cannot stop the westward movement of our people."

Matthew answered, "I think we can find Eli, but it will take some time. I don't know what view he will take of your proposal."

"When I send word to you that we need him, would you find him? Have him come here?"

"I'll try."

Again Madison paused. For a few seconds he sat with his fingers interlaced before he once again changed his train of thought. "Is your company carrying cargo in the West Indies? The Gulf of Mexico? Jamaica?"

"We were, yes."

"Were? You stopped?"

"We had to."

"Tell me about it."

"The sugar and rum coming out of the West Indies are highly profitable, and the manufactured goods—nails, bolts, kettles, utensils, pots, pans, flatirons, silks, wools, silverwork—going into those islands are also profitable, and slaves are a major commodity. Every nation in the civilized world wants that trade. The result is that pirates and buccaneers and privateers flying every known flag, and some flying no flag, have swarmed there. Hundreds of legitimate commercial ships have disappeared with crew and cargo and have never been heard from again. Most commercial lines now avoid that entire region."

"Have you lost any ships down there?"

"Four. That was a few years ago. We stopped going there."

"Where do these privateers—pirates—market their stolen cargoes?"

"Almost all at New Orleans."

"Louisiana Territory?"

"Yes. Merchants buy the stolen goods—including slaves—from the pirates at a bargain and sell them for four times what they paid. There are men down there making fortunes. It's all wide open. No one even tries to conceal it. It's accepted. A thriving business." Matthew paused for a moment, then continued. "Why do you ask?"

Madison leaned back. "We have some smattering of information that the British are taking an interest in that business down there. New Orleans. They might be considering moving in and declaring it a possession of England."

"Take New Orleans? Louisiana?"

"Yes. Take it and use it as a base to expand northward, up through the Louisiana Territory. Stop our people from the westward migration that seems to be taking shape."

Matthew reflected for a moment. "Am I hearing this right? The British have Canada on the north, Indians on the west, the pirates and Creoles down south on the gulf and in New Orleans, and domination of the Atlantic to the east? And they intend using it all against us? Is that it?"

Madison nodded slowly and for a time remained silent. "North, south, east, and west. By accident or design, it doesn't matter which, there is reason to believe they intend isolating us and attacking the United States from all sides. It is possible that's their plan."

For long seconds Matthew did not move. He stared at the little man while first fear and then anger rose within. He shifted as he spoke. "Do you have any plans to the contrary?"

Madison took a deep breath. "A few." In his quiet, dignified way, he leaned forward and continued. "But let me ask you one more question. Do I recall your brother—the one just younger than you—went down into the Gulf of Mexico several years ago to bring back one of your ship's crew? They were being held by the British?"

"Yes. Caleb. They were holding our youngest brother, Adam, and one of our crews in a British prison at Port Royal on the island of Jamaica. Caleb brought them back."

"Quite adventurous, if I remember it right."

"Caleb blew up the British prison and a fair number of redcoats with it, and sank about half a dozen British longboats and one of their big gunboats in making his escape. All during a bad storm." Matthew laughed. "It *was* adventurous. You'd have to know Caleb to understand."

"Is he still with your firm?"

"Yes. He married and is father of four and still with us."

"Would he be available to help?"

"Help how?"

"We don't know yet. Perhaps another adventure."

"New Orleans?"

"Possibly. We might need someone to go to New Orleans long enough to get an accurate description of how matters are conducted there. Pirates, British, Creoles, French—it is all a rather confused mess right now. We don't know who is really the power we should be dealing with down there. The American governor? The British? The pirates? The French? We may need someone who has the instinct for it to go down there and find out."

"Odd you'd ask, right at this time. We've been considering sending Caleb down there ourselves sometime in the next few months to find out if there's a way to get our ships back into the commercial trade without too much risk."

Madison jerked erect, ecstatic. "Send him! Would he be willing to do some investigative work for the government?"

"That would be for him to say, not me."

"Would you advise against asking him?"

Despite himself, Matthew smiled. "An adventure like that? No. Ask."

"Would you ask him for me?"

Matthew thought for a moment. "Give me a written request, signed by yourself or President Jefferson. He should hear it from you. I'll deliver it to Caleb." He waited for a moment before he continued. "You mentioned you had plans contrary to those of the British. What are they?"

Madison drew and exhaled a great breath. "For now, take the initiative. Don't wait for them to set their master plan in motion. Request Congress to expand our army and navy. Get ready."

Matthew reflected for a moment. "President Jefferson? What's his attitude on the possibility of war with England?"

Madison shook his head. "He prefers to avoid it."

"At any cost?"

"We don't know yet. In the meantime we confront England with a claim for the damage they did to the *Chesapeake*, and we demand compensation and the return of those four seamen they seized. Until we know their response, we wait, and we prepare. I will draft a written request for your brother Caleb. It will be signed by either the president or myself. I'll see that you get it."

Madison eased back into his chair and relaxed, and Matthew understood their business was finished. He waited for Madison to dismiss him. The little man smiled, and in his quiet voice said, "Well, Mister Dunson, you have been an immeasurable help. As always, I am in your debt. Do you have time for other talk?"

"All the time you want."

"Good. Tell me. How many ships do you now have in your commercial fleet? How is Billy Weems? How is his wife?—your sister? How many children? Tell me."

Notes

James Madison was appointed secretary of state by President Thomas Jefferson in 1801. Stagg, *Mr. Madison's War,* p. 16.

The startling and deplorable description of the city of Washington, D.C., in the early 1800s as set forth in this chapter is historically accurate. The construction of the city was a project very much in delay, due to lack of funding and national focus, as described. See Young, *The Washington Community, 1800–1828,* pp. 1–48.

Article I, Section 8 of the Constitution, regarding the provision for a parcel of land ten miles square to become the capital of the United States, is quoted verbatim. The first financial report of Alexander Hamilton, which triggered a division among the political leaders of the time; the dispute that arose as to where the ten square miles for the Capital city was to be located; the persons involved; Jefferson's preference of a "rural location"; the deadlock between Madison and Jay; the chance meeting between Jefferson and Hamilton on the street in front of the residence of the president; the banquet arranged by Jefferson that resolved the conflict; the naming of the French-born Major Pierre Charles L'Enfant to be the designer of the city; the selection of Benjamin Banneker, an ex-slave, to assist L'Enfant; and other related affairs are all accurate. See Bernstein, *Thomas Jefferson,* pp. 86–100.

The plethora of embargoes between the United States, England, and France, and the lust of Napoleon Bonaparte to rule the world as described in this chapter fall short of the actual ongoing undeclared commercial war between these countries that was occurring on the high seas and ports from 1790 until the end of the War of 1812. The "Rule of '56" had been in place since the year 1756, the second year of the Seven Years' War between France and England for ownership of the thirteen colonies; the Rule of '56 is explained in Hickey, *The War of 1812*, p. 10. For an exposure to some of the nearly unending embargoes between the three countries and Russia, see Stagg, *Mr. Madison's War*, pp. 3–47. The commercial war between Britain, France, Russia, and America drove insurance rates to prohibitive levels for all participants. See Hickey, *The War of 1812*, pp. 217–218.

The recollections of Matthew regarding the sea battle on Lake Champlain on October 11, 1776; the battle twelve miles off the eastern English coast on September 23, 1779 between the *Bon Homme Richard* commanded by John Paul Jones and the British gunboat *Serapis;* and the Chesapeake Bay battle between the French and British navies near Yorktown are described in Leckie, *George Washington's War*, pp. 297–306, 499–501, and 632–48, respectively.

The use by the British of Native Americans against the United States, including the Shawnee leader Tecumseh and his brother Tenskwatawa, also known as The Prophet, all as described herein, is set forth in some detail in Stagg, *Mr. Madison's War*, pp. 177–203; Hickey, *The War Of 1812*, pp. 24–26; and Antal, *A Wampum Denied*, pp. 19–25.

The thoughts of James Madison regarding the taking of Canada from England, first as secretary of state and later as president, are set forth in Stagg, *Mr. Madison's War*, pp. 3–47, and Wills, *James Madison*, 97–105.

The political conditions prevailing in New Orleans as described herein, including the positioning of Jean and Pierre Lafitte as persons of power and the nearly impossible task given to Governor William Claiborne to unify the various cultures found in the area, are described in Saxon, *Lafitte, the Pirate*, pp. 20–26.

CHAPTER III

*H*e was slightly taller than average, built strong, face tending toward square with a prominent chin and nose, middle aged, dressed in a quality business suit of deep brown broadcloth, and wearing a tricorn pulled low in front. He leaned against the chest-high railing of the south-bound Mississippi riverboat *Antoinette* as she nosed east on the river, toward the docks of New Orleans. The gather of ships was like nothing he had ever seen before. All along the black, ancient pilings and the worn, foot-thick planking, the wharves and piers were jammed with schooners, frigates, flat-bottomed freight boats, barges, longboats, rowboats, and great three-masted merchantmen flying flags from Europe, Africa, the Orient, South America—more than thirty nations. Some were working their way into the docks, some riding low in the water impatiently forcing their way out. Some were tied to the docks, unloading tea, silks, spices, ivory, opium, ebony, perfumes, and a hundred other exotic products from the world over. Others were taking on tobacco, baled cotton, indigo, nails, bolts, stoves, plows, and countless other American manufactured goods to be delivered to foreign ports.

Dockhands of every color and description swarmed, calling, shouting, jabbering in a dozen languages and dialects. Some with dusky skin and tattoos wore turbans and flowing robes. Some with a yellow cast were pigtailed, with broad pointed straw hats. Others were black, or white, or bronze, or a mix—barefooted, stripped to the waist, wearing only ragged, threadbare trousers that reached just below their knees and were held up by a piece of cord tied at their middles. Some were bearded, some smooth shaven, some sheared bald, some with long hair tied behind their heads by a bit of string. Children of all ages darted about, clad in worn clothing, some with no clothing at all. All were dripping sweat in the stifling heat and humidity that hung heavy over the river and the sprawl of the docks and the burgeoning town of New Orleans.

The tall man set his feet to take the jolt of the riverboat as it thumped into the dock. Hawsers were cast, and dockhands heaved into them and deftly looped them with the backhand figure eight to huge, black, iron cleats anchored in the planking. The man wiped at his face with a damp handkerchief and bent to pick up his two horsehide suitcases with the broad leather straps and buckles that bound them shut, then stood waiting with half a dozen other passengers while seamen lowered the gangplank. Etched into the tough, scarred leather beneath the handles of his luggage was the name M. E. HICKMAN. He waited his turn, then walked down the gangplank, feeling the slight give with each step. On the dock, he slowed for a moment, breathing shallow in the wave of odors that washed over him. Pungent spices, perfumes, the stink of decaying entrails from dead fish, raw sewage, and the sweetness of orange blossoms coming from the orchards on the far fringes of the city. From the south came the taint of ocean water.

Hickman moved on toward the place at the north end of the docks where men in sweated shirts or broadcloth jackets, some with turbans, others with soft, shapeless, broad-brimmed felt hats or dilapidated stovepipe hats that shaded their heads and faces, sat in the driver's seats of scarred hacks with eight-foot horsewhips in the sockets, and horses standing like statues, heads down, hipshot, half asleep. From the crowd a hand reached to seize the handle of one of his suitcases, and Hickman jerked back, looking. A small black boy with dirt on his face and his hands, not yet ten years of age, grinned up at him, wide-eyed, stripped to the waist, wearing only a pair of too-big, faded, dark-blue trousers held up by a piece of knotted string. The ragged, torn garment reached just below his knees.

"Carry for two-bits," the boy exclaimed. "Two-bits." He reached again for the handle of the heavy suitcase.

Instantly Hickman peered over the boy's head to a man in the crowd with a broken nose and a scarred face who was watching every move the boy made. Hickman shook his head. "No," he growled. "Get away."

The boy seized the handle and again looked up at Hickman, grinning. "Carry for two-bits."

Hickman pushed him back. "No! Move back."

The expression on the boy's face soured, and he kicked at the suitcase with a bare, calloused, dusty foot, then darted back into the crowd to the broken-nosed man behind him, head ducked, one arm raised for protection. The man struck the boy on the top of the head, then seized him by the shoulder and jerked him away and disappeared into the press of people.

Hickman watched until they were gone, all too aware that if he had allowed the boy to carry his suitcase, it would have disappeared with the boy and the man.

He pushed through the teeming mass and stepped across an open ditch filled with standing human waste to reach the place where the hacks waited for fares. He eyed the worn vehicles and their drivers, picked one that wore a black, dusty, battered stovepipe hat and was dressed most like an American, and stopped beside the front wheels.

"You speak English?" In Hickman's voice was the unmistakable nasal twang of an American Yankee from a northern state.

The man nodded.

"Can you take me to the Absinthe boarding house?"

"Absinthe? Yes."

"Is it far?"

"In distance? No. In time? Twenty minutes." The words were decidedly flavored with French.

"How much? The cost?"

The man eyed Hickman and his two suitcases and scratched at his whiskered jaw for a moment. "Two dollars, American. You are responsible for your baggage."

"Two dollars? Sounds like too much."

The expression on the man's face did not flicker. "There are other hacks."

Hickman glanced at the next hack, then loaded his bags in the rack at the back of the one before him. "Two dollars. Done."

The spiritless horse answered the reins and the pop of the whip, and the hack creaked as it moved toward the heart of the city. The dirt streets were crooked and narrow, with trash and refuse piled against the walls and near the doorways wherever people chose to throw it. Cul-de-sacs and dead-end side-streets shielded courtyards and buildings between which there was no break. Foot traffic paid little attention to the carts and wagons and hacks; everyone took their chances in the streets.

Men in doorways and shielded places covertly studied him, some with dirks and daggers hidden in their shirts or robes, and eyes that were shrewdly calculating how much gold he might be carrying in his suitcases or inside his coat. Other men in business suits seated in open-air restaurants peered, judging who and what he was, and whether he had come to buy silks or silverwork or slaves or perfumes or spices or opium from the dealers and the auctions, and if so, in what quantities. Women standing erect walked with filled baskets balanced on their heads. Incredibly beautiful bronze and golden girls in loose gowns, with painted cheeks and dark eyes that peered from beneath long, dark lashes, stood on balconies to watch who came and who went. Old men and old women with small tables set on the dirt hovered over objects of every description, calling out to come, buy their precious goods, come, buy. Catholic priests, two by two, walked the streets in their robes. A few British soldiers were there, always in small groups, obvious in their crimson tunics. There was no pretense. No dominant dress or appearance or standard or language. It was all wide open, a morass of saints and sinners, of cultures and dress, and of trades and professions, with very few pretending to be other than what and who they were.

Coming into the old section of the city, Hickman could not mistake the influence of the French in the stone buildings. Intricate facings, balconies, stairways, cafes and restaurants in proliferation, all built in the fifty-year span from 1718 to 1768, during which the French founded and laid the foundations of the city and built the core. Some buildings showed the dark stain of fires from long ago and pockmarks and jagged holes from muskets and cannon that remained from the Indian wars and the wars with pirates and between the countries that lusted after the wealth that was accumulating in the city. Others bore the marks of past hurricanes that had toppled chimneys and buildings and church steeples.

Hickman saw the subtle change that began in 1769 when the Spanish took New Orleans from the French by force, and for the next thirty-four years imposed its own culture and language on the French inhabitants. The architecture showed a shift from the delicate grace of the French to the more practical notions of the Spanish. Spanish officers found the French colonial girls irresistible, and intermarriages became common. The two cultures and the two languages became entangled and confused, and the Creole was born—a new blood, a new society, neither French nor Spanish but a jumbled mix of the customs and traditions of both, with its own new language. Then, in 1803, when President Thomas Jefferson bought the whole of the Louisiana Territory from the Spanish, hardheaded, impatient, practical American businessmen came flocking to the irresistible lure of land and riches, and the American influence spread quickly. Hickman could not miss the many newly painted business signs with American names at the entrances to the old buildings.

As for the people, they were all there—the aristocrats, adventurers, outcasts, criminals from the jails of Paris and London and Amsterdam, the nuns and priests, pirates, smugglers, and the solid, productive men and women from the middle class who had jumped at the chance of owning land. He saw the influence of the hard-headed, thrifty Germans who had come to settle the wilderness, to grow orchards and farms and to help build the levees that lined the riverbanks and crisscrossed the town to hold back the flood waters of the Mississippi.

The crooked, narrow street entered onto a large, open public square crowded with people and small shops, and the driver pulled the horse to a stop.

"The Absinthe House," he said without expression and pointed to a huge black wrought-iron gate set in an eight-foot-high stone wall, between two massive stone pillars. The gate was open, and through it Hickman could see into a spacious courtyard with magnolia trees in bloom and orange trees heavy with fruit, and the spider-web filigree of Spanish moss hanging from it all. Hickman drew a leather purse from inside his coat, handed the hack driver a five-dollar gold piece, took his change, and hefted his two suitcases from the rack. The driver clucked and slapped the reins on the rump of his dispirited horse, and the hack groaned quietly as it rolled away in the dirt street. Hickman pushed his way past the crowd, through the gate, and stopped.

The courtyard was paved with cobblestones. At the far end was a massive, two-story building that had been a thing of beauty and dignity eighty years earlier; but the hot, humid summers and the hurricanes and storms had taken their toll. The brick chimney was partly collapsed, and the building was weather-stained. But despite it all, the charm of the French architecture remained—worn, tired, eroded, but graceful still. People in dress from countries the world over sat at small tables, sipping tea or wine beneath awnings and umbrellas and shade trees that lined the courtyard. Some were absorbed in gestures and chatter, others leaned back, casually observing. Four British redcoats sat lounging at a table in one corner, a large pitcher of ale before them, their pewter mugs half empty.

Hickman continued through the spacious yard, to the great mansion that dominated all, and entered through the open double doors into the relative coolness of the parlor, where several people were milling about. He paused long enough to locate a small desk in the far corner, near the carved, dark-wood staircase that curved against one wall, leading up to the second floor. He stopped at the desk and faced a large black woman with a great round face, wearing a tent-like tan garment that hung loose from her neck to her ankles.

"May I help you?" she asked.

"You have a room for me. M. E. Hickman."

"Yes. Your letter asked for a room on the second floor. At the corner."

"Correct."

"One dollar a night, ten nights. Ten dollars. Payable in advance." She waited.

"My business might keep me here more than ten days."

"That will be all right. You can pay for that later."

Hickman laid a ten-dollar gold piece on the desk. The woman took it and reached behind the desk for a locked metal box. She produced a small key, opened the box, and dropped the coin inside. As she closed the lock she asked, "Receipt?"

"Yes. Business expense."

She nodded, and Hickman watched while she wrote a receipt, signed it, and slid it across the desk to him. "Is that acceptable?"

He read the brief document and noted her name. "Matsie." A single word. Hickman nodded, folded it, and thrust it into his inside pocket while the woman again reached below the counter for a large brass key. "Take the stairs over there"—she pointed—"and the room is at the corner of the hallway. There is a washroom and bath for the second floor across from your room. You can get water there for your washbasin." She leaned her bulk forward to glance down at his suitcases. "Shall I call someone to carry your baggage?"

"No. I'll handle it."

His leather heels clicked on the hardwood floor, and on the twenty-one curving stairs up to the second floor, and down the hallway to his room. Inside, he set his suitcases on the floor beside the bed and stepped to the window to peer down at the great courtyard. Satisfied, he opened his suitcases on the bed and began hanging his clothing in the wooden wardrobe, casually glancing at the appointments in the room. The walls showed age, and the paintings of ships at sea and pastoral scenes were fading. A nightstand with a kerosene lamp was on one side of the bed, and nearby, against the wall, was a second table with a large, flowered, porcelain washbasin and a matching pitcher inside—both old, chipped. A tall dresser with five drawers stood against the third wall, where he placed his shirts and underclothing and socks. He took a pistol from his suitcase, checked the frizzen, and slipped it beneath the pillow on the bed, then straightened the large comforter. Last, he picked a metal box with a lock from one of the suitcases and slipped it beneath his undergarments in the dresser drawer. Finished unpacking, he untied his necktie, hung it with his coat, rolled up his sleeves, and lay down on the bed to rest and consider what he had seen of New Orleans.

At six o'clock he walked back down the stairs into the huge parlor, to the desk. Matsie appeared from a door to his right.

"Yes?" she asked. "Is there something else?"

"I am to meet a man here. A Mister Ingersol. Amos Ingersol. Is he lodged here?"

Her brow knitted for a moment in thought. "Ingersol? No, but he comes here often."

"Can you tell me how I might find him?"

She pointed. "He has an office down the street. You'll find his name—"

A strong voice boomed from behind. "Mister Hickman? Are you Mister Hickman?"

Hickman swung around. "Mister Ingersol?"

"Yes." Ingersol, short, round-faced, sagging jowls, large, flat nose, thrust out a small, thick hand, and Hickman felt the power as he seized it. "I am delighted to finally meet you," Ingersol continued. "Been here long?"

Hickman studied the shorter man as he answered. "Arrived earlier this afternoon."

Ingersol gestured with his thumb over his shoulder. "My business office is just up the street. Would you care to accompany me there? Have you had supper?"

"No."

"Then you shall be my guest, sir. There is a fine restaurant just across the plaza. French. Excellent cuisine! Do you enjoy French cuisine?"

They walked across the cobblestones to sit in an open-air patio beneath a vine-covered portico and placed their orders. The swordfish was baked to perfection and covered with thick sauce that hinted of garlic, the mix of petite peas and diced new potatoes was drowned in creamed gravy, and the chocolate éclair was superb. The men exchanged small talk as they ate, each smiling amiably while he shrewdly studied the other as twilight settled into dusk. Candles and lanterns were lit to cast the dining area in a warm, golden glow. Ingersol wiped his mouth with his napkin, set his knife and fork clattering on his porcelain plate, leaned back, patted his well-padded paunch, and smiled.

"That will pass as a supper. Cigar?" he asked.

Hickman declined.

"Mind if I smoke?"

"Not at all."

Ingersol drew a cigar from his inside coat pocket, bit off the end, thrust it into his mouth and rolled it against his tongue, then leaned forward to light it from the candle on their table. With a cloud of gray-white smoke rising, he settled back in his chair.

"Coffee? Tea?"

Hickman shook his head. "I'm at my limit. The meal was delicious."

Ingersol worked on his cigar, and with his head wreathed in smoke he puckered for a moment while his eyes became serious.

"As I recall, you were interested in some merchandise, and it led you to me. I presume you still have an interest."

"I do."

Ingersol looked at his cigar, knocked its ash onto his plate, and went on. "How many?"

"Twelve."

"All male?"

"Yes. Young. In good health."

"Premium stock. Twelve, then?"

"Yes."

Ingersol slowly shook his head. "There are not that many for sale in the entire city, right at this moment. Nor can I predict when there will be. If you want three, perhaps four, I can provide them."

Hickman leaned forward, and there was a slight cutting edge in his voice. "I believe our correspondence called for twelve. Did it not?"

"Now that you mention it. What price are you prepared to pay?"

"Three hundred. The price stated in your letter."

Again Ingersol shook his head. "The market has changed. Prime males are drawing five hundred on the auction blocks, anywhere in the city. Partly because they are hard to find. The demand has gone up. I have standing orders for more than I can get."

Hickman placed his hands on the tablecloth, palms down. "Your letter said twelve, three hundred each. I have it in my room."

Ingersol drew on his cigar, then stared at the ash clinging to the end. "That was then. This is now."

Hickman's voice was brittle. "I've come from Massachusetts on the strength of your letter. Twelve. Three hundred dollars each, payable in cash. Upon arrival. I'm here with the cash."

For several seconds Ingersol studied the tablecloth, then his cigar, and finally raised his eyes. "Tell you what I think I can do. The public auctions won't have enough, and the price will be too high." He locked eyes with Hickman. "But there are other places I know of—have connections."

Instantly Hickman came to an intense focus. "Such as?"

Ingersol glanced both directions. "Take a walk with me. To my office. We can be there in five minutes."

The streets were dark, with lamps and lanterns showing in nearly every window of the buildings, jammed together. Costumes of every description were evident in the patches of light as people of every age— some toothless and bent with age, others just children—came and went, laughing, cursing, calling. Ingersol worked through the mix, stopped at a door with the legend INGERSOL painted on a sign beside the door, with the single word MERCHANT beneath. He thrust the cigar between his teeth, fumbled for a large key, opened the door, lighted a lamp, set it on a table, and gestured to Hickman to sit.

In the yellow lamplight that cast long, misshapen shadows on the old, plain walls, Ingersol leaned forward and tapped the tabletop with one finger. His voice was intense, quiet.

"There are places to get what you want. Not the public auctions." He paused, waiting to see if Hickman understood. Hickman did, and Ingersol went on.

"Four, five years ago, two brothers arrived here. French. Capable men. They made . . . arrangements . . . to acquire goods. Quality goods. All sorts. Silks, porcelains, spices, silverwork—all prime. Where and how they acquire these goods is a matter of interest, but no one around here cares to pursue that question."

Again Ingersol paused while he studied Hickman's face, searching for understanding.

Hickman nodded, and Ingersol went on.

"You're looking for twelve prime male slaves. It is probable these brothers have them, or can get them. You will have to pay more than three hundred dollars each, but not five hundred. I can make the connection for you."

"Their names? The brothers?"

Ingersol hesitated for a moment. "Lafitte. Jean and Pierre Lafitte. Businessmen."

Hickman studied Ingersol for a time before he said quietly, "The pirates?"

Ingersol shook his head. "Not pirates. Corsairs. They carry Spanish letters of marque from Colombia. They can legally seize ships flying foreign flags on the high seas and claim them as prizes." He paused for a time before he concluded. "They have never taken an American ship. Swear they never will. Seizing ships is not their general business."

Hickman asked, "What is?"

"They buy and sell anything, including slaves. No one asks how their suppliers get the merchandise. They've made fifty, maybe a hundred, merchants in this city rich. Their . . . enterprise . . . provides the base for a great deal of the growth and wealth in this city. The brothers are fair in their dealings. Men of their word. Trusted. Well thought of. I believe most people in this city would take their side if anyone tried to . . . disrupt . . . their business."

Hickman sat back in his chair and for a time stared at his hands, folded on the table. "Where do they live? How long to contact them?"

"They live here in town. In a little home. And they have a blacksmith shop. One contacts them through the blacksmith shop."

"When? How?"

Ingersol smiled. "Tomorrow, if you like. I can take you there."

"What time?"

"Tomorrow morning I will call for you at your room at Absinthe House at eight o'clock. We will have breakfast and then we will go to the blacksmith shop."

It rained heavily in the night, then stopped, and the heavens cleared. At eight o'clock the rap came at Hickman's door and Ingersol stood waiting. Outside, the streets were a quagmire of mud and humidity, with steam rising from the puddles under the hot morning sun. The trees and houses sparkled with droplets of clinging water. The two men stepped into Ingersol's waiting coach, and the old, round-shouldered driver gigged the horse into motion through the streets where the crush of people picked their way through the morass. They stopped at an open-air café for breakfast, then returned to the waiting coach.

They passed an ordinary cottage on a corner and Ingersol pointed. "The Lafitte home." Hickman studied the plain walls and thatched roof as they passed and was aware of a rather tall, dark, beautiful woman standing partially hidden in the open doorway. The coach rolled on until the driver pulled it to a stop before a building on a corner with but one street marking: Saint Philip Street. There was a huge door standing open, and another smaller one, closed. The two men stepped from the coach and Ingersol led his client into the shade of the large, single, dirt-floored room. The walls were lined with horseshoes and the clutter of metal workings of every description, some hung on pegs or stored in bins, some thrown on the floor at random. Central to the chamber was a huge brick forge, with a black man pumping a wheezing leather bellows to feed the white-hot fire, while he held a large calked horseshoe with tongs, carefully watching the black iron change to red, then yellow. In one corner stood a two-thousand-pound Percheron draft horse, skittish, stamping its feet that showed three new shoes. Hickman's mouth sagged open for a moment. The blacksmith was easily seven feet tall, built strong, thick in the shoulders and neck and arms. Hickman estimated his bulk at close to 400 pounds. The man glanced at Ingersol, then Hickman, then back to Ingersol.

"Need somethin', Mister Ingersol?" His voice was deep, resonant.

Ingersol said, "Thiac, this is Mister Hickman. He wishes to see Mister Lafitte."

The giant set the horseshoe in the fire and wiped his hands on his worn leather apron. "'Bout what?"

"A purchase."

"Of what?"

"Goods. Black goods."

Thiac studied Hickman, head to toe. "You the law?"

Hickman snorted. "No."

"Got money?"

"Yes." Hickman's voice became testy. "What's this all about? All these questions?"

Thiac used the tongs to seize the white-hot horseshoe and spoke to Ingersol as he reached for his smithy hammer. "Tomorra afternoon. Lafitte's house. You know where."

Ingersol nodded and turned on his heel to lead Hickman back to the street. He stopped beside his waiting coach. "That's Thiac. A legitimate smithy who handles contacts for Lafitte. He's had his trouble with the law, which is why he inquired of you. I'll take you to Lafitte's house tomorrow."

The coach swayed on its leathers as they climbed in, and the driver put it into motion in the mud of the crowded street. Ingersol leaned back, casually watching the kaleidoscope of people and dress and merchandise as the carriage moved along. He turned to Hickman.

"You have other business today?"

"Yes. A few matters I must take care of."

"Supper tonight?"

"I have an engagement. But I thank you for the invitation."

Ingersol grinned. "French, Creole, Spanish, or quadroon?"

"Neither."

"White! Now that's a novelty. A rare chance to dine with one of our Creole beauties, and you choose white!"

Hickman said nothing, and for a time they rolled on with the ground mist disappearing as the sun dried the streets. The driver stopped at the Absinthe House, Hickman shook Ingersol's hand, and Ingersol leaned forward as the New Englander stepped down.

"I will pick you up here tomorrow around two o'clock."

"I'll be waiting."

"May I offer you the services of my coach this afternoon or this evening, to keep your engagement?"

Hickman reflected for a moment. "Thanks for the offer, but I don't yet know how long I will be. I'll see you tomorrow."

Hickman took his midday meal at a small restaurant near the Absinthe House, then hailed a passing hack.

"Take me to the governor's mansion," he told the driver, who looked at him quizzically, shrugged, and snapped his whip over the withers of his bay horse. For a time he worked his way through the core of the city, then on out to the northeastern fringe where he stopped before a sizeable mansion set back from the road. Hickman paid him, then walked to the great double doors beneath the six-column portico, and rapped with the huge brass door-knocker. Moments later it was opened by a bent, elderly black man in a black suit with white knee-length stockings and white lace at the throat and wrists.

"Sir?" the man said.

"I have an appointment with Governor Claiborne."

"Come in. Your name?"

"Markus E. Hickman."

"I'll tell the governor you have arrived."

The servant's heels clicked as he walked down a long, broad hall to his right, to the second door. Hickman looked about the spacious room at the appointments, the old walls, the traditional staircase against one wall, the paintings of river scenes and of Creole celebrations. The servant emerged again into the hall and came tap-tapping back to face Hickman.

"The governor will see you now. May I have your hat, sir? Please follow me."

Hickman surrendered his hat and fell in behind the servant, remembering. *This is W. C. C. Claiborne—appointed territorial governor by Jefferson after we bought Louisiana—1803—a Virginian like Jefferson—family wealthy—educated—gentleman—politician—married a Creole woman—unable to unify New Orleans.*

Hickman stepped into the governor's inner office and closed the door. Across the room, behind a great, ornately carved French desk, Claiborne rose. He was a sparse man, with a demeanor that was nearly apologetic. His face was thin, with a long, aquiline nose. He walked around the desk and offered his hand. Hickman took it.

"Governor, I thank you for allowing me some time."

"Not at all. Be seated." His voice was high, with the soft drawl of Southern men of breeding.

They took seats on either side of a round table before a window and for a moment Hickman glanced about the room. One wall was shelved and filled with books. On a second wall hung a great painting of New Orleans in 1762, the year the French surrendered all claims to the United States to the British. The lamps in the room were ornate, the furniture leather upholstered, old, cared for.

Claiborne continued. "I received your letter. You represent a business firm in Massachusetts?"

"Yes. Hawkins and Delafield." Hickman handed him papers, and Claiborne peered at them for several seconds. They were official, under the seal of the city of Boston. Claiborne handed them back to Hickman, and Hickman continued. "We're investigating markets here in New Orleans. We concluded we should inquire what we're getting into here. You have a rather . . . unique city."

There was a wistful, conflicted twist in Claiborne's smile. "Like none other in the world. What, specifically, can I help you with?"

"Am I to understand that the merchandise being sold at the public auctions could be stolen? Booty taken by pirates and corsairs?"

Claiborne's answer was instant. "A great share of it, yes."

"The rightful owners allow this to go on?" Hickman's eyes were boring in.

Claiborne became defensive. His voice rose, and his gestures became exaggerated. "A long time ago they tried to stop it. Many disappeared and were never heard from again. Since I was appointed governor I have done everything in my power to correct it, but I tell you, sir, as I have told President Jefferson repeatedly, if the United States wants to rid New Orleans of the illegality and vice that is all around us, it will have to send an army and either imprison or drive out or eliminate about two-thirds of the population. The Almighty knows I've tried. Oh, how I've tried."

"That bad?" Hickman's voice sounded in disbelief.

"No! Worse! Be my guest for six months, and then tell me what to do. I would be forever in your debt."

For a time Hickman sat staring at Claiborne, working with his thoughts. "We have heard rumor that the British are taking an unhealthy interest in New Orleans. This is American territory. Have you had any indication the British might eventually try to take it?"

"Yes. I am convinced that one day—probably soon—they will send their military. I think they intend taking New Orleans and using it as a base to stop the westward movement of our people. I think they will try using the Indian tribes to do it."

"Do you have any hard evidence of that? Anything in writing?"

"Not yet. I can only tell you each day there are a few more British redcoats in our streets, and they are becoming insolent. Domineering."

"Are the British interested in the commercial trade that goes on here?"

"Extremely. The New Orleans harbor is probably the chief seaport in southwest America right now." Claiborne reached to open a large ledger, selected a page, traced a few lines with a finger, then raised his eyes to Hickman. "The last figures we have are nearly five years old now." He began to read. "At that time the annual export was about two million dollars, and the import was about two and one half million. Thirty-four thousand bales of cotton. Nearly five thousand hogsheads of sugar. Two thousand barrels of molasses. Rice. Peltries. Indigo. Lumber, about half a million. Fifty thousand barrels of flour. Three thousand barrels of beef and pork. A thousand tons of tobacco. Corn. Butter. Hams. Meal. Lard. Beans. Hides. Staves. Cordage." Claiborne paused to order his thoughts. "Yes, Mister Hickman. The British covet that commerce. Highly."

Hickman stared at his hands for a time. "One more thing. The Lafitte brothers. Pierre and Jean. Do they have an organization that deals in merchandise taken by pirates? Buying and selling?"

"The answer is yes. I've done all I can to stop those two. They came from the West Indies in about 1803, but are clearly French by birth and upbringing. Expert swordsmen. Dead shots. Charming. Handsome. They are insulted when called pirates and quick to declare they are honorable corsairs, authorized by letters of marque from the state of Colombia in South America. I've had them brought before me. They swear they have never bothered an American ship, and I can find no one to claim the contrary. It is an open fact they buy from pirates and sell to legitimate merchants. They have brought wealth and success and growth to New Orleans through their illegal dealings."

Claiborne leaned forward, eyes piercing. "They have made a hundred men wealthy in this town. They're generous with the poor. Common with common people, superior with the elite. I've threatened to drive them and their underground network out of New Orleans, but I tell you, Mister Hickman, if I tried it, there would be a bloody revolt. If they were eliminated, New Orleans would suffer a terrible decline. Perhaps fatal. The Lafitte brothers are admired by just about everyone."

Hickman slowly leaned back. "The Lafittes are the real power in this city?"

"From here to the Gulf of Mexico. Their organization—if you can call it that—is based at a place called Barataria, south, where the

Mississippi reaches the gulf. There are hundreds of islands down there, and only those who know the channels and the twists and turns dare venture. The Lafitte brothers control the passages one must use to get from the gulf to here, and no one passes without their notice and permission."

"Has anyone tried?"

"Yes. Most were never heard from again."

"Have you informed President Jefferson or Mister Madison of all this?"

Claiborne closed the ledger and opened a file on one corner of his desk. "Oh, indeed I have! Within months of my arrival I informed them in terms that cannot be misunderstood. Here. Read my copy of this letter. Notice the date."

Hickman turned the file and read aloud.

"Dated January 10, 1804.

"My Dear Mister Secretary:

"The credulity of the people is only equaled by their ignorance; and a virtuous magistrate, resting entirely for support on the suffrages and good will of his fellow citizens in this quarter, would at any time be exposed to immediate ruin by the machinations of a few base individuals, who with some exertion and address might make the people think and act against their interests. The population is composed of so heterogeneous a mass, such prejudices exist, and there are so many different interests to reconcile, that I fear no administration or form of government can give general satisfaction."

Hickman stopped and Claiborne exclaimed, "Can it be any clearer? And in the four years since that writing, things have not changed. If anything, they have become worse."

Hickman bowed his head in deep thought before he spoke. "I see." He shifted his weight forward in the chair. "Governor, I am indebted to you for your time. You've answered my questions. It now remains to be seen what comes of all this."

The two men rose, and Claiborne walked Hickman to the door. "Should your company decide to seek markets here, will you notify me? I will need your opinion on some things after you've been here a while."

"I will be happy to do so. Again, thank you for your time and advice."

The men shook hands, and Hickman walked down the polished hallway, nodded to the servant as he reached the door, accepted his hat, and stepped out into the hot, bright sunshine and the streets and the drying mud. He hailed a hack, gave orders, climbed in, and leaned back, absorbed in thought. The ride back to the Absinthe House was noisy and slow. He paid the hack driver and walked through the expansive courtyard into the parlor, still deep in thought. He nodded to Matsie at the desk and climbed the stairs to the second floor. Casually he noticed two men approaching in the hallway and nodded a greeting. One was slender, dressed as a businessman, the other shorter, burly, in clothes of the street, clearly of mixed blood. They were six feet from him when Hickman saw the small metal box tucked under the arm of the shorter man—the metal box that should have been in the dresser drawer in his room. He stepped directly into their path and stopped, feet spread slightly, arms loose at his sides, and spoke in a quiet, measured voice.

"Sir, I believe that box belongs to me."

The next five seconds were a blur. The short man's free hand disappeared inside his tunic and Hickman saw the flash of the blade of a dagger as he pulled it out. Hickman's right fist caught him flush on the point of his chin, and the man fell over backwards, rolling, his badly broken jaw dangling. The metal box clattered onto the hardwood floor, and the knife skittered away as the second man jerked open his coat to grasp the handle of a pistol. Before he could aim and fire, Hickman's left hand struck him just above his ear and he hit the wall with his knees sagging. To keep him from falling to the floor, Hickman grabbed his shirtfront and slammed him against the wall.

"Can you hear me?" Hickman rasped through gritted teeth.

The man stared through glazed eyes, unable to form an answer.

"Can you hear me?" Hickman repeated.

The words came slow and slurred. "I hear you."

"Who sent you?"

"No one."

Hickman's eyes were points of disciplined light, and he slammed the man into the wall again. "Who sent you?" he demanded.

The man's eyes cleared. "No one. Kill me if you want. I have nothing more to say."

Hickman released the man and picked up the pistol from the floor. "This is also my pistol," he exclaimed and thrust it into his waistband. He grasped the front of the burly man's tunic and hauled him to his feet. The man's eyes were flat, dazed, his legs wobbly. Hickman shoved him into the taller man and picked up the knife from the floor, then the metal box.

"Stand where you are until I can get a constable. Do you understand?"

A hall door opened to Hickman's left, and he partially turned toward it, instantly alert. A head appeared, there was a gasp as the eyes opened wide, and the head disappeared as the door slammed shut. The creaking of the staircase from the lower floor brought them all around, and Matsie appeared with two men close behind. She quickly took in the scene—the knife and the metal box and the two men cowering against the wall—and in the moment of understanding her hand flew to her mouth.

"Thieves?" she blurted, staring at Hickman.

"Yes."

"Anyone hurt?"

Hickman pointed. "I think his jaw is broken."

"He needs a doctor."

"In due time. We need a constable first. Know either one of them?"

She looked closely at the two, then shook her head. "There's men talked about in the streets. Thieves. Watch for rich folks and steals from them. They must be two of them."

"Did they come in through the parlor?"

"I was at the desk. They didn't come through."

"You have a back door?"

"Yes."

"They were in my room. How did they get a key?"

"Not from me."

Doors up and down the hall opened, and people cautiously stepped out, wide-eyed, silently asking the question. Hickman said, "We've had an accident. It's taken care of. Sorry for the disturbance."

Matsie gestured to her two men and they seized the thieves and started for the staircase while she followed Hickman to his room. He used his key, and they stepped inside and stopped short. The room was in shambles. The bed had been stripped and the mattress thrown aside. Clothing from the wardrobe and the dresser was scattered at random. Even the faded paintings had been pulled from the walls and flung to the floor. The porcelain basin and pitcher were in one corner, in pieces.

"Oh, my," Matsie murmured. "Oh, my." She turned to Hickman, eyes flashing, and he saw her blood was up. "I'll send someone to help straighten," she said. "You intend bringin' charges against these men? I am. Lookit this mess. Them two is gonna pay for this, one way or another. Why, this happen agin, and the Absinthe House will suffer. People ain't comin' to no hostel to be robbed. I'm chargin' these men! You want a different room 'til this one's fixed up?"

"No. It won't take long."

She turned, then stopped. "Someone'll be here shortly. Now, you don't put yourself out none. We'll take care of this." She put her hands on her broad hips and shook her head once more. "My, oh my, oh my!" She was still shaking her head when she disappeared through the door, then reappeared. "One more thing," she said, "'bout the festival tonight in the courtyard. Creole. Celebrating something—I don't know what. Doesn't take much for them to find somethin' to celebrate. Violins and coronets and dancin.' It'll be noisy and colorful but harmless. Might go on half the night. Wide open—you'd be welcome. Might be real entertaining. Thought you should know."

New Orleans was in deep dusk when men of every race and color, in clean shirts with lacy fronts and light colored trousers, and women of every blood, wearing dresses of all colors and descriptions, began gathering in the huge courtyard beneath Hickman's balcony. Japanese lanterns hung from the magnolia and orange trees were lit, and tables and chairs were set up. In the pale yellow light-and-shadow mosaic cast by the lanterns, musicians came with violins and coronets and castanets and maracas and flutes and small drums with pigskin drumheads. Huge guitars strummed. They tuned their instruments, and the music began. From his window Hickman listened to the wild syncopations and felt the allure of the driving rhythms and exotic melodies that spoke of far places and of people who lived in a different world. Dancers paired, and the courtyard filled with color and movement. Tall, dark bottles of wine and stemmed glasses were brought to the tables. Talk became loud, heady, and laughter rang.

On an impulse, Hickman turned from his window. In spite of the heat, he shrugged into his coat and left his room to descend the stairs, slowing as he passed from the parlor into the courtyard. The fragrance of the magnolias and orange trees was sweet, and men nodded their greeting while women with long, black, brushed hair ducked their heads to look at him from beneath thick, black lashes, and raise one eyebrow to smile at him. He took a seat, alone, at a small table in a corner of the courtyard and ignored the bottle and glass as he studied the celebrants. Blacks were stomping their feet in rhythm, gesticulating wildly with their hands to the beat of the music, while Creoles were writhing, heads thrown forward and back, arms in the air. The French were caught up in the intricacies of their native quadrilles, while the Spanish, hands on hips and feet flashing, were showing the hot passion of their native land.

Hickman let his thoughts run. *Claiborne was right—no city like this in the world—so many different cultures—forget unity.*

He shifted his feet and his thoughts ran on. *Fascinating—what is it that draws?—the disunity?—one of everything?—what is it?*

A familiar voice from his right brought him around to face Amos Ingersol with his cigar clenched between his teeth. He took it between two fingers before he spoke.

"Mister Hickman! I didn't expect you to attend a celebration like this. Did you finish your business of the day?"

Hickman gestured and Ingersol sat down, facing him.

"Yes."

"Successfully, I trust."

"Yes. In large part, at least."

Ingersol poured wine. "I heard about your . . . experience. Inside, this afternoon."

"You mean those two thieves?"

"Yes. You're a marked man, you know."

Hickman raised an eyebrow. "Marked? Marked how?"

"You broke Mister Potter's jaw, and knocked Mister Horne senseless. Word gets around. People know who you are. For better or worse." Ingersol laughed and sipped at his wine.

"Potter and Horne? Are those their names?"

"Horne does their thinking. Potter carries the knife. Local hoodlums. Been in trouble before, but no one ever caught them in the act. And no one ever disabled them in two blows. Yes, sir, you're a marked man. Where did you learn to use your fists like that?"

Hickman ignored the question. "Should I be worried? Where are they now?"

"Won't need to worry for a while. They're both in jail. Potter's jaw is wired shut. If Matsie inside"—he gestured toward the doors leading into the building—"has her way, they won't be getting out for years."

"What caused them to break into my room? Why me?"

"They watch the blacksmith shop. They concluded you were a businessman looking for the LaFitte brothers. If you were, they knew you'd have money. They followed you."

"How did they get into my room?"

"Picked the lock. Horne can do that in about ten seconds."

"Why hasn't the law put them away long before now?"

"Which law? United States law? French? Spanish? Creole? None of them are capable."

Hickman reflected for a time. "Many more like them around? Those thieves?"

"We've got at least one of everything here in New Orleans. Their kind? Hundreds." Ingersol drew on his cigar and blew smoke. He gestured broadly at the dancing throng. "Anyone here you want to meet?"

Hickman smiled. "I don't know a person here, outside of yourself."

Ingersol shrugged indifferently and rose and stretched. "Well, I've greeted all the right people here tonight—seen all I need. I think I'll go home. Nice seeing you. Pick you up at two o'clock tomorrow. I'll introduce you to the Lafitte brothers."

Hickman stood. "I think it is my bedtime, too. See you tomorrow."

In the wake of the fevered revelry, Hickman got precious little sleep. The dancing didn't even begin to wane until two o'clock in the morning, and it was five o'clock, with the eastern skyline showing the separation of earth from the heavens, before the last of the musicians packed their instruments and were gone. Still weary from lack of sleep, Hickman took his breakfast and midday meals at the little restaurant up the street. At two o'clock the Ingersol carriage squeaked to a halt before the huge gate into the Absinthe House courtyard, and Hickman took his place beside Ingersol. The carriage rolled on with Ingersol leaned back, his ever-present cigar clenched between his teeth, seemingly indifferent to the stifling midday heat and the usual press of people in the streets. They stopped before a modest cottage at the unmarked corner of an intersection, and as Ingersol stepped down he said to Hickman, "There will be a boy here—the child of a prior marriage of Pierre. The mother died. And there will be a woman—rather tall, quadroon Creole from Santo Domingo, beautiful. She is the house servant. Her name is Adelaide Maselari. She prefers to be called Maselari. She speaks little English."

The front door was standing open, and Ingersol rapped on the frame. A woman as tall as Ingersol was there in a moment. Her hair was long and black and made soft curls in the perspiration on her forehead. She was swarthy, dark-eyed, and utterly beautiful. Her modest dress was simple, and she wore no shoes.

The two men removed their hats and Ingersol spoke. "Good afternoon, Maselari." He gestured to Hickman. "This is Markus E. Hickman. Did Thiac make an appointment for us?"

The woman nodded and stepped back, gesturing, and the men entered the relative cool and the gloom of the small room. Hickman took note of the modest furnishings and appointments and peered out a window into the courtyard behind, where he could hear the rhythmic sounds of a saw. Maselari held up a finger and turned and disappeared. The sounds of the saw stopped, and the woman reappeared with two men following.

Given their resemblance to each other, Hickman knew instantly they were the brothers Lafitte, one of them noticeably older than the other. Both were six feet tall, each built well, strong, with a full head of dark hair that tended to curl. The older one was swarthy, the younger one somewhat lighter. Their eyes were dark, Roman noses, mouths generous, chins square. Their expressions were pleasant, innocent, and inquisitive. The older of the two rubbed sweating hands on his pant legs and wiped a sleeve across his dripping forehead, then thrust his hand to Ingersol. His voice was full, low, his accent French.

"Mister Ingersol, nice to see you again. Thiac was here."

Ingersol grasped his hand. "I am happy to see you again, Pierre. May I present Markus E. Hickman. He is here concerning business."

Pierre Lafitte offered his hand, and Hickman felt the raw power in the grip, and he saw the benign expression and sensed the dark eyes probing into him.

"I am privileged to meet you, Mister Lafitte."

"The privilege is mine. May I present my brother, Jean?"

The younger of the two men stepped forward, extended his hand, and bowed slightly from the hips in the best French tradition. "It is an honor to meet you," Jean Lafitte said. The accent was decidedly French, the voice low, vibrant.

Returning the man's firm grip, Hickman said, "The honor is mine, sir."

The expressions in the faces of the two brothers were open and friendly, but Hickman was aware that their every nerve was alive, probing, searching, and he was surprised as he calculated their ages—Jean perhaps less than thirty, Pierre edging more toward forty. Given their reputations, he had assumed they might be older than that.

Pierre gestured. "Here. Be seated. You must excuse our appearance. We were cutting wood. Would you care for some wine?"

When Hickman declined, Ingersol followed his lead, and they all sat down on modest, comfortable chairs around a table.

Pierre picked up the conversation. "I understand you've been here for a few days." His interest was genuine. "How do you like our city?"

Hickman smiled. "Like nothing I've ever seen."

Jean Lafitte smiled back. "It will possess you if you stay for a while. You are from the North?"

"Boston. Massachusetts."

"Ah, yes. I have never been there, but someday I shall visit."

"It would be my privilege to receive both of you. Show you my city."

"I thank you." Pierre's expression sobered. "You had a matter of business?"

"Yes. My company has need of twelve black men. Mister Ingersol informs me there are not that many available in New Orleans at this moment. He suggested you might be of help."

Pierre lowered his eyes for a moment and scratched at his sideburns. "What is your company?"

"Boston Mercantile, Incorporated." He drew the papers from his breast pocket. "These will explain."

For three minutes the brothers studied the papers. Boston Mercantile, Incorporated, was a legitimate Massachusetts corporation, verified by the seal of the State of Massachusetts and the signature of the secretary of the Department of Commerce. Pierre nodded and handed the papers back to Hickman.

"You say twelve? How soon?"

"When can you have them?" Hickman inquired.

"It is possible we have them now, but not here. Not in New Orleans."

Hickman waited while Pierre glanced at Jean, and in that brief, silent moment something passed between the brothers. Pierre turned back to Hickman.

"It will take two days for you to see them. One day going, one day returning. Do you wish to take the time?"

Hickman reflected for a moment. "May I ask where they are?"

Pierre hesitated for a moment. "Barataria. South of here."

Hickman maintained his casual appearance while his heart leaped. Barataria! The stronghold! The legend! The place where respectable corsairs and unrespectable buccaneers and some of the blackest cutthroat pirates in the world freely did millions of dollars in business with the Lafitte brothers. The name itself derived from the French word *barraterie* and translated into English implied theft and murder for plunder! The place he had come more than thirteen hundred miles to see!

Hickman smothered any reaction to the invitation, and said casually, "Would it be possible to bring them here?"

Hickman caught the flash of surprise in Jean, but did not look directly at him nor did he change expression as he waited.

Pierre answered, "It would be better if you went there. You can select the twelve you want."

Hickman cleared his throat. "What price?"

Pierre responded, "Four hundred each."

Hickman said, "I was told three hundred. I came prepared to pay three hundred."

Ingersol hastened to explain to Pierre, "I told him—that was the price seven weeks ago when there were slaves available in New Orleans."

Pierre's eyes narrowed at Hickman. "Markets and prices change. It is four hundred now."

Hickman countered, "And four weeks from now?"

Pierre smiled and shrugged. "Who knows? Supply and demand."

From the side, Jean inquired casually, "You have money with you?"

"No. Not here."

"In New Orleans?"

"Yes. In a safe place."

Pierre grinned. "In the little metal box?"

The question caught Hickman by surprise. "You know about that?"

Pierre chuckled. "It is common knowledge. The jaw was badly broken."

The four men laughed, and the tension eased for a moment. Hickman went on. "Do you accept credit?"

Jean replied. "Sadly, we cannot. Cash or gold." His face was casual; his eyes were not.

"I see. Then I cannot buy twelve slaves. I will have to get consent from my company. It will take at least four weeks for me to return to Boston and get the consent and the money."

Pierre tossed a hand in the air. "No matter. We can have them in four weeks." He started to rise, as though their business was done. Hickman raised a hand and Pierre settled.

"I will need to know where the slaves come from. It would be awkward if I were to deliver slaves to one of our clients only to find out they were stolen from him."

Pierre quickly responded, "We cannot tell you where they are from. We can only guarantee they were never owned by your client."

Hickman considered before he went on. "If I am to get authorization to pay four hundred dollars, I will have to report to my company that I have seen slaves of that quality. I will need to go to Barataria."

Silence held for a full five seconds before Pierre responded. "Mister Ingersol, are you available for the next two days?"

"I am."

"Then we will leave tomorrow morning at six o'clock. Is that agreeable?"

It was.

By six o'clock AM the top half of the sun had cleared the eastern rim of the world to cast long shadows westward when Jean Lafitte, Ingersol, and Hickman, dressed in loose white shirts and carrying their coats, stepped from a New Orleans dock into a large, flat-bottomed longboat and took their seats. Four silent black men with thick shoulders and muscled arms, stripped to the waist, sat in twos on either side of the boat with oars shipped, waiting. A fifth sat at the rear, arm resting on the tiller, a covered wooden box at his feet. On Lafitte's signal, the men sunk their oars into the muddy water and heaved into them to drive the boat away from the dock, out into the great Mississippi River. They felt the irresistible suck of the current swing the boat south, and with the oarsmen working in steady rhythm to keep the boat moving faster than the current, the man on the tiller brought her around, angling toward the center of the broad river, then due south, running strong. Within twenty minutes they had left the teeming docks of New Orleans behind and were moving downstream steadily, much faster than Hickman had imagined possible. He was much surprised that the shore had flattened to a gigantic, wet, level plain, with marsh grasses three feet higher than a man's head.

They passed bayous filled with what appeared to be stagnant water, and tiny lakes and small streams that emptied into the river. At noon Lafitte opened the wooden box and each man ate a lunch of bread and cooked shrimp and oranges. Small islands were everywhere. Palm and date trees stood high, and banana trees proliferated. Dangling from massive trees, webs of Spanish moss moved in the breeze. Water birds were everywhere—cranes with curled necks and matchstick legs, pelicans with their pouches on their chests, terns, seagulls, and flocks of macaws with plumage to challenge the rainbow. Insects buzzed and hummed as they rose in clouds with the passage of the boat. Crocodiles and caimans lay in the swamp grasses, unmoving, nearly invisible. Hickman studied the shores, suddenly realizing that he could not tell where land blended into marsh, and marsh into bayou. There was no clear demarcation to any of it. Lagoons and streams crossed and crisscrossed, turning, twisting back upon themselves, sometimes ending in blind cul-de-sacs that had swallowed up untold numbers of lost and unwary travelers. It came to Hickman why, and how, this place had been called "the trembling prairie." The blend of earth and water left almost nothing stable. The grasses and the trees could tremble in the wind and the storms and hurricanes that swept up regularly from the Gulf of Mexico.

Unpretentious two-room cottages began to appear in small clearings, half hidden among the cypress and palm and banana trees and the high swamp grass. There was no glass in the windows, only heavy batten blinds or shutters that could be closed against the pounding of rain and storms. Women were in the yards with children, pausing in their work to watch the boat pass. Some recognized Lafitte and raised a hand, and Lafitte waved back.

Hickman turned to Ingersol. "They live out here?"

"Yes. Been here for generations. Raise families who stay to raise their families. Fishermen, trappers, some smugglers, some outright pirates. They prefer it here. Total freedom. Responsible to no one for anything. They know these swamps and bayous like I know the streets of New Orleans. There are a hundred places they can hide within five minutes of their homes. They bring their hides or their shrimp or their stolen plunder up to New Orleans three, four times a year, buy what they need, and come back here."

By midafternoon the scent of salt sea became stronger and suddenly in the distance Hickman could see the green-blue of the open waters of the Gulf of Mexico. The coast broadened, and the islands grew larger, and the man on the tiller focused. Carefully he picked his way between the islands, following channels known only to a few, until he swung sharply to the west, into a large harbor, and before them was a cluster of small thatch-roofed cottages, gathered about one larger building that dominated. The longboat nudged into a low pier, where men of every blood and description came to tie it and stand waiting for their leader.

With every nerve alive to what he was seeing and hearing, Hickman followed Lafitte and Ingersol from the longboat onto the dock where the sweating men greeted Lafitte, and he slapped some of them on the back and returned the greetings before they all stepped back to let the small column of visitors file through to the big building. With its shutters open to facilitate a breeze, the dimly lighted, dirt-floored, single large room provided a welcome though slight respite from the unrelenting heat and humidity. There was one large, sturdy, scarred table close to one wall, with battered chairs surrounding it, a large desk in one corner, nine bunks in tiers of three against one wall, and a large wooden box in one corner. The strong odor of rum was everywhere, and Lafitte gestured and they all sat while he brought a large crockery jug of rum and three pewter mugs from the box. He poured two mugs full; Hickman declined.

For a few moments they sat quietly, Lafitte and Ingersol working on their rum, while they stopped perspiring and let their thoughts settle.

Then Lafitte stood. "I will return soon," he said and disappeared out into the dazzle of the late afternoon sunlight. In less than five minutes he returned to his chair and his half-empty mug of rum. He turned to Hickman.

"Soon my men will bring the Negroes for your inspection."

Within minutes Hickman heard the sound of men marching and the clank of metal on metal, and then a large, grizzled, bearded man appeared in the doorway. Lafitte led the others out into the yard where twelve tall, barefooted, well-muscled black men stood dressed only in frayed trousers that reached just below their knees. On the right ankle of each of them was an iron shackle, and a chain with heavy links bound all twelve of them together in a line. They stood silent, their defiant eyes shifting from Lafitte to Ingersol to Hickman.

Twelve men. Chained like animals. Bought like animals, and being inspected like animals to be sold like animals. Hickman bit down hard on the hot outrage that surged in his breast, and his hands trembled for a moment as he struggled to maintain an even expression on his face. He walked to the first man and looked into his face, then slowly walked down the line, then back, peering at each one, head to toe, front and back, looking for deformities that would limit the man's ability to work or diseases that could spread. He could see none. The men were all built strong—capable of the fourteen-hour days of backbreaking toil that would shorten their lives by twenty years.

Lafitte waited until Hickman finished his inspection, then asked, "They are suitable?"

Hickman shrugged indifferently. "They're acceptable."

Lafitte said, "You wish to have twelve such in four weeks, four hundred dollars American each? Delivered here?"

Hickman shook his head. "I must have consent of my company first. And we will need to take delivery in New Orleans."

Lafitte answered, "Then we will wait. If your company wishes to accept our terms, send a letter to Mister Ingersol. We will make delivery in New Orleans on the day you select. Agreed?"

Hickman reflected for a moment. "Agreed, provided the twelve have not previously been owned by any of our clients."

"That is guaranteed. These and fifty others come from the West Indies where they were born and raised for servitude. They have had but one owner. We know the man."

"Will you give me your written statement of that? Your word is good."

"I will."

"Done."

Lafitte bobbed his head and led the way back into the relative cool of the large building where the three of them sat back down at the table. Lafitte poured more rum, drank long, then went to the desk. Two minutes later he handed Hickman a written document.

"There is my statement of ownership of the slaves."

Hickman read the neat, scrolled handwriting and slipped it inside his shirt. "Thank you. May I inquire when we will begin the journey back to New Orleans?"

Lafitte smiled. "About four o'clock tomorrow morning the tides will come in, and we will ride them many miles back up the Mississippi. But tonight, we dine. My people have prepared a roast pig and sweet potatoes and some mangoes and papaya."

Dusk had settled when Lafitte led the way through the grasses and trees to a sandy clearing where twenty barefooted men had gathered around a fire pit. Firelight played off their faces and cast shadows into the gathering darkness. A small man with a huge beard and a deformed back slowly turned a spit on which a whole, wild pig had been skewered. Fat dripped from the blackened hulk to pop and sizzle in the fire. At Lafitte's arrival the men began digging into an earthen mound, removing steaming sweet potatoes they had buried over hot rocks at dawn, while others carried out a keg of rum and wooden cups and wooden plates, and still others brought out woven reed baskets filled with bananas and mangoes and papaya. The men used their belt knives to strip the hams and loins from the carcass, then the shoulders, and they sat cross-legged in the warm sand to eat it with their fingers with grease running into their beards and onto their bare chests. They broke open the steaming sweet potatoes and singed their lips and tongues eating the sweet flesh, and they dipped generous draughts of rum from the barrel.

When the eating and drinking finally slowed, the talk began, rough, raucous, between men who had seen and done the worst life can offer, and Hickman was surprised to see Lafitte talking, laughing, gesturing with his men, apparently carefree, as though he were one of them. Hickman sensed that among this gathering there was none who would yield his freedom, his independence, his fierce pride, to any other than Lafitte. It suddenly broke clear in Hickman's mind that if he had appeared here at Barataria alone, without the presence and the protection of Jean Lafitte, he would never have left alive. He remained silent, watching, listening, gauging, calculating, with the question foremost in his mind: *How has this man—less than thirty years of age—built this enterprise— and how has he taken command of such men as I see here?* He could only guess at the answer.

The moon had risen when the merriment dwindled, and it was approaching midnight when Lafitte and Ingersol and Hickman laid their heads on the pillows in their bunks inside the big house and drifted into sleep, stomachs full, weary from the long day.

Hickman awoke with the soft yellow light of a lantern casting misshapen shadows in the big room and Lafitte moving silently in his bare feet on the sandy floor. Hickman drew his watch from his trousers and turned the face to the light. It was half past three o'clock. Ingersol awakened with a start, and the three of them silently ate cold pork strips and mango, drank some tepid water, and with Lafitte leading, lantern held high, walked out into the black world of a moon already set and an overcast covering the vast expanse of stars. There was a fresh, light wind from the south, and Hickman smelled the coming storm. The oarsmen and the tiller were waiting in the boat, and the three men stepped off the dock into the longboat, rocking softly on the incoming tides. Hickman took his seat next to Ingersol in the midsection of the boat while Lafitte sat in the bow with the lantern. Between them the crew had mounted a mast with a furled sail. On Lafitte's signal, the oarsmen dug the oarblades into the black water and the boat drifted away from the dock. The tiller brought it around on a course due north, and two of the oarsmen shipped their oars long enough to unfurl the sail. It caught the south wind, popped and filled, and the boat sped north, pushed by the tides and the wind and the oarsmen.

The wind held and increased, and by five o'clock the rim of the world to their right, east, was separated from the dark heavens. By six o'clock the eastern horizon was a dull gray overcast, and due south, behind the boat, the deep purple of a storm coming in from the gulf was rising. Lafitte held his position in the bow, turning every few minutes, judging when the storm from behind would catch them. By ten o'clock the longboat was running before strong winds. The oarsmen had shipped their oars, unable to add to the speed. Every man on board was silently calculating how much time before they would have to beach the boat and wait out the storm. By eleven o'clock they saw the curtain of rain two miles behind, and forty minutes later the first huge drops came spattering. At noon, in a heavy downpour, Lafitte pointed, and the tiller leaned against the heavy oak handle, and the bow of the boat nosed to the right, toward shore and a small, abandoned cottage with the remains of a tiny dock on the river. With the boat tied to the rickety dock, the dripping men carried their wooden box inside the cottage and shared a lunch of cheese, oysters, steamed giant prawns, tough brown bread, and bananas, and waited. By one o'clock the overhead sun was a bright ball in the dwindling storm, and by half past one the wet, steaming world was sparkling under blue sky and a blazing sun.

The sun had set when they saw the harbor of New Orleans, and the lights of the city were beginning to wink on when they tied the longboat to a pier. The tired men stepped from the boat onto the old, worn planking, and Hickman turned to Lafitte.

"I thank you for your efforts and hospitality. I will write to Mister Ingersol as soon as my company has made a decision."

Lafitte smiled and bowed graciously. "I will be waiting."

They said their goodbyes and separated—Lafitte and his crew to his home, Ingersol to his, and Hickman back to Absinthe House. He took his supper alone and went to his bed to sleep the dreamless sleep of an exhausted man.

Morning found Hickman boarding a flatboat traveling north up the Mississippi, counting the days until he boarded a second flatboat moving northeast up the Ohio River, then on to the Delaware River, to Philadelphia. It was there he boarded a three-masted merchantman for the voyage down the Delaware to the Chesapeake Bay, out into the Atlantic, and north to Boston harbor. At noon, on the thirteenth day since leaving New Orleans, the big merchantman tied up to the Boston docks, and Markus E. Hickman walked down the gangplank with one suitcase in each hand into the familiar muddle of men and freight on the docks. He pushed his way through to the waterfront office with the sign on the door that read DUNSON & WEEMS, where he set one suitcase down long enough to open the door, picked it up, and walked into the office with the counter facing the door, and the six familiar desks behind, and the charts and maps on the walls.

Matthew Dunson and Billy Weems both raised their heads from the ledgers they were studying at their desks.

"Caleb! You're back!" Matthew exclaimed, rising to walk to the counter. "We were beginning to worry."

Caleb Dunson dropped the suitcases thumping on the floor as the two men reached him. "I was starting to worry a little myself."

Billy Weems, grinning, relief showing, asked, "How was it? Did you get what you went after? Anyone recognize you?"

Caleb nodded. "I think I got what Madison wants. I don't think anyone guessed I wasn't Markus E. Hickman."

"Lafitte? Barataria?"

"I was there. With Lafitte. Saw most of what was to be seen."

"The governor?"

"Spent an afternoon with him." Caleb glanced around the room. "Where is everybody?"

Matthew hooked a thumb over his shoulder. "Adam and John are delivering freight in Charleston. Jason's at the bank. Pettigrew's at home."

Caleb looked at Matthew. "Barbara and the children?"

"Fine. Checked with them every day. Annalee cut two more teeth. Anxious to have you home."

Billy interrupted. "How is it down there? As wild as we've heard?"

Caleb rolled his eyes and shook his head. "I don't know the words. I'll make up my written report for Madison. You'll read it all there."

"Lafitte," Billy continued. "What have we got there?"

"Two of them. Pierre, maybe thirty-six, and Jean, about thirty. Both capable. Dangerous." He drew the document Jean Lafitte had given from his pocket and tossed it on the counter. "Jean Lafitte guarantees twelve slaves at four hundred dollars each within the next four weeks. I have to write a letter to Ingersol telling him that Boston Mercantile has decided against paying that much. How long do you plan to keep Boston Mercantile alive as a corporation? You invented it just for this trip to New Orleans."

"We'll keep it as long as we need it to help Mister Madison," Matthew answered.

"Well, we don't need it any more for now," Caleb said. He hefted one suitcase onto the counter, opened it, and dug out the small metal box. "Here's the cash. Get it in the safe. It's all there, but there's a story." He pointed at the suitcases. "When I get home and unload these, I'll get them back to Hickman."

Billy asked, "What's the story? On the money box?"

Caleb exhaled a huge breath. "Two men tried to steal it."

Billy saw it coming and was grinning as he asked, "Where are they now?"

Caleb scratched at his chin. "I imagine they're taking the wires out of that one man's jaw about now. I don't know if the other one can think straight yet."

Billy laughed outright, and Matthew shook his head ruefully. "Caleb, when are you going to. . . ." He did not finish the sentence.

Caleb responded, "Well, now, don't jump to any conclusions. I met them in the hall at the boarding house and they had the money box. We had a brief discussion. I got the money box back and they went to jail.

Well, not exactly. They went to a doctor first, then jail. What would you have done? They had your money."

Matthew ducked his head to hide a grin and Billy laughed, then settled. "Did you have to buy the slaves?"

"No. When they raised the price from three hundred to four, I told them I couldn't do it without consent from Boston Mercantile. When I write to Ingersol, I'll tell him the hard-headed Yankee businessmen that run Boston Mercantile—which is you two—won't pay the higher price. The money's all there except expenses, and there's a list of what I had to spend." He stopped for a moment to gesture. "Anything happening around here I need to know?"

Matthew said, "No, business as usual."

Caleb grinned at them. "Then I think I'll get on home to Barbara and the children. Tell mother I'm back safe. Good to be home." He picked up the suitcases and walked back out into the sunlight and the dockhands and freight, worked his way west, and hailed a waiting hack.

Notes

The description of New Orleans in the time period in question, including the mix of Spanish, French, African-American, Native American, English, and American cultures, and many other nationalities, with the resulting new race called Creole, as well as the conditions in the streets, the cultural evolutions, the attitudes, the pirates, the black-market trade, and the wide-open auctions of slaves and all descriptions of merchandise taken by pirates on the high seas, is accurate. See Saxon, *Lafitte, the Pirate*, pp. 20–26. See page 23 for the list of stolen merchandise being sold in open auctions in the city, as set forth herein.

William C. C. Claiborne, a Virginian, was the first American sent to become territorial governor and bring law and order to New Orleans. The conditions he faced are as described herein, and the letter mentioned in this chapter dated January 10, 1804, is quoted verbatim. Governor Claiborne's wife was a beautiful Creole woman. See Saxon, *Lafitte, the Pirate*, pp. 22–23, 125.

The Lafitte brothers, Jean and Pierre, are accurately described herein, as are their business affairs. Barataria is accurately described. See Saxon, *Lafitte, the Pirate*, pp. 3–11, 34–43.

The old Absinthe House existed in New Orleans, as did the blacksmith shop of the Lafitte brothers and their cottage. See illustrations, Saxon, *Lafitte, the Pirate,* pp. 65, 8, 17.

Thiac, the huge African-American blacksmith and his part in the business affairs of the Lafitte brothers is accurately described herein. The tall, attractive, dusky-skinned woman described in the house of the Lafittes was named Adelaide Maselari, a woman brought with them from the West Indies. See Saxon, *Lafitte, the Pirate,* pp. 12–19.

Caleb Dunson is a fictional character.

Northeast Ohio Valley
Mid-October 1808

CHAPTER IV

*O*verhead, in deepening dusk, the night birds had begun
their silent, impossible pirouettes, taking invisible insects on the wing.
Squirrels and beady-eyed chipmunks with their winter hair coming thick
had gone to their lairs in the trees to escape the razor-sharp talons and
merciless beaks of great gray owls, and groundhogs had sought the safety
of their burrows, away from the coyotes and foxes. In the far distance an
owl spoke, and another answered. The crying of a great cat to the south
came echoing, so close to the sound of a human baby that it could
deceive experienced woodsmen. From the small streams and brooks that
worked their way down through the countless mountain ravines and valleys to the great Ohio River, and from the bogs and marshes, frogs began
their nightly songs.

Eli Stroud, tall, built strong, prominent nose and chin, regular features, long brown hair with streaks of gray held back by a buckskin tie,
glanced at the deep purple of the eastern rim of the world where the
evening star was faintly visible in the dying light of day. He was clad in a
buckskin Iroquois hunting shirt and fringed buckskin breeches that
reached past his ankles, partially covering his beaded moccasins. In his
right hand he carried a Pennsylvania long rifle. A rolled woolen blanket
was draped over his left shoulder, tied end to end on his right side, just
above the black tomahawk thrust through the broad leather weapons belt
about his middle. A knife in a beaded sheath was under the belt on his

left side. His powder horn and the leather pouch that held his shot and linen bullet-patches, and a small bag with cracked dried corn and chunks of dried fish and hardtack and salt hung on his left side on leather cords over his right shoulder.

Frost had come early in the fall, turning the woods into reds and yellows beyond imagination. Eli felt the chill coming in the night air, and the thought came, *more frost tonight.* He picked a place near a small brook where the deer tracks told him the water was safe to drink, and with flint and steel from his shot pouch kindled a small fire. With his rifle leaning against a tree, he gathered boughs for his bed and spread his blanket, and was on one knee beside the fire picking dried fish from his food bag when the sound of the frogs upstream stopped, then began again, first one, then another, and then many. He showed no sign of concern as he settled cross-legged beside his tiny fire and broke the fish between his fingers and put the first piece in his mouth. He sensed a silent movement in the forest upstream, to his left, and then another to his right, but still he gave no sign as he continued eating.

Scouts. Shawnee? Tecumseh's?

He finished the piece of fish, then for a time ground hardened kernels of corn between his teeth. In near total blackness he knelt beside the stream to dip cold sweet water with his hand and drink, then returned to the glowing coals of his tiny fire and covered them with dirt. With countless stars beginning to appear in the velvet blackness overhead, he unbuckled his weapons belt and reached for his rifle. For a long time he sat on his blanket with his rifle across his knees and his tomahawk loose at his side, unmoving, head tipped forward as he concentrated on the sounds of the night, waiting for an interruption that would tell him a human being was moving nearby. There was no interruption. With the moon rising over the northeastern rim, he lay down on his side with his rifle at hand, covered himself with his blanket, and within minutes was in the dreamless sleep of one who had covered fifty miles on foot since sunrise in the dense forest.

The morning star had faded and disappeared when he finished making a quarter-mile circle of his camp, rifle in hand, slowly picking his way through the knee-high forest undergrowth. Upstream he had found the bruised leaf of a wild cabbage and the faint impression made by a moccasin beneath it. Downstream were two moccasin imprints, close to the water.

Two. Moving north. Their village or their camp—whichever it is—can't be far. Tecumseh? Probably. With luck.

He took a trout from the stream with his hands and within twenty minutes cooked and ate it, and hung his rolled blanket over his shoulder. Sunrise found him three miles farther north, walking rapidly in crystal-clear sunlight, rifle held before him, ready, eyes moving constantly, watching for sign on the ground, concentrating on all movement and sound in the forest. The sun had not yet reached its zenith when he caught a flicker in the thick trees to his left and heard something brush against the undergrowth. Minutes later he sensed movement to his right.

It was high noon when the smell of cookfires reached him, and the two warriors who had been shadowing him finally showed themselves, one to the east, the other the west, both less than thirty yards away. They wore buckskins, and their hair was caught up in the swept-back pompadour of the Shawnee. Both men held their interval and said nothing, nor did he, as they moved on north.

The laughter of children and the ringing of axes cutting firewood reached him through the trees, and then he was out of the forest, into a large grassy meadow that bordered a clear, small lake, mirror-smooth in the still calmness of the day. It was not a permanent village with a great longhouse and dwellings in orderly rows for many families. Rather, it was a temporary village, with one small central building where government affairs and worship were conducted, and several lesser dwellings set randomly about it. Women and children moved among stew kettles hung above small fires on black iron chains suspended from smoke-blackened tripods. Some women were swinging axes, and they stopped to stare at the rare apparition of a white man in native Indian buckskins as he came into view from the forest. Responding to the village chatter, old men wrapped in blankets stepped from the dwellings into the sunlight to study him. A few held weapons. The shouts of the children at their games quieted, and some of them ran to stand beside or behind their mothers, waiting for them to bark the orders that would send them running if the intruder was a foe. Half a dozen deer hides were randomly stretched and staked to cure in the sun, prior to being scraped clean of hair and worked until soft, to become shirts, leggings, and dresses. The thick, tough hide of a bull elk lay nearby, to be cut into soles for moccasins. Two deer carcasses hung head-down from tripods, ready to be cut into thin strips of meat and hung on racks to be dried for winter. The golden pelt of a cougar was pegged to the ground, drying to become a blanket for cold nights. A great fur from a black bear was also being stretched in the sun. It would be a bed against the freeze of winter. Village dogs roamed, some gnawing on bones of animal carcasses. The odors of wild meat and hides, wood smoke, and cooking food hung in the still air.

Eli raised his hands to hold his rifle high above his head as he came on with the two scouts flanking him all the way. Women clad in one-piece doeskin garments that reached the tops of their moccasins, with long black hair braided down their backs, slowly closed in behind him, with the children following, intrigued, timid, wondering. He walked without hesitating to the larger building in the center of the clearing and stopped ten feet from the dark doorway. A man bent with age, and wrapped in a blanket, shuffled out into the bright sunlight. His face was craggy and pock-marked, and his long gray hair was in braids down his back. He stopped six feet in front of Eli and for several seconds silently studied him with watery black eyes. Many faces showed surprise as Eli spoke to him in the Shawnee dialect.

"I am Eli Stroud. I come in peace." He lowered his rifle. "I have traveled many days—to talk with the great Tecumseh and his brother Tenskwatawa."

He had called the name of Tecumseh's brother correctly, and he paused to let the startled expressions pass from the faces nearest him. Then he continued. "I come with a message from the American father far to the east. It is my hope that Tecumseh is in this village. I am honored if he will see me."

The old man answered in a voice raspy with age. The bitterness and hostility were like something alive.

"I know who you are. I was at Fallen Timbers and saw you there. I was at Greenville with all the others. Wyandot, Ojibwa, Ottawa, Miami, Delaware, Wea, Potawatomi—and the rest—when the chiefs—fourteen of them—all signed the paper with your great white father and gave to him our land south of the river. The Ohio. I saw you there. We gave you our land. What did you give us in return? Trinkets and rum and the white man's disease that killed many of us and left my face as you see it now. Marked forever with pits. I know who you are."

Eli answered. "If you were at Fallen Timbers, then you know that I did not take arms against your people. You know that it was I who stood between your people and the white people and that I tried to get them to sit down at a council of peace and come to a fair agreement regarding the land. Do you remember?"

"I remember that the white men would not council. Instead they shot at us. If you did not shoot at us, I did not know that."

"Tecumseh knows. You will ask him. With great respect I ask if he is here."

For a long time the old, watery, black eyes peered up into Eli's face before the answer came. "He is here. Inside."

"Will he see me?"

"He will. We have known of your coming for many days. Ojibwa and Miami messengers said you have visited their camps inquiring of many things. You inquired to find Tecumseh. We sent scouts to find you and protect you until you arrived." The old man turned and gestured. "Tecumseh is inside, waiting. You will follow me."

He turned on his heel and Eli ducked to follow him through the doorway into the dimness inside the windowless building. A fire burned in a pit at the center of the room, with the smoke rising in a straight line to disappear through a hole cut in the roof. Eli handed his rifle and tomahawk and belt knife to a man standing beside the door, then faced four men seated cross-legged on thick pelts of forest animals and waited while the old man took his place among them. They were dressed in fringed buckskins that were decorated with quills and beadwork and had blankets gathered about their shoulders—crimson blankets supplied them by the British. Half a dozen other men stood in the gloom away from the fire, near the walls, motionless, watching and listening. The only light in the room came from the doorway, the fire, and the single shaft of sunlight streaming through the hole in the roof, partially blocked by the escaping smoke.

The man in the middle of those seated stood and faced Eli. Tecumseh was slender, of average height, with coppery skin and a sharp face and piercing black eyes. His nose was long and pointed, as was his chin, and his voice was high and resonant.

"Eli Stroud. Informants told me of your coming many days ago. I sent two of my warriors to protect you. You are welcome here, but you have no promise of safety outside my camp."

Eli nodded. "I understand. I thank you for your protection and for allowing me to speak to you." He peered down at the man on the right of Tecumseh, still seated. "I am honored that your brother has joined in this meeting."

Tecumseh glanced down at his brother, who briefly bowed his head to Eli but said nothing, and Tecumseh spoke. "Tenskwatawa. The Prophet. You will remember the method by which he earned his title, 'The Prophet'? Two summers since?"

"I remember."

Tecumseh referred to the strange, startling event that had established him as a great leader of his people, and his brother as a great religious mystic who could command the sun and the moon and stars. It occurred two years earlier. William Henry Harrison, then the American governor of the Ohio Territory, was mortally afraid of Tecumseh, whom he saw as a threat and considered the greatest living Indian on the American continent. In a desperate effort to discredit Tecumseh, along with his brother Tenskwatawa, Harrison had thrown down a challenge. If Tecumseh was as powerful as his reputation implied, he could make proof of it by commanding the sun to stand still and the moon to change course. If he failed, they would be revealed for the frauds they were. It was known that Tenskwatawa had, to that point, lived the life of a wastrel, given to drunkenness and depravity. Governor Harrison saw no way his scheme could fail. But what he did not know was that many American scientists, and many Indians who had studied the heavens, were aware that an eclipse of the sun was to shortly occur. With that knowledge, Tecumseh accepted Harrison's challenge. He privately tore into his brother, condemning his profligate life, forbidding him the evils of rum and alcohol, ordering him to mend his ways or suffer exile. He carefully and patiently trained him for a performance that was calculated to utterly destroy the credibility of Harrison, and sent word to everyone within fifty miles of the coming event. On June 16, 1806, a great audience gathered. At the right moment, Tecumseh produced his brother in the center of the huge gathering, and, true to the training by Tecumseh, Tenskwatawa raised both hands to the heavens, threw back his head, and shouted to the sun, "I command your light to dim. Let darkness fall on this land for a time! Let it begin NOW!"

The eclipse began and gradually the northeast American continent fell into a twilight as though in obedience to the command of Tenskwatawa. Wailing broke out among the awe-struck audience, both white man and Indian, and they stood frozen, terrified that they were doomed! The eclipse began to diminish and again Tenskwatawa raised his arms and shouted, "Let your light return to save our land!" Minutes later the country was once again in full sunshine.

Tenskwatawa instantly became "The Prophet," and the brothers became two of the most powerful Indians in the northeast. Governor William Harrison became an object of ridicule.

Eli nodded. "I know of it."

Tecumseh sat down in his place among the council and gestured, and Eli sat down, cross-legged, facing them, waiting to be invited to speak.

The flickering firelight reflected off the lines of the dark faces of the council members as Tecumseh opened the exchange.

"You have come far. You carry a message from your white father in the east?"

"I do." Eli drew the written paper, wrapped in oilskin, from inside his shirt and offered it to Tecumseh. With dramatic patience he unwrapped it, unfolded the document, and for a time read the writing. Tecumseh spoke enough English to engage in conversation, but he did not like it, nor could he read it well enough to understand all that James Madison had written and Thomas Jefferson had signed. After staring without full comprehension at the document, he rewrapped it and handed it back to Eli. When he spoke again it was in Shawnee, and all too well did Eli grasp the significance of the shift in language. He was being told, not so subtly, that Tecumseh was distancing himself from Thomas Jefferson, the United States, and Eli Stroud.

"Your white father has given you power to inquire for him. What do you wish to know?"

Eli saw the flat, dead look in the black eyes of Tecumseh, and those seated around him, and he saw the set look in their craggy faces, and he felt their bitter loathing reach across to him.

He came directly to it. "What is in the heart of Tecumseh? War, or peace, with the United States?"

He saw a flicker of surprise in the eyes of those facing him. They had expected him to be indirect, to circle the core of his reason for finding Tecumseh. His bluntness had tipped them slightly off balance.

Tecumseh considered his words before he replied. "It is in my heart to protect the land that has belonged to my people as far back as memory can go."

Instantly Eli realized Tecumseh was not going to give a direct answer to the question regarding war or peace. Eli remained silent, waiting, and Tecumseh went on.

"White men came to our land in boats with wings nearly two hundred summers ago. We helped them live. We did not know they came to claim our land. We resisted them and they killed us. We treatied with them and they broke the treaties. We burned their villages and it did not matter. More came. Always more."

Tecumseh paused and for long moments stared into the firelight. There was a sadness beyond description in his face. "We could not stop them. They came with muskets and then with cannon. We could not fight their weapons. We retreated ever deeper into the forests but they came on. For many summers we tried to treaty with them but even while we were in council with them, they pushed us west. Ever west, into lands owned by other tribes. Finally they told us that it was now impossible to make the Ohio River the boundary between our lands and the United States. We were not willing to give them more land, and we met them in battle at the place called Fallen Timbers. That was fourteen summers ago."

Tecumseh stopped and locked eyes with Eli. "You were there. I was there. I know you tried to arrange a council in which we could settle our differences without war. I know you refused to bear arms against us. You acted with honor. If I did not know that, you would not be here. You would be dead."

Again he paused while the others shifted in their blankets. Then he went on.

"The Americans killed us with their rifles and their muskets and their cannon. We lost many. We lost the battle. And we learned that we must give yet more of our land to the Americans if we were to survive. So we met with them at the place you call Greenville. That was thirteen summers ago. You and I were both there, and we both know that my people gave to yours most of what land remained in our hands. Almost the whole of what you call the Ohio Valley. Prime land. Choice land. With the great river running through."

Again Tecumseh stopped, and for a time he stared into the firelight, remembering. "Stroud. I know your history. Raised Iroquois from your second summer until your nineteenth summer. A great warrior. I know you have sorrow in your heart when you see what the Americans have done to the Iroquois and to all the Indian nations. I know you see two sides of the trouble that divides us, and I know you have risked much and given much to try to bring my people and the Americans together. I know that. My heart is heavy when I think of the burden you have tried to carry."

He shook his head as if to clear his thoughts, then went on.

"We thought the British would become our ally. They brought

muskets for us and taught us to use them. They promised to join with us in pushing the Americans from our lands. We treatied with them, and we signed their papers, and we prepared for the war that would give us back our lands."

He drew and exhaled a tired breath before he continued. "But they did not keep their promises. After the battle at Fallen Timbers, they did not come. When we gave away our lands at Greenville, they did not come. Instead they abandoned their forts at Detroit, and at Michilimackinac, and at Niagara, and at Oswego up near the great inland sea that you call Lake Ontario, and they left us to face the Americans alone. It was then, only then, that we understood that we could not trust white men. Americans or British. What they said, what they promised, what they signed, meant nothing to them. They only wanted to use us for their own purposes, not for ours. We were nothing to them. If we wanted our lands, we would have to regain them alone."

For a moment Eli lowered his eyes to stare into the fire, knowing that Tecumseh had spoken the truth. Feelings of sorrow rose strong in his breast. He raised his eyes and waited for Tecumseh to continue.

"Do you know I have counseled this summer with the British at Amherstburg near the Detroit River at the west end of Lake Erie?"

Eli spoke softly. "I know."

"Do you know I told the British that if their king should be in earnest and appear in sufficient force, then our warriors of many tribes would hold fast with the British?"

"I was told. That is part of the reason I have come to counsel with you."

"And do you know the British agreed that if we would show restraint until the right moment, they would join with us to push the Americans back to the east? Retake the land that is rightfully ours?"

"I know of it."

Tecumseh continued in Shawnee, and his hands were working with signs as he spoke. "I have spent the remainder of this summer visiting Indian nations here and far to the south. It is my intention to continue to do so until I can bind them together in a confederacy strong enough to defeat the Americans, with or without the British."

Eli answered, "I learned of this on my way here. I visited the leaders of some of the other nations."

Tecumseh leaned forward and his voice raised. "It was them that sent messengers to me that you were coming. Wyandots, Ojibwa, Ottawa, Potawatomi, Miami, Delaware—others. They told me of your inquiries."

Eli nodded. "And they told me that you had come to them. Some—perhaps many—are in agreement with you."

Tecumseh raised a hand in gesture. "I know of them." His voice raised. "And I will continue to visit them until we are all united—until we are strong enough to reclaim our lands from the Americans!"

A low, guttural murmur arose from those seated beside Tecumseh. Eli sat in silence while it faded and the spirit of angry rebellion dwindled and was gone. Then Eli spoke.

"I know of the broken promises. I know of the taking of your land. I believe it was wrong. I can only say that the United States is a young country. The people have not yet learned the lessons necessary to take their place among nations. They have made mistakes and they will make more mistakes while they learn. I have come to seek your understanding. To ask you to overlook their errors. Find it in your hearts to come one more time to council with them. I am commissioned of our father in the east to arrange such a council. Here, if you wish. He seeks a peaceful solution to the problems now dividing us."

Eli stopped, and for a time the only sounds were those of the Indian village outside. Then he continued. "I do not believe Tecumseh wishes to have war. I believe Tecumseh sees the wisdom of a peace council. I ask permission to take the message back to the father in the east that Tecumseh will attend such a council if the hearts of the Americans are in favor of peace. Do I have permission to do so?"

Eli fell silent, and minutes passed while Tecumseh pondered his words.

Slowly he spoke. "My thoughts are troubled. I cannot force them to come clear and straight. I must counsel with my people, and I must seek the guidance of the Master of Life. I ask that you remain here for one night, and I will answer your question tomorrow in the morning. You will be under my protection while you are here."

Eli bowed his head. "I am honored that you will consider my request. I will remain here for the night. I thank you for your hospitality."

The old man with the pocked face stood, and Eli followed him to the door where the man who had taken his weapons returned them. He was led to a small dwelling less than ten yards from the central building. Inside was a bear skin to sleep on, and the stomach of a goat filled with water hanging on one wall. He laid his weapons down on the thick bear skin as the old man turned and disappeared, and then sat down beside them. For a long time he sat still with memories and scenes of the battle at Fallen Timbers passing before him, and the gathering at Greenville one year later in which he watched the Shawnee and other tribes sign away the rich beauty of the Ohio Valley, where they had lived free for as far back as memory and legend existed.

The sun was casting long shadows when a woman appeared in the doorway with a clay bowl of venison stew and a sweet potato roasted in the ground. He finished his supper, set the bowl beside the door, drank long from the skin of water, and resumed his seat on the thick bear hide, lost in thought, unable to judge whether Tecumseh would consent to one more meeting with a commission authorized by President Thomas Jefferson. The owls were talking when he stretched out full length and drifted into a troubled sleep.

The morning star was still bright when he walked silently to the lake to wash his face and work his hair, and he was aware that two warriors were in the shadows, following him. He returned to his dwelling and buckled on his weapons belt and waited to be summoned. The sun was half risen when the same woman brought the clay bowl filled with yellow corn mush and goat's milk and honey. He finished his breakfast and set the bowl by the door and sat back down, waiting.

More than an hour passed before the old man appeared in the door-way and led him back to the central building. Inside he was invited to sit, once again facing the council. This time Tecumseh did not rise, but remained seated to speak.

"The council talked far into the night. I sought the spirit of the Master of Life. My thoughts have cleared and my heart and mind are straight."

Eli's breathing slowed.

Tecumseh's words came slow and measured. "I cannot think of a white man that I can trust, except you. You have never spoken an untruth that I know of. You have risked much to seek peace many times. I know of no promise you have ever made that you did not keep. I believe you expect me to tell you the truth no matter the consequences. I believe you are a man of honor. It is for these reasons that I give you my answer true."

It ran through Eli's mind like a chant—*war—war—war—war.*

"It is my plan to bring my people to a confederacy that is strong enough to push the whites from our land. British or American, it is all the same to us. I will travel as far as I must, and I will talk to my people as long as I must to accomplish this. I will not meet with the Americans because I and others have met with them for nineteen summers that I know of and at no time have they ever kept their word or honored their own treaties. If the British care to join with us to drive out the Americans, then so be it."

Tecumseh stopped to take a deep breath and select his final words.

"If this means war between my people and the Americans, then we will go to war. That will be decided by the Americans. All we want is the return of our land."

Again Tecumseh stopped and ordered his thoughts.

"Stroud. I have given you the truth that is in my heart because I honor and respect you. You will always be under my protection in my camp, but I cannot protect you from others. Be careful. It would sadden me if others caught you and killed you. You are welcome to remain here for a time if you wish, but I advise you to return to your people now. Today. Do you understand?"

Eli looked him steadily in the eye. "I understand. I will carry your message to the father in the east. I thank Tecumseh for his words and for the honesty of his thoughts. I thank you for your protection. I will leave today, now."

Tecumseh stood, and Eli stood to face him as Tecumseh spoke. "So be it. Two of my warriors will accompany you to the limits of the land that belongs to the Shawnee. Is that agreeable?"

"It is agreeable. I thank you."

Eli stopped at the small dwelling in which he had slept and collected his blanket and his weapons before he walked back out into the sunlight, south, away from the lake, back into the woods. He saw the two warriors, each twenty yards away on either side, move into the woods with him as the sounds of the Indian village faded and were gone.

_____

Notes

The description of the Shawnee Indian chief and leader, Tecumseh, is accurate. See Antal, *A Wampum Denied*, pp. 72–74; p. 92; and see the painting, p. 73.

The British had in fact armed the American Indians and were stirring them to rise up against the Americans. See Antal, *A Wampum Denied*, pp. 14–20; Tecumseh sought guidance from his God, whom he called "The Master of Life," p. 19.

The battle of Fallen Timbers, referenced in this chapter, was fought August 20, 1794, on the Maumee River, near present-day Toledo, Ohio, at a place where a violent storm had uprooted trees. The Indian army consisted of Shawnees led by Blue Jacket, Delawares led by Buckongahela, and Miamis led by Little Turtle, as well as Wyandots, Ojibwas, Ottawas, Potawatomis, and Mingos. The Indians were outflanked and retreated to Fort Miamis where the British commander, who was not authorized to start a war with America, refused to open the gates to the Indians. See Sudgen, *Blue Jacket: Warrior of the Shawnees;* Antal, *A Wampum Denied*, pp. 18–20.

The Indian defeat at Fallen Timbers led to the Treaty of Greenville the following year, August 3, 1795, at a village called Greenville, in the territory of the United States northwest of the Ohio River. Fifteen Indian tribes signed the treaty, which gave to the United States much, if not most of the great Ohio Valley land, which had belonged to the Indians from time beyond memory.

See *Indian Affairs: Laws and Treaties,* Volume II (Treaties), compiled and edited by Charles J. Kappler, LL. M., clerk to the Senate Committee on Indian Affairs, Washington, D.C., Government Printing Office, 1904; Antal, *A Wampum Denied,* pp. 18–20.

The remarkable event wherein the wastrel brother of Tecumseh, Tenskwatawa, mended his derelict ways and was trained by Tecumseh to meet the challenge of Ohio Territory governor William Henry Harrison, who greatly feared Tecumseh, by causing the sun to darken, is accurately described. Few people knew that the loss of the sun was actually a predicted eclipse. Among the few who knew of the date the eclipse would occur was Tecumseh. Thus, on June 16, 1806, when Tenskwatawa ordered the sun to disappear, and it did, and then reappeared on his command, Tenskwatawa was immediately elevated to the position of one of superhuman powers and became The Prophet. See Drake, *Life of Tecumseh and of His Brother The Prophet.*

Eastport, Maine

March 1809

CHAPTER V

𝒯here was ice in her sails as the ancient American merchantman *Mona* turned southwest into the channel between Deer Island and Campobello Island in the Canadian waters of New Brunswick, not far south of the forty-eighth parallel that separated the British Dominion from the United States. Under lead-colored morning skies, a strong, freezing, northerly March wind held the stiff canvas sheets tight, while the seamen, bundled in woolens and oil-skins, worked the ice-slick ropes with hands that were raw and teeth that chattered. The morning wore on with the heavy, blunt-nosed, graceless ship, riding heavy and low, slowly plowing on through gray-black waters that were laced with two-ton chunks of ice, while the seaman in the crow's nest seventy feet up the mainmast hunched his back against the wind and kept his eyes moving, searching for the harbor of the small village of Eastport on the east coast of tiny Moose Island.

The crew had finished their midday meal of hot mutton stew and hardtack down in the relative warmth of the small galley, and were wiping at their dripping red noses as they reluctantly made their way to the steep stairs leading up to the slick deck, when the shout came down from the crow's nest, "Landfall. Eastport! Dead ahead."

It was midafternoon when the pilot boat left the *Mona* and she furled her sails and dropped anchor in Eastport Bay, and settled, rocking in the choppy water with the wind whistling in her rigging, to wait her turn among the gather of ships bobbing in the harbor. Dusk was falling when she thumped against the massive black timbers, and her crew cast the heavy hawsers to waiting hands on the nearly deserted wharf.

Captain Aubrey Tillotson, stocky, swarthy, square-jawed, impatient, waited while his crew lowered the gangplank. He marched down to the dock with the wind blowing his cape and whipping the vapor from his breath and continued directly to the old, unpainted, weathered line of buildings that formed the waterfront, to a small, unpainted one with a single grimy window and a battered sign above the door, BRISTOL LINES, and pushed through the front door. Inside, in the dull yellow light and misshapen shadows cast by two lanterns, a lone man seated at a desk raised his head. He was tall, slender, with a small wooden sign on his desk that read "Philip Driscoll." He stood and walked past the black, pot-bellied stove that showed dull red and fronted Tillotson. There was no greeting between the two men.

"Trouble?" Driscoll asked. "You're two days late."

Tillotson wiped at the ice in his beard. "Lost two days tacking into that north wind. Bad." He hooked a thumb over his shoulder, and there was deep concern in his voice. "I didn't see the *Liverpool* at the docks. Any news of her?"

Driscoll shook his head. "No. She's two days overdue, just like you. She'll likely be in tomorrow morning."

Tillotson paused to consider. "She's coming from Passamaquoddy. Running with the wind, not against it. She should have been here waiting." He took a deep breath, then went on. "There's no dockhands out there. When can we unload?"

"Couldn't get the dockhands to stay any longer in this weather. Tomorrow morning, unless it gets worse." Driscoll paused for a moment. "Any damage to your load?"

Tillotson saw the concern in Driscoll's eyes and shook his head. "No damage. I'll have my crew ready at daylight." He turned on his heel and walked back out into the deep twilight where he wrapped his cape tight and raised one hand to clamp his tricorn onto his bowed head. He marched back to his ship and up the gangplank where his first officer,

Eustus Keel, stood hunched against the wind. Tillotson gestured to Keel and led the way to his small, cramped quarters and tossed his tricorn onto his desk, working with the clasp on his cape as he spoke.

"We can't unload until morning. Raise the gangplank now and keep the regular rotation of deck watch through the night."

Keel remained silent and Tillotson continued, words measured, voice raised against the sound of the wind at the tiny windows. "If anyone comes in the night asking permission to come on board, make them wait. Awaken me at once. I'll handle them."

The first officer neither spoke nor moved. Tillotson tossed his cape onto his bunk and dropped into the plain, worn chair behind his desk. He gestured, and Keel pulled the only other chair to the desk front and sat down, waiting. Tillotson leaned forward on his forearms and began rubbing his hands together to warm them. Seconds passed before he spoke.

"I need to know more about one of our crew. Dulcey. Didn't he sign on at Philadelphia?"

"Yes."

"I've noticed him. Not the average seaman. Too polished. Too accomplished. How does he get on with the others?"

Keel shrugged. "Well enough. Seldom speaks. Keeps to himself. Watches everything. Does his duty. A natural leader. No trouble."

"What age?"

"I've never asked. I'd guess in his early twenties."

"Full name?"

"Robert. He signed on as Robert Dulcey."

Tillotson lowered his face and for a time concentrated on his hands, still rubbing them together. "Do I remember that name from something that happened in Philadelphia? Or was it Norfolk?"

"I've not heard of it."

A look of irritation flitted across Tillotson's face. "There's something . . . it bothers me. It'll come back."

Keel said, "Maybe someone in the crew knows. I'll ask."

Tillotson straightened. "Do that." He took a deep breath and went on. "We're here for the night. Arm the men on watch. Muskets and pistols. If anyone attempts to get on board by grappling hook or climbing the dock hawsers, shoot them. Do you understand?"

Keel's eyes narrowed. "Aye, sir."

"And bring me some hot soup. That's all."

Keel nodded and ducked to exit through the small door while Tillotson fed split white-pine kindling into a small stove. Keel brought the mug of hot chicken broth, and Tillotson wrapped it in his hands for the warmth, sipped at it until it was gone, then turned to his bed.

It was shortly past three o'clock in the black of night when Tillotson opened his eyes. It took him ten seconds to understand what had awakened him. It was the silence, and the lack of the rocking of the ship. The wind had died. He closed his eyes and within seconds was breathing slowly and deeply.

It was just past six o'clock when the crew of the *Mona* climbed the steep, narrow stairs from the galley to the main deck and stepped out into a world nine degrees below freezing beneath clear skies and no wind, with the first arc of the morning sun rising on the eastern horizon. Thin, ragged ice reached thirty feet from the rocky shores of Eastport harbor, and sea birds, heavy with their thick winter plumage, argued and fought over the dead fish and carrion left from the night. Bundled in worn and ragged coats, with tattered scarves wrapped tight and with their breath billowing in vapors, part of the crew released the locks on the hatches and lifted off the covers. Others swung the yardarms about and settled the loops of the heavy freight nets onto the hooks of the four-inch hawsers dangling from the yardarms to lift the cargo from the blackness of the hold and set it on the frozen dock. Down on the dock, bearded men with numb fingers were waiting to open the nets and move the heavy crates thirty yards further down the dock to the waiting freight nets of the *Liverpool,* and return with the crates from the *Liverpool* to the waiting nets of the *Mona.* The noise and bustle of a seaport grew as Eastport came alive.

Captain Tillotson, wrapped in his cape, vapor rising from his face, marched from his quarters onto the deck, and with Keel at his side stopped at the largest of the three hatches. Beneath his arm were three separate manifests attached to hardbacks. He glanced at the four men working with the hatch cover, then at Keel.

"Where's Dulcey?"

Keel pointed. "Over on hatch number one." Keel turned and called and motioned, and Dulcey came trotting, placing his feet carefully on the slick deck. He stopped and spoke to Keel. "You wanted me, sir?"

He was a little above average in height, well built, strong in the shoulders, brown hair, clean-shaven, prominent nose, regular features.

Keel said, "Cap'n Tillotson asked for you."

Dulcey's face was a mask, his eyes flat, noncommittal as he turned to Tillotson. For a few moments Tilllotson studied him before he spoke, vaguely sensing much was going on behind those calm, dead eyes.

"Mister Dulcey, can you write?"

"Yes, sir."

"Have you ever recorded the inventory manifest of cargo coming from the hold of a ship?"

"Yes, sir."

"You know the standard form? It must be accurate. You must sign off on it and if there are errors, you'll have to either explain them or perhaps pay for them."

"I know that, sir."

"We're exchanging our load of gypsum for the cargo in the hold of the *Liverpool.* That requires you to be responsible for what comes out of this hatch, and what goes into it. Am I clear?"

Dulcey raised one eyebrow. "Unloading and loading at the same time? Isn't that a bit unusual, sir? What if we find damage in our hold? Do we ignore it? No time for repairs?"

Tillotson's brows turned down. "There will be no damage. Do you understand?"

"Yes, sir."

Tillotson handed him one of the cargo manifest boards. "Make the record. Everything coming out, everything going in. Any questions?"

"Only one, sir. Why me?"

For an instant, surprise flashed in Tillotson's face at the impertinence of a common deckhand questioning his direct order. His answer came blunt, harsh.

"That's not for you to ask!"

There was no change in Dulcey's face as he nodded.

Tillotson continued, voice still raised, hard. "Where have you learned your seamanship?"

"At sea. And from my father."

"When did you go to sea?"

"I was fourteen, sir."

For a moment the three men stood in silence, vapor rising from their faces to disappear in the morning sunlight, and then Tillotson said, "I will need that cargo record tonight. I'll send someone. Understood?"

"Aye, sir."

Tillotson turned on his heel and strode to hatch number one to make the cargo manifest assignment to the waiting crew, then on to hatch number three. When he finished, he spoke briefly to Keel, then ordered the gangplank lowered, and descended to the dock. Five minutes later he was inside the small offices of Bristol Lines, facing Philip Driscoll across his desk.

"I haven't seen the *Liverpool.* Any news?"

Driscoll shook his head. "Nothing."

Tillotson thumped his fist on the desktop and exclaimed, "Three days overdue. We've got to have her cargo!"

Driscoll remained silent, and Tillotson continued, voice hot, angry. "Well, I have no choice. We're going to put our load on the dock. We'll wait one more day, and then we leave. We have loads scheduled from—"

The door swung open and the foreman of a dock crew, face white from the cold called, "The pilot boat's bringing the *Liverpool* into the bay right now. Be at the docks in less than an hour. Thought you'd want to know."

Driscoll raised a hand in thanks and the man walked back out into the bright, cold sunlight.

Tillotson rounded his mouth and blew air, then gave orders to Driscoll. "Have her tie up next to the *Mona.* We get her cargo and she gets ours. You handle it."

Driscoll nodded, and Tillotson walked back out into the freezing sunlight, where the yardarms were making their first lifts of the freight nets from the bowels of the *Mona.* At the large hatch, Dulcey stood back as the load cleared, and the crew began the slow swing of the net out over the dock, tight with twenty strong wooden crates, each with four-inch letters stenciled on the sides, TWO HUNDRED WEIGHT. GYP-SUM. TERRANCE, LTD. VERMONT. USA. The net was lowered, and the waiting dockhands cast the heavy loops aside, worked to stack the twenty crates to one side, then waited for the first load of freight from the *Liverpool,* thirty yards up the dock. Dulcey stepped to the rail to study what they were bringing. He counted fifteen medium-sized wooden barrels, sealed at both ends, girdled by three broad iron bands each. On the side of each barrel were large stenciled letters: ONE HUNDRED FIFTY WEIGHT. PRODUCE. BARTOLO, S. A. BARCELONA. SPAIN. There was a bung in the sealed top of each barrel. The crew loaded the barrels into the waiting net, dropped the loops onto the hook, signaled, and watched as the crew on the *Mona* raised the yardarm and lifted the cargo off the dock, over the rail, and to the open hatch, then slowly lowered it into the dim light inside the hold. Dulcey peered over the hatch railing to count the barrels again as the crew unloaded the net. He entered the figure, then counted the next twenty crates of gypsum that were loaded onto the net, and recorded the gypsum load as they raised it from out of the hold. All the while his thoughts were running.

Spanish produce in barrels? Spanish produce isn't shipped in barrels! Bungs in the barrel lids? Bungs for what? Produce doesn't require bungs!

The crews of the two ships settled into a routine of load, wait, and unload. By midmorning the sun had slightly warmed the still air, and the men had removed their scarves and unbuttoned their heavy woolen coats. At noon they sat in the ships' galleys to eat their thick beef stew and hard brown bread and drink from their steaming mugs. They shrugged out of their heavy coats before they climbed the stairs back onto the deck and set a pace for the afternoon work. At six o'clock, in deep dusk, with lanterns on the docks and on the decks of the ships, they emptied the last of the nets for the day and went to the galleys for their supper of halibut and boiled potatoes.

With the toil of the day behind them, the small room was filled with rough humor and tall tales and estimates of how many tons of cargo they had unloaded and loaded. Dulcey said little, and kept the manifest with his tally of what had come out of the hold of the *Mona,* and what had gone back in. He finished his supper, delivered his plate and utensils to the evening mess crew, and climbed the stairs back to the main deck.

He was halfway to the small door that led down to the sleeping quarters of the crew when he sensed movement to his right, near the quarterdeck. He slowed, and in the darkness saw two huddled figures and recognized the voice of Keel speaking softly. The words were muffled, and Dulcey understood but two of them. " . . . anything . . . Dulcey." Dulcey stopped in his tracks and strained to hear the response and recognized the voice of the ship's bos'n, a burly, thick man who went by the single name Peck, with a nose that had been badly broken long ago and a puckered scar prominent in the heavy, dark brow above his right eye. Only a few of Peck's words were discernible.

" . . . New Haven . . . eight, ten weeks . . . killing . . ."

The two indistinct figures had little else to say and separated, each to his quarters. Dulcey stood still for a time, frantically working with his thoughts while the remainder of the crew went to their small quarters below decks, with the hammocks strung between the pillars that divided the bunks, and settled in for the night. He was the last to descend the stairs and went to his hammock unnoticed. He stretched out full length, fully dressed, hands clasped behind his head, and waited. Twenty minutes passed before Keel descended the steps. All eyes turned to him as he gave a head signal to Dulcey, and Dulcey followed him back out onto the deck under the black velvet of the night sky.

"Cap'n wants to see you," was all Keel said.

Carrying the completed manifests, Dulcey followed him, aware that Peck had fallen in behind them. Keel ducked to enter the captain's quarters and held the door while Dulcey and then Peck followed. Tillotson was seated at his desk facing the door. Two lanterns were hung on hooks set in the ceiling, casting a dull yellow light and misshapen shadows. Keel stepped to one side of the desk, Peck to the other. For several seconds Dulcey stood facing Tillotson, still seated, and staring back at Dulcey with narrowed eyes. Tillotson's voice penetrated like a knife.

"A man named Robert Dulcey is wanted in New Haven for killing a man about eight or ten weeks ago. I will ask you once. Are you that man?"

Instantly Dulcey tensed, and he glanced first at Keel, then Peck, and moved one foot slightly backwards. Keel quickly moved toward the door and Peck moved toward Dulcey, and Dulcey stopped. Then he answered Tillotson.

"Yes."

Dulcey masked his worst fears. *He's bound by law to arrest me—will he?— will he?—I had to gamble—if he arrests me I've lost—lost it all.*

Tillotson sat up straight, staring down at his hands, and for a time the only sound in the room was the ticking of the clock on the tiny chest of drawers against one wall. The tension was becoming unbearable when Tillotson broke the thick silence.

"You said you are a navigator. Trained where?"

Dulcey's breathing started again. "Harvard College. Cambridge. Massachusetts."

Tillotson's eyebrows arched in surprise. "Harvard!" he exclaimed.

"Yes, sir."

Tillotson settled back in his chair, staring, saying nothing, and Dulcey spoke.

"Was there anything else, sir?"

Tillotson's eyes bored in. "Yes. What happened? Why the killing?"

Dulcey took a deep breath. "The man made unwanted advances to my fiancée. I warned him. He had a knife. He's dead."

Tillotson started, then settled and asked, "Self defense? You chose not to explain that to the New Haven constable?"

"Yes."

"Why?"

"I was with the crew of a ship from Philadelphia. The man was a member of the New Haven City Council. I thought it prudent to not find out how sympathetic a New Haven constable and jury would be toward a stranger who had killed one of their own."

Tillotson clamped his jaw closed for a moment, leaned forward on his forearms, and moved on. His voice resumed its blunt, domineering tone.

"So much for that. I will need those manifest forms you're carrying. Lay them on the desk when you leave. You will remain in your quarters for the night. I want you back here in the morning directly following mess. Do you understand?"

The thought flashed in Dulcey's mind—*Now I find out.* He cleared his throat.

"Am I under arrest, sir?"

For a time Tillotson looked into his face. "No."

"I'm certain you know, sir, that with my confession before you, maritime law requires you to place me under arrest and turn me over to the nearest law enforcement officers you can find."

There was anger and a cutting edge in Tillotson's voice. "I know that. I don't need instruction from the likes of you." He thumped a finger on the desktop. "I will expect you here in the morning."

"Yes, sir. Will I be under guard during the night?"

"No. Go to your quarters and remain there. Now. Mister Peck, accompany him, then return to your quarters."

"Yes, sir."

Dulcey laid the manifest forms on the desk, turned on his heel, and ducked to walk through the small door into the night, with Peck following. Behind them, in his quarters, Tillotson spoke to Keel.

"Warn the men who stand watch tonight. Watch for Dulcey. If he tries to leave the ship, they are not to challenge him. They are to shoot him on sight. Any questions?"

Keel shook his head. "None."

"You are dismissed."

Down in the second deck, in the cramped quarters of the crew, Dulcey sought his hammock and for a long time lay on his back, hands clasped behind his head, locked in deep thought. It was past nine o'clock when the seaman nearest the stairs blew out the last lantern, and their quarters were cast in total blackness. For a long while, Dulcey continued to lie on his back beneath his blanket, staring into the darkness, until he finally drifted into a restless sleep.

The morning mess was steaming oatmeal, and Dulcey was the first to finish. He rose from the crowded table with his empty bowl, delivered it to the morning mess crew, and made his way up the stairs to the deck. A breeze was stirring the flags on the ships in the harbor, and the tall masts were dancing with the rocking of the ships while gulls and terns and grebes hovered, bickering. Dulcey rapped on the door into Tillotson's quarters and waited until he heard the familiar voice.

"Enter."

He pushed the door open and stepped inside the small room to face Tillotson, seated across the desk. There was a tray with a pewter plate and mug and the remains of Tillotson's breakfast. Dulcey waited.

Tillotson gestured. "Sit down."

Dulcey drew a chair to the front of the desk and slowly settled, still silent, still waiting. He was surprised at the subdued sound in Tillotson's voice.

"With your education and experience, you know of the . . . ahhh . . . peculiar . . . predicament in which you now find yourself."

Dulcey did not move nor speak. Tillotson went on.

"You are wanted for murder. I hold your life in my hands."

Dulcey made no indication he had even heard.

"If we can . . ahh . . make the proper . . . arrangements, it is possible you can be much more useful here than stretching a rope in New Haven."

Tillotson stopped and slowly leaned forward, forearms on his desk, voice soft, eyes points of light. "Do you understand?"

Dulcey said quietly, "I can guess."

Tillotson continued. "I have substantial business holdings here. And elsewhere nearby. Substantial. I have need of a man with your education and experience. There are business records—critical records—that must be kept, correspondence, agreements, contracts. And there is money—large amounts of money passing through these businesses." He paused for several seconds, then continued. "It is all controlled by the office I keep here in Eastport. Am I making myself clear, Mister Dulcey?"

Dulcey nodded. "You are."

"The office is small. Insignificant. It draws little attention. I will continue using it until someone takes notice of the . . . ahh . . . traffic that comes and goes, and makes an inquiry. When that happens I will simply close this office and move my affairs to any one of half a dozen other offices I have in other ports. Passamaquoddy—Lake Champlain—Lake Ontario—and as far west as Lake Erie. Do you grasp the breadth of my . . . ah . . . affairs?"

Dulcey cleared his throat. "I believe so, sir. Sizeable."

"There are certain elements in my business that must be handled very . . . delicately. Cargo manifests—contracts—money—governments involved—all must be handled discreetly. A man with your education could be useful. Does this interest you?"

Dulcey looked down at his hands for several seconds. "Are you threatening me, sir? Either I do your bidding, or you turn me over to the local constable for trial at New Haven?"

Tillotson straightened in his chair, and there was mock surprise in his face. "Have I said anything about New Haven?"

"Not directly."

"Nor do I intend to," Tillotson exclaimed. He settled, and his tone became conciliatory. "Of course, you can see that if I have no need for you, I will have to surrender you to the local authorities. What I'm offering you is a chance to avoid the . . . ahh . . . unpleasant probabilities that might otherwise await you, and at the same time opening an opportunity for wealth and position. I see that as a decent, Christian thing to do for you. Do you agree?"

The thoughts flickered in Dulcey's mind—*Now—now—we make it or break it—now.* His voice was even, his words spaced. "What is your proposal?"

Dulcey saw the spark come into Tillotson's eyes as Tillotson answered.

"Take a position here in my Eastport office. Learn the business. Mister Driscoll will help train you. I will pay you full first-officer wages until you are competent. After that, there are other . . . compensations . . . we will discuss. Are you interested?"

Dulcey stared at the manifests on the desktop for a time with his mind racing—*Do it right, do it right, do it right.* He cleared his throat and spoke. "I will have to think on it."

Tillotson drew and exhaled a great breath before he answered. "You have until this afternoon, when we finish exchanging cargoes with the *Liverpool.*"

By seven o'clock, with the morning sun risen, Dulcey was back at the main hatch counting crates coming out and barrels going in. The crews broke the steady rhythm of handling the cargo nets for their midday meal, then returned to the established routine. At four o'clock the last net of crates came from the dimness of the hold into the sunlight, and swung over the side to be lowered to the dock. Dulcey entered the number of crates on the manifest, added the figures for the two days of work, wrote down the total, and checked it against the number of crates that had been counted into the hold at Philadelphia. They matched. He signed and dated his entries and waited for the last net of barrels from the *Liverpool.* He counted them into the hold of the *Mona,* entered the figure, added the load, and signed and dated it. Then he walked down the gangplank and made his way to the *Liverpool.* He walked the gangplank up to her main deck, to her large center hatch, and had begun to descend into the hold when the voice of a bearded seaman came loud and challenging from behind.

"Stop where you are! You got no business down there. Who are you?"

Dulcey turned to face him. "Dulcey. From the *Mona.* I handled the count at her main hatch." He held the manifests out before him, and the man took them. For several seconds he studied the figures, the totals, the signature, and handed them back.

"You still got no business down there." He pointed to the hatch into the hold.

"Who are you?" Dulcey asked.

"Bos'n."

Dulcey continued. "I want to see if any of our cases were damaged. Insurance. I need to know. For Tillotson."

"No damage," the man growled. "I watched."

"Then you won't mind if I go down. Come down with me if you wish. Won't take five minutes. That, or I'll have to tell Tillotson that you have refused me entrance."

The man stared for a moment. "Tillotson's orders? He never done that before."

Dulcey shrugged. "All I can tell you is this is the first time I've kept the manifests for him, and I intend letting him know I checked both cargoes for damage. Insurance."

Dulcey saw the reluctance in the man's face as he said, "Follow me. Five minutes."

Down in the hold, Dulcey quickly walked the narrow aisles between the stacked crates, jerked on some of the tie ropes that held them in place, counted rows and crates, made some mental calculations, and nodded to the bos'n, who was right behind him.

"Well done. Tillotson will hear about it."

The man bobbed his head and started back toward the stairs leading up to the main deck when Dulcey paused for one moment and turned. He drew a slow breath, eyes closed, while he tested the air in the hold for the last time. The scent of rum was unmistakable. He followed the bos'n out onto the deck, nodded to him, then walked down the gangplank and on to the *Mona.* On deck, he approached Tillotson's quarters, rapped on the door, and waited.

"Enter."

Dulcey ducked to pass through the small doorframe and stopped before Tillotson's desk.

"We're finished. Here's the record for the *Mona*. I checked the hold of the *Liverpool*. The gypsum we delivered was undamaged and well secured. I thought you would want to know. Insurance." He laid the manifest on the desktop, and for a time Tillotson studied it.

"Very good. Very good." He laid the manifest on his desk and leaned forward, eyes alive as he asked, "I need your answer. Are you interested in my proposition of this morning?"

Dulcey rounded his mouth and blew air. "Yes. I am."

Tillotson stood and reached for his cape. "Shall we go visit Mister Driscoll at his office?"

It was not yet half past five when Tillotson opened the door to the small, austere, worn office of Bristol Lines, and the two men entered. There was a front counter, two desks, a potbellied stove against the wall on the left, an old, scarred, black safe in one of the back corners, and four filing cabinets against the wall on the right, all of them locked. The walls were bare except for an ancient, yellowed map of the coastline of Maine on the wall behind the stove. Driscoll rose from his desk to meet them at the counter, eyes searching for the manifests. Tillotson handed them to him and was unbuckling his cape as he spoke.

"This is Robert Dulcey," he said. "He'll be with us for a time."

Driscoll reached to shake Dulcey's hand while the two exchanged perfunctory greetings, and Driscoll made a noticeable appraisal of Dulcey. Tillotson went on.

"Mister Dulcey is a Harvard-trained navigator. Knows ships and commercial shipping. He'll be here in this office while he learns the business. You will train him."

Driscoll's mind was running—*Harvard—navigator—what's he doing here?—what are they not telling me?*

Driscoll turned to Tillotson. "All of it? The entire business?"

Dulcey did not miss the implication, nor did he miss the fact that one wall was lined with four large cabinets, each under lock. It ran in his mind—*too many cabinets—all locked.*

Tillotson went on. "Start with the contracts and the various businesses we deal with. Later we'll open the financial records. Am I clear?"

"Yes," Driscoll answered.

Tillotson continued. "The *Mona* and the *Liverpool* will take on provisions tomorrow and sail the next day. Start Mister Dulcey with the contracts for those two loads. He can draw up the new manifests. Acquaint him with the customers who'll be receiving those loads. Show him the records of some of our other customers. I'll check on progress in about twelve days when I return. Do you have any questions?"

"No, sir."

Tillotson turned to Dulcey. "Any questions?"

"What hours am I expected to be here?"

Driscoll answered. "Eight o'clock in the morning until six o'clock in the evening, except for emergencies."

Dulcey asked, "Anything wrong with me being here evenings, after hours? Shouldn't take long to understand your office practices if I can get some uninterrupted time."

Tillotson looked at Driscoll, and Driscoll answered. "I don't see anything wrong with it. I'll give you some business records. Confine yourself to them."

It flashed in Dulcey's mind—*There are some records you don't want me to see?* He spoke to Tillotson. "Do you want me to stay with the crew on the *Mona* while she provisions?"

"No. Report here to Driscoll at eight o'clock in the morning. For now, go back to the *Mona* for the night. Tomorrow morning after mess you come here."

"Yes, sir."

Tillotson watched him close the door and listened until his footsteps faded before he turned to Driscoll. "He's wanted for murder in New Haven. You watch him while I'm gone. If he tries to get into any of the money records or the names of the people we're dealing with, don't ask any questions. Shoot him. Then get the local constable and tell him you've killed a felon who was burglarizing this office, and he's wanted for a murder in New Haven." He paused for a moment, then spoke forcefully. "If he gets those records, there's no end to what he could do. Extortion—bring in the authorities. Do you understand?"

"I understand."

"Watch like a hawk. If this all goes wrong, you'll answer to me."

Driscoll nodded, and Tillotson turned on his heel and walked out.

Lamps and lanterns were winking on when Dulcey arrived at the *Mona*. He went down into the galley to take evening mess with the crew, then sought his hammock to lay quietly, lost in thought until a seaman blew out the last of the lamps. More than an hour later he pulled off his trousers and shirt, reached for his blanket, and closed his eyes.

Dawn was breaking when Dulcey finished the morning mess of fried sowbelly and scrambled eggs, swallowed the last of his hard brown bread, and returned to his place in the hold. In minutes he had all his belongings stuffed into a seaman's bag and had it slung over his shoulder. He climbed the stairs into the full sunshine of a clear, cold day. Five minutes later he pushed open the door of Bristol Lines and found Driscoll at his desk, quill in hand, hunched over a great ledger, making entries from an open file. The two exchanged brief, sterile formalities of a greeting, and Driscoll hooked a thumb over his shoulder.

"Put your bag back there behind the cabinets." He tapped papers on his desktop. "There's the forms and numbers and the names of customers you'll need for the manifests Captain Tillotson needs before we close tonight."

Dulcey stowed his seaman's bag behind the filing cabinets and returned to Driscoll's desk. He picked up the papers, recognized his own accounting from the *Mona*, checked the figures from the *Liverpool* accounting, glanced at blank forms waiting to be filled out, and gestured toward the other desk near the stove.

"Can I use that desk?"

Driscoll shrugged and said nothing as he continued transferring information from an open file to the great ledger. Dulcey sat down at the desk, separated the papers, studied them briefly, and reached for the quill and inkwell to his right. He checked the papers once more before he began the task of preparing the two new manifests that could be required at the port of destination, and as he methodically entered numbers and weights on the papers, he was carefully memorizing the names of customers, the ports where they maintained offices, and how much of the cargo was to be delivered to each.

Andrews Ltd.—New York—eighty barrels Spanish produce—Stearns & Stearns—Philadelphia—Two hundred twenty barrels Spanish produce—LeBlanc Corporation—Quebec—two hundred cases gypsum—Dearborn Ltd.—Montreal— one hundred sixty cases of gypsum—gypsum going north on the Liverpool*—Spanish produce going south on the* Mona*—Spanish produce in barrels with bungs?—coming from a ship that reeks of rum?—Spanish produce doesn't come in barrels, it comes in crates.*

At noon Dulcey walked out of the office and west on the waterfront to a tavern with a sign declaring it to be the White Gull. He ate his midday meal of baked cod and potato and paid one week's rent for a small room on the second floor, then returned to the office. It was midafternoon when Dulcey leaned back, rubbed tired eyes with the heels of his hands, stood, and took the papers to Driscoll's desk.

"Here's the new manifests for both ships. *Mona* and *Liverpool.* Should I deliver them to Captain Tillotson?"

Driscoll took the documents and placed them in a file on his desk. "He's coming here later. He'll pick them up."

"Anything else I can do?"

Driscoll pointed. "Take those files. The ships should be here sometime tomorrow. They'll exchange loads. You prepare the new manifests."

Dulcey nodded, picked up the two files, and returned to his desk. He had just sat down when the front door opened and a small man dressed in a worn woolen coat walked in, glanced at Dulcey, and delivered a sealed envelope to Driscoll. Driscoll opened it and laid the enclosed papers on his desk, and the man turned on his heel and walked back out the door. Dulcey looked at Driscoll, waiting for an explanation, but Driscoll remained silent and continued work on his ledger. Dulcey went to work on the two new files, and half an hour later he laid the second file down and leaned back in deep thought.

Gypsum again? Going north? India tea? In barrels? Going south?

He flinched at the sound of the door abruptly opening and turned to see Tillotson close it and walk rapidly to Driscoll's desk.

"Are the manifests for tomorrow ready?"

Dulcey stood and walked to the side of Driscoll's desk and watched Driscoll hand the two prepared files to Tillotson. "Here they are. Ready."

Tillotson studied them for a time, then closed them and turned to Dulcey. "Do you know about the next two ships coming in? Two days?"

"I've seen the files."

"You'll have them ready?"

"Yes."

"Any questions?" Tillotson's eyes were focused, intent.

Dulcey shrugged casually. "None yet."

"I'll be back in about twelve days. Driscoll will give you what you need."

Dulcey stood beside the desk, arms folded, as he watched Tillotson march out the front door and disappear into the jostle of men and cargoes on the dock. He turned to Driscoll.

"Any more papers I can work on?"

"I'll get some." Driscoll went to the filing cabinets and drew a ring of keys from his pocket to unlock one of the drawers and draw out four files. "Here," he said, "study these. They are some of our regular customers. Get familiar with them. There are more." Dulcey took the files and turned to his desk, glancing back only to watch Driscoll thrust the keys back into his pocket and take his seat at his own desk.

Dulcey sat down, opened the first of the four files, and began the task of analyzing the papers. One hour later he laid the last of the four files on his desk and for a moment organized his thoughts.

Four separate companies, four different names—Peterson, O'Neil, Hoffman, Schaffer—all operating out of this office. India tea, Spanish produce, dried French fruit, Moroccan dates—all packed in medium-sized barrels with bungs in the lids—all being shipped south of here—New York—Philadelphia—Yorktown—Charleston.

He drew a deep breath and considered.

Pennsylvania gypsum. New York gypsum. Vermont gypsum. Packed in crates that

vary from eighty pounds to one hundred eighty pounds. All going north. St. Andrews—
on up to Quebec—Montreal—as far west as Kingston.

He stretched and settled, then glanced at Driscoll. He was hunched over an open file with one finger tracking information, while his other hand was making entries in the thick ledger. Dulcey gathered the files and walked to Driscoll's desk.

"Any others I should see?"

Driscoll started at the interruption, grunted, and pointed. "Right there."

They both turned their heads to look as the door swung open, and a hunch-shouldered man bundled in the garb of a seaman entered. He walked directly to the two men and stared at Dulcey while he laid a sealed document on Driscoll's desk. Insantly Driscoll picked it up, but not before Dulcey saw the name scrawled on the envelope. "M'sieu A. Tillotson."

Dulcey's thoughts ran. *Second one today—French—who are these men?*

Driscoll pointed to the two files on the corner of his desk. "Don't forget those files you asked for."

Dulcey nodded, picked them up, and walked back to his chair and settled in once again. For more than forty minutes the only sound was pages turning, the tick of the ancient clock on top of the nearest filing cabinet, and the muffled sounds of the traffic on the Eastport docks. Dulcey flinched when the clock struck six, stood, stretched, closed the file he was working on, and spoke to Driscoll.

"Think I'll go to the tavern for supper. I'd like to come back and work on more files afterwards."

Driscoll answered, "I'll wait until you're back from supper. I'll have to lock you in and let you out."

Dulcey lifted his coat from the hook next to the entrance and was putting it on when the door burst open and a corpulent man stalked in. He wore the hat of a sea captain. His hair was long, his beard full, and he paid no attention to Dulcey as he marched past him, straight to Driscoll's desk where he stopped and slapped the desktop with the flat of his hand. Driscoll jumped, and his chair moved back.

"I expected my pay yesterday," the man growled. "You didn't come."

"I couldn't leave here," Driscoll stammered. "Tillotson's gone, and I have a new man to train. I couldn't leave him here alone."

The man did not turn to look at Dulcey. "Then send him with the money! I have a ship loaded to leave in the morning. The policy is that I'm to be aboard that ship at all times, once she's loaded."

"I can't send the new man with the money. Tillotson's orders. I'll pay you now. You'll have to sign."

"Be quick about it."

Driscoll spun the dial on the heavy, black safe in the corner and removed a sizeable metal box. He set it on Dulcey's desk, used a key to open the lock, and quickly counted out sixty pounds, British sterling, in gold coins. He locked the box, replaced it in the safe, closed the door, and spun the combination dial. With the money on the desk, he unlocked the bottom drawer of the nearest filing cabinet behind his chair and removed a second huge ledger to set it thumping on the desk beside the money. Quickly he opened the old, worn, canvas-covered book, seized his quill, made a hurried entry, then spun the ledger and handed the quill to the man across the desk.

"Sign."

The man scanned the entry, hastily scrawled his name, picked up the stack of gold coins, and turned on his heel. For a silent moment he studied Dulcey, then stalked back out the door into the twilight of early evening.

Dulcey saw Driscoll's shoulders slump in relief before he looked at the signature, closed the ledger, and shoved it back into the drawer. He used his foot to push the drawer closed, then leaned forward to close the lock. Driscoll returned to his chair as Dulcey buttoned his coat and spoke.

"That happen often?"

There was a mix of fear and anger in Driscoll's voice, and his face flushed red as he answered. "With him? He's a part owner. A very small part. Thinks he runs it all."

Dulcey started for the door. "I'll be back as soon as I finish supper. What's his name?"

Driscoll shook his head. "It's not important. Get back soon. I'll be waiting."

Supper at the White Gull Tavern was roast mutton and boiled turnips. Dulcey ate thoughtfully, mechanically, paid at the desk, and walked back to the small office of Bristol Lines with the light of a lantern showing dull in the grime of a small window. Driscoll rose as he entered and shrugged into his coat.

"All cabinets and drawers are to be left alone. Don't touch the safe. There's some files on your desk to work on. I'll be back at ten o'clock to let you out."

Dulcey watched through the window until Driscoll was lost in the muddle of men and cargo still on the docks, then stepped to the yellowed map tacked to the wall behind the stove. For twenty minutes he traced the shoreline of Moose Island, then shifted north to Passamaquoddy Bay that was British territory, then back down to Cobscook Bay west of Moose Island. He held a lantern close to find the roads on the mainland, and carefully traced a winding line leading west from the coastline, then angling southwest and finally due south, down to Machias Bay. He traced the line again with his finger until he was satisfied he had it committed to memory.

Back at his desk, he noted that all the files he had worked on previously were gone—back into the locked filing cabinets. He went back to his desk and took quill and paper in hand. With the lamp turned low, he carefully wrote down the names of all the companies, all the men, the cargoes and destinations that he had committed to memory, and for a long time studied the list, trying to force an explanation that would answer all the questions that defied reason. He folded the paper and tucked it inside his shirt, then drew and released a great breath and settled into the four new files. At nine-thirty he closed the last file, stood and stretched, and was startled at the sound of the key rattling in the door. The door swung open and Driscoll entered, and without a word walked to the filing cabinets, where he inspected each lock.

Dulcey showed no emotion as his mind ran. *Returned early to see if he could catch me breaking into the files.*

Satisfied the filing cabinets were intact, Driscoll turned to Dulcey.

"We need to be out by ten o'clock. If the night watchman sees the light he'll stop."

Dulcey pulled his coat on and stepped out into the cold night air and waited while Driscoll locked the door.

"See you in the morning."

Driscoll nodded but said nothing and walked away.

In his room, Dulcey drew the paper from his shirt, and for a time carefully read the names and dates and cargoes, making mental notes of the companies he had known previously. It was close to eleven o'clock when he put out the lamp and went to bed. He awoke once in the night to the hum of wind and the steady drumming of rain on the roof.

Morning broke in a wet, gray world with a raw northerly wind snapping the flags on the mainmasts of the ships rocking in Eastport harbor. At eight o'clock Dulcey waited while Driscoll worked the key in the office lock, and the freezing wind came through the door with the two men to ruffle papers on both desks before they could turn and slam it shut. The two took off their coats and hung them on the wall pegs, and Dulcey kindled a fire in the stove while Driscoll opened one cabinet to select eight large files and drop them on Dulcey's desk.

"Start with these," he said, and returned to his own chair.

At noon, Dulcey clamped his tricorn on his head, turned up his collar, and hurried to the tavern for sausage and brown bread, then returned to continue reading the files Driscoll laid on his desk from time to time. Twice the work was interrupted by seamen who walked through the door, past the counter, to Driscoll's desk to leave documents. Both times the man making the delivery spent a moment studying Dulcey but asked no questions. By late afternoon, Dulcey was in a state of stunned disbelief.

Burlington—Plattsburgh—Cornwall—Crysler's Farm—Prescott Ogdensburg—Sacketts Harbour—Oswego—Charlotte—Buffalo—Fort Erie—Fort George—Presque Isle—Amherstburg—Detroit. Buyers in towns on the Canadian side of the lakes—towns that weren't there five years ago—built by Americans who left the United States to buy cheap Canadian land and get into this business of smuggling? Cargoes moving both directions from as far west as Detroit? Amherstburg? From Vermont, New York, Michigan, and Canada? Nineteen separate companies? British, French, American? Thirteen thousand tons of gypsum in twelve days, all traveling north? Gypsum? Enough gypsum to plaster every wall in Quebec and Montreal combined? Lumber—nine hundred tons of cured pine and oak going to England—enough to build a fleet of ships. Potatoes, wheat, flour, beef, pork, all coming from American ports to Canadian buyers? Spanish produce—India tea—Oriental ginseng root—all packed in barrels with bungs? Twenty-two hundred tons in sixteen days? All moving south? And the paperwork all crosses these desks in this office at Eastport?

At six o'clock Dulcey carefully closed the files on his desk, and Driscoll followed him to the front door. Dulcey paused.

"See you in the morning."

Driscoll grunted an answer, and Dulcey heard the key turn in the lock as he walked away toward the White Gull with the wind cutting through his coat. The small tavern was filling with seamen with white faces who wiped at dripping red noses with their coat sleeves. Dulcey took a small table in one corner to order roast ham and potatoes and a piece of apple pie. A thin woman with gray hair and sad eyes brought it on a tray and Dulcey picked up the knife and fork. The ham was dry and the potatoes overboiled, but it made a supper. He was starting on the pie, paying little attention to the rough talk of seamen at the tables nursing their steaming mugs of hot buttered rum, when he heard the words ". . . New Haven . . ." He slowed and glanced at four men, all in heavy coats and knitted caps, two tables to his right. He took the first bite of the pie and began to slowly chew, sorting out what he could of the conversation among the four sailors.

The youngest of them was talking too loud, gesturing, face twisted in loathing at a remembrance. " . . . caught him four weeks ago . . . trial . . . murdered a city alderman . . . hung him the next day . . . I saw it . . . worst thing ever . . . ever see a man hang? . . . worst thing ever."

For a moment Dulcey stopped breathing, then took the next forkful of pie and listened. A burly seaman snorted, sipped gingerly at his

steaming rum, wiped his beard on his coat sleeve, and spoke. ". . .
name . . ."

The younger man tossed a hand upward. " . . . Dorsey . . . Dulcey
. . . don't remember." He shuddered. " . . . remember his eyes when they
hung him . . popped wide open . . worst thing ever."

Dulcey's expression did not change as he finished his pie. He laid
down his fork, paid at the desk, and casually walked down the dim hall to
his room. Inside he turned the lamp wheel and sat down on his bed,
leaned forward, elbows on knees, hands clasped, as he battled to organize
his fragmented thoughts.

*If that man knows, who else knows?—how much time do I have?—must leave
now—tonight—got to get into the hold of the* Patrice *before I go—got to know what's
down there.*

With calm deliberation he packed his seaman's bag and drew the
strings but did not tie them. Then he sat down on his bed and forced
himself to wait for more than one hour before he walked back downstairs and out the front door onto the nearly deserted wharf. He stopped
with his shoulders hunched against the freezing wind, and for several
moments studied the ships that were tied to the docks. He glanced at the
heavens, where the moon and stars were hidden by thick, low, billowing
clouds, while the first wet snowflakes came stinging, slanting on the
wind.

Dulcey walked back to his room, put on his heavy coat, pulled his
knitted cap low, slung his seaman's bag over his shoulder, blew out the
lamp, and walked out into the hall. He did not go back into the tavern;
rather, he walked to the door at the end of the hall, out onto the landing
and down the stairs into the blackness of the alley. He backed up against
the building and waited, eyes closed, listening for any sound that he did
not understand, and there was none. He walked steadily down to the
slick, black timbers of the waterfront, and again stopped to listen, and
to peer intently into the sleet and the darkness, broken only by the dim
light of lanterns swinging in the wind from the bow and stern of ships
tied to the docks. The only sounds were the whistling of the storm in
the rigging of ships and the heavy thump of the hulls as they rose and

fell against the dock with the wind-driven waves. There was no one in sight. He moved quickly to the second ship.

The gangplank had been raised and was up on the deck. He hunched down where the big hawser held the stern of the *Patrice* against the dock and waited for the seaman on the first deck-watch of the night, to judge the time it took him to make one round. The lantern came past about each six minutes. On the third round, Dulcey watched it come, waited until it was past, then seized the hawser and climbed to the railing and over onto the deck of the ship. He crouched behind the main hatch and waited until the deck-watchman passed on his next round, and two minutes later had the hatch open far enough to slip inside and lower the cover back into place. He stood on the steep stairs in utter blackness for half a minute, eyes clenched shut while he waited for them to adjust to the darkness. He had just opened them and started down the steps when the scent registered, and he froze.

Sulphur! Two hundred tons of sulphur!

There was no need to go farther. Quickly he shouldered the hatch cover upward, stepped clear, and was crouched down behind the hatch when the deck-watch passed. He moved silently to the stern, slid down the hawser to the dock, scooped up his seaman's bag, and trotted, hunched forward, head ducked into the stinging wind and snow, to the office of Bristol Lines. He stopped to peer up and down the waterfront, and there was no one. He bowed one shoulder and rammed the door with all his weight, and the jamb splintered, and the door flew open. He quickly pushed it closed, and instantly the room was locked in blackness. By feel, he moved quickly to the file drawer where Driscoll kept the ledger that controlled the money and felt the lock. He worked his way to the stove, still warm, seized the soot-covered poker, rammed the point through the arch of the lock, and heaved upward. The poker bent, but held, and the hasp of the lock released. Dulcey grabbed the ledger and moved to the middle drawer of the second locked file. Again he drove the poker through the arch, heaved up, and again the poker bent, but the lock clicked and opened. He grabbed the big, heavy ledger with the names of customers, loads, dates, arrivals, and destinations and strode back to his seaman's bag. Two minutes later he was at the front door with the two ledgers inside the heavy canvas bag, the strings tied tight. He opened the door and stepped out into the howling wind and sleet, stood still for half a minute to be certain no one had seen him come, and then closed the door.

He did not go to the docks to stow away on a ship or take a long-boat. Rather, he headed northwest at a steady trot, toward the tip of the small island. He was gasping for breath when he stopped and waited in the darkness, watching for a lantern following and listening for a shout, but there was nothing. He ran on, stopping when he must, listening, watching, until he reached the wild coastline with the great granite rocks, where longboats danced at a small dock on the three hundred yards of choppy black water that separated the island from the mainland. He threw his seaman's bag into the nearest longboat, jerked the tie rope free, and dropped into it. He heaved on the right oar to turn the boat, then bowed his back and dug both oars deep to drive the bucking craft into the wind and the churning water. He took a heading due north, based on instinct and dead reckoning, with the map on the office wall bright in his mind. He missed the mainland docks by thirty yards, leaped into freezing water above his knees, and dragged the boat up into the rocks of the rugged Maine shore. With the seaman's bag over his shoulder, he took his bearings and started northwest once more, working his way through the scatter of granite boulders, searching for the winding dirt road he had traced on the map. In the storm and the darkness, he passed it and had to turn back fifty yards, searching. He found it and turned west, following it slowly, carefully, with the wind and sleet quartering in from his right. He trudged on in the night, peering downward, feeling his way in the freezing mud and slush of the road.

Twice in the night he saw the dull glow of lights just north of the road but did not stop. With dawn separating the gray overhead from the gray of the world, he followed the road southwest, clothes dripping, teeth chattering. Midmorning, the wind slackened and the sleet slowed. By noon there were patches of blue overhead, and an hour later the heavens cleared and the winds calmed. He walked on in chill sunshine, shivering, covered with mud to his knees, clothes soaked, listening to the drip of melting snow falling from trees and undergrowth to turn the world into rising steam and brown puddles and ponds.

The sun was casting long shadows eastward when he left the road to walk a quarter mile north on a path toward a plain, weathered farmhouse. In the farmyard, he paused at a slab-sided building connected to a pen with three Jersey cows grinding their cuds and two draft horses with their muzzles buried in dry grass hay. There was a second pen with a large black-and-white sow and nine weaner pigs. Beyond, there was a chicken coop with chickens clucking while their heads darted up and down as they snatched grain or insects from the ground. He stopped at the door of the building and rapped at the door, then opened it on creaking hinges. A hollow-cheeked old man with a week's growth of gray beard and one glassy eye sat on a one-legged milking stool, finishing the milking of a fourth Jersey cow into a wooden bucket. The man raised his head in surprise. His voice was high, raspy.

"Who are you?"

"Sir," Dulcey began, "I need a meal and a place to sleep for the night. I can sleep in this milking shed. I'll expect to pay."

The old man turned and buried his forehead in the flank of the cow for a time while he stripped the udder. Then he stood, pushed the milking stool back with his foot, and picked up the milk bucket by the rope handle.

"I asked, who are you?"

"Robert Dulcey. I've been walking since yesterday evening. From Eastport. I have to get to Port Machias."

The old man considered for a moment. "You in trouble?"

"Trouble? With the law? No, I'm not."

"Then why did you walk all night and all day, in the storm?"

"I have to be in Port Machias as soon as I can, sir."

The old man shook his head. "No, you're in trouble. When did you eat last?"

"Yesterday evening."

"How much?"

Dulcey's forehead wrinkled in question. "How much did I eat?"

"No. How much can you pay?"

"Whatever is reasonable."

"You said Port Machias?"

"Yes."

The old man scratched his beard with his free hand. "I've got the winter's cheeses in a root cellar. Got them sold in Port Machias. Got to get them loaded tomorrow and leave. Should be there in three days. Make you a deal."

Dulcey stood silent, waiting, and the old man went on.

"You help me load the cheeses tomorrow and deliver them in Port Machias, I'll give you lodging tonight. A hot supper of beef and turnip stew. Sleep in the bed in my son's room. He got married and left four years ago. My wife died last December. Buried just north of the house. Been hard, doin' everything around here alone. Hard."

"I'll help with your load of cheese," Dulcey said, and the old man bobbed his head once as he walked out of the milk shed with the bucket of milk, toward the low, log house. He stopped at a root cellar and set the warm milk to cool, then went on into the weathered log house with Dulcey following.

"Your clothes still wet?" the old man asked.

Dulcey set his seaman's bag against one wall. "No. They dried this afternoon."

"Supper's on in five minutes."

Dulcey could not remember anything tasting better than steaming beef stew that was too salty, with brown bread hardened by spending two weeks in a drawer, and a steaming mug of apple cider. With the meal finished and the table cleared, the old man gestured to the stone fireplace that dominated one wall and spoke.

"Set a spell and talk, if you've a mind. Name's Angus. Call me Angus."

Dulcey saw the need in the old face and sat down on a straight-backed chair while the old man settled into a battered rocking chair. He rocked back and forth with the old chair quietly groaning, hands clasped on his paunch, staring into the dancing flames of the fire. Minutes passed while the only sound was the popping of knots in Maine hardwood in the fire and the tick of the old clock on the plain mantle. Finally the old man spoke.

"Spring storm we had. Put some moisture in the ground. Good for the crops."

Dulcey nodded. "You grow crops?"

"Potatoes. Turnips. Cabbage sometimes. Apples. Maple syrup. Goin' to be hard this year, without Phoebe. Doin' all that."

Dulcey could not find the right words to say and remained silent, staring into the fire while the old man continued. "Might have to sell out. Go to a town somewhere." He shook his head. "Things is getting crowded around here. Towns growin'. People comin'."

Again he fell silent, and Dulcey did not interfere with his thoughts while the fire popped and sparks danced, and the dusty old clock continued to tick.

Dulcey cleared his throat. "Who takes care of your livestock while you're gone? Milks the cows? Feeds the sow? Collects the eggs?"

The old man raised one hand in gesture. "Neighbor up the road. Name's MacIver. We trade. I take care of his when he goes, he takes care of mine when I go. He'll be here day after tomorrow, early."

The fire dwindled and left the room in twilight before the old man stood. "I'll show you my boy's room. Name's Albert." He shook his head as he crossed the parlor and opened a door. "In here. I get up at five o'clock. I'll have hot water to wash. Breakfast before six. Outhouse is in back. Got morning chores and then fifty-two rungs of cheese to load. Thirty-six pounds each. Eighteen-hundred-seventy-two pounds. Near a ton."

That the old man kept such figures in his head surprised Dulcey. He said, "I can help with the morning chores. Where's the root cellar?"

"West side of the house. I'll show you in the morning. I'll bank the fire while you get the lamp goin' in Albert's room. Then I'll turn out the lamps in here. If you need the outhouse you better go now."

The old man returned to the fireplace and reached for the small shovel and poker to bank the fire while Dulcey closed the bedroom door and dropped his seaman's bag beside the bed and lighted the lamp on the simple dresser. He waited until he heard the footsteps fade and the soft closing of a door before he lifted the bag onto the bed and drew out the two ledgers. For nearly half an hour he studied the entries of each. In the larger one were the names of more than sixty-five companies, with a registry of dates of contracts, cargoes, points of origin, and points of delivery. The cargoes were generally gypsum going north and produce or tea going south. The ports of origin and destination ranged from the West Indies northward to Quebec, and west to Amherstburg, on the western tip of Lake Erie, in British Canada. The second ledger, the smaller one, was a line-by-line accounting of money; where it originated, and where it went.

Dulcey's breathing slowed. *Here it is! The names of all the men connected with this scheme! Half of them are representatives of governments—ours and Britain's! Millions! Millions of dollars changing hands to keep them quiet!*

His brow wrinkled in puzzlement. *Gypsum. Gypsum that smells like sulphur. Why sulphur going north?*

Bone-weary, he closed the two ledgers and replaced them in his seaman's bag and tied the strings. Slowly he dropped his shoes, changed to his nightshirt, and got into the bed, mind still puzzling. *Gypsum? Sulphur. Why sulphur?* These were his last thoughts as he drifted off to sleep.

They ate steaming oatmeal porridge and drank thick Jersey buttermilk for breakfast and walked to the milking shed in the gray of dawn. They finished morning chores a little after nine o'clock, and the two of them moved a great cart with seven-foot wheels to the root cellar. They stopped loading the large, yellow, wax-coated rounds of cheese at noon and ate hot ham and boiled potatoes, and the old man lay down before the fireplace and snored for twenty minutes before they went back outside in the chill sunlight to finish loading the cheese. By dusk they had finished with the livestock and carried the milk and eggs into the root cellar. They were in bed before eight o'clock.

Frost came in the night to turn the world into a sparkling wonder-land in the first arc of the rising sun. MacIver came rumbling up in his wagon, pulled by a single horse, while they were gathering eggs and emptying a bucket of whey mixed with grain into the pig trough, where the old sow grunted and nosed her nine weaner pigs aside to bury her snout in the thick mix.

MacIver walked to meet Angus. "Loaded?"

"Yep."

"Go on. I'll take over here."

Angus and Dulcey loaded their personal gear into the big-wheeled old cart and climbed up to the driver's seat. Angus slapped the reins on the rumps of the two horses, called "Giddap," and the wagon lurched into motion. The morning passed with the cart rumbling and lurching on the rutted road steadily southwest. With the sun high overhead, they stopped near a clear stream where the horses dropped their muzzles to drink, and the two men silently ate dried fish and cold, boiled potatoes, and drank from the stream while the horses pulled dried grass. Talk between the two was sparse as the afternoon passed. In early dusk, Angus pulled the team off the road to a small grove of maple and white pine trees. While Angus kindled a small fire, Dulcey unhitched the horses and led them to the stream to drink, then hobbled them in the trees, where they began pulling the high, dry, brittle grass. There was little said as the two men ate ham warmed on a spit, and potatoes sliced and fried in a cast-iron frying pan that was blackened by fifty years of hard use. They broke evergreen boughs to sleep on, and sought their blankets beneath unnumbered stars in the black heavens.

They broke camp and had the cart back on the narrow, rock-strewn, winding dirt road before the first arc of the sun cleared the eastern horizon. They nooned near a large lake to the east of the road, then pressed on. When Angus stopped the cart for evening camp, Dulcey caught the scent of the sea, far to the south, and at daybreak the following morning they were once again rolling, this time due south. Before ten o'clock they crested a gentle rise and there before them, far in the distance, was Port Machias, on the rocky northwest shores of Machias Bay. It was two o'clock before they reached the northern end of the small village and Angus clucked the horses down to the docks.

Dulcey waited with the wagon while Angus went to an office on the waterfront with a faded sign that read O'BRIEN & O'BRIEN. Minutes later he returned with a short, heavy man dressed in winter clothes, with the stub of an unlit cigar clenched between his teeth. The man climbed onto the back of the cart, jerked the knots from the ropes, and threw back the tarp that covered the cheeses. He examined half a dozen of them before he turned to Angus.

"Unload. Come to the office and I'll pay."

Angus moved the wagon to a warehouse at the west end of the waterfront and dropped the tailgate, and the two men began transferring the cheeses, one at a time, inside the cavernous room, while an agent of O'Brien and company counted them. At five o'clock, Dulcey placed the last one onto the carefully arranged stacks, the warehouseman made his receipt, and Angus and Dulcey walked back to the big cart, where Dulcey unloaded his seaman's bag and helped Angus raise and lock the tailgate.

Dulcey faced the old man.

"I think that finishes it." He saw the sense of sadness in the old, gray eyes, but there was nothing he could do. "Will you be staying here in town tonight?"

Angus shook his head. "Still good daylight. I'll make two, three hours yet today."

Dulcey didn't know what to say, and felt his face flush, embarrassed.

Angus broke the awkward silence. "Want to tell me the trouble you're in before I go?"

Dulcey shook his head. "No trouble."

Angus accepted it. "You be careful. You get up my way again, you come visit. Nice to have someone to talk to."

Dulcey was astonished. The old man had not spoken more than a hundred words in three days!

"I'll do that," Dulcey said. "Good luck to you."

There was nothing else to be said, and the two men parted, Angus to the driver's seat of his old cart, and Dulcey to the nearest tavern that had rooms for rent. The sign hanging on the wrought-iron arm above the door said RED DAWN TAVERN. Dulcey rented a small room on the ground floor for one night, locked his seaman's bag inside, and hurried back out onto the waterfront, down to the ships that were tied to the docks and loading.

The second ship, a two-masted schooner with the name *Martha* on her bow, flying an American flag, was finished loading, and her captain said he intended sailing for Boston harbor at high tide, which was four o'clock the next morning. And he had space for one paying passenger. Dulcey paid him in advance and returned to his room. He took his supper at the tavern and returned to his room to dig into his seaman's bag for the two large ledgers. It was close to ten o'clock when he closed them, mind reeling with the scope of what they told him.

For a time he sat still, concentrating on the single question—*Why the smell of sulphur in the hold of a ship carrying gypsum?*

Suddenly he sat bolt upright, eyes wide, the hair on his arms standing straight up.

Gunpowder! Gunpowder is made with sulphur and saltpeter and charcoal! They're shipping sulphur north to make gunpowder, in crates marked GYPSUM! He jerked to his feet and smacked one fist into the palm of his other hand. "Of course!" he exclaimed. "The British are making gunpowder up north! They're getting ready for *war!*"

Sleep did not come easy for Dulsey, and he awakened twice in the night, mind racing with the sure conviction that he had stumbled into a massive, hidden plot by the British to attack and destroy the entire northern American frontier. How far west did it reach? Detroit? How far north? Lake Superior? How many of the American forts on the southern shores of Lake Ontario? Fort Niagara? Sacketts Harbour? Oswego? Buffalo?

Dulcey was at the gangplank of the *Martha* in the four o'clock AM darkness and was admitted to his tiny quarters. The northerly winds held, and the little schooner was fairly flying as she took her heading due south out of Machias Bay into the Atlantic Ocean. Dulcey spent hours in his tiny cabin, poring over the ledgers, mentally marking the companies involved, the tonnage shipped both directions, and the names of the persons who had signed receipts for money. He came onto the deck for a little while in the morning and again in the afternoon, to clear his head and feel once more the gentle roll of the deck of a solid ship running with the wind. But he took his meals in his quarters and spoke little to any of the crew.

The second morning he sighted Cape Cod to the south and east and felt the little schooner lean to port as she turned to starboard, toward Boston harbor. By noon she had tied up to the docks, and Dulcey waited with his seaman's bag over his shoulder while the crew lowered the gangplank. The bos'n checked his name off, and he descended the gangplank in four steps and trotted through the men and cargoes on the docks to the office marked DUNSON & WEEMS, and threw open the door. Inside, three men raised their heads and stood instantly, the tallest of them trotting to seize Dulcey by the shoulders.

"John! Are you all right? We were . . ." Matthew Dunson clasped his son to his breast for a moment, and John threw his arms about his father.

"I'm all right," John answered. "Fine. Are things all right here?"

Matthew stepped back, checking his son from head to toe. "Yes, but we were worried."

Billy Weems stepped from behind Matthew and thrust out his hand. John grasped it and then threw his arms about Billy for a moment. "Good to see you. You can't know how good."

Captain Pettigrew thrust out his hand from behind Billy, and John shook it warmly.

"Laura?" John asked his father. "The baby?"

"Couldn't be better. Anxious about you."

"Mother?"

Matthew clenched his jaw for an instant. "Ailing a little. But fine."

Billy interrupted. "Any trouble up there?"

John rounded his mouth and blew air. "No real trouble. But you aren't going to believe what's going on."

Matthew sobered. "What is it?"

"Thousands of barrels of rum from the West Indies moving up to

British ports and from there back down to American buyers. The barrels are marked as Spanish produce and India tea."

Matthew was incredulous. "What? Rum in barrels marked Spanish produce and India tea? Ridiculous!"

"That's not all," John said. "Thousands of crates of sulphur marked as gypsum going north and staying there with British buyers."

The office went dead quiet for three seconds before Matthew exclaimed, "Gunpowder! The British are making gunpowder up there! They're preparing for war!"

John continued with every eye in the room boring into him, waiting. "Thousands of tons of cured white pine and oak. Peeled pine trees for ship masts by the thousand. All going to England. England is getting its navy ready!"

Billy cut in. "All of this in breach of the embargoes? Against the law? President Madison and Congress intend to stop it all with a bill they're working on. The Macon Bill."

John shook his head emphatically. "I know, but the Macon Bill isn't before Congress yet. I know about the embargoes and all the talk of shutting down commerce with Canada—crippling England because she can't get Canadian lumber to build a fleet. All I'm telling you is that right now, today, there's at least five times the amount of lumber and other materials flowing into and out of Canada and the northern sections of the United States—as there ever was. Smuggling! Almost no one up there is paying any attention to all the embargo wars between England and France and the United States. Americans have left the United States to buy cheap land on the Canadian side up there. Right now Americans have built at least three hundred new Canadian settlements, and they're producing lumber and potash and wheat, and making a fortune shipping it to England."

Matthew interrupted. "How strong is the French presence up there? Bonaparte intends being emperor of the world."

"Strong. The French stop ships of any nation on the high seas and confiscate whatever they want, just like the British. The only question is who is causing the most trouble, France or England?"

Billy asked, "In what quantities? How much of this is going on?"

John shook his head, eyes lost in disbelief. "At least fifty-two million dollars in the past twelve months."

Billy gaped. Matthew's mouth dropped open for a moment before he exclaimed, "What are the port authorities up there doing about it?"

John's words came slowly, spaced. "Apparently, nothing. Not the British or the Americans. A lot of them—maybe most—are part of it. Getting paid for their silence. A few said no to the bribery and soon found out they had far too few ships or men to stop it. And some of them disappeared. No one knows what happened to them."

Matthew broke in. "Names? Do you have names?"

"I've got two ledgers with most of the names the president will need."

Matthew's eyes widened. "How did you get them?"

"Stole them. Broke into the office and stole them."

"Tillotson's office?"

"Yes."

"Isn't he going to have a dozen men out looking for you?"

"I doubt it. Think about it. Once he thinks it through far enough to know where those ledgers are going, do you think he's going to be very quick to claim them? I doubt it. My best guess is he's a long way from Eastport by now, headed for the West Indies or maybe England in the fastest schooner he could find."

Billy said, "You're probably right. Even if he sends someone to get you, they'll be looking for a man named Robert Dulcey. So is the law in New Haven."

John shook his head. "I think you'll find out the New Haven authorities caught Robert Dulcey and hanged him about a month ago. That's why I had to leave Eastport. Some seamen were talking about it. If Tillotson heard about that while I was still there, he'd have had me dead overnight. As it is, when he finds out Dulcey is dead, who will he go looking for? He has no idea who I am. "

Matthew blanched. "It got that close?"

"It got a little tight there for one night."

"Where are those ledgers?"

"Here in my bag." He jerked open the strings and laid the two heavy ledgers on the counter. "Take a hard look at these and see if you can believe what's there. And be sure you don't lose them. If President Madison wants to know what's going on up there, he's got most of it right here."

"Bad?"

John shook his head. "I doubt you'll believe it, at least at first. There's grounds for war in those ledgers. And I need to ask, how is President Madison getting along? I left just about the time he was inaugurated, and I haven't heard."

There was a pause before Matthew answered. "He's in a battle. Political battle. He's finding out both the French and British have almost no regard for the United States. They see us as a newly arrived nuisance, not a newly arrived nation. They both stop American ships on the high seas for any reason they can think of, and they confiscate American cargoes in most of our ships they find in European ports. President Madison is getting advice from his own people that is contradictory. Some say negotiate, some say go to war and get it over with. No one knows where this will all finally come out."

For a moment John stared at the ledgers in thought. "I can tell you one thing. I can't see a way that negotiations will stop what those ledgers tell us."

Matthew laid his hand on the two books. "Enough of this for now. We'll lock these in the vault and talk later. You better go on home to Laura. She's concerned."

"I will. Let mother know I'm fine. I'll be over to see her tomorrow."

John retied his seaman's bag, swung it over his shoulder, and looked at his father. "Good to see you all again. I'll be back tomorrow to start a written report. When does President Madison want you there?"

Matthew smiled. "I'll find out. He wants you with me."

John Dunson shouldered his seaman's bag, grinned and nodded at his father, then at Billy and Pettigrew, turned, and hurried out the door.

Notes

As a result of the flood of embargoes and other orders that affected international shipping on the high seas, issued by the Americans, British, French, and Russians, the seaport village of Eastport, Maine, and the British-Canadian seaports in Passamaquoddy Bay, Nova Scotia, became notorious for trafficking in black market commodities from all nations, including but not limited to Britain and the United States. In a statement to Congress in 1811, President James Madison referred to the amount of smuggling as "odious." Fraudulent bills of lading, or manifests, became commonplace, showing American plaster of paris (gypsum) going north to Canadian-British markets, while Spanish produce was coming south into New England. In fact, the plaster of paris was sulphur, saltpeter, lumber, barrel staves, flour, wheat, and a long list of other products, and the Spanish produce was largely rum, shipped from the West Indies north to Passamaquoddy, then back down to the markets in New England. Between 1805 and 1810, the traffic into and out of these ports had increased five hundred percent, most of it illegal smuggling and black market. Because land was cheap on the Canadian side of the international border and smuggling was reaping astronomical profits, towns and villages had sprung up all along the northern international border where none had been before. In 1807, when America stopped supplying lumber to England, Napoleon induced Russia to close its trade from the Baltic states to England, which cut off that source of wood to maintain the English navy. As a consequence, the lumber trade from Canada to England leaped dramatically. When legal action was taken to prosecute the smugglers and black marketers, nothing could be done because of the "sudden absence of any experts to testify" against the criminal offenders. They were paid by smugglers to refuse to testify, or they disappeared under mysterious conditions. See Stagg, *Mister Madison's War,* pp. 22–31, 39–41.

The Macon Bill, as proposed by Congressman Nathaniel Macon, attempted to stop all trade with ships of the foreign powers until they recognized America's neutral rights, whereupon the United States would resume trade with that power. The bill was drafted and argued but defeated in Congress on March 16, 1810. See Wills, *James Madison,* pp. 87–88.

For the geographic locations of Eastport, Passamaquoddy Bay, and Machias Bay, see *National Geographic Map of Our Fifty States,* National Geographic Society, Washington, D.C., 1978, map of Maine, p. 37.

John Matthew Dunson is a fictional character.

Washington, D.C.
December 1809

CHAPTER VI

★ ★ ★

*M*atthew reached to grasp the thin, small hand of President James Madison while his mind recoiled from the shock of the appearance of the little man.

Haggard—white—eyes haunted—something's gone wrong—he's in trouble—England?—France?—war?

Madison shook Matthew's hand warmly, but his smile was wooden and his voice lacked vitality. "Welcome, Mister Dunson, welcome to my new home. Such as it is."

The Executive Mansion was less than half finished. Of the more than thirty rooms, less than half had been plastered, and of those, only a few were painted. Piles of stones for fireplaces were heaped about at random, and discarded bits and pieces of boards mingled with chunks of dried plaster and sawdust were swept into corners. The hardwood floors showed a thin spread of dust. Outside, in the clearing surrounding the huge, square structure, great piles of accumulated construction trash were scattered wherever the workmen had found it convenient.

"Won't you please come in," Madison continued, and stepped back to allow Matthew and John to enter. The room was large, square, plastered, and painted, and the fireplace that dominated one wall was finished nearly to the ceiling. There was nothing—no paintings, no murals, no draperies—to break the stark, white plainness of the room. Temporary bookshelves lined one wall, with books carefully arranged. A large leather upholstered chair stood behind a massive oak desk, with four matching upholstered chairs facing it. On the desk were papers and files, neatly stacked. Directly in the center were two huge ledgers with a bound document three inches thick. Both John and Matthew recognized them instantly as the ledgers John had brought back from Eastport and the report he had written.

Madison gestured. "I take it this is your son John?"

There was a light in Matthew's eyes. "It is. John, it is my honor to present you to President James Madison."

John bowed slightly and thrust out his hand. "I am honored, sir. You are a legend in our household."

There was genuine pleasure in Madison's face as he seized the hand and shook it warmly. "Being a legend is wonderful, but it begs the question, a legend for what? I have lately worried that my so-called legend is for bumbling and mismanagement. I can only hope you see it otherwise."

"I do, sir."

"I take it you have a son named James?"

"I do, sir."

"Is it possible I have the honor of his being named after myself?"

"You do."

"When I get to Boston next, I trust you will allow me the blessed privilege of meeting the little fellow."

"It will be my pleasure."

Madison gestured. "Let us be seated."

Facing Matthew and John across the desk, Madison gave no time for pleasantries or inquiries about his wife, Dolley, or conditions in the chaotic sprawl that was called Washington, D.C., or his election to the presidency of the United States, or the events of his inauguration. He tapped the file resting on the two great, battered, worn ledgers and spoke to John.

"I doubt you know what you did for me—and your country—by bringing these ledgers and making this report. I knew generally what was happening in the north, but I had no concept of the . . . *massive* . . . extent of it, or who was involved. I was appalled—frankly, stunned—with what those ledgers contain. Extending my thanks is far too little to make you understand what you have done. The United States stands in your debt, sir."

John nodded but remained silent, and Madison went on.

"I requested you be here with your father because you are the one who must answer a critical question. Should it become necessary, would you be willing to appear before the United States Congress to testify as to where you obtained these documents?"

John stiffened, caught by surprise, mind frozen for a moment. "Yes, sir. I would be willing to do that."

Madison raised a finger in warning. "Appearing before Congress is a very unique experience. Some senators on the committee will attempt to discredit you, and the rules of such inquiries do not provide much protection for the witness. It is not like a courtroom where objections can be made and a judge can maintain some semblance of order and fair play. Are you ready for that?"

"I'll answer their questions. Their conduct is up to them."

"Well said." Madison turned to Matthew.

"I need help, and I need it from other than these . . . politicians . . . who have difficulty rising above their paralyzing compulsion for power and position. I do not wish to get into the endless clash between the Republicans and the Federalists on just about everything. Most of it is rhetoric for public consumption, not a plan to resolve the problems of this country. Am I clear on why I invited you here?"

Matthew shifted in his chair, eyes locked with Madison's. "You are."

Madison drew and exhaled a great breath and paused for a moment to arrange his thoughts with the simple logic of the genius that had elevated him to the Executive Mansion.

"Let's start at the beginning. The Rule of '56."

Matthew's eyes narrowed for a moment, recalling the British policy regarding commercial shipping on the high seas. The British had declared it in 1756, the year after they entered the Seven Years' War with France for possession of the thirteen American colonies. With it they meant to cripple French shipping and wreak havoc with the French treasury.

Madison spoke rapidly. "The rule declared that trade closed to a neutral sovereign during times of peace could not be reopened in a time of war. The British meant it to stop American ships from carrying cargoes from France to her colonies in the West Indies at times when French ships could not do it."

Madison paused for a moment. "The policy was pretty much a failure because shipping companies found too many ways to avoid it, and for a time the British weren't diligent in enforcing it."

Matthew nodded understanding, and Madison went on.

"Then Napoleon Bonaparte rose to threaten the entire political and economic structure of Europe. That man intended becoming Emperor of the world! He established what is now called his Continental System, which was his plan to bring England to her knees by destroying her economically. The first step was Napoleon's Berlin Decree of 1806. It was a blockade of the British Isles altogether! Simply close down all shipping to and from the British Isles! It banished all ships that had touched a British harbor from entering a French harbor, and anything made in the British Isles was subject to seizure, no matter where it was found, even in ships of neutral nations. That included the United States!"

Madison's face was showing color as he continued.

"As you no doubt know, in 1807, the British retaliated with several of their infamous 'Orders in Council.' Collectively, those Orders declared a blockade of all ports that were closed to British trade, and required any neutral country that wished to trade in such ports to first stop in England and pay transit duties. Transit duties? Tribute! If American ships wanted to trade with France, they had to pay tribute to England for the privilege! Outrageous!"

For a moment Madison paused to collect his thoughts.

"Bonaparte retaliated. His 'Milan Decree.' Any neutral vessel submitting to the British Orders in Council was subject to seizure by any French vessel, wherever found. If American ships complied with the British Orders, they could be seized by the French. It left no choice for American ships. To obey the policy of either country laid them open to seizure by the other."

Madison stopped. For a moment he stared at his hands on the desk before him, and then leaned forward, eyes alive.

"Both of them—England and France—confessed that their decrees and orders were illegal—violated established maritime law—but each insisted they were only protecting their own interests from the ravages of the other. Both of them have attempted to minimize the devastation they're bringing down on the rest of the world with small concessions, but it isn't working."

He settled back in his chair. "We tried to strike back. Congress passed the Non-Importation Act of 1806, which wasn't enforced until 1807, and it was followed by the Non-Exportation Embargo that prevented all American cargoes bound for foreign trade from leaving American ports. It was a desperate measure, but President Jefferson signed it. We soon learned that it was being ignored. We passed the Enforcement Act of 1809 to enforce it, and gave unheard-of powers to our customs officials, including the use of the army and navy to enforce it, if necessary."

He paused to shake his head. "Imagine. Using our own military to enforce our own embargo against our own commercial trade."

He stopped to open a file and point to the top paper.

"Do you know what all these orders and embargoes have done to the United States? In 1807, two years ago, our exports were valued at one-hundred-eight million dollars. Last year, 1808, our exports were valued at twenty-two million dollars. It has cost us eighty-six million dollars in exports in one year! *One year!*"

He paused for only a moment and then went on. "In the midst of all this, do you know how many American ships have been seized by the two of them? Over seven hundred, as of now, with no end of it in sight!"

John sat bolt upright in his chair, shocked, wide-eyed. Matthew turned to look at him but remained silent. Madison peered at him, nodded his head slowly, then went on.

"This year we repealed both the Non-Importation Act and the embargo, and passed a non-trade act against both Britain and France. American ships can deal with all foreign ports except the ones belonging to those two countries. It has been of some small help but has fallen woefully short of being any real solution."

He cleared his throat, reflected for a moment, then continued.

"Rumors and wild stories began coming in that vessels of all flags were operating in the north, with smuggling and black-market trade reaching astronomical proportions. I asked for and received reports from various governmental sources. The reports came in, some from Republicans, some from Federalists, and badly inconsistent. Useless. I had to know first-hand from someone involved in maritime shipping—someone without a political agenda—what the truth is."

He reached to place a hand on John's report. "That's when I turned to you, and you turned to your son." He faced John. "Perhaps now you can begin to understand the value of these ledgers and your report. From them we know that all the embargoes and the orders issued to keep the seas open for free trade have done little more than make thousands of criminals."

He turned back to Matthew. "You know that during Jefferson's presidency, the war hawks in Congress raised a great hue and cry for war against England or France or both, as the means to restore our foreign trade. Jefferson refused, and we suffered. We are still suffering. When I assumed the presidency earlier this year, I likewise determined to find a resolution to this . . . disaster . . . on the seas, without war. I abhor the thought. Surely there has to be a way to restore common sense and civility to international trade without the evils of shedding blood in an all-out war."

Again Madison paused to clear his throat and wipe at his mouth with a handkerchief. "You have an advantage over me, Matthew. You have experienced war—seen what it does to men—the shedding of blood, the scarring of their lives. I have not. I have never borne arms against an enemy, never taken life, never seen men destroyed by musket or cannon."

Madison paused again, and Matthew shifted his weight in his chair with his mind moving ahead. *We're there—here it comes.*

Madison interlaced his fingers and leaned forward, forearms on his desk, eyes boring in. His words came spaced, quiet.

"Tell me. Were Jefferson and I wrong? Have we reached such a pass that war is necessary to preserve the Republic? Is it worth declaring war to restore sanity to our international trade?"

For a time the only sound in the room was the ticking of a carved clock on the mantel of the half-finished fireplace. Matthew's voice sounded oddly loud as it broke the silence.

"I think you're asking the wrong question."

Madison's eyebrows arched. "Explain."

"I think the right question is, can the Republic be saved and free trade be restored *without* war."

Madison's eyes half closed for a few seconds while he pondered the thought. "You think it is that simple? We live with what we have, or we go to war to change it?"

Matthew did not hesitate. "Yes. That simple."

"And what is your answer to that question?"

"No. I do not think free trade can be restored without war."

"You propose the United States declare war on England? Or France? Or both?"

"No, not yet. I think the United States has an obligation to two duties before it considers war."

Madison sat silent, waiting, and Matthew went on.

"First, do everything possible to settle our differences with the foreign powers. Exhaust every possibility. Pass whatever laws Congress thinks will restore free trade without bloodshed, and make it known to the world that you have done it. I think we're deep into a test of our morality. Our first test. The survival of the Constitution rests on the issue of whether we are a decent, moral people. We have a duty."

Madison's voice was scarcely above a whisper. "Go on."

"Second, prepare. If it must be war, we've got to prepare to protect our people in all circumstances. We have the duty to spare as many as we can, and that is best done by being prepared."

John sat mesmerized, speechless at what he was hearing between his president and his father.

Madison asked, "Do you think we can succeed by negotiating?"

Matthew shook his head. "I doubt it." He paused and for a time stared at the floor, then raised his head. "I know the evils of war. Men killed, maimed, crippled, blinded, lives shattered. Memories in their hearts and their minds that sicken them for the rest of their lives. Mothers, wives, children left alone. I detest it. It is an evil thing." He paused for a few moments to select his words. "But, finally, if evil is to be defeated, war will be necessary. I think we must be certain it is the last resort, and we must prepare."

Madison stared at his hands for a moment before asking, "In your opinion, why have negotiations failed so badly?"

"Because both England and France see us as more of a nuisance than a sovereign nation. Napoleon intends conquering England. England means to stop him. We're three thousand miles away and are going through the throes of learning to take our place among nations. They're never going to give us respect just because we're here. We're going to have to get it the same way they did. Stand up for ourselves. It usually takes a bloody nose to get respect from a bully."

Madison nodded. "What of the *Chesapeake* affair? I've demanded satisfaction, and they are paying no attention. Do I drop it?"

"No. They were wrong in that matter, and a dozen others. I would not yield on matters where they're wrong and we are right."

"That was my conclusion." Madison took a deep breath and exhaled it slowly, thoughtfully, before going on. "We spoke once before about Canada. In my view, taking Canada would accomplish two things. It would cut off an indispensable source of lumber and other commodities that England must have, and it would bring the British to the bargaining table to get Canada back. My question of you is, am I right?"

For several seconds Matthew closed his eyes in deep concentration before he spoke. "I doubt it. Our army is unprepared for a major engagement. And we don't know what to expect from the Indians. Worse, I doubt that taking Canada would stop the shipping trade from there to England. I think the smuggling would continue. It's too profitable, and there are too many people up there on both sides who have higher regard for wealth than anything else. I don't think taking Canada would stop what's going on."

"You think it would be a mistake, then?"

"I do."

"You mentioned the Indians. What of them? Should we consider them an enemy and engage them in war?"

"I would not. The Indians are only interested in getting back the land we have taken from them. They will side with the British so long as they believe the British can help them do it, and the British are using that as leverage to raise the Indians against us. The British have no intention of giving them the land. They will use the Indians against us, and if they win, that will be the end of it."

A puzzled look crossed Madison's small, heart-shaped face. "Are the Indians so blind they can't see that?"

Matthew answered slowly. "In times like these most of us get lost in anger over the injustices and insanity of lust for power and treasure. We lose sight of the violations of the fundamentals that caused it all. England and France each want to rule the world. Americans want lands rightfully belonging to the Indians. It's all wrong, but we all find justification for it, and the result is conflict. War. I don't think we can expect it to stop. We can only try to rectify our mistakes and move on. Maybe that's what America is all about. Maybe that's what the Constitution you created intended. Am I right?"

For a time Madison sat silent, without moving. "Before the Almighty, I hope you are. I hope you are."

John was frozen, his mind reeling with the depths into which it had been plunged. He glanced at his father, seeing a man he never knew existed.

Madison eased back in his chair. "Is there anything else you think I should hear? Anything at all?"

Matthew nodded his head. "Only one thing, Mister President. I would ask you to be certain there is no other option before you declare war. Some of us have much to lose."

Madison turned to look at John. The three of them remained silent, but none of them missed the portent in Matthew's request.

Madison looked back at Matthew. "You have my solemn promise." He rose. "I think I've covered the matters I intended. As always, I stand in your debt. We will talk again, I'm sure."

He walked around his desk and grasped John's hand, then Matthew's. "You will give my best regards to your wives and families? I think of you people often."

"We shall. Carry our regards to your wife."

Madison smiled and started for the door with Matthew and John following. "I shall. She is just becoming acquainted with Washington society. Seems to enjoy it, but she seems to enjoy society wherever she is."

There was genuine warmth and sincerity in his voice and a sense of relief as he reached for the large brass door handle.

"Have a safe journey home."

Notes

In the time period framed in this chapter, there were a great number of policies, embargoes, Orders in Council, and decrees issued by France, England, the United States, Russia, and other sovereigns, many of them illegal, most of them aimed at establishing superiority in the commercial trade at sea at the expense of all other nations. It would not be possible to list all of them in this chapter, or even in the remainder of this book. For that reason, only those most critical to an understanding of the commercial war then existing on the high seas have been referred to. The impact of this horrendous conflict resulted in the loss of eighty-six million American dollars in export trade from 1807 to 1808. For an explanation of these decrees and embargoes, as they are set forth in this chapter, see Hickey, *The War of 1812*, pp. 10, 18–21, with the loss figures to America's export trade appearing on p. 21; Stagg, *Mister Madison's War*, pp. 22, 28–29; Wills, *James Madison*, pp. 80–88; Roosevelt, *The Naval War of 1812*, p. 5.

James Madison was inaugurated president in March, 1809, Wills, *James Madison*, p. 80.

Boston
December 1809

CHAPTER VII

$\mathscr{T}$he temperature had risen in the still, wintry morning air of Boston town, and a little after one o'clock a thick, gentle snowfall of great, wet flakes settled over the peninsula to lock it in a quiet hush. By midafternoon the city had magically transformed from the gray of winter to a pristine wonderland of white. Citizens hurried through the streets with their hats pulled low and their coat collars turned up, smiling for no reason they could think of, spirits lifted by the rare beauty of trees and bushes and fences that had been naked and gray and stark now dressed in radiant white. Children coming from school shouted and cavorted, and threw snowballs at anything and anybody. People passing in the streets called at them to stop, and turned to take the frozen missiles on their backs, and laughed as they hurried on.

By late afternoon the Dunson family had gathered in the mansion once owned by Doctor Henry Thorpe, inherited from him by Kathleen before her marriage to Matthew. In the years following, it had become their home, and on special occasions the central gathering place for the children and grandchildren of the aging matriarch, Margaret Dunson. None knew why Matthew had called them all together for supper on this snowy night; they only knew it meant gathering at two great tables, one in the dining room, the other in the parlor, covered with white linen and porcelain plates and silverware and steaming bowls of meats and vegetables and condiments and cold buttermilk from the root cellar and hot cider from the stove. The grownups would sit at one table and the children at the other, teasing, pointing, creating an uproar, while their parents watched and scolded and gave up hope of stopping it. The house would be filled with aromas not to be forgotten and endless chatter. At the end there would be a great pudding, or stacks of tarts, or custards and pies, and endless talk. The babies would be taken to the master bedroom to sleep on the great bed, and no one would want to leave until the striking of the big clock on the mantle said the hour was late.

At six o'clock the tables were spread, and at Matthew's direction, they all knelt beside their chairs. Uncle Adam returned thanks to the Almighty for their blessings and the bounties of the table, and they all took their seats and dug in.

At seven o'clock Matthew pushed himself back from the table, patted his full paunch, raised a hand, and waited for quiet.

"Our thanks to all who prepared this. It was special. Now let's all help clear the tables."

In short order the leftover food was taken to the root cellar, the last of the dishes was dried and stacked in the heavy oak cupboards, the dishwater was thrown out the back door into the snow, and fresh water was heating on the stove to wash the bowls that would be used later to serve a piping hot custard. Matthew called to his two grown daughters.

"Linda. Louise. Would you gather the children into the parlor and tend them for a few minutes? Read to them?"

Margaret said, "Read them the story of the birth of Jesus. The book of Luke."

Matthew nodded. "That would be good."

The two girls called to the children, turned a deaf ear to their arguments, and herded them into the parlor to sit them down. Linda opened the huge, leather-bound family Bible, laid it on her lap, and opened it to the book of Luke. Louise pressed her fingers to her lips and whispered "Shhhhhh," and the children quieted as Linda began to read.

Matthew gave a head signal to the others. "The library," he said quietly and led the way. Two of the walls were covered with dark oak shelves, holding hundreds of books. A great stone fireplace dominated the third wall, with low flames dancing from hardwood logs. On the fourth wall were three paintings, two of great sailing ships, and one of George Washington. Matthew took his place behind the huge oak desk and gestured, and the ten adults took seats while Matthew remained standing.

"We won't be long. I asked you here tonight because I think we need to get ready for what is coming. You all know John and I spent time with President Madison in Washington, D.C., at his request, and got back two days ago."

He stopped and watched his family glance at each other, then settle.

"He did most of the talking. He reviewed the state of affairs as it now stands between England and the United States. He included France and Russia. He went into the embargoes and the decrees and the orders of council issued by just about everybody, which have made international shipping into a nightmare. Most of the shipping done by our company is confined to ports on this continent, so we haven't felt it like some other shipping lines have. We've lost a few ships as you all know, and insurance rates are cutting into profits, but we're surviving."

He stopped and drew a breath. "But that's not what I called you here for. He had John and me there to give the best answer we could on two questions."

The room became silent. No one moved.

"He wanted our opinion on the question of taking Canada. Invading. Conquering it. Taking it away from England. His reasoning was that for England to survive, it needs lumber and masts to maintain its navy, and all the embargoes stop them from getting it from the United States. They are getting it from Canada. It was his idea that if we were to occupy Canada and cut off that source, we could cripple the English navy and bring England to the bargaining table to end the commercial war."

There was murmuring for a time, and Matthew waited until it stopped.

"He wanted my opinion on whether taking Canada was the answer."

Billy interrupted. "You mean war?"

"Yes. War."

The women gasped, and Matthew stopped to wait while open talk dwindled.

"I told him no, I did not think it was. He had John's report and those two big ledgers John brought back from his adventure up north there on his desk, and in my mind there's no question. No matter who occupies Canada, the English or the United States, the profits coming from the sale of lumber and other commodities up there are so enormous that men and ships would go right on with the trade, no matter what the law says. The ledgers John brought back are filled with evidence that right now, today, there is a network of smugglers and black-marketeers operating up there who are making astronomical fortunes. I can see no way to stop it. So I told President Madison that taking Canada was not the answer."

Adam raised a hand. "Does President Madison understand the waterways up there? The St. Lawrence? The Richelieu? The Great Lakes? They connect thousands of miles of space with a thin population. Does he know how difficult it would be to occupy all of it?"

Matthew shook his head. "Remember, President Madison has never commanded an army. Or a navy. Never borne arms. Never been in combat. He is a master at theory and politics—even a genius—but is lacking in the practical. That's why he had me there."

Caleb rounded his mouth and blew air and muttered, "May the Almighty protect us from theorists, politicians, and geniuses."

Matthew could not stifle a grin, and Billy chuckled out loud. Matthew went on.

"He asked about the Indians. Should we attack and conquer them? I told him the Indians want only to get the return of their lands—the lands taken from them by us Americans. The British are making promises to them that if they will support the British against us, the British will get their lands for them. The truth is, the British have no such intentions, but they are willing to make the promises so they can use the Indians as a weapon against us. If we attack the Indians, we'll have to fight England."

Matthew stopped. For several seconds he labored with his thoughts and then continued.

"He wanted to know about war. Could we restore peace and common sense to our dealings with the British and the French without war?"

Instantly all six women sat upright, focused, waiting.

Matthew hesitated for a moment, and then laid it before them. "I told him no, eventually it will likely come to war."

Margaret jerked a hand up, her aged face alive, voice too high, eyes on fire. "No! No more war. It only leads to another war. I won't let you go. I watched my John go, and I lost him. You can't go, Matthew, nor Adam or Caleb or John. I won't let you go! Do you hear?"

Matthew's voice was filled with pain and deep compassion as he gently spoke to his mother. "I know, Mother. I know. I was there with Father. I've seen war. So have Billy and Caleb. I'll do everything in my power to avoid it. I promise. But if it must come, we have to be prepared."

Margaret shook her head violently. "No. It's evil. The Almighty will curse us."

"We'll do the best we can, Mother, I give you my promise."

Margaret mumbled under her breath and settled, and Matthew went on.

"I told President Madison what I just told Mother. We're a young country and just learning our way. France and England see us as a nuisance, not a sovereign nation. They're going to keep us under their hammer as long as they can. We must choose to accept that, or to stand up to them and gain respect. And that means going to war."

He looked at Kathleen, then his sisters, and his brother's wives, and continued.

"I also told President Madison we have two duties we must perform. First, we have to exhaust every possibility of avoiding war. That's what the United States and our Constitution are all about—honorable peace. Only as a last resort do we consider war. And I told him that if it becomes clear that's the only answer, we must prepare for it. The nation has a duty to save as many of its citizens as it can."

Margaret was sitting with her face set, unyielding. The five younger wives and mothers were erect, stiff, waiting.

"If it comes to it, I think much of the war will be fought at sea. If that happens, I don't think we have a chance. I've inquired, and right now, the United States navy has fewer than twenty ships that can carry cannon. The British have over six hundred gunboats. It's true that most of their navy is in Europe, engaged in trying to stop the French navy, but should war come with the United States, many of them would be sent here. If the contest between England and France comes to an end, the British could send their entire navy over here. Six hundred gunboats against fewer than twenty."

Laura gasped and went white with fear. "John? You're talking about taking my John to war against six hundred English war ships?"

Barbara seized Caleb's arm and exclaimed, "I won't let him go!"

Matthew raised a hand for silence and waited until the talk died.

"Let me finish. President Madison agreed with me. By that I mean he promised he would do everything in his power to negotiate this to a peaceful conclusion with those European powers before he would consider war. And I believe he will. There is hope that eventually, somehow, he will succeed."

Adam asked, "And if he doesn't?"

Matthew shook his head. "We must get ready. It won't happen soon. It may never happen. But if it does—when it does—we have to be ready. In this room are some of the best-trained naval officers in this country. There will be need for you. And perhaps for me."

Kathleen exclaimed, "You've done more than your share already!"

Matthew looked her in the eye. "My father has. I don't know if I have."

Kathleen swallowed hard and said no more. Matthew went on.

"I thought it was on my shoulders to bring you here and share this. Think on it. Get your minds ready. Each of you will have to decide what you'll do. Nothing will be worse than to find ourselves in a war unprepared. The cost of that would be more than any of us could bear."

He waited, and for a time those in the room were lost in their own thoughts, their own fears. Billy broke the silence.

"Anything else?"

Matthew nodded. "One thing. What I've said is only my opinion, and I could be wrong. I hope I am. All we can do is watch and wait and get ready."

Billy stood and reached to help Brigitte from her chair. "We'll know soon enough."

They all stood except Margaret. The men stood quietly for a time, thoughtful, saying little, reflective, while the women spoke all at once, hands thrust against their chests, voices raised. Matthew gave them time to vent their fears and gain their balance before he broke in.

"Let's get back out with the children. We've still got custard to serve, and I imagine Linda and Louise can use some help about now."

Margaret struggled to rise. "You tell Mister Madison that none of you are going to fight his war. You tell him!"

Matthew walked around his desk and leaned over to gently put his hands on his mother's shoulders. "I'll tell him, Mother. Let me help you up."

"Oh, fiddle," Margaret exclaimed. "I'm not dead yet. I can still get up out of a chair."

"I know you can. Now let me help you."

Caleb came to her other side to help her to her feet and spoke to Matthew. "Tell President Madison that if this comes to war we'll turn Mother loose on the British. That ought to put the fear into them."

Margaret took her first tentative step while she looked up at Caleb. "If they come to get my family, I'll give them a piece of my mind!"

They were through the library door and walking toward the parlor when Billy came up beside Matthew and spoke quietly.

"Did President Madison say anything about what's happening in the West? The British and the Indians at Amherstburg? The gathering of Shawnee at Prophetstown where the Wabash and Tippecanoe rivers meet? The Indians talking hot for war?"

"He knows, but he's not clear on what he should do about it."

Billy continued. "From what Eli said, it's only a matter of time before something ignites it. It could be bad."

Matthew looked him in the eye. "I think you're right. I think the die is cast. I doubt any of us—English, Indian, American—can stop the direction this is moving. The only question is, what will finally start it, and where?"

Billy nodded. "It will most likely start right off our coast. Too many British ships out there with the attitude they can do as they please, and too many American ships that won't take it much longer. One of these days . . ."

Notes

Members of the Dunson family are all fictional.

The tendency of President Madison to attempt to solve the critical problems of the presidency with theories and political adventures, rather than seeing them in the practical context of the realities of the harsh treatment the United States was receiving from both France and England, is accurately addressed in this chapter. See Wills, *James Madison,* pp. 7–8.

The tremendous imbalance of both naval and army power between England and the United States, with the Americans able to field fewer than six thousand soldiers and fewer than twenty armed naval vessels, while England could field about 250,000 soldiers and six hundred armed ships, is set forth in Stagg, *Mister Madison's War,* p. 3.

CHAPTER VIII

*I*n the still, warm calm of late evening, Commodore John
Rodgers, United States Navy, medium height, built strong, regular features, young, eager, laid his quill beside the inkwell. In the yellow light
of two lanterns he sat quietly at his desk in the captain's quarters while
he read the entries he had just finished in the daily log of the USS
President, a large, strongly built, three-masted ship-o'-the-line. The big vessel was tied to the New York docks on the south end of Manhattan
Island, loaded heavy and riding low in the quiet, still waters of the harbor, scarcely moving with the gentle rise and fall of the currents and
swells. She had been built for one purpose: carry forty-four cannon and
hunt British ships.

Commodore Rodgers glanced at the clock—just past nine o'clock—
adjusted one lantern, and tracked the carefully formed words with his
finger as he read.

"May 15, 1811 . . . took on dried beef, salted pork bellies, flour,
water, and other necessaries sufficient for two months service at sea . . .
fully provisioned . . . assigned crew arrived and is on board . . . appear to
be seasoned and reliable seamen . . . awaiting orders as promised . . ."

He nodded his satisfaction, plucked up his quill, dipped the split tip
in the ink bottle, and scratched his signature. He laid the quill down and
leaned back in his chair to stretch and dig the heels of his hands into

tired eyes. He was not expecting the rap that came at his door, and for a moment stared at it before he called, "Enter."

A young ensign, tall, slender, removed his tricorn, clamped it under his left arm, and ducked to enter through the small, low door. He bumped his head against the top of the doorframe once, winced, faced Rodgers, and quickly jerked upright to full attention. He whipped his right hand up to a salute and exclaimed, "Ensign Potter bringing a sealed letter to Commodore John Rodgers. Very important message. May I presume you to be Commodore Rodgers? Sir!"

Rodgers fought off a grin. "You may."

Ensign Potter shoved his hand inside his tunic and fumbled for several seconds before his hand reappeared with a letter.

"Here, sir, is the letter. From the secretary of the Navy. Paul Hamilton. Sir."

Rodgers stood to accept the document. "Thank you, Ensign Potter. That will be all." He looked at the scrolled writing on the envelope, then turned it to break the wax seal. He stopped to look at Ensign Potter, still standing as rigid as the mainmast on the huge man-of-war, and asked, "Was there anything else, Ensign Potter?"

"Sir, would the Commodore care to have me wait. In case there's a reply? Sir!"

"That will not be necessary. Thank you for your attention to this very important document."

"Sir, no thanks are necessary, sir. Am I dismissed, sir?"

"Yes, you are dismissed."

"Sir, thank you, sir."

The young ensign turned on his heel and marched back to the door, ducked his head, bumped it once again on the low door frame as he stepped through, and disappeared.

Rodgers chuckled out loud. "Hit his head both coming and going. Now *that* boy has the makings of a real naval officer!"

He sat back down on his chair, broke the seal, and smoothed the letter flat on his desk to read it carefully.

"May 6, 1811 . . . assigned to take command of the USS *President,* forty-four guns . . . crew assigned to arrive on or before May 15, 1811 . . . sail as soon thereafter as possible . . . patrol the waters off Cape Henry, New Jersey coast . . . seek British vessels . . . capture them if possible . . . bring them to nearest United States port . . . if capture not possible then engage them wherever found and destroy them if necessary . . . objective is to rid the waters off the American east coast of all British interference."

The signature was that of Paul Hamilton, secretary, United States Navy.

His eyes were bright as he contemplated his orders. *Finally! Finally!* He stopped and read the letter a second time, slowly, speaking each word softly to himself, to be certain the meaning was plain and unmistakable and could not lead to an unintended incident on the high seas.

There was but one message, and it could not be more clear: find British ships, capture them if possible. If not, sink them on the spot. Either way, get rid of them. Just find them and get rid of them. No questions asked.

He could not remember how long he had waited for these orders. He only knew he was sick to the bone of British warships that had been marauding the American coastline for too long, mauling American commercial ships, stealing cargoes, seizing American seamen on any pretext they could invent. He, and nearly every American in the tiny United States Navy, had taken just about all the humiliation from the insolent, arrogant, and condescending British they could swallow. Crew members had taken enough. The prevailing spirit had almost become: Forget orders! Forget protocol! Go find a British ship in American waters and capture it or blast it to the bottom of the Atlantic! That they had not done so was a tribute to their officers who would not tolerate disobedience to orders, at any cost.

He seized the letter, rose from his chair, picked his tricorn from its peg beside the door, and walked out into the night, to the quarters of his first mate, Alexander Buford. He knocked on the cabin door, waited for the muffled, "Enter," and swung the door open. Buford, swarthy, dark-eyed and dark-haired, clearly showing Spanish blood, sat on his bunk. He rose to meet his captain.

"Sir?" he asked.

Rodgers raised a hand. "Just received our orders. Signed by Paul Hamilton himself. We're to leave earliest, to patrol the waters off Cape Henry. We are to seek British gunboats wherever we find them. Capture them if we can, and if we cannot, we're to sink them."

Buford's head thrust forward for a split second. "Engage them?"

"If they resist capture."

"You're certain?"

"Certain. In writing." He slapped the written orders against his open palm.

"When do you plan to leave?"

"Tomorrow morning at four o'clock. I want to be out of New York harbor and into the Atlantic by sunrise."

Buford reached to wipe a hand across his mouth, eyes glowing, focused, intense. "Shall I inform the crew, sir?"

"Tell them to be on the main deck at four AM ready to cast off and set sail. Do not mention these orders. I want to read this letter to them all at the same time."

Buford was grinning in anticipation as he reached for his tunic. "Yes, sir. I'll have them ready at four o'clock tomorrow morning."

It was midnight before the last lantern went out in the crew's quarters, with every man instinctively sensing that something monumental was happening, and they were to be part of it. It was past one o'clock when Commodore Rodgers twisted the wheel on his lantern and settled into his bunk in the darkness, blood up, mind racing, caught up in bright images of what tomorrow could bring. It was a long time before he drifted into a restless sleep.

At five minutes before four o'clock, Rodgers walked from his quarters out onto the quarterdeck to peer down at the main deck, Buford beside him. The entire crew stood facing them, silent, faces turned upward, eyes gleaming in the dim yellow light of the lamps. Rodgers wasted no time.

"Gentlemen, I have received our official orders from the secretary of the Navy, Paul Hamilton."

He paused. No one moved.

"We are under direct orders to leave New York Harbor for patrol of the American waters off Cape Henry. We are to find British ships wherever they might be, and we are to take them captive and return them to the nearest friendly American port."

Again he stopped, and a breathless hush seized the crew as they waited for him to continue.

Rodgers' voice came calm, solid. "Should they resist capture, we are to fire on them and sink them if necessary. Rid American waters of all British ships."

Instantly the still of the early morning was shattered by a thunderous shout of approval from the crew of the *President*. For more than a full minute, Rodgers and Buford stood still on the quarterdeck, giving their men permission to vent the humiliation and outrage they had suffered at the hands of the arrogant and despised British, listening to the sounds roll out across the dark, glassy waters of the New York Harbor. As the cheering began to quiet, Rodgers raised both hands, and it died.

"We leave now. Cast off. We can be clear of the harbor shortly after sunrise and in open water before nine o'clock."

He turned to Buford. "Carry on, Mister Buford."

The men were scattering to their duty posts before Buford could give the orders. A gentle westerly wind caught the unfurled sails on the mainmast, and the big ship moved slowly south, away from Manhattan Island, down the channel, past Long Island and Staten Island, then turned to port to clear the cape, and was out of the bay by the time the top arc of the rising sun was turning the black Atlantic waters to dark green. By nine o'clock they were running south in open seas, canvas tight in the wind and the beauty of a warm, cloudless day. It was midafternoon when a shrill, excited shout came down from the crow's nest.

"Sail—due west off starb'rd! She's British! The British Union Jack! Certain!"

On the quarterdeck, Rodgers and Buford instantly spun and jerked their telescopes to full extension and stood with feet spread while they focused on the tiny speck on the distant horizon. On the main deck, every available seaman jammed the starboard rail, eyes slitted while they searched.

Rodgers bawled his orders. "All canvas! Turn to starb'rd—due west! Set a course dead on that ship!" His arm was extended, pointing.

The helmsman spun the huge wheel while seamen scrambled up the ladders to the arms with the wind blowing their hair and beards and walked the ropes crabwise, to jerk the knots loose. The great sails on all masts dropped fluttering in the wind, and quick hands seized the ropes dangling from the lower edges to haul them in and tie them off. In seconds the big man-of-war came alive, plowing a twenty-five foot curl in the dark waters, leaving a white wake of more than one-hundred-fifty feet behind.

For long minutes Rodgers and Buford stood motionless, studying the fleck on the horizon, calculating, hoping.

"Will we catch her before dark?" Buford asked.

"It will be close," Rodgers replied softly. "What time is it?"

Buford drew his watch from his tunic pocket. "Ten minutes until four o'clock, sir." He dropped the watch back into its pocket, and there was deep hope in his voice as he muttered, "Maybe. Maybe."

Time became meaningless as the *President* plowed on. Slowly the distant speck took shape, and then began to diminish.

"She's seen us," Rodgers exclaimed. "She's running." He turned to Buford. "Get the navigator!"

"Aye, sir." Buford left the quarterdeck at a run and within half a minute returned with a young officer and spoke.

"The ship's navigator, sir. Just assigned. John Dunson."

Rodgers wasted no time on formalities. "Mister Dunson, are you acquainted with these waters?"

John's answer was instant. "I am, sir."

"Do I remember correctly? Are there reefs dead ahead, this side of the capes?"

"There are, sir. Bad ones. If that ship continues its present course those reefs will take out her hull."

"You're sure?"

"Absolutely."

For a moment Rodgers stared into the intense eyes of John Dunson, judging whether or not he could trust this young navigator. He could. He spoke to Buford. "Steady as she goes."

He turned to John. "Stand by. I'll need to know when to expect that ship to turn."

"Aye, sir. She'll turn to port. Due south. If she turns to starboard she'll run into about six reefs that protrude this direction, maybe three, four miles. They're peculiar. Unexpected. They've wrecked a lot of ships that didn't know they were there."

Rodgers narrowed his eyes. "Think her navigator knows that?"

"My guess is yes, sir. They're on the latest charts." John pointed. "I will expect that ship to turn to port."

Rodgers considered for a moment. "Do I understand this correctly? If we catch up to her, and we turn to port before she does, we can trap her against those reefs?"

"Yes, sir, you can. She'll turn to port, or she'll try to turn completely around and run for the open seas, or she'll run aground on those reefs. The only problem is time. We'll have to catch her before full dark or we'll lose her."

Rodgers nodded. "All right. You stand by. I'll need to know when to start my flanking move to port."

"Aye, sir."

Rodgers turned to the helmsman. "Hold her steady."

The big ship plowed on with anxious seamen interrupting their duties to peer straight ahead, gauging whether they were gaining on the miniscule black fleck on the horizon. The sun settled toward the western horizon, and by evening mess they were shading their eyes with their hands to peer almost directly into the great golden ball.

It happened suddenly. The coastline was in the distance, and the black dot became square sails, stopped nearly dead in the water, and for several minutes the *President* raced on. John Dunson stood beside Rodgers on the quarterdeck, concentrating intently on the speed of the big ship, the distance to the shoreline, and the location of the British ship ahead. Suddenly his arm shot up.

"Turn!" he exclaimed. "West by southwest! She's just short of the reefs straight ahead and to starb'rd. Her captain will soon realize he has to turn her completely around, or try to outrun us in a race to portside. Turn!"

Instantly Rodgers gave his orders to the helmsman. "Sou'sou'west. Now!"

The big gunboat leaned slightly to starboard as she turned to port and continued. In just ten minutes the small ship ahead turned to port and held her course with all sails full, her British flag bright in the setting sun. Every man on the main deck of the *President* was at the rails, watching in awed silence as the chase unfolded. The crew below decks prepared the evening mess, then put lids on the steaming kettles to hold them warm until the crew came down. The sun touched the mainland with the *President* running hard at an angle, trying to intercept the smaller ship as she sped due south along the rough shoreline. The sun disappeared, and in the dusky afterglow Rodgers pounded the rail of the quarterdeck with his hand. His voice was high, excited.

"I think we'll catch her." He turned to Buford. "Recognize her?"

Buford shook his head. "Can't read her name. Not enough good light. I think she's the *Belvidera.*"

Rodgers concentrated for a moment. "If she's the *Belvidera*, she has thirty-six guns. A British man-o'-war. Fair game."

"Fair game, but this is going to be close. We'll be in full nightfall soon. The moon won't rise until close to midnight. If we don't catch her in the next thirty or forty minutes, we've lost her."

Every crewman on the main deck of the *President* was at the rail, silently calculating whether the speed and the course of the two ships would bring them together before nightfall robbed them of the fight. Dusk began to close in, and the men licked at dry lips and wiped at their beards, excited, impatient, ready.

Rodgers shouted his orders. "All hands to battle stations! Load your cannon!"

Seamen sprinted to grasp the two-inch hawsers holding the heavy guns in place, and strong backs heaved to pull them back from their closed gunports. Ladles with six-foot handles were plunged into budge barrels where they measured black gunpowder, and seasoned gunners drove the ladles down the gun barrels, then turned them upside down to dump the powder before they drew them out. A second pair of hands stuffed dried grass in the gun muzzle and drove it down with a long-handled ram to lock the powder in. A third pair of eager hands hoisted a cannonball upwards and shoved it into the muzzle, followed by a ram that drove it back against the dried grass, and a little more dried grass followed to lock the cannonball against the powder charge. At the rear of the big gun, a man stuffed the fuse through the touch-hole and stood with the smoking linstock, ready to touch the fuse that would ignite the blast.

"Open your gunports," Rodgers bellowed, and men jerked the clamps clear of the gunports and pulled them open, while others set their feet and bowed their backs to pull the hawsers that rolled the guns forward into firing position.

"Steady as she goes," Rodgers called, and Buford stood beside him, unaware that he was rhythmically pounding the railing with both clenched fists as he watched the two ships plowing through the black Atlantic waters on a collision course. At eight hundred yards the British ship was a clean silhouette against the last bright glow of a sun already set. At four hundred yards the Americans could see movement on the deck of the racing ship, fast coming up on the *President's* starboard side. At two hundred yards they could clearly make out individuals on the deck.

At one hundred yards Rodgers turned to the helmsman and ordered, "Turn due south, broadside."

The big gunboat swung to port and came alongside the smaller British ship at seventy yards, and Rodgers raised his horn to bellow, "I am Commodore John Rodgers of the United States Navy. Spill your sails. I am coming aboard."

There was no answer.

"Spill your sails, or I will presume you to be adversarial, and I will fire!"

Every man strained to hear the response, but the only sounds were the wind in the sails and rigging, and the curl being cut by the bow of both ships.

Rodgers took a deep breath and turned to his gun crews on the starboard side. They were turned to face him, nearly holding their breath as they waited for the order.

"Fire!"

The linstocks dropped, the fuses caught, and twenty heavy cannon on the starboard side bucked and roared. The muzzle flashes lighted both ships, and the billowing white smoke filled the void between the two racing vessels as the sound rolled out across the black water. The heavy cannonballs tore into the smaller ship, splintering rails, smashing into the two masts, cutting hawsers, knocking men down, some never to rise again.

"Reload!" shouted Rodgers and then turned his horn once more to the British ship.

"Spill your sails or suffer another broadside!"

Only three guns on the port side of the British ship had survived the near point-blank broadside, and they suddenly blasted an answer. Two cannonballs struck the *President* just below the second deck, harmless. The third cleared the main deck by ten feet and dropped into the sea beyond.

"Fire!" Rodgers shouted, and the second broadside roared. In the momentary light of the muzzle flashes, John Dunson suddenly jerked forward, staring.

"Reload!" Rodgers ordered, and efficient hands backed the guns from the gunports long enough to reload and roll them back into position.

"Fire!" Rodgers called, and once again the heavy cannon thundered.

John was at the rail, clutching it with both hands, head thrust forward, eyes wide as he concentrated on the image of the British ship in the light of the muzzle flashes. He saw holes smashed into her hull, and the shudder of the small ship at the impact of the third broadside, and watched both of her masts slowly topple, broken, shattered.

Suddenly he straightened and turned to Rodgers, face white, voice high, intense.

"Sir, I don't think that ship is the *Belvidera!* She's not big enough, and she doesn't have enough guns!"

Rodgers stared at him, dumbstruck. "Not the *Belvidera?* Who do you think she is?"

"I think it's the *Little Belt!* Seventy tons. Twenty guns, not thirty-six! The *Little Belt* has been seen in these waters in the past three weeks, and I think that's her! I think we're cutting a ship half our size to pieces! She had no chance from the beginning! We're outside the unwritten law!"

Rodgers voice was furious, filled with outrage. "Why didn't she answer my challenge? Why? She knew better!"

"Maybe she thought she could outrun us," John exclaimed. "Maybe her captain is under orders not to allow us to board. Pride—arrogance—who knows?—but whatever the reason, the report that captain will make to England will crucify us for what we've done. We might have committed an international incident that will start a war!"

Rodgers turned on his heel to face Buford. "Mister Buford?"

He shook his head. "She's smaller than I thought, sir. I think Mister Dunson is right. I think it is the *Little Belt.*"

Rodgers stared at him. "Do we withdraw?"

"I would challenge one more time. If she does not answer, I would withdraw, sir."

For several seconds Rodgers stood stock still, staring out across the narrow void between the two ships, then he cleared his throat and raised his horn.

"Identify yourself. Identify yourself. Are you the *Little Belt?*"

Every man in the crew of the *President* held his breath, waiting.

There was no answer.

"Do you need help? If you need help, spill your sails. We have a ship's surgeon and medical supplies. If you need help, spill your sails. Answer. Answer!"

Again they waited, and there were only the sounds of the wind and the sea.

For a full thirty seconds Rodgers paced, slamming one fist into the palm of his other hand over and over again, grinding his teeth, face livid red. He stopped and barked orders to the helmsman.

"Hard to port. Due east. Withdraw. Withdraw."

Then all the air went out of him and his shoulders slumped. He turned to Buford. "Order the gun crews to stand down. Close the gun ports. Make for open water."

"Aye, sir."

The big ship made the turn with Rodgers, Buford, and John all standing at the railing at the stern of the ship, staring silently through the darkness at the disappearing ship. There were a few fires on her deck, and lanterns began to wink on. In their minds the three men were seeing the carnage and the destruction they had inflicted on a once-proud ship and crew.

How many dead? Crippled? Is she seaworthy or mortally wounded? Will she get home to England?

On board the wreckage of the *Little Belt,* her captain wiped at the blood running from the bone-deep cut on his forehead into his eyes, trying to focus on the shattered pieces of his ship, and count his dead and wounded.

Nine dead. Twenty-three wounded. Both masts down. Hulled nine times. Taking on water. Fires. Low on provisions.

He straightened, and a light came into his eyes. *We'll survive. We'll survive, and I will make my report to London. There is not one man in the Admiralty Department who will let this pass unpunished. They will pay, and the price will be more than they can bear. Much more.*

Notes

On May 6, 1811, Paul Hamilton, secretary of the United States Navy, issued orders to the USS *President* to active duty patrolling American waters off the New Jersey coast at or near Cape Henry. Commodore John Rodgers was to be in command of the big American man-of-war that carried forty-four cannon. His orders were to clear the waters of marauding British ships. On

May 16, he sighted and took chase of a British ship that eluded him all day, into the early evening. In fading light he caught the British ship and believed it to be the *Belvidera*, a British gunboat carrying thirty-six cannon. In fading light he delivered three devastating broadsides, only to realize it was not the *Belvidera*, but a much smaller ship named *Little Belt*, only seventy tons and carrying only twenty cannon. Realizing his mistake he withdrew, but his attack had killed nine British sailors and severely damaged the much smaller ship. When the incident was reported to the British admiralty in London, the outrage was overwhelming. The incident later became one of the direct causes of the War of 1812.

See Wills, *James Madison*, p. 112; Hickey, *The War of 1812*, p. 24; Horsman, *The Causes of the War of 1812*, p. 220; Stagg, pp. 45, 70, 144; Malcomson, *Lords of the Lake*, p. 42; Roosevelt, *The Naval War of 1812*, pp. 80, 83, 99, 144, 150, 154, 157, 244.

For a description of loading and firing a cannon as described herein, see Peterson, *Round Shot and Rammers*, p. 30.

Southwest Indiana Territory

Late October 1811

CHAPTER IX

★ ★ ★

n overnight heavy frost and a brilliant sunrise turned the forest on the Wabash River in southwestern Indiana Territory into a world of sparkling prisms that caught the golden rays and changed them to yellows and reds and blues, and mixed them with the unending colors of the crisp leaves of summer to make a forest wonderland.

In a small clearing four miles south of the village of Vincennes, and one quarter mile east of the river, Eli Stroud finished his simple breakfast of oatmeal mush and cider, rinsed the wooden bowl and mug and spoon, set them on the shelf to dry, and shrugged into his sleeveless deerskin vest. He walked from the small cabin out into the yard and flexed both shoulders against the twinges and rubbed at his elbows.

Getting old—cold raises the rheumatism—got to cut winter kindling—that'll raise some warmth.

His moccasins left tracks in the frost as he walked to the smoke-house just west of the cabin, on the shady side, head turning as he marveled at the kaleidoscope of colors on all sides.

No man can ever match that—no paint to compare with Nature's.

He opened the door to the smokehouse and stepped back to let the build-up of smoke and heat escape before he stepped close. He reached to touch the four venison hind quarters and four front quarters carefully hung above the small, smoldering hardwood fire in the pit below.

Done. Ready. Ned should be here today.

He partially closed the draft, then closed the door and walked back through the yard to the east side of the cabin, bright in the sunlight, to the wood yard. He flexed his hands to get past the stiffness, picked up a large, double-bitted ax, set the first rung of pine on the chopping block, and swung. By nine o'clock he had his vest laid aside and was swinging in a rhythm, and the stacks of split kindling were growing at random on the ground all around the block. At midmorning he stopped to wipe the sweat from his face and go into the cabin to drink water from the wooden dipper in the water bucket. With the sun overhead he drove the ax bit into the chopping block and began to gather the kindling to stack it against the east wall of the house. An hour later he stood back and made his estimate.

Close to two cords. Three more before dark. Ten more before the first big freeze.

He walked back into the cool dimness of the cabin, added wood to the small fire in the fireplace, and swung the arm out to place the pot directly above the flames. Then he went to the root cellar behind the house for cider and the remains of an opossum stew he had cooked two days earlier, and returned to set the cider on the table and the stew in the pot. He was reaching for a wooden plate when he felt the vibrations through the boards of the floor. He set the plate on the table and walked back out into the sunshine with one hand raised to shade his eyes while he studied the crooked path to the river. There was movement, and then the team of horses pulling the small, light-freight wagon took shape through the trees.

Eli raised a hand to wave, and the deep voice came booming, "Hallo, the house! Is that you, Eli?"

"Ned, come on in," he called.

"Don't shoot me for an Indian," came the answer.

"Then what shall I shoot you for?" Eli was grinning.

A laugh echoed in the forest. "You shoot me, and you'll pay the devil trying to deliver all I got in this wagon."

The wagon rolled on into the yard and Ned Preece, short, paunchy, round, bearded face, noisy, dropped to the ground grinning.

"Well," he exclaimed, "I see the bears didn't get you."

"None tried," Eli answered. "They're all gone. Things are getting too civilized around here."

Ned sobered. "Yeah, it worries me. A day like this! What's a day like this going to be worth when all the trees is gone and all we got is towns and roads and people?"

Eli shook his head. "It's a worry." He pointed. "Got some things for me in there?"

"Sure do. Here. Give me a hand."

Together they untied the ropes and threw back the heavy canvas, and Ned dropped the tailgate.

"You want this pork in the root cellar?" Ned asked.

Eli nodded. "Yes. I'll brine it later." Each man seized a wooden box covered with canvas and walked around the cabin to the small root cellar to put two fresh pork legs, two bellies, two loins, and two shoulders on the shelves. They walked back to the wagon and pushed the empty boxes into the wagon bed, and Ned pointed to a thirty-pound rung of cheese and two smaller crates of dried, shelled corn.

"Root cellar?"

"Yes. All of it."

They finished unloading, and Eli pointed with his chin. "The venison's in the smoke house."

Twenty minutes later the smoked venison was laid out in the wagon box, still uncovered, still hot.

"Come on in," Eli said, "and we'll have some stew while it cools."

Ned hitched at his pants and a grin divided his beard, with his square, gapped teeth showing. "Thought you'd never ask. Don't mind if I do." He followed Eli through the low door into the warmth of the small cabin and waited a moment while his eyes adjusted to the loss of bright sunlight before he sat down at the table. He thumped his foot on the floor.

"Surprises me every time. Not many out here have wood floors."

Eli used a pad to lift the stew pot from the arm above the fire and set it smoking on the table beside the cider and a half loaf of dark bread. Both men bowed their heads while Eli returned thanks, and Ned reached for the stew. He heaped his plate with the steaming chunks of meat and potatoes and carrots, and tore a piece of bread from the half-loaf. He blew on the first spoon-load to cool it, then gingerly took it in his mouth, sucking air against the heat.

"Now, that's edible!" he exclaimed, stuffing a chunk of bread in his mouth.

"You can thank the 'possum," Eli replied.

For a time they ate in thoughtful silence. Each broke bread to wipe their plates clean, then reached for their wooden cups of cider. Ned had his elbows on the table, his cider cup held between the palms of his hands.

"Heard about what's happening up north? Harrison? The Prophet?"

Eli reflected for a moment. "I know Tecumseh's down south trying to get the tribes down there to come north. I know Governor Harrison's been drilling the militia all summer, right here in Vincennes. I know there was shooting up north between some of The Prophet's warriors and the army there where they're building Fort Harrison. That was three weeks ago. Governor Harrison's under orders from Eustis in the War Department in Washington, D.C., to avoid confrontations with the Indians unless there's no other way. I heard the territorial bank account was down to three dollars, and Harrison asked for help from the federal government, and he got it. I put all that together, and I get an uneasy feeling."

Ned nodded. "Did you know Harrison asked Scott—Governor Scott in Kentucky—for help? I'm told Scott sent one hundred riflemen. With Harrison's militia and four hundred more army regulars from Washington, D.C., Harrison can field near twelve hundred men. He's got them marching north from Vincennes right now."

Ned sat back and watched Eli's mind reach some conclusions.

Eli said, "I knew that Harrison left Vincennes marching north, but I didn't know he had a force of twelve hundred. It didn't make sense until now. If he's got a force of twelve hundred armed men, he's marching toward Prophetstown. He intends doing something with Tenskwatawa. The Prophet. Tenskwatawa is not Tecumseh. Tecumseh could handle

Harrison and keep the peace. I doubt Tenskwatawa can handle Harrison, and it's certain he won't care too much about keeping the peace. Are we looking for real trouble up there?"

Ned nodded vigorously. "That's how I read it. It's been building for six, eight years. I think Harrison knows Tecumseh's down south, and I think he knows Tenskwatawa can be sucked into a war over almost nothing. I think Harrison intends to give him an excuse, and when Tenskwatawa makes the wrong move, I think Harrison intends putting him away. Him and all his people. I think Harrison figures that will remove the last obstacle, and he'll have a free hand to survey the entire Wabash River Valley for settlement. I think that's what's going on up there." He stopped for a moment, then raised a hand. "Oh. One more thing. It looks like Tenskwatawa read this whole thing the same way and about a month ago sent a message down to Harrison in Vincennes, declaring his peaceful intentions, but I think he did it to make sure everyone knows that if trouble starts, it wasn't his fault. I know Harrison ignored it. He's marching up there anyway. He wants the Indian land and power." Again he stopped for a moment, then shook his head. "Land and power. How many wars has that caused? How many lives lost?"

Eli studied his mug of cider for a time. "Too many. Harrison's going to put the spark in the tinder box, and something bad's going to happen."

Ned's eyes narrowed. "When it explodes, I don't know where the end of it will be. This whole territory could blow up."

"Maybe someone ought to go up there and take a look."

Ned drew a huge breath and exhaled it slowly. "I'll keep an eye on your place while you're gone. Thanks for the victuals. They was good. Let's go cover that venison, and I got to go. More deliveries before nightfall. Won't get back to Vincennes before midnight. That venison'll taste good to Alice and the kids when the snow flies."

"I owe you any money?" Eli asked.

"None. The trade was even. But you got to get civilized. Get some pigs and chickens and a milk cow. Plant a garden. If the bears are gone, it won't be long until the deer and 'possums are gone too, and then where'll you be? Starving. That's where." He bobbed his head emphatically. "Let's finish the wagon."

With the venison covered by the canvas tarp and tied down, and the tailgate up and locked, Ned heaved himself up the step into the driver's seat and threaded the long leather ribbons between his fingers. He turned serious eyes to Eli and spoke with intensity.

"Eli, you be careful. You hear me? Be careful."

"I will. I will. You get a chance, stop by and take a look at the place while I'm gone."

"Every chance I get. You be careful."

He slapped the reins on the rumps of the two horses and hauled hard to turn the wagon to the left, back around and down the trail to the winding dirt road leading back four miles to Vincennes. He turned once to nod a goodbye to Eli, who waved back to him, and he was gone.

For a time Eli stood quietly, mind working with the news delivered by Ned, studying the picture that was developing between the United States and the Indians, from the Great Lakes to the bayous and swamps of Louisiana. Tecumseh and his brother Tenskwatawa, The Prophet, dedicated to forming an alliance of all tribes to force the return of the lands taken from them by the whites; the muddled William Eustis, secretary of war in Washington, D.C., trying to contain the Indians; the belligerent, hard-headed Indiana territorial governor William Henry Harrison lusting for a chance—an excuse—to wipe the red men from the face of the earth.

Eli reached his conclusion. *Harrison will find his chance, or he'll force an excuse, and one side or the other will start the shooting. Maybe it can be avoided, maybe not. But someone has to try.*

He walked back to the chopping block, jerked the ax free, set up the next rung of pine, and swung. The sun had set and dusk was closing in when he drove the ax back into the block and began the work of stacking the kindling against the wall. It was full darkness when he finished and went inside the cabin. He finished the stew, drank from the water dipper, and in the pale light of two lanterns picked his long Pennsylvania rifle from the pegs above the front door. Within twenty minutes he had his powder horn, shot pouch, patch pouch, tomahawk, and belt knife on the table, ready. With a lantern in hand he walked to the root cellar to return with a block of cheese, a sack of dried corn, hardtack, and dried apple slices. The three-quarter moon was up, shining through the filigree of tree branches, and frost was forming when he banked the fire, went to his bunk, turned the lamps out, and pulled the blankets to his chin.

The morning star was still high and bright when he rolled and tied his blanket and looped it and his other belongings over his shoulder, slipped his tomahawk through his weapons belt, picked up his rifle, and walked out the front door. He checked the root cellar, then the smokehouse, and paused for a moment to stop and listen for any interruption of the stillness of the dark, and there was none. He turned west down the winding trail to the main road with his breath forming vapors, walking stiffly at first, then, as warmth came and the reluctance left his joints, he swung into his usual free, open stride.

The eastern horizon was purple when he passed Vincennes, with lights glowing yellow in some of the windows of the scattered log homes. He continued north on the winding, rutted dirt road with the Wabash River on his left and the pristine forest on his right. The frosts of October had touched the leaves, and he gloried in the incomparable colors. He nooned next to the river on dried corn and cheese and clear, cold, sweet water, sat with his knees high and his back against a tree trunk for ten minutes, then continued on through country unspoiled by white men until the sun settled in the west to cast long shadows eastward, and then disappear to leave a dying afterglow in a cloudless sky. He took a fish from the river and roasted it on a spit over a low fire, ate more corn, drank, and went to his blankets with his rifle and tomahawk inside his blankets, to keep them from the frost.

Morning found him moving north again, following the river, holding his steady stride. He greeted and passed a solitary man and then two men driving a two-wheeled freight cart pulled by an ox. He slowed as he passed a clearing that had not been there before, with fresh wood chips scattered about many tree stumps, and a cabin half built with no one around. He wondered who had spent the summer swinging an ax and sweating, then abandoned their work. What, or who, had stopped them, and why? There was no answer, and he moved on, stopping occasionally to eat the wild berries that were fat for harvest, digging the roots that were heavy from summer growth, and broiling them for his supper.

The third day a six-hundred-pound brown sow bear waddled across the trail ahead of him, fat, winter hair long and heavy, face smeared with juice from the berries she had been taking for the past three weeks. She scented him and paused to rear up on her hind legs, weak eyes probing for what she could not see while her superior nose told her everything she needed to know. It was the scent of the two-legged creatures, not native to the forest, who were little more than a nuisance. She dropped back to all fours and disappeared into the forest to gorge once again on the rich berries that would fatten her for her long sleep through the winter snows that were coming. Later that day Eli took a rabbit in a snare and roasted it with some roots for his supper.

Each day he saw sign on the road, and on the river, and in the clearings, of a large body of men moving north, and understood the tracks had been left by Harrison and his army three weeks earlier. On the fifth day the river made its turn to the northeast, and he followed it. It was late on the eighth day that he crested the familiar hill at the southwest rim of a valley and stopped. In the cup of the valley, far in the distance, was the village called Prophetstown, home of Tenskwatawa and his Shawnee followers. Beyond, coming from the north, was a faint, meandering line in the forest that was the Tippecanoe River, flowing to converge with the Wabash not far from the settlement.

Eli had arrived, but there was something strange, different, about the village he had seen so many times before. For several seconds he stood still, eyes narrowed as he studied it, and suddenly he understood. There were too many buildings. It had grown. Carefully he counted the buildings and made his calculation. There were more than two thousand Indians. His breathing slowed as he realized the gathering of warriors from other tribes had begun. He was looking at a force preparing for war.

He raised his eyes to study the distant Tippecanoe River, and in time he saw the many thin wisps of smoke rising dimly from the treetops.

Evening—campfires—Harrison's army—two miles from Prophetstown—too close—Tecumseh's not there—there's going to be trouble.

He shouldered his rifle and began the descent into the valley. In full darkness he stopped to make camp for the night, his thoughts running with questions he could not answer.

What's Tenskwatawa's mind—will he parley with Harrison?—will he have the sense to avoid a fight?—and what of Harrison?—will his lust for the Wabash Valley push him to war?—or will he follow his written orders from the Department of War?

He shook his head, heaped dirt on the coals of his cookfire, and went to his bed with his rifle and tomahawk under the blankets with him. His last clear thought before sleep was—*Tomorrow will tell.*

Sunrise found Eli half a mile from Prophetstown, walking steadily on frosty ground, in the open, watching everything, both right and left. He saw the movement in the trees and raised his rifle high above his head with both hands as the Shawnee scouts angled in to within ten yards on either side of him and kept pace with him, silent, muskets at the ready, watching his every move. He walked directly into the village and watched the children run to their mothers, who hid them behind their deerskin skirts and turned hate-filled eyes toward a white man. He reached the center of the village, where the longhouse stood, and stopped, rifle still above his head, and waited. Half a minute later an aged Indian with a blanket wrapped about his shoulders came from the darkness inside the long building and stopped six feet from Eli. There was a look of contempt in his face as he spoke in the Shawnee dialect.

"You are Stroud. What is your purpose in coming?"

"I come in peace. I wish to counsel with Tenskwatawa. It is important. I do not mean to cause trouble."

When Eli spoke in their dialect, surprise flashed on the faces of every Indian near enough to hear.

The old Indian continued. "Do you come from the white man's camp to the north? The army that has come to destroy us?"

"I do not come from the camp. I come from Vincennes, to the south. I have not been in the camp of the white army. It is my wish to talk with Tenskwatawa about the camp."

Open murmuring was heard among the gathered Indians. It quickly died, but the dark expressions on their faces were changing to curiosity.

"Who sent you?"

Eli shook his head. "No one sent me. I came when I was told many days ago that Harrison was bringing his army. I fear for the Shawnee. I do not wish to see blood shed. Either Shawnee or white."

The watery old eyes bored into Eli. "Why should I believe you?"

"I am here. It speaks for itself. I would be thankful if you would tell Tenskwatawa I am here and wish to council with him. I have sat with him and with Tecumseh many times before. He will receive me."

Eli lowered his rifle and set the butt on the ground.

Without a word the old Indian disappeared back into the dim light inside the longhouse and returned in one minute.

"Tenskwatawa will see you."

Eli followed him through the entrance into the dim light. The traditional fire burned in the pit in the center of the floor with the smoke rising through the hole in the roof and bright sunshine coming in. There were no windows. Tenskwatawa was seated to one side with but one other Indian beside him. He did not rise. Eli handed his rifle to a younger man standing beside the door, followed by his black tomahawk.

Tenskwatawa opened the talk. "Stroud. You have come to council with us. You may sit." He gestured, and Eli took his place on the thick bearskin eight feet in front of the seated Indians. Their faces were a mask that covered their inner thoughts. Eli held his silence according to Indian custom, waiting until Tenskwatawa invited him to speak, and Tenskwatawa wasted no time.

"You are here to council about the white army two miles north? Where the Wabash and Tippecanoe rivers meet?"

"I am."

"You have not been to the white man's camp?"

"I have not."

"You were not sent here?"

Eli took a deep breath and spoke the plain truth as he knew it. "I was not. I learned that Harrison marched from Vincennes to this place with twelve hundred soldiers. I believe Harrison wishes to have the land bordering the Wabash River. I do not know if he is here to claim it. If he is, I believe he is wrong. I wish to tell him. Before I do, I need to know the mind of Tenskwatawa. I know Tecumseh is far to the south. You are the leader here. May I ask you of your mind?"

"What is your question?"

"Do you wish war with Harrison?"

The three Indians exchanged brief glances, startled by the directness of Eli's question. Then came the answer.

"I sent my message to him some time ago, before the frosts began. I asked him to parley. He did not answer."

Eli nodded. "I know that. That is behind us. Do you wish war with Harrison now?"

There was a long pause in which Eli brought every sense to a focus on the Indian, watching every muscle twitch of his face, the flat look in his eyes, the angle of his head, the timbre of his voice, the spirit that came from him.

The answer came firm. "I do not."

It flashed in Eli's mind—*dishonest*—*saying what he wants me to hear*—*hiding his intentions*—*trying to deceive.*

Eli did not change his expression as he continued. "Do I have your permission to carry that message to Harrison? Now? Today?"

"You intend holding council with Harrison today?"

"I do."

The Indian's eyes narrowed. "Have you come here to count my warriors? See if we are prepared for war? To tell Harrison what you have seen?"

"No. I have not. Stroud has counseled with Tenskwatawa and Tecumseh before. Stroud has never lied. Never deceived. You know that. I am insulted that you would accuse me of deceit now."

All three Indians gaped for a moment at the shock of a white man accusing Tenskwatawa of insulting him. They settled, and Tenskwatawa replied, "I meant no insult. I trust Stroud. I do not trust Harrison. I do not trust white men. You ask if you may carry my words to Harrison.

Yes. I ask only that you return to me today with the words of Harrison after you have spoken. Do I have your promise?"

Eli's answer was instant. "You do. Do I have your permission to leave your camp now, and to return with the words of Harrison before the sun dies?"

"You may go. You have my protection until your return."

Eli rose and bowed to the three Indians. "I thank you. I will return."

He walked away from them and took his rifle and tomahawk at the door and walked through the camp, northeast, following the Wabash to its junction with the Tippecanoe. The smell of the morning cookfires from Harrison's camp filled the crisp, cool air, and he trotted the last quarter mile. A picket challenged; Eli answered and raised his rifle above his head and waited while the picket walked toward him, musket cocked, at his shoulder, and aimed at the center of Eli's beaded buckskin shirt. Eli saw the puzzled look cross the picket's face at the sight of a man who was obviously white, dressed in buckskins that were obviously Indian.

"Who are you?"

"Eli Stroud. Here to see Governor Harrison."

The picket gaped. "A white man? Dressed like that? To see Harrison?"

"I don't have time to waste. Is he here?"

"Well, yes, right down there in his tent, but I don't know . . ."

Eli ignored the confused young man and trotted past him, rifle held loosely in his right hand.

"Hold on there," the picket shouted. "I'll take you in." He ran to catch up with Eli and pointed. "Over there. I'll announce you."

Five minutes later Eli was seated inside a huge white canvas tent, facing an impatient, grumpy Harrison seated behind a battered table. Harrison, tunic open at the throat, unshaved, hair rumpled, dour expression, eyed Eli head to toe.

"You're Eli Stroud? I've heard about you, but I didn't expect you here, dressed like an Indian."

Eli ignored it. "I just left Prophetstown. I've talked with Tenskwatawa. There are things you need to know."

Harrison's eyes narrowed in question. "He send you here?"

"No. I came here—"

Harrison waved a hand irritably. "Wait a minute. Who *did* send you here? Why have you come? Do you have orders for me from Eustis? Or President Madison?"

"No. I came—"

Again Harrison waved his hand broadly. "If you don't have written orders for me from someone in Washington, you're wasting my time. Nice to see you, Mister Stroud, but I don't need advice from—"

The palm of Eli's hand smacked the tabletop, and the scatter of papers jumped as Eli half rose, leaned forward, face not two feet from Harrison's. Harrison recoiled as though he had been struck. Eli's eyes pinioned him to his chair and his voice purred quietly.

"You're sitting on a powder keg and don't seem to have the brains to know it. You mishandle things here, and the probabilities are that sooner or later, one way or another, there'll be a war. There'll be blood from here to Canada and Louisiana. And you'll be responsible. If that's what you want, you tell me that in plain terms and I'll be gone in one minute. I'll carry that message back to Washington, D.C., and you can deal with the consequences."

Eli stopped, and Harrison fought to regain some sense of composure. Eli went on.

"One more thing. Three years ago, I'm the one Madison sent into this country to counsel with Tecumseh. He had to know what the Shawnee thought about the battle at Fallen Timbers and about the Greenville Treaty. I talked with Tecumseh, and I took my report back to Madison. He was secretary of state then, but he's president now. He's the man I go to with this report. I think he'll listen."

Eli settled back into his chair and brought himself under control. "You have about one minute to decide. Are you going to talk sense, or do I get up and walk out of here?"

For half a minute Harrison gaped and stammered and tried to bring his shattered mind under control. His voice was high, cracking, insecure.

"I didn't mean to . . . I didn't know what . . ." Finally he stood and walked to one corner of the tent, and Eli watched him battling to bring himself under control.

He turned back and sat down.

"What do you want to know?"

"Is it your intent to attack the Shawnee? Prophetstown?"

Harrison shook his head. "I don't know how the land lays between here and there. I don't know how many fighting men they have. Until I know that it would be foolish to make an attack." He stopped for a moment and raised one eyebrow. "How many fighting men does he have over there?"

Eli shook his head. "That's not the question. Do you intend an attack on the village? Yes or no?"

"Not right now."

Eli clenched his jaw for a moment, and the quiet purr came back into his voice. "One more chance. Yes or no. Do you intend an attack?"

Harrison fought to retain control. "I do not intend an attack. What happens depends on them. If they provoke it, I will defend myself. Tecumseh's not there. I can't trust that brother of his. How do I know what they're going to do? I came here to keep the peace." He raised an arm to point accusingly at Eli. "But I'll tell you this. Sooner or later, those Indians have got to go. We're going to have the Wabash Valley. One way or another."

Eli sat back in his chair. "By whose orders?"

Harrison blustered. "Madison. The secretary of war. It doesn't matter. It's going to happen."

"Not here. Not now. You say you do not intend an attack. I'm carrying that back to Tenskawatawa. He may want to counsel with you."

Harrison waved a finger. "You're not carrying that back to him. If he needs to hear it, he can hear it from me. Maybe it's time he did."

Startled, Eli leaned forward in his chair. "You'll go there?"

"Yes."

"Today? Now?"

Harrison was caught up in his own bravado. "Yes. I'll take a detail of men, and I'll go settle this with that savage right now. When I finish, he'll understand he better take his people somewhere else."

Eli rose. "It's a start. There's risk if you try it alone. Take only a few men and go unarmed. I'll take you in. I guarantee your safe return."

"All right," Harrison snapped. "Give me fifteen minutes to tell my officers and put together a detail." He thrust the tent flap aside and strode into camp while Eli waited. Twenty minutes later Harrison pushed back into the tent, his face flushed, teeth clenched.

"I informed my officers. Most of them came near mutiny. Major Daviess—Joseph Hamilton Daviess from the Kentucky regiment—all but demanded we attack those savages today. Now. The word is spreading through the camp. I'm going to have to deal with it when we get back. Do you understand what this insanity is going to cost me?"

Eli's answer came quietly. "Do you want them angry, or dead? Your choice."

"All right. I've got a squad of ten out there waiting. Let's go."

Eli led the column through the camp in single file, aware that most of the other soldiers stopped to stare as they passed, and he heard the murmurings of disgust and anger. They took the narrow, winding trail through the two miles of forest separating Prophetstown from the American camp, and as they approached the Indian camp, once again Eli raised his rifle high above his head and walked steadily forward. Half a dozen scouts appeared on either side of the trail, and each American felt the Indians' black eyes searching them for weapons. They walked into the clearing, to the longhouse, and Eli stopped them. The old man came out, still wrapped in his blanket, and spoke in Shawnee.

"You brought white men with you." It was almost an accusation.

Eli answered in Shawnee. "I gave Tenskwatawa my promise. I bring the leader of this territory. He represents the white father in the east. He is Governor Harrison. He wishes to settle many things with the Shawnee. He requests council with Tenskwatawa."

Without a word the old man turned and disappeared into the longhouse, and returned half a minute later.

"You may enter."

Eli led them inside, left his rifle and tomahawk with the young warrior at the entrance, and approached the six seated Indians, Tenskwatawa among them. Harrison looked about, then at the Indians, and no one could mistake the contempt in his face.

Tenskwatawa spoke. "Be seated."

Eli gestured, and the Americans sat down cross-legged, facing the Indians. Eli held up a hand to hold them silent, waiting for Tenskwatawa to open the conversation.

"I am honored that Harrison has come. It is my desire to counsel in peace. I will be happy to hear his proposals."

Harrison looked at Eli for translation and Eli said quietly, "He understands some English but prefers Shawnee. He said he wants to counsel in peace. He wants your proposals. I will translate."

Harrison's voice rang loud, and Eli translated his words into the simple sentences preferred by the Indians.

"I am here to represent the great father in the east. He is concerned that you are gathering warriors here. He is concerned that Tecumseh is now far to the south to gather more. He sent me here to learn your intentions. We wish to have peace. We do not know if that is your wish, too."

Tenskwatawa studied Harrison for several seconds before answering. "We wish peace. Our only desire is to keep the land where our people have lived since beyond memory. It is right that we keep these lands. We wish to make a treaty."

Harrison shook his head. "That is not possible. We have settled this land. Built towns and villages. Roads. Farms. You are welcome to become part of this great thing, but you must give up your claim to the land as your own."

Tenskwatawa shook his head. "We do not understand. By what right did you come and take our lands for your towns and your farms?"

Harrison could not answer the question and avoided it. "It is impossible to undo what is already done. The Shawnee must leave. Find new land to the west, where they can live in peace. You must leave Prophetstown. I am here to request that you leave tomorrow. The seventh day of November."

Not one Indian moved, but the air was suddenly filled with a tension that was nearly physical. Tenskwatawa broke the deadly silence.

"You said you request that we abandon our land. What is to happen if we deny your request?"

There was no hesitation in Harrison's answer. "You will be forced."

Eli turned to Harrison and spoke quietly. "You said you wanted to come to counsel, but you just threatened the whole Shawnee nation. In their eyes, you have all but declared war. Do you want me to tell him what you said, or do you want to change it?"

There was rage in Harrison's face as he answered. "Tell him we request him to leave Prophetstown tomorrow. If he chooses not to, we must counsel with him again. But in the end, the Shawnee will need to move farther west where they can once again be a free people."

Carefully Eli delivered the message, but he was watching the face of Tenskwatawa, and he knew The Prophet had understood both what Harrison had said in English, and the meaning of it. If Harrison were to have his way, it would only be a matter of time until the Shawnee would be a scattered, lost people.

Tenskwatawa bowed his head to Harrison. "I thank you for coming to counsel. I must discuss these matters among my own people. You have safe passage back to your camp. I will send a message soon, when my people have spoken."

Harrison refused to say anything more, and Eli answered for him. "It is my great hope that this is the beginning of talks that will settle the differences between our people peacefully. I believe that what has been said today has opened a door. It remains to be seen if both sides have the wisdom to keep it open and to find a way to avoid war. I thank you for your protection."

Tenskwatawa nodded to him, and Eli stood. Harrison and the ten soldiers stood with him, and without another word Eli took his rifle and tomahawk at the door and led them single file out of the camp, with silent Indians watching them until they disappeared along the trail into the forest. Little was said during the two-mile walk back to the sprawling

American camp, where Eli followed Harrison into his tent. Harrison sat down in his chair and turned to face Eli, who remained standing.

"Well," he exclaimed, "we counseled with your Indians. What good did it do?"

Eli spoke evenly. "You didn't counsel. You dictated. Maybe Tenskwatawa will understand it enough to think that you took the first step toward trying for a peace treaty, but I doubt it. If it had been Tecumseh, he would have seen it for what it was and probably overlooked the fact you went over there to serve notice they were to leave or get pushed off their land. He would likely have set things up for a major council and spelled out his side of it in detail and asked you to do the same. But Tecumseh is down south, and you're dealing with Tenskwatawa, and my guess is he's over there right now making plans for a fight. Either he'll start it, or he'll defy you and you will." Eli paused, and a look of sadness crossed his face. "I think you're in trouble."

Harrison tossed a hand upward. "Let it come! Let's get this thing settled, the sooner the better."

Disgust and fear were plain in Eli's face as he answered. "I'm going to make my camp out in the woods. In the night I'm going back to Prophetstown for a look. I'll be back before morning if anything happens. You better post extra pickets all around your camp and tell them to stay out of sight. Indians favor an attack just before dawn."

Harrison brushed it off. "I know that. Good. Fine. See you in the morning."

Eli turned on his heel and ducked to pass through the tent entrance into the sunlight of late afternoon. At dusk he was a mile north of Prophetstown, partially hidden in the decayed remains of a great, ancient sycamore tree, sitting quietly in the twilight, with no fire, grinding corn between his teeth and eating dried fish. He gathered boughs to lie on, and in full darkness wrapped himself in his blanket and let his thoughts run before he drifted into a restless sleep. In the frosty chill of three o'clock, beneath a nearly full moon that cast a faint silvery light in the forest, he awakened, rolled his blanket and slung it over his shoulder. He gathered his gear and silently started south, toward the Indian village, stopping every hundred yards to listen. The only sound was owls asking, "Whooo?" He was still half a mile from the village when he passed through a small clearing and for the first time saw the glow of light in the night sky ahead of him, where the village had to be, and he stopped, brow knitted in puzzlement.

Light? Fires? In the night?

He went on with his rifle held before him at the ready, crouched, every nerve, every instinct alive, placing his feet with care, brushing nothing that would make a sound.

At a distance of four hundred yards, through the trees, he could see glimpses of light from fires in the camp and dropped to one knee. With his head bowed and his eyes closed to concentrate, he listened for any sound that would tell him of a nearby sentry, but there was nothing.

An enemy camp two miles away and no pickets? Fires where there should be none?

He moved on slowly, stopping every ten yards, poised, ready to move any direction instantly if he came upon a hidden sentry. At two hundred yards he could see two large fires burning in the center of the village, near the longhouse, and see the silhouettes of people gathered and moving about it. The sound of a single shrill voice reached him. He stopped to listen but could not make out the words that were being shouted in Shawnee. Crouched low he moved on, one careful step at a time, waiting for the tell-tale sound of a moccasin on the forest floor or the guttural challenge of a surprised sentry. At the place where the forest yielded to the clearing, he lay down flat on his belly and studied what was before him.

Nearly every Indian in Prophetstown was gathered near the longhouse. Two huge fires sent sparks soaring into the black heavens, turning them all into a circle of black, moving images. In the center of the circle, on a crude platform, stood Tenskwatawa, one arm raised to the heavens as he shouted his message to his people. Eli turned his head and concentrated to catch fragments of the words.

". . . the white men have lied from the beginning . . . broken every treaty . . . sent an army now camped nearby . . . come to drive us away

. . . destroy us . . . the Master of Life has spoken . . . they must be destroyed . . ."

Eli studied the crowd of more than one thousand Indians and for the first time noticed that in the center of it were warriors, and they were armed. Their long British muskets were thrust high, thin black lines in the firelight. The oration of Tenskwatawa went on.

". . . I have seen a vision . . . it has been revealed to me . . . it is on us to rid our sacred lands of the white men . . . we must obey . . . we will meet Harrison's army . . . tonight . . ."

The voice stopped, and Eli peered at Tenskwatawa as the Indian drew himself to his full height and then slowly raised both arms high above his head, fingers spread. His voice became firm, vibrant, resolute.

"I tell you now . . . do not fear battle with the white men . . . they will fire their muskets and their rifles but the bullets will not touch you!"

Eli's head jerked forward in disbelief. Tenskwatawa continued.

"You will be protected by the Master of Life! The weapons of the white men will harm none of you. Their bullets will be guided away from you. I am The Prophet. I give you this promise as it has been given to me by the Master of Life!"

It struck Eli like a thunderbolt, and he raised to one knee, ready. *That Indian intends attacking Harrison's camp tonight! Now! Just before dawn! Like they always do.*

He remained still for one more minute, waiting, and then it came. Tenskwatawa's voice was like thunder. "Prepare yourselves! We leave at once! We strike before the sun rises!"

A deep, guttural, thrilling sound came from seven hundred warriors who had been raised to a blood-lust fever. They separated from the crowd and formed themselves into a column, and on the signal from The Prophet, started at a trot toward Harrison's camp, two miles distant.

Eli came to his feet, spun, and broke into a run, heedless of the sound and the branches and underbrush that tugged at him. He came to the small clearing and sprinted through, on into the forest. Half a mile from Harrison's camp he began shouting, "White man coming in! White man coming in! Hold your fire! Hold your fire!" He was less than one hundred yards from the camp when he saw the smoldering campfires through the trees and suddenly understood there were no extra pickets posted, nor was there anyone awake and on his feet in the camp. The tents were there, but the campground was deserted.

That fool! That fool!

He sprinted halfway through the camp directly to Harrison's tent, threw the flap back, and burst in, panting, sweating in the cold. Harrison's eyes opened just as Eli seized his shoulder and shook him hard, his voice raised, nearly shouting in the darkness of the tent.

"On your feet! You're under attack!"

Harrison raised his head and opened his eyes, trying to focus on the dark shape above him while his brain struggled to come back to the world.

"Wha . . . who . . ." he stammered.

"Stroud. Eli Stroud. The Shawnee are coming. You're under attack." Eli threw Harrison's blanket back and grasped him by both shoulders. "Get up. On your feet. You haven't got ten minutes!"

Harrison struck at Eli's arms. "Get your hands off me. What are you doing here?"

"Can you understand me?"

"Yes. I can. What are you doing here?"

"I just left Prophetstown. About seven hundred warriors are coming here at a trot. They're going to strike this camp in less than ten minutes. Unless you want a massacre, you better get your men up and armed and ready. Kill those campfires! Get your men positioned in two lines, facing south, one behind the other so they can put up a sustained fire! Move! *Move!*"

Harrison was dressed in his long underwear and trousers, still sitting in the dark, brain fumbling, reeling to understand what he was hearing. He spoke sharply.

"Stop. You come in here in the middle of the night with some wild story about an attack! What attack? I don't hear an attack."

"Where are your pickets? Why aren't there extra pickets out there?"

"What for? Those Indians aren't going to take on this army."

"You fool! They'll be here in less than five minutes!"

"All right, all right. I'll get dressed and we'll see about an Indian attack."

Eli spun on his heel and darted out the flap into the center of the camp and ran to the nearest tent. He threw back the flap and thrust his head inside. "On your feet," he shouted. "Wake up. You're under attack. Get your weapons. Now!"

Six groggy militiamen raised on one elbow to squint at the dark shape at the tent flap. None spoke, and Eli ran to the next tent, shouting all the way. The camp began to stir and men began coming from the tents in their long underwear, still fumbling with their trousers, hair messed, wide-eyed, waiting for the sleep fog to clear from their brains. A few of them had reached their racked weapons when the first blood-curdling, warbling war cries were heard from the forest to the south, and then the bronze bodies were there, dodging through the trees in a long line, muskets raised and ready.

Eli held his breath, waiting, and the Shawnee broke into the camp, and the first volley blasted from more than four hundred muskets. Silhouetted against their own campfires, the Amerians made perfect targets, and at near point-blank range, the musket balls ripped into them. In an instant, the sleeping camp was thrown into pandemonium. Men burst from their tents in their long underwear, racing for their stacked muskets and rifles, and the second volley of three hundred Shawnee muskets roared, and more Americans went down, some unmoving, others groaning, writhing on the frosty ground. Some Shawnee stopped to reload their muskets while others threw them down and jerked tomahawks from their belts and plowed into the crowd of disorganized, terrified soldiers. Eli backed to the edge of the clearing, away from the Indians, unwilling to kill them.

Then an American musket cracked out, and then another, and then more. Eli stared, unable to believe what he saw next.

The Shawnee paid no heed to the American muskets! They charged straight into them, and Eli heard the rifle balls smack into the bare flesh and saw the Indians crumple, and still they came, showing no fear of the

American weapons, taking the wounds and going down with astonishment on their faces.

Eli gaped. *They believed him! He told them the American musket balls would not hit them, and they believed him!*

Then Eli saw Harrison, half-dressed, working through his men, shouting, "Buckshot! Load with buckshot! Use buckshot!"

Slowly at first, then more rapidly, the Americans rallied. The Kentucky riflemen were loading fast, with only gunpowder and buckshot—no greased linen patch—and firing from the hip, to reload as fast as they could. The other militiamen saw it, and soon the Americans were blasting buckshot into the swarming Indians as fast as they could reload and pull the trigger. The sound of musket fire crescendoed into one sustained explosion, and it rang and echoed for miles in the forest. Dead bodies of half-dressed Americans were mixed with those of the Indians as the hot, hand-to-hand battle raged on in the dark, unreal world of dwindling campfires and muzzle flashes. Tomahawks and belt knives flashed in the firelight, and dozens of Americans and Indians groaned and fell to the ground. Almost as though someone had given a signal, the Shawnee musket fire decreased, became more sporadic, partly because some had no more ammunition, partly because the others had stopped in their tracks and were retreating, stepping over the dead and crippled bodies of their own warriors, cursing, bewildered, the heart gone out of them.

The Prophet had lied! Fallen! Sacrificed them for his own gain! Had he not told them the American musket balls could not hit them? That they need have no fear of them? Ignore them? Had they not done exactly what he told them? And were not many of these fallen bodies Shawnee, dead because they had obeyed their revered Prophet?

He is a fallen prophet! Abandon him! Abandon him!

Some backed into the forest and disappeared while others held their ground, and the battle raged on. The sun rose in the east, and in the gathering light of a cloudless, calm day, both sides could see the carnage that surrounded them. The American camp was littered with men, white and red, who were dead and dying and crippled, bloody, maimed. Gun smoke hung in the forest and over the battlefield like a pall. Tents were ripped, torn from their pegs. Americans were barefooted, with only their trousers to cover their long underwear. There was little pretense of military formation on either side; rather, it had been a wild, disorganized, disoriented fight for survival, man to man.

The momentum had shifted. With ammunition gone, the Indians retreated into the forest and within moments had disappeared. Behind them, the Americans reloaded and waited, silent, watching, rifles and muskets at the ready. The firing died, and an awful silence seized the camp. Harrison, sword in hand, picked his way through the bodies to the edge of camp where the Indians had disappeared, then turned and gave orders.

"You fifty men, take up positions here in a line with your weapons at the ready. The next fifty, start the cookfires for morning mess. Where's Major Daviess?"

A barefooted private clad only in his long underwear called back, "Right over here, sir. He's dead."

Harrison flinched, then continued. "The rest of you start looking for the wounded. Do what you can for them. We'll bury the dead later."

By noon they had done what they could for the wounded. After midday mess, they silently set about the mournful business of burying their dead. Eli joined the great body of men assigned to dig the shallow graves. By dusk they had covered the last of the bodies and tallied their losses. Eli was standing near Harrison when his officers made their report.

"Two hundred casualties, sir. About one hundred Indian casualties."

The air went out of Harrison. "Two to one?"

"Yes, sir."

Harrison could not raise his eyes for a time. "All right. Get the evening mess finished and get the men to bed. Post double pickets for the night."

Eli followed Harrison to his tent and stepped inside. Harrison sat down at his desk and looked up at him defiantly.

"You wanted something?"

"What is your plan from here?"

Harrison's words came loud, sharp, cutting. "This isn't the end of it, if that's what you're asking. I'm going over to Prophetstown tomorrow and finish it. If that scum thinks he can promise us to counsel just so they can make a sneak attack, he's badly mistaken. Tomorrow we set this right."

"You've already lost two hundred men. Are you willing to lose more?"

Harrison's eyes were flashing. "If that's what it takes."

Eli heaved a sigh. "As you wish." He turned and walked from the tent. He took mess with the soldiers who ate without tasting, each lost in his own remembrance of the gun flashes in the dark and the wild melee of men going down, moaning, screaming, dying, in their desperate fight for their lives against Indians who were swinging tomahawks and belt knives.

He went to his blankets at the edge of camp but was awake and working his way through the forest toward Prophetstown by three o'clock, beneath a myriad of stars and the full moon. He came silently to within eight hundred yards of the village, waiting for a sound or a challenge from an Indian sentry, and there was none. At two hundred yards he saw nothing through the trees. At fifty yards he could distinguish the black shapes of the orderly rows of buildings, but there was no light. The entire village was utterly dark. He waited and watched in the moonlight, and there was no movement. No village dog barked. No sound. Nothing.

Abandoned! Why? What happened?

On instinct alone, he stood and walked straight into the Indian village, to the longhouse. The fire that burned constantly in the big fire pit was cold. The great buffalo and bear skins on the floor for ceremonies—gone. All decorations for worship—gone. The longhouse, the center of the Indian religion and government, had been stripped to the walls! Quickly he trotted back out into the village, rifle loose in his right hand, and moved up the street, approaching one doorway after another, to find the dwellings hollow, stripped.

Why? Why would Tenskwatawa . . .

It hit him, and he stopped in his tracks, stunned. *It wasn't Tenskwatawa! It was his warriors! His people! He promised them the American musket balls would not hit them, and they trusted him, and a hundred of them died. The Prophet! Fallen! They had lost faith in their fallen prophet! He did not order them to leave. They could no longer trust him, and they left in spite of him, and he had to follow!*

Eli left the ghostly village at a trot. The eastern horizon was deep blue with a sun not yet risen when he encountered the first picket at Harrison's camp. The two men walked to Harrison's tent, which showed light from a lantern inside. The picket reluctantly asked permission, and Eli heard Harrison answer, "Enter."

Inside, Eli stood before the desk, rifle in hand. Harrison looked up and waited in silence.

"I just returned from Prophetstown. It's abandoned."

Harrison reared back in his chair. "Abandoned? What do you mean, abandoned?"

"Not one person. Stripped. Abandoned."

"The whole village?"

"The whole village."

Harrison lunged from his chair to pace for a moment. "Well! I guess we did a better job of it than we thought. They attacked us, which puts the blame on them, and we beat them so bad they fled." His entire countenance had changed. His face was flushed, smiling, jubilant, as he went on. "Abandoned the field yesterday and their whole village overnight. Now, that's as complete a victory as can be had! I imagine President Madison will find *that* report encouraging."

It flashed in Eli's mind. *Power lust! He's lost in power lust!* He raised a hand and Harrison stopped his pacing, waiting to hear Eli's reply.

"You didn't beat the Shawnee. Tenskwatawa did. I was there yesterday morning before the fight. He told his warriors he had a revelation from the Maker of Life. He told them your American musket balls would not hit them, that they did not need to fear your weapons. They believed him. They walked into your guns, knowing they would be protected. A hundred of them died. The survivors lost faith in their prophet. They could no longer trust him. They revolted and left. Packed everything and left the village behind. He had to go with them or face you alone. The truth is, if Tenskwatawa had not begun to believe he had powers that no man has, and convinced his own people he was right, those Shawnee would not have overrun your camp yesterday. That's the report that President Madison will hear from me."

Harrison sobered and for a time stared at Eli while his mind raced to create a defense. "Make any report you want. I'm going over to Prophetstown this morning and burn it to the ground. My report will state that they attacked us, we drove them back, they abandoned their village, and we burned it. The Shawnee threat is gone. The Wabash Valley is ours. That's the truth, and the whole of it."

"Do you intend reporting that your own staff of officers came very close to a mutiny over your actions? That Major Daviess is dead because of it? That your losses in battle were double that of the Shawnee? Will that be there?"

"Men die in battle. The point is, we won! We won! We've turned the tide!"

"You better think deeper. Tenskwatawa has fallen from grace. That leaves Tecumseh. When he hears what happened here, what will he do? It's my guess what happened here will harden him against us. Right now he still might be willing to council with us for a peaceful treaty. When he hears about this, it is more likely he'll conclude the only way to deal with white men is war. If that happens, there will be no end to the blood."

"That's for him to decide. If there's nothing else, I have to get this army ready to march to Prophetstown."

By ten o'clock Harrison's men were moving through the abandoned Indian village with torches in their hands. On his command, they systematically touched fire to every building, then backed away to the perimeter to watch Prophetstown in flames. By noon not one structure remained standing. What had been a proud Indian settlement was reduced to smoking black ashes.

Harrison gave orders and led his men back to their campground. In the late afternoon he rallied them to deliver his victory speech and commend them for their heroic action in defeating the Shawnee nation. At evening mess the men sat cross-legged with their wooden plates of venison stew, silent, conflicted, divided against themselves at the memory of what they knew they had done, and what Harrison had tried to convince them they had done.

The following morning Eli watched them strike camp, get their wounded onto everything they could find that had wheels, and fall into a column. At midmorning Harrison gave his orders, and they started their march southward from the junction of the Wabash and Tippecanoe rivers, following the Wabash as it wound through the unparalleled beauty of the wide valley. He moved out ahead of them, covering both sides of the narrow trail, watching for any sign of ambush, and there was none. They arrived in Vincennes, from whence they had started, and on November 18, 1811, Harrison quickly disbanded his army, sent the men home, and set about carefully but quickly drafting his written report to James Madison. His had to be the first to reach the president.

In early December, Harrison's sensational account reached the desk of President James Madison in Washington, D.C. An elated Madison read it several times, each time finding something new that would aid his upcoming reelection campaign in 1812. Clearly, the "reduction of the Shawnee threat on the northwestern frontier" would be a monumental achievement for his campaign committee to crow about. On December 18, 1811, Madison contacted the most influential newspapers in the United States and issued his official press release.

The Battle of Tippecanoe had been a monumental, pivotal event in the history of the United States! President Madison had restored peace to the northwestern frontier and opened the great Wabash Valley to the westward expansion of the United States! It was, in his judgment, an unparalleled accomplishment in the history of the fledgling country.

With his announcement still on the front pages of most newspapers, other reports began to reach Madison's desk, one from Eli Stroud, others from Harrison's own officers and soldiers. Madison read them, and it slowly came clear in his mind. They had been there for the battle, and their recitals of it gutted Harrison's claims. The newspapers discovered the reports and instantly published them, and suddenly what had been a bonanza for President Madison was a matter of hot debate. Was Madison a hero or a liar?

Senator Thomas Worthington of Ohio described the whole thing as "a melancholy affair" that never should have occurred.

A shaken Madison called in his secretary of the War Department, William Eustis, a man who went whichever direction the current political winds were blowing, and laid it out before him.

"What's to be done?" Madison demanded.

Eustis replied, "Well, now, Mister President, I really don't see any gain at all in prolonging public debate over the merits of the contradictory versions circulating in the newspapers. I suggest you ignore it and move on."

Shaken, Madison turned to a new tactic to blunt the cutting edge of the rising controversy. Arm and equip companies of volunteer militia to serve as frontier rangers, then appoint three commissioners to meet with the Indians, investigate their claims against the Americans, and settle the whole matter without bloodshed.

Slowly the furor faded as new and dramatic events surfaced between the United States and England.

As for William Henry Harrison? In January 1812, Mr. Harrison's request for a commission in the regular army reached President Madison's desk. Included in his documentation was his claim that "no officer in the army can maneuver a battalion with more exactness than myself."

President Madison took up his quill, and in his neat, cursive handwriting, carefully wrote across the face of the document, "Request denied."

Then he moved on to other, more pressing matters on his agenda.

Notes

The events described herein are accurate. In the summer of 1811, the Shawnee Indian leader Tecumseh left his home ground in Indiana Territory to go south in an effort to rally support for his stand against further white encroachment on Indian lands. He left his brother, Tenskwatawa, also known as The Prophet, in charge of their village, Prophetstown, near the junction of the Tippecanoe and Wabash rivers in what is now northwestern Indiana. William Henry Harrison was the territorial governor at the time, and he was ambitious to rid his territory of the Shawnee threat. Learning that Tecumseh had left Tenskwatawa to preside over Prophetstown, he decided to amass a fighting force and require the Shawnee to vacate Indiana. He sought help from Ohio governor Charles Scott, who sent him one hundred riflemen. As late as September 25, 1811, Tenskwatawa sent messages to Harrison stating his desire to counsel in peace. Harrison ignored his pleas, and with his combined force of about 1,200 soldiers, marched north from Vincennes, Indiana, up the Wabash and established his camp two miles from Prophetstown.

Not knowing the terrain or the strength of the Indian forces, he hesitated in attacking, choosing rather to visit them at their village and demand that they leave. On November 6, 1811, he made the visit with no result. Harrison failed to post proper pickets and in general was not efficient in handling his command. Harrison's own officers came close to mutiny when they understood what Harrison had in mind.

Tenskwatawa, fearing Harrison's intentions, organized his fighting force that night, promised them American musket balls could not touch them, and led them into an attack before dawn on November 7, as described herein. The battle was strongly in favor of the Shawnee until they realized the American musket balls, followed by buckshot, were in fact killing the warriors. Their faith in Tenskwatawa shattered and their ammunition low, the Indians retreated back to Prophetstown. The battle concluded with about two hundred American and one hundred Indian casualties. Major General Joseph Hamilton Daviess, one of Harrison's chief critics, was killed in the fight.

Incensed at the pre-dawn attack, Harrison marched his army to Prophetstown the following morning to find it abandoned. The Shawnee had lost faith in their leader, The Prophet, because his promise regarding the American musket balls had proven fraudulent. Unable to trust their leader, the Indians had abandoned their village.

Harrison declared total victory and marched his army back to Vincennes where he disbanded his soldiers on November 18, 1881. Then he wrote a glowing report to President James Madison in which his role was much exaggerated. Madison, facing re-election in 1812, used the report to enhance his own standing with the voters in his press release of December 18, 1811, declaring the battle to be a great American victory, obviously to his credit since it had happened during his presidency.

Shortly thereafter, other reports from participants in the battle, including some of the officers, strongly contradicted Harrison's account. The newspapers pounced. Politicians were divided and had a field day with the conflicted affair. Ohio senator Thomas Worthington declared the Tippecanoe fight to be "a melancholy affair." Madison was deeply concerned. He conferred with his weak War Department secretary, William Eustis, who advised him to ignore it. Madison shifted his emphasis to a peaceful resolution, and the matter slowly faded from public memory, and Madison moved on.

In January 1812, Harrison requested a commission as a regular officer in the Continental Army, claiming, among other things, that he could maneuver a battalion of men better than any other man in the army. Madison and members of his administration rejected the application.

See Stagg, *Mister Madison's War*, pp. 184–93; Wills, *James Madison*, p. 91; Hickey, *The War of 1812*, pp. 25, 294; Horsman, *The Causes of the War of 1812*, pp. 158, 206–228; Antal, *A Wampum Denied*, 16; Barbuto, *Niagara, 1814*, pp. 4, 5, 339. The Indiana territorial bank account was down to three dollars, Stagg, *Mister Madison's War*, p. 183. For the count of the Indians at Prophetstown, in excess of two thousand, see Stagg, *Mister Madison's War*, p. 182.

For a map of Indiana showing the location of the places described herein, see *National Geographic Picture Atlas of Our Fifty States*, p. 151.

For a description of the longhouse and the general appearance of the Indian villages of the times and of the rites and ceremonies conducted therein, see Graymont, *The Iroquois*; Graymont, *The Iroquois in the American Revolution*; Hale, *The Iroquois Book of Rites*; Morgan, *League of the Ho-de-no-sau-nee or Iroquois*; all pages and all illustrations in these references.

The reader is advised that there are many, many other persons involved in the politics and conduct of this event and many other minor occurrences that occurred in conjunction with it; however, they are far too numerous to be set out in detail. For that reason, only the core characters and events are included herein.

The "Tippecanoe Affair" is included in this book in such detail because it later became one of the two most prominent causes of the War of 1812.

Eli Stroud is a fictional character.

Washington, D.C.
June 1, 1812

CHAPTER X

*I*t was uncertain whether the high ceiling and the massive oak desk with the great, overstuffed chair behind and the four large matching chairs in front made the man seem small, or whether the smallness of the man made the room seem large. It was only known that when President James Madison, diminutive at scarcely over five feet and one hundred pounds, slender, delicate, heart-shaped face, blue eyes, soft voice, sat behind the desk in his private study in the Executive Mansion, he somehow seemed dwarfed, misplaced, overpowered. The illusion soon faded when one engaged him in discussion on any topic the visitor might choose. Then his visitor discovered him to be a giant among men. The range and depth and the orderliness of his mind and his logic startled men who perceived themselves as being among the wise and learned of the world, and left them less sure of themselves, struggling to match the loftiness of his intellect. His strength lay in his rare ability to reduce the chaotic mess of world affairs to a simple, logical, organized, understandable whole, and lay a plan filled with hope. It was also his weakness. The chaotic, messy world did not function on principles of logic, simplicity, rightness, and organization. It functioned as it had from the dawn of time—a chaotic, messy stew of sinners and saints, heroes and villains, and the unpredictable whims of the human race. The world respected no human plan. Rather, it ran over men's plans in its relentless march into the future, and the saints and sinners of the next generation were left to struggle and win and lose.

The early morning hours of June 1, 1812, promised a hot, muggy, summer day. Breakfast with Dolley, his wife of eighteen years, had been a bright spot. Seventeen years his junior, widowed in 1793, with one young son, attractive, tending toward plump, dark-haired, blue-eyed, already a legend in the city for her warmth and charm and generosity, she had glowed as they talked at the breakfast table. She had listened to him with her heart, then embraced him, and watched as he paced down the hall to his duties, leather heels clicking a quick, measured cadence. He had stopped at the door into his study to look back and raise a hand to her before stepping inside and closing the door against the world.

Madison sat down in the great chair with the window behind and the filled bookshelves on the two sidewalls. He squared his shoulders and settled back, fingers interlaced across his sparse middle, making a slow survey of the myriad documents on the desk before him. For days he had been gathering them, reviewing them, selecting, discarding, organizing. Some were in neatly stacked files, others in orderly piles with no file. In the center of the desk, near the edge closest to him, were twenty-six pages, filled with his small handwriting, which he had created line upon line from his meticulous research of the circumstances and recent events that would weigh heaviest in what was coming.

This was the day he would reduce it all to one document for secret delivery to the United States Congress, aimed at persuading the members of those houses to two conclusions—conclusions that would likely change the history of the world: first, the United States must declare war on England, and second, he, James Madison, must be reelected to a second term as president of the fledgling nation.

With half-closed eyes he began the labor of organizing his thoughts.

First issue? Power in Congress. We Republicans: seventy-five percent in the House, the Federalists, twenty-five. In the Senate: eighty-two percent Republican, eighteen percent Federalist. How will they vote on the sole issue of war with England? Our Republicans are rampant with hawks who are openly campaigning for war with England, but not all. The trouble is we Republicans are divided—a few of the Clintonian followers will vote against it. The Federalists? Their vote will be nearly unanimous against it. Will there be enough votes in favor? Probably yes. Probably.

He shifted slightly in his chair. The uncertainty of *probably* was not well received in the meticulous mind of James Madison.

Can we pay for a war? He shook his head in frustration. *The debt remaining from the war for independence was staggering, and the purchase by Mister Jefferson of the Louisiana territory—eleven million dollars of borrowed money—pushed the country to the limit. The Federalists and Mister Jefferson and the secretary of the treasury—Mister Albert Gallatin—repealed enough taxes—including the salt tax—to leave us drowning with eighty-two million to repay, and an annual income of ten million to do it! And of the ten million, three-fourths of it must be used to pay the debt, and will be for the next sixteen years, if Mister Gallatin's plan succeeds. That leaves us with two-and-one-half million annually to pay all other costs of running the United States. Insanity! As of now, in our current state of peace, the cost of maintaining our army and navy, meager as they are, is four million per year, and the diplomatic service alone is costing one million. Five million total—double what's left after we pay on our annual debt—and not a cent left to pay for everything else. If we go to war with England, costs will soar! We are going to have to raise taxes, and that will cost us votes!*

There was no other answer, and Madison grimaced in his discomfort.

What are the current tides of politics? The election is nearing. The temper of the country generally favors war with England, and I think the people are right. If we Republicans can succeed in committing the United States to such a war before the election, our chances of winning the election will be much improved. The question is timing. When do we make the move? Now? July? August? September is too late. Is June too early? If we declare war in June and things go badly before the November election, will we have undone ourselves?

For a moment Madison stared at his desktop in frustration. His loathing of uncertainty was not well suited to the fluid, shifting, vicious world of politics.

And what of France? Thus far the French have been as arrogant as the British toward us. Seized our commercial ships—imprisoned our seamen.

He reached for three documents and for a moment scanned each. *Napoleon's Berlin Decree—and the Milan Decree—both promising French withdrawal of their blockades of all ports where our ships are found—and their Rambouillet Decree that undid all they had promised us.*

He tossed the papers on his desk and picked up a fourth document. *Our Macon Decree Number Two. Weak as it was, it was all we could do to find a way of opening the high seas for our ships of commerce—offered to begin trading with whichever of the two belligerent powers—France or England—would open trade with us and continue our embargoes against the other.*

He tossed it back on his desk and shook his head slowly. *All for nothing. Years of maneuvering with both France and England, and finally it comes down to war. And what is to become of France and England in the event we declare war on England? With France just across the English Channel, England must assign the majority of its navy to the task of keeping the French navy in check. So long as that persists, England will have scant little time or ships to consign to its difficulties with the United States. It is apparent that now is a propitious time to move against England.*

The little man leaned forward, elbows on the huge desk. *How does one organize all this into a document that will persuade Congress that we must declare war on England or forever accept the idea that we are a very small pawn in international affairs? What are the British offenses that our Congress most despises? How far back should this listing of those offenses go?*

He picked up his quill, dipped it in the ink bottle, and began writing notes as his thoughts continued.

In the past several years Britain has taken nine thousand American seamen from our ships—away from their native country—wives—children—all they hold dear—pressed them into service in the British navy and forced them to fight against their own! Over six hundred American ships—gone! Barbarous! The Chesapeake affair in 1807—Congress is still infuriated over the arrogance of that heinous affair.

British ships have invaded American waters. Their ships are seen from the mainland, patrolling our waters, looking for any vessel flying our colors. Willing and anxious to intercept them—board them—seize cargoes—seize American sailors—all contrary to centuries of the natural laws of traffic on the high seas. Closing our ports, stopping the very foundations of American industry and commerce. The insult is intolerable!

They have issued endless Orders in Council. How many of them? Twenty? Thirty? All of them with but one intent—suppress American commerce. For thirty years the British have been unable to rise above the concept that we are still their little, belligerent colonies. They cannot conceive of the United States as an independent, sovereign nation, with the natural rights and powers commensurate with that position in the affairs of the world.

Our ports, their ports, neutral ports worldwide—all blockaded against American ships on pain of confiscation of the cargoes and the crews and the ships. By what right? They admit they have no such right, but still they persist!

They have committed piracy against us on the high seas. They refuse to acknowledge it as piracy, but how else can it be described? They take our ships in free international waters, seize the cargoes, imprison the crews, and claim the ships as prizes.

He put the quill down for a moment and reached for two documents. For a time he scanned them, then set them aside as his thoughts continued:

For years they have incited the Indians in the northwest to rise against the United States—supplied the tribes with muskets and powder and shot and taught them to use them efficiently, with but one thought. Arm them, train them, hold them in check until the right moment, and then send the red horde to crush the Americans that have settled the great northwest sections of the United States. What could be more clear and convincing evidence of their plan than the Tippecanoe event of last November? The Shawnee promised to counsel with Governor Harrison, then immediately attacked him in the darkness before dawn, carrying British muskets and firing British powder and shot.

He sat back in his chair, meticulously, methodically working in his mind with the basic concepts, selecting some, abandoning others, and then choosing the words best calculated to make his case.

Then he squared a fresh piece of paper on the great desk and picked up his quill, and for a time the only sound in the room was the quiet scratching of the split tip on the paper.

"Washington, June 1, 1812

"To the Senate and House of Representatives of the United States:

"I communicate to Congress certain documents, being a continuation of those heretofore laid before them on the subject of our affairs with Great Britain.

"Without going back beyond the renewal of 1803 of the war in which Great Britain is engaged, and omitting unrepaired wrongs of inferior magnitude, the conduct of her Government presents a series of acts hostile to the United States as an independent and neutral nation.

"British cruisers have been in the continued practice of violating the American flag on the great highway of nations, and of seizing and carrying off persons sailing under it, not in the exercises of a belligerent right founded on the law of nations against an enemy, but of a municipal prerogative over British subjects. . . .

"The practice, hence, is so far from affecting British subjects alone that, under the pretext of searching for these, thousands of American citizens under the safeguard of public law and of their national flag, have been torn from their country and from everything dear to them; have been dragged on board ships of war of a foreign nation . . . to risk their lives in the battles of their oppressors, and to be the melancholy instruments of taking away those of their own brethren. . . .

"Against this crying enormity, which Great Britain would be so prompt to avenge if committed against herself, the United States have in vain exhausted remonstrances and expostulations . . . to enter into arrangements such as could not be rejected if the recovery of British subjects were the real and the sole object. The communication passed without effect. . . .

"British cruisers have been in the practice also of violating the rights and the peace of our coasts. They hover over and harass our entering and departing commerce. . . .

"Under pretended blockades . . . our commerce has been plundered in every sea, the great staples of our country have been cut off from legitimate markets, and a destructive blow aimed at our agricultural and maritime interests. . . .

"To our remonstrances against the complicated and transcendent injustice of this innovation the first reply was that the orders were reluctantly adopted by Great Britain as a necessary retaliation on decrees of her enemy proclaiming a general blockade of the British Isles. . . ; that retaliation, to be just, should fall on the party setting the guilty example, not on an innocent party which was not even chargeable with an acquiescence in it. . . .

"When deprived of this flimsy veil for a prohibition of our trade with her enemy . . . her cabinet, instead of a corresponding repeal or a practical discontinuance of its orders, formally avowed a determination to persist in them against the United States until the markets of her enemy should be laid open to British products. . . .

"Abandoning still more all respect for the neutral rights of the United States and for its own consistency, the British Government now demands as prerequisites to a repeal of its orders as they relate to the United States . . . the repeal of the French decrees nowise necessary to their termination . . . not . . . a special repeal in relation to the United States, but should be extended to whatever other neutral nations unconnected with them may be affected by those decrees. . . .

"It has become, indeed, . . . certain that the commerce of the United States is to be sacrificed, not as interfering with the belligerent rights of Great Britain . . . but as interfering with the monopoly which she covets for her own commerce and navigation. . . .

"Anxious to make every experiment short of the last resort . . . the United States have withheld from Great Britain, under successive modifications, the benefits of a free . . . market, the loss of which could not but outweigh the profits accruing from her restrictions of our commerce with other nations. . . . To these appeals her Government has been equally inflexible. . . .

"If no other proof existed of a predetermination of the British Government against a repeal of its orders, it might be found in the correspondence of the minister plenipotentiary of the United States at London and the British secretary for foreign affairs in 1810, on the question whether the blockade of May 1806 was considered as in force or as not in force. It had been ascertained that the French Government, which urged this blockade as the ground of its Berlin decree, was willing in the event of its removal to repeal that decree, which . . . might abolish the whole system on both sides. . . . The British Government would, however, neither rescind the blockade nor declare its nonexistence. . . . the United States were compelled so to regard it in their subsequent proceedings. . . .

"There was a period when a favorable change in the policy of the British cabinet was justly considered as established. The minister plenipotentiary of His Britannic Majestic here proposed an adjustment. . . . The proposition was accepted with the promptitude and cordiality . . . of this Government. A foundation appeared to be laid for a sincere and lasting reconciliation. The prospect, however, quickly vanished. The whole proceeding was disavowed by the British Government without any explanation . . . and it has since come into proof that at the very moment when the public minister was holding the language of friendship . . . a secret agent of his Government was employed in intrigues having for their object a subversion of our Government and a dismemberment of our happy union. . . .

"In reviewing the conduct of Great Britain toward the United States our attention is necessarily drawn to the warfare just renewed by the savages on one of our extensive frontiers—a warfare which is known to spare neither age nor sex and to be distinguished by features peculiarly shocking to humanity. It is difficult to account for the activity and combinations . . . developing . . . with British traders and garrisons without recollecting the authenticated examples of such interpositions heretofore furnished by the officers and agents of that Government. . . .

"Such is the spectacle of injuries and indignities which have been heaped on our country. . . .

"We behold, in fine, on the side of Great Britain a state of war against the United States, and on the side of the United States a state of peace toward Great Britain. . . .

"Whether the United States shall continue passive under these progressive usurpations and these accumulating wrongs, or, opposing force to force in defense of their natural rights, shall commit a just cause into the hands of the Almighty Disposer of Events . . . is a solemn question which the Constitution wisely confides to the legislative department of that Government. In recommending it to their early deliberations I am happy in the assurance that the decision will be worthy the enlightened and patriotic counsels of a virtuous, a free, and a powerful nation. . . .

"James Madison."

The president put his quill down and flexed the fingers of his writing hand, stiff after four hours of continuous writing. He heaved a great sigh and stood to stretch and walk from the desk to the window, where he peered out at the green world of Washington in the early summer. Then he walked back to the desk and sat down. For half an hour he read his work slowly, meticulously, nodded his approval, and carefully inserted the several pages into a large white envelope. He slipped the whole of it into a leather pouch and snapped the two buckles before he placed it in the left bottom drawer of his desk.

I will let it rest overnight—final reading tomorrow morning—then send it to the House of Representatives for congressional action.

The morning of June 2, 1812, broke clear and humid, and eight o'clock found the diminutive Madison hunched over his desk with the document spread before him. He inserted it back into its envelope, dropped melted wax in three places on the flap, and pressed the presidential seal into it as it hardened. With a sense of firm resolve he delivered it to his private courier.

"Deliver this to the acting chairman of the Foreign Relations Committee in the House of Representatives immediately. John C. Calhoun. For his eyes only. Do you understand?"

The pudgy little courier bobbed his head emphatically, jowls jiggling. "I do, Mister President."

Madison watched him disappear down the long hallway before he walked back to his desk with the familiar, unsettling feeling washing over him that his work, no matter the merit, was now in the hands of others who would accept it or change it or reject it, and there was nothing he could do about it.

John C. Calhoun read the document four times, then converted part of it to language he felt more persuasive than that of the gentleman James Madison. He finished his work and sat back in his chair to read it.

"The mad ambition, the lust for power, and commercial avarice of Great Britain, have left to neutral nations an alternative only between the base surrender of their rights and a manly vindication of them. I plead most vigorously an immediate appeal to arms."

The Calhoun report was delivered to Attorney General William Pinckney. When the text was read by the Federalists they recoiled in horror and sought to have the veil of secrecy lifted for open public debate. The Republicans, a strong majority in the House, voted them down, and the debate proceeded behind closed doors. Two days later—a near record for such a shocking matter as a declaration of war—the Republicans forced the vote. Those in favor, 79; those against, 49.

The matter went to the Senate, where debate raged hot and heavy, with attempts made to limit the declaration to maritime war only, and to include France in any declaration of war. The members of the House of Representatives were riveted with the split they were seeing in the Senate, and James Madison hardly slept or rested.

On June 17, 1812, the vote was held on the original bill, which had survived all proposed amendments. The senators in favor, 19; those against, 13.

That night, President Madison slept soundly for the first time in seventeen days. The following morning, June 18, 1812, he sat once again at his desk with quill in hand and carefully read the simple document Congress had delivered to him. It lacked some things he would have included had it been his creation, but he was satisfied with it as it was. He carefully signed his name, and the bill became law.

For the second time in his lifetime, the United States had declared war on England.

Notes

On June 1, 1812, President Madison drafted and then submitted a secret document to the United States Congress with the intent of delivering his views on the question of war with England. Included in Madison's reasoning was the political setting of the time, with the majority of Americans openly favoring such a war. The American populace was divided into two parties at the time, the Republicans and the Federalists, with the Republicans decidedly the larger and more powerful of the two. Madison, a Republican, saw need to prepare for the election that he would be facing in November and calculated correctly that his hopes for reelection would be considerably enhanced if the nation was at war when the election arrived, since the voting public would be prone to favor retaining the acting president in office to perpetuate the national effort to win the war. He also had the serious problem of lack of money as a result of the staggering debt inherited from the Revolutionary War some thirty-five years earlier, combined with Jefferson's purchase of the Louisiana Territory in 1803 with borrowed money—eleven million additional dollars. The document Madison created was many, many pages longer than what appears in this chapter; however, the parts of it as they appear herein are direct, verbatim quotations of the document he produced. In this manner, the writer of this book attempted to capture the intent of the document, and any shortcomings are the fault of the author. The document was delivered to the House of Representatives on June 2, and John C. Calhoun, acting chair of the Foreign Relations Committee, added his words to make it slightly stronger than Madison's effort, and delivered it to the House on June 3. It was passed by the House on a 79–49 vote within two days and went to the Senate. The Senate became embroiled in attempted amendments and argued it hotly, but finally, on June 17, passed the bill as originally received, by the narrow margin of 19 to 13. On June 18, President Madison signed it into law, and it was made known to the public. The addition of the comments of John C. Calhoun, as found herein, are direct, verbatim quotations.

The United States had declared war on England.

For the complete text of Madison's secret message to Congress, see *Messages and Papers of the Presidents, Volume II*, pp. 484–490. For the responses to the secret message and additions of John C. Calhoun, see Hickey, *The War of 1812*, p. 44; for the vote count in both the House and Senate, see Horsman, *The Causes of the War of 1812*, pp. 260–262; for the financial condition of the United States at the time in question, see Stagg, *Mister Madison's War*, pp. 130–135, and generally, pp. 130–176; for the five points on which Madison accused the British of illegal and insulting acts, and which five points form the basis of his secret message to Congress, see Hickey, *The War of 1812*, p. 44; Barbuto, *Niagara 1814*, p. 6. In general support, see also Wills, *James Madison*, pp. 69–96; Barbuto, *Niagara 1814*, pp. 6–11.

PART TWO

CHAPTER XI

A soft, steady, warm, summer morning rain was falling beneath a gray, overcast sky to seal Boston into a hot, humid day that slowly diminished the spirit of the town and left people wilted, quiet, glancing at clocks as they counted the hours until they could be home, out of their damp clothing, into something cooler and less confining.

The waterfront had much the appearance of a dying thing, with ships tied to less than half the docks, and none standing at anchor in the harbor with their sails furled, waiting for their rotation to load or unload a cargo. dockhands and ship crews, including captains and officers, and the men who owned the ships and cargoes labored in worried silence, preoccupied with the single question that dominated the entire Boston peninsula: When will the blockades be lifted and the rights of free commerce on the high seas be restored; When will Boston become once again a bustling seaport with ships and crews and dockhands straining to handle the cargoes, both coming and going? When will prosperity return? Or, with an all-out war with England in the making, are Boston and the sea commerce of America doomed?

Just before noon, John Dunson stepped into the White Pearl tavern near Fruit Street and walked to the desk where an elderly man with a useless leg sat on a high stool, spectacles at the end of his nose, thin gray hair pulled back. The old man peered at John over his spectacles.

"Mail?"

"Yes. Anything for us?"

The gnarled fingers shuffled through a stack, drew out half a dozen sealed envelopes and a newspaper and handed them to John.

"Here it is. Say hello to Matthew and Billy."

John nodded, and as he turned toward the front door, he unfolded the four-page newspaper. Eyes wide, he stopped and quickly scanned the first page, then barged on through the door and out into the rain, to trot back east along the waterfront to the office of Dunson & Weems.

Inside the office, the sound of the door being thrown open brought the heads of Matthew Dunson and Billy Weems up from the documents spread on their desks, and Matthew stared at his son, silently asking the question.

"War!" John exclaimed.

Matthew and Billy both stood and strode to the front counter where John spread the newspaper for them to read.

"France or England?" Matthew asked. "Or both?"

John's voice was high, excited. "England! Last week. Congress declared war on England. President Madison signed the declaration. Announced it to the newspapers on Thursday the eighteenth. We're at war."

For a moment Matthew and Billy stared at John in disbelief, and then Billy rounded his mouth and blew air. "It finally happened. We're there."

The three men clustered to silently read the great, bold headlines. "WAR DECLARED ON ENGLAND."

"I knew it was coming," Matthew murmured, "but it's still a shock when it happens."

John pointed to the two-column article. "That's not all. It looks like Madison intends invading Canada."

Billy's eyes narrowed, and his forehead creased in doubt. "Canada? He thinks we can take Canada?"

Matthew was shaking his head. "Are you certain?"

"Yes. Read it!"

For thirty seconds the room was silent as Matthew and Billy read the article.

"I don't think we stand a chance of taking Canada," Matthew said. "Not now, not with the army we have."

Billy stepped back to the huge map of the world that was attached to the wall of the austere office. His finger traced a line from the Atlantic ocean to the left end of Lake Erie. "Fourteen hundred miles of lakes and rivers and almost no roads through those forests. Ten years ago Jefferson thought we could take it just by marching up there. Today? There are as many Canadians and English and Indians up there as there are Americans, and they're a lot more familiar with the territory than we are. That newspaper article says President Madison thinks we can take Canada and use her for a bargaining pawn. If England will give us freedom of the seas and ports, we'll return Canada to her." He shook his head. "I doubt it can be done."

Matthew spoke. "The key to that whole area is not by land. It's by water. You can reach all of it—from the Atlantic to Detroit—by the rivers and the Great Lakes, and right now the British navy controls them all." He tapped the map with a forefinger as he recited. "Quebec, Montreal, Prescott, Kingston, York, Stoney Creek, Fort George, Fort Erie, Moraviantown, Amherstburg—all on Canadian soil, all distant from each other, all accessible from the water—the St. Lawrence, Lake Ontario, Lake Erie. To take them all by land and hold them, we would have to divide our army into units so small there's no chance of success. I think we do it by water, not land, and that means we'll be fighting a naval war, not a land war."

Billy looked at Matthew, then John, then at the floor for a moment before he spoke. "Eli's up there trying to forestall a war. I hope he hears about this before the Canadians do. I doubt they'll hesitate to shoot him if they find out first."

For a moment the men stared at each other with the growing awareness of the danger he was in and the fact that there was no way to warn him.

John broke in. "Congress has authorized money to expand the army. Maybe that will be enough."

Billy shook his head. "To go fight in those woods? Territory the enemy knows, and we don't? The trouble is that President Madison has never been in battle, and neither have most of our congressmen. Their notions of what will work up there fall far short of the reality. They just don't know."

Matthew picked up the half dozen pieces of mail and walked back to his desk and sat down, and Billy and John followed. Matthew leaned forward on his elbows.

"We've got to remember, this is all going to be decided by politics. The Republicans and Federalists in Washington, D.C., will collide, and what finally comes out of it could be disastrous. Good sense will take a beating, maybe get lost altogether. Did Congress authorize money to expand the navy? Not just the army?"

John shook his head. "No. Matter of fact, I think they reduced the number of ships we have."

Matthew shook his head. "Who's doing the thinking down there?"

Billy responded, "Politicians. I think General Washington had it right back in '78 when he wrote to the old Continental Congress. Come on out here where we are at Valley Forge. Starve with us. Freeze. Get sick with us. Die with us and help bury our five hundred we lose each month. Maybe then you'll learn enough to understand how a war is fought."

John watched the hot light in Billy's eyes recede and disappear.

Matthew reached for the mail. "Well," he said, "there's not much we can do about it right now." He handed four of the envelopes to Billy. "Payments from customers." He set the other few pieces on his own desk. "New contracts for business." He went on. "John, on your way home stop and tell Mother I'll be over to see her tonight. She'll need to talk with someone about this declaration of war."

"She'll ask about Adam and Caleb."

"Adam's due back from Charleston. Caleb's not due back from Philadelphia for a few days. Tell her not to worry. I'll explain when I stop there on my way home."

It was after one o'clock when the three hurried back to the White Pearl for their midday meal of chowder and bread, then ducked their heads against the rain to return to the office and the unending work of keeping accounts, answering correspondence, making contracts, tracking the maintenance records of their fleet of ships, hiring seamen and officers to sail them, negotiating for insurance. In the late afternoon the first breaks overhead showed patches and slivers of blue sky, and by five o'clock the sun was casting shadows eastward and tiny wisps of steam were rising from the puddled water. The three men were setting their desks in order when the door opened and Adam entered, satchel in one hand, his tunic in the other.

Not as tall as Matthew, built somewhat more thickly, dark hair and dark eyes, steady, tending to speak little, regular, strong features, Adam was a born leader. The three rose to meet him, relief showing as always when one of their ship captains returned from the open seas.

"Back safe," Matthew exclaimed.

Adam smiled. "Good to be home." He laid his tunic and satchel on the counter. "Too warm out there. Humid."

"Could be worse," Matthew answered.

"Any trouble?" Billy asked, grinning.

"None to speak of." Adam pointed at the satchel. "Ship's log's in there. Payment for the last load with it."

John took the satchel and walked back to the large, black vault.

Matthew asked, "You get the load of cotton?"

Adam hooked a finger over his shoulder. "In the ship, safe. I let the crew go for the night. They'll be back tomorrow to unload. Is Brewerton ready to receive it?"

Billy nodded. "Yes. Right on time."

"Good. Can you pay the crew tomorrow?"

"Got it in the vault," Billy answered.

Adam leaned against the counter. "Did I hear it right? Congress declared war on England? President Madison's talking about invading Canada?"

Matthew pointed at the newspaper. "It did. Last Thursday. And Madison is talking about invading Canada."

For long moments Adam stared down at the countertop while his thoughts ran. He slowly exhaled. "David and Goliath. What is Madison going to use for the stone to put in his sling? The one that will hit England in the forehead and end this thing? Is he thinking of the army or the navy?"

Billy cut in. "No one knows yet. But either way, the stone won't be big enough."

Adam looked at them, first Billy and then Matthew, and then John. "It's going to come down to the navy, one way or another." He pointed at the map. "It will take an army twenty times what we have to occupy and hold all that land. And right now the British navy has total control of the rivers and Great Lakes."

Adam fell silent, and a quiet fear arose in each man that everything they had had suddenly been plunged into a war that was going to demand it all. Their ships, their crews, their fortunes, their lives, their skills with men and the sea—everything they had built was at risk. None of them had the faintest hope that the United States could prevail against England's vastly superior army and navy. For long moments they stood at the counter, struggling to rise above the sick knot that had risen in their chests.

"Well," Matthew finally said, "it appears we have some plans to make. Adam, there's no need to hold you here any longer tonight. Charlotte and the children are waiting. See you in the morning."

Adam reached for his tunic. "How's Mother?"

A cloud crossed Matthew's face. "All right. We check on her every day. You might stop on the way home to let her see you. It does something for her to see us."

Adam shook his head and a smile crossed his face. "Why won't she come live with us? Take turns at our homes?

Matthew grinned. "Mother? Dependent?"

Adam grinned back. "Pardon me for asking. I'll stop to see her for a minute. See you in the morning."

He was at the front door when Matthew called, "Good to have you home. Say hello to Charlotte."

The sun was touching the western rim when the three men walked out the door into the stifling, sweltering heat and the familiar sounds of seabirds squawking and quarreling and tides working against the pilings of the wharfs. They separated, Billy going home to Brigitte, John to Laura, and Matthew to Kathleen. Matthew struggled with his thoughts, trying to restore some sense of dependable structure to a world that had been shattered by a declaration of war, but there was nothing left for a foundation. The very existence of the United States was in doubt! David and Goliath? At least David had a sling that he had mastered, and a smooth round stone. What does the United States have? An army and a navy that are impotent against the mightiest military power on the earth—no sling, no stone. If England were to crush the United States, what would become of everything they had fought for since that morning of April 19, 1775—thirty-seven years ago? Their wives—families— children—Dunson & Weems? His mind could not imagine it, nor could he force his thoughts to invent it.

He glanced up at the beauty of the sun catching the tops of the green trees that lined the streets as he came to the white picket fence he had known from earliest memory, and he pushed through the gate and onto the walkway to the front door. He did not knock, but pushed it open and stepped into the parlor.

"Mother?" he called.

The answer came from the open back door. "Matthew, is that you?"

"Yes. What are you doing out there?"

"Getting some ham from the root cellar."

"You wait for me. I'll get it." He hurried through the house.

"Too late," Margaret answered, "I've already got it. I'm coming in."

"Mother," Matthew scolded, "you know you shouldn't be lifting that door and going up and down those stairs. What would happen if you fell? You wait until one of us is here."

"Oh, fiddle," Margaret said. "I can still go up and down stairs."

She walked in, a little flushed, puffing, swaying slightly, carrying a chunk of ham on a wooden plate. "For supper," she said, and Matthew took it from her and set it on the cupboard. He took her by one arm.

"Sit down for a minute. We need to talk."

They sat down at the dining table, Matthew beside her. He did not sit at the head, where his father had presided until he took the British musket ball in his right lung that day in April, thirty-seven years earlier.

"Talk about what?" Margaret asked. "The war?"

"You know? Adam came by?"

"Adam and John. Yes. Told me all about it." She threw both hands up. "Nonsense! Utter nonsense! Why can't people just sit down and reason these things out?"

Matthew avoided the question. "Caleb will be home soon. Is there anything you need? I can have the twins here whenever you need something."

"No, not a thing. I'm worried about Adam. Did he look a little peaked to you? Is he getting enough to eat?"

Matthew snorted. "Mother, Adam's strong as a bull. He's fine. That isn't what I want to talk about. It's the war. It's here. The chances are strong that this country is going to need every man it can find, and every ship, to fight the British. That might include most of us at Dunson & Weems."

Margaret's face clouded. "You? At your age? Why, you're sixty! Too old for such things!"

"Not quite sixty, and I doubt age will matter anyway. Listen to me."

She used a handkerchief from her apron pocket to wipe at the perspiration on her forehead, then became still. "I'm listening."

"We're going to need your help."

Her eyes opened wide. "Me? What can I do?"

"Think about it. This trouble with the British didn't start last Thursday. It started a long time ago. The Mayflower Compact. The Confederation Congress. Lexington. Saratoga. Valley Forge. Yorktown. Our Constitution. A new country. We thought it was over with England, but it wasn't. It won't be over with them until they understand we are a separate nation. That's what this is all about. We have to fight them one more time to prove it. Father knows that. It has to be."

He watched the face that had been there for him from birth. He saw the beauty; he did not see the wrinkles or the creeping age. She worked her handkerchief with her hands for a time, face downcast, and he saw her eyes fill with silent tears at the remembrance of her John and the thirty-seven years she had yearned for him in the aching emptiness. She wiped at her eyes with her handkerchief, then raised her face to him.

"I remember. I understand. You need me to give you my blessing and let you all go back to war. One more time. I understand." She gazed for a moment at her hands, then said quietly, "I'll do that."

Matthew left his chair and went to one knee beside hers. He wrapped his arms about her and pressed her close to him. "Thank you, Mother. Thank you."

He released her and stood.

"But I'll worry the whole time," she declared.

Matthew laughed. "I know you will. Bless you for it. But you'll make it through."

She struggled to stand, and he helped her up.

"I have to go now," he said. "I'll have the twins here in less than an hour to help you with the supper dishes and get ready for bed."

"No need," she exclaimed. "I can manage."

"I know you can. But they'll be here all the same."

Notes

For the letter George Washington wrote in high temper to the Confederation Congress in February 1778 from the ravages of Valley Forge, chastising them for their neglect of his starving and dying army, see Leckie, *George Washington's War*, pp. 433–34.

All other characters in this chapter are fictional.

Washington, D.C.
Early July 1812

CHAPTER XII

$\mathcal{T}$ he President will see you now."

Tiny beads of perspiration glistened on the foreheads of Matthew and Billy as they rose from the upholstered chairs in the huge entry area of the Executive Mansion where they had been waiting in the dead, sweltering July midmorning heat of a mosquito-infested Washington, D.C. They both wiped their faces with handkerchiefs as they followed the quick, clicking steps of the small man in the starched black suit down the hallway, past framed paintings of men who had made history and scenes of the struggle for independence, to the large library. The little man held the door for them while they entered and slowed and stopped. Three walls of the room were lined with bookshelves stocked with orderly, organized rows of books and memorabilia. The fourth was a great window with heavy draperies and sashes and sunlight streaming through to cast a bright, misshapen rectangle on the polished floor. In the center of the room was a massive table surrounded by eight chairs with leather upholstery and brass studs. Spread on the table was a great, detailed map of the American continent, with President James Madison leaning over it, arms stiff, palms flat, as he studied the contours. At their entrance, he raised his head, and his smile was genuine as he strode to greet them.

"Mister Dunson and Mister Weems! Welcome to my humble quarters. Or should I say my humble *temporary* quarters?"

They all smiled as Matthew and Billy reached to shake the small, thin, firm hand, and Madison continued.

"You received my letter, then?"

"Yes, Mister President, we did." Matthew touched the breast of his suit coat where the letter was held in the inside pocket.

"Was it a great inconvenience for you to come? Leaving your business for several days?"

Billy answered, smiling. "It is a blessing to be away from it for a little time."

Madison smiled back. "I understand. Oh, yes, I understand."

Again the three of them smiled, and Madison continued.

"Your wives? Families? They are well, I hope."

Billy spoke. "Yes, thank you. They're in good health. The children are growing."

For a split second a wistful look crossed Madison's face. "They grow up so fast. So fast."

Too late Billy remembered that Madison's marriage to Dolley had been childless. Widowed with an infant son after three years of marriage to John Todd Jr., she had married Madison, and together they had raised the boy, Payne. He had been unsettled and erratic as a youth, and a frustration to Madison, and now, as a mature man away from them and making his own way, his life remained as it had been—in turmoil.

Billy made no answer. Madison went on, wasting no time or words.

"I'm certain you are aware Congress declared war on Great Britain."

"Yes," Matthew replied. "Two weeks ago."

Madison gestured to the table. "Good. I need help. Advice. And I need it from someone who has borne arms and who has no political ambitions or axes to grind."

He led them to the table and within seconds both men were oriented to the huge map.

"Let me be specific," Madison declared. "Congress is firm in its conclusion that the key to defeating the British at the earliest possible time is taking Canada."

He paused, and Matthew and Billy exchanged glances. Madison went on.

"In large part I concur. Right now Canada is the source of lumber and other necessaries to keep the British navy afloat. If that source is denied them, their navy will decline rapidly and they will very abruptly lose dominance of the high seas. And when that happens, they become vulnerable, first to France, then to us. The question becomes, what is the most efficient way to take Canada?"

He pointed to the map. "From the Atlantic on the east, to the west end of Lake Erie, travel is almost exclusively on water. Hudson's Bay, the St. Lawrence River, Lake Ontario. Nearly fifteen hundred miles. I'm informed roads on either side are little more than wagon ruts and nearly impassable about half of the year. It follows that whoever controls that waterway controls Canada."

He glanced at both men, who were intently studying the map, waiting for him to continue.

"If control of the water is the key, then I propose that we accomplish that in three ways." He tapped the map. "Here. Montreal. At the east end of the corridor. Take Montreal, and we control all shipping, both directions."

He shifted his hand and pointed again. "Here. The central section of the corridor, at the west end of Lake Ontario. Take York and Fort George and Stoney Creek, and our Fort Niagara can control the Niagara River. We can stop all that comes and goes from Lake Erie to Lake Ontario."

He shifted his hand once more, pointing. "Here. Detroit. The west end of the corridor, on Lake Erie. From our Fort Detroit we can cross the Detroit River and take Fort Malden and Amherstburg from the British. Once in possession of all three of these locations, we can control all traffic from the Great Lakes to the Atlantic. All of northeastern Canada."

He straightened and cleared his throat.

"I propose we attack and take all three locations immediately. Take control now. If we're successful, Canada's commerce is paralyzed, and England is crippled. She'll come seeking terms soon enough."

He straightened and faced the two men, a very small man looking up at two large ones. "Mister Dunson, you are a seasoned combat naval officer. Mister Weems, you were a lieutenant in the Continental Army. Your advice would be invaluable. What is your reaction to all this?"

Matthew exhaled slowly. "How do you propose taking these three locations?—Montreal and Niagara and Detroit? Water or land?"

"Almost entirely by land. We will march armies to the locations. Once they arrive, they'll have to cross the Niagara River to take Fort George, and the St. Lawrence to take Montreal, and the Detroit River to take Fort Malden and Amherstburg. But none of those rivers are an insurmountable obstacle."

Matthew shook his head. "The problem isn't the size of the rivers. The problem is that all three of those locations can be reached by gunboats—Montreal, Fort Niagara, and Detroit. The question is, who's in control of the Great Lakes and the St. Lawrence River right now? We or they?"

"Right now, they are."

"Do you have a plan to change that? Take control from them?"

Madison frowned. "No. I asked Congress for more gunboats, but they see no need for them. In fact, they reduced what little we have up there."

Matthew's voice came quiet. "What *do* we have up there?"

Madison was slow in answering. "Two vessels. A small army transport named the *Detroit* on Lake Erie, and a navy brig named the *Oneida* on Lake Superior."

Matthew dropped his eyes for a moment. "Do you have any idea how many they have?"

"One ship of the line, nine frigates, and twenty-seven lesser gunboats, stationed at Halifax and Newfoundland, available to the Great Lakes and the waterway. Thirty-seven vessels that are armed and available."

"Congress can't see the problem?" Matthew exclaimed. "We have two ships to face thirty-seven? We can't take control and maintain it without ships!"

Madison nodded. "I agree. Unfortunately, it is not in my power to change it. It is in the hands of Congress, and for their own reasons, they refuse. They see this entire plan in a very simple light. They have convinced themselves that if we just go through the formalities of marching up there, the Canadians will surrender without a fight."

Matthew would not let go. "Congress is responsible for this plan? What committee? Who?"

"William Eustis—secretary of war—asked the advice of two of our generals—Hull and Dearborn. General Hull insisted we needed a stronger naval force up there, but Eustis disagreed. Mister Eustis agreed with the three-pronged approach and presented the plan to Congress. With a few adjustments, they approved it."

For a moment Matthew stood in silence with the muscles of his jaw making tight ridges. "I don't recall ever hearing that William Eustis has had combat experience. Has he?"

"He was a surgeon in the Revolutionary War, and later in Shay's Rebellion."

Matthew's face clouded. "Who are you sending up there to lead the campaigns? Which officers?"

"General William Hull is already marching there with about two thousand men he gathered in Ohio. He is under orders to cross the Detroit River, take Fort Malden and Amherstburg, and move east. Major General Henry Dearborn will command a second army that will be divided. One section will be under orders to cross the St. Lawrence far to the east of Lake Ontario and subdue Montreal, and at the same time the second section will cross the Niagara River at our Fort Niagara and take the British Fort George at the western tip of Lake Ontario, and on around to take Stoney Creek and York. Then the two armies, one under General Hull, the other under General Dearborn, will join, and we shall be in control of the entire region."

Billy spoke. "Did you say they are the same two generals who Eustis called on for advice?"

"Yes."

"Do I remember General Hull from the war back in '76? Wasn't he an officer? And Dearborn?"

"Yes. Both were officers in the Continental Army during that war."

Matthew interrupted. "Isn't Hull the governor of Michigan Territory?"

Madison nodded. "Yes. Why? Is there a problem?"

Billy cut in. "Maybe, but not because he's the governor. How old are those two men?"

Madison reflected for a moment. "Sixty years, perhaps a little over. They've had experience commanding men in battle. Is age a concern?"

Billy ignored the question and wiped at the perspiration on his forehead. "How is their health?"

There was a pause before Madison spoke. "Hull has had a stroke, but he's reported to be completely recovered. I believe Dearborn to be in good health."

"Have both men accepted these commands?"

"Finally, yes. When I offered the Detroit command to Hull, he refused at first because of his view that we must have a greater naval presence up there. I then offered it to Colonel Jacob Kingsbury, but his health is failing, and he could not accept. When I went back to General Hull, he had changed his opinion about naval power. He now thinks that a strong army in Detroit will be able to defeat the British and hold the west end of the water corridor. He accepted the commission and was actually marching before Congress declared war. Dearborn accepted the position of commander of the force that is to take Montreal and the Niagara area. Why? What are you seeing that I am not?"

Billy spoke slowly. "Age. Old men to plan wars, young men to fight them. Age brings experience, and experience makes men cautious. All too often there is no place in battle for caution. Officers have to take chances. Make decisions almost instantly. They don't have the time to reflect. To be cautious. I see a strong probability of problems." Billy abruptly changed direction. "Who is the secretary of the navy right now?"

"Paul Hamilton."

Billy reflected for a few moments. "Haven't I heard things about him? He has a weakness for strong drink? Undependable?"

"Both. Regrettably. And there's little I can do about it."

Billy went on. "If this plan is put in motion, you're going to need a clear mind that you can depend on to make it work."

Madison's face dropped. "I could not agree more, but I repeat: There is nothing I can do about it. Anything else?"

Billy pointed. "Yes. I don't recall a road from Indiana to Detroit. Is there one?"

"No. Hull is building a road as he moves north."

Billy made calculations from the map. "Two hundred fifty miles?"

"Approximately."

Billy asked, "If Hull gets to Detroit, and the British cut that road and trap him, how does he get out, or how does a force get up to relieve him?"

"He'll have to make his own way out."

Billy shook his head slowly. "With Tecumseh's Indians up there, that could become a massacre. A tragedy."

"Hull knows that. He'll be responsible to avoid it."

"If the British use Indians, Hull won't know they're there until they come jumping." Billy shifted his hand to point. "Over here—Detroit and Niagara—the same problem. If the British cut the roads, how do those men escape, or how do we get relief up there?"

There was defensiveness in Madison's soft voice as he made his answer. "We will have to be certain the force we send there is large enough that they can defend themselves in any event."

Billy went on. "Supplies?"

"They'll have to take sufficient with them to stand a siege."

Billy broke off and remained silent. Matthew picked it up.

"Do you know who the British have in command up there?"

"Yes. Major General Isaac Brock."

For a moment Matthew closed his eyes, probing his memory. "He's a competent officer. Even brilliant."

"That is our estimate of him, yes."

"Do you intend sending more ships of the line up there?"

"Yes. The *Constitution,* and the *President.*"

Again Matthew reached into his mind. "Two more ships? That brings it to four of our ships facing thirty-seven of theirs? The *Constitution* and the *President* will add about eighty-eight more cannon to our forces—forty-four each—but that will still leave us about six hundred short of what the British already have up there. The odds against us are heavy." He turned to tap the map. "How do you plan to keep the three locations in full communication? By land or water?"

"Water, if we can. Land if not. Is it critical?"

"It could be. The success of all this depends on taking all three locations at about the same time. If we fail at one location, we'll be in trouble. If we fail at two locations, we're doomed. The reason is, the British will have to split their forces to cover three locations, and when they do, they will have weakened themselves. If they have only two locations to cover, or one, they can consolidate their forces to better advantage."

He paused and watched Madison until he saw understanding, then went on. "The result is that our three forces must be in constant communication so that if one or two fail, the others can get braced, or get out of it altogether. You're going to need a plan and a schedule and a secret code for communications so each will know what's happening with the other two."

"That can be done."

Matthew straightened to his full height. "May I give you my worst fears?"

"That's why you're here."

Matthew's hand swept across the map. "Close to fifteen hundred miles, east to west. The enemy knows the territory better than we do because they've been there longer. They have Indian allies who know it in close detail. Those Indians can move through the woods eighty miles in one day and fight the next without a problem. Our forces would be lucky to cover a fourth of that."

He paused and looked Madison in the eye. "What Congress has

planned is the war Billy and I fought thirty-five years ago, but in exact reverse. Then, we knew our own territory. The British did not. We could move through it quickly, and they could not. We could cut their supply lines with twenty men, and they could do nothing about it. There were a thousand places we could hide in ambush and then disappear, and we did. The territory they were trying to take was simply too big, too strung out, too vast, too complicated for them. It took them six years to realize they were never going to force us to a stand. They were the most powerful military in the world, but they didn't have enough to take all the vast territory we held and occupy it. They finally simply gave up and went home."

He paused, and for several seconds the room was caught up in an intense quiet. Then Matthew went on.

"That is my worst fear for the plan as I understand it." He pointed at the map. "Look at the territory you intend taking. Big. Vast. Complex. Empty. They know it better than we. We will never be able to push them to a battle they don't want because they'll just disappear in those woods, and we'll never catch them if they don't want us to. How many places up there can they lay an ambush? A thousand? Ten thousand? If we take Montreal and Niagara and Fort Malden and Amherstburg, do you think they'll surrender? Or will they simply disappear and wait us out?"

Again he stopped and turned to Billy. "How do you see it?"

Billy's answer was short. "Remember Burgoyne at Saratoga? Cornwallis at Yorktown? They both tried to force us to a stand and couldn't. We caught them at a place of our choosing, and they lost. Burgoyne surrendered his entire army of six thousand. Cornwallis surrendered over six thousand. They learned too late what Matthew's talking about. We didn't beat the British. They gave up. The United States simply wasn't worth the cost in British lives and money."

Billy stopped, then went on. "If William Eustis and Paul Hamilton are the two men who must make this work—our secretary of war and secretary of the navy—there's reason to fear. I doubt either is up to it."

For a time Madison looked into the face of one man, then the other, then turned to pore over the map again before he spoke.

"I know about the problems with both of them, but I have no alternative."

He heaved a great sigh and raised his face to them. "You've done me a tremendous service. You don't know how I needed to see this through men who know and who are willing to say the hard things." He gestured. "Take a seat. I need answers to one or two more things."

They sat in the upholstered chairs with Madison facing them across his desk. "If it comes to it, will you be available to help?"

Matthew looked at Billy, then back at Madison. "In what capacity?"

"Any you choose. Battlefield commanders if you wish."

Matthew shook his head. "Billy was right. We would both run the risk of being too cautious. Too unwilling to make the instant decisions that will get men killed. You'll need younger men for that. But speaking for myself, I am at your service to give you the best I have to advise your commanders." He turned to Billy. "What's your answer?"

"The same. I wouldn't trust myself. I've seen too many men dead and crippled. I'm not sure I would make the right decisions while men were dropping all around me. But I will deem it an honor to give you my best advice, any time."

Madison looked at Matthew, and there was pleading in his eyes. "You have men in your business who are outstanding in their naval abilities. Navigators. Captains. Would they be available?"

Matthew's eyes narrowed. "You mean my brother and my son? Adam and John?"

"Yes, and your brother Caleb."

"That's for them to decide. Write them a letter and make a proposal. They'll give you their answers."

"And there's one more matter. Would Mister Stroud be available? His services among the Indians would be invaluable."

Billy cut in. "Write a letter to him but send it to me. I'll see that he gets it. He can make his own answer."

Madison drew and released a great breath and rose and thrust out his hand, and the two shook it warmly. "There is no way for me to extend an adequate thanks," Madison exclaimed. "I'll write those letters soon. And one more thing I must say."

Matthew and Billy looked at him, waiting in silence.

"We have war hawks in Congress from all sections of the United States. Henry Clay and John C. Calhoun, and others, some from the north, some from farther south. Each has his own views on all this, and the debates that develop in the hallowed halls of both houses are all too often ridiculous. The plan I have explained is almost entirely the work of General Dearborn and Congress. There is absolutely nothing I can do about it. I have no idea how many times I've wished that persons such as yourselves could speak to Congress assembled and call down thunder from heaven to make them understand what you've told me here today. I will do my best with what I have."

He led them to the door. "I won't hold you longer. Give my best wishes to your families, will you?"

They shook hands warmly as Matthew spoke.

"It has been an honor to come. If there is anything else we can do, you have only to ask."

The little man held the door for them as they passed out into the long, polished hardwood hall floor. He watched them walk away, and he heard the door close behind them. He remained standing, silent, unmoving, for a long time, with a growing alarm rising in his breast as their words rang in his brain.

The War of Independence in reverse—too big—too vast—can't control the waterway—Eustis and Hamilton incapable—commanding officers too old—too cautious.

He straightened and squared his shoulders and walked resolutely back into the library and closed the door.

There is an election coming. I have no choice. We must move. Now.

Notes

Immediately after the American declaration of war against England was made public, President James Madison began a plan to take Canada, reasoning that England could not survive without Canadian timber to support her massive navy. He turned to his secretary of war, William Eustis, who was not prepared for his position and somewhat of a bumbler, who in turn sought advice from General William Hull, who at that time was governor of the Michigan Territory and Major General Henry Dearborn, both men above sixty years of age who had served well in the Revolutionary War. Dearborn proposed the three-pronged plan as herein described, of taking Montreal, the Niagara area, and the Detroit area, simultaneously. At the time, the United States could commit fewer than seven thousand troops to the cause and only seventeen ships. The British navy consisted of six hundred ships and its army of about two hundred fifty thousand men. At the time, England and France were at war, and England had to divide her armed forces between the conflict in Europe and that in America. Despite the horrendous imbalance of military power between the United States and England, the consensus of Congress was that it would require only that we march north and seize control of the great waterway, and the Canadians would surrender without a fight. General Hull saw the need for a massive overhaul of our naval presence on the waterway, but Congress did not agree, and in fact reduced the naval presence. President Madison offered command of the three-pronged plan to Hull and Dearborn—Hull to the Detroit area, Dearborn to the other two. Hull refused at first, so Madison offered it to Colonel Jacob Kingsbury, whose health would not permit him to accept. Madison went back to Hull and persuaded him to take the position. The secretary of war at the time was Paul Hamilton, who was openly addicted to alcohol and incompetent. Eustis and Hamilton were unqualified to handle the proposed invasion and taking of Canada. The addition of the two American frigates *President* and *Constitution* to their shadow navy on the Great Lakes would add eighty-eight cannon to American firepower, since each was armed with forty-four cannon. The reasoning presented herein of Matthew Dunson and Billy Weems, both fictional characters, represents the reaction of the better-qualified veterans to the whole plan. The area was too vast and United States forces were too sparse to carry it.

See Stagg, *Mister Madison's War*, pp. 3–7, 181–192; Hickey, *The War of 1812*, pp. 80–92; Malcomson, *Lords of the Lakes*, pp. 15–16, 39–41; Wills, *James Madison*, pp. 97–100; Barbuto, *Niagara 1814*, p. 57.

Fort Malden, Canada

July 3, 1812

CHAPTER XIII

f the links that formed the great highway of water that reached west from the Atlantic Ocean nearly halfway across the North American continent, none were more strategically located nor critically important than those that connected the lower four Great Lakes. There were two such links, both relatively small rivers. The Detroit River at the south end of Lake Huron drained Lake Michigan, Lake Superior, and Lake Huron into Lake Erie, to connect the upper half of the great waterway with the lower half. The Niagara River at the east end of Lake Erie drained into Lake Ontario, thence into the mighty St. Lawrence River and on eastward to Hudson Bay and the Atlantic Ocean, making the chain complete—from Lake Superior to the great ocean. The result was that whoever controlled the Detroit River or the Niagara River, had the power to stop the commerce that fed and sustained most of the northeast section of the continent.

To protect their claims to the rights of navigation on the two rivers that were the indispensable keys to the northern sections of the continent, the Americans had built Fort Detroit on the west side of the Detroit River at the west end of Lake Erie, on United States soil in the territory of Michigan; and the British had built their opposing Fort Malden on the east side of the Detroit River, on English soil in what was called Upper Canada. At the other end of Lake Erie, the east end, the Americans had built Fort Niagara on the west side of the Niagara

River on soil belonging to the state of New York, and the British had built Fort George on the east side of the Niagara River on Canadian soil.

Twenty miles south of Fort Malden, on the Detroit River, the village of Amherstburg had sprung up, where the British had created a small shipyard for construction of their gunboats that patrolled the Great Lakes.

Thus, in the early months of 1812, with unbearable tension gripping those on both sides of the entire waterway, Great Britain and the United States stood toe to toe and face to face across the two key rivers in what had suddenly become a stand-or-fall confrontation for possession and control of the Detroit River and the Niagara River, and, consequently, the great waterway and Canada.

In early July, Fort Malden stood wilted and sweltering in the hot, dead, midmorning humid air. The proud Union Jack with its royal blue field and red and white crosses hung limp and unmoving from the seventy-foot flagpole at the huge gates into the square, efficient fort with its log buildings constructed around the great parade ground in the center. Sweating soldiers in proper British rank and file cursed their crimson wool tunics and their ten-pound Brown Bess muskets as they mechanically executed the barked orders of their drill sergeant. The drill field was planted in grass that was thick and green in April and May, but with winter and spring past, was now fast disappearing under the relentless tread of British boots in daily drill. The firm steps of the marching soldiers raised tiny curls of dust as they marched on.

Along the north wall of the east-facing fort, women with cloths tied to hold their hair back and clothed in ankle- and wrist-length dresses and high-top black leather shoes that were soaked, perspired as they carried water in wooden buckets from the fort well to steaming, blackened kettles hung from chains on nine-foot tripods for the weekly washing of the clothing of the entire fort. Some fetched armloads of split kindling to feed the fires beneath the kettles. Some scrubbed clothing on corrugated washboards in heavy wooden tubs filled with hot water and strong, homemade lye soap that left their hands raw and cracked. Some hung the dripping, laundered clothing on wires strung between posts. Others gathered those already dried to make way for the wet ones coming. All paused from time to time to wipe at the perspiration and steal a moment to watch the soldiers make their oblique movements and their left and right flanking maneuvers, before they turned back to the unrelenting, sweaty work of keeping clean clothing available to a disciplined, orderly military presence in the wilderness.

None wished to suffer the consequence of dereliction of duty that would provoke Major General Isaac Brock, the commander of the fort and of British subjects in the area. Tall, hair golden in the sunlight, powerful in the shoulders and arms, with strong, regular features, Brock was a fair man, and a just man, who gave rewards when earned and punishment when deserved. He never asked a soldier or a civilian to do a thing he would not do himself and had earned the respect of every man in his command. Perhaps not their friendship, but always their respect. In battle, he was brilliant to a fault, leading his men into combat where his peers would not go, inspiring them, driving his command on to victories that made them the envy of the British army.

Just days earlier, an exhausted messenger on a weary horse had delivered a message to General Brock that left him shaking his head in stunned disbelief. On June 18, the United States had declared war on England! For long minutes he had sat at his desk, reading the message over and over again as the stark realization settled in. *The Americans have invited their own demise! They've thrown the spark into the powder barrel. When and where will the explosion come?* Then General Brock had stood and squared his shoulders and set his jaw and made his resolve. *If it comes here, we'll be ready. We'll be ready.*

He was seated at his plain desk in his office reading the morning sick-call report when a loud, rapid, urgent knock at his door brought his head up. He closed the report and leaned back in his chair.

"Enter."

His eyes narrowed at the sight of the slender, sweated, red-faced, winded, wide-eyed lieutenant who pulled up short and jerked his hand up in a salute, then dropped it as Brock recognized him.

"Sir," the man panted, "I have just come from the river. There's an enemy ship out there coming this way. She's—"

Brock held up his hand and smiled calmly. "Slow down, Lieutenant Webb. Start at the beginning. Something's happened. Tell me."

The young man took a deep breath. "Sorry, sir. It caught us by surprise. Captain Morton thought you should know and sent me. It's an American ship. A schooner. The *Cuyahoga.* Commercial, we think. Not carrying cannon we can see. She's moving north in the Detroit River. She'll be under our guns in a few minutes. If I understood it right, sir, the United States has just lately declared war on us. We are not quite sure what to do about a civilian ship moving north. It's certain she's headed for Detroit, most likely to bring supplies to the Americans there. Respectfully, sir, what are your orders?"

Brock's forehead wrinkled in question. "An American commercial schooner? Voluntarily coming under our guns?" For a moment he stared at his desktop. "I would almost wager her captain doesn't know about the declaration of war." He paused for just a moment. "Board her and bring her to our docks. Do not use cannon or muskets unless absolutely necessary. Bring her war chest and all paperwork here to me. I want to know if they're aware America has declared war on us."

"Yes, sir," the young lieutenant blurted and turned on his heel and fairly ran from the room, then turned left to sprint down the boardwalk to the great gates. He seized the reins of his horse from the startled private who had been holding the bay gelding and vaulted into the saddle. He pulled the head around and jammed his blunted spurs into the flanks of the animal, and in three jumps the horse was at a dead run down the narrow dirt trail that wound through the dense forest to the British gun emplacements dug into the banks of the river. He hauled the winded horse to a sliding stop and was shouting General Brock's orders to Captain Morton before he hit the ground, pointing to the light schooner, still four hundred yards to the south, steadily moving up the river under a light breeze.

"Sir, General Brock orders us to take the *Cuyahoga.* Bring her to our dock. Get the war chest and all the papers of her captain and take them to the general. Do not use cannon or musket if it can be avoided."

Instantly the captain turned and trotted down to the dock on the riverbank to drop into a longboat with six seamen in position on the cross-benches, oars shipped, and a helmsman seated at the rear, hand on the tiller, all ready and waiting. The captain used his horn to bellow his orders to the gun crews on shore. "Guns one, two, and three. I'm going out there. At my signal, each of you fire one shot over the bow of the *Cuyahoga.* I will demand they tie up at our dock peacefully. If she refuses or if she shows cannon that we have not seen, all batteries open fire at once and continue until she is disabled. Do not sink her if it can be avoided. We want her crew alive and all her papers." He lowered his horn and then raised it again while a wry grin crossed his face. "Should any of your cannonballs come within twenty yards of this longboat, that crew will be hung just before evening mess. Am I clear?"

Chuckling gun crews reached for powder ladles and budge barrels and commenced loading their cannon.

Morton lowered his horn and gave orders to the longboat crew. "Cast off! Take us out into the mainstream, well ahead of the American ship."

The long oars dropped from their upright position and rattled as they were shoved into the oarlocks. The three men on the right held their oar blades above the water while the three on the left dug theirs deep and grunted as they threw their backs into it to turn the boat. On the fourth stroke all six oars were in the dark waters of the Detroit River, and the boat was skimming out into the smooth current. Morton waited until he was directly north of the oncoming schooner before he turned to face his waiting shore batteries and raised his horn.

"Numbers one, two, and three. Fire!"

Three seconds later white smoke leaped from the cannon muzzles. The booming blasts and the concussion came rolling across the open water and an instant later three geysers erupted twenty yards past the bow of the oncoming ship. Morton raised his telescope to study the scramble of confusion on the deck of the little ship and waited until the echo of the cannon roar died before he raised his horn.

"Hello, the *Cuyahoga*," he shouted. "I am Captain Reginald Morton of the British Royal Navy. I command you to change course and dock your schooner at the pier on the east bank of the river. If you refuse I have ordered my cannon crews to destroy you immediately. Do it now or bear the consequences."

While Morton watched, a man pushed his way through the shaken crew on the little schooner and stood spread-legged at the railing on the ship's bow. His voice came high, shocked, belligerent, defensive.

"This is not a gunboat! We are commercial! By what right have you fired on us? By what right do you demand our surrender?"

"Sir," Morton went on in his steady monotone, "the United States has declared war on Great Britain." He paused and saw the entire crew on the *Cuyahoga* come to a standstill, silent, unbelieving, and then he went on. "Do you understand? A state of war exists between the United States and Great Britain. I am taking your ship as a prize of war and your crew as our prisoners. Turn to starboard now, or my shore batteries will reduce you to kindling. Should you elect to destroy any part of your cargo, or your war chest, or your manifest papers, you will all be hanged before nightfall. You have ten seconds."

Morton counted slowly to ten and was turning with his horn to shout orders to the shore batteries when the helmsman called, "Sir, they're coming about to starboard."

On Morton's command, the six oarsmen turned the longboat, and with Morton watching like a hawk, they led the schooner back to the docks that served Fort Malden, where Morton waited while the schooner cast her hawsers and British hands looped them in the inverted figure eight to secure them to the cleats on the heavy planking. Morton waited impatiently until the gangplank was lowered, then marched up to the deck of the ship.

"Your name, sir," he demanded of the captain, an aging, bearded, burly man who had shed his tunic in the heat of the morning and was standing in a white shirt damp with perspiration. His face was a red mix of anger, disbelief, insult, and terror. He ignored Morton's question and his words came hot, fast, with an unmistakable New England inflection.

"What do you mean, a state of war? What declaration of war? I own this ship, not the United States. We're unarmed! I was hired to bring possessions and personal belongings north to Fort Detroit! I got no part of any war!"

Morton's expression did not change. "I understand, sir, but the fact remains, we are in a state of war. This ship now belongs to Great Britain, and you and your crew are our prisoners. Your cargo is ours. My men will inspect it immediately, and we shall do with it as we see fit. You will order your men to follow mine to the fort just behind us, where you will be placed in cells and extended every courtesy afforded prisoners of war. I will have your name, sir."

There was hatred in the man's eyes and voice as he answered. "Beltran. Andrew Beltran."

"Thank you, sir. If there is nothing else, let us move. Now."

Captain Morton led up the winding trail from the river to the gates of the fort with Beltran behind, followed by his bewildered crew, muttering blasphemies against England, Captain Morton, and a world that had turned hostile in an instant. The ramparts were filled with both officers and enlisted who had heard the cannon blasts and were peering over the top of the fort walls, waiting to see what had happened. Lieutenant Webb threw open the gates, excited, face flushed with the thrill of action and the capture of an enemy ship, choosing to ignore the fact that the American crew had blundered into a war of which they knew nothing and the ship was a small commercial schooner filled with someone's personal belongings and not one cannon.

Morton hooked a thumb over his shoulder. "Lieutenant, this is Captain Andrew Beltran. Take charge of him and his crew. Extend every courtesy due prisoners of war, but be certain they're locked up."

"Yes, sir," Webb exclaimed. "Captain Beltran, you and your crew will follow me."

Morton walked on to the headquarters of General Brock, was

cleared by the general's assistant at the front desk, rapped on the door, and was ordered to come in.

Morton stepped inside, saluted, and waited for Brock to speak.

"Report."

"The ship is a commercial schooner owned by a man named Andrew Beltran. The crew is American. Beltran said he did not know America had declared war on us, and I believe him. He claims his cargo is personal belongings he contracted to carry north to Fort Detroit."

Brock considered for a moment. "Whose personal property?"

Morton smiled. "That, sir, I thought might be most interesting. May I have a squad of men to find out?"

"Immediately. Report when you know."

Less than one hour later, Morton and two enlisted men carrying heavy wooden crates were back at Brock's office in the low, square, sparse office building.

Morton held the door while the two enlisted men entered, wondering how they were going to salute their commanding officer without setting the boxes down, and if they did put the boxes down, where was the proper place. Morton rescued them.

"General," he explained, "we have here some documents which I think will be of interest to you. May we set them on your desk?"

Brock nodded and pointed, and the enlisted men quickly set them on the desk, stepped back, and snapped a salute. Morton said, "You are both dismissed," and they both heaved sighs of relief as they hurried back out the door and closed it behind them.

The top document in the nearest box was a large ledger, and Brock had it open on his desk before the door thumped shut, reading the first page of scrolled handwriting. He raised his eyes to Morton.

"A daily log made by Governor William Hull of Michigan." His forehead wrinkled in question. "This has to be the same William Hull who fought in the Revolution thirty years ago. He must be sixty by this time."

He laid the ledger down, lifted a file from the box, opened it, and for thirty seconds studied the first few pages.

"This appears to be records of an army he's been commissioned to command."

Morton broke into a broad smile. "It is, sir. And it gets better." He lifted a document from the near box and handed it to Brock, who studied it for a few moments.

"Are these what they appear to be?" he asked. "Orders from the United States Congress directing Hull to march an army up here to Fort Detroit? And what's this about Niagara? And Montreal?"

"General," Morton exclaimed, "I think we have intercepted the entire plan of the United States for their conquest of Canada. All of it! The commanding officers, their orders, the number of men they will command, the timing of their movements, their objectives, their strategies—all of it."

Brock suddenly sat down in his chair, confounded by what he considered the incomprehensible stupidity he was seeing before him.

"You mean," he said quietly, "Hull trusted all of this to be carried on that schooner right under our guns, on to Fort Detroit? Is the man insane?"

Morton shook his head. "No, sir, I doubt it. I think he received his marching orders before the declaration of war was signed and was well on his way to Fort Detroit before it was made public. I think he was ignorant of it when he put all this on the schooner to take to his new headquarters at Fort Detroit, and most likely still doesn't know the United States is in a state of war with us. From what little I've seen of those documents so far, it is my guess we have the entire American offensive spelled out in detail. If we act quickly, it is probable we can hand General Hull and his Americans some very disheartening surprises."

Thoughtfully Brock asked, "Did you see what else was in the hold of that ship?"

"Generally, yes. Clothing and personal property. I think we are in possession of most of the personal property of General Hull."

For a time Brock sat in silence while his mind raced. "Captain Morton, leave these things with me. Do not speak of what we have to anyone else until I've had time to put this all together. I'll call you when I have finished. It may be tomorrow."

"Yes, sir," Morton replied. "Would you like to have the other items brought from the ship and locked in storage here?"

Brock shook his head. "Not yet. Post sentries to guard the ship round the clock, and wait."

"Yes, sir." Morton turned to go, and Brock stopped him.

"Captain, well done."

"Thank you, sir."

The afternoon passed with Brock seated at his desk, poring over the ledgers and papers taken from the *Cuyahoga*. He set them aside to take his evening meal at the officer's mess, where he invited Captain Morton to be at his office at eight o'clock the following morning. At precisely eight, the rap came at his door.

"Enter."

"Reporting as ordered, sir."

"Take a seat." Brock pointed to the two stacks of ledgers and papers on his desk. "You were correct, sir. We have intercepted the entire plan by which the Americans intend reducing Canada to an American territory. That includes this fort and this command."

Morton leaned forward in his chair, eyes narrowed as he concentrated. Brock went on.

"General William Hull is leading a force of about two thousand from Ohio to Fort Detroit, across the river. They left weeks ago. They are cutting a road north from Urbana to Fort Detroit. I expect they will arrive within the next two or three days. Their orders give Hull authority to cross the river and take possession of this fort, in any manner he deems appropriate. At about the same time, to the east of us, General Dearborn is under orders to cross the Niagara River and take Fort George, and further east, cross the St. Lawrence River and take Montreal."

He stopped speaking to watch the changing expressions on Captain Morton's face as he considered the information, and then went on.

"They intend to supply these armies by land, over the roads now in existence, with the new one from Urbana and a few others they intend building."

Morton stiffened. "Through the woods? The forests? Not by water?"

"Yes," Brock answered, "through the woods. It appears the thought just entered your mind as it did mine yesterday evening. Tecumseh. Am I right?"

"Yes. He's back, and he's ready. Tecumseh and about eighteen hundred of his warriors."

Brock nodded. "Correct."

"May I inquire, sir," Morton exclaimed, "what is your proposal in all this?"

"Wait. Let them come to us. Let them cross the river and make the march down here. With a little thought and preparation, I intend giving them a warm welcome."

Notes

General William Hull, Governor of the territory of Michigan, was appointed to assemble a fighting force consisting of soldiers, state militia, and Indians, and march north from Ohio to Fort Detroit. He assembled about two thousand men and began the march in early June, prior to the declaration of war by the United States against England. He cut his own road through the woods. When he reached the Maumee River, a tributary of the Detroit River, he hired the small commercial schooner *Cuyahoga* to transport all his personal belongings, including the critically important papers from both Congress and President Madison in which the entire offensive plan of the American armed forces were defined in detail, ahead of him to Fort Detroit. At the time, he did not know that the United States had declared war. The British at Fort Malden, under command of Major General Isaac Brock, one of the finest in the British military, knew of the declaration of war and took the *Cuyahoga* as a prize of war on July 3, 1812, along with her crew and the entire cargo of General Hull's personal property and official government papers. The papers gave the British the entire American plan, including the number of troops, their condition, their proposed supply and communication lines, the timing of their attacks, and all other critically important information.

See Hickey, *The War of 1812*, pp. 80–81; Stagg, *Mister Madison's War*, pp. 200–201; Wills, *James Madison*, pp. 100–102.

CHAPTER XIV

★ ★ ★

ith the sun just reaching its zenith, General William Hull, United States Army officer, Governor of the territory of Michigan, and commander of a force of close to two thousand army regulars, Ohio militia, and volunteers, all strung out on the narrow, crooked wagon ruts that wound through the forest behind him, gritted his teeth against the ache in the muscles of his back and the sweat from the insufferable humidity and heat that sapped the strength from a man by midmorning. Before him was the south wall of Fort Detroit, with cannon muzzles showing in the notches near the top.

The weight of his sixty years bore down as he swung his leg back from the far stirrup and dismounted his horse. He stood stiff-legged to put his hands on his hips, and he straightened, then leaned back hard to relieve the tension and the pain in muscles that had grown stiff in the seven hours he had remained in the saddle since four o'clock AM. While his column broke ranks to hunker down in the shade of the thick, dense forest that came within yards of the walls on three sides of the fort, Hull studied the structure he had been ordered to command.

The fort was constructed of lumber cut from the surrounding forest. The four walls would have formed a near-perfect square had they been straight, but they were not. Each wall slanted slightly inward from the corners to make a shallow V at about the midpoint, with a small projection outward near the center, all to afford a clear field of fire in all directions for the cannon mounted inside the walls. The structure had been built with the huge gates facing the Detroit River to the east. On the north, west, and south sides the guns came to bear on the forest, so thick Indians or redcoats could be within yards of the walls and still be invisible. Between the entrance and the river was the small village of Detroit, built of rough-cut logs, with less than ten streets laid out east-west and north-south to form rectangles in which the business and the living of Detroit were carried on. On the east edge of the village a single dock projected out into the river; all who were familiar with survival in this wilderness understood that the river was the lifeline that connected them to the world and sustained them, and the dock was indispensable. The guns in the east wall of the fort covered the tiny village and the river beyond.

Hull removed his black tricorn and used a damp handkerchief to wipe at the wet leather sweatband, then his forehead, before he settled the hat back on his head. He was turning to his horse when he suddenly stopped dead and stared at the dock with a knot of fear rising in his midsection and his thoughts racing.

Where's the Cuyahoga? My personal belongings. My orders. The plans for the campaign? The inventory of resources? Where? Sunk? Pirates? The British?

He called to Colonel Duncan McArthur, the senior officer in his command, and McArthur came trotting.

"Mister McArthur, have the men start making camp. I'm going inside the fort. I'll return when I've settled matters there."

McArthur nodded, turned, and walked back to the lounging men while Hull remounted and trotted his horse around the southeast corner of the fort and on to the front gates. They were standing open, and he paused long enough to identify himself to the sentry before he passed through into the enclosure. He walked his horse in while he studied the walls and the parapets and the guns and the low log quarters built against the walls. Clusters of silent people—soldiers and civilians and white men dressed in buckskins and beaded moccasins and stone-faced feathered Indians—had gathered to stare at the arrival of the great column. He reined in before the building that housed the headquarters of the fort, dismounted, handed the reins of his mare to a private, and walked through the door into the relative cool of the square, plain room. A sergeant and two corporals were on their feet, standing at rigid attention, and they saluted while Hull stood still, waiting for his eyes to adjust to the lack of bright lights. He returned the salute and started to speak when the far door opened and a short, stocky man with a round, jowled face strode into the room, uniform rumpled, long hair pulled back. On his shoulders were the epaulets of a colonel. He spoke.

"General Hull, I presume."

Hull nodded stiffly. "Correct. I am under orders to assume command of this fort. I trust you received notice."

The man stepped forward and offered his hand. "Yes. I received the notice. Welcome to Fort Detroit. I am Colonel Waldo Everton. We have been expecting you ever since we were advised of the war with Great Britain."

Hull shook the hand perfunctorily, and then his face suddenly clouded. "War?"

Everton showed surprise. "You didn't know? June 18. By vote of Congress the United States declared war on Great Britain."

It took Hull three seconds before he blurted, "Did a schooner named *Cuyahoga* arrive here? With my personal belongings?"

Everton raised a hand. "Your personal belongings? You had cargo on that ship?"

"Yes! All my papers. My personal belongings. You know where she is?"

Everton stumbled for words. "I . . . uh . . yes. I'm sorry to say, the British intercepted the *Cuyahoga* two days ago. She's about fifteen miles downstream, tied to the docks of Fort Malden."

Hull recoiled. "Her cargo? Her crew? Do they have it all?"

A look of puzzlement crossed Everton's face. "Of course! We are in a state of war with them. They took the ship and the cargo as prizes of war, and they still have the entire crew. Prisoners of war."

Hull felt his thoughts disintegrating and for a moment stood mute, unable to force a coherent sentence. "I must have . . ." He stopped and started again. "There were papers that . . ."

Everton stared, aware that Hull's grasp on reality had been shaken. He stood silent, waiting.

Hull tried once more. "Have you made any effort to negotiate a recovery of the ship? Her cargo? Her crew?" There was near panic in his face, and his voice was too loud, nearly out of control.

"No, sir. I repeat, we are at war with Great Britain. They have a force at Fort Malden far superior to mine. I refused to provoke them into an armed conflict that I would lose." He drew himself to his full height. "And I might add, sir, I had no notice that your personal belongings and papers were on that vessel. Had I known, I could have intercepted her before she reached Fort Malden and made other arrangements."

Hull blustered, "Had someone—anyone—notified me of the state of war I would *never* have separated myself from my papers and belongings. *Never!*"

"Very unfortunate," Everton said. "Very."

Hull straightened and glanced at his uniform, sweated black beneath his arms and down the center of his back. "Well, we'll deal with the *Cuyahoga* matter later. My men are making camp to the south and west of the fort. I will need quarters here for myself and my staff. And I'll need a bath. Change of clothing. I trust you have suitable quarters?"

"Yes, sir. May I escort you?"

Everton led Hull out the door back into the fierce sunlight, while the sergeant and two corporals remained behind, exchanging puzzled glances at what they had seen and heard of their new commanding officer.

The two officers walked down a covered board walkway with their boots thumping, to stop at a door built of rough-cut pine planking, and Everton used his key to open it. The parlor was dimly lighted by two small windows, one on either side of the front door, with coat pegs in the front wall and a table with four chairs hand-crafted by some long-forgotten settler who understood the first rule of the wilderness. Sturdy. Sturdy men, sturdy women, sturdy rifles, sturdy cabins, sturdy beds and tables. Beauty was a long afterthought. A pot-bellied stove stood in one corner, cold in the summer, glowing hot in the harsh winters. The kitchen was a study in stark efficiency. There was a black, cast-iron stove with an oven and four plates for cooking and a pipe reaching upward through a hole in the low ceiling. Cupboards on two walls for pots and pans and table service, an empty water bucket and dipper on a counter beneath one cupboard, and nothing more. The bedroom was large enough to accommodate a wardrobe on one wall, a large double bed on the other, a nightstand with an unlit lantern, and a desk and chair in one corner. In the entire fort, Hull had not seen one wall, inside or outside, that was finished. Rather, they were all logs, most of them with the bark still on, chinked with gray clay to seal them against the heat and rain of summer and the cold and snows of winter.

Hull turned to Everton. "This will do. I will return to my men to settle them for the night. I'll take midday mess with them, and then I'll be back with my staff. What time do you serve the evening mess for officers?"

"Half past six o'clock."

"There will be four of us."

"Very good, sir."

Hull walked back up the boardwalk, and gathered the reins to his horse. Carefully he held the left stirrup while he raised his foot and inserted it firmly, then leaned forward to grasp the pommel of the saddle and strained to lift himself aboard. Everton watched with growing questions about his new commanding officer. Was the simple act of mounting a horse all that difficult for a man whose life had required horsemanship for over thirty years?

What Everton did not know was the memory burning all too brightly in Hull's brain of that morning less than four months earlier when Hull had led his command on parade to show them off before leaving on his march northward. Riding at the head of his men, proud, erect, he had lost control of his prancing mount. He also lost both stirrups, his hat, and his composure, as he frantically lunged forward to grab the horse's mane in a wild effort to stay mounted. He could not have picked a worse time or place to show his age and his infirmities of mind and body. His entire command was embarrassed, humiliated, at the performance of their leader, and the quiet, subtle murmuring grew. "Too old . . . that stroke he had has done him in . . . lost his nerve . . . his head won't work right . . . an old woman . . . unfit for command." Hull was aware of the criticisms, but his fierce pride would not let him seek help among his staff. He had lately learned that they had joined in the murmuring campaign against him.

He reined the horse around and walked it past the small clusters of frontier people still gathered to watch, out through the gates, then south to the corner of the fort, and west to his command of men. He awkwardly dismounted and handed the reins of his horse to his waiting orderly, Sergeant Daniel Wellington.

"Mister Wellington, have Corporal Tunstall see to the horse, and then bring colonels McArthur, Cass, and Findlay at once."

"Yes, sir." The sergeant turned and led the horse away while Hull took a grip on himself at the thought of facing the three colonels. Too well did he recall the history that resulted in all three of them being advanced to the rank of a full colonel, when none should have received such a commission, and the humiliating, grotesque mess that ensued. All three were from Ohio, where Governor Return Jonathan Meigs had been requested by the federal secretary of war to form a fighting force of 1,200 men. Meigs, overly anxious and fearful of raising such an army, had handed out high commissions to unqualified men, including Duncan McArthur, Lewis Cass, and James Findlay, making all three of them full colonels. Shortly after their appointments, the three got embroiled in an open quarrel over which one of them should be senior. Further, the three of them, along with far too many of their Ohio volunteers, saw Hull as a newcomer, a stranger, in whom they had little confidence. Their squabble was placed squarely before Hull, who referred it to regular army officers for resolution. The army officers' answer was simple and immediate: none of them should have been commissioned colonels—they should all have been only lieutenant-colonels; reduce their rank to lieutenant-colonels and that's the end of it. When the three men were

informed, they all reared back and swore they would resign their commissions and leave if anyone tried to cut back their rank. The entire matter, now out of hand, was sent to the War Department. Secretary Eustis
told Governor Meigs he had erred, to which Meigs replied, nonsense, I
acted within my powers according to the state constitution. A compro-
mise was proposed—advance one of them to brigadier general—but
President Madison bluntly refused to surrender the principle of federal
supremacy in all such matters. This bounced the whole mess back into
Hull's lap, and his reaction was that the very organization of his army
was " . . . peculiarly calculated to create distrust." The proposal was then
made that the three of them should draw straws to resolve the argument,
and they refused. Reluctantly, Hull put an end to the ludicrous tempest
in a teapot. He determined that McArthur had been appointed two
weeks prior to the others, and was therefore afforded the position of
senior colonel.

But there was no way Hull could stop the acrimony between them
or their distrust of him as an interloper, an outsider, or their subtle,
destructive influence among the rank and file of his small army.

While he waited for the three colonels to appear, Hull stepped from
the road into the shade of the thick forest and sat on the decaying trunk
of a downed pine tree. He was weary to the bone, sick in his soul that
the British had in their hands the entire plan of action for the United
States to take control of the great waterway from the Atlantic Ocean to
the northern reaches of Lake Superior. He removed his hat and sat with
slumped shoulders, working the black felt tricorn slowly in his fingers,
unable to control his rampant fears. *They know the count of men in this army,*
the officers—the dates—times—places of the timetable, the inventory of supplies—
reinforcements—and that we must keep the road open back to Ohio for our exchange of
communications with my superiors. His teeth were on edge as his thoughts ran
on, independent of his struggle to control them. *How could Congress declare*
war without informing me at once? Why didn't Madison sent a special messenger? They
knew I was marching straight into a trap! Monstrous insanity! Why? Why?

He was still seated, deep in thought, when McArthur arrived, with
Cass and Findlay following. The three officers stopped in front of him.

They did not salute. Their eyes were downcast, or peering at the forest, or the sky; they would not look him in the eye. Hull stood, set his hat on his head, and spoke.

"On June 18, the United States Congress declared war on England."

Instantly the three men came to a focus, staring at him in disbelief. He went on.

"The British intercepted the *Cuyahoga* two days ago. The ship with her entire cargo and crew are at Fort Malden in the hands of the enemy. They know everything concerning our presence here—the purpose, the numbers, the supplies, the intended attacks at Niagara and Montreal— all of it."

The faces of all three colonels went blank and they cursed under their breaths. Hull went on.

"So much for that. Have the men establish campsites near the fort, off the road. I will take midday mess with them. Have them load all our personal necessaries in a wagon. This afternoon we will take our places at the headquarter offices inside the fort, and our personal quarters. Have Sergeant Wellington and Corporal Tunstall come with us. They will serve as our orderlies. Am I clear?"

McArthur nodded curtly and spoke. "Anyone say anything about the British? Are we expecting an attack?"

"No one spoke of it, but my estimate is that our forces far exceed theirs right at this moment. Our first priority will be scouting out their positions to determine their strength. See to it. Is there anything else?"

All three colonels shook their heads and turned, and Hull watched them walk away and disappear in the forest.

Midday mess had been served and the clean-up was complete when McArthur led the other two colonels to the shaded spot where General Hull was waiting. Behind the three officers, Sergeant Wellington hauled back on the long leather reins to pull the two horses and wagon to a stop. Corporal Tunstall was seated beside him, silent, waiting. Tied behind the wagon was the general's saddled mare, moving her feet, nervous. Behind the horse were four privates, standing loose, bored, disinterested. Wellington held the reins while McArthur pointed and spoke to Hull.

"Here's our personals and our orderlies. We brought four enlisted men to help unload. When did you want to move on into the fort?"

Hull nodded. "Very good. We will leave now."

The three colonels and six enlisted men stood transfixed, watching while Hull untied the reins to his horse, waiting to see if Hull would embarrass himself again, and them, in trying to mount the mare. Hull had his left foot in the on-side stirrup when the big bay shied, and Hull reached to seize the cheek strap on the bridle and jerk her head around, then swung his leg over and slid into the saddle. He hauled back hard on the left rein and turned her in a tight circle twice, then straightened her, and she settled. He reined her around the wagon, past the three colonels, and started forward at a walk, tall, erect in the saddle. He did not look back as he led his small column around the fort, through the entrance, and stopped in front of the headquarters building to dismount. He gave them orders to wait, and while he was inside the building the nine-man detail remained in the bright sun, studying the walls and the gun emplacements and the crude buildings and the odd assortment of people staring at them in stony-faced silence. Minutes passed before Colonel Everton walked out into the sunlight with General Hull following.

"Gentlemen," Everton said, "welcome to Fort Detroit." He pointed down the covered boardwalk. "Your quarters are down there. General Hull has agreed to take you. Should you have any needs, you have only to ask. We serve evening mess at half past six."

Hull led his horse with the wagon rumbling behind and the three officers and four enlisted men following. They stopped before the officers' quarters, and Hull pointed to the doors where McArthur, Cass, and Findlay were to be, then the single door where Wellington and Tunstall were to bunk together. The six enlisted men drew a deep breath and settled into the task of unloading the wagon, sorting the luggage, and carrying the freight into the quiet cool of the dimly-lighted rooms, where the officers opened the crates and boxes to hang uniforms and shirts in closets and lay socks and underwear in dresser drawers. They were deep into the afternoon when Hull gave orders, and the four enlisted mounted the empty wagon. Two took the driver's seat, and one threaded the reins between his index and middle fingers and gigged the drowsing horses. The four officers watched the high-walled wagon make the wide turn to the left and angle back through the fort gates and disappear beyond the walls of the fort.

Evening mess for the officers consisted of boiled corned beef and turnips, and with the last rays of a sun already set catching the treetops and the red, white, and blue of the flag, those in the fort stood at attention while the drum rattled and two enlisted men retired the colors. In deep dusk, lamps and lanterns winked on, and at ten o'clock the drummer sounded taps, and all lights disappeared as those within the walls of Fort Detroit sought their beds.

The banging of the reveille drum at dawn brought bare feet to the cool floors, and soldiers and civilians rose from their blankets to settle into the unrelenting sameness of another day in a military fort. Wash in cold water, dress, make your bunk, morning mess that followed a predictable daily menu of mush one day, fried sowbelly and biscuits the next, sick call, drill, take your squad's rotation at cutting firewood, cleaning cannon, policing the grounds, shoeing and caring for the horses, and standing picket duty. Always picket duty—marching endlessly back and forth on the wooden parapets that graced the inside of all walls of the fort, fourteen feet above the ground, with covered towers at each corner.

In the early afternoon, Hull had Wellington and Tunstall saddle horses for the four officers, and they rode out of the fort to inspect their command. They returned late in the day with Hull acutely aware of a growing undertone of impatient criticism. *We came to take Fort Malden. Why are we camped here?*

The second day a lieutenant with a five-man escort and a bearded guide, a white man dressed in buckskins with a tomahawk and two black scalps at his belt, arrived with a pouch of documents from Washington, D.C. Hull spent half the day in his quarters poring over the papers before he sent Wellington to gather the three colonels to his headquarters office. From the set of Hull's white, drawn face, they knew the moment they entered the dimly lighted room that something was wrong. They took their places on the plain chairs, facing his plain desk, waiting.

"Gentlemen," Hull began, "I have received information and orders that you need to know."

McArthur glanced at Cass but said nothing. Hull went on.

"The United States Indian agent for this area, Benjamin F. Stickney, has reported to our secretary of war, William Eustis, that there are now assembled in the area of Fort Malden approximately eighteen hundred Shawnee and other belligerent Indians under the leadership of Tecumseh."

Hull stopped and watched the three officers straighten in their chairs, and their faces go dead. He went on.

"The execution of the plan of attack to the east of us—north of New York and New England—is not going well and has faltered."

Tension was rising in the square, austere room. Hull tapped a document with a finger.

"Secretary Eustis is of the opinion that current conditions require us to use our best discretion in attacking and seizing Fort Malden at once, and then to broaden our conquests, as he puts it, 'as circumstances may justify.'"

For a time Hull sat hunched forward, forearms on his desk, staring at his hands.

"Let me put this in perspective," he said. "Our military is in trouble to the east of us. To draw pressure off them, we're being ordered to take the offensive. Across the river is a regiment of British regulars at Fort Malden, with eighteen hundred savages lusting to massacre all of us. We are to cross the river and subdue them all, and then move east to relieve our failing military forces there."

Hull stopped and for a moment stared into the eyes of each officer. Then he leaned back in his chair and went on.

"I need not explain to you that should those Indians cross the river to this side and cut our communication line with our support from the south, we would be caught in a trap from which we would most likely never escape."

He waited until he saw understanding in their faces and went on.
"I will acknowledge these orders, and we will execute them, but I will not hesitate to inform Secretary Eustis that the force I now have is going to be very hard-pressed to accomplish what those men in Washington seem to regard with such little concern."

For the first time, the three officers moved in their seats, then settled.

"Gentlemen, you will prepare your commands to cross the river within the next five days. Once there, we will prepare to attack Fort Malden. These orders will be in writing by tomorrow, in full detail. Are there any questions?"

There were none. He handed each of them a copy of a document.

"That is a proclamation I am having printed for distribution to all Canadians and Indians in the area. I invite you to read it." He sat back while each of them silently pored over the page.

" . . . I offer protection to the peaceable unoffending inhabitants . . . I issue a warning that Canadians choosing to fight with the British will be considered and treated as enemies and if fighting as allies to the Indians will face instant destruction . . . the United States offers you Peace, Liberty, and Security—your choice lies between these and war, slavery, and destruction. . . ."

He waited until all three of them raised their heads with blank stares before he went on. "It is my opinion that document will persuade many Canadians to abandon any thought of continuing with the British, and either surrender or flee. It will be distributed immediately. Do any of you have advice on the matter?"

Each of them shook his head and remained silent.

"Very well. You are dismissed."

The three officers were outside Hull's office, in the headquarters foyer, before Cass turned to McArthur.

"You expect that proclamation will turn this whole thing?"

McArthur answered, "A piece of paper? It might scare a few Canadians. But it won't scare the British army."

Cass continued, "You reckon this general can lead in battle?"

McArthur answered quietly, "I have my doubts."

Behind them, in the privacy of his office, Hull dipped quill in ink, drew and released a great breath, and began scratching.

"Secretary of War William Eustis:

". . . I acknowledge your orders received this date directing me to lead my force across the Detroit River and reduce Fort Malden and surrounding area to our possession. I must state that I am in doubt that my forces are equal to the demand your orders place on them, and advise the administration that it must not be too sanguine. . . ."

He laid the quill on his desk and read what he had written. For a time he leaned back, staring at the document. Then he resolutely folded it, addressed it, reached for the wax and sealed it, then walked to the door and out into the foyer where Sergeant Wellington stood to face him.

"Sergeant, would you see to it this message is delivered at once?"

"Yes, sir." Wellington took the document and watched Hull walk back into his office before he read the address. He raised his eyes and stared at the closed door with a strong feeling of concern rising in his chest.

Secretary of War William Eustis? Washington, D.C.? What's happened?

Notes

General William Hull, who was also governor of the territory of Michigan, was commissioned by Secretary of War William Eustis to lead a force of close to two thousand to Fort Detroit. The force was largely constituted of Ohio volunteers, appointed by the Ohio governor Return Jonathan Meigs, who in his eagerness awarded too many officers' commissions to his Ohio volunteers, resulting in three full colonels, among them Lewis Cass, James Findlay, and Duncan McArthur. These three fell into hot debate about who should be senior, and the matter was referred to the secretary of war, the president, Governor Meigs, and finally back to General Hull for resolution by Hull, who determined McArthur had been appointed two weeks prior to the others and would serve as the senior colonel. The Ohio volunteers quickly decided that General Hull was too old, too disabled by his recent stroke, and far too indecisive to lead them into battle, and their dim view of their commander soon spread throughout most of the command. Their opinion was much enhanced when the entire command saw the debacle of Hull nearly falling from his horse during the parade review just prior to their marching, in which he lost both stirrups, his hat, and his dignity by lunging to clutch at the horse's mane to save himself. Hull's column cut a new road from Ohio to Detroit and arrived July 5, 1812, still not knowing the United States had declared war on England. The description of Fort Detroit, the village of Detroit, and the river are accurate. General Hull never recovered all the papers lost to the British when they captured the schooner *Cuyahoga* on July 3, 1812, which papers acquainted the British general Brock, commanding officer at Fort Malden, across the river, with the entire plan for taking and occupying Canada. The orders General Hull received from Secretary of War Eustis directed him to immediately cross the Detroit River and take Fort Malden, then extend his conquests "as circumstances may justify," all of which was an attempt by the inept Eustis to take pressure off the failing assault that was underway hundreds of miles to the east, at Niagara and Montreal. At about that same time, Hull received notice from the American Indian agent at Fort Wayne that there were already about eighteen hundred Indians from various tribes gathered at Fort Malden, under the leadership of Shawnee chief Tecumseh, willing to join the British in the war against the United States. Despite the frightening news, Hull determined to follow his orders, but in a confirming letter back to Eustis on July 9, 1812, Hull served notice that he doubted whether his forces would be equal to the demand and that the "administration therefore must not be too sanguine."

See Stagg, *Mister Madison's War*, pp. 194–201; Hickey, *The War of 1812*, pp. 80–81; Wills, *James Madison*, pp. 100–103; Barbuto, *Niagara 1814*, pp. 27–28.

CHAPTER XV

★ ★ ★

*M*idday mess for His Majesty's Ship *Shannon* was two hours past, and her officers and crew were at their stations, quiet, squinting in the fierce afternoon sun, studying the flat line where the green-black Atlantic met the pale blue of a cloudless July sky. Due west twelve miles, just beyond the horizon, was Barnegat Bay in the southern reaches of the state of New Jersey. To the north, south, and east was the open sea. Under orders of British vice admiral Sawyer, Captain Philip Vere Broke had led a squadron of British frigates to cruise the east coast of America with the object of attacking any seagoing vessel flying American colors and creating as much havoc as possible. The squadron assigned the task consisted of the *Shannon* with thirty-eight guns, the *Belvidera* with thirty-six cannon under command of Captain Richard Byron, the *Africa* with sixty-four cannon under command of Captain John Bastian, the *Aeolus* with thirty-two guns under command of Captain Lord James Townsend, and the *Guerriere* with thirty-eight cannon under command of Captain James Richard Dacres. They were five frigates flying the British Union Jack, carrying two hundred eight cannon, ranking among the best in the most powerful navy in the world and commanded by some of the finest seagoing officers in the king's military service.

The crews felt no panic, since the entire American navy consisted of less than twenty fighting ships, and most of them were scattered far to the north, some in the Great Lakes. There wasn't the faintest possibility that there were enough American gunboats within two hundred miles to make a fight of it against the firepower and the skill of the British squadron. For the British crews, it was just a matter of finding another American ship, taking her crew and cargo captive, and burning her at sea. The British crews remained calm, watchful, ready to pursue and destroy.

In his small quarters high above the water at the stern of the *Shannon*, squadron commander Broke sat at his small desk, leaning forward, rereading his entry in the ship's log for the previous day. Slender, dark-haired and dark-eyed, hawk-nosed with a cleft chin, he followed the words with one finger.

"July 16th '12.

". . . sighted, pursued, and captured United States brig *Nautilus*, 14 guns . . . Lieutenant Crane commanding . . . he attempted flight to avoid capture . . . threw all cannon overboard to lighten her . . . took entire crew prisoner with all items of value . . . set her afire . . . confirm that she sank . . . no casualties in our squadron. . . ."

Satisfied, he plucked up his quill and signed his name. He salted the wet ink, blew the crumbs into a small basket for waste, set the log in its desk drawer, and turned to open the two small windows behind him, hoping for a stir of air in the heat of the summer afternoon. He was settling back into his chair when the call came from the crow's nest, seventy feet up the mainmast.

"Sail ahead to the windward! American!"

Broke grabbed his telescope and was buttoning his tunic as he trotted up the few stairs from his cabin onto the main deck, then up to the quarterdeck. He jerked his telescope to full extension and carefully scanned the horizon to the southeast, and it was there—the small pyramid of sails on two masts, with the tiny flag of red and white stripes, and the blue field with specks of white, fluttering in the mild breeze. For ten seconds he tracked her to take a reading on her bearing and anything that would tell him that the American ship had seen his squadron.

The British ships were traveling southwest, angling toward the New Jersey coast. The American frigate was traveling northeast, out into the open Atlantic.

Broke lowered his telescope. "She's heading for the open sea! I think she's seen us. I think she intends trying to sail around us." A smile tugged as he gave his orders to his first mate, Gerald Laughlin.

"Mister Laughlin, I think the Americans are going to try to go around us. Make a chase of it. Signal the *Guerriere.* Captain Dacres is to take a heading to the east by northeast. Get to the east of the Americans and cut off their attempt to escape."

"Aye, sir." Laughlin, sandy-red hair, long, bright-red sideburns, round, ruddy face, built strong, clearly and proudly Irish, turned and trotted away. Within minutes the signal flags were run up the mainmast, and the *Guerriere*abruptly changed course from southwest to southeast, angling to force the oncoming American ship back into the trap that was being laid with four British gunboats on one side, and a fast frigate with thirty-eight guns on the other.

Broke cupped his hand to call up to the crow's nest. "When you can, get a count of her guns, and identify her."

"Aye, sir."

All eyes in the British squadron were on the American ship, straining to get out into the open Atlantic to escape the five gunboats. Minutes became one hour before the call came from the crow's nest.

"Frigate, sir. I count forty-four guns, all on the top deck. If I read it right, sir, she's the *Constitution.*"

For a split second every man on the *Shannon* stopped dead in his tracks to stare at the distant sails with the tiny flag fluttering, and Captain Broke took a deep breath with his thoughts running.

If that's the Constitution, *she's a Joshua Humphreys frigate. That Yankee Quaker designed the best in the world—all guns on one deck—more armor in the hull than any other frigate—more canvas—smaller draft—carry four hundred fifty men and supplies and armament and still outrun and outmaneuver any other gunboat afloat—our parliament tried to get him to build frigates for us, but he refused—took them to the United States instead.*

He turned to Laughlin. "Do you recall who might be in command of the *Constitution?*"

The first mate's brow knitted down as he concentrated. "Seems to me it was Hull. Captain Isaac Hull."

For several seconds Broke reached into his memory. "Isn't Hull the one they sent to Detroit? To take Fort Malden?"

"That was *General* William Hull, sir," Laughlin replied. "Isaac Hull is his nephew. William Hull is army. Isaac Hull is navy."

"What is his reputation? Isaac Hull?"

Laughlin drew a deep breath. "Very good, sir. At times, brilliant. If that's a Joshua Humphreys frigate out there, and Isaac Hull is in command, this could become most interesting."

For a moment Brock clamped his mouth, and his eyes were alive as he said quietly, "We'll see about that. We'll see."

Both men turned to peer to the northeast for a time, judging the speed of the *Guerriere,* calculating when she would pass to the east of the *Constitution* and force her back to the west, into the four British ships that were waiting to spring the trap. Minutes passed before Laughlin turned to Broke.

"Sir, it is going to be close. Perhaps the *Constitution* will win the race for position."

Broke shook his head. "She won't escape, but the two of them might be on a collision course out there." He glanced at the sun. "I think Hull is playing for time. Hopes to stall this pursuit until dark."

Laughlin wiped at his mouth. "Outmaneuver five of us? Most unlikely, sir."

While they watched, the *Constitution* changed course to due east with the *Guerriere* straining to intercept her. With the westering sun hot at his back, Laughlin's arm shot up to point, voice high, excited.

"I think the *Constitution* is squaring for a fight."

Broke nodded but remained silent, while the thought flickered in his mind. *I wonder what Captain Isaac Hull plans to do—how he sees this—one American frigate against five British gunboats—he can't fight us all—his only chance is to beat us in a race for an American port—how does he plan to do it?—what's in his mind?*

Three miles to the east, Captain Isaac Hull stood on his quarterdeck, telescope extended, studying the *Guerriere* coming in two miles ahead of him, to the north. Then he turned to watch the other four British gunboats due west. Medium height, nose too long and pointed, eyes wide-set, chin slightly receding, dark-haired, Hull's voice was steady, controlled, as he gave his orders.

"Helmsman, steady as she goes for two more minutes, then hard to port."

"Aye, sir."

The two minutes seemed too long before the frigate turned left, leaning right, and the crew leaned opposite to keep their footing. While they watched, the *Guerriere,* almost dead ahead, made a hard turn to starboard to take a heading to the west that would bring her directly across the course taken by the *Constitution,* but far out of gun range. Half an hour later the *Guerriere* was past the *Constitution* and slowing, and Hull called to his helmsman, "Steady as she goes." He turned to his gun crews. "Open all gun ports and prepare to load."

He called to his young navigator, twenty feet away on the quarterdeck silently watching everything. "Mister Dunson! What is our depth? Are we clear to maneuver without fear of reefs or sandbars?"

The answer came instantly. "About sixty-five fathoms where we are, sir. It reduces to about fourteen fathoms to the north of us, but there is no danger of reefs or sandbars or shallow water within about two hundred miles. To the west, near the coast, there are reefs."

"Stand by on the quarterdeck. See to it you keep me advised if there is danger."

"Aye, sir."

On board the *Guerriere,* Captain Dacres stared at the oncoming *Constitution* in amazement. *She's not turning! She intends engaging us if she must! One against five? What is she counting on?*

He glanced at the sun, half set, catching the sails and the flags to set them glowing like fire, casting long shadows eastward.

Darkness? If he intends slipping away in darkness, why is he coming dead on to engage us? Dacres suddenly turned to peer behind the *Guerriere,* then carefully swept the horizon in all directions for distant sails beneath American flags. There were none.

Are there other American gunboats coming? Does the Constitution *have a squadron out there in waiting, listening for cannon fire? Or is he bluffing?*

He spoke to his helmsman. "Hard to port. Take a new heading due north, parallel with the *Constitution* but one mile west of her. We will come alongside her within gun range gradually."

"Aye, sir."

With the ship turning, Dacres called up to his crow's nest, "Keep a sharp eye in all directions. Report immediately if American ships come into view."

"Aye, sir."

Cautiously the *Guerriere* took up a position just over one mile west of the *Constitution,* and with the sun already set and dusk setting in, began to close the distance slowly, watching for unexpected sails or lights from any direction. The afterglow of the sun faded and was gone. The evening star rose prominent in the east, and still the two ships held their course north, with the four ships companion to the *Guerriere* lost in the distance and the darkness. The light breeze began to dwindle. The sails fell limp, and both ships slowed to a near standstill.

In the full darkness of ten o'clock, Captain Isaac Hull, on the quarterdeck, called for his first mate, Erling Strand, blonde, blue-eyed, jutting chin, ponderous, speaking English with a strong Swedish accent.

"Get the signal lanterns and start sending messages so the *Guerriere* can see them."

Strand stared at him in the darkness for a moment. "What messages, sir?"

"'We are engaged with the British. Come immediately.' Repeat it until I give orders to stop."

A slow smile crossed the big man's face. "Aye, sir."

Within minutes the lanterns were on the quarterdeck in the hands of a bos'n's mate who could send and read the signals of both navies. The shutter began to click, and the light reached out across the black waters.

On board the British *Guerriere,* Dacres and Laughlin both stopped dead on the quarterdeck, their heads thrust forward in disbelief. *Light signals? For whom?*

"Can you read them?" Dacres exclaimed.

For a full five minutes, both men, and most of their crew, stood at the rails of the scarcely moving ship. Then Laughlin's Irish brogue came, too high, excited.

"She's calling for help! From ships out there somewhere in waiting!"

"That's how I read them," Dacres exclaimed. Instantly he shouted up to the crow's nest, "Do you see those signals?"

"Aye, sir."

"Can you read them?"

"Aye, sir. They're calling for help."

"Have you seen anything of more ships?"

"No, sir. None. Been watching steady."

Dacres turned back to the helmsman. "Do not close with them until I give the direct order."

"Aye, sir."

The two ships moved slowly on north, side by side, less than one mile apart, in a wind that was nearly gone. Forty minutes later, aboard the *Constitution,* Hull gave orders and the message lantern shut down. At midnight the crews on both ships changed, and the silent vigil continued with Hull and his first mate and navigator remaining on the quarterdeck of the American frigate.

At three o'clock, Captain Dacres on the *Guerriere* spoke to his helmsman.

"Take a heading that will close the gap. Slowly. I do not want to be within gun range before good light."

"Aye, sir."

Slowly, almost imperceptibly, the distance between the two scarcely moving ships lessened, with each crew watching the other in tense silence. Then, at half past three o'clock, in the blackness, the strained shout came down from the crow's nest on the *Guerriere.*

"Lights! Astern! Four ships approaching!"

Dacres and Laughlin had not left the quarterdeck since sunset.

Instantly they raised their telescopes and in twenty seconds counted the running lights of four ships, spaced out behind them in a line. Battle formation!

Before Dacres could give the order, Laughlin broke for the main deck and down into the seamen's quarters. Two minutes later he shoved a bare-footed man still in his underwear and struggling to come awake, up onto the quarterdeck. Laughlin lighted a signal lantern, shoved it into the hands of the seaman, and turned to Dacres, waiting.

"Challenge those ships," Dacres ordered, pointing.

The man shook the cobwebs from his head, and the shutter started clicking. Five times he sent the message, "Identify yourself. Identify yourself. What is your flag? What is your flag?"

There was no response. The ships came on slowly, running lights dim, but no answer to the challenge of the *Guerriere.*

Dacres faced Laughlin. "Who are they?" he exclaimed. "John Rodgers and his American squadron have been active in these waters lately. Is it them? Have they laid an elaborate trap for us? We have no chance if those ships are frigates under command of John Rodgers."

"I'm aware of that, sir. But what if they are not Rodgers? Could they be the *Belvidera* and the rest of our own squadron?"

Dacres shook is head. "Then why didn't they answer my challenge?"

"I don't know, sir. I have no explanation."

Dacres took a deep breath and by force of will brought his thoughts under control. *I cannot risk loss of this ship—until I know what I'm contending with out there I cannot commit to battle—two more hours until daylight—the* Constitution *will still be there—we wait—we stay with her and we wait.*

Dacres gave his orders, the helmsman obeyed, and the *Guerriere* changed her heading and held it until she was more than one mile from the *Constitution,* and then straightened to run parallel with her, moving northward with the other four unidentified ships following. The wind had died to a gentle breeze, scarcely disturbing the sails of the strange, scattered procession, moving almost imperceptibly north in the darkness before dawn.

The morning star was fading, and the eastern sky was a deep purple against the black of the Atlantic when Hull, on the quarterdeck of the American frigate, again extended his telescope and searched for the five British ships. One by one he found them. Astern of his port side were the *Belvidera* and the *Guerriere*. Directly south, behind him in the far distance, came the *Shannon, Aeolus,* and *Africa.* He brought his telescope back to the *Belvidera* and *Guerriere,* making his best calculations of their speed compared to his, with the stand-or-fall question bright in his mind.

Can they catch me?

His eyes narrowed, and a look of defiance came across his face. *Not if I can help it. Come on—all five of you—and we'll see who wins this race. Come on. Come on.*

Three miles south and east of him, Captain Dacres stood on the quarterdeck of the *Guerriere* with his telescope to his eye, straining to identify the four ships that had loomed up in the night and refused to answer his signal lantern asking them to identify themselves. Suddenly his head jerked forward and he brought the telescope down, mouth gaping open, staring in disbelief. *Those four ships are my own squadron! Not Rodgers!* He exclaimed aloud, "Those fools! Those fools! Why didn't they answer my challenge?"

His face was flushed with hot anger when he turned to Laughlin, "Get the signal lantern! Ask those ships why they didn't identify themselves three hours ago when I challenged!"

Three minutes later, in the twilight before sunrise, the signal lantern blinked out the question. Within seconds the signal lantern on the *Belvidera* answered:

"We were certain you knew who we were. Saw no need to answer."

There was outrage in Dacres's voice as he barked orders to Laughlin. "Make a record of this entire incident, and do it today! Be certain it includes the fact I challenged in the night, and they did not answer. The result is that this morning that American ship ahead of us—the *Constitution*—is still afloat and it will be a close question if we can catch her." He raised a fist in anger. "By the Almighty, there will be courts-martial over this, and I want a record that leaves no question as to who failed in their duty! Am I clear?"

"You are, sir."

The first arc of the rising sun laid a sparkling golden path to the west across the shimmering waters beneath a cloudless blue sky, with the heat from the great burning ball following, while the odd procession worked its way north, the lone American ship straining for its life, followed by the five British gunboats intent on her destruction. On the quarterdeck of the *Constitution*, Captain Isaac Hull stood transfixed, his eyes never leaving the five men-of-war whose sole objective was to take his ship, her cargo, and her guns, and imprison his crew.

The sun was half risen when he felt the deck beneath his feet settle, and the frigate slow, then stop dead in the water. He peered over the stern to see water in which there was no movement, then turned to look east. The Atlantic had become a sheet of glass. There were no waves, no whitecaps in the water, no movement. The sails hung limp, useless, and their flag hung down unmoving. The *Constitution* would not answer her helm—she was adrift.

They were becalmed.

Hull set his teeth. *If we're becalmed, so are they. Now we find out who has the will and the seamanship to win this contest!*

He turned to Strand. "Load the longboats—all of them—with towing hawsers and get them into the water. Break the crew into squads and man the longboats to tow the ship!"

"Aye, sir."

While Strand set the crew scrambling to throw tied coils of two-inch hawsers into the ten longboats and lower them on ropes and pulleys into the calm water with their crews, Hull stood on the quarterdeck with his telescope extended, studying the five British warships far behind. They, too, were lowering their longboats, but there was one crucial difference. Nearly all the longboats from all five British ships were taking a position ahead of the *Shannon*, and falling into orderly lines to tow her! Calmly, Hull made a count. There were twenty-two British longboats towing one frigate; he had ten to tow his own.

The *Shannon* began to steadily gain.

Hull turned to shout orders to Strand. "Get a twenty-four pounder from the main deck and the forecastlechaser. Move them to the stern. Cut away the railing to give them freedom of movement. Then get two more of the twenty-four pounder long guns from the main deck into my cabin and line them out through the windows to cover our stern! Get the gun crews ready."

Minutes passed while Strand and two dozen men jerked the four guns from their mounts and moved them to the stern of the ship, two on the main deck, two in the captain's quarters, muzzles thrust out through the windows. Strand was sprinting back to the quarterdeck to report to Hull when the first stir of a breeze fluttered the sails, and it held. For more than ten minutes the *Constitution* gained speed moving north, and then the wind died and did not stir again.

While the crew of the American frigate watched in tense silence, the *Shannon,* with the crews of the twenty-two longboats putting their backs into it, gained with each minute, steadily closing the gap.

Hull turned to Strand. "Have all gun crews load. Get ready."

"Aye, sir."

Strand turned to shout his orders when the first blossoms of white smoke spewed from the muzzles of the four cannon in the bow of the *Shannon,* and Hull held his breath. *Too far—too far—she's out of range!*

Five hundred yards short of the *Constitution,* four geysers of water leaped fifteen feet into the air, and a moment later the sound of the four cannon blasts rolled past the frigate. Through his telescope, Hull watched the gun crews on the British ship wheel the cannon back while four men rammed the soaking wet swabs down the barrels to kill all sparks before the next four men rammed the powder in to reload.

Hull turned to Strand and Dunson, face set, a mix of fear and defiance in his eyes. "We have a choice. We can fight and risk the crew and the ship, or we can surrender and save the lives of our men."

The navigator broke in. "Sir, may I make a recommendation?"

Hull looked into his face. Dunson was too young to have experienced battle at sea in the war for independence. He had come on board as a volunteer while Hull was refitting and resupplying in the Chesapeake River six weeks earlier. He had been quiet, watching everything, a constant unassuming presence, responding quickly and with amazing accuracy when asked for advice on any questions of navigation.

"Yes, Mister Dunson, what is it?"

Dunson's voice was steady, intense, controlled. "At this moment we are in waters that sound at not more than fourteen fathoms. Running north, that reduces to about twelve fathoms, then back to fourteen, and holds at that depth for nearly one hundred miles."

He stopped and Hull stared for a moment in puzzlement. "Go on."

Dunson pointed over the stern at the oncoming *Shannon.* "I think we can outrun the British by kedging, sir—at least stay far enough ahead that their cannon can't reach us."

For an instant Hull did not move, and then he exclaimed, "Kedging! Of course!" He turned to Strand. "Get all the hawsers we can spare tied together in two continuous lines and get the main anchor and the reserve anchor into the nearest longboats!"

Strand turned on his heel and was gone at a run, down onto the main deck, shouting orders, watching while startled seamen leaped to search for hawsers, and began tying them together, end to end, coiling them into two gigantic lines as they went. Then he grabbed his horn and ran to the bow of the ship to bellow to the two strings of longboats ahead, connected to the lines towing the ship, "Hello, the longboats! The nearest four! Return to the ship. Return to the ship!"

The four longboats nearest the *Constitution* released themselves from the lines and turned about with the sweating seamen on board pulling strong on their oars, puzzlement showing clear on their faces at the peculiar order to return. Dunson was standing beside Hull, both watching, first the *Shannon,* then their own crews in the four longboats as they came alongside. The nearest crew chief cupped his hand to shout to Strand, "What's the reason to call us back?"

"Kedging," Strand answered. "Come alongside. We're going to lower the anchors into the first two longboats and a line into the other two. You're going ahead as far as the line will allow to drop the anchor and we'll pull the ship to it."

Instantly the crews of all four longboats nodded their heads and came alongside, two to receive the heavy anchors, the other two to receive the great coils of hawsers tied together to form two lines more than half a mile in length. Then all four boats turned, and the crews strained to race forward ahead of the frigate while Hull and Dunson stood on the quarterdeck judging speed and distance, first between them and the *Shannon* behind them, and then between them and their own longboats ahead of them. The single question had once again risen to the top: could they stay far enough ahead of the British squadron to avoid its cannon?

They watched with held breath as the longboats reached the end of their tethers, and the first one dumped its anchor overboard. The crew on the *Constitution* waited one minute for the anchor to sink fourteen fathoms and hit the bottom of the sea, and then twelve men leaned into the four arms of the winch anchored to the deck and began reeling in the tether rope, leg muscles knotted as they drove with all their strength. The tether rope came singing tight and the frigate suddenly plowed ahead, gaining speed as the winch groaned and the drum turned to reel in the rope. When the first kedge was under the bow of the ship, the longboats assigned to it were there waiting to take the anchor and the line back out, while half a mile ahead, the two longboats assigned to the second kedge dropped the second anchor, and the crew on the winch aboard the ship began reeling in the second line. The rotation had begun: first one kedge, then the other, to maintain a continuous towing. The *Constitution* slowly began to widen the gap between it and the *Shannon*, despite the fact that twenty-two British longboats were straining to catch her.

The sun was one hour above the eastern horizon when a whisper of breeze fluttered the sails, stopped, then rose again, and held. Hull trimmed his sails to catch all the wind he could, and watched while the British did the same. With her twenty-two longboats towing, and wind in her sails, the *Shannon* held pace with the *Constitution*, and then Hull thought he saw them gaining. For half a minute he stood with narrowed eyes, then turned to give his orders to the four gun crews at the stern of the ship, two on the main deck, two in his own quarters with the gun muzzles thrust out of the open windows.

"Load!"

Sweaty hands rolled the guns backwards, ladled the black gunpowder down the muzzles, then the straw, the cannonball, more straw, primed the touch-hole, and held the linstocks poised, ready, waiting for the order.

"Fire!" Hull ordered, and the four guns bucked and roared. For several seconds the white cloud of gun smoke hung in the dead air and then began to thin and rise. Half the crew watched with held breath, knowing the distance was too great, hoping only that the British would understand the warning: if you come within gun range, we'll fight!

The four geysers of water leaped short of the *Shannon*, while Hull, Strand, and Dunson, and most of their crew, watched, scarcely breathing. The British ship began to fall back, but her companion, the *Guerriere*, changed course to the west. It was clear the British squadron meant to close the American ship in a box.

For over two hours the cluster of ships moved north, longboats towing, kedging, while the seamen stood fast on the ropes overhead waiting to trim their sails to catch every wisp of wind possible. The sun was high when the first promise of a small, lasting breeze fluttered the flags and the ships all changed their sails to catch it. The moment the ships could respond to the helm, the captains called in their longboats. Hull, on the *Constitution,* ordered his held suspended on ropes above the water, to be available for instant use should the breeze fail again. All crews on all ships were at the rails, silent, intense, each calculating when, or if, the British could catch the American frigate. There was a mounting sense of a classic sea-chase on all six vessels as it continued, the British smelling blood, the Americans determined to elude them.

Midmorning, the gun ports on the starboard side of the *Guerriere* belched their white smoke, and sixteen geysers erupted on the port side of the *Constitution,* four hundred yards short.

Hull and Strand and Dunson watched with one common thought. *She's testing the range. They mean to force us to take a stand and fight.*

Abruptly Dunson turned to Hull. "Sir, I believe we could add a little speed if we wet the sails and lightened our load."

"Lighten the load how?"

"Use some of our drinking water to wet the sails. Dump some of it overboard. I think we can make a friendly port within five days. Hold back just enough to keep the men alive and dump the rest. Over two thousand gallons. Eight tons. It will increase our speed by about two knots."

Hull looked at Strand, and Strand nodded. Hull turned back to Dunson. "You're certain about your five-day estimate?"

Dunson's expression did not waver. "Certain. Boston. We can make Boston in five days."

Minutes later wooden buckets with rope handles were being passed up the rope ladders to seamen waiting to empty them onto the sails to capture every slight hint of wind. The crew watched in silent amazement while six of them manned the pump handles, and they watched their drinking water spray overboard to disappear in the salt sea. They wiped at their bearded mouths, and they looked at their captain, and then they understood.

The *Constitution* picked up speed, and then something undefined, something powerful, crept into the entire four-hundred-fifty-man crew. They stood ready with the water buckets and sent them dripping up the chain of men to those standing on the ropes, leaned against the spars, waiting, and they kept every square inch of the sails wet. When the wind failed, they were lowering the longboats before Hull's orders came loud, and they were into the boats and straining to kedge and tow with every pound and every ounce of energy they possessed. A light was in their eyes, and their jaws were set, determined. *We can do it! We can beat the British! We can!*

On deck, Dunson did not ask permission. He jerked off his tunic and tossed it onto the nearest hatch cover, and took a place in a line, passing the dripping buckets upward. Within ten seconds Strand was there beside him, sweating, watching, shoulder to shoulder, officers with their seamen. In that moment, Hull knew. *We're going to win this race!*

It was nearing noon when Hull saw the *Belvidera* draw ahead of the *Shannon* and lower her anchor into a longboat, followed by a heap of hawsers into a second one. He lowered his telescope. *Kedging. Towing and kedging. They may come within gun range.*

While he watched, both the *Shannon* and the *Belvidera* slowed and then held steady, just yards out of cannon range. Hull studied them for a time before a hint of a smile came. *They're afraid of our stern guns. They're waiting for the others to box us in. And that isn't going to happen.*

The day wore on under the heat of a late July sun, with the ships maintaining their interval as they moved north. On board the *Belvidera*, Captain Richard Byron watched the deck crew of the *Constitution* like a hawk, studying their every move as they used every device known to seafaring men to maintain speed and position on a windless sea of glass. He saw sweating, exhausted men lay down on the decks and sleep near their stations while the next crew took their place. Weary gun crews slept with their backs leaned against their cannon carriages when the next crew replaced them. The officers had stripped off their tunics with the gold bars on the shoulders and were right in among their men, sweating, rowing, working the bucket chain up on the ropes and spars. A grim smile flickered for a moment, and a look of admiration came into his eyes. *Flawless. The officers mixed right down among the seamen—every man refusing to leave his station—sleeping on the decks—how does one defeat such men?*

The day wore on with seamen, both British and American, straining at the oars, rowing, kedging, passing buckets of water up into the sails with every whisper of breeze that might help. Down in the galley of the *Constitution* the cooks prepared food that could be carried up onto the main deck, and came from their kingdom down below, up into the blazing sun to serve it. The sun set. Twilight, then deep dusk, and finally full darkness came to change the race into a series of five sets of running lights pursuing a single set that doggedly refused to be caught. Dawn came, then sunrise, with the American frigate using every stitch of sail she had, still kedging, still with her longboats out towing, and the British behind, just out of gun range, still unable to gain the four hundred yards that could have forced a fight.

The sun was three hours high when the shout came down from the crow's nest of the *Belvidera*.

"There! Nor'east! An American merchantman coming straight in!"

Captain Richard Byron came to a startled standstill, and for long seconds peered through his telescope before his arm shot up to point.

"There she is!" He turned to his first mate. "Quickly. Lower the Union Jack and raise an American flag! We must decoy that ship into us. Maybe the *Constitution* will come to her defense!"

Within three minutes the American stars and stripes was dangling from the mainmast of the British *Belvidera*, the only British ship within sight of the American merchantman, and Captain Byron was watching, waiting to see if his deception would succeed.

On board the *Constitution*, the sunburned seaman in the crow's nest had called down to Captain Isaac Hull, "Nor'east! American. Merchantman." Hull swung around to watch the oncoming, unarmed ship with the words running in his mind—*Veer off—veer off—can't you see the British flags?—veer off.*

Then Hull turned about and watched in stunned silence at the sight of the American flag going up the mainmast of the *Belvidera*. In one second, understanding hit him, and he gaped. *Decoy! They're trying to decoy that merchantman.*

He jerked around to bark orders to Strand, but he was too far down the deck among the gun crews. Then Hull saw Dunson already frantically undoing the figure-eight windings of the flag rope on the mainmast. Under Dunson's arm was a British Union Jack flag, and while Hull watched, Dunson lowered the American flag and unsnapped it from the cable, then mounted the British flag and instantly started it up the mainmast as fast as his hands could work. The British Union Jack hit the top of the mainmast, and below, Hull, Dunson, Strand, and every man on deck froze as they peered at the oncoming American merchantman, waiting to see if she understood.

The heavy freighter, loaded and riding low in the water, hesitated, then stopped. On board the *Constitution* the entire crew and all officers raised fists and a shout at the sight of the big vessel turning east out into the open waters of the Atlantic, well out of range of the British squadron, and they watched as she steadily grew smaller and disappeared.

On board the *Belvidera,* Captain Byron slowly shook his head, ruefully grinning. *They could not have performed better!*

The day wore on with the American crew sweating in the pounding heat of the sun, refusing to leave their duty posts, snatching sleep on deck, taking their rotation in the back-breaking work of rowing the long-boats on the tow lines and the kedging lines, the officers with their tunics off, sweat dripping as they worked among their men. Sunset came with the ships still locked in place, the British no nearer nor farther than they had been at sunrise. The sun was reaching for the western horizon when the *Constitution* slowly began to distance the five British pursuers. By evening mess the gap had extended to nearly four miles, and Hull called for his navigator, John Dunson.

"How many more miles do we have at fourteen fathoms?"

"At least forty, sir."

Hull gestured to the heavens. "I feel a squall coming."

Dunson nodded. "I agree, sir. Within half an hour. If we're careful, we can use a squall to gain distance."

"I agree."

At fifteen minutes before seven o'clock PM, the squall rolled in, and with it came gusting winds and rain in sheets that drenched everything on the top deck of the frigate. Grinning men with water running from their hair and beards and clothing waited, poised, until the last second before they pulled all the longboats and kedging boats in, and the blustering winds billowed the dripping sails of the *Constitution,* and she leaped ahead.

Behind them, Captain Byron once again shook his head in admiration. *Used every second they had and then caught the squall squarely—I don't think we have a chance.*

It took minutes for the squall to reach the British, but in those minutes the American frigate had gained more than half a mile on them. The squall held until full darkness, then moved on to leave the ships soaked and dripping beneath countless stars in the black velvet overhead. The only difference was, the *Constitution* had gained an invaluable lead, and she was not going to relinquish it back to her pursuers. All night the Americans held their frantic pace of rowing and kedging, passing water buckets up into the rigging to get every inch they could out of each passing draft of breeze. By six o'clock, with the sun rising in the east, the British ships were but faint flecks far behind the *Constitution,* with the *Belvidera* leading, then the *Shannon, Guerierre, Aeolus,* and *Africa* following. Slowly, one by one, the British ships dropped from sight.

On board the *Belvidera,* Captain Byron drew a deep breath and turned to his first mate. "Break off the chase. Let them go."

A wistful look crossed the man's face. "Aye, sir." He started to turn to carry out the order when Byron stopped him.

"Commend our men. They've done well. Just tell them those Americans earned it. They were superb."

On board the *Constitution,* Captain Isaac Hull drew his watch from his tunic pocket. It was fifteen minutes past eight AM. He drew a deep breath and turned to Strand and Dunson. In the entire engagement, none of the three men had slept more than a total of eight hours. They were unshaven, sweated, bone-weary, rumpled, and grinning.

"Gentlemen," Hull said quietly, "I believe the British have abandoned the chase. Mister Strand, tell the men. We'll hold this pace for one more hour and then we'll fall back to regular routine. Tell them their performance was . . . remarkable. Every man will receive a commendation. And extra rations."

Strand bobbed his head. "Aye, sir."

Hull turned to Dunson. "We're on short water rations. When will we make Boston?"

"Tomorrow morning at about this time, sir, if the wind holds. Our water ration will get us there."

"Very good. Carry on."

Not one man in the crew of the *Constitution* could recall a feeling on board any ship in their experience to compare with that which had crept into them. They had met the best the British had to offer—five to one— and they had come together as one man in a chase that had no equal in history, and they had won! They had sweated and strained together, sleeping and eating at their posts on deck, with their officers stripping away their tunics and becoming one of them—every man had contributed to do the impossible. They stood a little taller and talked a little louder and laughed too much. No matter who else did or did not hear of it, they were the ones, and they would have that memory for the rest of their lives. They were the crew the British could not catch.

They settled back into their duties, and in late dusk the call came from the crow's nest, "East'nor'east. Sail."

On the quarterdeck, Hull raised his telescope, then lowered it. "Can't tell her flag. I think we should find out if she's British or American. Change course to northwest until we know if she's an enemy."

Through the night they tracked with the ship. In the gray before sunrise they closed with her, close enough to identify her as an American merchantman. The *Constitution* corrected course to northeast toward the Massachusetts coast, with all canvas out.

In the late afternoon they again sighted an unidentified ship, large, heavy, low in the water, but were unable to read her flag.

Hull turned to Dunson. "Do we have enough water for one more day?"

Dunson reflected for a moment. "We'll be on short ration, but we can make it last one more day. We're half a day out of Boston right now."

Hull considered. "We'll have this one identified by midnight, then turn back due east."

It was shortly before past midnight when Hull gave orders to Strand. "Get the gun crews ready on the starboard side. We don't have time to wait for morning. I'm going alongside that ship now to identify her. If she's British, we'll know shortly. If they fire, don't wait for my order. Fire back."

"Aye, sir."

In full blackness, Hull brought his frigate alongside the larger ship and raised his horn.

"Captain Isaac Hull. USS *Constitution*. Request permission to board for purposes of identification."

The answer came back with an unmistakable New England inflection. "We are the *Cornelius.* Commercial. Dunson & Weems, shipping out of Boston."

Hull turned to John Dunson. "You know anything about Dunson & Weems out of Boston?"

John was grinning. "I know them. My father and Billy Weems own it. That's Captain Bertram Walters. Can't miss that voice."

Hull chuckled out loud, then turned back to the big merchantman. "Identification accepted. I extend a warning. We were pursued by a British squadron of five armed frigates. They abandoned pursuit yesterday, south of us. Watch."

"Understood. If you are the *Constitution,* do you have a navigator on board named John Dunson?"

"We do."

"Greetings to John from all of us. And his father."

Laughter rolled out across the gap in the darkness between the two ships, from both sides. John ducked and shook his head in embarrassment, then joined in the ringing laughter while those nearest him clapped him on the back.

The merchantman continued on her course, and Hull turned to his navigator.

"Mister Dunson, take us home."

"Aye, sir."

John took his place beside the helmsman, spent a moment taking his bearing from the stars, and began giving his instructions—"East by northeast—due east—east by southeast—due east" guiding the frigate through the reefs and shoals through the night toward the coast of Massachusetts. At dawn they picked up the lighthouse marking the northernmost tip of Cape Cod and angled eastward, in a direct line for Boston harbor. It was shortly past noon when the *Constitution* tied up at the dock designated for United States gunboats on the Boston waterfront.

Captain Isaac Hull gave orders that the crew could take shore leave in rotation, and gave John Dunson direct orders for a six-day leave, to report back for duty on August first.

Hull turned to Strand. "Would you go ashore and find contractors to resupply us? Water, flour, salt pork, hardtack—the things we'll need for our next cruise? I have some things to do on board until you return. We'll go together tomorrow to make the purchases."

"Aye, sir."

Strand left the ship, and Hull remained on the quarterdeck long enough to be certain all matters were under control before he went to his cabin. He stepped in and stopped short. He had forgotten the two long, heavy cannon set squarely in the center of his small quarters with their muzzles out the rear windows.

I'll get those moved later, he thought. He sat down at his tiny desk, which had been pushed to one side, and drew out the ship's log. He opened to the page with the latest writing, and for a time sat still, pondering how to write the conclusion to the wildest sea chase he had ever known. Then he plucked up his quill and for a long time sat with the sounds of its scratching his only companion.

On deck, with his seaman's bag packed and on his shoulder, John Dunson thumped down the gangplank to the heavy, black planking of the dock, glanced up once at the familiar sight of countless seagulls and terns and grebes scolding overhead, and trotted east through the heat of the half-deserted waterfront to the familiar office with the sign DUN-SON & WEEMS. He pushed through the door and dropped his heavy canvas bag on the countertop. Inside, Matthew and Billy raised their heads from their desks, and both instantly came to their feet to stride quickly to meet him.

Matthew spoke first, relief and a question in his eyes. "You're home! Too early! Are you all right?"

"Fine."

Billy reached to shake his hand. "We've missed you. Run into trouble?"

John nodded. "A little. Is Laura all right? The baby?"

Matthew smiled. "Both fine. The baby's cutting more teeth." He paused for a moment. "A little trouble? What happened?"

"We met a British squadron off the New Jersey coast. Barnegat Bay. Five of them. All frigates, all armed. Two hundred eight cannon against our forty-four. About five to one, both in ships and firepower."

Instantly Matthew tensed.

John continued. "Captain Hull—Isaac Hull—decided saving the ship and crew was more critical to the U.S. Navy than losing both, so we turned and made a run. Nine days. Most of it just out of gun range." A grin spread on John's face. "Got quite exciting. They quit. We won the race. We came on in to get water and resupply."

Matthew's brow drew down in question. "You ran out of water?"

"No. We dumped eight tons to lighten the load."

"The race was that close?"

"It was close." John chuckled. "We were towing and kedging and soaking down the sails most of the time to catch whatever wind came our way. They were doing the same. It turned out our crew was just a little more . . . inspired . . . than theirs. If they had caught us, we wouldn't have had a chance."

Billy was smiling, shaking his head. "Inspired? Sounds more like frightened. Scared."

"Whatever it was, our crew beat theirs. It was pretty tense."

Matthew said. "We heard the *Constitution* was in the harbor. I'm sure the word got to both Laura and Mother. Take your bag and go on home. Stop at Mother's on the way and let her know you're all right."

John bobbed his head. "I'll be back tomorrow to make a full report. Good to be home."

He shouldered his seaman's bag and walked back out the door into the sweltering heat of the afternoon sun and turned east, toward home.

In his quarters on board the *Constitution,* Captain Isaac Hull continued his careful work on the ship's log, pausing to remember and record the detail. He came to the closing lines, wrote them slowly, then set the quill down and read them to himself.

". . . the unwavering obedience of the crew—the ingenuity and selflessness of the officers—the remarkable contribution of our navigator John Dunson—all require that every man aboard the ship receive a commendation which I shall gratefully write . . ."

He closed the big ledger, rose, smiled at the incongruity of two cannon in his small quarters, tucked the ship's log under his arm, and walked out on deck to the bos'n's mate standing at the gangplank.

"I will be gone about one hour. You are in command until my return."

"Aye, sir."

It took Captain Hull fifteen minutes to locate the Boston newspaper office. Inside he asked for and was introduced to the owner and chief editor. Behind the closed office door, he laid the ledger on the desk, amid a disorganized clutter of papers.

"Sir," Hull began, "I am Captain of the USS *Constitution.* My name is Isaac Hull. I have a ship's log here. In it is what I believe to be the most remarkable story in written history of a sea chase. Would you be interested?"

On the open waters of the Atlantic, far to the south, British captain Richard Byron sat at his desk, sweating in the July heat of his small quarters on the *Belvidera.* Before him was the ship's log, with the ink still wet from his last entry. He laid down his quill and silently went over his last sentence.

"The American crew performed to perfection. Their escape from the best we had to offer was earned. Their effort was in every detail, elegant."

He looked at the word *elegant* and for a time pondered. Then he closed the ledger and put it back into its drawer. He could find no word better suited to the need than the word *elegant.*

The following day, in the late afternoon, the Boston newspaper published its front-page article of the feat of the Americans, quoting liberally from the log of the USS *Constitution.* Within seventy-two hours the story of the chase had swept every newspaper in every major city in the United States. The story became the talk of the nation. The *Constitution* and her crew became instant legends. The intrepid navigator—John Dunson—the one who saved the ship by suggesting kedging to his captain and recommending dumping eight tons of water to lighten the load and then running a British flag aloft to save an American merchantman, was the talk of Boston. The office of Dunson & Weems was flooded with mail and seamen and officers who came to shake his hand and congratulate him.

On the sixth day after their arrival in Boston, John Dunson strode up the gangplank of the *Constitution.* First mate Strand stood at the top, on the deck of the ship, with a ship's roster in his hand.

"Reporting for duty," John said.

A big grin creased Strand's large, homely face as he checked off the name, John Dunson, Navigator. "Nice seeing you again. We sail with the tide, about four o'clock in the morning. Think you can get us out of Boston Harbor?"

Notes

On July 17, 1812, at about 2:00 PM, Captain Isaac Hull, in command of the USS *Constitution,* a forty-four cannon American navy frigate, was four leagues, or about 12 miles, off the New Jersey coast, east of Barnegat Bay. Isaac Hull was the nephew of Army General Hull assigned to command Fort Detroit in the Michigan Territory. Isaac Hull had resupplied his ship in the Chesapeake River just weeks earlier. His vessel was designed by the most celebrated shipwright of his time, a New England Quaker named Joshua Humphreys. Many foreign governments, including England, had sought the services of Humphreys, who chose to share them with the United States. A Humphreys frigate was the best of its kind—larger, faster, and stronger than any other. On that day in July, Hull encountered five British frigates whose names and captains and gun count were as described herein. Two of the British captains were the finest in the British navy, and their frigates were excellent, but no match for the Humphreys frigates. Recognizing that he had no chance in a fight with five British frigates, whose combined firepower was about five times his own, Captain Hull ordered his ship to turn and outrun them. The British came in hot pursuit, and the race began, as described. Captain Hull used every device known to seamen in his retreat, including towing, kedging, dumping excess water to lighten his ship, and soaking the sails to catch all possible wind.

John Dunson is a fictional character, used herein for the purpose of maintaining the story line. The crewman who suggested kedging to Captain Hull was not John Dunson, but actually Lieutenant Charles Morris. The pursuit continued basically as herein described, with the American frigate able to stay just out of gun range the entire time, with crewmen sleeping and eating on deck, exerting themselves to exhaustion to maintain their lead, and the officers mixing with the ordinary seamen in the harsh work.

An American merchantman appeared, and the British attempted to decoy it within gun range by raising an American flag to trick the merchantman into thinking they were American ships; however, the *Constitution* foiled the ploy by raising a British flag to warn the merchantman away. On the night of July 18, the British ship *Guerriere*, commanded by Captain James Richard Dacres, drew near the *Constitution*, leaving the other four British ships behind. The *Guerrierre* slowed, and her four companion ships came closer. Captain Dacres saw their lights, but did not know who they were in the dark and signaled to them to identify themselves. They made no return signal, and he presumed them to be a squadron of American ships under command of American Captain Rodgers.

He withdrew and waited until morning, when he discovered they were his own ships. They had failed to return his signal in the night, presuming he knew who they were. He was furious and later demanded a court-martial to clear his name. Hull had two heavy cannon brought to the stern of his ship and tore out some of the railing to give them free access to fire at anything behind. He had two other heavy cannon brought into his tiny quarters with the muzzles thrust out the windows for added firepower at the British behind them, should it be necessary. The race continued, until finally a rain squall passed over the ships, giving the Americans enough wind to pull away from the British. The morning of July 20, the British withdrew from the chase. On his return to Boston for resupplying his ship, Hull sighted two separate merchantmen and paused to investigate both. Each was found to be American. Hull arrived in Boston on July 26. The entire episode appeared in newspapers throughout the United States, to become one of the most celebrated events of the War of 1812. The British Navy did in fact describe the actions of the Americans as "elegant."

See Roosevelt, *The Naval War of 1812*, pp. 47–50; Hickey, *The War of 1812*, pp. 91–93; Wills, *James Madison*, pp. 112–114.

For a painting of Captain Isaac Hull, see Hickey, *The War of 1812*, p. 95.

CHAPTER XVI

*T*he deep, faint rumble that was felt more than heard came rolling north from Lake Erie, up the Detroit River, to turn the heads of those who had lived in the thick woods or in the tiny village of Detroit long enough to know the signs. They paused in the fierce, humid heat of the midmorning sun to peer south at the low purple hedge of clouds, billowing, shifting, moving steadily up the river, with the flashes inside that for an instant lighted the clouds to all shades of blue, then were gone.

The village blacksmith, white-hair, white beard, face lined with age, stepped from beneath his three-walled lean-to into the dead air and raised one hand to shade his eyes while he studied the horizon to the south.

Been too hot—big 'un comin'—hit here about noon. He glanced west at the high walls of Fort Detroit. *Wonder if those soldier boys know they're in for a lot of noise and a good soakin'.* A wry grin crossed his face as he turned back to the large brown mare tied to the post near his forge, nervous, moving her feet, ears twitching. Beyond the mare were three geldings, tied to a hitch rack, unsettled, shifting. *They feel 'er comin'—better git the shoes on these animals this mornin' if them Ohio officers figger to cross the river tomorrow.*

Inside the fort, within the headquarters building, General William Hull paced in his small private office, sweating in the stifling heat, hands clasped behind his back, staring unseeing at the floor. For the fifth time in ten minutes he looked at the wind-up clock on the crude mantel above the small, smoke-blackened, stone fireplace.

Nine-fifty, he thought, *ten minutes—have they prepared for the crossing?—where are the supplies we were promised?—are the south roads open?—where are the Indians?—what does Brock . . .?*

He started at the sudden knock on his door and exclaimed, "Enter."

The door burst open, and the corporal on duty in the foyer barged in, eyes wide.

"There's a messenger here, sir. Civilian. Has a paper he says you must see."

Hull started. "A messenger? Get him in here."

The corporal turned and signaled, and a young man strode into the room. He was average height, hair awry, sweating, breathing hard, face grim. In his right hand was a paper.

"I'm Thomas Atwater." He pointed west. "I got a farm out there. This was handed to me this morning by British soldiers. I thought you should see it." He offered a crumpled paper, and Hull took it and read the signature.

General Isaac Brock, Commander, Fort Malden, His Majesty's Army.

There was a slight tremor in Hull's hand as he read the message.

" . . . I feel it my duty to remind you that the prosperity you have enjoyed is the result of British naval superiority, which has thus far guaranteed Canadians access to world markets. . . . Further, it is but too obvious that once exchanged from the powerful protection of the United Kingdom you must be reannexed to the dominion of France, not the United States. . . . Finally, I respond to the proclamation recently uttered by General William Hull of the United States Army . . . should he, or the United States, undertake to summarily execute Canadian citizens found in alliance with the Indians, it will be deliberate murder, and I give my oath that I will exercise retribution in every quarter of the globe . . ."

Hull blanched, then exclaimed, "Where did you get this?"

Atwater raised one eyebrow in question. "I thought I mentioned it. British soldiers. Came by my farm about an hour ago. They're handing those out all around."

Hull brought himself under control. "I see. You were right to bring it here. Is there anything else?"

Atwater shrugged. "Only that a lot of us are caught in the middle of this whole thing. We got your paper saying we should join you, and now the British want us to join them. Looks like we're in trouble no matter what we do."

"Return to your farm," Hull said. "Prepare to assist us when we liberate Fort Malden and Amherstburg."

Atwater turned and walked out into the foyer, shaking his head all the way. He was reaching to open the front door out into the sunlight when it swung open, and he stepped aside to allow three uniformed colonels to enter, the gold epaulets bright on their shoulders. The corporal at the desk stood and saluted as Atwater walked out and closed the door.

The corporal faced the officers. "I'll tell the general you're here," and his boot heels tapped on the hardwood floor as he hurried to the private office with a crude sign GENERAL HULL at eye level. Two minutes later the three colonels, McArthur, Cass, and Findlay, were inside the private office, seated opposite Hull, facing his desk.

Hull was ramrod straight, voice firm, controlled. "Gentlemen, we cross the river tomorrow morning. I trust your men are prepared."

There was a silence, and McArthur reached to scratch under his chin.

Hull cleared his throat. "Are your men prepared?"

McArthur shook his head. "Some. Not all. We've had a . . . sort of mutiny. Two hundred of them from Ohio say they're not crossing the river. That would put them out of the United States into foreign territory, and they say they were never authorized to leave the United States. They won't go."

Color came into Hull's face, and his voice raised. "What do they mean, they won't go? They can be arrested! Shot!"

McArthur shrugged. "They know that. They doubt you'd shoot two hundred of your own men. They won't go."

For several seconds Hull sat in unmoving silence, unable to force his thoughts to a conclusion. Then he drew a deep breath and continued.

"Very well. We'll leave them behind." He handed the paper he had received from Atwater to McArthur. "Are you aware of this?"

McArthur took it and sat in silence for several seconds reading it. "I heard about it. This is the first I've seen it."

"It's bound to have an effect," Hull said. "All of you see to it your men are told of it, and inform them that it has absolutely no bearing on our actions. We cross the river tomorrow, and we will move on Fort Malden and Amherstburg as planned. Do you understand?

McArthur glanced at Cass and Findlay. "Yes, sir."

Hull bobbed his head once. "Very good. The basic purpose in crossing the river is to be certain the British are not gathering there to attack us."

He paused for a moment, then went on. "Now, as to our actions after we've crossed the river. We have a substantial superiority in numbers over the British, which gives us time to make all preparations for an attack on Fort Malden. We must build cannon carriages if we are to place their fort under siege. You will assign men to construct the carriages and the wheels."

He paused to look into their faces for some sense of acceptance, support. Their expressions were passive, nearly blank.

Hull continued. "Once on the other side we will establish regular patrols to keep the roads open and to forage for supplies. And we will assign some men to construct a temporary dock and maintain enough longboats to control all traffic on the river."

He reached for another document and pushed it across the desk. None of them reached to receive it. "That message was received late yesterday. It states that a column of two hundred men left Ohio with loaded supply wagons to be delivered here. They've stopped at the River Raisin, thirty-five miles south. They are concerned that Tecumseh and his hostiles will attack them if they come any farther north. They request help. I am dispatching a relief column of one hundred fifty men under command of Major Thomas Van Horne to go there immediately and escort the supply wagons on to this fort. Is there any discussion?"

McArthur casually asked, "When does Van Horne leave?"

"Today." Hull stopped and drew a heavy breath in the silence, frustration showing in his face and his movements at the indifference he was seeing in his officers. Finally he placed both palms flat on his desk and leaned forward, eyes too bright, voice too high.

"Do any of you have anything to say about all this? We're surrounded by British redcoats and Indians; we've got a supply train stopped thirty-five miles south; we're dividing our force to go down there to rescue them; we cross the river in the morning into British territory; two hundred of our men have refused direct orders to leave United States soil—there's nothing you have to say about all this?"

Cass responded. "Not much to be said. We've got our orders. Let's get on with it."

For a moment Hull looked at McArthur, then Findlay, who remained silent, and Hull tossed one hand into the air. "Very well," he exclaimed, "you're dismissed."

The three officers walked out into the late-morning sunlight and heard the rumble far to the south. They slowed to look above the rough walls of the fort at the purple line that was slowly rising, and to listen to the distant thunder. "Going to have a wet afternoon," was all they said, and continued on to their quarters for a few moments before walking out through the big gates to their commands, camped in the woods.

The wind rose before eleven o'clock, blustering and heavy, to rip leaves and branches from the thrashing trees. They lost the sun half an hour before noon mess, and the world darkened as the bellies of the thick purple clouds rolled over them. The soldiers at the head of the food lines were filling their pewter plates when the first great drops of rain came slanting. By ten minutes past twelve o'clock the lightning flashes were turning the twilight into brightness, and thunder shook the walls of the fort and every building inside, while the driving rain came so thick men had to bow their heads to breathe. Within minutes the drill field was a morass of mud and water, and everything inside the fort was drenched. Soldiers broke from the food lines to sprint for cover under the eaves of the buildings and the parapets overhead. Cooks abandoned the steaming kettles of stew to crouch beneath wagons or carts and watch as the stew pots filled with rain water. For half an hour the summer cloudburst raged with lightning strikes so close they left the air smelling burned and brought thunderclaps that jolted the ground and deafened the men and left their ears ringing.

The storm rolled on north, toward Lake Huron, and the thick clouds gave way to patches of blue overhead, and then shafts of golden light came streaming through. Within minutes the skies were brilliant, and the sun was turning the world into a wet, steaming mass with endless tiny droplets of clinging water sparkling. Soldiers came from cover to silently survey their ruined midday meal, the mud-spattered, rain-soaked tents and bedrolls and firewood. They sighed and wondered how they were going to set their camp and the fort in order and still be ready to cross the river at four o'clock in the morning. They hitched at their belts and set their teeth, mumbling curses against the harsh reality that ninety-five percent of soldiering was the monotony and dirty work that filled the gap between the battles that were five percent of their lives.

Midafternoon, the knock came at Hull's door, and he stood at his desk and called out permission to enter.

Major Thomas Van Horne, fully uniformed, with boots muddy halfway to his knees, pushed through the door and saluted.

"We're prepared to leave, sir."

Hull reflected for a moment. "I presume you have my written orders."

"I have a pouch, sir, with your orders inside and paper and quill for sending messages and letters the men might write."

"Keep the mail pouch available. You may need it. Be alert for Indians. That is all."

"I shall take personal charge of the mail pouch. Thank you, sir." Van Horne turned and walked from the room. There were spots of mud from his boots on the floor as he closed the door.

Hull opened the center drawer in his desk and drew out a plug of tobacco and a small knife. He folded the blade out, cut a piece of the pungent brown tobacco, and put it in his mouth, then replaced the knife and tobacco and closed the drawer. He worked the cud between his teeth as he glanced down to locate the shining brass spittoon on the floor at the corner of his desk, then spit a stream of brown liquid and wiped at his mouth and beard before calling the corporal from the foyer.

"Have my brown mare brought from the blacksmith and saddled."

"Yes, sir."

Ten minutes later the corporal reported back, and Hull walked out the front door to the hitch rack where the mare was tied in front of the headquarters building. He stooped to raise each hoof to inspect the new shoes, then mounted and rode slogging through the muck of the camp outside the walls of the fort. Sweating soldiers, stripped to the waist and muddy to the knees, were chopping fresh firewood or washing mud-speckled uniforms or hanging them on lines or tree limbs or bushes to dry, while others worked on roasting whole pigs for evening mess. They raised their heads to see the general coming, then paused in surprise. He was among them alone, unannounced. This was not a regularly scheduled inspection, nor was it a surprise inspection with the general escorted by his junior officers. This was a man driven by compulsions that were rapidly reducing him to an enigma that did not conform to the unwritten code governing military leaders. At first it had puzzled the soldiers. Quiet talk had begun around the evening campfires. Then the puzzlement faded, and open concern had crept in. *Is this officer fit? Can he lead in battle? We cross the river in the morning—will he attack Fort Malden? Will he?*

Few saluted as he passed, ramrod stiff in the saddle, face severe, head turning from side to side, probing. They watched him for a few moments, then went on with their duties, wondering, their concerns bordering on fear of what this man would do when the muskets began rattling and the cannon booming.

The afternoon wore on with the command sweating as they steadily put the camp in order for their river crossing. They went to the evening mess lines to eat hot roast pork and boiled potatoes, then back to their campsites to roll and pack their own clothing, most of it still damp, into their forty-pound backpacks, and count their paper cartridge ration, fifty rounds per man, into the cartridge cases mounted on their belts. Lanterns burned for a time after the ten o'clock taps drum sounded, and no officer came to order them extinguished. It was midnight before the camp and the fort were dark and silent and without movement, save for the pickets who took their rotation at their posts.

By three o'clock in the morning the lanterns in the headquarters building inside the fort walls were casting misshapen rectangles of light out onto the ground while General Hull sat at his desk inside, poring over his notes for the river crossing. *Boats—crews—barges for the horses— freight-boats for the cannon—food—gunpowder—cartridges—is the camp prepared?— what if the Indians come swarming?—the British attack?—another summer cloudburst strikes with winds that make crossing the river impossible?—if a boat capsizes?—if . . .*

He suddenly straightened, staring at the three-page list as though it were something alive and deadly. *What am I doing?—we've crossed rivers before—we'll make this crossing successfully—what am I doing?*

He shoved the list aside and rose from his chair to walk from his small private office into the foyer, then on out into the night. He stopped to stare upward at the unending points of light that gleamed in the eternities overhead, and he stood still as a sense of stability and rightness came into him and grew. He turned and walked back into his private office to collect the papers he would need in the next few weeks and pack them into a leather valise ready for the crossing and what would follow.

At four o'clock, the reveille drum rattled, and the camp came alive as men began their morning toilet and then struck their tents to fold them and bind them closed. By six o'clock they were walking to the breakfast lines with bowls and cups for hot oatmeal and steaming coffee. They ate in near total silence, washed their utensils, packed them in their backpacks and tied them shut, and then reported to their squad leaders to begin the massive work of moving more than sixteen hundred men across a river, with all their horses, cannon, tents, and food.

Major Thomas Van Horne reported to General Hull, then led his one-hundred-fifty-man detail south along the crude road the army had cut from Ohio to the fort as they came. General Hull watched them out of sight with one thought bright in his mind. *Indians. What happens if Tecumseh finds them?*

At the riverbank, where men were systematically loading crates of food and cannon into longboats, half a dozen wild-eyed horses reared and fought the ropes as they were being led onto the barges, terrified at leaving solid ground to step onto a shifting, rocking thing that was somehow connected to the water. Men grabbed the cheek-straps of their halters while others blindfolded the plunging animals. Then they threw the quivering horses off their feet, tied their legs together, and picked them up like a huge bundle to lay them on their sides atop the barge, still tied and blindfolded. The loading went on hour after hour, with the men shedding their tunics and wiping at the sweat that ran from their faces into their beards. They paused for midday mess and to collapse in shade wherever they could find it, then went back to the heavy labor of loading boats and barges that worked their way across the river, unloaded, and returned, time and time again.

They took their evening mess and returned to the boats for the last two crossings, to finish the long, weary day in late dusk. Tired men built their campfires on British soil and rolled into their blankets to sleep the dreamless sleep of the exhausted beneath the stars, with their tents still tied and stacked.

With smoke from the morning cookfires rising straight up in the still air, General Hull gathered his staff of officers into his tent, where they sat in canvas chairs while he faced them on his side of a small, scarred table. He spat into the spittoon and wiped his mouth and beard before he spoke.

"Gentlemen, commend the men for their performance yesterday. So far as I know we did not lose a man or a horse or any of our freight."

He glanced at them, waiting for a grin or a smile, or any response at all. There was none, and he went on.

"We have previously detailed the assignments that will be carried out for the next several days. Specifically, Mister McArthur, you will take your men out into the local vicinity to forage for food and observe any activities that might be detrimental to our effort."

McArthur nodded but said nothing, and Hull moved on.

"Mister Cass, you will maintain your detail here at the river. They will construct a temporary dock and maintain the longboats and intercept all traffic on the river. They will allow passage, up the river or down, only to those vessels friendly to our cause. All others will be confiscated and their crews held until it is determined what shall be done with them."

Cass said, "Yes, sir."

"Mister Findlay, your command will construct cannon carriages, and at least every other day a small party will approach Fort Malden to the south to be certain they are not preparing for an attack on us. Be very astute. Do not provoke a fight."

"Yes, sir," Findlay said quietly. "We're prepared."

"You all understand that it is our intent that our presence here will persuade the Canadians and the Indians that with our force near double that of General Brock at Fort Malden, we will have little trouble subduing him and then all others who oppose us. If they see us preparing for such an attack, it is possible they will desert, and perhaps even surrender without need for firing a shot."

For a few moments Hull waited for any response, but there was none. He fumbled for a few seconds, knowing what he wanted to say but not knowing how to say it. He cleared his throat and finally asked, "Now that we are here, do any of you have any response to the plan?"

McArthur raised and dropped a hand. "When do we attack Fort Malden? The men want to know."

Hull locked eyes with him. "That is undetermined. If the Indians and Canadians do not join the British at Fort Malden, we will attack soon. Otherwise, we will have to wait until our own reinforcements arrive. That is all I can say at this time."

"May I tell the men that?" McArthur asked.

"You may. Is there anything else?"

The officers shook their heads.

"You are dismissed."

The officers pushed through the tent flap and each went his own way to his command to give orders. For a long time, Hull sat in his chair with a rising knot of fear in his middle. *Can those men be trusted in an emergency?—what happens if the Indians do join the British?—will they fight?*

He stood and gathered his papers with his thoughts running. *What is General Isaac Brock doing at Fort Malden at this minute? His patrols have reported our crossing by now—what's in his mind?—what does he mean to do about it?—how will he strike back?*

Twenty miles south, on the banks of the Detroit River, British general Isaac Brock sat at his desk facing Major Dennis Courtney. Between them was a large map of central Canada. Brock spoke.

"You're aware our scouts reported the Americans have crossed the Detroit River. They're camped twenty miles north of us on Canadian soil. They're making cannon carriages and doing all they can to influence the citizenry up there against us. It's obvious they're getting ready to attack."

"I know about it, sir."

"Good. Let me tell you why you're here. General Hull is depending on his ability to get help from both north and south." Brock leaned forward to tap the map with a finger, and Courtney rose to lean over the desk, studying the Great Lakes intently.

"Here," Brock said. "Right here. At the top of Lake Huron. Do you see this small island?"

"Yes, sir," Courtney replied.

"The Americans have a fort up there. Fort Michilimackinac. Some call it Mackinac. Hull is certain that in an emergency he can bring troops from there down to here. I intend removing that possibility."

Courtney began to smile, and Brock continued.

"You will pick two hundred men who can travel light and fast, and lead them on a forced march from here to Fort Michilimackinac. As you go, gather as many Canadians and Indians as will volunteer, and attack the fort and subdue it. That will cut off any hope General Hull and his Americans have for help from the north."

"I understand, sir."

Brock went on. "Right now there is an American supply train camped at the River Raisin, across the river and thirty-five miles south."

"I know of it, sir."

"Yesterday a detachment of American soldiers started south to escort them on into Fort Detroit."

"I know of that, too, sir."

"I have already sent a detachment to catch that American relief column and stop them. If we do, Hull is going to conclude that he is trapped. He can't get help from either north or south. From there, we'll just have to wait and see what he does. If necessary, we'll cross the river and attack Fort Detroit."

Courtney was beaming. "Very good, sir. Very good. When do you want me to leave?"

"As soon as you can get your men picked and supplied."

"I can be ready by morning, sir."

"Good. Avoid being seen by the Americans if you can."

"I shall, sir."

"Excellent. Carry on."

In the black stillness of four o'clock AM, the gates of Fort Malden slowly swung open and Major Dennis Courtney sat his gray horse to lead two hundred picked men out into the starry night. Each had his backpack stripped to the bare essentials and his musket and wore the crimson tunic known to every nation in the world. They moved rapidly due east, then north to pass the American camp unnoticed, then back west to cross the St. Clair River into the United States territory of Michigan. As they traveled, they sent men scouting ahead, stopping at the log cabins and the tiny villages, with a single message: Come with us! We're going to drive the Americans from Fort Michilimackinac. Come join us!

As if by magic, armed Canadians began to appear from nowhere to fall in behind the column, eager, ready. On the third day, half a dozen buckskin-clad Indians appeared, followed by others in twos and threes, solemn, stone-faced, armed, some with scalps dangling from their belts. They spoke little English, but it was plain they meant to be rid of the Americans up north.

Courtney's line of march corrected to northwest for two days, then due north in a straight line toward the northern tip of Lake Huron and Michilimackinac Island, just east of the junction of Lake Huron and Lake Michigan. The morning their advance scouting party sighted the shores of the huge lake, the two-hundred-man column that had left Fort Malden had grown into a one-thousand-man column, nearly half of them Indians with tomahawks in their belts and a fierce light in their eyes.

The main column caught up with their scouts by noon. Before dusk, Courtney had scouted the shoreline and knew the concentration of Americans and the location of the fort on the island and had gathered canoes and longboats for twenty miles up and down the lake. All night men cut and stripped trees and lashed cleats to the trunks for use in scaling the walls of the fort, while others silently made the crossing to the island, back and forth. In the dark before dawn the entire force was crouched in the woods facing the American fort, scaling ladders in place.

The Indians talked to each other with bird calls so authentic the British soldiers looked about to locate the birds, with Courtney waiting until his Indian scouts nodded to him that everything was in place. With the eastern sky just beginning to show a sun not yet risen, Courtney took a deep breath and broke from cover.

"All right," he shouted. "Follow me, lads! Follow me!"

Instantly the night was filled with the battle cry of five hundred fighting men and the terrifying screams of nearly five hundred Indians, and within seconds they hit the front gates of the sleeping fort. The scaling ladders came banging against the wall, and with stunned pickets staring in stark disbelief, the first of the redcoats and Indians were over the top and on the parapets and then swarming inside the fort. Within minutes the defending Americans were waving the white flag of surrender, with their muskets on the ground and their hands in the air. Half an hour later, Courtney handed a written message to a sergeant and a picked squad of four enlisted men.

"Leave now and take this back to General Brock. It is critical that he knows we have taken this fort and that we are leaving a small detachment here to hold it while we return with the prisoners of war and about eight hundred Indians and Canadians who have joined us."

The sergeant, still heady from the brief fight, took the document and shoved it inside his tunic. "Yes, sir."

Within the hour the small detail was on its knees in a large, light, birchbark, Huron Indian war canoe, digging the paddles deep into the waters of Lake Huron as they sped south, one mile from the Michigan shoreline. Two days later they beached the canoe on the Canadian side of the Detroit River, six miles above the fort, and disappeared into the forest. The following morning they hailed the pickets at Fort Malden and the gates swung open. Two minutes later they were standing at attention before General Brock. They were disheveled, unshaven, in uniforms that showed days and nights of traveling fast, but their shoulders were square, their chins were sucked in, their heels were clacked together, and their eyes were bright with pride as they stared straight ahead.

"Sir," the sergeant said, "Major Colonel Courtney wished to have this delivered to you earliest." He drew out the document and General Brock took it eagerly. He broke the seal and read it twice before he raised his eyes back to the sergeant.

"You know the contents of this message?"

"No, sir. It was sealed."

"It says your force took Fort Michilimackinac in less than half an hour. You had hundreds of Canadians and Indians join you."

"Yes, sir." The sergeant could not repress a grin. "Good fight, while it lasted, sir."

"I would like to have been there," Brock said. A quizzical look crossed his face. "You came from Michilimackinac in three days?"

"Yes, sir."

"How?"

"Canoe most of the way, sir. Colonel Courtney suggested you were waiting for this report."

"I was. It's vital. When did you eat last? Sleep?"

For a moment the sergeant pondered. "We ate yesterday morning, sir. We slept two days ago. I think."

Brock pointed. "Take your detail to the mess hall and tell the officer in charge I said to prepare anything you want. Then go on over to the barracks and tell the officer you're to be given bunks to sleep. Get a bath. Have the laundry clean your uniforms. You have done well, Sergeant, you and your detail."

"Yes, sir. Thank you, sir." The five-man squad turned on its heels and marched from the room.

Brock stepped back to his desk and spread a map of the area to study it, tracing roads and rivers with a finger. *All right, General Hull—you've lost Michilimackinac to the north. Now we'll see how matters develop here.*

Twenty miles north, on Canadian soil just east of the Detroit River, the American cooks were setting the tripods and great black kettles on chains over cookfires to boil cabbages and turnips for evening mess when a shout came from the men assigned to control the river.

"Longboat approaching from Fort Detroit!"

Inside his tent, General Hull sat bolt upright, then listened as the call came a second time. "Longboat approaching from Fort Detroit!"

Longboat? Who is it? No one was ordered to make the crossing. He stood, clamped his tricorn on his head, and pushed the tent flap aside to walk out into the late afternoon sunlight. He strode rapidly to the makeshift dock his men had built and shaded his eyes against the western sun, studying the oncoming boat. It was thirty yards from the dock before Hull recognized Major Thomas Van Horne sitting on the middle bench. Hull met him as he stepped from the boat onto the dock. Van Horne came to attention and saluted but could not bring his eyes to meet Hull's.

Hull stammered when he asked the fearful question. "Did you bring the column and the supplies from the River Raisin?"

Van Horne glanced about at the silent men staring at him, waiting for his answer. "Sir," he began quietly, "this matter should be handled in your tent."

Hull's face went white, and he ignored Van Horne's plea for privacy. "I'll take your answer here and now. Did you bring them?"

Van Horne straightened and looked directly into Hull's face. There was an edge in his voice. "No, sir. I did not. We had not yet reached them when we were surrounded and attacked by Shawnee Indians with a force far in excess of our own. We think Tecumseh led them. We took cover and formed ranks and returned fire. The battle carried into the second day, when we regrouped and broke through their lines to return to Fort Detroit. We were in a running fight with them for twenty miles before they withdrew and disappeared. There was no possibility of our reaching the supply column. We sustained thirteen casualties. My command is across the river at the fort."

For long seconds Hull stood in shocked silence, his mind paralyzed, unable to function. Then he suddenly came to himself and looked about at the men gathered around, watching, listening, visibly shaken by one of their greatest fears.

Tecumseh! The Shawnee have gathered! How many? When do they strike us?

Only then did Hull realize why Van Horne had requested that he make his report in the privacy of Hull's tent. Within minutes every man in camp would know that Tecumseh and his warriors had surrounded the Ohio supply column and had ambushed Van Horne's relief force— driven them back in a running fight. What had happened to the two hundred men and the supplies south of them on the River Raisin? Did they escape? Make a run—a retreat—for Ohio? Dead? Massacred?

For several seconds the only sounds were of birds in the woods and the lapping of the river against the longboat and the dock. Then Hull said, "I will take your report in my tent." He turned, and Van Horne followed him back up the incline to the camp, and on into Hull's tent where both men took chairs on either side of Hull's small table.

"Give me the details," Hull demanded.

"They caught us at dawn. Came from nowhere. Half a dozen of my men were down before we knew what was going on. For a time it was hand-to-hand before we drove them back into the woods and regrouped and took cover. We could hear them all around us, but we couldn't see them. For most of the day it was them firing from cover and us shooting back at the musket smoke. We tried twice to form and break out of the circle, but each time they were there in numbers at least double ours. We finally broke out the second morning and made a run with them following. We lost thirteen men. Four of them we had to leave behind."

Van Horne stopped and for several seconds looked down to study his hands, working them together, while in his mind he was seeing what Indians do to the bodies of their enemy dead. He raised his eyes. "That's about all. Sir."

"Did you bring back your mail pouch with my written orders in it?"

"No, sir. It was lost in the ambush. The bag and some notes I entered in a log, and a few letters written by the soldiers, and your letter to Secretary Eustis."

"Do the British have it, then?"

Van Horne shook his head. "I don't know. It was there. I don't know if they found it."

Van Horne saw the panic enter Hull's eyes as he spoke. "Return to your command at the fort and make a written report. I will expect it by tomorrow afternoon."

"Is there anything else, sir?"

"No. You are dismissed."

Van Horne walked from the tent and down to the waiting longboat, aware of the men who slowed from their work and eyed him, murmuring quietly. He saw the fear in their faces and the question in their eyes.

Evening mess was finished when General Hull sent a written message to Lieutenant Colonel James Miller.

"Come to my tent at once."

Lanterns were glowing in deep dusk when Miller appeared at the flap of Hull's tent, and Hull invited him in.

"Colonel Miller, you are ordered to lead a force of six hundred to find the supply column now waiting at the Raisin River. As circumstances will allow, either bring them here, or return with them to Ohio. In any event, they must be rescued. Am I clear?"

Miller's pulse raced. "When, sir?"

"Tomorrow, before noon. You can begin selecting your men and supplying them yet tonight."

"Yes, sir."

At midmorning the following day, Miller's hand-picked column marched down the slope to the dock, and the longboats began the monotony of crossing the Detroit River to the Michigan side loaded, to return empty, reload, and repeat it over and over again. It was late afternoon before the last boat emptied on the Michigan side and Miller formed his command into a column, four abreast, each man with his backpack and musket. With Miller mounted on a bay gelding, they had marched six miles before he stopped them in the dusky light and ordered them to build their cookfires for evening mess.

Sunrise found the column five miles farther south, and four hours later Miller reined in his horse to call a fifteen-minute halt. The men left the wagon-ruts they called a road to drop their backpacks and lie flat on the ground, eyes closed, not caring about the mosquitoes and biting insects that came swarming to the scent of their sweat.

The sun was past its zenith when Miller stopped the column for their midday mess of biscuits and fried sowbelly from their backpacks. They drank tepid water from their canteens and once again sprawled in the green undergrowth to rest muscles that had labored for eight hours. Twenty minutes later Miller came to his feet and mounted his horse, and his orders rang in the trees.

"Form the column. We're marching."

Mumbling curses against heat, mosquitoes, officers, and marching, the men stood and reached for their backpacks. An instant later the first high, warbling Shawnee war whoop froze them in their tracks, and then the forest was filled with musket fire while painted Indians came leaping, screaming invectives, stripped to the waist, tomahawks high and swinging. Behind them came red-coated British regulars, muskets firing and bayonets flashing in the sun, cutting down and scattering the Americans in the forest. In the first volley, Miller heard a musket ball strike and felt the give as his horse stuck its nose into the ground and went down with a broken neck, sending Miller rolling.

He scrambled to his feet shouting, "Into the road, into the road! Form in battle ranks! Into the road! Battle ranks!"

The Americans gathered in the road and formed into four ranks, two facing each direction. The two outside ranks took the kneeling position while the two inside ranks remained standing, and they began a rotation, the kneeling ranks firing their volley and then reloading while the standing ranks fired their volley over their heads and reloaded while the kneeling ranks fired their next volley.

As quickly as they had appeared, the Indians and British fell back into the forest, and then the deadly sniping began. The only thing the Americans saw was the blossom of white smoke in the deep green of the thick forest, and then they heard the sharp report of the musket and the whack of the musket ball hitting. In fear and frustration they returned fire at targets they never saw.

Miller was crouched behind the carcass of his dead horse, sword in one hand, pistol in the other, seeing the hopelessness of being caught in the open roadbed by an enemy force that might be double the count of his own. For seconds that seemed an eternity, he watched in the desperate hope the Shawnee and British would fade and disappear as quickly as they had struck, but the cracking of their muskets settled into a steady stream of deadly fire tearing into his men. He saw the terror and the panic rise in their faces, and he knew that within minutes they would bolt and scatter and run—the worst thing they could do.

He made his decision. He leaped to his feet shouting, "Fall back, fall back! Hold your ranks and maintain your fire! Hold your ranks! Walk! Do not run! Keep your heads! Fire in volleys! Steady. Move north, back up the road. Move! Do not break ranks!"

Time was forgotten as the column gave ground, retreating north, firing in volleys, reloading, firing again. Slowly the musket blasts from the forest dwindled, and then became sporadic, and then died altogether. Miller moved among his men on foot, sword still in his hand, bellowing orders.

"Keep moving! Leave the dead! Forget your backpacks! Keep moving!"

Daylight faded into dusk, and dusk yielded to the black of night beneath a quarter-moon, but Miller refused to halt his column. They moved steadily north on the twisting road, afraid to stop, muskets at the ready, listening to the sounds of night in the forest, eyes straining in the darkness, seeing and hearing Indians and redcoats that were not there. The march continued until the eastern skyline changed from black to deep purple and then gray, and when Miller could see individual branches on the trees flanking both sides of the narrow road, he called his first halt. Nervous men held cocked muskets in one hand while they drank from their canteens with the other, and they ignored the gnawing hunger in their bellies and stayed on their feet, waiting for the order to move on. Miller judged time and distance to Fort Detroit and then the mood of his men. Morning cookfires and a hot morning mess were both forgotten; they wanted only to be out of the forest, away from any possibility of the world erupting in their faces with screaming Indians wielding tomahawks and knives.

After a brief rest, Miller called out, "Form the column!" and the weary and wary men moved on into the sunrise. At noon they rounded the last turn in the road. Less than a quarter mile before them was the huge American camp and beyond were the south and west walls of Fort Detroit. Miller led his men into camp, where soldiers gathered to meet them and stare in wide-eyed silence as the incoming column slumped to the ground, dirty, sweated, many of them bloodied, beaten in body and soul. Miller stopped long enough to give orders to the camp cooks to feed them, then walked on to the fort to get the fort surgeon and every nurse he could find to tend his wounded. Then he walked down to the dock and ordered a longboat and crew to carry him across the river, where he went directly to the tent of General William Hull. The corporal standing picket at the tent flat stared in disbelief as he approached.

Miller spoke first. "Is General Hull inside?"

"Yes . . . uh . . . he's . . . yes, sir, he's inside."

Miller did not wait for the corporal to inform Hull of his presence. He pushed the tent flap aside and stepped inside to face Hull, who was seated behind his desk.

General William Hull gaped. "What are you . . . you're supposed to be . . ." He caught himself and started again. "I presume you succeeded in bringing the supplies in from the River Raisin."

Miller shook his head emphatically. "No, sir. I did not. We were ambushed by Shawnee and redcoats."

Hull came to his feet. "You defeated them?"

"No, sir. We returned to the fort."

Hull's head thrust forward. "Retreated?"

"Yes, sir. We were outnumbered and surrounded. It took us overnight to break out. We returned without stopping. We had to leave our dead behind. The men are across the river at the fort right now, being fed. The fort surgeon and nurses are among them, doing what they can. I came here to make this report."

"What of the supply train at the Raisin?"

"I do not know, sir. We never got there."

"How many dead?"

"I don't have an accurate count. Several. Too many."

"Was it Tecumseh? Do you know if it was Tecumseh?"

"They were Shawnee. That's all I know. I don't think we saw more than one hundred of them. They were in the trees. We saw some British regulars with them."

"Do you know the size of their force?"

"No. They were on both sides of us, the full length of our column. It had to be several hundred. Perhaps more than a thousand."

Hull started. "A thousand?"

"It could have been."

Hull licked dry lips and said, "I need a written report. Today."

Miller shook his head. "All due respect, sir, I can't have it today. I've got men across the river that I'm responsible for."

Hull's voice was strained. "By morning. You must have it by morning."

"I will, sir."

"Very well. You are dismissed."

Hull watched Miller disappear through the tent flap, and he stood there with his mind reeling, thoughts running wild. *Thousands! Surrounded by thousands of those savages! Led by Tecumseh! If they attack Fort Detroit . . .*

His thoughts were cut off by the picket at the tent flap. He rapped on the pole and waited until Hull called, "Enter."

"Sir, there's a messenger from up north. Fort Michilimackinac. Says it's urgent."

Hull recoiled. "Send him in."

The bearded civilian was dressed in buckskins and beaded moccasins. He carried a Pennsylvania long rifle, and had a tomahawk thrust through his weapons belt. He faced Hull without saluting, his deep-set eyes steady, firm.

"Yes," Hull said, "what is it?"

"I come to tell you Fort Michilimackinac fell. British and Indians. They got prisoners up there."

Hull's head jerked forward and for a moment his mouth trembled as though he were trying to speak and could not. Finally he muttered, "When?"

The man shrugged. "Six, seven days ago. I lost track."

Hull's mind locked. His thoughts disintegrated and for several moments he could not speak. He forced out the words, "Your name?"

"Samuel Laughlin. I was a scout up there. Hid in the trees. Got out in a canoe at night. Came here. Figgered you ought to know so you can send a force up there to take the fort back. Or at least get the prisoners released."

Hull could not force coherence to his thoughts and shook his head. "You are dismissed."

Laughlin peered at him. "You all right?"

Hull repeated, "You are dismissed."

Laughlin raised a hand and dropped it. "As you wish." He ducked through the tent flap and walked away, down toward the river and his canoe.

For a time Hull stood still, struggling to force some sense of logic and reason into his thoughts. Finally, he straightened and called the corporal at his tent flap.

"Bring colonels Findlay and Cass and McArthur here at once."

"Yes, sir."

While he waited for their arrival, Hull opened the desk drawer and carefully cut a small cud of tobacco. He was just tucking it into his cheek when the three officers entered. He gestured, and they sat in crude chairs opposite him. They could not miss seeing the controlled panic in his face.

"Gentlemen, a scout just reported that Fort Michilimackinac to the north has fallen. Our northern support is gone."

The three colonels remained motionless, their faces dead, and Hull went on. "I've also been informed that a large force of Indians and British attacked and routed Colonel Miller's command, preventing him from finding and rescuing the supply column now waiting at the Raisin River. With Michilimackinac gone, a hive of Indians has been loosed and are swarming down in every direction. My purpose in calling you here now is to receive your advice on a proposal."

He took a deep breath and continued. "As it now stands, the total force of British and Canadians and Indians opposing us is larger than our own—much larger. They are on all sides. To the south at Fort Malden, across the river to the west and north, gathered here to destroy us. The supply train we were depending on is still on the River Raisin. Two columns I sent to relieve them—Van Horne and Miller—were driven back with casualties."

He paused long enough for the information to sink in then proceeded: "I have heard nothing of the efforts of General Dearborn to take control of the Niagara River or Montreal to the east of us and must presume the worst for them. Had that operation succeeded, I would surely have been told. I can only conclude we have no support from the east. We are simply surrounded by hostiles, and must look to ourselves for relief. We must reopen our communication and supply lines back to Ohio. To do that I propose we build blockhouses at Brownstown and on the River Raisin."

He stopped, and a tension began to build among the colonels before he went on.

"When we crossed the river, it was our intent to attack Fort Malden. It is still my intent, but I cannot do it under present conditions. I have no wish to lead a bayonet charge of undisciplined militia to storm walls fourteen feet high, and with twenty-four cannon to protect them. I conclude we have two choices. We must wait until we have sufficient of our own cannon available and in place to breach those walls before we send our troops in, or we must consider a full retreat back to Ohio until we are ready. I need your response."

McArthur glanced at Cass and Findlay for a moment, then turned to Hull. "I have my doubts, sir. The men are sullen. They don't know why we didn't attack Fort Malden the day after we crossed the river. If a full retreat is ordered, clear back to Ohio, I think this entire command will melt away and be gone. They're of the opinion they can't rely on their officers."

Hull caught the thinly veiled insinuation that his command had lost confidence, that they would not support him. For a moment the tension was electric, and then Hull asked, "What are you suggesting? Can you guarantee the obedience of your men to direct orders?"

McArthur hesitated for only a moment. "No, sir. I cannot." He turned to Cass and Findlay, who both shook their heads but remained silent.

Hull leaned forward. "Are they cowards? Afraid of battle?"

"No, sir," McArthur replied, heatedly. "They are not cowards."

Hull went on. "If a retreat to Ohio is unacceptable, then we must get on with the plan to attack Fort Malden. I propose that we cannot consider it until we have artillery in place to breach those walls. Are we agreed?"

"Yes, sir."

"Very well. We will continue preparations to put our artillery in place, and then we will proceed. We'll find out if those men are soldiers or cowards. Am I clear?"

"Yes, sir."

"There is one more matter. Twice I have tried to reach the supply train down on the Raisin. We *must* reopen that road and bring those men here at the earliest time possible. I intend assigning four hundred picked men to try one more time, under command of yourself, Colonel McArthur, and Colonel Cass. Do you agree with me?"

There was a pause before McArthur answered. "Yes."

"Pick your men as soon as possible and leave. Are there any questions?"

There were none.

"All right. Carry on with your assignments. You are dismissed."

Hull watched them leave his tent, and for a time sat without moving, sick in the feeling that he no longer had the respect or the support of his command. With bowed head he pondered, *What of General Brock and his redcoats and Indians—what are they doing?—do we have time to get our artillery ready?*

Twenty miles south, in the headquarters building of Fort Malden, General Brock raised his head at the sound of the knock on his door.

"Enter."

"Sir, there's a Lieutenant Richardson here to see you. He has a bag."

"Send him in."

Short, muscular, uniform rumpled and stained from days in the woods, Richardson approached Brock's desk and saluted. Beneath his left arm was a dirty, tattered canvas bag.

Brock stood. "Yes, Lieutenant?"

"Sorry about my appearance, sir. I just returned from the River Raisin. We found this bag among the things left behind when the Americans retreated. I think it's a mail sack, sir. I thought you might be interested."

Brock reached for it. "Have you looked inside?"

"No, sir. We thought that was for you to do."

"Very good. Is there anything else?"

"No, sir."

"Your force performed admirably. Thank you for delivering the bag. You are dismissed."

Brock was opening the pouch as Richardson closed the door. Among the documents was a sealed letter written by Hull. It was addressed to the Honorable William Eustis, Esq. United States secretary of war, Washington, D.C. Brock puzzled for a moment before he understood that Hull had intended the letter to be delivered by Van Horne to a mail carrier among the Americans stranded on the River Raisin, to be carried back to Ohio, thence on to Washington, D.C. Eagerly, Brock broke the seal and carefully read it, then reread it.

"... troops dispirited ... rebellious ... openly talking against myself ... officers discussing plans to replace me with one of their own ... only the refusal of Colonel Miller to cooperate with them avoided an incident in which I would have been required to hang some of my own officers ... the enlisted are talking of wholesale desertion ... never seen morale so low in any military unit ... I believe they will mutiny if changes are not made immediately ..."

Brock closed his eyes to concentrate, then picked up his quill and began to write. He finished, signed the document, dropped melted wax onto the flap and pressed it with his seal. He closed it inside a leather message satchel, and called to his aide.

"Could you bring an experienced mail rider?"

He sorted through the remainder of the American mail pouch until the mail rider rapped at his door, and Brock called for him to enter.

"You wanted me, sir?"

"Yes. You've carried the mails?"

"Yes, sir."

"You know the routes?"

"Yes, sir. Just about all of them, from Amherstburg to Fort George."

"You know the places to expect American patrols?"

"Yes, sir. And I know just about when the patrols are active. I can avoid them, if that's what you mean."

Brock smiled. "That's exactly what I'm looking for. Only this time, don't avoid them. Time it so you will meet one of them. When you do, turn your horse and make a run, but be certain you lose this leather satchel in plain sight. Can you manage that?"

A puzzled look crossed the rider's face. "Do I understand this right, sir? You want me to lose that satchel so they can find it?"

"Exactly. The trick is, don't get shot doing it."

The rider shook his head. "I don't know what this is all about, sir, but if you want that satchel in their hands, I can do it. And I most certainly intend to keep from getting shot!"

"Good. Excellent. Leave in the morning and report back when you've completed the assignment. And by the way, tell no one of this."

"I understand, sir."

Late the following afternoon, while the redcoated troops were lining up for evening mess, the mail rider rapped on Geneal Brock's door and entered on command.

"Sir," he said, "I just returned and I'm reporting as ordered. The American patrol saw me and I dropped the satchel and made a run. I stopped in the woods long enough to see them pick it up. They have it, sir."

Brock raised a fist in triumph. "Good. Excellent. Was there any trouble? Shooting?"

"Yes, sir. They shot, but me and my horse was moving fast enough I don't think the musket balls caught up with us."

Brock chuckled. "Thank you. Go get in line for evening mess."

"That I can do, sir."

Brock was still smiling as the door closed and he sat down. *Well, General Hull, you should have that fake letter sometime soon. What are you going to do about it?*

He pondered for a time, then called his aide.

"Would you bring the war council here for a brief meeting?"

Within twenty minutes, six officers were gathered around Brock's desk, wondering at being summoned without notice.

"Gentlemen," Brock explained, "get your men ready. It is my guess we are going to march north soon. We'll cross the river about two miles south of Fort Detroit and move on up to surround it and attack."

Smiles appeared, and murmurs of approval were exchanged.

"I don't know precisely when, but soon. Have your men ready to march on half an hour's notice. With artillery. Any questions?"

"No, sir."

Twenty miles north, General Hull watched as the last of four hundred men loaded into the waiting longboats and pushed off into the smooth flow of the Detroit River. They made the crossing, and for a time Hull studied them with his telescope as they unloaded their baggage. In fading twilight they fell into a column and disappeared on the road leading south. Hull turned and walked back to his tent, keenly aware that there was a large, vacant gap in the campground where four hundred of his fighting force had been.

Too few remain, he pondered. *If Brock and the Indians were to come now . . .* He shuddered and did not finish the thought.

The following day, with the heat of the sun directly overhead, a winded sergeant with the leather satchel in his left hand stood impatiently at the flap of General Hull's tent, waiting until the picket gave him permission to enter. Inside, he saluted the general, surprised at the tobacco stains in the man's beard and the spots on his tunic. The general did not stand.

"Yes, Sergeant, what is it?"

"Late yesterday we intercepted a British mail carrier. He dropped this satchel. I thought you might want it, sir."

"What's in it?"

"I don't know sir. I didn't open it."

"Lay it on my desk. Is there anything else?"

"No, sir."

"Dismissed."

The sergeant turned and walked out without looking back, aware there was something very wrong inside the tent.

General Hull spat tobacco juice into the spittoon before he opened the satchel and drew out the single sealed document. It was addressed to Major General Henry Montgomery. Hull's hands were trembling as he broke the seal and read the signature of General Isaac Brock, Commander, Fort Malden. His breathing came shallow as he read.

" . . . advise you that Chief Tecumseh is gathering three thousand

Indian warriors from the Shawnee, Miami, Ojibwa, and Wyandot tribes to arrive here within three days . . . request that you bring your sixteen hundred regulars immediately, primarily to create a fighting force of at least five thousand, and secondarily to help control the Indians . . . it is impossible to predict what they will do once we have taken the force presently on the west side of the Detroit River under command of General William Hull and also Fort Detroit itself, on the east side of the river . . . we must do all possible to prevent a wholesale massacre of the Americans and those friendly to their cause . . . we will move north imminently with our artillery to commence the attack . . ."

It did not occur to Hull that he had never heard of a British Major General named Henry Montgomery, nor did he consider the possibility that no such person existed. Hull sat in shock before he leaped to his feet and charged out the flap of his tent to confront the first officer he saw.

"Assemble the war council in my tent immediately," he ordered. Tobacco juice oozed from the corners of his mouth as he talked. "Get them here. Go! Now!"

The officer backed up one step, staring at the wild look in the eyes of his commanding officer.

"Yes, sir," he stammered and turned to run.

They came singly, until seven of them were in the tent facing Hull. Not one of them saluted. Hull stood rigid on his side of the desk as he spoke. His voice was high, nearly out of control.

"The British are gathering three thousand Indian warriors. Shawnee, Miami, Ojibwa, Wyandot. Sixteen hundred British regulars are joining them. They are going to attack us here, then Fort Detroit. With artillery. Our force is reduced by one third. We must—*must*—get a message to Colonels Cass and McArthur to return! Immediately. Select two riders on the best horses we have and dispatch them within the hour. They are to ride without stopping until they have delivered the message and returned to inform us of it."

He paused to wipe the tobacco juice onto his sleeve. "While the messenger is gone, prepare your men to cross back to Fort Detroit! I do not know if such a crossing will occur, but should it become necessary, time will be against us. We must prepare, *now!*"

In the late afternoon, American patrols returned to make reports. *There's activity out in the woods—saw Indians—red-coated regulars—some horses—six cannon—they're coming!* Reluctant officers carried the messages to Hull, who began to mutter under his breath, spraying tobacco juice, wiping it on his sleeves, giving incoherent orders.

He took evening mess in his tent, ate none of it, and paced the floor, pointing, gesturing, exclaiming to no one. Outside, the pickets and the officers who passed his tent paused in wonder, then continued, fearful their commander had lost his sanity.

The moon had risen and the nighthawks were darting overhead when the messenger hauled an exhausted horse to a stop before Hull's tent and the picket gave him entrance.

"Sir," the winded messenger blurted, "I delivered your message. To Cass and McArthur, personal. Both said to tell you they will not be returning to this camp."

"What!" Hull stood stock still. "Refused to return? Refused a direct order? A written order?"

"All I can tell you, sir, is they said no, and ordered me to return."

"Rouse the camp," Hull shouted. "Everybody. Get the officers here!"

Without a word the messenger fled the tent and ran to his regimental officer. "General Hull's in trouble, sir. He wants the entire camp roused. Now. I have no idea why."

Half an hour later Hull stepped out of his tent to face his war council in the flickering yellow light of great fires.

"Colonels Cass and McArthur refuse to return. We are being surrounded by Indians! Break camp. Now. Tonight. Cross back to Fort Detroit! In the name of the Almighty, we have women and children over there! We cannot leave them to be massacred!"

By morning the crossing was completed. Hull cowered inside the walls of the fort, mumbling incoherently. A woman found him crouched beneath a stair casing, hands thrown over his head to avoid incoming cannonballs that were not there. The woman shook her head and walked away. Talk against Hull was no longer subdued, it was open, rampant.

Within the hour, pickets on the walls shouted, "British and Indians are in the woods. They have artillery!"

Then came the thunder of cannon and the white smoke, and cannonballs ripped into the walls of Fort Detroit. Some cleared the walls, landing on the parade grounds and smashing into the buildings. For thirty minutes the shelling continued, then ceased. When the white smoke cleared, two British soldiers under a white flag marched to the gates of the fort.

"A message from General Isaac Brock," they announced, and delivered it to the American officers waiting at the gate.

Hull was cowering in his private office when the knock came at his door. He did not answer, and the two officers walked in. Hull was on his knees in the corner, his back to the door, his head held in his hands.

"From General Brock, sir."

Hull jerked upright. His hands were shaking so hard he could hardly open and hold the document, and he slumped into the chair behind his desk to hold the message flat while he read it, mumbling incoherently.

" . . . It is far from my inclination to join in a war of extermination, but you must be aware that the numerous body of Indians who have attached themselves to my troops will be beyond control the moment the contest commences . . ."

He read it again, then sat with his head tilted forward, staring at the document. A full minute passed before the officers before him moved, then spoke.

"Sir, are there any orders?"

Hull did not move, nor did he give any sign he had even heard them. One officer looked at the other, and the two of them turned and walked out of the office. They had no sooner reached the parade ground than Hull came barging out behind them.

"Get a white flag!" he raged. "Get it now!"

One officer, a captain, turned to confront him. "A white flag? For what? Are we surrendering the fort?"

"Get it. Now!"

"A white towel? Will that do?"

"A dirty towel?" Hull exclaimed. "Not a dirty towel! A sheet. A clean white sheet!"

Again the officer asked, "Sir, are we surrendering the fort?"

Hull roared, "Get a clean white sheet!"

Minutes later, while Hull knelt in the corner of his office with his back to the door, trembling, talking to the wall, incoherent, three officers opened the gates of Fort Detroit and marched out under a clean white bed sheet, held high on a pole. They were met by a detail of British officers who accepted their swords in surrender, including the fort and every soul within, as well as the men under command of Cass and Findlay, who were not present. Those men were hidden in the woods nearby, close enough to have come to the aid of those inside Fort Detroit, but refusing to do so.

The moon was up, and Americans were on the parade ground outside the headquarters building, openly accusing General Hull of cowardice and treason when Isaac Brock sat at Hull's desk by lantern light with his daily log before him. Thoughtfully he dipped Hull's quill in the ink well and wrote:

"August 16, 1812. This date General William Hull of the United States Army surrendered Fort Detroit and all personnel, present or in the field, to British and Indian forces. The battle was minimal and casualties were light. General Hull is thought to be suffering from mental and physical exhaustion, due to a stroke suffered by him some two years since, with possible effects of alcohol or narcotics. The occupation of Fort Detroit and vicinity brings control of the western front of the American offensive into our hands . . ."

Notes

The very complicated chronology of events by which the United States lost Fort Detroit and dominance on the western front of the three-pronged American invasion of Canada to the British is virtually as herein described. The command of the American force sent from Ohio to Fort Detroit with the intent of crossing the Detroit River to capture the British Fort Malden and then the town of Amherstburg was first offered to General William Hull, governor of Michigan Territory and aging Revolutionary War hero, who refused, then to Jacob Kingsbury who also refused. Finally, President Madison persuaded William Hull to accept it. Hull marched north with a force of about two thousand troops, cutting a new road as he went. The circumstances of that expedition and the misfortune of Hull's papers being seized are accurately represented herein, as is the incident of a supply column being sent, with the subsequent ambush by Indians. The events of this period in the War of 1812 are historically accurate, including the derision in which Hull was held by his command. General Hull's mental and physical collapse is accurately described. His surrender was completed on August 16, 1812. Many of the messages sent by both sides, as they appear herein, are verbatim quotes, or abridgements of verbatim quotes.

See Hickey, *The War of 1812*, pp. 80–84; Stagg, *Mister Madison's War*, pp. 196–205; Wills, *James Madison*, 100–103; Barbuto, *Niagara 1814*, pp. 28–29.

For a painting of British General Isaac Brock see Hickey, *The War of 1812*, p. 83.

The reader may be interested to know that later, after General Hull was returned to the United States in an exchange of prisoners of war, he was tried by a court-martial for cowardice and neglect of duty, convicted, and sentenced to death, with a recommendation, however, for mercy, because of his "revolutionary services and advanced age." President Madison approved the sentence and remitted the punishment. See Hickey, *The War of 1812*, p. 84.

CHAPTER XVII

 $\mathcal{T}$ he sound of the front door opening and closing brought Kathleen Dunson to a standstill in her kitchen as she listened for the familiar sound of Matthew's footsteps quietly crossing the parlor floor.

"Matthew?" she called softly.

"Me," he answered in a whisper. "Children sleeping?"

"Yes. All but the twins."

She twisted the handle to close the grate-setting on the stove firebox and walked to the archway into the dining room as Matthew came from the parlor. For a moment she felt the slight rise inside, as she always did when he appeared, and in the same moment she saw the tiny signs that more than twenty years of marriage had taught her. He had come home pensive, preoccupied, troubled.

She spoke first. "Sit down. There's warm ham and potatoes in the oven."

"Good. I could eat."

She turned back into the kitchen. "Small wonder, coming home this late."

"Things happened," he replied. He took off his coat and hung it on the back of one of the chairs at the dining table, then tugged the knot loose on his cravat and draped it over the coat. He sat down at the great table, silent, listening to the sounds of the oven door and plates and silverware, and then she walked back into the dining room with a plate of steaming ham and potatoes in one hand and a pitcher of buttermilk in the other. She set them before him and for a moment took deep satisfaction in the light that came into his eyes.

"Be right back," she said and moments later returned from the kitchen with sliced bread, butter, and a bowl of applesauce.

"That enough?" she asked.

He looked at her with the beginnings of a smile. "For starters."

She stood beside him while he bowed his head and returned thanks for the bounties of life, then sat down in a chair beside him, feeling that rare joy known only to wives and mothers, of seeing the pleasure in his face as he gratefully ate what her hands had prepared. He was spreading home-churned butter on home-baked bread when the sound of a single chime came from the large, engraved clock on the parlor mantel, crafted by Matthew's father thirty years earlier.

Matthew paused. "Nine-thirty?"

A wry smile crossed her face. "Nine-thirty PM."

He understood the gentle reprimand. "Sorry. Things happened. Where was it the twins were going tonight?"

"The theatre. *Hamlet.*"

"With those two young men?"

Kathleen nodded. "Linda with Robert Littlefield, Louise with Charles Penn. All four together. They'll be all right."

"Home by midnight?" Matthew asked.

"I told them. They'll be here."

Kathleen leaned forward to straighten her gray ankle-length housedress and rub her feet through her knitted woolen slippers. "It's been a long, hot day."

Matthew bit into the bread.

Kathleen continued. "Brigitte came by. She'd been at Margaret's. Said your mother had another of those spells today. Couldn't keep her balance."

Matthew paused. "Get her to the doctor?"

"The doctor came to her. Gave her some medicine—I don't know what. Told her to stay off her feet as much as she could for a day or two."

"Someone with her now?"

"Brigitte for tonight. My turn tomorrow night if she needs it."

Matthew asked, "Should I go over to see her? Now?"

Kathleen shook her head. "She's sleeping. I think the doctor gave her medicine to help her sleep."

Matthew continued eating, and Kathleen waited for a time before she interrupted. "Got a minute to talk?"

Matthew stopped eating, waiting, and Kathleen went on.

"Part of you is still at the office. Something wrong?"

Matthew laid his knife and fork on his plate and straightened in his chair. For a moment he looked into her eyes and then spoke.

"It's Adam. You know he left about three weeks ago. To go north, up to the Great Lakes. Converted our ship *Margaret* to a gunboat and sailed up to help on Lake Ontario. We haven't heard from him. That's not like Adam."

She shrugged. "There has to be a good reason. Maybe the mail was lost. Things happen in war."

Matthew leaned back in his chair. "There's more. There was talk down at the docks this afternoon. A crew just back from the Great Lakes. They said the British overran Fort Detroit three days ago. Fort Detroit is far to the west. East of Fort Detroit, our troops at Niagara and Montreal are in trouble. Bad. If that's all true, Adam could be a prisoner of war right now. I doubt it, but it's possible."

Concern came into Kathleen's face. "Isn't there something our army can do about it? Send someone up to find out what's happening up there?"

Matthew drew a deep breath, and Kathleen saw the look in his eyes that said he dreaded what had to be said next.

"That's not all. You know that John's been gone since August second with Captain Hull on the *Constitution*."

Kathleen stopped moving, waiting for Matthew to continue.

"Their orders were to seek and destroy British men-o'-war. He's been as far north as Newfoundland and the Gulf of Saint Lawrence. If it's true we've lost Fort Detroit, and the campaigns for Niagara and

Montreal are in trouble, was he up there when it all happened? And if he was, did the British take the *Constitution?* I'm worried about what might have happened to him."

Kathleen's breathing slowed, and Matthew saw the mortal fear leap in her eyes as she spoke with words that came slow, measured. "Matthew, are you telling me everything? Is John dead?"

He shook his head and raised a hand. "No one on the docks said anything that even suggested that. I think he's all right. I know the captain of the *Constitution. Isaac* Hull. One of our best. Remember? Five British frigates couldn't catch him. It's near certain the *Constitution* is all right. It's just a worry."

Kathleen sat in silence watching Matthew finish his supper, then stacked the dishes to carry them into the kitchen, Matthew following. She poured steaming water from the stove into a small wooden basin and washed them while Matthew wiped them one at a time and set them in their place in the cupboard. He carried the tub of dishwater out the kitchen door to throw it into the dark backyard while Kathleen carried the buttermilk and ham to the root cellar.

Back inside the house, in the light of the lamps, Matthew yawned. "Getting late."

"You go on to bed. I'll wait for the twins."

"I'll wait with you."

"No need. I'll knit."

"Sure?"

"You go ahead."

"I'll bank the fireplace before I go," he said. In the cold of winter or the heat of summer, the fire in the fireplace had to be maintained if there was cooking to be done. It was there the pots were hung from arms that swung out or in. Matthew used the small brass shovel to heap the coals in a single pile against the rear wall of the parlor fireplace, replaced it in its rack with the brush, tongs, and poker, straightened, and called back to Kathleen, still in the kitchen.

"Want to come for evening prayers?"

They walked quietly down the hall into their bedroom and knelt together at the side of their bed with their heads bowed and hands clasped before them while Matthew softly prayed.

"Almighty Father of us all, we thank thee for the blessings of this day. . . ."

He leaned to gently kiss his wife, and she rose as he sat down on the bed to remove his shoes.

"I'll wake you when the twins get home if anything's wrong," she said.

He nodded, and she turned to walk out the door and close it behind, then on down the shadowy hall to the parlor. She opened the bottom door of the great china hutch to get her knitting bag and sat down in her overstuffed chair to draw out the two long bamboo needles and the half-finished set of tiny blue booties for her grandson, James. The needles began to click in a steady rhythm as she mechanically continued, unconsciously counting as she looped the yarn on the needles—knit three, purl two—with her thoughts running.

Adam—up where the British are in control—John—somewhere on the Atlantic Ocean hunting for British warships to fight—has his ship found them?—has there been a battle?—is he all right?—is he wounded?—dead?

She swallowed against the anxiety in her mother's heart. *Where is he tonight? Where?*

At ten o'clock, beneath clouds gathering in the black Atlantic sky seven hundred fifty-two miles due east of Boston, John Dunson stood on the quarterdeck of the USS *Constitution,* feet spread slightly for balance against the gentle undulations of the ship, face tipped up, intently studying the position of the stars. It all hinged on the two stars that formed one end of the big dipper. Extend the straight line formed by the two, and it pointed directly at the North Star. Always. All other constellations in the summer sky in the northern hemisphere—Scorpius, Orion—related to the North Star.

John made his reckoning of where the ship was, then stood for a time feeling the freshening wind quartering in from the northwest and felt the rise and fall and roll of the ship as she sped southeast, sails full. He listened to the whisper of the wind in the rigging, and the murmur of the thirty-foot curl the frigate was cutting in the dark water, and he felt the rise of spirit that binds men to the sea.

He flinched at the unexpected sound of the voice of Captain Isaac Hull behind him.

"Mister Dunson, where are we?"

"Just about seven hundred fifty-five miles due east of Boston, sir."

Hull walked up beside him, hands clasped behind his back, peering into the heavens. He raised one hand to point. "North Star. Interesting. Locate that star and all other things in the heavens fall into place."

"Yes, sir."

A little time passed with both men silent, studying the black vastness above, conscious of the profound and fragile smallness of themselves and their ship on the wide ocean, beneath the eternity overhead. Hull once again gestured to the North Star, and there was a quiet reverence in his voice.

"A little like life, wouldn't you say?"

For a time John did not answer, and then he said, "I would, sir. If you can find your own North Star."

"Hmmm," Hull murmured. "Well said."

For a time the two men stood together, not as captain and navigator, but as companions. Two small men on a tiny ship, unexpectedly caught up in the riddle of who they were, from whence they had come to arrive in this life, and whither they were going when they left it. They understood that in the mortal world all around them there was good and there was evil, and each had its champion; and every human being on earth must choose between them in the time they were allowed to remain. But what then? The Almighty would judge their lives, and they would be consigned to either heaven or perdition? For all eternity? What would they find in heaven? Loved ones? Would they recognize them? And what of perdition? Burning in eternal flames, but never consumed?

The power of it held them in silence for a time before it began to recede, and as it dwindled John's arm suddenly shot up, pointing.

"Lights! There! Dead ahead!"

Instantly Hull was at the railing, searching, and suddenly he exclaimed, "There. I see it." He shouted up to the watch in the crow's nest, "Ship dead ahead! Can you see her?"

Seconds later the answer came from seventy feet above. "Yes, sir. Less than two miles. Coming in dead on the bow."

Hull called to the helmsman, "Hold course until we intercept that ship."

"Aye, sir."

The deck crew on duty crowded the rail, watching the running lights of the distant ship draw closer, straining to see the flag she was flying, knowing they could not in the black of night. First mate Erling Strand, tall in the darkness, bolted up the few steps to the quarterdeck, still buttoning his tunic, wide-eyed.

"Trouble?" he exclaimed.

Hull pointed. "Unidentified ship."

Strand bobbed his head and took his place beside Hull.

Steadily the two ships closed, with Captain Hull watching, judging time and distance. He spoke once again to the helmsman.

"Port for about three minutes, then starboard. Bring us across her bow at fifty yards."

"Aye, sir."

He turned to the deck crew. "Get ready to spill the sails."

"Aye, sir." Barefoot sailors climbed the rope ladders in the blackness and walked the ropes on the arms crabwise, ready to loose the sails and spill the wind. The *Constitution* leaned as she made the left turn, then straightened to resume her course due south, then leaned again as she made the right turn that brought her in from the starboard side of the oncoming ship. Hull judged the two vessels to be about one hundred yards apart when he called up to the men in the rigging, "Spill the sails!"

The sails shifted to empty the wind, and the frigate slowed in the water. It was fifty yards in front of the unidentified ship when it stopped, and the oncoming vessel also slowed to a stop.

Hull raised his horn. "Hello the unidentified ship. I am the USS

Constitution. Captain Isaac Hull. Recently out of Boston. Identify your-self. Identify yourself." The shout seemed strangely loud in the darkness.

Seconds passed before the answer came. "I am the *Trinidad.* Captain Theodore Pullman. Privateer. Salem, Massachusetts."

Hull looked at Strand, then John, and both men nodded their heads. The voice was decidedly Yankee. The ship was friendly.

"Do you need assistance?" Hull called.

"No. We are sound. Are you?"

Hull answered, "Yes. We are sound. Have you seen British ships to the south?"

"Yes. One. Yesterday. Due south. We avoided her. Are there British ships to the north?"

"We have seen none in the past two days."

The *Trinidad* answered, "We shall proceed north to our home port."

On Hull's orders, the *Constitution* shifted her sails, and they caught the wind, and she made her turn south. Without further exchange the two vessels passed in the night, traveling opposite directions. Strand turned to Hull.

"Sir, is it our intention to find that British ship to the south of us?"

"If we can."

The deck crew changed twice in the night, while Hull and Strand relieved each other on four-hour intervals. John remained by the helms-man, taking his bearings by the stars, holding the ship on her course due south. The morning star faded, and the eastern sky brightened to give definition to a world with a fresh northwest wind, driving the frigate south on a choppy sea. Morning mess was finished when the first clouds appeared, moving fast in the wind. By midmorning the gather of clouds covered the sun, and the crew of the *Constitution* glanced upward, judging whether they were to have heavy weather. The midday mess was finished and the deck crew was changing when the shout came from the crow's nest.

"Sail! Two miles south. Bearing east southeast!"

Every man on the main deck of the *Constitution* jammed against the railings at the bow of the ship, shading his eyes to peer south.

Hull called to the crow's nest, "Can you make out her colors?"

"No, sir. She's not flying colors."

John exclaimed, "She has to be the British gunboat the *Trinidad* reported!"

Hull pursed his mouth for a moment. "We'll find out. Mister Dunson, can you give me our exact location?"

"Yes, sir. I shot the sun ten minutes ago. Latitude forty-one degrees thirty minutes north, fifty degrees west."

"Very good." He turned to Strand. "Add another reef to the top sails. Let's see if we can catch her."

Within minutes, her bow knifing through the rough, wind-tossed Atlantic, masts creaking under the pressure of sails full and billowing, the fleet American frigate was gaining on the distant ship. Time passed without notice as the gap between the racing ships shortened. The hidden sun was slipping toward the western horizon when the leading ship suddenly sent her colors to the top of her mainmast.

The Union Jack! The red, white, and blue crosses of the Union Jack!

A spontaneous shout erupted aboard the *Constitution,* and Hull called his orders to Strand.

"Hoist our colors!"

Within minutes the stars and stripes were snapping in the heavy wind at the top of the mainmast, and there was controlled excitement in Hull's voice.

"Mister Strand, have the gun crews stand by for loading. Solid round shot."

"Aye, sir."

The men were sprinting to their guns before Strand could repeat the order. John was standing on the quarterdeck, between Hull and the helmsman, extending his telescope to study the movement of the crew on the British ship and trying to make out her name, carved beneath the small windows into the captain's quarters in the stern. Both Hull and Strand extended their telescopes, straining to make out the name.

"*Guerriere,*" John exclaimed. "She's the *Guerriere!* Captain James Dacres! She's one of the five that couldn't catch us four weeks ago!"

A light came into Hull's face. "So she is," he said quietly. "Let's see how well she does in a fair fight."

For a time the American frigate held its pace, slicing through the whitecaps, gaining on the British gunboat, with Hull, Strand, and John watching every move of the crew and the changes in heading taken by the ship. First port, then starboard, then back to port. Then suddenly the cannon on the stern of the *Guerriere* blasted and the white smoke billowed and the cannonballs came humming to raise fifteen-foot geysers in the sea, forty yards short of the *Constitution*, with the American frigate holding her pace, closing fast. The British gunboat turned hard to bring the cannon on her port side to bear, and again the guns roared and the shot came whistling. Two struck the hull of the *Constitution*, while the remainder passed over her decks to punch a few holes in the rigging while the American crew involuntarily ducked and instinctively turned to watch the shot fall into the sea beyond them.

The British ship turned sharply to starboard, this time to bring her starboard cannon to bear, and again her guns roared and the smoke billowed, but none of the cannonballs hit. Again she turned sharply, back to port, to bring her reloaded cannon to bear, and Hull watched intently as they fired, and again the shot plowed harmlessly into the rough sea.

Hull turned to John and his helmsman. "She's setting a course that swings back and forth to bring her guns to bear, first port, then starboard, to rake us. Set a course to counter her moves! When she turns to port, we turn to starboard."

"Aye, sir."

He spoke to Strand. "Have the gun crews fire only occasionally, when our guns come to bear. Let them think we are inept with our cannon."

"Aye, sir."

Light was beginning to fade beneath the dark clouds with Hull hunched forward, watching every move of the British vessel when suddenly he pointed. "A mistake! She made a mistake! We can come broadside from her port beam!" He spun in the wind to shout, "Mister Helmsman, bring us broadside on her port beam."

The *Constitution* cut sharply to starboard, then straightened, and her port side passed the stern starboard of the British ship, with the twenty-two American port-side guns coming to bear in order as they passed. As they did, the heavy cannon blasted in sequence, and the few British guns that could be brought to bear, answered. The *Constitution* raced ahead, passing the *Guerriere* broadside, and again the great guns on both ships bucked and roared and the shot came humming through the white smoke that was whipped to the south by the wind whistling in the rigging. An American seaman saw two twenty-four pound British cannonballs slam into the reinforced side of the Humphreys frigate and rebound to fall harmlessly into the sea.

"She's got sides like *iron*," he exclaimed. The seaman next to him turned to stare at him, then shouted to others nearby, "Old Ironsides! The British can't sink Old Ironsides!"

The crews on both ships were frantically reloading, but the American crews were ten seconds faster than the British, and they delivered their second broadside at near point-blank range. The shot tore into the railing and the British gunports and crews, and three thirty-two pound cannonballs smashed into the mizzenmast to cut it nearly through. Captain James Richard Dacres watched white-faced as the mast toppled over the starboard quarter to knock a huge hole in the deck and swing the crippled ship around against her own helm. The British ship slowed, unable to maintain speed, only partially responding to the rudder.

Quickly Hull turned to see the damage to his own ship, and his shoulders slumped in relief. The *Constitution* was sound, virtually unharmed. Hull shouted to his helmsman.

"Hard to port! Bring her around with the starboard guns coming to bear!"

The American frigate swung hard, and the starboard guns came to bear in raking order, and once more ripped loose in sequence. The cannonballs cut the arm on the mainmast in half, and the main sails ripped free to flutter in the wind.

"Hard to starboard," Hull shouted, and the *Constitution* swung past the bow of the crippled *Guerriere* to once again rake her with her port guns, so close that the bowsprit of the British frigate passed over the quarterdeck of the American ship, and as the *Constitution* turned away, her rigging caught foul in the fallen mizzenmast of the British ship. The hawsers snapped tight and held, and the American frigate was jerked to a halt in the wind-driven seas with the *Guerriere's* starboard bow slammed tight against her own port stern. Both ships were wallowing in the heavy seas, side by side, unable to separate.

The British guns opened up on the stern of the American ship, and in minutes the windows of Captain Hull's quarters were blasted away and the interior of the small quarters was burning. John leaped from the quarterdeck to the main deck and grabbed two seamen by their shirt fronts. They quickly filled four buckets with water before he led them down into the smoke and flames of Hull's tiny quarters. They threw the water and then beat the flames with blankets until they were gone, then sprinted back to the main deck to hear the cracking of muskets from the decks on both ships as the crews faced each other, each trying to board the other ship, both finding that the pitch and roll of the ships in the heavy seas made it impossible. Seamen on both ships were staggering back, hit, wounded, dying, from the banging muskets.

It happened suddenly. One moment Captain Dacres was shouting with his sword held high above his head, and the next moment the sword clanged onto the deck as he staggered back and slammed into a hatch cover, then fell forward to his knees and slumped face down onto the deck of his ship, an American musket ball lodged in his back. His life hung in the balance. Within moments the wind and the wallowing seas had turned the ships to tear them apart. As they separated, the shattered mizzenmast on the British frigate fell into the sea, and as it did, the ship tilted violently to starboard. Her main-deck guns could not hold in the gun ports. They rolled to the starboard side and smashed through the railing to fall into the sea with the mizzenmast. The *Guerriere* was mortally wounded, a defenseless hulk at the mercy of the harsh Atlantic and the guns of the American *Constitution*. Her captain was down, unconscious, battling for his life.

Hull drew the *Constitution* to a stop a scant fifty yards from the stern of the British frigate to get a damage report to his own ship and start repairs, and to give the *Guerriere* time to take stock of her defenseless position. The report came quickly. The ship was sound. Some of the yards had taken damage, but all were still functional. All masts were sound. The hull was unharmed. He had lost seven of his crew, with seven others wounded. The *Constitution* was in all particulars seaworthy and her crew sufficient to man her in all weather.

Aboard the *Guerriere,* almost every officer on the quarterdeck had gone down in the first volley of musket fire from the American marines. Twenty-three were dead, fifty-six wounded. Captain Dacres was unconscious. His first lieutenant, Bartholomew Kent, and his master, Robert Scott, were down, along with two master's mates and their young lieutenant midshipman—all from American musket fire. None of the officers were coherent, nor could they take command.

At seven o'clock PM, the *Guerriere* struck her colors. It was over.

Cautiously, Hull brought the *Constitution* alongside and attempted to board the dying ship with medical help but was driven back by the wind and the surging seas. He remained close to the British ship through the night, watching her running lights, ready to try the impossible should she begin to sink, calling to her with his horn every half hour. The wind lessened during the night, and by four o'clock the ships were riding on smoother waters. Dawn brought the realization that the *Guerriere* was sinking. She would not remain afloat through the day.

Hull gave his orders, and morning mess was forgotten as his crew tied the two ships together and began the transfer of prisoners and the ship's log and other important papers and the war chest from the *Guerriere* to the *Constitution.* By three o'clock in the afternoon, beneath clear skies, they had completed their work. Hull sent a squad of ten men onto what was left of the British man-of-war with torches, and waited while they disappeared below decks for ten minutes, then reappeared to come back aboard the American ship. They released the hawsers binding the ships together, the *Constitution* unfurled her sails, they caught the wind, and she distanced herself from the column of black smoke rising from the burning hulk.

Fifteen minutes later, what was left of the *Guerriere* exploded to blow shards of metal and wood two hundred feet in the air and scatter it for half a mile on the sea. Hull gave all British seamen the right to stand at attention on the deck of the American ship to bid their own ship farewell.

It was in the evening, after mess, that Captain Dacres opened his eyes. It took several moments for him to understand he was in the burned-out quarters of Captain Hull, in Captain Hull's bed, with the American surgeon seated by his side, watching his every move, counting the slow regularity of his breathing.

Dacres cleared his throat and tried to speak.

"You lie still," the old, gray doctor said.

"Bring Captain Hull," Dacres murmured.

Five minutes later, Hull entered the quarters with John Dunson at his side and knelt beside his own bed to look into Dacres's eyes.

"You wanted me, sir?"

The wounded captain's voice was faint. "Yes. Should I not survive, I want you to know. You have treated us as a brave and generous enemy should. We have had the greatest care. You have seen to it we did not want for the smallest trifle that was in your power to provide. My log and my letter to His Majesty's Navy shall so state, if I am allowed to live long enough to make the entries."

Hull looked into his face. "I gave you nothing you did not deserve. Nothing you would not have done had the fortunes of battle fallen in your favor, sir."

A faint smile formed on Dacres's lips, and his eyes closed as he drifted into sleep. Hull waited until the surgeon nodded that Dacres would survive, then made his way back to the quarterdeck with John following. The second night crew had taken their stations when John Dunson took his bearings from the stars, with Captain Hull standing next to the helmsman.

Hull spoke. "May I know where we are, Mister Dunson?"

"Yes, sir. Just about seven hundred sixty miles east and a little south of Boston."

"In miles, not far from where we were this time last night."

"No, sir, not far."

"In life? Experience?" He shook his head gently. "We came a long way in the last twenty-four hours. Thirty brave men dead. Sixty-three wounded. A great ship on the bottom of the Atlantic."

John's answer came quietly. "Yes, sir. A long way."

Hull cleared his throat. "Mister Dunson, is the North Star still there?"

"As always."

"Interesting. Wouldn't you say?"

"Yes. Interesting."

Notes

On the night of August 18, 1812, the United States naval frigate *Constitution*, under command of Captain Isaac Hull, was on a mission to search the Atlantic seaboard for British warships and engage them. He had been as far north as Nova Scotia and Newfoundland and the Gulf of Saint Lawrence before returning to waters off the American coast. That night he sighted an American privateer that was out of Salem, Massachusetts, who reported a British man-of-war to the south. Captain Hull sailed south in search of the British frigate, and at two o'clock PM on August 19, sighted her two hundred fifty miles due east of Boston, in overcast, windy weather that caused heavy seas. He engaged her. The longitude and latitude of the *Constitution* at the time is as recorded in this chapter.

The battle between the two warships is as described herein, with the *Guerriere* traveling what would be called a zigzag course, with the *Constitution* countering her moves. The ships fired a few rounds at each other with little damage. Then the American ship came alongside the British ship and they both fired broadsides. The British ship took much the worst of it, with her mizzen-mast destroyed, lying at an awkward angle on her deck. The American ship came back around and continued with broadsides that cut the British ship to pieces and toppled her mainmast; however, the two came into such close proximity that the bowsprit of the British ship was thrust over the quarterdeck of the American ship. Shortly thereafter, their riggings became entangled, locking the British ship against the American ship, toward the stern. The British cannon blasted the captain's quarters and set them afire. The flames were not extinguished by John Dunson, who is a fictional character, but by an American Lieutenant Hoffmann.

During the time the ships were locked together, musket fire from both crews was exchanged, with losses and wounded on each side—seven Americans dead, seven wounded, twenty-three British dead, fifty-six wounded. An American seaman saw a British cannonball bounce off the side of the *Constitution* and exclaimed, "Her sides are made of iron!" Others heard it, and the legend of "Old Ironsides" was born.

Among the severely wounded on the British ship was the captain, James Richard Dacres, who took an American musket ball in his back. All officers on the British quarterdeck were hit by American musket balls. Then the ships were torn apart by the heavy seas, and the *Constitution* drew off a short distance to take stock of her losses. The ship was sound, and her dead and wounded did not affect her ability to man the ship. The *Guerriere*, however, had two of her masts shot off, and one of them finally fell into the sea, tipping the ship so violently that her cannon fell overboard. She was a mortally wounded, helpless hulk. Because of the heavy seas, it was impossible for the *Constitution* to transfer the British crew to safety after the battle, but Captain Hull stayed close to the sinking *Guerriere* through the night, and when morning brought smoother seas, he transferred the entire British crew to the safety of his own ship.

Captain Dacres survived his serious back wound, and his official report to the British navy of his loss of the *Guerriere* included praise for Captain Hull for his care of the British crew. The statements appearing in this chapter by the wounded Captain Dacres to Captain Hull are very close to a verbatim quotation of how they appeared in his official report.

For a definition of the nautical terms used herein, such as *frigate, topsail, quarterdeck,* etc., see the glossary in Malcomson, *Lords of the Lake,* pp. 343–52.

See also Roosevelt, *The Naval War of 1812,* pp. 51–54, and for a detailed diagram of the strange zigzag route of both ships, see page 53; Wills, *James Madison,* p. 115; Hickey, *The War of 1812,* pp. 93–94.

CHAPTER XVIII

*E*li Stroud sat rigid in an upholstered leather chair. Nearing sixty years of age, he was still uncomfortable in a black suit with a white ruffled shirt and black cravat, and black, square-toed shoes with silver buckles. Uncomfortable to be in a private library with four walls of books in the Executive Mansion, waiting for President James Madison. Uncomfortable to be in a teeming city, uncomfortable among politicians and government personnel who shared the common façade of wooden smiles and forced pleasantries in their desperate compulsion to be all things to all people. He moved uneasily in his chair, then slipped his hand to his inside coat pocket to touch the letter he had received from Billy Weems telling him that President James Madison had urgently requested him to come to Washington, D.C. There was no reason given.

The sound of rapid footsteps made by small feet in the long hall-way brought him from his chair, and he turned to face the door as President Madison entered the room—small, quick, his delicate hand thrust out to Eli.

"Mister Stroud! I can't tell you how grateful I am to have you here. How are you? Your family?"

Reaching to shake the thin, small-boned hand, Eli nodded. "We are all well, sir." The president's handshake was surprising firm. "And you?"

"I'm well, thank you." Madison gestured. "Would you care to be seated?"

They sat down in matching leather upholstered chairs on the same side of a large, ornately carved desk, and Madison did not waste words.

"The war effort to the north of us is not going well. I'm sure you know of the surrender of General Hull a month ago at Fort Detroit."

Eli was leaned slightly forward, watching every expression, listening to every inflection. "I do."

"Since that time I've learned of some problems within our military forces up there that could become catastrophic. Are you aware of the strategy Congress approved for the conquest of Canada? Did Mister Weems inform you?"

"In general, yes. So far as I know, it was intended that our military move north at Niagara to take Fort George and probably Queenston, and at the same time to move across the St. Lawrence to take Montreal."

"That is correct." Madison moved in his chair and for a moment collected his thoughts. "The trouble we're having concerns the officers that were appointed to carry out the plan." He rose abruptly from his chair to stride around the desk, open a drawer, and draw out a large map. He spread it on the desk and gestured to Eli, and the two men hunched over the map. It took Eli just a moment to recognize the great north waterway—the five Great Lakes and the Saint Lawrence drainage to the Atlantic Ocean.

Madison set his finger firmly on the Niagara River, connecting Lake Erie with Lake Ontario, with Canada on the west side, and the state of New York on the east side of the river. At the north end of the river, British Fort George stood on the west side, facing American Fort Niagara on the east. The British town of Queenston Heights stood on sheer bluffs that dropped two hundred forty feet to the river, six miles to the south of Fort George. Opposite Queenston Heights, on the American side, was the village of Lewiston. At the south end of the river, British Fort Erie on the west side faced Buffalo, New York, on the east side.

"The root of the problem is here," Madison said, tapping his finger on Fort Niagara and then on Queenston Heights. "Let me try to explain it." He paused to collect his thoughts and his words.

"The man selected to take command of the entire operation is Henry Dearborn. He is a retired major general in the Continental Army and has served as secretary of war. Months ago he was ordered to coordinate attacks on the British Fort George on the Niagara River, and a second attack further east on Montreal." Madison stopped for a moment, then tossed one hand in the air to let it drop. "Nothing happened!" he exclaimed. "We could not understand his failure to take action until we learned that he misunderstood his orders and thought his only responsibility was Fort George. Somehow, he thought someone else was to have responsibility for the attack on Montreal. Then we learned that on August 8 he had struck an armistice with the British, which gave him time to do some things he thought necessary."

Eli raised a hand in alarm, and Madison stopped as Eli spoke. "Dearborn made an armistice with the British?"

Madison answered, "We were absolutely shocked! I found out about it and disavowed it altogether on August fifteenth, and ordered Dearborn to organize and execute the attacks according to his previous orders."

Madison stopped and watched Eli's eyes until he saw understanding, then went on.

"The man chosen to lead the attack at Niagara is General Stephen Van Rensselaer. He is the forty-eight-year-old commander of the state militia up there. He has had no combat experience, but he has brought in one of his kinsmen by the name of Colonel Solomon Van Rensselaer to advise him. The kinsman has had years of experience in the Indian wars up there and served as adjutant general for the state of New York."

Again Madison paused, and Eli waited as the president chose his words.

"The man who shares command of the military forces up there with Solomon Van Rensselaer is named Alexander Smyth. He is a general in the army and has command of all federal troops. I am sorry to say, General Smyth tends to be . . . vain, shall we say? Vain and a bit pompous. He has declared that he will not place himself under command of General Van Rensselaer under any circumstance for the reason that Van Rensselaer is a commander in the state militia and Smyth is in command of United States regulars. Smyth is insulted at the thought of subordinating federal troops to state control. The United States War Department ordered him to do so, but he defied the order."

Glancing at Eli, Madison saw the disbelief in Eli's eyes. "You have it right, Mister Stroud. Our General Alexander Smyth defied the United States government." He gestured, and the two men returned to their chairs before Madison went on.

"Are you beginning to understand my concerns?"

Eli nodded. "It sounds like you've got a few problems with your officers up there. Dearborn doesn't understand his orders and thinks he can make armistices for the United States. Stephen Van Rensselaer doesn't have the combat experience he needs, and he's relying on Solomon Van Rensselaer. Smyth sees himself as superior to his commanding officer and the U.S. War Department." Eli shook his head. "I doubt I've ever heard of a worse arrangement among men who are preparing to invade a foreign country."

Madison nodded. "You see the core of the problem, but I haven't told you how it all came about. The one word answer to that is, *politics.* Dearborn is a Republican. General Van Rensselaer is a Federalist. The New York continental soldiers are largely Republicans. The New York militia are almost all Federalists. Need I say more?"

A look of amazement crossed Eli's face. "No. The Federalists are strong against the war and the Republicans are in favor of it. You say you've got a Republican general in command of a Federalist general, who is in command of both Republican and Federalist troops? Can anyone explain that?"

Madison shook his head ruefully and repeated himself. "Politics. Now let me get to the worst of it. The army we have up there has become all too aware of the dissention among its commanding officers. A division is rapidly developing, with some troops supporting one officer, some another. Some are openly calling General Dearborn "Granny" because of his age and his health. He is sixty-one years of age and has become fat and complacent. There is talk that some soldiers will not leave United States soil to fight. Some predict a wholesale mutiny."

Madison drew and slowly exhaled a great breath. "That brings us to why I've asked for you. I have two sealed documents, bearing my signature, to be delivered by someone independent of all the politics. I believe you are the man. The documents are orders for General Dearborn at Albany and for General Van Rensselaer at Fort Niagara. Then I will need you to stay at Fort Niagara for a short time to watch developments and return with a written report that I can depend on."

He stopped and his eyes were pleading. "Can you do this?"

Eli stared at his hands for a moment. "How soon?"

"Immediately. As you well know, winter in those north woods is approaching. Time is critical."

Silence held for a time while Eli considered. "I'm a civilian. I doubt military generals will respond."

"I have prepared a written order giving you full standing."

For long seconds Eli pondered before he answered. "I will try."

For a moment the air went out of Madison in relief. Then he stood and walked back to the map on the desktop.

"What route will you take?"

Eli asked, "Dearborn is in Albany?"

"Yes."

Eli traced with his finger on the map. "I'll likely go north on the Chesapeake, on over to the Delaware and up to Trenton, cross over to New York, and move up the Hudson to Albany and on north to Lake Champlain—the Richelieu River—the St. Lawrence—then west to Lake Ontario and on to the Niagara River. Much of it in a canoe. It's longer, but faster than going cross-country."

Madison looked into his face. "You will likely be in sight of the British once you are on the St. Lawrence. They control the Great Lakes."

"I'll move mostly at night. Should be no trouble."

There was gratitude in Madison's face as he opened a desk drawer and drew out three sealed documents and handed them to Eli.

"Two of those bear the names of the generals. The third one has your name. It's your authorization." Madison looked up into Eli's face, aware that while his genius was in the world of matters politic, Eli's genius was in the secrets of battle and of the forest. Madison went on. "Do you need money? Anything? Can I pay you for your services?"

"No."

"Do you want anyone to accompany you?"

"No."

"Is there anything else you need? Want to say?"

"No. I'm prepared to leave. I can get passage as far as Philadelphia on a schooner sailing this afternoon. I'll work my way north from there. I'll have a written report as soon as I can get back."

Madison reached to shake his hand. "I hope to find a way to repay you. In the meantime, my thanks and gratitude is all that I can offer."

With Madison following, Eli walked to the door and turned the handle. He paused to look down into the earnest face of the little man.

"With luck I'll be back before the snow flies. I hope you succeed in all this."

Madison bobbed his head once and walked out into the hall with Eli, down to the Executive Mansion foyer, and held the door while Eli strode out into the bright September sunlight with the recently sculpted grounds of flower beds and flowering trees and grass all around.

He made his way through the afternoon traffic of pedestrians, scurrying preoccupied from one building to another amid the ringing of iron horseshoes on cobblestone streets. He walked four blocks to a tavern with a sign EAGLE'S NEST above the door, up to his room on the second floor, where he changed out of his formal clothing into a pair of leather breeches, moccasins, and tunic, and packed his clothing into a battered valise. He checked to be certain he was leaving nothing behind, then walked downstairs to the front desk to count coins to a small man with nervous eyes who was overly impressed with his own importance. He waited while the little man disappeared into a back room, to reappear gingerly carrying a long, fringed, beaded buckskin scabbard with Eli's Pennsylvania long rifle inside. He handed it to Eli, and Eli walked out the door to a waiting hack. Less than an hour later he was on board a small schooner named *Nancy*, waiting for her to cast off from the navy yard dock for her trip to the top of Chesapeake Bay, thence northeast up the Delaware River, bound for Philadelphia.

For three days he suffered the confinement of the little ship, sometimes impatiently pacing the deck as she pushed on up the waterway. Occasionally he stood at the rail to study the small towns and settlements that had sprung up along the shore. The last day he gathered his belongings and walked down the gangplank to the docks on the east side of Philadelphia. He bought passage on a Durham freight boat hauling sixteen tons of iron ore upriver to the Bordentown smelters, and the captain held the boat steady while Eli jumped ashore at Trenton. For more than one hour he walked in the streets of the little village—King Street, Queen Street, Quaker Street—seeing once again in his mind the muzzle flashes and hearing the roar of muskets and cannon of the desperate battle fought in the howling blizzard of December 26, 1776, and hearing once more the cries and moans of men mortally struck. He paused to stare at the wheat field on the east edge of town, near the Assunpink Creek—white, ready for the harvest, still bordered by the peach orchard, heavy with the last of the summer crop. Eli saw it as it had been that December morning, stark and barren in the flying snow, when he and Billy and a sick, starved, shoeless, scarecrow American army under command of General George Washington surrounded nine hundred Hessian soldiers and took them prisoners of war.

He paid passenger fare to the owner of three freight wagons bound for New York, loaded with wheat and dried fish, tied his bag and rifle on top of the load, and climbed a huge spoked wheel to take his place beside the plump driver of the lead wagon, who spent the next three days in meaningless chatter and laughter, spitting huge jolts of brown tobacco juice and wiping his mouth and beard on a shirt sleeve already stained from elbow to wrist.

At New York, Eli hauled his valise to the waterfront where he paid to ship it to Billy Weems at Dunson & Weems Shipping Company in Boston. With rifle in hand and his weapons belt buckled around his middle, tomahawk in its place, he bartered money and a hunting knife for a canoe made by the Iroquois and waited for the Atlantic tides to come rolling in. They came, and the Hudson River changed directions, flowing from south to north, upstream, as it had from time immemorial when the tides came in. He placed his rifle in the canoe and pushed off Manhattan Island into the waters of the river to paddle north with the current.

Late the following day he beached the canoe at Albany, inquired, and walked into the foyer of the military headquarters of General Henry Dearborn. The bald corporal at the desk glanced up, then half stood, wide-eyed, gaping, startled at the old, tall man before him dressed in Iroquois buckskins, carrying a long rifle in a beaded scabbard, with a tomahawk through his belt.

"Who . . . what is it you want?" he stammered.

"I'm Eli Stroud. Special messenger sent by President James Madison. I have a sealed message for General Henry Dearborn. Is he here?"

The corporal's head jerked forward in disbelief. "President James Madison? You've got a message from President James Madison?"

"I do. Is Dearborn here?"

The corporal's arm shot up to point. "He's right in there, but you're not going in. Give me the message. I'll deliver it."

Eli shook his head. "Can't do that. My orders are to deliver it myself and wait for any answer." He walked to the plain, scarred desk and laid his rifle down, then drew his tomahawk and belt knife and laid them beside the rifle. He stepped back and said quietly, "I suggest you inform Dearborn. Now."

The corporal glanced down at the tomahawk, then back at Eli, and strode across the room to knock on a door. A voice from within called, "Enter," and the corporal pushed on through. One minute later he came back out, stood to one side, and motioned to Eli, who walked into the small, austere office to face an average-sized man with deep-set eyes, a near lipless mouth, and a prominent nose.

"Yes?" Dearborn said.

Eli nodded. "I have been sent by President James Madison to deliver a message to you and wait for a reply, if you want to send one."

Dearborn stared at his face, then examined him from head to toe with skepticism rampant on his face. "President Madison sent you?"

"He did. I have his letter giving me commission to carry the message to you." He drew the document from his shirt and offered it to Dearborn. The general broke the seal, read it, refolded it, and handed it back to Eli.

"Let me see the message for me."

Eli drew the sealed message from his shirt and handed it across the desk to Dearborn and watched as the man broke the seal, read it, then slumped into his chair to read it again.

" . . . must assemble your army and march on Montreal earliest . . . coordinate your attack with General Van Rensselaer's attack on Fort George . . . you are aware of the surrender by General William Hull of Fort Detroit on August 16, 1812 . . . we must—repeat must—have a victory to announce to Congress when it meets in November . . ."

A sense of indignation swept over Dearborn as he thumped the letter flat on his desk and raised his eyes to Eli. His words came too loud, defensive.

"Do you know the contents of this document?"

"No. It was sealed."

"Tell President Madison I will follow my orders. Tell him that as soon as my command is prepared, we will proceed to Montreal. Tell him—"

Eli raised a hand to stop him. "I'm sorry, sir. Any response must be in writing with your signature. President Madison has to be certain you received that message."

Dearborn rose abruptly. "All right! Take a seat in the foyer. I will call you when I have the message completed."

For twenty minutes Eli sat patiently against one wall in the small foyer with the nervous corporal seated behind his desk alternately glancing at the rifle, the tomahawk, and Eli, his discomfort obvious at having what he thought to be an Indian facing him.

Eli stood when the door opened and Dearborn strode to him to hand him a sealed letter. "There's my answer. I trust you will deliver it to President Madison."

"I will." Eli took it and thrust it inside his shirt. "If there's nothing else," he said, "I'll be on my way."

"There is nothing else," Dearborn said with finality.

Eli walked to the corporal's desk and picked up his tomahawk to thrust it through his belt, then took up his rifle with both the corporal and Dearborn staring as he walked out the door and down to the docks on the Hudson River to his waiting canoe. Dusk found him nine miles upstream, seated beside a small brook and a campfire with an opossum roasting on a spit. He finished his simple supper and for a time sat back against a massive oak, watching the stars appear, and then the rise of a quarter moon. After a time, he heaped dirt on the fire and went to his blanket with his rifle and weapons belt nearby.

He was back on the water before sunrise, kneeling in the light birch-bark canoe, settled into the rhythm of the paddle stroke that drove the canoe steadily north through the mist rising from the river. He paused for a few moments as he passed Saratoga, remembering the cataclysmic collision of the British army commanded by General John Burgoyne with the patched-together American army consisting of regulars, militia, and volunteers who appeared from nowhere in the battle that was turned in favor of the Americans by Benedict Arnold and which resulted in the surrender of more than six thousand British redcoats, including General Burgoyne himself.

Further north, he slowed to study the walls and gun turrets of five-sided Fort Ticonderoga and to look at Mount Defiance just to the southeast. He remembered the humiliating shock that forced the Americans to abandon the fort without firing a shot when it was discovered that somehow the British had dragged cannon up the back side of Mount Defiance and positioned them on top—guns capable of reducing the fort to rubble while American cannon could not reach them.

He reached the headwaters of the Hudson, made the eleven-mile portage to the south end of Lake Champlain, and continued north on the lake to the place where it joined the Richelieu River. Then on north to the Saint Lawrence River, where he waited for moonrise before he turned southeast to make the journey in four nights that would take him past the British outposts at Cornwall, Crysler's Farm, Prescott, and Gananoque before he entered Lake Ontario, where he could hold to the south shore on the American side in daylight. He passed Oswego and Sodus before he made camp, and the following morning stopped for a short time to eat cheese and hardtack near Charlotte, where the Genesee River emptied into the lake.

The next day, with sunset casting long shadows eastward, he rounded a small, jutting point of land and there in the distance, shining in the yellow glow of a setting sun, was the tiny peninsula on which stood Fort Niagara. He brought the canoe to the docks of the fort, paused to study the British Fort George across the width of the river, and beached his canoe.

With rifle in hand, he walked the twenty feet to the docks to face a young, slender picket with a long, narrow face, a hunch between his shoulders, and the beginnings of a beard. The picket jerked his musket up and exclaimed, "Halt! Or I'll shoot! State your name and your business."

Eli stifled a smile. "I am Eli Stroud. President James Madison sent me to deliver a message to General Stephen Van Rensselaer. Is he here?

The picket stared at him with narrowed, suspicious eyes. He could not recall ever hearing of a tall white man wearing what was clearly Indian buckskins, carrying a Pennsylvania rifle and a tomahawk, asking for an American general.

"You want to see the general?" he blurted.

"I have a message for him. Written. From President James Madison."

The picket's head jerked forward in disbelief, and he exclaimed, "You're carrying a message from the president? Madison?"

Eli answered calmly, "Yes. I am. I suggest you take me to the general."

For a moment the picket stood in shocked indecision, unable to decide whether he would be a hero or a buffoon if he took this man to the general. Seconds passed before he exclaimed, "Show me the message."

Eli drew the sealed document from his shirt and held it up for the picket to see. "It's been about seventeen days since I left Washington, D.C.," Eli said quietly. "President Madison wants this in the general's hands now. I don't know what will happen to you if you prevent that."

The picket recoiled, licked at dry lips, and shifted his feet, struggling. "All right. You move ahead of me on up toward the fort and don't make a move with that rifle. Or tomahawk."

Eli shrugged and strode up path to the gates of Fort Niagara where the picket answered the challenge, the gates swung open, and he followed Eli inside.

Eli turned. "Where is the general's office?"

The picket pointed. "Over there."

The picket still had his musket at the ready when Eli pushed through the door and stopped while his eyes adjusted to the lack of light, with the picket right behind him, still clutching his weapon. The corporal behind the desk jerked to his feet at the sight of a white Indian followed by a soldier with a musket and stammered, "Who . . . what . . . who are you?"

The picket's answer spilled out. "Says he's got a message. Written message. From President James Madison in Washington, D.C. He says he has to deliver it to General Van Rensselaer."

The corporal gaped, eyes narrowed, forehead furrowed. "A message from *whom?*"

Eli held up a warning hand against the picket and spoke to the corporal.

"I am Eli Stroud. I have a sealed message from President Madison for General Van Rensselaer. Is he here?"

All three men turned at the sound of the general's office door opening, and the general, average size, square face, generous mouth, stood in the door frame, surprise showing as he peered at Eli.

"Did I hear someone mention President Madison?"

The picket and the corporal burst into a confusion of exclamations at the same moment, and the general raised a hand to stop them. He looked at Eli.

"Are you the one who spoke of President Madison?"

Eli was studying the general as he answered. The man was younger than himself and had the feel about him of one whose mental abilities exceeded his maturity to handle them.

"I am Eli Stroud. I have a written message from President Madison."

"May I see it?"

Eli drew the letter from his shirt, and the general took the parchment from him. Still standing in the doorway, he broke the seal, unfolded it, and quickly examined the signature at the bottom. There was no questioning the small, neat handwriting of President Madison.

"Leave your weapons here and come inside," the general said.

Eli laid his rifle and tomahawk on the corporal's desk and followed the general into his office where they took seats on opposite sides of the plain desk, with the door closed. For a time the two sat in silence while Van Rensselaer read the document, then read it again.

" . . . must prevail on General Alexander Smyth to follow his orders and join with your forces when you make the attack on Fort George . . . critical that you coordinate your attack with the assault of General William Dearborn on Montreal . . . must proceed at once before the winter closes in . . . must have a victory to announce when Congress convenes in November . . ."

He laid the letter down on his desktop while he leaned back and spoke.

"You know what's in that letter?"

"No. It was sealed."

Van Rensselaer nodded. "Was there anything else? You need food? Rest?"

"Yes. There is something else." Eli drew out the document with his own name on it and handed it to the general. "My orders are to remain here for a time and then return with my report and with any letter you wish to send to President Madison."

Van Rensselaer accepted the letter and sat upright to read it, then leaned forward, temper beginning to show in his face. "President Madison wants your personal report on matters up here?"

"Yes."

"He doesn't trust us to tell him?"

Eli's face was without emotion. "He did not tell me his reasons. I intend following his orders."

Van Rensselaer straightened, then leaned forward. He hesitated for a moment, then said, "I'll tell you what's happening here. General Smyth—Alexander Smyth—has refused to submit to my orders because he's regular army and I'm state militia. We're into October, and snow could shut us down any time. I haven't heard from Dearborn for weeks, and there's no time to argue with Smyth now, or to coordinate with Dearborn."

He stopped, suddenly realizing what he was saying was probably meaningless to Eli. "Do you have any idea of the plan Congress came up with to invade Canada? Fort Detroit, Fort George, Montreal?"

Eli nodded. "I know of it. President Madison took the time to explain it to me. Fort Detroit fell about six weeks ago."

Van Rensselaer's eyes came alive with a fire from within. "I've heard. We're not going to have a repeat of it around here! Not while I'm in command." He took a deep breath and plowed into it.

"Let me get to what's happening. My scouts tell me we outnumber the British at Fort George right now, at least three to one. Twice I ordered Smyth and his command to cross the river here and attack Fort George while I take my command six miles south to cross the river and take Queenston Heights, to protect Smyth's flank. Smyth refuses. I'm going ahead with my command, independent of him. We make our crossing in two days to take Queenston Heights, then on north to take Fort George without Smyth."

The general stopped and straightened in his chair while he brought his anger and passion under control. "I'll inform General Dearborn as soon as possible, under the circumstances. I'll also give you a written report signed by me for President Madison."

He leaned forward and his words came spaced, loud. "After I've taken Fort George!"

Eli paused for a moment. "You intend attacking Queenston Heights?"

"I do."

"You have a plan to scale those cliffs? They're nearly two hundred fifty feet high—almost a sheer drop to the river."

"We know."

"How do you plan to scale them?"

Van Rensselaer avoided the question. "That's a problem for my officers. We'll manage." He stood, and it was clear he was finished with Eli. "You need a bed for the night? Supper?"

"I could use a warm meal. I prefer to sleep in the woods."

Van Rensselaer walked to the door and followed Eli into the foyer, where Eli gathered his rifle and tomahawk while the general said, "Tell the mess sergeant you're to have mess privileges as long as you're here, on my orders."

Eli nodded. "Thank you." The corporal was still staring at the tomahawk in Eli's weapons belt as Eli walked out into the sunset and the general closed the door.

The boiled fish and cabbage was too salty, and there was mold on the hard, black bread. With dusk coming on, Eli delivered the wooden plate and cup to the cleanup detail and walked out of the enlisted mess hall into a fort shutting down for the night. He stood to listen to the drum pound out taps as the flag was lowered, then walked out of the fort and into the nearby woods to the banks of a small stream that fed into the immensity of Lake Ontario. He leaned his rifle against a tree, unbuckled his weapons belt and laid it on his spread blanket, and sat down with his back against a ninety-foot pine tree and his knees drawn up. He let his thoughts run.

A divided command at odds with each other. . . . those cliffs at Queenston Heights . . . no plan to scale them . . . taking Fort George . . . too fragile . . . too fragile . . . one thing goes wrong, it could bring down all of it. . . . another disaster . . . like Fort Detroit . . .

The moon was risen when he pulled his blanket to his chin and rested his head on his arm and drifted into the sleep of a weary man.

With the incomparable colors of sunrise in the October forest all around, Eli knelt beside the small stream and dipped with his hand to drink, aware of the stiffness and the tinges of pain in his joints. He wiped his dripping chin on the sleeve of his buckskin shirt, then raised it to shade his eyes against the brightness of the morning sun while he studied the knot of men gathering at the dock, pointing, gesturing wildly, voices raised in hot argument. He could hear the clamor but could not make out the words. He rolled and tied his blanket and fastened it over his shoulder, then gathered his rifle and weapons belt and tomahawk and walked the forest path down to the dock to stand to one side, trying to make sense of what he was hearing.

A young lieutenant was gesturing wildly, pointing out into the lake, face red with anger, voice raised to a shout as he berated a white-faced sergeant.

"Who did it? Someone had to see! Who was it?"

The befuddled sergeant stammered, "I don't know, sir. I don't know. It happened in the night. Ask the officer in charge of the docks."

"Fine," the lieutenant blustered. "Which one?"

"I don't know, sir. I didn't come on duty until four o'clock."

The lieutenant paced for a moment, furious, then stopped, and his voice rang. "All right! I'll find out which officer is responsible! You and your squad stay right here until I return. Whoever's responsible will be tried by court's martial, and I'll see to it they're *hanged!*"

Eli watched the lieutenant trot up the trail to the fort, muttering to himself, then walked over to the sergeant.

"Something wrong?"

The sergeant's eyes popped wide at the sight of an aging white man in Indian garb, carrying a rifle and tomahawk. "Who are you?" he demanded.

"Eli Stroud. Here under command of General Van Rensselaer. What's gone wrong?"

The sergeant's eyes narrowed, and he cocked his head. "I've never seen you around here before. You sure you didn't have something to do with this?

"With what?" Eli asked.

"The oars! We were supposed to move up the river tomorrow

morning to cross the river for the attack on Queenston Heights. Most of the boats are already up at Lewiston right now. The oars were loaded into eight of them. A messenger showed up this morning before sunrise to tell us the eight boats with the oars are gone! Disappeared! We can't cross the river! We can't make the attack! No one knows who took them or where they are!"

Eli stood still, incredulous, appalled at the near total breakdown at Fort Niagara of every military principle he had ever learned, starting with the shambles that Smyth and Van Rensselaer had made of unity of command, and now ending with soldiers who could let someone steal eight longboats filled with oars, without which the entire fighting force of Van Rensselaer was landlocked, crippled, unable to make the attack that had been ordered by the president of the United States!

Eli closed his eyes and bowed his head, unable to make his brain accept the stupidity and the paralyzing dysfunction that had seized the entire American fighting force at Fort Niagara. The sergeant sputtered and fumed, cursing the corporals and privates who had been on picket duty during the night and who had failed to see eight longboats stolen from the Lewiston docks and brought past the Fort Niagara dock unde-tected, and cursing the company of men six miles upstream who allowed someone to steal the boats less than forty feet away. The corporals and privates stood silent, afraid to interrupt, not knowing how to respond to the hysteria of their sergeant.

One thing was clear to Eli. The sergeant and his squad were terrified of what could become of them should a court-martial find them guilty of dereliction of duty. Because the assault had been ordered by Congress and the president, this was no minor blunder. If they were found guilty, it was entirely possible they could spend life in prison or be hanged or shot!

Without another word, Eli walked up the path to the fort to learn what Van Rensselaer was going to do. The answer came quickly. Inside the fort, officers of the rank of lieutenant colonel and above were emerg-ing from command headquarters at a trot, while civilians stopped in wonder and enlisted men stared in bewilderment, unable to remember when so many of their superiors were moving so fast at the same time.

Eli was near enough to hear a captain shout to a sergeant under his command, "Down to the dock! Every man in your platoon! Take two longboats and move out onto the lake! Search for eight of our boats that were stolen from Queenston Heights in the night!"

The startled sergeant stammered, "Now, sir? We were assigned—"

The captain cut him off. "Forget that! Move!"

"Yes, sir!" The sergeant bellowed orders, and his twelve-man platoon dropped everything and followed him at a run, through the gates and down to the docks.

A lieutenant colonel shouted to four majors to come at once, and waited, pacing, until they were facing him.

"You have new orders. Stop everything your men are doing and order them to get tools and start making oars. Longboat oars. Two hundred forty of them. From any lumber they can find."

One astonished major asked, "Oars, sir?"

"Oars!" the colonel bellowed.

"The oars are all upriver, sir, for the attack tomorrow. May I inquire what's happened?"

The colonel hesitated, undecided for a moment if he should give the answer, then realized the news would be rampant throughout the entire command within minutes.

"Someone stole them all!" he exclaimed. "Eight boatloads, overnight. The attack planned for tomorrow is delayed. We must have oars before we can cross the river. Now do you understand?"

"Yes, sir."

Eli watched the majors trot to their commands to bark orders and make explanations that drew stunned silence, followed by a torrent of exclamations as sergeants and corporals scattered to assemble their men and lead them to the carpenter's shop for tools.

Thoughts came to Eli as he watched. *Van Rensselaer sent men onto the lake to search for the boats, and he's making more oars, but he didn't send a detail south to find out what happened at Lewiston or give them new orders.*

Quietly Eli left the fort, shaking his head as he walked down to the dock to watch the two longboats push off out into Lake Erie, searching for eight longboats they would never find. Minutes later he quietly disappeared into the forest and turned south, silently passing through the dense woods, pausing from time to time to listen for any break in the sounds of the birds and the chatter of the long-haired squirrels and chipmunks that would tell him someone or something not of the forest was near. He did not want some frightened, lost American picket from the Lewiston camp to fire on him first and challenge him after.

The sun was directly overhead when he dropped to his haunches on the east bank of the Niagara to study the sheer granite cliffs on the west side of the river, rising two hundred forty feet straight up with the small village of Queenston Heights on top. He watched the flow of the river where the channel narrowed between Queenston Heights and Lewiston to force a fast, heavy current with half a dozen swirling eddies. A British flag flew over the distant camp, and he could see movement, but not the detail.

How many, he wondered, *and who are they? Redcoats or Canadians or Indians? Or all three? Who's in command over there?*

He peered upriver, then down, but there was no sign of either a British or an American patrol or boat.

Where are the American pickets? I should have seen a picket or a patrol long before now. He pushed on south, every nerve, every sense alive, searching for any sign of the Americans who were assigned to guard the boats for the river crossing to attack Queenston Heights. He had covered three hundred yards before he heard the bickering voices of Americans, and then he saw their camp, fifty yards ahead through the trees and foliage. He stopped to study the woods between himself and the arguing Americans, and it was then he saw the picket leaned against a pine tree, nearly hidden, dozing in the shade. Without a sound he came in from the side of the tree and reached to seize the musket held loosely by the sleeping hands. The picket's head came up and his eyes opened as he came back to the world, and he lunged for his musket as he exclaimed, "Halt or I'll shoot!"

Eli quietly said, "Stand easy. I'm friend, not foe."

"You got no right . . ." The picket caught himself as he came fully awake and realized he had been asleep. The penalty could be hanging. He wiped at his mouth and tried to arrange his thoughts.

"You ought not to have come in like that. I could have shot you."

Eli let it pass. "I've just come from Fort Niagara. We were told someone stole eight boats loaded with oars from here last night. Know anything about it?"

The picket bobbed his head, fearful of being reported for sleeping on picket duty. "Yes, oh yes!" he exclaimed. "Some officer. Stole them all!"

"What officer? What name?"

The picket shook his head. "No one knows. All our officers were here this morning. We thought they might have caught them at Fort Niagara when they tried to pass the docks down there."

"They didn't see them in the night."

"Well," the picket blurted, "neither did we! I been up since four o'clock this morning, watching. Nothing happened until you came. Are they still planning an attack for tomorrow?"

Eli grunted a laugh. "Not likely. They're making oars. You should be getting orders soon." He handed the musket back to the picket. "You better watch for a messenger from the fort."

"Oh, yes, sir, I will, sir."

Eli started on south, toward the camp when the picket called after him, "You're not . . . are you going to report that I was asleep?"

Eli paused and turned to look back at the man, pleading in his eyes. "No. Stay awake."

He walked on south, into the camp, where a dozen men stopped to stare at him. A paunchy captain emerged from the cluster of soldiers to face him.

"Who are you?"

"Eli Stroud. From Fort Niagara. We got your message about the stolen oars. I thought I'd come see what happened. Could I know your name?"

Instantly the captain became defensive. "Captain Jacob McCown," he said. "General Van Rensselaer send you?"

"No. President Madison. Would you care to see his letter of commission?"

The captain's face drained of blood. "President Madison?"

Eli remained silent.

The captain took a breath, and his words came as though they had been carefully selected and memorized. "I don't . . . we don't know what happened. All we know is that we had double pickets out all night to protect the boats and the oars, and with daylight eight boats and all the oars for tomorrow's attack were gone. No one heard a thing and no one saw it. We can't find a sign of who did it. Maybe one of our own officers, maybe the British, maybe Indians. We thought it might have been an officer from the fort, but we don't know. We just don't know."

"Are the rest of the boats still here? Ready to cross the river?"

"Yes. We've tripled the pickets."

Eli thought about the picket he had found sleeping and understood how such a thing could happen, right under their noses. "Are your men ready?" he asked.

"Yes."

Eli looked about at the faces of those who had gathered. There was a mix of fear of what their loss of the boats and oars would bring down on their heads, and of anxiety over what Van Rensselaer planned to do about the attack still scheduled for the next morning.

Eli spoke to the captain. "I better get back to the fort. Anything you want me to take back? Any message?"

The captain struggled for a few moments. "Tell the general—"

Eli cut him off. "In writing. Put it in writing."

The captain shook his head. "I'll make a full written report shortly."

Eli turned, and a path opened through the crowded men, and he walked into the woods moving north. He was within the walls of Fort Niagara to share evening mess with the enlisted, and moonrise found him at his small campsite wrapped in his blanket with his rifle and weapons belt at hand.

A touch of frost came in the night, and morning broke clear with a cloudless sky. At the fort, the stack of newly crafted oars grew throughout the day, with men working feverishly, waiting for orders they knew had to come, setting a new day for the attack. In late afternoon the general officers were summoned to headquarters for half an hour, and when they emerged, each went directly to their command to assemble their men and read from the written orders of General Van Rensselaer. Eli stood quietly on one side of a regiment of militia, listening carefully.

"The oars will be loaded onto longboats and moved up the Niagara River to Lewiston tonight at nine o'clock PM. At one o'clock AM all commands heretofore ordered to participate in the attack on Queenston Heights will march to Lewiston where they will board the longboats and cross the river under command of Colonel Solomon Van Rensselaer. They will make the assault on the Heights at first light tomorrow morning, October 13, 1812. Following the occupation of the Heights, they will proceed north to Fort George where they will launch a second assault and reduce Fort George to American occupation."

Caught by surprise, Eli pondered the questions. *Colonel* Solomon *Van Rensselaer in command of the assault? Not General* Stephen *Van Rensselaer? Is the general incompetent? Afraid? Or is it that his kinsman is battle trained and the general is not?*

There was no answer.

The troops were dismissed for evening mess, and Eli sat quietly with the enlisted men, listening, watching, studying their expressions as they ate. He saw in them the rising dread of knowing that they might not survive the next twenty-four hours, or worse, that they could be maimed and crippled for the rest of their lives, and he remembered the many times the same sick feeling had risen in his breast on the eve of battle.

He finished his supper, delivered his utensils to the cleanup detail, and walked across the parade ground to the headquarters of General Van Rensselaer in the long shadows of sunset. The corporal gave him entrance, and Eli walked into the private office of the general, seated behind his desk, his face a mask of determination.

"Yes?" the general said.

Eli remained standing. "I wondered if you sent word south to the camp at Lewiston. Do they know about your latest orders? For an attack tomorrow morning?"

Van Rensselaer tried to cover his error. "They'll know soon enough. This command will begin arriving there in the next eight or ten hours."

"The captain down there—McCown—has some pretty jumpy men. Might be a good thing to let them get ready for what's coming."

Van Rensselaer started. "You know Captain McCown?"

"I was there yesterday."

Van Rensselaer came to his feet. "You what?"

"I was there yesterday."

"What did you tell him?"

"Not much of anything."

"Did he send any message back with you?"

"No. I told him he'd have to do it in writing. He said he'd file his report later."

The general sat back down, face drawn in thought. "Is there anything else?"

"No."

Van Rensselaer's words came sharp, with a cutting edge. "Mister Stroud, I do not want you interfering in the affairs of this fort again. Am I clear?"

Eli looked steadily into his face. "I'll try to not interfere, but I intend completing what President Madison sent me here to do. Am I clear?"

The general's face went blank. Eli waited for one moment before he turned on his heel and walked out of the room, across the foyer, and out into the parade ground. He stopped at the sound of the drum sounding taps and watched the two soldiers lower the flag. He was walking toward the fort gates when the corporal from the foyer came trotting from behind.

"The general wants to see you."

Eli followed the man back to the headquarters building and into Van Rensselaer's office.

"You want to see me?"

The general's face was a mask, unreadable. "Yes. I have written orders for Captain McCown at the Lewiston camp. Would you deliver them tonight?"

It took Eli a few seconds to consider. "Yes."

Without a word Van Rensselaer handed him a sealed letter. Eli took it and pushed it inside his shirt.

The general's words were crisp, formal. "You are dismissed."

Eli walked out into the gathering dusk, across the parade ground, out of the fort into the forest. He gathered his belongings and turned south to disappear into the forest. Dusk became deep twilight, and the stars began to appear. Stopping from time to time to listen, the aging woodsman worked his way south, staying in sight of the black ribbon to his right that was the river, glancing at the nighthawks darting overhead, listening to the occasional question asked by owls, "Whooo?"

An hour before midnight he was half a mile from the Lewiston camp. He saw the glow from the campfires, and he came the last quarter mile standing upright, rifle held over his head, calling out, "Eli Stroud. Friend. From Fort Niagara." Two hundred yards from the camp, a picket challenged him, he answered, and the picket fell in behind to follow him into the flickering light of the campfires.

"I have a written message from General Van Rensselaer for Captain McCown," he told the lieutenant on duty. Minutes later McCown came, buttoning his tunic, hair awry.

"You have something from General Van Rensselaer?"

Eli handed him the sealed orders.

McCown broke the seal and opened it while he turned to catch the light of the fire. He pored over the orders before he raised his head and turned to the young lieutenant.

"Everybody awake," he exclaimed. "The troops from the fort are on their way with boats and oars. We make the attack at seven o'clock in the morning. Forty cartridges for every man. Check all weapons. The cooks are to have morning mess ready at three o'clock AM."

Three minutes later a half-dressed, sleep-fogged drummer hammered out reveille. Barefooted soldiers in their long underwear stumbled out of their tents, squinting against the light of the campfires while they struggled to understand the shouted orders of their officers.

Eli stood at one side of the sprawling camp, watching it come alive. He shared hot mush and burned sowbelly with the enlisted, then watched while they stood in line to receive their forty paper cartridges, counting them into the small leather cases on their belts.

In the faint light of the quarter moon, the longboats carrying the oars from Fort Niagara arrived at the docks while the cleanup crew was washing the huge mush pots and taking down the nine-foot tripods on which they were mounted. More than one hundred men crowded to unload 240 oars, and others counted them out, six for each of the long-boats that had been tied to the dock for the last ten days.

The eastern sky was gray, and the stars overhead were fading when the sounds of the army marching from Fort Niagara reached them through the woods, and twenty minutes later they were in camp. They dropped their backpacks and sat down, breathing hard from their five-hour forced march through the dead of night. Within minutes Colonel Solomon Van Rensselaer called them to attention.

"We will load into the boats immediately and start the crossing on my command. The two hundred men I previously designated will lead. When they have reached the west bank, the balance of the regiments will follow in the order of the march." He stopped, gave hand signals to his regimental officers, and walked briskly to the longboats with the troops following, piling into the boats, crowding to take seats, cursing their backpacks.

The first arc of the sun was rising behind them when Colonel Van Rensselaer shouted his order, and his boat pushed off into the river, with others on both sides. Eli watched with held breath when the big boats hit the fast-flowing main channel and were suddenly swept downstream sideways, out of control. The frantic oarsmen dug deep and hard and slowly the longboats corrected, bows pointed upriver, working toward the west bank and the steep granite cliffs. Eli lifted his eyes to study the rim on the far side of the river, and they were there—British regulars, Canadian civilians, Indians—with their muskets, waiting for the oncoming Americans to come within range. The lead boats were less than thirty yards from shore when the popping of the muskets high above them commenced and held. Some of the men in the longboats slumped, struck. Oarsmen groaned and fell back and others pushed them aside to take their place, heaving on the oars with all their strength. Behind them, on the west bank of the river, General Stephen Van Rensselaer and the waiting soldiers stood silent, unmoving, staring at the longboats and the men inside them that were caught beneath the enemy guns, without cover, without the possibility of retreat. They flinched when the first longboat hit the far bank and the troops leaped ashore to sprint for the nearest rocks for a shield, and then all the other boats were on the bank and men were running in all directions to escape the deadly fire from above. Eli saw Solomon Van Rensselaer stumble and go down, then struggle to his feet as a sergeant grabbed him and jammed him down behind a huge boulder at the base of the cliff.

The oarsmen pushed the boats back into the river and turned them to recross the river with the dead and wounded, while those behind them among the rocks raised their muskets to fire upward at the British. The return was faster than the crossing, and waiting hands lifted the wounded and the dead from the boats to lay them on spread blankets while the surgeon and his aides began their frantic, heartbreaking work of deciding which ones were fatally wounded and which ones they might save.

The second regiment loaded into their longboats, and Eli saw the need. He stepped into the lead longboat and sat on the first bench, hunched forward, rifle between his knees. He felt the current suck the boat downstream and then heard the grunt of the oarsmen behind as they strained to correct their course, and he watched as the far bank came into clear definition with the Americans crouched behind anything that would shield them while they fired upward at the barrage coming down from the British on top of the cliffs. He heard the hits and the groans behind him and he saw the two-foot geysers of water leap around the boats when the .75-caliber British musket balls struck the river. The boat was ten feet from the rocky shore when Eli leaped into the water and waded in, waiting to hold the bow of the boat steady while the others jumped into the river and slogged their way onto the bank and into the rocks to cover.

Eli ran, crouched, dodging, to the place where Colonel Van Rensselaer was slumped against the sheltering boulder, with his head bowed, eyes closed, his jaw clenched against the pain, blood running from his forehead and shoulder and right side. The white-faced sergeant who had saved him looked at Eli and shook his head.

"Six hits."

Eli gently shook the colonel by the shoulders. "Can you hear me?"

The colonel managed to raise his head to look Eli in the face. "Yes."

"Can you stand it if I take you back to the longboat?"

"I can try."

As gently as he could, Eli picked up the stricken man and turned back toward the boats with the sergeant beside him, trying to bear some of the weight. They reached the longboats with musket balls ricocheting off the rocks around them, and Eli waded into the river up to his waist to lift the colonel into the reaching hands of the waiting oarsmen in the nearest longboat.

"Get him back across," Eli shouted as he turned back to shore and the safety of the rocks where the sergeant was waiting.

Above the rattle of the musket fire, Eli shouted, "Who's next in command?"

The sergeant pondered for a moment. "Captain Wool. John Wool. I saw him over there." The sergeant pointed, and Eli sprinted. Captain John E. Wool saw him coming and was waiting when Eli dropped beside him in the shelter of a rock, breathless.

Wool spoke. "The colonel?"

"Alive," Eli exclaimed. "Barely. Are you in command?"

"As far as I know."

"What are your orders?"

Wool was struggling to recover from the shock. "We've got to get these men off this riverbank."

"Do you know the trails up the cliffs?"

Wool shook his head. "No. No one ever showed us."

There was anger in Eli's voice. "Wait here. I'll be back."

For more than five minutes Wool waited, shouting what encouragement he could to his men, before Eli came running to once again crouch beside him.

"There," Eli exclaimed, pointing south. "Maybe one hundred yards. There's a trail leading up. I think it's one used by fishermen."

Wool bobbed his head. "Let's go."

With Eli leading, the two men ran, dodging among the rocks, shouting, "Follow us, follow us." Those who could broke from cover to run from the field of fire to the place where Eli stopped, and they gathered at the base of the cliff. Eli pointed to a place where a rocky path made its crooked way upward across the face of the steep rock wall, partially sheltered from above by an overhang. He turned to Wool who stood pasty-faced and panting, and he pointed.

"That leads to the top. We've got to get these men up there before the British figure out what we're doing."

Wool nodded, and Eli started up the path at a trot, hunched low, with Wool behind and the troops following. The musket fire overhead dwindled and became sporadic and had nearly stopped when Eli broke out on top of the cliff, breathing hard, sweating, with the soldiers right behind. He paused only long enough to turn to Wool and point.

"I don't think they know we're here yet. Keep moving!"

They came charging in from the right flank of the startled British, muskets blasting, bayonets flashing. Red-coated soldiers and Canadians and Indians went down, and suddenly those still on their feet broke into a scrambling retreat with the screaming Americans scattering them in all directions. Within minutes the small advance party of Americans held the crest of the cliffs and the village of Queenston Heights.

Eli dropped to his haunches beside a dazed British soldier who was trying to tie a tourniquet around his right thigh, sweating, teeth gritted against the pain and blood of a ragged hole made by an American musket ball.

"Let me," Eli said, detaching the bayonet from the British musket lying beside the wounded man. He thrust it through the bandage loosely looped around the leg and began rotating it until it came tight, and the flow of blood quit pulsing from the wound. Eli took the soldier's hand and placed it on the bayonet and said, "Hold that until someone comes to help."

The soldier looked him in the eye. "Thank you," he said, his voice barely audible.

"Who's your commanding officer?"

"Brock, sir. General Isaac Brock."

Eli started. "The one who took Fort Detroit?"

"The same."

"He came here?"

"On orders."

"Where is he?"

A look of pain came into the eyes of the British soldier. "I believe I saw him fall in your first volley. Over there." He pointed east, toward the bluffs.

Eli walked through the white gun smoke hanging in the air, the American soldiers giddy with relief, and the wounded and dead British, looking for the one with the gold on his shoulders. He was just yards from the bluffs when he saw him, on his face, arms thrown outward, hat with the gold braid lying beside his golden hair. Eli knelt beside the still body and gently felt at the wrist, then the throat, and knew he was dead. One of the best.

For a moment Eli felt deep sadness at the waste, and he looked about at the others who were dead or writhing in pain, and an anger came welling at the evil of wars and the sickness of the human race that left it unable to stop them. In his life he had seen too much of it, and he rose and walked on to the crest and stood with spread feet, watching the next command of longboats working their way through the current to unload, followed by another. Within half an hour there were six hundred Americans assembled on the heights, among them Lieutenant Colonel Winfield Scott, who was the highest ranking officer and who took command.

He called together his war council and Eli listened as he gave them his orders.

"They have about twice our number in reserve just to the north of us, and we can expect a counterattack as soon as they rally. General Van Rensselaer will bring the balance of our command across the river at once, but we've got to hold here until they arrive. Use anything you can find for breastworks. Form four battle lines facing north."

The Americans seized the British supply wagons, British backpacks, and discarded shipping crates and began forming barricades facing north. Eli walked to the bluff once more to watch twelve longboats crossing but could not understand why thirty others remained tied near the dock, empty, while soldiers stood on the banks, muskets in hand, doing nothing. He watched the twelve boats unload and the soldiers start up the path to the top, and he walked to meet them. He fell in beside the officer in charge.

"Isn't the general coming with the others?"

The officer stopped to look down at the river. "That was the plan."

"What's holding them? There's a counterattack coming, and we need them."

A blank look crossed the officer's face and he shrugged. "I don't know what's happened."

The sure knowledge struck Eli like something physical. He trotted down the trail to where men were unloading cased ammunition and crated medicines and stopped the nearest lieutenant.

"Are the others coming across to reinforce Colonel Scott?"

The lieutenant turned to peer back across the river. "I thought they were."

"Are you going back?"

"Yes. To get another load of supplies."

Eli climbed into the longboat to help with the unloading, then settled onto a seat while the six oarsmen rowed back across the river. Eli was the first out of the boat, searching for General Van Rensselaer. He found him standing before a huge gathering of the New York State militia, red-faced, neck veins extended, ranting his condemnation of the entire force. The few soldiers who were not militia were crowded behind the general while his voice rang in the woods.

"Mutiny! Treason! Cowardice in the face of the enemy! I will personally see to it you are hanged if it is the last act of my life! Each and every one!" His arm shot up to point across the river. "We have a thousand men over there who will be lost if you do not go to reinforce them! For the last time, I give you a direct order! Enter the longboats and cross the river and go to save your fellow soldiers!"

Not one man among the New York militia moved. They stared at the ground, or the sky, or each other, with blank faces, and said nothing.

The general was close to hysteria. "May the Almighty forgive you, because neither I nor the United States ever will!" He stopped and for a moment did not know what to do next. He had no words, no one to turn to, no way to force a thousand men to board the longboats. He backed up two steps and then turned to stalk off to his tent.

Eli asked the nearest officer, "What's happened?"

There was outrage in the officer as he answered. "When the first boatloads of dead and wounded came back across the river, the militia took one look at them and got about half sick. When the second load got here, they started talking. When the general ordered them to load into the boats to make their crossing, they told him to his face that they were state militia, and they were not authorized to cross onto Canadian soil. They had not joined the army to fight on foreign soil. They refused. You know the rest."

For a full five seconds Eli stood in stunned disbelief. Foreign soil? The idea was insane! Beyond ridiculous! How could half an army sacrifice the other half? How could these men bear the shame? How could they ever hold their heads up again?

From across the river came the deep boom of a single cannon, and then five more cannon, and then an eruption of the rattle of muskets. Eli ran to the dock to shade his eyes while he watched the great granite bluffs. A soldier blurted, "What's going on over there?" and another answered, "The British counterattack just began."

Time passed unnoticed as they stood there, staring, not knowing what was happening up on top of the bluffs. No one knew how long they were there before they saw the movement of men at the crest, and no one knew whether they were Americans or British until the Union Jack was hoisted with its blue field and red and white crosses, unmistakable in the bright fall sun.

For a time the New York militia remained huddled together, afraid of the simmering rage in the small remainder of the soldiers. For a long time Eli stood at the dock, hoping against hope to see some of the American soldiers making their way down the trail to the river to be picked up, but there were none.

A thousand men, dead or captured. A thousand men!

Never had Eli been in, or heard of, a camp as violently divided as the one in which he now found himself. For a long time the few soldiers who had been willing to make the crossing stayed together with hatred and utter contempt that leaped from their eyes and faces like something alive, to reach and condemn the great gathering of New York militia who had refused to save their comrades in arms. The New Yorkers remained gathered, fearful of what would happen to them if they disbursed to their individual commands and tents.

General Stephen Van Rensselaer refused to leave his tent, and his officers could hear him heaping venom on the New York militia, his voice rising and falling while he paced. In the camp, the tension and bitterness rode like a great, black pall. Camp discipline was forgotten. Without their commander, the soldiers degenerated into two groups, aimless, without focus. Finally the lesser officers gave the orders to prepare evening mess and be prepared to march back to Fort Niagara at four o'clock in the morning. Slowly the troops separated and walked back to their own tents.

Evening mess was served to a tense, silent line, with the entire New York militia coming behind all others, to sit in the forest, away from the camp, raising their heads to peer into the woods, nervous, watching. The other soldiers turned their backs on them and let them go. Taps and the lowering of the flag was a mournful thing, with the smaller group of men staring at the larger group with an expression that could suggest only one word—*traitor, traitor, traitor.*

Eli remained near the large fire in the center of the camp until midnight, when the last of the lamps in camp went dark, and then he walked to the tent of General Van Rensselaer to wait silently nearby for more than half an hour before he walked to his own campsite a short distance into the woods. The lamp inside the general's tent was still burning. Eli pulled his blanket to his chin and listened to the sounds of the forest for a time until he drifted into a restless, troubled sleep.

He was at the tent flap of the general twenty minutes before reveille. The lamp inside was burning, casting grotesque shadows on the yellow tent walls. Eli rapped on the post supporting the front end of the ridge pole.

There was surprise in the general's voice. "Who's there?"

"Eli Stroud."

There was a pause, then, "Come in."

Eli stepped through the flap and was instantly aware the general had not slept. On his small desk were his inkwell and quill, and a scatter of papers with scrawled notes and markings. On one corner was a document, folded, with the general's seal pressed into the wax.

"Yes?" the general said. His face was unreadable.

"I thought you might want me to cross the river and find out what became of our men yesterday."

Van Rensselaer's answer was curt. "They're obviously dead or prisoners of war."

"Maybe something can be worked out with the British."

"Excellent idea," Van Rensselaer sneered. "Go tell the British I'll exchange those cowards out there for the prisoners they took yesterday."

Eli drew a huge breath and said quietly, "I understand. I do not blame you. I'll be leaving soon. Is there anything I can do to help? Shall I stop at the fort and tell them what happened here?"

Van Rensselaer took control of his outrage. "Yes. Tell them the truth." He took the sealed document from his desk. "I was going to ask you to deliver this to President Madison."

Eli tucked the letter inside his shirt. "I will."

The general looked him in the face. "Do you have any idea what it is?"

Eli shook his head. "That's between you and the president. It will remain sealed."

Van Rensselaer waited for a moment, considering. "It is my request that I be relieved of my duties. Immediately. I refuse to go one day longer than necessary with those . . . traitorous cowards."

"I will make my written report for President Madison," Eli said. "I'll tell him what happened here. All of it. I'll deliver it with your report."

A brief look of gratitude crossed the general's face, and he said, "Do you want an escort? Anything I can give you?"

Eli shook his head. "No. I'll manage."

"Good luck to you. Tell the president. Tell him what you saw. What you know."

Without a word Eli walked out of the tent into the blackness of the night. Minutes later the camp drum sounded reveille. It echoed in the dark woods, sounding too loud, as though it did not belong, and lamps began to glow inside tents as the troops came to life. Eli did not wait. He was half a mile north, working through the woods, before the troops shuffled into line for their morning mess.

The morning sun was an hour high when Eli stopped at Fort Niagara to report the Queenston Heights disaster to the shocked lieutenant colonel in command. Half an hour later he was on Lake Erie in his canoe, gliding on glassy water into the brilliant autumn sun.

Notes

With the national election set in November 1812, President James Madison realized he needed a strong victory in the ongoing war to maintain himself and his Republican party in office. The plan to gain the strong victory included conquering Canada by taking Fort George on the west side of the Niagara River where it empties into Lake Erie. Directly across the river was American Fort Niagara. Six miles south of Fort George was Queenston

Heights; across the river was the American settlement Lewiston. The American officers selected to conduct the attack were General Stephen Van Rensselaer, his kinsman Lieutenant Colonel Solomon Van Rensselaer, General Alexander Smyth, and General Henry Dearborn. The army Congress sent north to accomplish it consisted of a large number of New York militia, mixed with some United States Army regulars.

The entire operation was to be under command of General Henry Dearborn, but he misunderstood his orders and failed to perform. Dearborn did make an unauthorized armistice with the British on August 5, 1812, which was discovered and quickly repudiated by President Madison on August 15 and rescinded by Dearborn on August 25, 1812, at which time Dearborn was ordered to get on with the plan. When Dearborn failed to do so, Van Rensselaer exercised his own initiative and formulated a plan to have Smyth and his regulars attack Fort George while Van Rensselaer and his kinsman went south to attack Queenston Heights. Smyth and his regulars refused to follow any orders issued by a state militia officer. The result was a conflicted, fragmented army as described herein.

Knowing he had numerical superiority over the British, General Stephen Van Rensselaer decided to attack Queenston Heights alone, then proceed north to attack Fort George. The day of the planned attack on Queenston Heights the oars necessary to row the longboats across the Niagara River went missing. It has never been determined who stole them. The Americans postponed the attack for two days, got more oars, and two days later, October 13, 1812, made their assault on Queenston Heights with Lieutenant Colonel Solomon Van Rensselaer leading the attack. He suffered six wounds but survived. Captain John E. Wool took command.

The first two hundred Americans to cross the river were pinned down by British musket fire from the sheer cliffs of Queenston Heights, two hundred forty feet above the river. The invaders found a fisherman's trail leading up the cliffs and climbed up to successfully drive the British back. Among the British dead was General Isaac Brock, hero of the battle of Fort Detroit the previous month of August and one of England's best officers. Other Americans followed across the river and joined those on top of the bluffs, totaling about nine hundred fifty, among them Lieutenant Colonel Winfield Scott, who took command. The Americans expected a British counterattack, and Stephen Van Rensselaer ordered the New York militia to cross the river to reinforce the Americans over there waiting. The militia refused, claiming they were not authorized to leave New York to fight on foreign soil. Van Rensselaer did everything in his power to try to force them to cross to save the men on the west side of the river, but did not succeed. The British did counterattack, and the entire force of nine hundred fifty Americans at Queenston Heights was either killed or taken prisoner. General Stephen Van Rensselaer submitted his written request to be relieved of command.

See Hickey, *The War of 1812*, pp. 86–87; Stagg, *Mr. Madison's War*, pp. 244–49; Wills, *James Madison*, pp. 103–05.

Eli Stroud is a fictional character.

The reader is advised that many of the major characters who were involved in this entire action against Canada are not included in this chapter simply because the numbers would make the chapter impossibly long and complex. Further, there were a number of minor skirmishes and battles that are likewise omitted for the same reason. Only those events that were of major importance in the War of 1812 are described herein.

CHAPTER XIX

★ ★ ★

*T*he President will see you now."

John Armstrong, the newly appointed secretary of war, stood quickly and strode into the library of President James Madison, leather satchel under his arm. Aging, balding, strongly built, strong face, large, penetrating eyes, nose tending to be slightly bulbous, he walked with the certainty of a man with unwavering confidence in himself, his views, his place in the affairs of the United States government, his ultimate ambition to become president, and the fact that his long-standing and well-known differences with Secretary of State James Monroe had been vindicated by his recent appointment to the office of secretary of war. Since his arrival in Washington, D.C., three days earlier, in a whirlwind of energy he had charmed, coerced, and cajoled the control of army patronage from Congress, made much of his reorganization plan for the entire War Department, and seized direction of the war away from James Monroe. After all, he was the "Old Soldier" who had written the book *Hints to Young Generals from an Old Soldier,* which, right or wrong, had catapulted him into the position of a leading authority on the business of war. No matter the "Old Soldier" had gained his experience thirty-five years earlier in the war for independence. No matter that the office of secretary of war had been first offered to both William H. Crawford and Henry Dearborn, but each had refused. Armstrong's sense of politics assured him that success in the office would give him footing to seek the presidency, and he was resolved that simple success was not acceptable. His success was going to be spectacular.

James Madison rose from his chair and walked around the great desk, smiling, congenial, hand extended.

"Secretary Armstrong! Thank you for coming. I'm aware of the . . . vigor you've demonstrated since your arrival here, what, three days ago?" Armstrong reached to shake the president's hand. "Yes, sir."

Madison sobered and wasted no time. "I take it you are prepared for tomorrow's cabinet meeting?"

"I am." Armstrong's eyes were glowing.

"Good. Take a seat. May I give you a brief synopsis of where we are politically?"

Madison did not wait for a response. As both men took seats, Madison began, and Armstrong could see the quiet, controlled fear in the eyes of the small man.

"The war campaign for 1812 did not go well. You know we lost Fort Detroit and the battle at Queenston Heights and Fort George. In November, Dearborn tried to redeem the entire Canadian effort by attempting to take Fort Erie. He failed and ordered Smyth to attack. Smyth printed and distributed several bombastic warnings to the British of the calamities he would bring down on them if they did not surrender, which the British saw as comical at best. Smyth made two token attempts to take Fort Erie, failed both times, and simply disbanded his army and returned home."

Madison stopped long enough to see Armstrong nod understanding, then went on.

"As a result, our Republican party paid the price. In the last election we lost seats in both the House and Senate. We still have a majority, but we lost twelve percent in the House and four percent in the Senate. And we lost our majority in three states—Massachusetts, New Jersey, and Maryland. Add those three to Rhode Island, Connecticut, and Delaware that were Federalist to begin with, and we now hold a bare majority of states."

Again Madison paused, watching Armstrong, then went on.

"You're aware that in the recent election in New York, our Republican senator John Smith lost to Federalist Rufus King. You are also aware that on April twenty-seventh—just seventy-nine days from now—New York will return to the polls to elect a governor. If the same forces that got Rufus King elected are able to get a Federalist elected governor, we will have lost one more very important state. That could become a disaster. Do you understand?"

Armstrong was clear, firm. "I do, sir."

Madison sat back for a moment, gathering his thoughts. When he spoke he was making small gestures with his hands. "To give some vital support to our Republicans in New York we very badly need to show some strength—some initiative on the Canadian front. We need to bring to the whole country some inspiring news about some victories."

Armstrong was nodding vigorously.

Madison smiled woodenly. "Now, sir, I will be happy to hear the plan you propose delivering at the cabinet meeting tomorrow to accomplish this."

Armstrong stood, quickly unbuckled his satchel, and drew out a sheaf of papers. He laid them on the leading edge of the desk and began to speak as he unfolded a large map. As Madison rose to stand over the map, Armstrong squared it with the compass, then tapped his finger firmly on the St. Lawrence River where it was marked "Montreal," midway between Quebec and the east end of Lake Ontario.

"For some time now the administration has been aware that the key to taking Canada is seizing control of the Great Lakes. If we intend driving the British from Canada altogether, this is the place we should start. Take Montreal and place fifty cannon batteries on the riverbanks, and we can stop anything the British send up the St. Lawrence to sustain their military on the Great Lakes. Every British outpost, every British fort, will be trapped without communication or support and could eventually be taken systematically, in order!"

Armstrong paused, intensely watching Madison for a change of expression. There was none, and he went on.

"To take Montreal would require us to assemble a large military force in the state of New York, train it, equip it, and move it north on the Richelieu River to the St. Lawrence, then west to Montreal. At the same time we would move what gunboats are available east on the St. Lawrence to take up positions facing Montreal. A coordinated attack— the army on land, the navy on the river—would bring Montreal under our control."

Again he paused, aware of the growing sense of frustration and impatience in Madison. He took a breath and continued.

"At best, it would take the entire summer to accomplish such a plan. And we do not have the entire summer. It is seventy-nine days until the pivotal election that will decide whether the Republicans lose the state of New York to the Federalists."

He stopped, then spaced his words for dramatic impact.

"We *must have* a military victory that will help swing the New York election to the Republicans, and we must have it not later than the first day of April. It must reach all newspapers in Albany and New York City and in other towns in time to persuade the voters that the Republicans and this administration have turned the course of the war in our favor, and can win it."

For the first time, Armstrong saw faint hope in Madison's eyes. Armstrong shifted his finger on the map, following the St. Lawrence west to the point where it joins Lake Ontario, to stop at the place marked Kingston.

"Taking Montreal is the most strategically important objective we can undertake to defeat the British, but at this moment the strategy of the war must yield to the political realities. Before the New York election, the Republican party must bring to this country a victory that will lift the spirit of the nation—revive a sense of patriotism—restore confidence that we can rise above our mistakes of last year and win!"

Madison cut in. "How do you propose we accomplish that?"

Armstrong tapped his finger on the map. "Take Kingston!"

Madison's forehead drew down in question. "Take the British base of naval operations on the Great Lakes?"

"Exactly! At this moment it is poorly defended. Vulnerable. Land our army on both sides while our gunboats engage their shore batteries, and attack the naval base from both sides and the rear. The meager force they have there now would surrender within twenty-four hours or be completely destroyed. If such a victory could be announced in this country in the first week of April, the election would be assured in our favor."

"If we do take Kingston, what is our next step?"

Hastily Armstrong traced with his finger. "York. Here. At the other end of Lake Ontario. Then on to Fort Erie. Here. On the British side of the Niagara River. Across from Buffalo. Once we have Kingston, York and Fort Erie will quickly fall. That will give us the political advantage we must have immediately. We can follow that with a military victory at Montreal that will give us control of the Great Lakes. And once the Great Lakes are ours, the British hold on Canada is doomed."

Madison nodded, and Armstrong saw the light coming into his eyes. He went on.

"You remember that last September orders were given to Captain Isaac Chauncey to assume control of American naval forces on Erie and Ontario, and to do whatever necessary to bring them under our control."

Madison reflected for a moment. "Yes. I remember. Chauncey is a younger man, but capable. Am I right?"

"Yes. He has spent the winter gathering ships wherever he could, and getting others built. He has them moored at Sacketts Harbor, here, on Lake Ontario, and at Presque Isle, here, on Lake Erie. He also contacted and brought in a twenty-seven-year-old naval officer named Oliver H. Perry—a very promising young officer. He's ordered Perry to take control of our Lake Erie forces while Chauncey continues with Lake Ontario. There's a third man Chauncey has included. Adam Dunson. Dunson's a middle-aged man of experience in commercial shipping. He's commanded commercial ships on the Great Lakes many times in the past twenty years for a company named Dunson & Weems out of Boston. Knows every port on the lakes. Intimately. Chauncey needs Dunson's experience."

Madison asked, "Is Dunson going to command one of our naval gunboats?"

Armstrong shook his head. "No. He brought his own ship, the *Margaret.* His own crew. He converted one of his commercial ships to a gunboat—thirty-eight heavy cannon—and has offered it—himself, his crew, and his gunboat—as a volunteer."

Madison suddenly straightened, eyes wide. "Did you say Adam Dunson?"

"Yes. Know him?"

"Not him, but I know Matthew Dunson! Matthew Dunson and Billy Weems own that shipping company. Matthew is one of my most trusted confidants! If Adam Dunson is of that family, Chauncey has chosen well!"

Armstrong went on. "This entire offensive is to commence the first day of April. Twenty-two days from now. We don't have one day, one hour, to waste."

Madison stared in question. "April first?"

Armstrong nodded vigorously. "April first."

"The ice?" Madison asked.

"It will be far enough gone that it should not be a hindrance. What's left of it we can handle." Armstrong paused for an instant, then continued. "Now, I have arranged for the two prominent newspapers—the *Albany Argus* and the *National Advocate*—to prepare news articles for release the first week in April. The articles will trumpet our successes on both the lakes—Erie and Ontario."

Madison peered into Armstrong's face in question. "Odd that you're preparing news articles before the event. What becomes of all this if the campaign fails? The Republican party would be the laughingstock."

Armstrong passed it off casually. "The plan will work. Even if we experience problems, the election will be completed before it becomes an issue."

Madison straightened at the terrible risk Armstrong was proposing and raised a hand as if to speak, then dropped it and remained silent, caught between his inner sense of right and wrong, and the terrible need to be reelected to the presidency.

Armstrong went on. "The man I propose to take charge of this entire campaign is General Henry Dearborn."

Madison recoiled. "Dearborn? After his failure at Detroit and Niagara and Montreal last fall? He very nearly lost the war for us! A total disaster!"

Armstrong paused for a moment to let Madison settle. "I'm well aware. The sole reason I suggest him is that in my opinion there is no one else available right now who would accept the position. Do you have someone else in mind?"

Madison turned and paced a few steps, then returned to the desk, torment in his eyes. "Dearborn."

"Good. The only remaining formality is to have your approval of this plan at the earliest time possible. You intend presenting it at the cabinet meeting tomorrow?"

"Yes. Tomorrow. You will present it, not me."

Armstrong bobbed his head. "Very good, sir. I shall be prepared." He folded his map, assembled his papers, slipped them all back into his satchel, bid goodbye to Madison, and walked out, leaving the president standing alone, hands clasped behind his back, head tipped forward as he stared at the polished hardwood floor, struggling with the rising fear that the entire campaign was too fragile.

Too many assumptions. Too many uncontrollable contingencies. What if the ice on the lakes holds until the end of April? What will the British do when they see the buildup of American naval forces on the Lakes? What of this twenty-seven-year-old Commodore Perry?—too young—too young. What of Adam Dunson—unproven—he knows the Lakes, but what will he do in battle? Dearborn! What will the country say when we put Dearborn in command?—the one who led us into that disaster last fall? Newspaper articles to be published before the event, announcing great and glorious victories? If those articles appear and then Dearborn bungles the whole campaign, who will ever again trust the Republican party!

Half a dozen times throughout the day Madison rose from behind his desk to pace while he battled with his growing fears. *Chauncey— capable? Perry—too young? Dunson—untried in battle. The British—what will they do? Dearborn! The worst of it!*

It was late when he turned out the lamps and went to his bed to spend a sleepless night tossing and turning while the darkness played havoc with his mind.

Morning broke bleak with ice on the Potomac, a blanket of frost covering Washington, D.C., and a dull gray overcast. Madison's cabinet arrived on the porch one at a time, bundled in capes, vapors rising from their breath. They hung their winter wraps in the cloak room and took their places at the long, oval, polished oak table in the luxurious room with paintings and murals and gold lamps on the walls, where Armstrong had placed maps and a written outline of his war campaign for 1813. At nine o'clock Madison entered the room, called them to order, made a perfunctory statement of agenda, and turned the meeting into the eager hands of John Armstrong.

His presentation was crisp and precise, but he was not five minutes into the meat of it before every man at the table had studied the map and the outline, and was caught up in silent skepticism, and then in abject pessimism at the growing number of dangerous contingencies that became all too apparent. Debate opened, and the challenges came, frank and strong. Armstrong answered, dodging and turning, but in the end it all came down to the simple question that was the foundation on which life in Washington, D.C., finally came to rest: What must I do to get reelected and maintain my power?

Every concern, every objection to the plan would fade and die if the men gathered in the luxury of the Executive Mansion cabinet room could believe it would permit them to remain in office.

Very artfully Armstrong reached his blunt conclusion. "The New York election is seventy-eight days away. If any man in this room can conceive of a better plan to swing it to the Republican party, now is the time to lay it on the table."

A tense silence continued for ten seconds before Armstrong concluded.

"Thank you, gentlemen." He turned to Madison. "Mister President, I have nothing further."

Madison said, "Gentlemen, your reactions? Do you approve Mister Armstrong's proposal?"

Murmurings were exchanged, then the men quieted.

Madison stood. "Very well. Mister Armstrong, start immediately. Notify General Dearborn of his appointment to take command of the campaign. Time is against us. This meeting is concluded. Please leave all papers and maps on the table."

There was little talk among the cabinet members as they rose and took their leave while Armstrong gathered up his maps and paperwork and buckled them into his satchel, while Madison watched, silent, caught up in his own reservations.

"Mister President, I'll notify General Dearborn of his appointment today."

"Thank you."

In the cloak room, Armstrong buckled his winter cape about his shoulders and set his tricorn on his head. His boot heels clicked a steady cadence in the long hallway as he made his way to the heavy door. He scarcely noticed the hush that had settled in the streets, or the large, lazy snowflakes that had begun drifting in the gray, dead air. He walked the two blocks to his own small, austere office, hung his wraps, and took his place at his desk.

It was midafternoon before he called his assistant with a sealed document in his hand.

"It is imperative that this reach General Henry Dearborn in Albany as soon as possible. Send it by courier."

Four days later a light, two-masted schooner broke through the ragged ice that reached fifty feet from the wharf at Albany out into the Hudson River. The gangplank thumped into place on the frigid docks, and a man with a small suitcase in his hand and vapor trailing from his nose and mouth stepped gingerly ashore. Twenty minutes later Henry Dearborn raised his head at his desk, startled at the loud, insistent rap at his door. The courier, short, wiry, with nervous eyes, handed him the sealed document and stood waiting, shifting from one foot to the other while Dearborn read it twice before he looked up.

"Wait in the foyer. I'll have an answer within the hour for you to deliver back to Secretary Armstrong."

For a time Dearborn arranged thoughts and words in his mind before he reached for a sheet of paper and his quill and began to write.

" . . . I understand I am to immediately assemble four thousand troops at Sacketts Harbor for an assault on Kingston, and an additional three thousand troops at Buffalo for the subsequent assault on York and the Niagara Peninsula. I further understand that I shall have available the services of naval forces under command of Captain Isaac Chauncey and Commodore Oliver H. Perry, and their ships, to transport troops and lend firepower should it be required. I must voice my principal concern in the plan as I understand it. The British will observe that we are concentrating large forces and supplies at Sacketts Harbor and shall correctly conclude that we intend attacking their facility at Kingston. My deep concern is that should they do so, we will once again find ourselves lacking in men and material in sufficient supply to take possession of Kingston. However, notwithstanding my concern, I shall proceed at once . . ."

For days Dearborn buried himself in the endless paperwork that politics and war demand. Sealed orders were sent by courier to Isaac Chauncey and Oliver Perry, ordering them to gather their ships and crews—Chauncey at Sacketts Harbor on Lake Ontario to prepare for the assault on Kingston, Perry on Lake Erie, at Presque Isle. Commissary and supply agents were sent to contract for the purchase of the massive stockpiles of materials necessary to support ten thousand men through the last months of winter and into the spring. Through the remaining days of February and deep into the month of March, troops arrived to take up camp at the naval base at Sacketts Harbor, along with mountainous stockpiles of uniforms, shoes, muskets, rifles, cannon, mortars, gunpowder, shot, shells, blankets, wheat, dried fish, barrels of salt pork and beef, potatoes, rice, sugar, coffee, medicines, and bandages.

From his office in Washington, D.C., Armstrong was watching Dearborn in Albany like a hawk, to be certain he did not repeat the fatal performance that had cost the United States the entire campaign of

1812. When bold leadership had been the critical need in the assaults on Fort George and Montreal, Dearborn had hidden behind paperwork and protocol and abandoned any pretense of uniting and leading his men into battle. The result was disaster. It was not going to happen again, if Armstrong could stop it. He arranged contact with picked officers and purchasing agents, under orders that they were to keep him abreast of every development among the troops and their supplies, and Armstrong read and reread their incoming messages daily.

It was late in March when he sensed it. With the date to commence the assault on Kingston just days away, Dearborn was still in Albany, vacillating, spending his days in bookwork and communications, ignoring the crying need for him to step up and lead! Armstrong sent him a direct order.

"You are hereby ordered to travel from Albany to Sacketts Harbor to command the American forces *in person!*"

Reluctantly, almost fearfully, Dearborn made the wintry journey up the Hudson River the few miles to the Mohawk River and then west on the water to Rome, and on northwest overland to Sacketts Harbor. The day he arrived at the naval base he took his first shock.

The harbor was still frozen with ice thick enough to march an army to Canada, or for the British to march an army to the United States! Chauncey and his boats had no chance of reaching Kingston.

Two days later Dearborn took his second shock. An exhausted messenger with a great brown wool coat and a beard with icicles hanging banged on his door to hand him a message scrawled by one of the captains out on patrol.

"The British have assembled between six and eight thousand regulars at Kingston . . . they intend marching on Sacketts Harbor."

Dearborn recoiled as though struck. His worst fear—the one he had stated so clearly to Armstrong months before—had come to pass. British patrols had reported the buildup of men and materiel at Sacketts Harbor, and the British war council had correctly concluded the Americans meant to attack Kingston. Their response? Gather their own forces and strike Sacketts Harbor first!

Eight thousand British regulars at Kingston, poised for an attack? How could his own four thousand American soldiers survive such a battle?

Behind the closed door of his office he paced back and forth, near distraction, unable to force his shattered thoughts to any sense of logic or reason. In his panic, it never occurred to Dearborn to send out other patrols to confirm the number of British troops actually gathered at Kingston, nor to determine their state of readiness to make an all-out march and attack on Sacketts Harbor. He would never know that had he done so, he would have learned that the British forces at Kingston were not eight thousand. Far from it! They were less than three thousand, and they were not prepared to march anywhere, least of all across ice where they would be visible for miles, to make an attack on Sacketts Harbor!

Within one hour he had issued grim orders to his war council.

"You will immediately make all preparations to receive and resist an attack from the British at Kingston."

The following day he summoned Chauncey and his naval commanders, among them Adam Dunson, to his office for a session to be conducted behind locked doors. Agitated, hands trembling, he wasted no time in spreading a map before them and the usual formalities were forgotten as he jammed a finger on the map at the place marked Kingston.

"Gentlemen, reports reached this office yesterday that the British have about eight thousand troops gathered at Kingston and that they intend making a full-scale attack on our facility here at Sacketts Harbor."

The room went silent, and Dearborn droned on.

"I have no reason to doubt the reports. I have ordered our army to prepare for a massive assault. If it comes, we have no choice other than to engage the British here, which we shall do."

He paused while the alarmed officers exchanged open exclamations, then settled. Dearborn continued. "If the British do not attack, we have the option of completing our attack on Kingston as planned. However, with eight thousand British regulars there to defend their facility, there is little chance of our success with only four thousand to make the assault."

Adam Dunson sat still, only his eyes moving as he watched Chauncey, then the other lesser naval officers and then Dearborn, and Adam saw the near-panic in Dearborn's eyes.

"My orders," Dearborn continued, "are to deliver a victory, and I will not engage in a battle we cannot win. It is clear to me that we must reconsider the standing orders to take Kingston. I brought you here to discuss an alternative plan. I am open to suggestions."

There it was, plain, simple, ugly. With no confirming reports, with no definition of how the British forces were disbursed, or the number of their cannon, or the officers in command, Dearborn was once again in full-blown retreat from horrors that existed only in his mind.

Chauncey sensed it and was the first to speak. "If that's true, then may I suggest we reverse our plan. Take York first, then back to take Fort George, and on east to take Kingston last."

Adam saw the first light of hope come into Dearborn's eyes. "Yes, go on."

Chauncey continued, his voice rising, hands gesturing. "York is the capital of Canada. Small, but the capital nonetheless. There is only a small British force there to defend it, less than one thousand. It is accessible from the lake. Once the ice is gone, we can make an amphibious landing. Our gunboats can give cannon cover to the troops as they march on the town."

Adam saw the relief coming into Dearborn's face. "How do you propose getting our troops from here to the York harbor and then ashore?"

Chauncey considered for a moment, then turned to Adam. "Mister Dunson, you've been inside the York harbor before, correct?"

"Yes. Many times. Picking up and delivering shipped goods."

"How would you go about attacking the town?"

Adam rose from his chair and for several seconds studied the map. Then he moved his finger along the Canadian shore of Lake Ontario, east of the York harbor, as he spoke.

"Scarborough Heights are here. The British have picket posts about every three or four miles with semaphore flags to pass messages. If there is no fog, they'll see our squadron coming long before we get to the York harbor, and they'll relay the message on to Fort York. They'll be waiting for us."

A tense silence settled over the officers as Adam paused, then went on.

"But I think there's a way to surprise them. Track with me."

He placed his finger on the west side of the harbor, near the top. "The blockhouse and the legislative buildings are here."

He moved his finger down, speaking as it went. "The naval dock yards are in this area."

He stopped about halfway to the mouth of the harbor. "Fort York and the village are here. The governor's house is right here, and next to it is a powder magazine. A huge one."

He moved his finger a short distance farther down. "There is a battery of cannon right there. Those guns can reach anything approaching Fort York and the village from the water, before it gets there."

He shifted his finger further south, on the west side of the very mouth of the harbor. "There is an old fort here, built years ago by the French. I doubt there are any guns still active there, but there could be."

He moved his finger around the curving mouth of the harbor to the shoreline of Lake Ontario and moved it west and stopped.

"If I were to do it, when the ice will allow, I would not take the squadron into the harbor to face the British guns that will be waiting for us. I would put my men ashore here. From Lake Ontario, outside the harbor. It's about one and one half miles from the town. From there, they can march northeast *behind* the old French fort and *behind* that battery of guns, directly to the town. They can hit the town from the west side and the rear at the same time. While they're marching, we can send gunboats into the harbor and pin down the defenders with our cannon to keep them from preparing to meet the land attack. For a short time, the British are going to be in a state of confusion, trying to decide whether they should engage the soldiers coming from the west on land, or the ships coming into the harbor from the south."

There was excitement in Chauncey's eyes as he responded. "You would not attempt an amphibious landing from the harbor directly on the town? If we land troops on both sides of the town, we can trap the defenders. Leave them no way out."

Adam nodded his head. "It is my guess they will be expecting us to do that. If they do, they will divide their force, most of them on each edge of the town, facing outward. That will reduce their forces by about one half, either direction. If we can get our troops ashore quickly enough down here to the west, and if they can cover the ground fast enough while we open fire from our gunboats with all available cannon, it is my opinion we can pin down the British long enough for our troops to overrun the defenders on the west side of town before the other half of their fighting force can get there to help them. We can be into the town before they get organized."

Chauncey looked at Dearborn, waiting for a response.

Dearborn cleared his throat. "Does anyone have other options?"

Experienced eyes went over the map again and again while comments and proposals were put out on the table, discussed, dismembered, and discarded. Slowly the talk died.

Chauncey seized the moment. "I propose we agree on Mister Dunson's plan. There is risk, but it is acceptable risk, and if it succeeds we will have accomplished our major objective. We will have our victory, and the nation will be lifted!"

Adam raised a hand in caution, and the room became silent as he spoke. "There are two remaining questions. Do we have a commander capable of getting our troops from the ships to the shore in longboats and bateau, and then leading them to Fort York at double-time and taking the town? And who are the British officers we will be facing? How capable are they?"

Every eye turned to Dearborn, expectant, waiting in the silence.

He shifted his feet before he spoke. "I will have to consider which army officer should lead the attack. As for the British officers we will be facing, my information is that their commanding officer is Sir George Prevost. He is capable. Sir Roger Sheaffe leads their army troops. His military record is very good. Commodore James Lucas Yeo is expected to become their naval commander but has not yet arrived. He is a cautious man, but competent."

Meaningful glances were exchanged around the table with a few comments before they all turned back to Dearborn.

"If there is nothing else, this meeting is concluded. Mister Chauncey and Mister Dunson, remain here to assist in drafting the new proposal for delivery to Secretary Armstrong and President Madison."

It was late afternoon before an exhausted Dearborn signed the six-page document addressed to Secretary of War John Armstrong, then leaned back to dig the heels of his hands into weary eyes. He drew a great breath and released it slowly before he stood.

"Gentlemen, I shall personally deliver this to Secretary Armstrong. While I am gone, Brigadier General Zebulon Pike will be in command of the army here. He will be under orders to prepare for the British attack."

There was no attack. On April first, the ice was still thick on the lake. Strain and raw nerves at both Sacketts Harbor and Kingston took its toll on soldiers and sailors who waited and watched through day after day of bleak, freezing cold, and storms with gale force winds that cut through their heavy coats to chill them to the bone. By mid-April the ice had begun to turn rotten, and by April nineteenth only patches remained along the shoreline. On April twentieth, Dearborn returned from Washington, D.C., to Sacketts Harbor and resumed command of his forces. The morning of April twenty-first he called both Chauncey and Pike to his office.

"Secretary Armstrong approved our plan. We attack York immediately." He turned to Pike. "Start loading your troops onto Mister Chauncey's boats and bateaux tomorrow morning."

Chauncey raised a hand to cut him off. "We have a storm coming in. A big one. I strongly recommend we wait until it passes."

Dearborn shook his head emphatically. "We're already three weeks late. Storm or no, we load tomorrow and proceed."

The morning of April twenty-second broke dismal gray with thick, purple clouds riding low, driven by heavy winds. Captain Chauncey bit down on his need to wait out the storm, and General Pike gritted his teeth against his innermost fears as he ordered his men to board the ships and the bateaux for the attack.

The loading began. In an unending procession the longboats left the docks filled with soldiers from Pike's army, rowed out to the waiting ships with the bateau tied behind, and tried to hold steady in the rising swells while the soldiers climbed netting up to the rocking decks above. Then they broke away from the ships to make way for the longboats waiting behind, and returned to the docks for the next load. They continued through the afternoon, with the winds rising, whistling in the rigging of the ships, whipping spray from whitecaps onto the huddled troops.

The ships steadily filled, with soldiers jammed into every compartment, every corner—in the hold of the ship and crammed onto the main deck, standing shoulder to shoulder. On the USS *Madison,* more than six hundred men were squeezed together in a space designed for one hundred fifty. On every ship, no more than half the men could go below deck at one time, so they began a rotation—half above and half below deck—to avoid freezing that could cost fingers and toes and noses.

Dusk came gray with the winds holding strong, singing in the rigging, kicking up swells and whitecaps that drenched the men and swamped the longboats and slammed them into the sides of the pitching, rolling ships and bateaux. With full darkness upon them, Chauncey shouted the orders that stopped the longboats, and they returned to shore to wait for morning.

The winds held through the night, and with dawn approaching the rain squalls came freezing, driven, slanting, to soak every man and the rigging of every ship, whipping the water as it ran from their beards and blankets and coats and the sails of the bucking vessels.

On the *Margaret,* Adam ran flags up the mainmast that told Chauncey, "There is danger to men and vessels. Do we continue loading?"

Chauncey answered. "Danger recognized. Will inquire."

Quickly he sent a written message ashore to Armstrong with an officer in a departing longboat.

"Imperative that we cease loading and wait for the storm to abate . . .
there is risk of longboats or ships capsizing."

The answer came back. "Continue loading. Make sail for Kingston
when finished."

Chauncey silently cursed Armstrong for a fool and sent flags up the
mainmast with the message to Adam and all other ships.

"Ordered to continue loading."

Adam shook his head in disbelief, and the *Margaret* continued battling the treacherous winds and rains with the crew holding its breath,
desperately straining to avoid a mistake on the swamped decks that
would kill or maim the men coming aboard from the longboats.

Shortly before noon the last longboat was unloaded, and it broke
away from the ship to fight its way back toward the docks. Obedient to
his orders, Chauncey ran the signal flag up the mainmast, and commanders of the thirteen ships, each with one or more bateau lashed on
behind, stared for a moment in stunned amazement, then weighed anchor
and followed Chauncey on the flagship, with the *Margaret* right behind,
out of the partial shelter of Sacketts Harbor into the full fury of the
storm.

The masts of the schooners creaked and groaned as the freezing,
howling winds from the southeast stretched the sails to their limits, and
the great, surging whitecaps came sweeping over the railings to bury the
decks of the overloaded ships and the bateau, and send them wallowing,
pitching, leaning violently, first to port, then starboard. Time had no
meaning as Chauncey stood stony faced on his quarterdeck, conscious
of but one thing. Every ship in his squadron was loaded double and
triple beyond its design, with hundreds of huddled men and far too
much weight on the main decks. They were unstable, leaning fifteen and
twenty degrees beyond their limits. The question was not, would one or
more of them capsize? The question was, *when* would one of them
capsize?

He had reached Stony Point before he overrode Armstrong's orders.

He barked his own orders to his first mate, and the man ran signals up the mainmast, "Return to port immediately."

One by one the ships made the turn and fought their way back to Sacketts Harbor to drop anchor and ride out the storm while the troops remained on the decks with their soggy blankets pulled about their shoulders to hold in what heat they could. The following day the storm blew itself out, and by evening the clouds separated to a glowing sunset. At dawn the next morning, beneath clear skies, with a steady southeast wind, the entire squadron weighed anchor and once again took a bearing due west, out of Sacketts Harbor into the open waters of Lake Ontario with the *Julia* leading, the *Growler* in the rear, and the *Madison*, *Oneida*, and *Margaret* in the center. The wind held, and the line of ships, each towing its flat-bottomed bateau, sped steadily west, watching the distant shoreline of the lake slip past throughout the day.

The sun was low in the west when Adam extended his telescope and for a time stood on his quarterdeck studying the faint, dark line to the north that was Scarborough Heights on the shore of the lake. He could not see them, but he knew there were British outposts on the heights, and that red coated pickets would be there with their own telescopes, intently watching for the first sighting of the sails of the approaching American squadron.

Have they seen us yet? What will their General Sheaffe do when the report reaches him? Will he set up his defenses the way we expect? Or are we sailing into a surprise? A trap? Time will tell. We'll see.

Onshore, a British sergeant at a picket post near the top of the Heights raised his telescope to his eye to scan the lake on his regular fifteen-minute interval. Suddenly he tensed, and his arm shot up to point. "There!" he exclaimed to the three startled soldiers beside him. "A squadron! It has to be the Americans! The ones we were told about."

"How many?" blurted the corporal next to him.

Seconds passed while the sergeant slowly moved his telescope, counting.

"Thirteen ships, and it looks like they're towing bateau! It's them!

Their main force! On a heading for York harbor! Send the message. Now!"

The corporal snatched up his semaphore flags and raced up the ladder rungs to the small platform at the rear of the post. He faced due west and with the flags fluttering in the wind, spelled out the warning over and over again, "Thirteen enemy gunboats with bateau approaching York harbor—thirteen enemy gunboats approaching York harbor."

Four miles farther west, with the sun setting behind, the next picket post read the message, waited for it to repeat, then turned and relayed it to the next picket post. In early dusk, the message reached Major General Sir Roger Hale Sheaffe at his desk in the government building at York. Sheaffe, aging, balding, heavy-lidded eyes, long tapered nose, calmly rose from his chair and called for his assistant.

"The American squadron is approaching. Assemble the war council."

Within minutes the six officers were gathered around the plain pinewood table in his small conference room, waiting in apprehensive silence.

"Gentlemen, there is a squadron of thirteen American gunboats with bateau approaching from the east. The total firepower of their cannon is about triple what we have here, and their complement of soldiers is more than double our total fighting force."

Wide-eyed silence gripped the room while Shaeffe spread a map and tapped his finger on Scarborough Heights, east of York harbor. "They were seen here less than half an hour ago. I expect them to be in the harbor about sunrise. I am open to suggestions of how we deploy our forces to meet them."

For more than one hour the officers leaned intently over the map, gesturing, debating, exclaiming in the give and take that slowly shapes a plan the majority can agree with. The moon had risen before they shrugged into their capes and clamped their tricorns on their heads and walked out into the freezing wind and hurried across the parade grounds to the barracks to give the orders that brought groans and murmured cursing. In the blustering cold, red-coated regulars shouldered their backpacks and slung their muskets over their shoulders and marched to follow their officers to their assigned positions to face the attack. One half of them took positions on the east end of town, around the legislative buildings and the old blockhouse, while the other half went west, to positions near the lone cannon battery. The gray of approaching dawn found them hungry, shivering in the cold, wiping at dripping noses, peering west toward the entrance to harbor, still hidden in the dark. The black silhouettes of the sails of the American gunboats came with first light, and then the rising sun caught the tops of the masts with the American flags snapping in the southeast wind about one mile west of town, not far from the ruins of the ancient French fort and nearly one mile off shore. There, in the frigid wind, the red-coated regulars watched as the American flotilla dropped anchor.

On board the American ships, the captains gave the orders, and soldiers went over the sides into the more than thirty bateaux, hunched down while the seamen rowed to gather around the *Madison,* waiting for the signal to start for the distant shore where General Sheaffe had positioned the Eighth Infantry to oppose them, supported by the Glengarry Light Infantry, a few Newfoundland Fencibles, and a scatter of Canadian militia.

American general Zebulon Pike, thirty-four years of age, a rising star in the United States Army, whose brusque leadership had irritated some of his fellow officers, had been assigned to lead the assault. He was in the lead bateau with a company of Benjamin Forsyth's riflemen when the signal was given to start for the distant Canadian shore, watching for the first glimpse of movement that would mean British troops waiting, or for a British Union Jack flying in the stiff wind that was blowing hard from the right, driving the bateau to their left, west, out of line with the place picked for the landing.

They were two hundred yards from the shore when the first cloud of white smoke erupted on the shoreline, and the first musket balls came whistling, and then the rolling blast from the first volley of the British regulars. They were fifty yards closer to shore when the second volley came whining, and some men in the leading bateau groaned and sat

down. Two paddles in the first bateau shattered while the others continued to dig into the choppy waters, oarsmen straining to cover the last
distance to shore to get off the water where they were prime targets.

They were yet fifteen yards from shore when the riflemen in the first
two bateau went over the side into water up to their belts to get ashore,
rifles high above their heads to keep the powder dry while musket balls
kicked up geysers two feet high in the water all around them. Then, as in
a dream, the first of them were on the land, dripping, kneeling, some
going down while the others fired back with their deadly Pennsylvania
long rifles, and British redcoats were going down and any sense of time
was lost as the two major forces collided in hand-to-hand fighting and
then the British lines began to buckle, then bent and backed up and
broke, and the Americans stormed after them into the trees, leaving the
invaders in control of the beach and the forest while the British beat a
full retreat back toward the town.

Back on the water, Adam stood fast on his quarterdeck while the last
of the bateau broke away from the *Margaret* and started for the shore
amidst the continuous rattle of musket and rifle fire. Adam raised his
telescope and studied the collision of the two armies, and watched with
growing hope as the British wavered then suddenly began their retreat.

He turned and barked his orders, pointing ashore. "Weigh anchor!
All canvas! Move west to that open ground between the woods and the
town! Full speed! All gun crews! Load with canister. Stand by to fire!"

Seamen threw their weight against the windlass, and the anchor chain
rattled on deck as it came reeling in. The gun crews banged the gun ports
open, jerked the knots loose, and backed their cannon away to jam the
sacks of gunpowder down the muzzles, followed by the pouches filled
with canister, then strained on the ropes to drag the cannon back into
firing position. Seamen on the arms high above the deck unfurled the
sails, and they dropped to catch the wind, popped full, and the big ship
came alive, cutting a thirty-foot curl as she plowed east, toward the town
and the open ground through which the British had to pass. The red-
coated regulars broke from the trees at the same moment the *Margaret*
came abreast of them and Adam shouted, "Fire!"

The nineteen heavy cannon on the port side of the ship bucked and roared in unison, and the wind whipped the great cloud of white smoke aside. Adam and his gun crews saw the British soldiers buckle and go down as the canister shot spread to rip through the trees and into the running soldiers.

As fast as seasoned hands could move, the gun crews on the *Margaret* reloaded and sent a second broadside of canister shot whistling ashore to knock the fleeing British rolling. The companies Sheaffe had stationed on the other side of York, the east side, came at a sprint, intending to meet those running the gauntlet of the cannon on the American ships, but they stopped in the town, hesitant at first, then refusing to be caught on the open ground being raked by the heavy cannon on the American ships, now two hundred yards off shore, delivering a near continuous barrage of grape and canister shot.

The lone British battery belatedly returned fire at the ships, and two American schooners held back, fearful of the heavy explosive cannonballs that came at them. It was on the third volley that someone in the British crew made the fatal mistake of allowing the smoking lanyard to touch the budge barrel, and the keg of powder exploded. When the smoke cleared, the gun had been blown off its mount, and the gun crew was yards away, lying dead or dying. The British battery never fired another shot.

In the town, at the governor's residence, Sheaffe saw it coming. His forces had no chance of surviving the driving attack coming from the west, led by Pike and the crack riflemen, in combination with the American gunboats now relentlessly pounding the retreating British regulars and the village with continuous cannon fire. Quickly he rallied his officers and turned to Colonel William Chewett.

"Set fire to the main powder magazine. The gunpowder and munitions must be kept out of American hands. Then march your command to Kingston, on the Kingston Road. Do it now!"

Chewett gaped. "Sir," he stammered, "there are more than two hundred barrels of gunpowder in the magazine, besides other munitions. Enough to blow half the town away!"

Sheaffe raised a warning finger. "Set it on fire and get away from it."
"Yes, sir."

Sheaffe turned to Major William Allan. "Set fire to ship—the *Sir Isaac Brock*—and all the stores at the dockyard storehouses. We cannot let the ship or the supplies fall to the Americans. Then order your command to follow Colonel Chewett on the Kingston Road. Save your men. Do you both understand?"

There was no time to argue the order. Chewett and Allan both turned on their heels and trotted out of the building, back to their command.

Within twenty minutes, gray smoke was rising from the powder magazine, while the *Sir Isaac Brock* was in flames that were spreading in the wind, and the British regulars were east of town on the Kingston Road in full retreat. In the small village, the American soldiers had stopped among the crude log homes and buildings, in the dirt streets, winded, fighting for breath after their sprint from the forest across the open ground and into the town. They saw the smoke rising from the powder magazine and the ship at the far end of the docks, and from the huge piles of crated supplies on the wharves, and some of them were trotting toward the powder magazine to stop the fire.

Suddenly the magazine blew with a roar. Fire and rocks and stones and chunks and splinters of wood and a column of smoke were blasted three hundred feet into the air to rain down on everything within half a mile. Thirty-eight of the nearest American soldiers were blown back ten yards to hit the ground rolling and lay still, the life blown out of them. Two hundred twenty of those farther away were knocked off their feet, stunned, groaning, disoriented, bleeding where rocks and debris had ripped into them, crippling them, disabling them. The blast rattled windows as far away as Fort Niagara, across Lake Erie. The shock waves hit the American ships in the harbor to set them rocking and shiver their sails while chunks of stone twice the size of a man's fist rained down on the decks.

The instant General Pike saw the flash he spun to take the shock on his back, and a rock the size of a cannonball hit him at the belt line to knock him ten feet, sprawling. Dazed, he tried to rise and realized he could not move his arms or legs. When they could, his troops gently laid him on a blanket and carried him to a longboat where waiting seamen rowed him back to the *Madison.* He died minutes later of a broken spine, with his head resting on a British flag his men had sent with him in tribute to his heroism and the victory that had cost him his life.

On the quarterdeck of the *Margaret,* the concussion of the blast hit Adam head-on and swept him back two full steps. In utter amazement he stared at the smoke and flame that leaped one hundred yards into the sky, and he hunched his shoulders and raised his arms above his head against the rocks and debris that came raining down. He raised his telescope to study the town and read the battle, and he saw the red-coated British gather at the east end of the village and then disappear on Kingston Road in full retreat with the Americans in hot pursuit. In the town, more smoke began to rise where Americans had set fires, first from the blockhouse at the east end of the dockyards and then at the governor's residence facing the harbor. Then other smudges of smoke appeared among the homes, and Adam realized some of the soldiers were looting residences under any excuse they could invent, taking what they wanted and burning the buildings. The jails were raided and emptied and set afire. Amid the smoke and flames and the wreckage of much of the town left by the powder magazine explosion, Adam saw the British Union Jack hauled down from the battered flagpole, and moments later, the stars and stripes ascended to the top. The battle was over.

It was late in the day when Chauncey rapidly wrote and sealed a message describing the actions of the day, dramatically declaring a complete victory. York had fallen! The Americans had taken the capital of Canada! He sent the message by a special courier under instructions to sacrifice his horse if need be to reach Sacketts Harbor and the newspapers in New York before the polls closed two days later to end the politically critical election of the governor.

The exhausted messenger delivered the message in record time. The news spread as though carried on the wind. Euphoria seized the state of New York. *We have taken the capital of Canada! We beat the British on Lake Ontario*

and on their own ground! Land and sea! We won! We won! The Republican administra-
tion has been vindicated. Vindicated!

The election ended, and the polls closed with a shaky President
Madison awaiting the results. Two days later it was clear that Daniel
Tompkins, the Republican candidate, had won the election by a resound-
ing margin. Unending praises were heaped upon Chauncey and his
squadron, and upon the brilliant leadership of President James Madison.

Chauncey sent written messages to each of the American ships
anchored in the harbor.

"To be certain the British do not return with a counterattack to
retake York, we will remain anchored for more than one week in York
harbor. You will hold your gun crews at the ready while our forces on
shore set up defenses at the blockhouses and at the battery west of the
small village. Scouts and patrols will make daily reports on any British
forces in the area."

For more than a week the American ships remained at anchor, while
patrols on both land and water maintained a continuous watch for the
return of the British. None were seen. The British had accepted the loss
of York.

On the sixth day of May, Chauncey lowered himself into a longboat,
and his crew rowed him to the nearby *Margaret,* where he met with Adam
behind the closed door of the captain's quarters. With the two of them
seated at the small desk inside the tiny room, Chauncey spoke quietly.

"I have sent a message to President Madison describing in detail the
entire assault. Your name is prominent, as it should be. Your contribution was irreplaceable. You are not an officer in the United States Navy;
however, I am recommending that you receive congressional acknowl-
edgement of your action."

Adam's expression did not change. "Thank you, sir."

Chauncey's eyes dropped for a moment, then came back to Adam's.
"You have heard me speak of Captain Oliver Hazard Perry, a naval officer presently in command of our forces on Lake Erie, to the west of us."

"I have, sir. I know something of the man."

Chauncey went on. "The British have lately sent their Commodore

Sir James Lucas Yeo to take command of their forces here on Lake
Ontario, and I am under orders to remain here to prevent him and the
British from controlling this lake. At the same time, it is clear the British
mean to maintain their present control of Lake Erie. Our Captain Perry
is to drive them out if he can. To do that, he will need all the assistance
available."

Adam saw it coming and remained silent.

Chauncey concluded. "This squadron is going to leave York in two
days to return to Sacketts Harbor because I expect the British will
attempt an all-out assault there to try to redeem their loss here at York.
Now, Mister Dunson, I cannot order you, so I am asking you on behalf
of the United States Navy and the American people. When I weigh
anchor and make sail for Sacketts Harbor, would you take your ship and
crew south across this lake, up the Niagara River, to Lake Erie. Find
Captain Perry at Presque Isle and deliver this document to him?"

Adam took the sealed document and studied it for a few moments.
"What is the document?"

"My orders to Perry to accept your services in helping to secure Lake
Erie."

Adam's eyes narrowed. "You're asking me and my ship and crew to
volunteer to help hold Lake Erie? For how long?"

"Until there is no question that we are in control."

"That might be next fall, or early winter."

Chauncey bobbed his head. "It might well be."

For several seconds Adam weighed it out in his mind. Food, ammunition, his obligation to Laura and his children, the obligations of his
men to their families, and the terrible burden of taking them all into
harm's way.

"Yes, sir," Adam replied quietly. "The *Margaret* will be ready. And her
crew."

For a long moment Chauncey stared into Adam's eyes, and in the
silence something passed between the two men that would remain with
each of them forever. Chauncey nodded and reached to shake Adam's

hand, then turned and ducked out of the small door to return to his longboat.

Notes

The badly bungled military campaigns of 1812, under the command of the aging and inept General Henry Dearborn, brought serious political losses to Madison's Republican Party in the national election of November, 1812: twelve percent in the House of Representatives, four percent in the Senate, and the loss of governorships in six states. Madison understood he must deliver some victories to the voters if he did not want to lose the pivotal Republican governorship of the state of New York in the state election of April 27, 1813.

As described herein, he appointed John Armstrong his secretary of war and requested him to create a plan that would succeed. Armstrong arrived in Washington, D.C., February 4, 1813, moved into the political scene with much energy, and had audience with President Madison on February 7 to receive his approval for a plan to be set before Madison's cabinet February 8. The plan was as described. Captain Isaac Chauncey, a rising American naval officer, was selected to take command of the ships. The date set to commence the campaign was April 1, 1813, and was totally dependent on the ice on the Great Lakes being gone by that date. At the same time, Armstrong had arranged for newspaper articles to be delivered to the prominent newspapers in the country on April 1, declaring victory for the Americans in the April campaign.

The ice did not recede until April 19. The attack was postponed until April 22, then postponed again when a great gale made it impossible to land troops at Kingston, and Chauncey had to override Dearborn's specific instructions by ordering his squadron to return to Sacketts Harbor. The ships and bateaux, loaded double and triple the number of men the vessels were designed for, finally made sail on April 25. They were seen by British outposts at Scarborough Heights on the Canadian shores of Lake Ontario, and the message was sent on to Fort York by semaphore flags. British General Sir Roger Hale Sheaffe divided his command to defend York, placing one half on each side of the village, east and west.

The American ships arrived at the mouth of York harbor two days later, and the all-out attack was made April 27. The American ships carrying the troops set them ashore west of York harbor, on the shores of Lake Ontario. While the troops made a hard run for the village, the ships entered the harbor and immediately began shelling the British troops that were sent to meet them.

The British troops had to move through an exposed field to meet the Americans, and the troops on the east side of the village had to move through the village to reinforce those on the west. But with the American cannon on the anchored ships raking the field with canister and solid shot, the British refused to move. However, as the lone British cannon emplacement began to return fire, a careless crewman accidentally touched off the powder barrel and it blew the British gun and crew out of commission. The Americans stormed the village of York. The British officer in command, Sheaffe, ordered his troops to set fire to the British ship *Sir Issac Brock*, all supplies in the ship dock area, and the huge powder magazine next to the governor's residence, and then retreat by marching out on the Kingston Road. The Americans had followed them into the town, when the gigantic powder magazine exploded. The blast shook the ground for miles and rattled windows across the lake at Fort Niagara and rained rocks and debris on every American ship in the harbor. The explosion killed thirty-eight Americans outright and disabled and crippled 222 others.

Among the American dead was General Zebulon Pike, commander of the American land forces, who was fatally wounded when a huge rock broke his spine as reported by one authority, or a stone hit his forehead, as reported by another. He was taken to his ship, the *Madison*, where he died with a folded British flag beneath his head, a tribute by his men to his bravery and leadership.

The Americans raided the town, pillaging and burning some homes, emptying the jails, and taking property at will. The Americans remained at York until May 8, 1813, when they loaded the troops back onto the waiting ships and set sail for Sacketts Harbor, fearing the British would retaliate with an assault there. News of the victory was sent to Sacketts Harbor immediately and on to New York newspapers, where it played a significant role in the election of Republican Daniel Tompkins in the governor's race.

See Malcomson, *Lords of the Lake*, pp. 103–08; Stagg, *Mr. Madison's War*, pp. 282–333; Hickey, *The War of 1812*, pp. 127–30; Barbuto, *Niagara 1814*, pp. 71–75; Wills, *James Madison*, p. 123.

For a diagram of York harbor, or bay, as described herein, see Malcomson, *Lords of the Lake*, p. 102.

Adam Dunson, his ship the *Margaret*, and his crew are fictional.

Boston
Late August 1813

CHAPTER XX

*T*he dead midafternoon air in Boston was hazy with humidity, and the pounding sun had turned the town into a sweltering oven. Only those who had need were in the streets; all others were inside the buildings—any building—sweating, working with fans, doing anything for relief.

On the waterfront, dockhands were stripped to the waist, sweat dripping as they loaded and unloaded the cargo that was the lifeblood of the town, onto and off of ships while gulls and grebes wheeled and squawked and paraded in the shade beneath the docks, snatching up bits of dead carrion washed up by the sea and garbage thrown overboard by the ship crews.

The office door of the shipping firm of Dunson & Weems stood open while those inside yearned for a breeze to stir the air, but none came. Inside, Billy Weems sat at his desk hunched over one of the large company ledgers making the never-ending business entries of payments received, billings sent out, contract balances, business costs, insurance, payroll, taxes, and the myriad smaller records that had to be kept current. He wiped at the sweat on his forehead, dipped his quill in the ink well, adjusted his bifocals on his nose, and continued transferring figures from the bills and invoices to the various sections of the ledger where they needed to be.

Behind Billy, Matthew sat at his desk, his shirt damp with perspiration, poring over insurance claims, sorting them out by company, type, and amount. To his right, across the aisle, against the far wall, Adam's desk was vacant, and behind it, the desk used by John had stacks of records listing the crews of the eighteen commercial ships owned and operated by the company. Keeping the ships manned by competent seamen was an unending challenge. John's chair was pushed back, vacant; it was his day to go to the tavern two hundred yards up the waterfront where the mail was delivered and sorted.

Billy heard the rapid footsteps approaching the front door and raised his head as John walked into the room, past the counter, and back to his desk, carrying the mail. He dropped it in a heap and slumped into his chair, wiping at the perspiration on his face with his shirtsleeve.

"Hottest day of the summer," he complained.

"Anything in the mail?" Matthew asked.

"Yes. You have a letter from Adam, and Billy has one from Madison."

Billy's head snapped up. "Madison? President Madison?"

"President Madison."

Both men came to John's desk to get their letters while John began breaking the seals and opening the other business letters.

Billy was back at his desk before he broke the seal and spread the letter flat on his desk. He pushed his bifocals up his nose with one finger and concentrated as he read.

" . . . and I have confirmation of the fact that Tecumseh is leading many of his Shawnee and also warriors from other tribes north . . . It is my conclusion he intends joining British forces somewhere at the west end of Lake Erie to drive out all Americans and reclaim lands previously ceded to the United States by treaty . . . I deem it imperative that we attempt to deter him from such a course of action . . . It is for that reason that I inquire if you can find Eli Stroud and persuade him to contact Tecumseh with the objective of preventing the bloodshed that will surely follow should he join the British in their attempt to recover their loss of control of Lake Ontario . . ."

Billy pushed the letter away and leaned back in his chair and rounded his mouth to blow air. *Find Eli and ask him to walk into that nest of hornets up in Canada?*

From behind, Matthew asked, "Bad news?"

Billy turned his chair. "Madison wants me to find Eli and ask him to go up to Lake Erie to talk Tecumseh out of a war."

Matthew came to a focus. "Tecumseh! Is he up there? Does Madison know?"

"Says he does. Somewhere near the west end of the lake."

Matthew leaned back in his chair. "Think you can find Eli?"

Billy shrugged. "That's not the question. The question is do I want to try? What about my obligations here at the office? And at home— Brigitte and the children. Finding Eli could take weeks."

Matthew wiped at his face with his handkerchief. "We can make do around here if you decide to go."

Billy studied his quill for several moments before he responded. "Madison wouldn't ask without need. I think I better go. I'll talk to Brigitte."

John stopped working with the mail to interrupt. "Anything to get out of work." He shook his head. "Two old men out there in the woods. You'll get lost, certain. Maybe I better go along just to—"

Matthew cut him off. "You're staying right here."

John was grinning at his father. "What did Adam have to say?"

Matthew gestured to the letter. "He'll be a while on the lake with Perry. He's expecting a major engagement up there on the water. Wanted us to know. He's written Laura about it."

John continued. "You ever read that commendation Madison sent to him? For his part in the York harbor fight?"

"Laura showed me. Things got pretty lively in that battle. Adam did well."

Billy cut in. "You'll be all right here if I go?"

"We'll get by."

Billy began putting his desk in order. "I think I better go home and talk with Brigitte. If she agrees, I might leave tomorrow. No way to know how long it will take to find Eli, and the summer's about gone."

It was five minutes past six o'clock, and the sun was reaching for the western horizon when Matthew stood and stretched.

"Let's lock up for the day. Been too hot. Going to storm soon."

Billy called John to his desk and pointed at the stacked documents and ledgers as he spoke.

"There's the shipping schedules for the next four weeks with the cargoes and the ports listed. There's the contracts and insurance papers. There's the ledgers with the customer accounts." He pointed at the west wall, where a huge chart was fastened with the detail of customers, contracts, cargoes, pick up and delivery dates and destinations, ships assigned to each, captains, and number of crew members required. "Keep the ledgers and records current. Make sure they are consistent with the chart, and keep the chart updated every day."

"I'll take care of it. Let's go home."

Matthew held the door while the other two walked out onto the ancient black timbers of the Boston docks and waited while he locked the door. They went west together, away from the waterfront, and had just reached the intersection where they would separate when Billy stopped and looked at Matthew.

"What's the best way to the Ohio Valley right now? The lakes or down across New York and Pennsylvania?"

Matthew reflected for a moment. "I think I'd take the land route. We're in control of Lake Ontario and have been since the British attacked Sacketts Harbor and lost the battle last May. But they still control Lake Erie. An American ship might run into trouble. I'd go cross-country."

"That's what I think." Billy paused for a moment. "I could be gone in the morning. If I am, would you write a letter to Madison? Tell him I received his. Tell him I'm looking for Eli.

Matthew nodded. "You be careful. Hear? We're both too old for this business of war."

Minutes later Billy walked through the front door of his home and Brigitte called from the kitchen, "Billy, is that you? Supper in ten minutes. Get washed."

Supper was finished, the dishes washed, dried, and in the cupboard, and the remains of a leg of lamb were in the root cellar when the large clock on the mantel sounded half past seven o'clock. Billy led Brigitte into the library and invited her to sit opposite him. She sat erect, focused, aware something had happened.

She spoke first. "Is it Adam?" she asked, and he saw the dread in her eyes.

"Not Adam. I received a letter today from President Madison. He asked me to find Eli and tell him to meet with Tecumseh. The Shawnee are gathering up north, and Madison believes they intend joining with the British to drive us out of Canada. Madison wants Eli to persuade Tecumseh to give it up."

"He wants you to find Eli? That's all? Not go to war?"

"That's all the letter said."

"How soon?"

Billy drew a deep breath. "It has to be done soon. I'd like to leave in the morning."

Brigitte stiffened in surprise. "So soon? When will you return?"

He looked her full in the face. "There's no way to judge. It could be two or three weeks. I'll come home as soon as I can."

He saw her shoulders slump and the air go out of her. For a time she sat with her head bowed, looking at her hands folded in her lap. "When will it ever end?" she murmured.

Billy sat back in silence, giving her time. Finally she raised her head, and he saw the resolution in her eyes. "I'll help you pack," was all she said.

Clouds had covered the moon, and a breeze was coming in from the Atlantic to stir the curtains at the open windows when Billy finished rolling clothing and cheese and cooked mutton and hardtack inside a blanket and tying it. The mantel clock struck ten times as Billy blew out the lamps and the two of them sought their bed to kneel while Billy offered their nightly prayer. In the quiet darkness they heard the first sound of raindrops through the open windows, and moments later the soft, steady pelting of a summer rain. Brigitte rose to close the windows far enough to hold out the rain, and still leave an opening large enough to let the breeze clear the heat from the house. She returned to the bed, and moved close to Billy with her back to him.

"Hold me," she said quietly. He could hear the strain in her voice, and he reached to gather her to him, to drift to sleep.

The dawn came gray, and the soft rain was still falling when Billy tied his blanket behind the saddle and mounted a bay gelding with his rifle across the saddle bows. He moved west, away from the dripping town to the narrow neck that connected the peninsula to the mainland, sharing the muddy, rutted dirt roads that wound through the thick forests with great two-wheeled farm carts drawn by horses, moving steadily past him toward Boston, loaded with the summer's harvest for the markets of the city. He stopped to noon beneath the sheltering arms of a tall pine and hobbled the horse to let it graze while he ate cheese and hardtack and drank from a rain-swollen stream. The heavens cleared in the late afternoon, and at dusk he spread his blanket beneath a huge oak tree and built a small fire over which he heated mutton for his supper with the hobbled horse feeding in tall grass nearby.

With the days growing cooler as he moved inland, away from the humidity of the coast, he angled south of due west to cross the Hudson River thirty miles below Albany, then paid the fare to ferry across the Delaware River into Pennsylvania, well north of Philadelphia. The fourth day he crossed the Susquehanna River and turned just north of due west, winding through the incomparable beauty of the Appalachian Mountains to the Allegheny River, where he rested the horse one day before taking the ferry across to continue into Ohio, and on to the Sandusky River. There he turned north, directly toward the southern shore of Lake Erie.

It was late in the day when he reined in his horse at a trading post in a clearing carved out of the thick woods. One outside wall of the old, weathered log building was covered with a lion pelt and half a dozen out-of-season beaver pelts. Near the front door about twenty rusty beaver traps hung from pegs. A tired old gray mare stood at a hitch rack near the entrance, and Billy tied the bay next to her before he pushed through the rough plank door. He stood for a moment on the dirt floor with his

rifle in hand while his eyes adjusted, then walked to his left where two
heavy planks were supported by two barrels to form a counter. Behind
the counter was an old, thin, gray-haired man with a straggly beard and a
withered left arm that hung limp. Seated towards the rear of the room
at a rough-cut table with a jug before him and a pewter mug in his hand
was a round man with a jowled, bearded face and suspicious eyes.

Billy walked to the old man behind the counter and nodded to him.
"I'm in need of some direction. I wonder if you might help."

The old voice was high, scratchy. "Lost?"

"No. I need to find the nearest place where the military has an
outpost."

"Which army? British or American?"

"American."

The aged man pointed through the wall behind him. "Straight on
north. Can't miss it. They been gatherin' up there for days."

"Who's been gathering? For what?"

"Soldiers. Militia. Heard they're expecting a fight up there on the
lake. British and Americans."

"Navy? Ships?"

The man bobbed his head. "Navy and army. Ours against theirs."
He pointed at his useless arm. "It was a fight like that cost this arm. Back
in '81."

"Where? Which battle?"

"Yorktown. Heard of it?"

For a moment Billy was back thirty-two years at the edge of the
small tobacco-trading village of Yorktown in the dark preceding dawn
on that October day when the French and American soldiers stormed
the British redoubts numbers nine and ten on the banks of the York
River. He was Lieutenant Billy Weems, hearing the roar of the cannon
and seeing the flash of the muskets as he led his company leaping over
the ditch and sprinting up the rise to the abatis and then over the top,
plunging in among the British soldiers. He saw his sergeant, Alvin
Turlock, go down in the deadly hand-to-hand melee, and then the British

threw down their arms in surrender, and he gathered Turlock into his arms and ran to find the surgeons.

He nodded to the old man in the trading post. "I've heard of it." He paused, then asked, "You've seen soldiers passing here going north?"

"Several. Come in bunches. Some stop here. Goin' up for a battle."

"See any Indians going north?"

"Don't hardly ever see 'em on the roads. They move through the woods. Don't hardly ever see 'em."

Billy nodded. "Thanks. I better be going on."

The man asked, "You need supplies? Salt? Gunpowder?"

"No," Billy answered, then reconsidered. "You have any brown sugar?"

"Got some. Gone lumpy."

"I'll take about a pound. And carrots. Got any carrots?"

A quizzical look crossed the old man's face. "You're askin' for carrots?"

"Got a few?"

"A few. In that barrel over there."

Minutes later Billy walked out to his waiting bay with a threadbare cloth sack holding lumpy brown sugar and twelve unwashed carrots. He held a large lump of sugar in the flat of his hand and lifted it to the nose of the bay. The long upper lip reached to grasp it, and Billy smiled as the horse worked it in its mouth and then lowered its head looking for more. He fed the horse two more lumps before he mounted and rode on north until dusk, when he set up his camp near a small stream, built a small fire, caught a trout with his hands, cleaned it, and set it on a spit to roast. He spread his blanket nearby and fed the horse three carrots before he hobbled it and let it go to graze through the night.

With the moon rising in the east and the hush of night all around him, he leaned his rifle against the trunk of a sycamore tree and sat down with his knees drawn up, staring into the last, low flames of the dying campfire to work with his thoughts.

If American soldiers and seamen are gathering at some military post up by Lake

Erie, they're expecting a major action, and that means the British are up there waiting. If they are, Eli's most likely already up there or on his way.

Forty feet across the campfire, two large yellow eyes appeared in the blackness of the woods, and Billy stopped all motion to watch them. In his mind he was unconsciously judging how many seconds it would take to reach the rifle, cock it, bring it to bear, and fire. For three or four seconds the eyes did not move, and then they were gone as suddenly as they had appeared. Billy remained still, watching, listening for more than one minute for any sign of the big cat, and there was nothing. He continued with his thoughts.

If there is a major battle taking shape up there between the Americans and the British, the Shawnee are bound to get into it, and that means Tecumseh will be there. That's where Eli can find him. The question is, can Eli find him before the fight, and if he does, can he talk him into staying out of it?

Billy pushed dirt over the coals of the fire and sat for a time in the black of the forest, listening for any sound that would tell him a great cat was circling, waiting. The only sounds were the frogs, the soft whisper of the stream, and the ruffle of silken wings of the night birds overhead. He went to his blanket with his rifle at hand and slept the sleep of a tired, aging man.

He awakened with the morning star fading and saddled the bay, hungry to ride north until the sun was directly overhead, when he stopped near a stream to eat what was left of the fish with some cheese and hardtack, and to drink from the stream and let the horse graze for half an hour. It was late afternoon when he caught his first glimpse of Lake Erie, shining in the sunlight in the far distance. He camped on the bank of a river and was up the next morning and mounted on the bay with his rifle across his thighs before sunrise. By late afternoon he was approaching the south shore of the lake, riding through a sprawling camp of men camped in clusters, some in uniform, some in homespun, some in buckskins, a few stripped to the waist, splitting wood or washing clothes or tending huge smoke-blackened kettles dangling over fires from twelve-foot tripods and filled with steaming soup. Some paused in the confusion to watch him pass while he made his way to a large tent with a flagpole and an American flag hanging limp in the still, warm air. He dismounted and approached the tent flap to rap on the front support pole. From inside a voice called, "Wait," and a minute later a young, blond-haired man with blue eyes and a saber scar on the left side of his neck pushed the flap aside, still buttoning his tunic, with the gold bars of a captain on the shoulders. The man studied Billy for a moment and with narrowed eyes asked, "You wanted to see me?"

"Yes. My name is Billy Weems. I've been sent to find a man named Eli Stroud. He ought to be somewhere nearby."

"Who sent you?"

"President James Madison."

The young officer's mouth dropped open for a moment, and then he laughed. "President Madison sent you?"

Billy drew the letter from inside his shirt. "Yes. He did. Would you care to read his letter?"

The officer stopped laughing. For long seconds he stared before he reached for the letter. For a time Billy stood quietly while the man read it, and read it again, then raised his eyes to stare in disbelief.

"Who wrote this?"

"President Madison. I need to find Eli Stroud."

The officer refolded it and handed it back to Billy. He rounded his mouth to blow air for a moment. "Well, that may or may not be a letter from President Madison, but whatever it is, it looks authentic to me. Who is this man? Describe Eli Stroud."

"Tall. About sixty years old. Raised Iroquois. Should be wearing buckskins. Moccasins. Carries a Pennsylvania rifle and a tomahawk. Fought with distinction thirty-five years ago in the Revolution. Sparse with words. Knows the woods. Good man."

"He can speak Shawnee?"

"He speaks seven languages."

The officer gaped. "Seven?"

"Including French and English and all Iroquois dialects."

"He knows Tecumseh?"

"He knows him well."

"How do you know this Eli Stroud?"

Billy paused for a moment. "I fought beside him in the Revolution. I was a lieutenant in the Continental Army."

Surprise showed in the young officer's face. "What's your name?"

"Billy Weems. From Boston."

"Well, all right, Weems. I've not seen Stroud but that doesn't mean I won't. If I do I'll tell him you're here looking for him. You might go on over to command headquarters about half a mile west of here and ask. Someone might have seen him."

Billy nodded. "Thank you, Captain."

"Good luck."

Billy remounted the bay and reined it west at a walk, studying the men and the camps on both sides as he went. Halfway to the headquarters tent he passed the largest rope horse corral he had ever seen. He judged there must be fifteen hundred saddle mounts inside, and camped next to it was a great spread of tents on the lake shore and in the woods, and men in homespun and buckskins with a flag declaring them to be from Kentucky. Some stared as he rode by. He passed smaller camps with flags from Pennsylvania, Ohio, New York, and Michigan. He stopped in front of the largest tent, with an American flag hanging from a sixty-foot flagpole to one side. He rapped on the support pole and waited until a man wearing the gold epaulets of a colonel opened it to stare at Billy, impatient, scowling.

"What is it?"

"I was sent here by a captain in this camp to ask about a man named Eli Stroud."

"A soldier? An officer?"

"No. A civilian."

The colonel shook his head. "I don't have time right now. Wait here." The tent flap closed, and Eli heard brusque orders given inside, and a young lieutenant emerged.

It took Billy five minutes to explain himself, in which time the young lieutenant read Madison's letter, looked skeptically at Billy, returned the letter, and said, "I am Lieutenant Uriah Ellington. You're looking for this man Stroud?"

"I am."

"I have not seen him. The best I can do is inform all the other officers and hope one of them will see him. Where will you be if that happens?"

"I'll check with you every day, if that's all right."

"I'll be available. Was there anything else?"

"Yes. How many men are gathered here?"

"About five thousand. More coming."

"For what?"

Lieutenant Ellington took a deep breath and launched into it, pointing north across the lake.

"Weeks ago we cut off the supply routes to the British forces across the lake. There are thousands of Indians over there—men and women and children—all dependent on the British for food, and since we stopped the supplies, the British can no longer feed them. They're starving—getting unruly. Captain Barclay—Robert H. Barclay—is the naval commander of the British warships on the lake. He lost one arm in a sea battle years ago, but he's capable. Right now his sailors are on half rations. He's desperate. We're expecting him try to reopen the British supply lines, and to do that he'll have to defeat our naval forces on the lake. We think he'll attack sometime in the next twenty-four hours. Does that explain what's going on here?"

"Most of it. Who commands our naval forces?"

"Captain Oliver Hazard Perry. He's young, but he's good. He has nine gunboats, and they're out there right now, waiting for Barclay."

Billy came to a focus. "Do you know the names of the American ships out there? Is there one named the *Margaret?*"

The young lieutenant's forehead wrinkled. "Is she a commissioned naval ship?"

"No. A volunteer. Civilian."

"I only know about the commissioned ships. There isn't one named the *Margaret.*"

Billy shifted his feet. "Thanks. Ask your officers about Eli Stroud. I'll check back."

The lieutenant disappeared back into the tent, and Billy led the bay away, further west to the fringes of the great camp, where the tents and the men thinned. He stopped just inside the woods to unsaddle the bay and buckle on the hobbles to let it graze while he sat down to eat what was left of his cheese and hardtack. Finished, he arranged the saddle beneath a tree with his blanket next to it, led the bay to a tiny brook to let it drink, then led it back to his saddle and hobbled it nearby in the grass, tied to a twelve-foot picket rope.

With the sun setting, he watched the men gather for their evening mess and took his wooden bowl to stand in the line with the Pennsylvanians, listening to the excited talk of the battle that was coming. He saw in them the rise of tension that was a strange, contradictory mix of impatience to get into the shooting and a fear of the death and destruction the shooting would bring.

The man ahead of him in line turned to ask, "New in camp?"

"Just arrived."

"From where?"

"Boston. I haven't seen a Massachusetts flag. Hope you don't mind me being in your mess line."

The man shrugged. "Don't matter much. Some of our boys are over with the Kentucky bunch right now, in their mess line."

Billy asked, "Where are our ships? Where's this big battle to take place?"

The man pointed due north at Lake Erie. "Our ships are right out there at Put-in-Bay in the Bass Islands. Can't see 'em from this side of the lake. On over on the British side, Barclay and his navy is about starved out. He's got to do something, and it looks like tomorrow is the big day."

The cooks didn't even look up when they shoved a piece of hard brown bread into Billy's hand and dumped a large dipper of odorous, brown, steaming stew into his bowl, and he moved on. He returned to his saddle and blankets to sit with his back against the tree while he gingerly poked at the steaming stew with his wooden spoon, then blew on it before he took the first taste. He could identify possum, wild turkey, raccoon, and wild boar in the mix, along with strong turnips and cabbage, and the bread was stale and unsalted, but he ate it all and it stayed down.

With the stars coming alive overhead, he checked the horse, then sat down with his back against the tree, working with his thoughts.

What day is this? He paused to count from the morning he left Boston. *Thursday. September 9. How long will I be here?—no way to know—big battle on the lake tomorrow—is Adam there?—will he be all right?—where's Eli?—how do I find him?—Indians over there starving—is Tecumseh there?—will he talk with Eli?*

His thoughts came to Brigitte. *When will I see her again?—when will women be spared seeing their men go off to war?—they're the ones who pay the real price—at home—not knowing if we're alive or dead—or crippled—how do they bear it?*

The great, sprawling camp slowly settled and quieted, and lanterns inside tents began winking out. In the solitude, Billy sought his blankets and for a time lay on his back studying the vastness of the heavens and the stars overhead, and drifted to sleep awed, humbled by his own smallness.

He was up at dawn to feed the horse the last of the carrots, rubbing its neck while he listened to it grind them between yellow teeth and bump Billy's chest with its head for more. He led it to the stream to drink, then back to hobble it on a picket rope in the grass. He stood in the line for morning mess of mush and burned sowbelly and was washing his wooden bowl in the stream when the shout came high and excited from near the lake.

"They're coming! They're coming!"

Within minutes, the lake shore was jammed with men standing tall, hands raised to shield their eyes against the morning sun as they peered north across the still waters of the lake, straining to see sails that were not there. The officers came among them, giving commands.

"Back to your companies. Back to your duties. There's nothing to see. The British ships are on the lake but you can't see them from here."

Reluctantly the soldiers turned back to their campsites, talking, pointing, turning to peer back at the lake, anxious, apprehensive. Billy waited, then stopped a captain who was returning to his command.

"How many British ships?"

"The message said six. Against our nine."

"Where?"

"Last seen moving south from somewhere around Fort Malden, towards Put-in-Bay."

"How much time before they meet? Ours and theirs."

"Soon."

Billy walked back to his campsite and leaned his rifle against the tree, then sat down on his blanket cross-legged, with his elbows on his knees. *Is Adam out there? Will he be in the fight?* He stared north, knowing the Bass Islands and the ships were too far away to be seen, but unable to stop looking.

Out on the lake, under clear morning skies and bright sunshine, a light wind was quartering in from the southeast to ruffle the dark waters as it moved from the American shore northwest, past the Bass Islands and Put-in-Bay, on to the British shore. The American fleet lay anchored just north of the islands, rocking gently on the slow swells, waiting, with men and extended telescopes in every crow's nest, intently scouring the north horizon, waiting for the first fleck that would be a British ship leading a squadron from Fort Malden harbor to do battle. Neither side had illusions of the stakes at risk. Both understood only too well that control of the entire northern waterway, from Lake Superior to the Atlantic Ocean, was to be decided that day; and whoever controlled that waterway held the fate of the war in their hands.

Perry was ready. He had taken command of his largest man-of-war, the *Lawrence,* and had given command of his next largest ship, the *Niagara,* to Lieutenant Jesse Elliott. Behind the *Niagara,* at the request of Captain Adam Dunson, came the *Margaret,* the volunteer commercial ship converted to a gunboat, and behind the *Margaret,* in order, came the smaller, flat-bottomed gunboats with but one deck, that Perry had built during the summer under the direction of Noah Brown, master naval architect. Perry had spent months scavenging for ship crews, and had gathered an odd, rag-tag assembly of ex-soldiers, civilians, Negroes, and a few trained seamen.

In the dark hours of early morning, when the message reached him that the British squadron had left Fort Malden during the night, sailing south, Perry had divided his men among the ships and ordered them to spread sand on all decks to avoid slipping when the decks were drenched with water or blood. Then he ordered every gun to be loaded, with the gun crews at the ready.

And he had given clear, emphatic orders to his captains that he, Perry, commanding the *Lawrence*, would lead them into battle, with the *Niagara* right behind, the *Margaret* following, and the lesser ships in order. Under no circumstance were they to break the battle line.

With hands shading their eyes against the bright morning sun, the American crews crowded against the railings, peering north, nervous, anxious, quiet, waiting through the morning. It was approaching noon when the man in the crow's nest of the *Lawrence* shouted, "Sail. Due north. Two . . . three. . . . six sails! Looks like the whole British squadron!"

Perry barked orders to his first mate, and instantly he ran the prepared signal flags up the mainmast with the message: "British approaching. Follow me."

Perry turned to shout commands to his crew. Seamen threw their weight against the windlass, and the anchor chain rattled as the anchor left the bottom of the lake and started to rise. Barefoot sailors scrambled up the ladders to the overhead arms to walk the ropes outward. They jerked the knots loose, and the sails unfurled to catch the wind quartering in from behind. They billowed and popped, and while the deck crew secured the anchor, the ships became as living things, falling into their places in the battle line, gaining speed as they moved north, directly toward the oncoming British.

Adam stood in the bow of the *Margaret*, telescope extended, his view partially blocked by the two ships ahead of him while he watched every move of the British ships as they tacked into the wind, moving into their battle line.

Our nine against their six, and we have the wind in our favor. What's going through Barclay's mind? He's got courage, but the odds are strong against him.

On the quarterdeck of the HMS *Detroit*, the flagship of his command, Captain Robert Barclay counted the sails of the approaching American squadron, then studied the build of each of the ships.

The first three—men-o'-war—heavy guns—but the last six—only light schooners—few guns—single deck—if we can disable the first three, the last six are ours.

He ran the signals up his mainmast. "Wait for my command to fire, then broadside the first three when you can."

As in a dream, the distance between the two enemy fleets was suddenly half a mile, then six hundred yards, and Barclay ran the signal high on his mainmast.

FIRE!

The heavy, long-range British guns blasted, and the white smoke was swept away by the wind to reveal most of the cannonballs raising fifteen-foot geysers in the sea around the first three American ships. A few punched holes in the sails; one or two hit the railings to blow them to kindling.

Instantly, the long-range guns on the *Lawrence* and *Niagara* and *Margaret* answered. With the deafening roar of the cannon and the smell and sight of the white smoke and the whistling of incoming cannonballs, the crews on both the British and American ships moved past their frayed nerves and fears into the strange world of calm precision, loading and firing mechanically, without thought.

The lead ships were less than three hundred yards apart when suddenly the *Niagara*, just ahead of Adam on the *Margaret*, began to slow, then angled to port, leaving the battle line. Ahead of the *Niagara*, Perry held the *Lawrence* at full speed dead ahead, on a collision course with the oncoming *Detroit*.

Stunned, Adam's thoughts raced. *What is Elliott doing leaving the battle line—abandoning the* Lawrence?

While Adam watched, Captain Elliott spilled his mainsails. The ship slowed and came to a near stop, with its long guns still blasting. Adam held the *Margaret* behind the *Niagara* with his cannon firing, torn between a compulsion to break away to support Perry and the *Lawrence,* and his direct orders to maintain his place behind the *Niagara.* Heat waves were rising from the gun barrels, and frantic crews were throwing buckets of lake water on them to cool them enough to keep them from igniting the gunpowder while they were ramming it down the muzzles.

In the next minute, the *Lawrence* disappeared in the thick cloud of gun smoke hanging between the *Detroit* and the *Queen Charlotte,* and the sound of the cannon became one continuous roar, echoing to both shores of the lake as the lone ship traded broadsides with both of the British ships, one on each side.

Adam stood horrified. *He hasn't got a chance! They'll cut him to pieces!*

He could take no more. He pivoted and shouted to the helmsman, "Hard to starboard!" He used his horn to shout to his first mate, "Make all sail! Now!"

Men leaped to the rope ladders and scrambled up the three masts to the arms, and out on the ropes to release the sails. They caught the wind and snapped tight, and the *Margaret* surged ahead in a hard turn to starboard, breaking from behind the *Niagara,* directly toward the British ships that were pounding the *Lawrence* into rubble.

Adam shouted to his gun crews, "Fire when you come to bear!"

Behind him, Elliott stood on the quarterdeck of the *Niagara,* startled to see Adam and the *Margaret* break from the battle line and set all sails to close with the British ships, cannon blasting as she went.

What is Dunson doing? He knows his orders! What's he doing?

Then Elliott stopped short. He suddenly realized that, for reasons he could never explain, he had suffered a mental lapse that had sent Perry and his ship and crew into the heart of the British squadron alone, without support. *He* had broken the battle line! *He* had sent Perry into a death trap! Shocked, sick in his heart, Elliott shouted his orders. Within minutes the *Niagara* was in a hard turn to starboard, all sails unfurled and full, following the *Margaret* straight at the British men-of-war.

The *Margaret* swept past the bow of the *Detroit,* with every cannon on the port side of the *Margaret* raking the British ship in order, and Adam saw the *Lawrence* for the first time since she had disappeared between the two large British warships. Her masts were shattered, her spars on her deck, her sails shredded and dragging. Her railings were blasted to splinters, her quarterdeck strewn with wreckage, and her hull showed more than twenty black holes where British cannonballs had smashed through.

For ten seconds Adam searched through the smoke and wreckage before he saw Perry. He was there on the quarterdeck, with the blood and carnage of his dead and wounded all around, still shouting to his gun crews to load and fire. Adam groaned and then shouted to his own helmsman, "Hard to port!"

The *Margaret* leaned hard to starboard as she made her turn to port, coming in between the *Queen Charlotte* and the *Lawrence,* all nineteen guns on her starboard side loaded and waiting, and as he came alongside the British ship, fewer than forty yards to his starboard side, he watched the British crew frantically reloading their guns.

In the instant before the British crews seized the ropes to pull their cannon into the gunports, Adam shouted to his gun crews, "Fire!"

All nineteen of the heavy cannon bucked and roared, and the white cloud of smoke hid the British ship for several seconds as the American cannonballs and canister shot hit broadside at point-blank range. Two of the masts on the British ship slowly tilted and then toppled, and the broken spars and riddled sails hit the wreckage that littered the deck, among the dead and dying British seamen. The smoke cleared as the *Margaret* passed the crippled *Queen Charlotte,* and Adam saw the quarterdeck on the British ship, shot to pieces, with her captain down, not moving.

Instantly he turned to find the *Detroit,* off his port stern, on the far side of the *Lawrence.* Beyond the *Detroit,* he saw the *Niagara* coming under full sail, closing with the British ship, and Adam shouted orders to his helmsman.

"Hard port! Come about between the *Lawrence* and the *Detroit!*" Then he turned to his gun crews. "Reload! Stand ready!"

Again the *Margaret* leaned as she came hard to port, around the bow of the battered *Lawrence,* on toward the *Detroit,* yet three hundred yards distant.

Onboard the British ship, Captain Barclay saw the *Niagara* coming from his starboard and the *Margaret* coming hard on his port stern, and gave the command he thought would avoid the trap.

"Hard to port!"

The British ship was far into its left turn before Barclay saw the *Queen Charlotte*, crippled, her captain and first mate dead, only one mast standing, less than fifty yards away, on a collision course with the *Detroit*. In desperation he shouted at his helmsman, "Hard to starboard—hard to starboard!" and the big man-of-war straightened, then began its turn, but too late. The *Queen Charlotte* plowed into the *Detroit* amidships, and her masts and spars and tattered sails caught in the splintered railings. The *Detroit* continued her violent turn to starboard, trying to break from the *Queen Charlotte*, but the ropes and the sails would not disengage, and Barclay felt the jolt as the *Detroit* was jerked to port and slowed to a near standstill by the dead weight of the crippled ship clinging to his port side.

Adam saw it all, and beyond the two fouled British ships, he saw Elliott bringing the *Niagara* alongside the *Detroit* at less than one hundred yards. He turned to his own helmsman.

"Hold your bearing, dead ahead."

Less than one minute later the cannon on the *Niagara* blasted a broadside to the starboard of the *Detroit*. The sound had not died when Adam shouted orders to his gun crews, and his starboard guns delivered a broadside that caught the *Queen Charlotte* and the *Detroit* on their port sides. When the smoke cleared, the two British ships were still entangled, and Adam turned once more to his helmsman.

"Pass them and turn to starboard around the bow of the *Detroit*."

While he watched, Elliott circled the *Niagara* around the stern of the two British ships to come in on their port side. Adam was counting seconds in the hope that both the American ships would be in position before the British ships could separate and bring their guns to bear. With fewer than fifty yards yet to go, he saw the hawsers snap and the sails rip, and the two ships begin to drift apart. The British gun crews had their cannon half loaded when both the American ships came into position and their cannon fired. Solid shot and canister tore into the two British ships and their crews from both sides. Adam saw Barclay stagger back and topple over, then try to rise to his knees before he slumped forward, trying to support his body with his one arm. But even at eighty yards, Adam could see that it was shattered. Instantly four British seamen raised their captain to his feet and carried him to the nearest hatch and disappeared below decks.

For the first time in half an hour, Adam turned to peer at the *Lawrence,* less than one hundred yards over his stern. She was a battered hulk. Her masts were cut in two, her spars broken and lying on the decks, her sails ripped and torn by solid and canister shot, almost of all her crew down, but she had not struck her colors. She was still in the fight. He searched for Captain Perry, but he was not there, and then Adam gaped at a sight that would remain with him forever.

Captain Perry was lowering himself into a longboat with six oarsmen waiting. The moment his feet hit the bottom of the boat the oarsmen threw their backs into it, and Perry wrenched the rudder around to set a course for the *Niagara.* Some of the smaller British gunboats believed that the *Lawrence* must be sinking and that Perry had surrendered her, and made ready to attach hawsers to claim their prize. When they saw Perry in the longboat trying to reach the *Niagara,* they brought their ships around to fire on him. With cannonballs and grapeshot raising geysers all around the longboat, Perry remained on his feet, holding the rudder, pointing, while the oarsmen set their oars deep and pulled with all their strength.

Adam found himself muttering, "Pull—pull—you can make it—pull!"

No one in the fight could believe it when Perry's longboat slammed into the side of the *Niagara,* and he leaped to catch the netting thrown to him and pulled himself up and onto her deck. Seconds later he was on the quarterdeck, in command, and the ship came around the bow of the *Detroit* to rake her from bow to stern, while the *Margaret* came in from the stern to blast both the *Detroit* and the *Queen Charlotte.*

The four lesser British gunboats made a brave attempt to rescue the two heavy ships, but the seven small American gunboats met them head-on. For three minutes the cannons roared before the British realized it was hopeless. The captains and first mates on all six of their ships were either dead or totally disabled. Their two largest gunboats were shattered, floating hulks. Barclay was below decks in delirious, fever-ridden pain while his ship's surgeon futilely worked to save his one arm, then conceded it could not be done.

Four of the British ships struck their colors, and the Americans came in beside them to claim them. Two of the smaller gunboats turned north, trying to run with the wind to escape surrender, but Adam was there, ahead of them, broadside, waiting. The fleeing ships slowed, then turned back, struck their colors, and surrendered.

It was over.

With the battle ended, the crews on all ships came back to reality. Four of the English ships were shot to pieces. Every English officer was either dead or critically wounded. More than half of all British crew members were dead or wounded. The American *Lawrence* was hardly recognizable, and eighty percent of her crew were dead. Every ship in the battle had holes in its hull and sails, with spars and arms broken and dangling and shattered railings and hatches. When the Americans boarded the British *Detroit,* they faced a pet brown bear that was licking at the blood on the decks. In the hold they found two Indians cowering in a dark corner.

While the ships made their way south toward the American base at Put-in-Bay, seamen gathered the dead to cover them with canvas, while others did what they could to stop the bleeding and give comfort to the wounded. The sun was setting when the ships dropped anchor amid the cheers of hundreds of men who had listened to the distant rumble of cannon for more than three hours, not knowing who had won and who had lost when the guns fell silent.

On board the *Niagara,* Captain Perry rummaged in the captain's quarters until he found an old, rumpled letter and a lead pencil. He pondered for a moment before he turned the letter over and wrote on the back side:

"We have met the enemy and they are ours: two ships, two brigs, one schooner & one sloop." He stuffed the report into his pocket for delivery to William Henry Harrison, commander of the northern forces of the United States.

The battered ships entered Put-in-Bay at sunset and dropped anchor close to the docks. Through dusk and twilight the longboats carried the wounded ashore to the surgeons and nurses, and then the bodies of the dead to be placed side by side in any buildings where space could be made. On Perry's orders, every military courtesy was extended to the British. Their wounded were taken ashore along with the American wounded, and their seamen were allowed to carry their dead officers ashore with British flags covering their remains. The camp cooks had roasted quarters of beef on spits, and they held evening mess hot until the somber work of caring for the wounded and dead was finished, and the remainder of the ship crews came to the mess lines, quiet and bone-weary.

Adam had finished his evening mess and was rinsing his plate in the officer's mess hall when a rangy sergeant approached him.

"Cap'n Perry wants you at command headquarters."

Adam put his plate and utensils in the large wooden tub for the cleanup crew and walked out into the soft night air. Mosquitoes were in the air, and frogs on the small streams nearby were well into their nightly chorus as he walked past men moving among the tents with lanterns glowing inside. He entered the log headquarters building, and the corporal at the front desk pointed. Adam walked to the door and knocked.

"Enter."

He stepped inside and closed the door. Seated on the far side of a worn desk, in the small, crude office, Perry, young, charismatic, eager, raised his head from a document he was drafting, laid down his quill, stood, and gestured.

"Please have a seat, Captain."

Adam sat down on a simple hard-backed chair facing the desk, and Perry sat back down facing him. In the yellow lamplight, Perry came directly to it.

"Captain Dunson," he said quietly, "I felt it appropriate to tell you.

Out there on the lake today, we gained control of the northern campaign in the war. Already the fight is being hailed as the pivotal battle of the war. We now command the northern waterway, from Lake Superior to the Atlantic Ocean. It means our military forces can now turn their full energies on the southern campaign."

He stopped to gesture at the unfinished document before him. "I am writing my report. In it will be the detail of the battle. Captain Elliott's mistake—leaving the battle line and leading seven ships astray—would have been fatal. It was your ship, the *Margaret,* that saved us. If you had not broken away from the *Niagara* and attacked both the *Detroit* and the *Queen Charlotte* as you did, the entire affair would have gone against us."

He paused to order his thoughts. "I have talked with Captain Elliott. He has no explanation for why he disobeyed his orders. I trust you understand, such things happen in the heat of battle. Elliott frankly asked that he face a court-martial for his lapse. I told him no, he had redeemed himself when he came to his senses. He requested that I tell you, he knows you gave him his chance for redemption and saving his career. He is most grateful. So am I."

Adam dropped his eyes for a moment but said nothing.

Perry went on. "Your name will appear prominently in this report. I speak for myself and for a grateful country when I tell you we are beholden. Accept my deepest thanks. It has been my honor to serve with you."

Perry stood and extended his hand across the old desk, and Adam stood and reached to grasp it.

"Thank you, sir," Adam said. "The honor and the privilege are mine."

That rare thing that sometimes passes between men who have faced death shoulder-to-shoulder and won, was silently exchanged between the two of them, and Adam nodded and turned and walked out of the room, back into the night.

It was later, after the drum had rattled taps and the lamps were turned off, that Adam lay on his back in his bunk in the officers' quarters, hands clasped behind his head, staring into the blackness.

We won—reports will be sent—newspapers will make headlines of glory—honors will be given—the country will make much of it—but little will be said about the price—the hundreds of men who died out there today—the hundreds who are crippled and maimed for life—the women and children with fatherless homes—the mothers with sons they will never see again—the pain—the suffering—who will tell it the way it was?—the way it is . . .

He turned on his side and closed his eyes. His last conscious thoughts were of Laura, at home, waiting, not knowing if he was dead or alive, and he felt the deep yearning to be there with her, away from the horror of war—just Adam Dunson, a citizen quietly helping his brothers and Billy Weems to run a shipping company.

It was much later that he drifted into a troubled sleep, seeing the flash of cannon and the destruction of ships, and men falling, crippled, mortally wounded.

Notes

On September 10, 1813, the pivotal sea battle of the War of 1812 was fought on Lake Erie between nine American ships anchored at the American port at Put-in-Bay in the Bass Islands at the west end of Lake Erie, under command of Captain Oliver Hazard Perry, and six British ships anchored at or near Fort Malden on the Canadian side of Lake Erie, under command of Captain Robert Hale Barclay. The names of all ships in this chapter are actual, except the *Margaret*, which is a fictional ship.

The Americans had taken control of Lake Ontario to the east and cut the British supply and communication lines. Thousands of Indians, including women and children, had gathered at Fort Malden, and the British were responsible to feed them. When supplies ran out, the Indians were starving and threatening revolt. British regulars were on half rations. Barclay had but one choice, and that was to break out, take control of Lake Erie, and reestablish the supply lines. To do so he would have to defeat Perry and the American fleet.

That Friday morning he left Fort Malden to engage the Americans. The two forces met in the open water, and Perry, commanding the *Lawrence*, sailed straight into them. Captain Jesse Elliott, commanding the second ship, the

Niagara, failed to follow him into the battle and contrary to orders, held back, using his long-range cannon. Elliott never did give an explanation of what caused him to fail to follow Perry into the midst of the British ships. As a result, Perry's ship was shot to pieces; however, in the process, he badly damaged both British gunboats, the *Queen Charlotte* and the *Detroit*. It was only then that Elliott realized what he had done and came into the fight head-on. Between the two American ships, they succeeded in taking both the large British ships out of action.

In the process, Perry lost eighty percent of his crew, and his ship was reduced to a shattered hulk. He did in fact board a longboat, and a crew rowed him to the *Niagara*, where he took command. Some of the smaller British ships thought he had surrendered and were prepared to board the *Lawrence*. During the same time, the *Queen Charlotte* and the *Detroit* collided and became entangled, and before they could completely separate, the Americans shot them to pieces.

Musket fire was given and received by every ship. Every British captain was either killed or badly disabled. Barclay, with one arm missing from a prior sea battle, lost his remaining arm. Four of the British ships struck their colors and surrendered. Two made a run for freedom but were stopped and surrendered. When the Americans boarded the *Detroit*, they in fact observed a pet bear licking the blood on the decks and found two Indians in the hold, who had been brought on board as marksmen but had hidden when the gunfire became unbearable.

Perry found an old letter and on the back of it wrote the message he would later send to William Henry Harrison, commander of the American northern forces: "We have met the enemy and they are ours; two ships, two brigs, one schooner & one sloop." The first nine words of the message became immortalized, and Perry instantly became a shining hero. The battle is regarded as the single most important sea battle in the war, since it gave complete control of the northern waterway, from Lake Superior to the Atlantic Ocean, to the Americans, allowing all military forces to be concentrated on campaigns to the south.

See Hickey, *The War of 1812*, pp. 131–35; Wills, *James Madison*, pp. 124–25; Malcomson, *Lords of the Lake*, pp. 196–98; Stagg, *Mr. Madison's War*, pp. 328–30; Roosevelt, *The Naval War of 1812*, pp. 141–56; Antal, *A Wampum Denied*, pp. 286–88.

Adam Dunson and the ship *Margaret* are both fictional. Most of the action ascribed to them in this chapter was actually performed by Captain Elliott and the *Niagara*, only, however, after Captain Elliott finally came to Perry's rescue.

For a likeness drawn of Captain Perry by artist George Delleker, see Hickey, *The War of 1812*, p. 134.

Fort Amherstburg, Detroit River, Canada
Mid-September 1813

CHAPTER XXI

*T*he five British officers came to the large, rustic headquarters building inside the high walls of Fort Amherstburg in the late afternoon, one at a time, silent, with a deep sense of dark foreboding. They entered the battered door, and the uniformed sergeant at the foyer desk pointed each of them into the plain, square, private council room of General Sir Henry Procter, commander of British forces in northwestern Canada. They took chairs on two sides of the rough table to sit rigid, quiet, in scarlet uniforms that were slightly faded and threadbare at the cuffs and the tops of their erect, rigid collars. Their black boots lacked luster, and the gold epaulets on their shoulders had long since become dulled by the harsh Canadian winters and the sun and storms of summer.

They flinched at the sound of the foyer door closing too hard, and moments later they watched Matthew Elliott enter the twilight of the singled-windowed room. All nodded to him, but none spoke as Elliott slowly walked to the end of the table, laboring under the weight of his eighty years. Bent, wrinkled, white-haired, hands gnarled and twisted with age, the old man eased himself painfully onto the chair, then looked up at the officers and returned their nod. As head of the British Indian Department, he was dressed in the garb of a civilian, not a military officer. The British Parliament had ordered him to Amherstburg in a desperate attempt to save the tenuous, trembling alliance between England and the Indians. Each man at the table understood that should the

Indians turn on the British, the six of them would be witness to the most horrifying massacre in the history of the North American continent. They sat in silence, nervous, moving their hands, eyes downcast, waiting.

They heard the foyer door open and close once more, then listened to the sound of leather heels on the floor planking, and General Procter entered. The five officers came to their feet and stood at attention.

Average height, blocky build, face unremarkable and square, dark wavy hair combed straight back, sideburns prominent, Procter took his place at the head of the table and laid a rolled map and several documents to one side. His eyes were dead, a mask covering the turmoil and fear that were destroying him inside. A tension began to grow in the austere room.

Procter cut through the usual protocol of greeting.

"Be seated. Gentlemen, I believe a review is in order for what is coming." He paused long enough to pick up a sheaf of hand-written notes, which he glanced at as he spoke.

"You know about the naval battle on Lake Erie four days ago. Two days ago I sent an agent from the Department of Indians with four natives in a canoe to determine the results. They returned. The news is disastrous. Captain Barclay and his entire squadron were defeated and captured by the Americans. There are four American ships at Put-in-Bay being repaired from the battle. All other American ships are anchored at the mouth of the Portage River on the American side of Lake Erie. It is obvious they are preparing to transport General Harrison and his army to this side of the lake."

He paused to watch the officers' breathing slow and their eyes widen.

"We are cut off. Isolated. All water routes are closed. We have no communication from the east. No supply line on land or water. No reinforcements can reach us. The last message I received from General Prevost in the east was that I should 'call forth the combined discipline and gallantry of the troops to cripple and repulse the enemy.' He did mention the possibility that a withdrawal from the area might become desirable, if done with 'order and regularity.' He encourages me to meet this catastrophe with 'fortitude.'"

He paused, and the officers saw the disgust and contempt in his face at the ridiculous advice from his superior.

Procter went on. "Four days ago I sent several bateaux to Long Point for food. They got nothing. Yesterday our flour ran out. Our commissaries are bare to the walls. Our soldiers are on short rations of potatoes and wheat, and there is no way to acquire more. Our men are wearing tattered uniforms. Some are barefoot. Within thirty days we can expect the storms of approaching winter."

He paused to collect his thoughts, then went on.

"You know that yesterday I declared martial law in this entire area. That gives me the authority to requisition all foodstuffs from all civilians, if we can find it. It is already obvious that they are hiding their stores. We will never collect enough of it to be of any help."

He stopped and took a great breath and released it.

"Food and supply shortages, lack of communication, and oncoming hard weather are matters we could most likely survive."

All six of the men seated at the table saw it coming, and they braced themselves.

"The Indians are another matter. Lacking a solution to the Indian problem, our entire army in this sector is lost."

He stopped and waited for a time before he went on.

"My latest count of our own forces places them at something around twelve hundred. Latest reports on the Indians say there are ten thousand adults gathered in this area. At least one third are warriors. In addition, there are wives and children. I do not need to tell you that we have been making them promises of food and blankets for more than fourteen months, and each month our supplies coming from the east became more and more meagre until there were none. To stay alive, the Indians spent part of this past summer killing deer and opossum and raccoon for food—even a bear—and when they were all gone, they ate whitefish and parched corn and maple sugar. When that was gone, they turned to crab apples and chestnuts. That is now gone. They're starving."

Not one of the officers moved or spoke as Procter went on.

"I have today received what amounts to an ultimatum from their chiefs. They flatly accused us of lying to them, using them. We promised them food, and there is no food. We promised we would drive the Americans from their ancestral lands and restore to them what was theirs, and we have failed. We promised them we would deliver muskets and ammunition to them and that we would be their allies in the battle. We have not delivered the arms, and there has been no battle. We have done none of it! Instead, we have lost control of both Lake Erie and Lake Ontario, and they know we are now preparing to retreat east, overland. They have made it very clear that if we do not now live up to all we've promised, they will rise against us in bloody revolt. If that happens, there will be nothing left of any of us."

There it was! Procter and the entire British command on the west end of Lake Erie would either deliver what they had promised or face the tomahawk and scalping knives of three thousand enraged warriors. The tension in the room became almost palpable.

Procter reached for the rolled map and spread it out on the tabletop, oriented it, leaned forward, and spoke as he pointed.

"We are here at Fort Amherstburg on the Detroit River where it drains into Lake Erie. North of us about five or six miles is Sandwich. Here, about twenty-five miles east of Sandwich, is the place where the Thames River drains into Lake St. Clair, between Lake Huron and Lake Erie."

He moved his finger east, up the Thames River. "Here, about twenty miles or so east of the mouth of the river is the fork where McGregor's Creek joins it, and it is a natural defensive position." His finger continued up the river. "Here, about twenty miles farther east, is Moraviantown. There's a church there, and about sixty homes—the largest settlement on the river. It has high ground and some natural cover for defensive positions. By far, the best route for our retreat will be east on the Thames River."

Procter straightened. "I arrived here fourteen months ago by schooner on the lake. I have never been out in the wilderness in this area. I do not know the terrain along the river. I will have to depend on what information I can gather, and so far that information has been seriously flawed and lacking. I can only assure you, I will do what I can."

The officers saw his pain as he made his confession.

He continued. "In determining my course of action, I intend abiding by three principles. First, I must preserve our alliance with the Indians at all costs. Second, I have no choice but to order an all-out retreat. Third, the Thames River is the only course that affords such a retreat."

He paused to let the officers' minds accept the three foundation principles before he went on.

"The result is we must persuade the Indians of two things. One, the retreat we are planning to the east is our only hope of survival. Two, that making such a retreat does not mean we are abandoning them, or that we do not intend keeping our promise to drive the Americans from their ancestral lands and restoring to them what is theirs."

For the first time, Elliott moved. He leaned back on his chair and slowly shook his aged head in silent, hopeless resignation. The five officers looked at him for a moment, then turned back to Procter, who cleared his throat and continued.

"It is one thing to make an orderly retreat with trained soldiers. It is another thing to try it with Indians. General Brock put it rather succinctly a year ago when he told General Prevost that he would be unwilling in the event of a retreat to have three or four hundred of them hanging on his flanks. Brock was of the opinion that if the Indians imagine that we are deserting them, the consequences would be fatal."

Procter stared at his officers for a moment. "If General Brock was concerned about three or four hundred of them in a retreat, what would he have thought of ten thousand of them?"

There were audible groans from the officers, then silence, and Procter went on.

"I trust you all know the rules of conduct among the Indians. No chief has the power to give orders. Every Indian is a law unto himself. Should one of them, or a hundred, or a thousand, decide to simply leave, they will leave, and there is no way to stop them. If they decide to march, they march; if they decide to stop, they stop. I do not know how we are going to manage a retreat in which we are responsible for thousands of them. I only know we must try."

He stopped to reroll his map and place his notes on the papers. There was quiet murmuring among the officers, and Elliott sat hunched forward, elbows and forearms on the table, face a blank.

Procter concluded. "You are aware that tomorrow morning at ten o'clock the chiefs of all the Indian tribes in the region will meet with us in the council house. I will attempt to persuade them that there is no choice other than to abandon Amherstburg and Fort Detroit, and to make a full-scale retreat east on the Thames."

For the first time, Elliott spoke. "You plan to burn them both? Amherstburg and Detroit?"

Procter said, "Yes."

Elliott muttered something under his breath and then fell silent.

Procter reached to gather his papers. "If there is nothing else, you are dismissed."

The six men stood and silently filed from the room, Elliott last, swaying slightly as he favored the stiffness and the rheumatism in his aged legs. Procter stood still for a time with his papers under his arm, staring at the closed door, caught up in a premonition of impending doom. After a time, he opened the door, and the sergeant at the desk stood while he passed on out into the great parade ground where the golden light of the setting sun caught the tops of the trees and the top of the east wall of the fort to set them glowing.

Procter was halfway across the open expanse, on his way to his quarters, when he was seized by the strongest impression of his life. For an instant he was a small speck inside a fragile, meaningless, walled structure, tiny and ridiculous in the vastness of a Nature that was both offended and contemptuous of the insanity of mankind. Soon—too soon—everything about him, and every human being connected with it, would be gone. They would be remembered for a time, and then slowly forgotten. The fort, the roads, the conflicts, the pain, the wins, the losses, would drift into nothingness.

By force of will he drove the melancholy impression from his mind. *I am a British officer—I have my orders—I will carry them out—There is meaning— There is purpose.*

He picked at his evening meal and, with the drum sounding taps, went to his bunk to a restless sleep filled with visions of his red-coated regulars, thin, emaciated, terrified, surrounded by crazed, screaming Indians, brandishing tomahawks and scalping knives.

It was still dark when he swung his feet out of his bed and curled his toes against the cold floor to sit in the darkness, silently rehearsing again and again what he had to say to the Indians at the council meeting, struggling to control the fears that rose in his breast. *What will Tecumseh say? What will the chiefs do? If they revolt, what do I do? Shoot them? Arrest them?*

There were no clear-cut answers; he could not remember an event in British military history that even approached the muddled, soul-wrenching duty he now faced. He lighted a lamp and heated water to shave and wash himself, then dressed and sat at his desk for a time, mechanically going over the map and the notes he must use. At dawn, the reveille drum he had heard ten thousand times sounded strangely loud, and on a sudden impulse he walked to the door and opened it to stand in silence, watching the fort awaken to the bright sun of a day in which the fate of every soul within its walls, and thousands outside its walls, could be determined. While he buttoned his tunic he glanced at the calendar on the wall above his desk. September 15, 1813.

It was approaching ten o'clock when he walked from his quarters into the dead air, onto the parade ground, and slowed in stark disbelief. A company of regulars under command of a sergeant barking orders was marching in rank and file on the drill field, and the women were hunched over their wooden washtubs scrubbing laundry, and the chimneys of the twelve ovens at the bakery were sending gray smoke upward in straight lines, as they had been doing each workday for more than a year. But every soldier, every wash woman, every baker, was staring in white-faced fear at the Indians. Hundreds of them were gathered, milling about, gesturing, pointing, black eyes narrowed, glowing. They were not wrapped in their blankets as was their custom, and there was not a woman or child among them. They were warriors, clad in buckskin breeches and beaded buckskin shirts and moccasins. They wore necklaces of bear teeth and eagle talons. Their thick, black hair was pulled and tied behind their heads, and feathers hung loose. In their belts were tomahawks and scalping knives. Some carried muskets and rifles. A few had pistols. The huge gates of the fort were open, and Procter could see hundreds more gathered outside, and he could hear the guttural undertone of their voices and see the hatred in their faces.

He squared his shoulders, raised his chin, and walked steadily toward the great council building with those in his way sullenly stepping aside to give him passage. The large room on the ground floor was crowded with a mix of soldiers with muskets and fixed bayonets and Indians with tomahawks and knives. Procter paused long enough to find the ranking officer and give the order.

"Clear this room."

"Yes, sir."

Procter watched as the officer gave blunt orders, and the soldiers locked shoulder to shoulder to move everyone out the door, onto the parade ground.

Procter waited until the door was closed before he climbed the stairs to the huge council room with the high, pitched roof on the second floor. The conference tables had been arranged in the shape of a large U, with chairs at the head for Procter and his council of officers. Along the tables to the left were chairs for the Indian chiefs, and along the right, for the lesser British officers. Most of the Indian chiefs and British officers were already present, standing in groups, Indians on one side, British on the other, each locked in subdued conversation while they covertly eyed each other. It took Procter three seconds to locate Tecumseh in one corner, listening to six sub-chiefs while his eyes never stopped moving about the room.

Procter masked his shock at their dress. They were not clad in their chiefs' robes, with the British medals given as gifts on golden chains about their necks. They wore instead the battle garb of a warrior—

buckskins, with feathers and deer antlers and heads and teeth of wild-cats in their hair, and tomahawks and knives in their belts. Their belts were decorated with eagle feathers, an open declaration of their bravery and fearlessness in battle.

The British had their swords in scabbards fastened to their belts—standard for a British officer in dress uniform.

Procter took his place, checked his pocket watch, and at ten o'clock raised his hand for silence. All took their seats, Indians to his left, British officers to his right. Seated at the head table immediately to his left was an Indian interpreter, and on his right was a British interpreter, each to be certain the other was translating correctly. Beside the interpreters were the five officers of Procter's war council. Procter turned to the British interpreter, nodded, then turned back to the Indians and spoke loudly.

"I speak for the Father across the great water. I welcome the great chiefs who honor us with their presence."

He stopped, waiting for Tecumseh to rise and return the greeting, as was the custom. But Tecumseh did not move or speak. Instantly the room was locked in silence, and the tension became electric.

Procter licked dry lips and took a deep breath while he made the pivotal decision. *Stop the platitudes. Come directly to it.*

"Our ships on the big lake have been taken by the Americans. Our food is gone. The Americans are coming to drive us from this place and from Detroit. They have great numbers. We have only a few. We cannot get more food from our people in the east. We cannot get more soldiers. We cannot stop the Americans."

He paused. No one moved or spoke, and he went on.

"We must leave this place. We must leave Detroit. We must destroy everything so the enemy cannot use it. We must move east on the Thames River to Niagara to escape the Americans. We must do it now. I am ordering the redcoats to prepare for it."

The Indians erupted. The room rang with their shouted threats. A few reached for their tomahawks. British officers had their hands on their swords, ready. Then Tecumseh came to his feet and raised both hands, and slowly the chiefs settled back onto their chairs. The British officers shifted their weight to keep their sword handles free, ready, and sat, waiting, hardly breathing.

Procter sat down, showing the proper respect to Tecumseh, the leader of the Indians. For several seconds Tecumseh's long, narrow face remained without expression before he took a deep breath and began.

"More than thirty seasons ago the redcoated soldiers came to us. They said the Father across the great water had declared war with the Americans. They gave us the tomahawk and told us he was ready to strike the Americans. The Father wanted our assistance. He would get us our lands back which the Americans had taken from us. He would feed us. He would give us muskets and ammunition. He would care for us. We listened. We believed the Father across the great water. We took up the tomahawk against the Americans for him."

He paused, and his black eyes were glowing like embers.

"The red-coated soldiers did not drive the Americans from our land. They made peace with the Americans and did nothing about the land. They did not feed us. They did not care for us. They abandoned us. They lied to us."

A low rumble rose and died on the Indian side of the table. Tecumseh went on.

"Two seasons ago the Father across the great water sent his soldiers to us again. The Americans had declared war. He wanted our assistance. Again he told us to take up our tomahawks against the Americans. If we would, he promised he would get our lands back. He would feed us. He would give us muskets and ammunition. He would take care of us. Again we listened. Again we took up the tomahawk to fight the Americans.

"Now we have come here to listen. You are telling us again that you cannot drive the Americans from our lands. You cannot get food for us. You cannot get muskets and ammunition. We are starving. Our women cannot suckle their babies. We are sick with white man's disease. We have no blankets against the winter that is coming. You tell us that we must leave this place. We must burn it. We must move far to the east, away from our ancestral lands that you promised to restore to us. Again you have lied to us. We cannot trust the Father across the great water. He is a liar. He makes promises that he will not keep. He uses us to kill Americans and then abandons us."

Tecumseh turned to face Procter directly, eyes boring in like daggers.

"You speak for the Father. You are also a liar. You have done nothing you promised us more than one season ago. We have done everything we promised. You now plan to abandon us to the big knives of the Americans. You refuse to meet them here and fight them on the shore of the lake."

Procter sat rigid, frozen, silent in the face of the truth that Tecumseh was spewing against the British government and against him personally.

Tecumseh hunched slightly forward and raised a long, bony finger to point directly at Procter.

"Your conduct is that of a fat animal that carries its tail upon its back, but when affrighted, it drops it between its legs and runs off."

Tecumseh had just called Procter a pig! The Indians pounded the table in approval while the British officers sat stunned, unable to believe what they had heard. Some looked at Procter for orders, but Procter's eyes never left Tecumseh's.

Again Tecumseh raised his hands for silence and continued, with scorn in his face and in his voice.

"If you wish to go from this place, then leave your arms and ammunition with us. We will continue to fight the Americans without you. That is better than to retreat with you, knowing that you will abandon us if the Americans catch you."

For a time Tecumseh stood facing Procter, eyes flashing, face drawn in utter contempt. Then he sat down, and instantly bedlam filled the hall. Every Indian chief in the room leaped to his feet and jerked his tomahawk from his belt to wave it high above his head, shouting oaths, uttering high, warbling war whoops that echoed from the high ceiling to chill the blood, cursing Procter and the British officers.

In the next instant every British officer was on his feet, white-faced, reaching for his sword. Procter jerked erect and pointed to his officers, shouting, "No swords! No swords! Sit down. Sit down. Do not show fear. Do *not* show fear. Keep your chins up. Be officers! British officers!"

For a moment the officers looked at their commander as though he had lost his mind, then slowly settled their swords back into their scabbards and sat down on their chairs with their chins up, staring straight ahead at the Indians on the far side of the room. Procter remained standing and turned to face Tecumseh, who remained seated. Procter's hands were steady, his head high, his face set, determined, unafraid, and he did nothing to stop the wild melee before him. Minutes passed before the war whoops and the cursing and the threats diminished and stopped. Only then did Procter raise a hand to speak. His voice was calm, controlled, without rancor.

"There is much truth in what the great Tecumseh has said. I speak for the British Father when I say we regret our failure. It was not our intent to fail. We could not stop it. I ask you to understand. I ask you to overlook it."

The unbearable tension began to diminish, and Procter continued.

"I can only repeat what I have said. I must leave this place with the red-coated soldiers. I have no other choice. We must move east on the Thames River. I promise you that if the Americans catch us we will find a place and we will fight them. That is in my power to decide, and I promise it."

He stopped for a moment to order his thoughts.

"The great Tecumseh has asked that we leave arms and ammunition here for you to fight the Americans when they are on the lake shore. I see the wisdom in it. I ask that you give me a few days to consider it. It is in my power to decide, and if we have the arms and ammunition, I will do it. I give you my promise."

In that moment, Procter sensed the slightest softening in the eyes of the Indians, and the thought flashed in his mind—*Stop—Now.*

He spoke directly to Tecumseh. "Will you grant me a few days?"

For several moments the bloodiest massacre in history of the British army hung in the balance.

Tecumseh drew a deep breath. "Granted. A few days. Here in this place."

Procter nodded deeply. "I thank the great Tecumseh. If there is nothing else, this council is adjourned for a few days. I will give notice to all of our next meeting."

Chairs scraped on the plain pine floors as everyone stood, and the British officers came to attention while the Indians filed out, down the stairs, and out into the parade ground. When the downstairs door closed, every British officer released held breath and for a moment their shoulders slumped while the color slowly came back into their faces. They remained in the great council room for a time, talking quietly in groups, milling about, reluctant to go back out onto the parade ground until they were certain the chiefs had left the fort. Procter slowly gathered his papers, watching his men, gauging their mood, judging how close they were to their breaking point.

Procter remained at his place while the officers quieted and fell into a line to descend the long flight of stairs to the main floor, and out into the bright sunlight of the late morning. Elliott was the last man, and as he hobbled to the head of the stairs, Procter fell in beside him.

"Mister Elliott, I'm leaving for Sandwich this afternoon. I have to put things in order there for our withdrawal. I'll be back in three days. While I'm gone, take some officials from your department and talk with Tecumseh. Reason with him. Draw him away from his belligerence."

Elliott looked up at Procter. "I'll do what I can, but after what happened this morning, I doubt it will be of any benefit."

Procter took the old man's elbow to steady him as they descended the stairs and walked out of the building onto the parade ground. They both stopped for a moment, startled that not one Indian was in sight. They glanced at each other before the old man walked away and Procter went to his quarters.

Noon mess was finished when Procter went to the stables where his staff was waiting with their horses saddled, including a tall, rangy, brown mare that Procter preferred for travel. With them was a squad of armed regulars, waiting to ride escort duty. Within minutes the small column was mounted and pacing their horses toward the gates of the fort and out onto the two crooked wagon ruts that were called the road to Sandwich, less than two hours north. They rode in silence, listening, watching all movement in the forest on both sides of the road, waiting for the first glimpse of bronze shadows moving in the trees, but there were none.

They arrived at the tiny settlement in the late afternoon and rode past the great, random scatter of lodges and tepees of the Indians who had gathered during the summer on the broken promise that they were joining the British to drive the Americans from their ancestral grounds. The mounted British held their horses to a steady walk as they rode, aware of the sullen faces and the muttered curses of the Indians who stopped to watch them pass.

They continued on to the British camp, past the nervous pickets in full uniform carrying muskets and bayonets, to the orderly rows of tents and the forty-foot flagpole with the Union Jack hanging limp in the still, dead air. They dismounted before the low log command building, and were tying their horses to the wooden hitch rack when the commanding officer and his aide pushed through the front door and came to attention, saluted Procter, waited for the salute to be returned, and invited the general and his aides inside, while the armed escort squad waited outside.

They took their places at the long table, and for more than half an hour Procter spoke while the camp commander and his staff listened in stony silence, mouths set in a straight line, faces expressionless as they began to grasp the fact that they, and every British soldier within two hundred miles, would be under the tomahawk and scalping knife within minutes of the moment the Indians, for any reason, or for no reason, turned on them. Their lives now hung on the whim of a volatile, unpredictable people they neither understood nor knew how to control.

Procter continued.

"Have your officers assembled here at nine o'clock in the morning. We must plan a full retreat west on the Thames River. Every building here, everything we cannot carry, must be burned. We can leave nothing the Americans can use. Have your entire command on the parade ground at ten o'clock, full uniform. They must hear it from me. I will spend the balance of the day inspecting any supplies you have left, all arms, all ammunition, to decide what goes with us and what we must destroy.

I will remain here tonight and tomorrow night, and return to Amherstburg the following morning. Are there any questions?"

There were none.

General Procter took his evening meal in his small quarters, while his staff took evening mess with the camp officers. As they ate, they were aware of the furtive glances from the camp officers and the conversations that were carried on in quiet undertones.

"Did you hear what happened at Amherstburg this morning? The Indians went wild in the council room! Got out their tomahawks and scalping knives! War whoops you could hear clear outside the fort!"

"Tecumseh called General Procter a liar! He called the British Parliament liars!"

"A liar? I heard he called Procter a pig! A fat pig!"

"Tecumseh told Procter and the whole British staff that if they were too cowardly to stand and fight, they should leave the arms and ammunition for him. He'd stop the Americans without us."

Procter spent a restless night and was cleaned and in full uniform well before morning mess. The mood of the nine o'clock meeting with the staff was somber, quiet, and apprehensive. The ten o'clock meeting with the entire command in rank and file on the parade ground left the red-coated regulars staring in disbelief when Procter informed them they were to abandon everything they could not carry and burn the entire camp. The afternoon inspection was quick—perfunctory, since the food stores were almost entirely gone—and there were not enough arms and ammunition for the regulars, and none for the Indians.

Procter spent the evening in his small quarters, pacing in the light of a single lantern, sick in his heart at the stark realization that the life of every man in his entire command depended on how he conducted a retreat the likes of which the British army had never experienced, and which had suddenly become a gigantic powder keg, waiting for the smallest spark to set off an explosion that would be heard in London.

Before he sought his bunk, he sent word through his aide to his staff and escort squad. "Be prepared to leave immediately after morning mess is concluded."

The sun had scarcely cleared the trees on the eastern horizon when Procter mounted his horse, and with half his armed squad leading and the other half following, the column took the rutted road south, winding through the dense woods, every man silent, watching, listening for anything that interrupted the sights and sounds of the forest. It was midmorning when they rode through the thousands of Indians camped outside Fort Amherstburg and through the gates and stopped at the headquarters building.

Procter thumped across the boardwalk, through the door, and slowed at the sight of Elliott sitting slumped in a chair against the wall, white head bowed. Procter closed the door, and Elliott raised his head, then stood. Fear was plain in the weathered face, and his hands and legs were trembling.

Procter studied him for a moment, with dread rising in his chest. Quietly he asked, "You're waiting to see me?"

"Since dawn."

Procter gestured, and Elliott shuffled into Procter's private office to take a seat opposite Procter, at his desk.

"What is it?" Procter asked.

The old man wiped at his mouth, and his voice croaked. "I took all the agents from my department I could gather and we talked with Tecumseh and some of the other chiefs."

Procter saw it coming. Elliott continued.

"They wouldn't listen. They got more hostile. There's open talk of rebellion—turning on us—killing us all and plundering everything within hundreds of miles—taking all our arms and ammunition and fighting the Americans any way they can. I have never seen Tecumseh in such a mood. He is capable of becoming most terrible—beyond anything we have ever imagined. The only thing that stopped him yesterday was the Ojibwa and Sioux leaders. They told him it was a matter of honor—he had to stay and continue to be their spokesman because he said he would, and it would be dishonorable to break his word."

Elliott raised a hand to point at Procter. "I warn you, if you do not meet their demands, you will be facing consequences unimagined."

He dropped his hand, and Procter swallowed, and the old man went on.

"You know about the wampum belt. The one the Indians made more than fifty years ago. The one with the heart in the middle and the hands on each end. The one that represents the bond between the Indians and England. Tecumseh has had that belt for the past eight years, and he swore to me that if you try to retreat, he will produce that belt in council, and he will cut it in half! When they cut that wampum belt in half, they are severing all ties with England. All promises, all that has gone before is ended. They will be free to butcher us at will." Elliott paused long enough to lean forward, eyes wide, face white, and thump the desk with an index finger.

"And I promise you, General, they will! William Caldwell fought on the side of the Indians in the Revolution and at Fallen Timbers. He knows those people better than anyone else around here. Yesterday, he packed his family and sent them south. He stayed, but he said he wasn't going to have his wife and children here for the bloodbath he sees coming!"

Procter rose above the dread that was ripping him inside and spoke calmly.

"Tecumseh and the other leaders agreed to give me a few days to make my decision. I want to meet in private with Tecumseh before that final council. Arrange to have Tecumseh here in two days. Only Tecumseh and not more than three or four of the other chiefs. Ten o'clock next Monday morning. September 20."

For the next two days, no British subject dared go outside the walls of the fort without a squad of armed regulars. The pickets on the walls stayed low, avoiding the rifle slots where they could be seen by the Indians camped below, fearful of the moment they would hear the crack of a rifle from the woods and one of the pickets would drop.

Monday morning broke with an overcast, and a light rain held for less than ten minutes before the clouds cleared and the sun came streaming. By ten o'clock, Tecumseh of the Shawnee, and the leaders of the Ojibwa and Sioux and two other tribes, were in their places in Procter's council room, seated at the single huge table that Procter had arranged. Seated opposite them at the same table were Elliott; his chief field inspector, Augustus Warburton; William Evans of the Forty-First Infantry; members of Elliott's headquarters staff; and two British officers. Procter presided at the head of the table with the translators and his aides beside him. The Indians were dressed as at the last council meeting, in buckskins, with their tomahawks and knives in their belts, attired for war. The British officers had their swords in plain sight, handles ready.

Procter stood and bowed to Tecumseh. "I thank the great Tecumseh and his chiefs for honoring us once again with their presence. I have journeyed to Sandwich to determine conditions there. I have reports of matters as they are now on the Thames River. I have other reports regarding what the Americans are doing. I wish to share this information with you, our allies."

The Indians exchanged glances, and Tecumseh nodded.

Procter spread a large map on the table and waited while everyone present oriented themselves to place and direction.

For more than one hour, Procter leaned over the map while he moved his finger, identifying every location of importance, and noting why it was important. He patiently, carefully explained that Barclay's loss of the entire British naval squadron on Lake Erie had left Fort Amherstburg and Sandwich and the entire western half of the lake defenseless, isolated, without food, arms, or ammunition. They could get no reinforcements from Niagara, far to the east. He pointed to the Portage River on the south side of the lake and told of the great number of American soldiers now gathered there, getting onto ships to cross the lake and attack. He shook his head when he told them that the heavy cannon on the American war ships could shoot two cannonballs at one time, with a chain between them, and with such weapons the Americans could not be stopped.

He straightened and paused to allow the Indians to examine the map, tracing rivers and calculating distances, and he remained silent while they began to understand that he had told them the truth. With the loss of the British ships, there was no way to stop the Americans. Fort Amherstburg and Sandwich, and all British troops and Indians with them, were doomed if they stayed where they were. They had no choice: flee, or be killed.

Procter waited until he saw the reality come into their eyes, and then he went on.

The retreat would follow the Thames River. The British had a great supply of picks and shovels in the hold of two small ships, the *Mary* and the *Ellen,* enough to prepare a defense at places on the river that would give good position against the oncoming Americans—Dolsen's Farm, the Forks, McGregor's Mill, Cornwall's Mill, Moraviantown. In solemn terms, Procter promised the chiefs that at one such place the retreat would end. He would halt the army, and they would build breastworks and dig trenches, and they would stop the Americans.

The Indians fell into a sober silence, and Procter moved on.

"I request that the great Tecumseh bring all his chiefs to a council in the great council room tomorrow. I wish to share with them the matters we have talked about. I wish to have their consent to all that we must do."

With stoic silence the Indians filed from the room and out across the parade ground, through the gates, to their own people. Procter spent part of the day on the parapets inside the high fort walls, telescope extended, watching the chiefs sit with their people, gesturing, signing with their hands, pointing. He saw heads nod in agreement, and he watched the leaders all gather at the great evening campfire, where they sat while Tecumseh stood among them, talking. For the first time since Procter could remember, all heads nodded in agreement before Tecumseh sat down, and the council ended.

At ten o'clock the following morning, with the Indians dressed in their buckskins and war decorations and their tomahawks and knives at their belts, seated in the great council room inside Fort Amherstburg, and the British officers seated opposite them, Procter called the council to order and faced the chiefs.

He began by saying, "I thank you all for honoring us with your presence. I wish to counsel with you on the matter we spoke of six days ago."

He did not hesitate. In brief, succinct terms he repeated the harsh facts he had laid before Tecumseh only twenty-four hours earlier: to remain where they were would be suicide. They must retreat. They would find a place on the Thames River, and they would stop, and they would drive the Americans back.

Then he concluded.

"I will not do these things unless you agree. I ask for you to answer my question now. Do you agree?"

Tecumseh rose and looked into the face of each of the tribal leaders, then turned to Procter.

"We agree, with the understanding that you will stop at the proper place, and we will fight the Americans."

Procter nodded. "It is agreed. This council is adjourned."

The Indians filed from the room, down the stairs, and out of the building, and the British officers exhaled held breath in giddy relief. They waited for a few minutes, nearly jubilant, talking too loud, while the Indians left the fort, and then they walked down the stairs and out across the parade grounds to their quarters.

Elliott waited until the room was cleared before he spoke to Procter alone.

"Let me see the map."

Procter spread it before him, and the old man pointed with a crooked finger.

"Some of the worst is yet to come. See these streams and rivers? Seven of them. Petite River, Pike's Creek, Riviere aux Puces, Belle River, Carp River, Roscom River, Indian Creek. All with bridges you're going to have to cross. When you do, you should burn them to slow down the Americans. But with two or three thousand Indians behind you, you don't dare burn them. And when the Indians finally get across, it will be too late. With those bridges in place, the Americans are going to have no trouble catching you."

He took a deep breath and went on.

"And you had better understand that some Indians will go with you, and some will not. Tecumseh is headed for Sandwich right now, thinking to make a stand there. He'll be back, but I'm telling you certain. Don't count on the thousands that are here now. They all said yes this morning, but they're shaky. It will take next to nothing for most of them to disappear. You will be fortunate to have a few hundred left when the Americans catch you and you have to fight."

The old man stared into Procter's eyes for a time and then turned on his heel and left the building.

Procter gathered his map and his papers and walked down the stairs, out onto the parade ground where a brisk, chill south wind was blowing heavy clouds due north. He slowed and peered at the south wall as though he could see through it, down to Lake Erie, and across to the mouth of the Portage River where American General Harrison had ships and men. Procter could not stop his thoughts or his fears.

The storms of fall are soon here. Where's Harrison and his army? When is he coming? How many men? Ships? What is his plan of attack?

Across the lake, on choppy, wind-driven waters at the mouth of the Portage River, an unending concourse of small boats and flat-bottomed bateaux continued making the trip from the rocky shore out to the anchored ships under command of Captain Oliver Hazard Perry, where they unloaded the soldiers, cannon, food stores, and horses of the largest American army ever seen west of the Appalachian Mountains, and turned back to shore to take on the next load. Volunteers from Ohio and Pennsylvania had arrived, and the tough, eager Kentucky horsemen were there with their long rifles, impatient to get on with the war.

Billy Weems stood on the shore with his rifle in hand, watching the smaller craft bucking the swells and whitecaps as they labored out to the ships to unload and return. In the distance, on the far side of Perry's anchored fleet, Billy studied the familiar silhouette of the one ship he knew so well—the *Margaret*—and he watched them using belly slings to lift horses from the bateaux onto the top deck of the big vessel.

She's still afloat. Got all her masts. Adam? Still with her? Is he all right?

He walked west to where the Kentucky cavalry was loading and faced a young, hawk-faced, bearded lieutenant who was caught up in getting nervous horses to walk up a gangplank and into the pitching hold of a large bateau.

Billy pointed. "You loading onto the big ship out there—the *Margaret?*"

The answer was short, irritated, perfunctory. "Who wants to know?"

"I do. I have family out there."

The lieutenant paused. "Family?"

"The captain is my brother-in-law."

"Captain Dunson?"

"Adam Dunson. I haven't seen him in months. I'd like to talk to him."

The change in the young lieutenant was instant. "Get on here with us. After what he done in that fight out there on the lake two weeks ago, we'll get you out there and back."

Billy boarded the bateau, stacked his rifle in one corner with those of the crew members, and took a place among them, talking low and gentle to the frightened, wild-eyed horses, trying to calm them in their distrust of standing on the deck of a rocking, pitching boat.

The south wind held the sails full and tight and drove the flat-bottomed boat pitching and rolling past the squadron of anchored ships to the *Margaret,* where the crew cast hawsers down to waiting hands on the bateau and tied the two vessels together. Then the risky business of earing down terrified horses began with experienced hands passing the big canvas slings beneath their bellies and dropping the loops over the hooks that would lift them up to the deck of the ship.

In the noise of the wind and the snorting of the horses and the sound of their hooves on the bottom of the bateau, the young lieutenant turned to Billy and pointed upward. Billy nodded, picked up his rifle, and climbed the netting hanging down the side of the *Margaret,* over the railing to the main deck. There he stopped in the clamor to study the quarterdeck, and Adam was there, absorbed in the loading of his ship. Billy walked to the steps and climbed them, and quietly came up beside him.

Busy directing the loading process, Adam was not immediately aware of him. When he finally turned his head in Billy's direction, he froze in disbelief and then exclaimed, "Billy! Billy! What are you . . ."

Billy was grinning broadly, and he thrust out his hand, and Adam grasped it and shook it, and then they seized each other in a strong embrace. Adam released him and took one step back, eyes still wide in disbelief.

"What are you doing here?"

Billy could not resist. He shrugged. "Your mother was worried. She sent me."

Adam grinned as he asked, "How are you? Are you all right?"

"Fine. You?"

"Good." He grasped Billy by one shoulder. "Come down to my quarters where we can talk."

Adam ordered his first mate to carry on, and they walked quickly down the stairs to the main deck, turned and passed down the few steps and through the low door into Adam's small quarters in the stern of the ship, and both sat down on chairs by Adam's desk.

"Truly, what brings you here?" Adam asked.

Billy sobered. "President Madison asked me to find Eli Stroud. I have a message for him."

Adam's eyes narrowed. "Eli? You're looking for Eli?"

"Yes. Know anything of his whereabouts?"

Adam shook his head. "No. I've thought he might come here when he heard of what's happening, but I haven't seen him. Or heard anything."

Billy went on. "I understand Tecumseh is over at Sandwich right now."

"That's the last we heard. General Procter's preparing to retreat. The Indians are apparently going with him."

"How many men does General Harrison have here at this camp?"

"We were told about five thousand. We're under orders to move them to East Sister Island, not far from the north shore, and wait for further orders to make a landing at Bar Point, three miles south of Amherstburg."

Billy's eyes narrowed in amazement. "Five thousand? With horses?"

"Only the Kentuckians have horses."

"Once you unload at Bar Point, what are your orders?"

"Nothing, yet. We wait."

Billy remained in thoughtful silence for a moment, and Adam went on.

"How is Laura? And the family?"

Billy saw the need in his eyes. "Fine. They're all anxious for you to come home. Laura has all the newspaper articles about the battle you had with Barclay's squadron."

Adam shook his head. "The war isn't over. We did what we had to. It took all of us. Perry—just twenty-seven years old. Remarkable man."

Billy said, "If we heard it right, he'd have been lost if you hadn't broken from the battle line to save him."

Adam stared at his hands for a moment. "I was fortunate."

Billy stood. "No, you were Adam Dunson." He reached for the door. "I better get back up there. I have to go back on that bateau. If you hear anything of Eli, tell him I'm looking for him. President Madison needs him."

"I will."

The two made their way back to the main deck and watched as the last of the horses was hoisted over the side of the ship, dangling in the belly sling, to settle on the deck where skilled hands released the hooks and the huge booms raised the hawsers clear. Adam and Billy shook hands and said their goodbye before Billy went over the side and climbed down the netting into the pitching bateau below.

The vessel had to tack almost directly into the south wind, back and forth, to reach the south bank of Lake Erie close to the mouth of the Portage River, where Billy thanked the young lieutenant and waded ashore. He paused for only a moment before he started east, toward the tent being used by the officers in command of the massive operation of moving thousands of men and hundreds of horses from shore to ships.

He had not covered twenty feet when the familiar voice came from behind.

"Billy. Billy Weems."

Billy turned on his heel, and Eli was there, smiling, a light in his eyes, walking rapidly toward him.

Billy said nothing as he reached to grasp the hand and shook it warmly. For a moment the two men stood in silence, feeling the surge within their breasts of old comrades who had stood shoulder-to-shoulder in battle, and in life, and shared it all, and won. In that instant, the war and the soldiers and the ships were gone. They stood alone, conscious only of the bond between them.

The moment passed, and Billy said, "I've been looking for you."

"I know." Eli hooked a thumb over his shoulder. "An officer back there—a captain—told me."

"Did he tell you why?"

"Something about President Madison."

Billy pointed. "Come with me to my camp. We need to talk."

They walked to the shelter of a great pine, away from the mass of soldiers and militia moving down to the ships, and sat cross-legged on the ground. Billy drew President Madison's letter from his pack and handed it to Eli. For a time Eli studied it, then handed it back.

"I've been across the lake near Fort Detroit for four days, among the Indians. They've agreed to support the British. I doubt it will do any good to talk with Tecumseh now."

"What's the mood of the Indians?"

"Bad. Three days ago there was talk of them turning on the British."

"Our patrols say Procter is going to abandon the lake. Go east up the Thames, on to Niagara."

"That's what the Indians said. They also said he's promised to stop and fight if the Indians follow them."

"Will they fight?"

"They will."

"Do you intend going to talk with Tecumseh for President Madison?"

For a time Eli bowed his head in deep thought. "Yes. But I'll need that letter to show him."

Billy handed the letter back to him, and Eli folded it and slipped it inside his shirt as he spoke.

"How is Laura? And your family?"

Billy smiled. "Fine. Laura's as beautiful as ever. The children are all well. Laura made me promise to tell you the children are anxious to see their grandfather."

Eli smiled at the thought, then pointed out onto the lake. "Is Adam on one of those ships? I heard he might be."

"The *Margaret.* Our company owns it. We converted it to a gunboat. Adam was in the fight on the lake two weeks ago."

Eli straightened. "Is he the one?"

Billy grinned. "Broke the battle line to save Perry. Turned the battle. Might have turned the war."

Billy saw the light come into Eli's eyes as Eli nodded. "Fine man. Fine."

Billy remained quiet for a time before he continued. "When do you think you'll leave to find Tecumseh?"

"As soon as the wind will let me. I'll go by canoe."

Billy nodded. "I'll be waiting when you come back."

Notes

The loss of the British ships in the Lake Erie naval battle on September 10, 1813, left British general Henry Procter Sr. landlocked and isolated at Fort Amherstburg on the west end of the lake with a small command of regular soldiers and several thousand Indians. For more than a year the British had promised the Indians they would feed and arm them, provide for them, and drive the Americans from their ancestral lands, if the Indians would support the British in the war. By September 12, with winter coming on, the Indians were starving, without arms, and for the first time understood that Procter intended to abandon the lake to the Americans.

September 13, Procter declared martial law so he could commandeer provisions wherever he could find them. When the Indians threatened revolt, Procter arranged a council with them for September 15 and in the day preceding informed his own staff of his plan to retreat west on the Thames River. The council took place as described herein. Most of the speech made by Tecumseh, in which he cursed the British, called them liars, and called General Procter a pig, are taken verbatim from the best reports available. At the conclusion of the speech, every Indian in the council room leaped to his feet and conducted a demonstration with his tomahawk and scalping knife and war whoops, terrifying the British officers. Procter was able to get the Indians to leave without bloodshed and persuaded Tecumseh to promise to return soon for a second council meeting while Procter was working out the details of the planned retreat.

Procter visited Sandwich, a British outpost six miles north of the fort, told them of the plan, and returned on September 18 to find William Elliott, the eighty-year-old head of the British Indian Department, terrified, reporting that Procter could expect a massacre like none other in British history. William (Billy) Caldwell, a lifelong friend to the Indians, packed his family and sent them south, fearing a massacre. Procter called Tecumseh and his main chiefs into a private council with Elliott and his agents Warburton and Evans in an effort to persuade the Indians that the retreat was absolutely necessary. They partially agreed. Thereafter a second major council was arranged among all British staff and officers and all Indian chiefs. The Indians agreed to continue to support the British, and to join the retreat, on the promise of Procter that he would pick the first appropriate place and set up defenses to stop the Americans if they followed.

By September 22, the Americans had their ships and bateaux at the mouth of the Portage River on the south side of Lake Erie and were loading the largest army ever seen in that sector onto the vessels to cross the lake and attack. Again Elliott warned Procter that if he ordered a retreat and abandoned the Indians, Tecumseh would produce the wampum belt that had served as the peace treaty between the Indians and the British for more than forty years, and he would cut it in two and throw it away. With the wampum belt destroyed, all ties between the British and the Indians would be severed, and the Indians would consider themselves free to turn their tomahawks and scalping knives on the British.

See Antal, *A Wampum Denied,* pp. 297–310, 331; Stagg, *Mr. Madison's War,* p. 329; Wills, *James Madison,* p. 125; Hickey, *The War of 1812,* pp. 136–37.

The reader is advised that in the time period presented herein, there were more battles fought at different locations than reported here; however, it would be impossible to include in the confines of this book all the battles and all the events. For that reason, only the pivotal battles and events are presented.

Billy Weems, Eli Stroud, and Adam Dunson and the parts they played in these events are fictional.

CHAPTER XXII

A chill wind was moaning in the pines and the forest beneath rolling clouds that covered the moon and stars and left the Indians camped at Sandwich in a world of thick blackness. Their supper fires had long since turned to glowing embers and then to black ashes. A few lodges and tepees glowed dully from tiny fires within; only those with great need were outside their crude dwellings in the cold of a late-September night.

Alone inside his lodge, Tecumseh sat cross-legged on the great, gray pelt of a silvertip grizzly bear, staring at the dwindling flames of his tiny fire. A crimson blanket given him long ago by a British general was wrapped about his shoulders, and he clutched it at his breast to hold in the warmth. In his face was an immense, hopeless sadness as he pondered again and again the sixty years his people had given their lifeblood in their struggle to save their ancestral lands and their homes and their way of life with honor, and they had lost. Always, always, the answer was the same. White men had come, and they had taken the land, and they had held it. It made no difference whether they were British or American. They were white, and there had been no way to stop them. The Shawnee, Ojibwa, Iroquois, Potawatomi, Ottawa, Miami, Sac, Fox, Mohawk, Huron, Seneca, and the other tribes—all doomed. Their chiefs—Main Rock, Five Medals, Walks-in-the-Water, and others—abandoning all hope—returning to their lands as beaten subjects of whoever won the war, willing to accept whatever pittance the greedy white men offered, watching the white men violate that which they held most sacred—the valleys and forests and rivers that had been theirs from beyond memory.

Soon he would leave this place and he would follow where Procter led, east on the Thames River, doing once again the bidding of the white men, leaving behind the graves and the land of his ancestors to go to a strange, new country to live where he and the Shawnee would be told where to live, eat what they were given, and live without honor.

He started when the low, narrow door to his lodge opened, and in the next instant he was staring at Eli Stroud who stood before him, rifle in his hand, tall in the dim light, face shadowed, eyes peering at him steadily.

Tecumseh did not move.

Eli spoke. "I have come to counsel with Tecumseh. I regret that I was forced to come in secret, in the night. I ask your forgiveness."

For a time Tecumseh stared, and then he gestured, and Eli sat down opposite him, rifle across his knees. Eli went on.

"I am sent by the American Father, Madison. He has great desire for your safety and that of the Shawnee. I have a writing. I hand it to you."

Eli held out the letter, and Tecumseh reached to accept it. Slowly he unfolded it and turned it to the dim light of the remains of the fire to read the words he knew. Minutes passed while he studied the document, and then he handed it back.

"The letter is not to you. It is to a man named Weems."

"That is true. Weems traveled from Boston to deliver it to me. The letter requests that I come here. I am here."

"What is the message from the American Father?"

"He wishes me to make peace with you and your people on terms that are acceptable to you. He does not wish to fight you when the Americans come to drive the British out of the lands owned by America."

Tecumseh raised a hand. "It is a lie. The Americans do not own the lands. They stole them from us. They are *our* lands."

Eli took a deep breath. "Tecumseh speaks the truth. I regret that it is not possible to undo what has been done. A change must be made. The white men and the Indians must learn to live together. It is not necessary that one must die that the other might live. Tecumseh knows I was born white. I was raised Iroquois. I have now lived white for forty years. It is possible. The Indians can learn to live with the whites. The Father in Washington has given me authority to settle this with Tecumseh."

Tecumseh slowly shook his head. "Live without honor? Accepting the charity of the whites to stay alive? Our lands gone? Our customs gone? Our religion gone? Our pride gone? Stroud knows that it is better to be dead than to live in such a way."

Eli saw the terrible sadness in the man, and his heart ached for him as he continued.

"The Great Spirit has seen all that has happened. The Great Spirit will not abandon his Shawnee children. He will protect you and provide a way for you to live with honor and dignity. It is on your shoulders to do all you can. He will do for you what you cannot do for yourselves."

Tecumseh's black eyes were points of light. "The Great Spirit has turned his back on us. I have fasted for days many times and sought him, and he does not answer. I believe he is punishing us because we did not drive the white men out when they came in the time of our fathers. We extended our hand to them and we taught them to live in the forest. They came in numbers—ever greater numbers—and they took our forests from us. We did not drive them out, and now the Great Spirit is silent. He will not help us."

Eli cut him off. "Will Tecumseh fast with me? For five days? And then two days in a sweat lodge? The Great Spirit will answer us if we fast and sweat and seek him."

Tecumseh lowered his eyes to stare into the glowing embers for a time before he answered.

"It is no use. We offended the Great Spirit when we did not protect our lands. He will not hear us because he has turned his back to us and will not listen."

Eli knew in his heart that there was no power on earth that could reach deep enough into Tecumseh's soul to lift him, inspire him to save himself and his people. He went on.

"What message do you wish me to carry back to the American Father, Madison?"

"We will fight with the red-coated soldiers against the Americans. That is all."

"You refuse to counsel?"

"Yes. He cannot give us back our lands. Our honor. Of what use would it be to counsel?"

Eli bowed his head and sighed. When he looked up, he said, "I will carry your message. I thank you for your courtesy. With your permission I will leave."

Tecumseh raised a hand. "You do not have my protection."

"I came without your protection. I can leave without it."

Eli stood and looked down at Tecumseh as if to memorize the long, narrow face and the pointed nose and the eyes, and he turned to go.

Again Tecumseh raised a hand, and Eli stopped, waiting.

"If I meet you on the field of battle, I will have to kill you."

Eli nodded. "I know."

He walked through the door into the wind and the blackness, and he left the Indian camp as silently as he had come, to make his way through the forest the short distance to the Detroit River, to his waiting canoe. He paddled west across the river, then turned south with the current to follow the shoreline to Lake Erie. The wind died, and the clouds opened to show the stars and a half moon overhead. With dawn approaching, he passed the mouth of the Raisin River and continued, following the bank where it turned east, past the mouth of the Maumee River. It was midmorning when he beached the light birchbark craft at the mouth of the Portage River. He studied the vast emptiness of the lake for a moment, then the litter and refuse of the huge, nearly deserted campground, and walked steadily toward the place in the trees where Billy had made his camp. Billy was waiting with a small fire, roasting a trout on a spit. He gestured, and Eli sat down, tired, weary, hungry, and reached for the fish. He held the spit away from the fire, waiting for it to cool.

Billy sat down facing him. "Did you find Tecumseh?"

"Yes. He refused to talk. He will remain with the British." He shook his head, and Billy saw the deep sadness in his face as he went on. "Tecumseh, Main Rock, Five Medals, other chiefs, have accepted the fact they are doomed. All of them. They blame the white men—British, American, it makes no difference—for taking their lands and their way of life. They will not try to learn to live with the whites. They accuse all whites of being liars—without honor."

He stopped and broke a piece from the fish and put it in his mouth while Billy waited. Eli went on.

"He sent a message back to President Madison. They will fight us. Tecumseh knows there is no hope, but they will fight anyway. He said it is better to die with honor than to live without it. Their struggle is over. It now remains only to watch them be destroyed."

They sat in silence while Eli continued to eat the fish. Finally, he wiped his hands in the dried grass and pointed out to the lake where the great armada had been anchored.

"When did they leave?"

"Over the past three days. They had to wait until the wind died. They're too heavy. Might have capsized."

"How many were there?"

"Sixteen heavy ships and well over one hundred bateaux and small boats."

"How many men? Horses?"

"About five thousand men and twelve hundred horses. They were going to stop at East Sister Island to scout the shoreline. If they're on Harrison's schedule, right about now they ought to be landing at Bar Point, just south of Fort Amherstburg."

Eli peered out over the lake and reflected for a moment. "I think we better go on over there."

Billy nodded. "I agree. In the canoe, when the wind dies."

Across the lake, the largest American armada ever assembled on the North American continent was dropping anchor at Bar Point on the Detroit River, three miles south of Amherstburg. Hungry soldiers hitched their forty-pound backpacks higher, lowered themselves over the sides of the smaller craft into water up to their waists, and waded ashore with their muskets held high above their heads. Others jumped snorting horses over the sides of the boats into the water and led them bucking and fighting ashore. Still others began the back-breaking process of unloading barrels of flour and dried fish, dried beef, and salted sowbelly.

On shore, Major General William H. Harrison sat his horse, watching the bateaux come to shore, riding low in the water and returning to the ships riding high. Satisfied, he signaled to his aides, and they followed him on their saddle mounts to the tiny village of Bar Point and reined them to a halt to sit staring. The large blockhouse was a heap of smoldering timbers. Half the houses were burned-out shells. Cast-off litter was blowing in the dirt streets. There were no human beings or horses in sight.

Harrison's eyes narrowed as he judged what had happened, and he turned to his aides. "Procter's gone, and his army with him. They burned everything here. Keep our men moving on into Amherstburg. I'm going to ride ahead to see what's left there. Find our scouting patrols if they've returned, and gather the war council. Bring them to the big council room at the fort. I'll be waiting."

With one aide at his side, Harrison raised his horse to a ground-eating lope and held it on the winding, rutted road until the high walls of the fort came into view, and with them, the haze of smoke that hung low in the dead air. Most of the public buildings outside the fort were charred ruins, along with a great pile of lumber. A few Canadian citizens stood away from the road, silently watching him pass. He rode through the fort gates into the abandoned parade ground, where he brought his horse to a stop. For a moment he sat in the late afternoon sun while an odd feeling of disquiet washed over him at being in a place that should be filled with people and sound and action but was not. It was as though a great hand had stripped the fort of everything and left it as in a dream. There was not a sound, not a movement.

He led his aide to the great council building and walked in. Desk drawers were open and discarded papers were scattered on the floor.

Everything that had been attached to the walls was gone. He briefly looked at the papers, knowing he would find nothing of value, and dropped them on a desktop to climb the stairs. His steps echoed hollow, and he stopped at the head of the stairs and studied the huge council room. Only the great table remained. He descended back to the main floor and walked out into the parade ground, across to the officers' quarters. Nothing remained—no uniforms, no boots, nothing. He strode to the commissary, and it was stripped to the walls. There was no food, nothing of value to be used by his men.

At that moment he paused, head cocked, listening, and the sound came faint at first, then stronger. The regimental fife and drum corps was playing "Yankee Doodle" as they led the army to Amherstburg. Harrison and his aide remounted their horses and rode out to bring them on in.

With the soldiers building their cookfires and setting up their camp, Harrison assembled his scouts and war council in the big council room. Lacking any chairs, they stood around the table. He wasted no time.

"General Procter has gone, and he has burned everything we might have used. I expect him to burn the bridges he crosses, and I expect him to be traveling fast. I judge he has over one thousand horses, and with the lead he has on us right now I doubt we have a chance to catch him."

"Beggin' your pardon, sir," exclaimed a bearded, disheveled sergeant. "I just come back from scout. He don't have a thousand horses. He don't have a hundred horses. The Injuns took most of 'em. He's walkin'. His men got sixty-pound backpacks, and right now they haven't ate in two days and they're about finished. It won't take no week to catch 'em."

Harrison saw a glimmer of daylight. "The bridges?"

"He don't dare burn 'em. The Injuns—more'n a thousand of 'em— are moving with him, most of 'em behind, and they're movin' slow, way behind Procter. They got two boats with equipment way up the Thames River, not far from Moraviantown, but they won't catch up to those boats for maybe a week. They didn't make a full five miles today. Procter don't dare burn the bridges because the Injuns need 'em, and if he burns 'em that's about all it would take to turn the whole lot of 'em on the

British. Right now the Injuns don't much care who they massacre, us or the British."

"You're certain?"

"Yes, sir. Certain."

"You said more than a thousand Indians. My report says close to five thousand of them."

The sergeant turned to his corporal. "Dobbins, you made the count. You tell the general."

Dobbins, short, lean, young, bobbed his head. "Sir, there were over five thousand, but that was a week ago. Most of the Potawatomi, and the Ottawa, Ojibwa, Wyandot, Miami, Kickapoo, Delaware—most of 'em has deserted already. I doubt Procter's got more'n twelve hundred left, and they're mostly Shawnee. I counted 'em."

Procter looked at his officers. "If all that is true, can we catch them?"

The response was instant and raucous. They could catch them.

Harrison turned back to Dobbins. "Did you get a count of the British soldiers?"

"Yes, sir, I did, sir. Including all of 'em—officers, sick, wounded, cavalry, seamen—all of 'em, it counted out just about seven hundred ninety. Short of eight hundred."

Harrison turned to his aide. "What's our count of effectives right now?"

"Sir, deducting those we left behind to control Sandwich and Bar Point, we have over three thousand effectives. Among them are the mounted Kentucky infantry led by Colonel Richard Johnson and James Johnson and Elisha Whittlesey and Governor Shelby. We also have about two hundred Shawnee and Ojibwa Indians with us."

Harrison reflected for a moment. "Nearly four to one in our favor." He bowed his head and closed his eyes in deep thought, then spoke with finality.

"Gentlemen, we're going after the British. If those bridges are still up, and they don't have horses to pull wagons, we can catch them in about four days. Are there any questions?"

For the next hour the council pored over the map with the officers ignoring rank as they asked the scouts the questions that had to be answered: how are the roads?—if the weather goes bad are they passable?—does Dolsen's farm have good defensive ground?—is there natural cover at the Forks, where McGregor's Creek joins the Thames?—can they make a stand at Bowles' farm?—at Arnold's Mill?—Dover?—Chatham?—at Cornwall's Mill?—is there good ground for a defense at Moraviantown?

Full darkness was upon them long before Harrison issued his orders for the following morning, and they filed out of the big building to take their places with their men.

In the night a cold wind arose once more, and by dawn, dull gray clouds came rolling in. The reveille drum pounded, and anxious soldiers had finished their morning mess and were packed to travel light well before eight o'clock. With Harrison mounted and leading, they marched north on the road that bordered the Detroit River, then angled east to the place where the Thames River emptied into Lake St. Clair. They made their evening camp in the chill wind and glanced at the billowing purple clouds overhead before they sat down with wooden bowls of steaming stew to eat while they bragged on the twenty-five miles they had made the first day and vowed they'd catch the British within five more days.

A steady rain came in the night, and morning found them up and marching on muddy ruts, soaked, shivering, shoulders hunched against the cold, determined to make another twenty-five miles before evening mess. They raised their heads from time to time to peer ahead, searching for the first sign of the British, and by midafternoon they were passing discarded canteens and worn-out clothing thrown from the backpacks of the red-coated regulars.

Sixteen miles ahead of the Americans, in the early evening, with the rain still steadily falling, Procter called his scouts and his war council into his tent for the evening reports. They were all too simple. The Americans are coming. They will catch us if we do not burn the bridges and leave the Indians behind.

Procter shook his head. "We cannot burn the bridges, and we cannot abandon the Indians. We must continue. We will scout the American progress daily, and when it is clear they will overtake us, we will pick a place and make our stand." He spread his map on the table and pointed. "Where are the best places for us to establish ourselves, should it become necessary?"

The nearest place with good defensive ground was Moraviantown. Short of that, there was no place where Procter's one thousand men could stop more than three thousand American infantry and Kentucky cavalry. Procter gave his orders. They would continue to move east on the Thames as fast as the Indians could keep pace and hope to reach the town before the Americans caught them.

For two days the rains held while the exhausted British slogged on. In the forenoon of the second day a mud-splattered, dripping, white-faced sergeant came splashing through the black muck to catch Procter, mounted, at the head of the column.

"Sir, I was sent to tell you. More than half the Indians are gone. Left sometime in the night. There are only about six hundred remaining with us."

Procter's shoulders slumped for a moment. "Tecumseh?" he asked.

"He's still with us. With maybe four hundred of his Shawnee."

"Thank you, Sergeant. Return to your regiment."

He turned to his aide who was sitting in a soaked uniform, on a wet saddle, on a wet horse. "Find Warburton and bring him to me. I've got to know how close the Americans are."

Forty minutes later the aide reined his horse in beside Procter with Warburton beside him. Procter looked him full in the face and asked, "Mister Warburton, when did you receive your last report on the position of the Americans, and how far behind us are they?"

Warburton's words were spaced, firm. "Half an hour ago they were twelve miles behind us, still on the road, and gaining. You know about the Indians? The ones that left?"

"I know about that. How are the Americans traveling?"

"Light. Fast. No artillery, no wagons. Light backpacks."

"Cavalry?"

"Right with them. About one thousand Kentuckians. The best they have."

For a time the three men continued at the head of the column, with the steady rain falling, listening to the suck of the hooves of their horses in the black morass of the rutted road. Warburton and the aide waited in respectful silence until Procter spoke once again.

"We must send an advance force to prepare defenses at Moraviantown. Mister Warburton, take your regiment to the river near Bowles's farm and get the picks and shovels from the *Ellen* and the *Mary*. Put them in flatboats and move them up the river to Moraviantown. Then burn the two ships and all the stores and ammunition that are with them. Leave nothing the Americans can use. Proceed to Moraviantown and pick the best place to build breastworks and trenches. In this rain, be certain it is on high ground. We can't fight in mud."

Warburton reined his horse around and spurred it to a lope, muddy water splashing with every step.

Procter twisted in his saddle to watch him go, then peered long into the wind and freezing rain, probing for the first sign of an advance American scouting party. He saw nothing but his own soldiers shaking in the freezing rain, some barefoot, all silent, sullen, and he straightened in his saddle with the single question burning in his mind.

Sixteen miles behind us yesterday—twelve miles behind us half an hour ago. Will they catch us before we reach Moraviantown? Will they?

Eleven miles behind the British column, General Harrison held his mud-splattered horse to a walk at the head of his column. Rain was dripping from his hat and his clothes, and he was shaking with cold, but there was a light in his eyes as he passed the burning hulks of the two ships, *Mary* and *Ellen* in the Thames River, between Dolsen's farm and the Forks, where McGregor's Creek entered the river. Far to his right, across the Thames, he could dimly see Indians—hundreds of men, women, children—standing still, staring at him through the rain.

They've deserted the British—they're beaten—out of the fight.

He set his jaw to stop the shivering and moved on.

The raw wind held, and the freezing rain came and went for the next two days, tension mounting each hour with the British constantly peering over their shoulders, cursing the black clay muck that sucked at their boots, the Indians that could not hold the pace, the lack of food, their wet backpacks that were breaking them down, and their commanding officers whose orders were draining them of strength and the will to fight.

Behind them, the Americans were coming strong, grinning as they passed discarded packs and burned carts. They passed the charred hulk of the ship *Miamis* in the river. They crossed the river at the Forks to reach McGregor's Mill on the south side in time to put out the fires that were burning in two buildings and recover one thousand British muskets, together with more than fifteen hundred bushels of wheat. They hesitated only long enough to stuff their mouths full of the wheat and scoop what they could into their backpacks as they moved on to make their evening camp.

The rain stopped in the night, and a hard frost firmed the mud in the road. By midday the British were on King's Road, six miles ahead of the Americans as the exhausted redcoats passed Arnold's Mill, and only four miles ahead when the British made the turn at Cornwall's Mill, where the road turned south for two miles before it turned to run east again to Moraviantown, just four miles distant. Procter reined his horse from the road to watch the leading regiment pass in uniforms that were disheveled, muddy, ragged, and his heart sank.

They won't make it in time. Four more miles, and they won't make it in time. We'll have to make our stand this side of Moraviantown.

In the late afternoon, behind the lagging British, General Harrison crossed the Thames back to the north side at Arnold's Mill and had just passed Cornwall's Mill and was making the turn to the south when two men stepped into the frozen road twenty feet ahead of him and stopped, rifles held high above their heads. The shorter one, thick shouldered, built strong, was dressed in colonial homespun. The taller one with the hawk nose was in beaded Indian buckskins and moccasins.

Harrison had his hand on his sword as he called, "Identify yourselves."

"Friends. Billy Weems and Eli Stroud. Americans."

Harrison's aide murmured, "Watch out, sir. Most likely British agents. Might even be assassins."

Harrison's hand did not leave his sword. "Lay your rifles on the ground and don't move."

He dismounted and led his horse to the two men. "What are you doing here? Can you prove you're Americans? Friendly?"

Billy drew Madison's letter from his coat. "A letter from President Madison."

A dumbstruck Harrison seized the letter. "President Madison?"

He opened and read it, then reread it, then handed it to his aide. "I know Madison's signature. The letter looks authentic to me. You can pick up your rifles." He looked up at Eli. "You're Stroud?"

"I am."

"Did you talk with Tecumseh?"

"I did."

"What result?"

"He'll fight. Most of the others have deserted, but he's there with about five hundred of his Shawnee and a few Ojibwa, and they'll fight."

"You want to join us?"

Eli went on. "There's something you need to know. We've been out ahead of you. The British are about three miles away, and they know you're going to catch them before they reach Moraviantown. Right now they're deploying their troops at a place just over one mile this side of the town."

Instantly Harrison came to an intense focus. "You've been there?"

"Yes."

Harrison turned to his aide. "Stop the column! Get the war council up here with my maps."

"Yes, sir." The aide handed the letter back to Harrison, who passed it on to Billy.

While the American column made their camp for the night, Harrison had his table unloaded near the great campfire and gathered his war council and his chief scouts around while he unfolded and laid out his map. He shifted it to lay consistent with the river and began, pointing and moving his finger as he spoke.

"We're here. Moraviantown is here." He turned to Eli. "Where are the British, and how has Procter prepared their defenses?"

With Billy at his side, Eli took a moment to study the detail, when Harrison interrupted.

"First, has he begun digging trenches and throwing up breastworks?"

Eli shook his head. "No. They don't have their trenching tools. Their picks and shovels were moved from two ships into in two flat-bottomed boats that are behind us on the Thames. They didn't get them. They can't build defenses." He paused for a moment, then went on. "They also forgot to unload their ammunition boats. Most of their gunpowder and shot are on the river, behind us, near Arnold's Mill."

"What?" Harrison exclaimed. "They left their trenching tools and ammunition behind? Procter? Ridiculous! Are you certain?"

"Certain. They're behind us on the river. Yours for the taking."

Harrison plunged on. "What's wrong with Procter? How could he let that happen?"

"It wasn't Procter. It was Warburton. Procter left his command and is in Moraviantown right now."

Harrison recoiled in disbelief. "Abandoned his men at a time like this?"

Eli said, "I don't know what he's doing, or why. All I can tell you is Warburton is in command, and Procter is in Moraviantown right now."

Harrison thumped his finger on the map. "Where are the British, and how are they deployed?"

Eli dropped his finger on Moraviantown and moved it west. "Right about there. Just over a mile this side of the town. There's a wedge-shaped piece of high ground there with a few birch trees, just a few feet from the road." He turned to Billy. "How wide and how long is that strip of ground? Two hundred yards wide, north to south, and half a mile long, east to west?"

Billy answered, "About two hundred fifty yards wide, and just less than a half mile long."

Eli moved his finger north. "Over here, away from the road, at the north edge of the high ground, is a bog. A marsh—a bad one. It's called Backmetack Swamp. No one can put troops there."

Eli paused for a moment, then went on. "From what we saw before we came to you this afternoon, the British intend forming a line with their regulars that runs from the road pretty much north towards the swamp. At the end of that line, near the swamp, they're going to form the Indians in an adjoining line that curves somewhat towards the west. They'll most likely put Tecumseh and his Shawnee at one end of the Indian line, and Oshawahnah and his Ojibwa at the other end."

Eli stopped and turned to Billy. "Have I missed anything?"

"Only that they don't have artillery. Maybe one gun, but no more."

Harrison looked carefully at both Billy and Eli. "Have you two had battle experience?"

There was a hint of a smile when Billy answered, "A little."

Harrison looked at Eli, dressed in Indian buckskins with his toma-hawk and his sheathed knife thrust through his weapons belt. "You speak any of the Indian dialects?"

Billy spoke for him. "Seven."

Harrison's jaw dropped open, and he clacked it shut, then took a deep breath and moved on. "Is there anything else we need to know?"

"I don't think so," Eli said. "You might want to send a detail of men back to Arnold's Mill to get those trenching tools and ammunition before Procter does."

Harrison asked, "Will you two stay with us? We might need you in the morning."

Eli looked at Billy, and Billy answered. "We'll stay, but we might be gone for a while. Someone ought to take a look at the British lines tomorrow morning in the daylight just to be certain what they're going to do."

Harrison bobbed his head. "Done." He turned to one of his officers. "Send a company of men back to get those trenching tools and ammunition from the boats on the Thames, now, tonight." He spoke to the remainder of his staff. "I'll spend some time working out a plan of attack. All of you be back here at seven o'clock tomorrow morning to approve it and receive your orders. No fires tonight. Double pickets. If there's nothing else, you're dismissed."

Billy and Eli shared a sparce evening mess with the officers and went to their blankets beneath a lean-to they made from pine boughs. It was close to two o'clock when they were awakened by the return of the men sent to get the trenching tools and ammunition from the British boats on the river. At four o'clock they left their blankets beneath a clear, star-studded sky and silently made their way through the camp and disappeared onto King's Road, traveling east toward the British camp.

Frost was on the ground, and the eastern horizon was showing deep purple when Harrison roused his camp. He allowed his men to build fires to cook their morning mess, then gathered with his war council at the table and laid out his map. He tapped the high ground where the British were camped and began.

"I propose we attack the British lines with Mister Henry's infantry division. The British will not have breastworks or trenches because we have their equipment. The result is, we will meet them out on open ground, and we have at least twice the numbers they do. As for the Indians, I propose that Mister Desha and his division face them and hold them over by the swamp. Once the British are defeated, we can send all our forces against them until they are defeated or have fled."

He stopped while the simplicity of the plan was accepted by his officers, and he was about to continue when movement on the road stopped him. He peered up the winding ruts and suddenly recognized the two men coming at a trot. He waited until Billy and Eli reached the gathering of officers before he spoke.

"You've been scouting the British?"

Billy was breathing hard as he answered. "We've been there. They've changed their lines. It looks like they might form the British regulars in two lines, not one. The larger line in front, facing us, with a second one about two hundred yards behind it. That means that front line is not going to be shoulder to shoulder, the way they usually form. There's going to be a fairly large gap between each of the soldiers, in both lines. It doesn't make sense. To leave gaps like that will weaken both lines bad enough that they're going to fold in the face of a head-on infantry charge."

He stopped to catch his breath, then went on. "It doesn't look like they're going to change the Indian line. They're still out by the swamp, with Tecumseh and Oshawahnah and the Shawnee and Ojibwa warriors."

Eli cut in. "Seems to me we should move on over there soon, and let them see us. Then watch what they do. As it is now, Billy's right. They seem to be forming two loose lines, one behind the other. I don't know what Procter is thinking."

Harrison asked, "Is Procter back from town?"

"Yes. Got there about two hours ago."

Harrison turned to his officers. "Get your men into ranks and check their ammunition. We march in thirty minutes." He turned back to Billy and Eli. "Go on down to the officer's mess and tell them I said to get something hot for you. Will you two stay with me? No telling when I'll need you next."

"We'll stay," Eli replied, and the two of them made their way through the scurrying ranks to the officer's mess where a tall, rangy, profane sergeant was in charge of clean-up. He handed them wooden bowls and pointed, and two minutes later Billy and Eli were standing by one of the cookfires, gingerly working on steaming mush made from the wheat confiscated at Arnold's Mill the day before.

Twenty minutes later, with Billy and Eli mounted nearby on army horses, Harrison mounted his mare, called his orders, and the column moved forward amidst the din and jostle of more than two thousand men marching and one thousand more mounted on horses with vapor rising from their belled nostrils, feeling the cold, throwing their heads, fighting the bit. Four hundred yards ahead of the main column rode twenty bearded Kentuckians, cocked rifles across their knees while their heads and their eyes never stopped moving, probing everything on both sides of the road and dead ahead for the first sign of a British patrol or an ambush.

The sun was three hours high when the road slanted to within twenty yards of the river, and in the far distance, through a break in the forest, Harrison and Eli and Billy caught their first glimpse of the high white church steeple above the treetops in the settlement of Moraviantown. The thought ran through their minds, *They're waiting— one mile this side of that church.*

The column kept moving on the hard-crusted ruts that wound on through the woods, searching the left side of the road for the field Eli had described. It was shortly before noon that the forest suddenly opened, and the gentle rise was there, less than one mile ahead, and on it were the crimson-coated British regulars with their Union Jack flag high on a pole. Harrison halted the column long enough to extend his telescope and study the position of the British and the Indians and identify Procter, very close to the road. He handed the telescope to Billy.

For one full minute Billy studied the red-coated lines, then handed the telescope to Eli and waited until Eli lowered the instrument.

Harrison spoke. "Looks like they still intend forming one line, not two. Let's move out in the open and see if Procter changes his mind."

With Harrison mounted, near the road, flanked by his aide, and Billy and Eli, the Americans came by rank and file, steadily, methodically. The two thousand American infantry marched onto the west end of the open field, eyes riveted on the British less than eight hundred yards due east. Then, behind them came the Kentucky volunteers, mounted on their horses, rifles across their knees, to form lines behind the infantry. The last of them were taking their places when Harrison suddenly jerked forward in his saddle, and his arm shot up, pointing.

"They're shifting! About half of their line is falling back!" Instantly he had his telescope up, watching, scarcely breathing as half the men in the long line fell back two hundred yards to the east and reformed in a second line.

"They've got Warburton in command of that first line and Muir in the second. Procter's clear off to one side, next to the road. What are they doing?" Harrison exclaimed and looked at Billy.

Billy shook his head in amazement. "I don't know. That front line will never survive a head-on infantry charge, and the second line is too far back to give support."

Harrison took a deep breath, and his face settled. "All right. Let's get on with it."

He turned and was raising to give his signal to William Henry at the head of his command of Kentucky infantry when his aide pointed and shouted, "Sir, wait! The Johnsons are coming."

Harrison reined his horse around to the sound of two horses coming in from behind at a high run, their riders hunched low over their withers, rifles held high above their heads. He waited while the two brothers, Colonel Richard Johnson and Lieutenant Colonel James Johnson, who had gathered the Kentucky cavalry and now had command of them, came pounding in and hauled their mounts to a sliding halt, stuttering their feet, wanting to run.

Harrison peered at them, waiting.

Richard paid no attention to formalities. He pointed with his rifle. "There's too much ground between us and them. If we use the infantry for the attack we're going to lose some men. We've got a thousand mounted Kentuckians back there, and they can cover that half mile horseback in about one minute." He stopped to lick his lips, and Harrison saw his eyes shining. "Our men are ready. Most of 'em came with us from Kentucky because they remember the fight at the River Raisin—the one where some of their friends and families were massacred, even after they surrendered. These men are ready. They'll cut those British to pieces in less than three minutes." He turned to his brother James. "What do you say?"

James came loud and firm. "My men are beggin' for the chance. The last thing they said to me before I came here was that I had to tell you, remember the Raisin."

Harrison made his decision in five seconds. "Get your cavalry up here. Now!"

The two Johnson brothers jerked their horses around, and in two seconds were gone at stampede gait.

Harrison shouted to Major General William Henry and then to General Shelby and waved his arm violently for them to come at once. They arrived at the same moment, and Harrison didn't wait for questions.

"Hold your infantry right where they are. The Kentucky cavalry is going to take a position in front of you, and they're going to lead the attack. James Johnson and his regiment are going straight at that line of redcoats while Richard Johnson is charging the Indian line to the north. It's going to happen fast, so get back to your positions and order your men to hold. Don't move until I give the signal. The cavalry goes in first. Do you both understand?"

Billy and Eli watched the two officers spin their horses and gallop back to their commands, shouting Harrison's orders over and over again.

The Kentucky cavalry came trotting up the road and with Harrison pointing and shouting orders, they formed their lines in front of the infantry, with every man among them waiting for the order to launch the attack. Harrison thought to draw his watch from his pocket to check the time. It was 3:45 on the bright, chill day of October 5, 1813.

Harrison jammed the watch back into his pocket and shouted his last order to the two brothers.

"See that cannon on the right of their line? Try to get it first. Don't let them get that gun going."

Both brothers nodded and held their eyes on Harrison, waiting for his signal.

Harrison looked at his aide, who nodded his head, then at Billy and Eli, who both nodded, and he straightened in his saddle. He raised his arm high and dropped it.

The dead quiet was shattered with the war cries of one thousand mounted Kentuckians as they drove their spurs home and the horses leaped out to a hard run in three jumps. The men held their rifles high above their heads, and in their weapons belts they carried tomahawks and knives and hatchets, ready for what was coming.

James Johnson's command swept across the open field like an avalanche, to fire their first volley at fifty yards, and all up and down the line, British regulars groaned and went down. The tide of horsemen was only thirty yards from the British lines before the stunned regulars could recover from the shock enough to raise their muskets, and the oncoming horde was less than five yards from the first British line before the British fired their first volley, ragged, without aim, without effect. The Kentuckians hit them head-on, swinging their tomahawks and hatchets, running over them, knocking them sprawling. They overran the lone British cannon and its crew before it could fire a single shot, and the British threw down their muskets and sprinted in all directions, done, wanting only to be away from the demons that were killing them. The Kentuckians held their mounts at stampede gait straight on through the first line, across the two hundred yards, and hit the second line of regulars with their tomahawks and hatchets and knives working. The terrified second line also threw down their muskets and wildly fled, heedless of anything that got in their way.

The Kentuckians pulled their mounts to a skidding stop and spun around to descend on the scattering British, driving them in all directions, a beaten, devastated, undisciplined mob. The total time from the moment James Johnson's command had dug spur to horse and started its run across the open ground, to the time the British were a disorganized, destroyed army, was just under three minutes.

North of James Johnson and his command, his brother Richard had led his regiment at a full gallop into the line of Shawnee and Ojibwa warriors who had their backs to the Backmetack Swamp, with some of them hidden in the trees to the west of the bog. With Tecumseh shouting his defiance, the Shawnee stubbornly held their ground while the mounted Kentuckians stampeded among them, slashing with their tomahawks and hatchets, shouting, "Remember the Raisin!" South of them, on the open ground, Joseph Desha shouted to his waiting regiment of infantry and led them in a sprint toward the embattled cavalry. Behind Desha, James Johnson turned his horse and led half his command at a run to reinforce his brother. James was thirty yards from the battle line when he gasped and sagged in his saddle and toppled to the ground, rolling, hit hard but still alive.

Back at King's Road, Harrison sat his horse with his aide and two officers beside him, and Billy and Eli slightly behind and to his left, all standing in their stirrups, caught up in the fury and unbelievable speed of the battle.

Suddenly Billy pointed east on King's Road and shouted, "There— Procter! He's running! Deserting his men."

Harrison stared, shocked that a British officer would desert his men in the worst crisis they had ever seen. He turned and barked orders to Major Devall Payne. "Get him! Take a company and get him!" Payne and a company of his infantry left at a run.

Harrison and those with him watched them running up the road, then turned back to the battle raging four hundred yards to the north, where the Indians were slowly backing toward the swamp, giving ground, taking devastating losses.

Billy saw Eli tense, and then Eli raised a hand to point, and Billy saw Tecumseh in full battle dress, alone, tomahawk raised, shouting his defiance and hatred at two Kentuckians. While they watched, both Americans raised their rifles, and the yellow flame and white smoke spewed from the muzzles, and Tecumseh's slender frame shook as he staggered backward and stumbled and fell and did not move.

All the wind went out of Eli, and he sat for a second, staring, unable to believe, and then turned to Billy.

"We need him! If we're ever going to make a treaty with the Shawnee, we will need him."

Eli dug his heels into his mount, and in three jumps the gelding was at a full run, out across the open ground, neck stretched out, mane flying, with Eli low over the withers, rifle still in hand, heels pounding the horse's ribs with his heels. Two seconds later Billy was behind him, his horse stretching to catch Eli, shouting, "Stop! Wait!"

Eli sawed on the reins to bring his blowing mount to a sliding stop ten feet from the fallen Tecumseh. He leaped to the ground and had taken two steps when he stumbled and went to one knee, tried to rise, and toppled over onto his right side and rolled partially onto his face.

Behind him Billy heard himself scream, "Eli!" as he hauled his horse to a stop and hit the ground, running toward Eli, and his heart burst when he saw the great gout of blood on the buckskin shirt in the center of Eli's back, and he dropped to his knees beside him and turned him and felt him limp and he cradled his head on his arm and he was muttering, "Eli, Eli, Eli," when the blue-gray eyes opened and slowly focused. Eli swallowed and his mouth moved as if he were trying to speak and then he smiled up at Billy and relaxed and Billy felt Eli leave.

Billy sat down, still holding Eli in his arms, and he closed the vacant eyes. He gently laid his hand on the cheek and turned the head onto his chest and he began to rock back and forth with the scalding tears running, and he did not care. He did not know how long he sat holding Eli. He only knew that finally Harrison was alone by his side, his hat in his hand, silent, waiting. Billy looked up at him and wiped his eyes on his sleeve and said, "He's gone."

Harrison's voice was choked. "Is there anything I can do?"

Billy shook his head. "No. I'll take care of him."

Harrison silently turned and signaled to his aide and escort and led them quietly away.

It was well past evening mess when Billy rapped on the door of the Mayor's house in Moraviantown, where Harrison and his staff had established command headquarters. He was taken to the library, where Harrison stood when he entered.

Billy said, "I would like to take him home. I will need a few things. A surgeon to prepare the body. A coffin. A wagon and a team of horses and an ax and shovel."

"When?"

"Tomorrow."

"Where is he now?"

"Outside. Wrapped in canvas. Tied across his horse."

"Would you like to bring him inside for the night? Here? You can stay here."

Billy reflected for a moment. "That would be good."

"I'll send a detail to bring him in."

"No, I'll do it."

"I'll send for the surgeon. The coffin and wagon and team will be ready tomorrow. Anything else?"

"No. That will be enough."

"Where are you taking him? Where is his home?"

"Ohio. But I'm taking him to Vermont. He'll be beside his wife."

Harrison's eyes widened. "He was married?"

"Yes. One child. A daughter. Married to my nephew. Lost his wife over thirty years ago."

"I'll have the things you need ready when you want to leave."

"Thank you." Billy started to walk out when Harrison stopped him.

"Just a few things you should know. Tecumseh is dead. His warriors took his body. We could not catch Procter. We won today. The United States now controls the entire northwest section of the country. We turned the war in our favor. Was it worth it?"

Billy drew a deep breath. "He'd say it was."

"You?"

Billy stared at the floor for a time before he answered.

"We won a great battle. We lost a rare man. Higher powers will have to decide if it was worth it."

Notes

All locations identified in this chapter, such as East Sister Island, Sandwich, Bar Point, Fort Amherstburg, Dolsen's farm, the Forks, Kings Road, McGregor's Mill, Cornwall's Mill, Arnold's Mill, Moraviantown, and the scene of the pivotal battle west of Moraviantown, and all others, are historically accurate. The location of the rivers and streams, such as the Portage River, Raisin

River, Detroit River, Thames River, McGregor's Creek, and all others, are accurate. See Antal, *A Wampum Denied,* maps on the fly leaf, and p. 322.

Eli Stroud and Billy Weems are fictional characters; however, all other persons named in this chapter and the parts they played in the sequence of events, are real persons, and their names are accurate.

This chapter traces the fast-moving and startling events in which American general William Henry Harrison and his army of more than five thousand infantry and cavalry pursued British general Henry Procter and his much smaller British army with ten thousand Indians, from the west end of Lake Erie eastward, up the Thames River, where the Americans caught them, and the crucial battle now called the Thames Campaign, or the Battle of Moraviantown, was fought just over one mile west of Moraviantown on a parcel of land relatively clear of trees and forest, with the Backmetack Marsh on the north border. The chapter follows the route, the daily developments, and the weather patterns accurately. The rapid desertion of thousands of the starving and disillusioned Indians is accurately described, with only six hundred remaining for the battle, under the leadership of Shawnee chief Tecumseh and Ojibwa chief Oshawahnah. The capture by the Americans of the British trenching tools and most of their ammunition, from boats the British unintentionally left behind on the Thames River, is accurate. The names of all ships are accurate, except for the *Margaret,* which is fictional.

The battle fought at 4 PM on October 5, 1813, is accurately described, beginning with the arrival of the American troops to find the British formed in a single battle line, waiting. Harrison had planned to send his infantry against them, but when Procter suddenly moved half his men back two hundred yards to form a second line, leaving the first line much weakened, Robert and James Johnson, colonels of Harrison's Kentucky cavalry, advised Harrison they could reach the British far quicker than the infantry. Harrison agreed. Half the Kentucky cavalry under James Johnson made their charge, shouting, "Remember the Raisin!" and decimated the British in just under three minutes, while the other half, under command of his brother Robert Johnson, charged into the Indians, who stubbornly resisted. Desha then led his infantry from the field to support Robert, as did James Johnson and some of his cavalry.

James Johnson was wounded but survived. The British, and then the Indians, broke and scattered in total defeat. Procter escaped and was not caught. Tecumseh was killed and his body removed by his warriors. Harrison instantly became a national hero, celebrated in every state in the union. It will be remembered that Harrison became the ninth president of the United States but died of pneumonia about one month after he was inaugurated.

For a complete chronological summary of the crucial events described in this chapter, see Antal, *A Wampum Denied*, pp. 315–53, and see particularly the diagram on page 343 showing the battle site, with the dispersement of both the British troops and Indians and the American troops.

In support, see also Hickey, *The War of 1812*, pp. 136–39; Stagg, *Mr. Madison's War*, p. 329–30; Wills, *James Madison*, p. 125; Barbuto, *Niagara 1814*, p. 85.

Billy Weems and Eli Stroud are fictional characters.

The reader is again reminded that many less significant events occurred in the time frame and the area presented in this chapter; however, it would be impossible to include them all. Only the significant ones are presented herein.

Boston, Massachusetts

August 1814

CHAPTER XXIII

$\mathcal{T}$he distant rumble of thunder rolled over Boston, sweltering in the still, muggy, late-afternoon heat of mid-August, and citizens in the cobblestoned streets paused to peer west at the low line of deep purple clouds steadily moving across the neck that connected the peninsula to the mainland. They made their calculations of when the storm would engulf the town and hurried on to be certain it would not catch them unsheltered.

On the waterfront, Jeremiah Skullings walked steadily from his small insurance office on the east end of the waterfront, moving west, past Long's Wharf, toward Fruit Street, eyes squinted against the western sun. Short, corpulent, Skullings carried his suit coat and a large brown envelope in one hand while he wiped at his round, sweated face with a handkerchief held in the other. To his left were the docks, and beyond them the harbor, where he was accustomed to seeing the masts and riggings of hundreds of ships of every flag in the civilized world—coming, unloading and loading thousands of tons of freight, and going—the lifeblood of Boston town and much of the state of Massachusetts and the northeastern region of the United States. He studied the long, empty piers where only a few ships were tied, most of them with their decks deserted, their hatches sealed, their holds empty, riding high on the incoming sea swells. On the entire waterfront he saw fewer than ten ships with dockhands, stripped to the waist, sweating while they operated the arms and nets, loading or unloading the crates and barrels. The clamor and jostle and loud, raucous sounds of hundreds of dockhands of every description and language were gone. Skullings hurried on, unsettled at the quiet and the uncharacteristic inactivity of the Boston waterfront.

He angled toward the long row of buildings to his right, where offices of shipping companies and warehouse owners faced the docks, and walked through the open door with the sign above, DUNSON & WEEMS. He tossed his suit coat onto the counter, wiped at his face again, and watched the five men inside rise from their desks and walk to the counter, faces blank, waiting.

Skullings's attitude was a mix of anger and frustration as he pushed a large envelope to Billy Weems.

"There they are. Just arrived from Philadelphia." He shook his head. "Bad."

Billy opened the envelope, laid the twelve-page document on the counter, and silently read the bold print at the top.

"MONTBANK INSURANCE, LTD. PHILADELPHIA, PENNA U.S.A."

Beneath, in smaller letters: "Revised Insurance Premiums. Effective midnight 31 August 1814."

Billy glanced at Skullings for a moment, and Skullings shook his head, apologetic, frustrated, hating it.

"I'm sorry, Billy. Nothing I could do. The board of directors in Philadelphia decides all these things. I only follow them."

Silence held for thirty seconds while Billy scanned the heavy print at the headings of each section and the first few lines. Matthew stood behind him. On Billy's left was Adam; on his right were John and Caleb, all standing still, silent, waiting.

Billy drew a deep breath and said quietly, "We're in trouble."

Matthew asked, "Up?"

"Every one of them."

"How much?"

Billy turned pages and followed lines on the schedules with his finger as he answered.

"They won't insure anything to do with weapons. Cannon, muskets, bayonets, gunpowder, sulphur, flints—any of it."

Matthew shifted his feet but remained silent. Billy went on.

"Tripled the rates on just about everything made of steel or iron. Stoves, plows, nails, chains, saws, tools, needles, screws, bolts—everything."

He moved his finger to the next page.

"Doubled the rates on flour, rice, dried fish, salt beef, sowbelly—most food items—tobacco, cotton, spices, salt. Raised rates on cloth, buttons, just about everything made of wood."

He raised his eyes to Skullings. "Any discounts for regular customers? We've been with you for nine years."

Skullings shook his head. "I asked. I told them if anyone's earned a discount, it's you. But their answer was no. No discounts to anyone."

Matthew interrupted. "If those rates hold very long, we'll have to close our doors."

Skullings's answer came instant, hot. "If those rates hold for ninety days, we'll have to close the Boston office of Montbank Insurance Limited! I'll be dismissed. Nobody can afford those rates. The Buford Insurance Company across the back bay in Charlestown? Their rates got so high they closed their office four days ago. Their central office in New York is declaring bankruptcy. There was even some talk of bankruptcy in our Philadelphia office."

Adam broke in. "How much commercial shipping is there right now here on the east coast?"

Scullings turned to him. "Our company figures show a sixty-eight percent drop since May of this year, and it's getting worse." He threw up a hand. "It was Napoleon! When he surrendered to the English last April, the British had hundreds of ships and thousands of troops they'd been using in Europe to fight him. They sent most of them to put a quick end to the war here! Have you seen Chesapeake Bay? Delaware Bay? New York Harbor? Filled with British ships and soldiers."

Adam continued. "Does your company have any estimate of how long this will go on?"

Skullings shook his head. "None. No one does."

"Why haven't the British shut down Boston Harbor?"

"They don't need to. The biggest harbors are New York and Philadelphia and Baltimore, and when they closed them down, business stopped at just about every other harbor from Maine to the West Indies. They'll get around to Boston if they think it's necessary."

Billy pointed out the open door. "Nine of those empty ships out there are ours. Crews are gone. Our customers can't pay the insurance rates, and they won't risk shipping without insurance for fear of losing it all to the British." He tapped the twelve-page insurance schedule on the countertop. "I think this just about finishes it."

Caleb was leaning on his elbows on the counter as he spoke to Skullings. "You sure they're after the big shipping ports? Washington, D.C., is just south of Baltimore."

"Yes, but there's no commerce in Washington, D.C. Government, but no commercial value worth going after. It's Baltimore they want. Baltimore and maybe Annapolis."

Caleb answered, "Don't be too sure. If they take Washington, the federal government stops. That might end the war in a hurry."

Skullings shrugged. "Could be. I'm no expert on war. My only interest in all this is insurance, and as of right now, that's almost gone." He drew a great breath, and his cheeks ballooned as he exhaled. "I need to get back to my office. I'm going to have some upset shippers coming in." He pointed at the document. "I brought this to you to give you notice as quick as I could so you'd know what to do with your customers." He shook his head, jaw set in disgust, and picked up his coat. "I hope you understand."

Billy said, "Thanks. Not your fault. We'll be in touch."

The five men stood silent in the stifling heat of the Dunson & Weems office, watching Skullings disappear east on the nearly deserted waterfront, coat in hand, wiping sweat.

Matthew broke the silence. "I can't see a way out."

Billy heaved a sigh. "I don't think there is one."

There was fear and defiance in John's face and his voice. "We just sit here in this office and go bankrupt?"

Caleb cut in. "Who's in command of the British down there on the Chesapeake and Delaware Bay?"

Adam answered. "An admiral named Alexander Cochrane. A second admiral named George Cockburn, and a general named Robert Ross. All competent. A little arrogant, and they all dislike Americans. Why?"

"Who's in command of our forces?"

Again Adam answered. "Commodore Oliver Perry is near the top of the naval command. He's outstanding. Our ground forces? Right now it's General William Winder. I doubt he's qualified for what he has to do. He answers to John Armstrong. Secretary of war. John Armstrong is likely the most incompetent man in Washington. He's caught up in politics—compromised—beyond all hope. He has his yes-men in critical positions, and when you put them all together, they don't stand a chance of defending this country. Why are you asking?"

Caleb straightened. "It looks like Dunson & Weems is going to close its doors if our military doesn't clear the British off our coast."

Adam replied, "I doubt John Armstrong is even aware of what's going on. The man seems to think inspecting troops and making padded reports is the key to winning the war."

Matthew spoke from behind Caleb. "What are you suggesting?"

Caleb shrugged. "Nothing. I was thinking about Adam up on Lake Erie. He helped Perry beat Barclay. Maybe there's something we could do to help him on the Chesapeake."

Matthew shook his head. "Send Adam and the *Margaret?* One ship? I doubt the British would let the *Margaret* get past Cape Charles into the bay, and if they did, it would only be to trap her. The British have more than two hundred gunboats down there. If we armed every one of our ships and sent them in to help Perry, they wouldn't last two days."

Caleb turned and started back to his desk. "Just a thought."

Matthew picked up the new schedule of insurance rates and said, "Get your chairs around my desk. There are some things that need to be said."

Chairs scraped on the worn floor, and Matthew took his seat facing the four other men.

He pointed at the schedule of insurance premiums. "These are the insurance rates we'll have to start quoting tomorrow. I doubt we're going to find one customer who can pay them. I think our business will be at a standstill by this time tomorrow afternoon." He turned to Billy. "If that's true, how long can we keep our doors open? How much cash do we have in reserve?"

Billy pondered for several moments. "If we anchor all our ships, lay off all the crews, pay the debts we now owe, and collect our accounts receivable, we'll have enough cash in reserve to keep the five of us and our families alive for about six months. Next February. If the British are still here, we'll have to start selling the ships to feed our families. There will be no market for the ships in the United States. We'll have to sell them to some foreign company. French. Dutch. Spanish. Anywhere we can, for whatever we can get."

Matthew leaned back in his chair, eyes narrowed as he worked with Billy's opinion. He turned to Adam and went on.

"Caleb raised a question. Is there any way we can use our ships to help win this war? Arm them? Provide crews? Tell Perry they're available?"

Adam studied the floor for a time, then raised his head. "I don't think so. If this were out on the open sea, or even on a lake the size of Erie, there might be a chance we could help. But this is going to be decided within the confines of the Chesapeake and the Delaware. Two narrow bodies of water. There's no place to run, and I can promise you, we aren't going to take on two hundred British gunboats without space to run. I can't think of a way to help Perry. Matter of fact, we'd be a hindrance. He'd be worried the whole time about getting us killed."

John suddenly leaned forward. "What's Madison doing? He's our commander. He should know what all this is doing to commerce. He should have a plan."

A look of frustration crossed Matthew's face. "President Madison is caught in a web of politics. He saw what was coming as far back as last June and called a cabinet meeting. He told them they needed more ground troops and a plan for defending Washington, D.C. The cabinet told Congress, and Congress ignored it. Madison tried to appoint competent men to head up the military, but Congress disagreed. He got John Armstrong. The others are split by political loyalties and shot through with incompetence."

He stopped long enough to set his thoughts in order.

"Right now most of the British troops are still on their ships out on the Chesapeake and the Delaware. We don't know where they intend coming ashore or where they plan to make their attack, and we won't know until they do it. That means we're going to have to have armed troops—a lot of them—waiting at every major city and seaport, and they have to be ready to move fast in any direction. With the inexperienced militia and the mediocre military leadership we now have, I think we're set up for a disaster."

Matthew stopped and for a time the five men sat staring at nothing while their minds searched for anything they could do to save Dunson & Weems, and there was nothing. So long as the British dominated the shipping lanes of the east coast, commercial shipping was doomed. The only sounds in the sweltering room were drifting in from the gulls and seabirds outside who were frantic in their search for the refuse that had disappeared when the ships ceased to sail, and the oncoming rumble of distant thunder as the storm steadily rolled in from the west.

Then, in less than thirty seconds the bright sunlight was gone and all shadows disappeared as the thick purple clouds rolled in. Suddenly there was a stir of breeze, and within seconds the wind came to set the ships rocking. Thunder boomed on the west edge of the town, and then the winds were howling and a bolt of lightning turned Boston town white, and in the same instant a thunderclap shook every building on the peninsula.

The five men in the Dunson & Weems office all ducked involuntarily, then peered out the door as the rain hit like a torrent.

John stood and walked toward the front door to close it, and Caleb called to him, "Leave it open. It's only water. Can't hurt anything in here."

John returned to his chair, and the five men sat watching in silence, humbled once again at the realization that the struggles of mankind fade into insignificance in the face of the supreme power of Nature and the Almighty.

Within minutes the wind quieted and the cloudburst passed as quickly as it had come. Shafts of sunlight came through to set the wet town sparkling. Matthew spoke as he stood.

"I think we're finished for the day. It's past closing time. We all better go home and see how bad our roofs are damaged and which of our trees have branches down."

He was the last to leave, and as he locked the front door he was struck by the quiet on the nearly vacant docks and the lack of carriages and people in the streets. He walked west, picking his way around the puddled rain and the leaves and small branches that had been stripped from the trees that lined the streets and scattered against fences and bushes and on the cobblestones. He walked with a growing fear in his heart that the shipping company he and Billy had built with grit and daring and hard work over nearly thirty years was in mortal trouble, doomed by the British ships and troops that had paralyzed the major American seaports. He slowed to peer southwest, as though he could see past the green, rolling hills and valleys to the Delaware and Chesapeake, with his thoughts running.

What's happening down there? Does Madison understand the danger? Can he rise to it? Lift Congress and the military to it? Can they find a way?

Four hundred miles distant, with the setting sun casting long shadows eastward, President James Madison, a small, sweated, dusty man on a large bay mare, surrounded by an escort of uniformed cavalry and some members of his cabinet, reined in his mount at the aging residence of the mayor of Old Field, eight miles north of Washington, D.C., near Bladensburg, in the state of Maryland. Beside him secretary of the navy William Jones and secretary of war John Armstrong gathered the reins of their horses, and as Madison made the long reach to the ground, they dismounted with him. Minutes later they were seated about a square table in the simple, plain library of the old home.

While two of Madison's aides were ordering subordinates to arrange an evening meal appropriate for the president of the United States and half his cabinet, others were out at the well drawing fresh, cold water for the thirsty party.

Madison turned to his assistant.

"I was expecting General Winder and Secretary of State Monroe. Do we have word of their arrival?"

"I'll find out, sir," the aide said and quickly left the room.

The cold well water arrived, and Madison poured from a porcelain pitcher and passed it around while the weary men gratefully drank their fill and wiped at their brows with handkerchiefs. They finished drinking and were setting their empty glasses on the table when the door opened and the aide reported.

"Both General Winder and Secretary Monroe will arrive here early in the morning, sir."

"Thank you," Monroe responded. "Would you give notice we will expect their presence here for a cabinet meeting?"

"Immediately, sir."

The aide turned and was gone, and within minutes a portly woman with her hair drawn behind her head in a bun and a huge apron covering most of her front side knocked and timidly entered.

"Mister President, sir, supper is prepared in the dining room. I do hope you gentlemen like roast mutton and sweet potatoes. Let me show you your rooms so you can wash."

The rooms were comfortable, the meal was rewarding, and the talk was relaxed. The men thanked their hostess and went to their rooms to hang their coats, remove their black ties, open their shirt collars, and sit at their small desks with papers before them, preparing for the impromptu cabinet meeting to be held the following morning.

They were up with the sun, washed, shaved, and dressed for their breakfast of bacon, eggs, home-baked bread, jellies, and buttermilk. They were wiping their mouths with napkins and pushing away from the table when an aide entered the dining room.

"Mister President, General Winder and Secretary Monroe have arrived."

Madison rose and walked through the archway and across the large parlor to the front door, where the two men stood with their hats in their hands. They nodded their greeting to their president, he gestured, and they followed him to the library where the others had gathered around the table, papers before them, waiting.

"Gentlemen," Madison began in his soft voice, "I appreciate your presence here this morning. Events led me to believe I should receive first-hand reports from each of you." He turned to Winder.

"I understand you have redeployed your troops from Wood Yard to here—Old Field. I am not clear on the reason. Would you enlighten me?"

Winder cleared his throat and began his defense. "Two days ago my patrols reported the British landed forty-five hundred troops at Benedict. Yesterday they reached Upper Marlboro, and there were massive British troop movements in the general direction of Wood Yard and Bladensburg—far too many for my command to resist. I withdrew to consolidate my troops here at Old Field because it is closer to Washington, D.C., and has access to all roads. I have just ordered General Tobias Stansbury to return to Bladensburg with his command and prepare a defense there. I believe the decisions are sound."

Madison reflected for a moment. "Do you have information that the British intend attacking Washington, D.C.?"

"None directly, sir."

Madison's blue eyes were boring into him. "What is your opinion regarding their intentions?"

"Annapolis, sir. Everything I have seen indicates they intend taking Annapolis."

Madison turned to James Monroe, secretary of state. "Mister Secretary, am I to understand you have been reconnoitering? On scout? Horseback?" A smile flitted across Madison's face at the thought of his fifty-six-year-old secretary of state, a long-time friend, out on scout, on horseback, alone.

Monroe's answer was immediate. "Yes, sir. I needed to see the British lines myself. They are gathered in force north and east of the capital, and I doubt our militia can stop them. On General Winder's orders, most of the bridges up there have been destroyed in an attempt to slow the British, but there are enough left for them to reach the city almost at will."

"Do you believe, then, that their objective is Washington, D.C.?"

Monroe pondered for a moment. "I don't know, sir. There is no strategic value to Washington. From a military standpoint, Baltimore and Arlington are more valuable. But taking Washington would be a powerful symbolic defeat for the United States."

Madison reflected for a moment, then turned to Winder and Monroe. "If they do intend moving on Washington, we must be certain all heads of governmental departments have read the evacuation plan and know what their responsibilities are. They must get the vital government documents out of the city to the selected destinations in Virginia and Maryland, and they must protect all government secrets."

He paused, then turned to John Armstrong. "I trust the printed plan has been distributed to those who had need to see."

"I circulated it among the military commanders with orders to study it. I presume it was done, sir."

Madison turned back to Winder and Monroe. "You recall that should the British attack Washington, the entire cabinet is to meet at Bellevue. That's the residence of Secretary of Navy Jones in Georgetown."

Both men nodded.

"When we arrive this afternoon, would you be certain the department heads have reviewed it? Know what to do?"

"Yes, sir."

Madison turned to William Jones, secretary of the navy. "What success have we had with our naval forces?"

Jones shook his head. "Limited. I assigned Joshua Barney and a squadron of our gunboats to prevent British raids on targets in the Chesapeake. He had some success—limited as it was—until the British sent a sizeable flotilla of heavy war ships to eliminate him. Barney escaped by hiding in the headwaters of the Patuxent River. That's where he is now. We simply do not have sufficient naval forces to resist the British."

Madison paused for a moment. "Do you have an opinion of where the British intend to strike in the Chesapeake?"

"No, sir, I do not. Taking Baltimore or Annapolis would make military sense. Taking Washington would make political sense. It all depends on which the British believe to be the most important at the moment."

Madison spoke to Armstrong, the secretary of war. "Do you have any information concerning where the British intend to strike?"

"No, sir. In my *opinion* it has to be Baltimore. Or Annapolis."

Madison fell silent for a time while he mentally constructed the current position of the British and American forces and evaluated the differing, sometimes conflicting opinions of the men before him of where the British intended to strike. Washington? Annapolis? Baltimore? Until he knew, he could not set up defenses, and it was clear that none of them would know until the British made their move.

Talk broadened to include some of the detail of supplies and morale of the American forces, and it was late in the morning before Madison shuffled his papers together.

"I believe we have done all we can. It's obvious that for now we can only remain prepared to move rapidly when the British commit themselves. Until then, be certain that the major roads to Washington are well defended. Be prepared to burn the bridges behind you. Keep patrols out constantly. If there is nothing more, thank you for your efforts. Return to your commands. I and the cabinet members present are departing for Washington immediately."

With his armed escort both leading and following, Madison and his cabinet members made the eight-mile ride back to Washington, D.C., in temperatures above one hundred degrees, on horses showing sweat on their hides and white lather at the saddle girths. They entered the city and had reached the Executive Mansion when a sweating rider on a winded horse came pounding up behind them.

"Sir," the man panted, "General Winder sent me ahead to request a meeting with yourself and the cabinet immediately. He'll be at the navy yard within the next half hour."

A startled Madison exclaimed, "What's happened?"

"The British, sir. They're marching on Bladensburg. General Winder needs a conference with yourself and your cabinet."

Madison and his confused cabinet members and escort remounted their horses and made their way across town to the headquarters of Dr. Andrew Hunter in the navy yards on the Anacostia River, which had grown to be the largest naval station in the United States. Ten minutes after their arrival, General Winder knocked on the front door, and with his escort, entered, breathing heavily, wide-eyed. He was invited into the library, where Madison and some of his cabinet members stood to face him.

Madison wasted no words. "You asked for a conference?"

"Sir," Winder blurted, "the British are marching. Just minutes after you left this morning the shooting started near Bladensburg. I believe the plan we discussed is no longer feasible. We must redeploy our troops to cover the roads into Washington. To do that, I will need your permission. If you could, sir, it would be most advisable for you to come back and see what's happening for yourself."

Beside Madison, secretary of state James Monroe, a veteran of many of the critical battles of the war for independence, who had been a shining hero in the miracle of the fight at Trenton that stormy morning of December 26, 1775, turned his head to hide the disgust in his face. *If Winder's in command of the troops at Bladensburg, what's he doing back here, begging the President to come hold his hand when the shooting starts?*

Madison stared back at Winder for a moment, then remounted his horse, and with his escort and cabinet members around him, rode back through the city, to the road headed north. They held their horses to a lope for a time, then slowed to a walk in the heat and humidity and kept moving. They crossed the bridges spanning the Anacostia River and held to the main road cut through the thick forests, and were yet three miles from the town of Bladensburg when the first boom of distant cannon and then the rattle of muskets, were heard. Every man in Madison's party came to full alert, watching for the first flash of red tunics on the road ahead or in the forests on both sides of the road. As they came into Bladensburg, they were met by retreating Americans, abandoning the town, moving south, back toward the capital city.

Madison led his party to the crest of a knoll east of the road, above the river, where they could see more than one mile to the north. Within seconds they saw the orderly lines of the British infantry in their crimson tunics, marching across the green fields, almost unopposed, and they saw the white smoke of the cannon and the muskets. The red-coated regulars marched onto the bridge spanning the river north of the town and slowed at the hail of musket and rifle fire from the Americans lining the riverbanks, but did not stop. It was the American lines that broke and retreated, crossing to the safety of the west bank, with the British following undeterred, six abreast as they passed the bridge and spread out into Bladensburg.

Madison's enclave sat their horses on the knoll, spellbound by the sight of the British descending on Bladensburg from three sides, while the Americans steadily gave ground, falling back. The British artillery was moving forward, while the American cannon answered, firing, moving back, firing again. The entire scene was laced with the glitter and the howl and the smoking trails of the British Congreve rockets, arcing high to fall onto and behind the American lines, crippling men, setting fires.

Madison's horse tossed its head and stuttered its feet, nervous, fearful, wanting to be away from the growing noise of explosions and the rockets, and within seconds the other horses in his party were straining at their bits, backing away from the crest of the knoll.

Without a word Madison reined his mount around, and with his uniformed escort and party following, raised her to a run, down the slope to the main road curving south toward the city, across Tournecliffe's bridge, past the Washington, D.C., militia on the west side of the road and the Annapolis militia on the east. They held the pace until the sounds of the guns were well behind before they pulled their lathered, heavy-breathing horses to a walk. Every man in the party turned in the saddle to look back, fearful of what they would see, but there were no red-coated cavalry or infantry in sight.

They rode on, southwest, toward the nation's capital, passing Maryland and Virginia militia trotting north, gripping their muskets, sweating, heedless of the president and his party. They rounded the long, slow curve of the road that brought them in view of the city, and Madison slowed, shocked at what lay before him.

The bulk of Washington consisted of about nine hundred buildings, some government, many residences, most of them clustered between the proud Capitol building under construction on the hill that dominated, and the huge Executive Mansion on Pennsylvania Avenue. The entire city was in a state of confused, panic-driven chaos! The streets were jammed with civilians and government workers and militia running from office buildings and homes with armloads of government papers and family heirlooms and treasure to throw them into anything on wheels—wagons, carriages, carts—all hitched to jumpy, frightened, snorting horses. The broad arterial streets—Pennsylvania Avenue, New York Avenue, Massachusetts Avenue, South Capitol Street, Constitution Avenue—were clogged with fleeing vehicles and pedestrians. The traffic on the bridges crossing the Potomac into Virginia was at a near standstill. The Capitol building was swarming with politicians and civilians milling about, confused, indecisive, torn between fear of what the British would do to them if they remained at their duty offices and fear of what the United States would do to them if they did not. Boxes of papers by the ton were moving out of the great building into waiting wagons.

Madison and his group reached the fringes of the city before the president halted and gave orders.

"Mister Winder, take the armed escort and give support wherever you feel needed." He turned to his cabinet members and pointed west, toward the road to Georgetown. "We were to meet at Mister Jones's residence in Georgetown and move on to Frederick in Maryland. There is no chance of our getting there. I'm changing the plan. We will meet instead at Wiley's Tavern near Difficult Run on the Virginia side of Great Falls. As soon as possible. Each of you get to your offices the best way you can and announce the change. Are there any questions?"

There were none.

Winder wheeled his horse around and started back north toward Bladensburg with the armed escort following. Madison and two aides continued on into the city, working their way through the jumble of horses and wagons and carriages and pedestrians, moving constantly toward the Executive Mansion with fear rising in the president's breast for Dolley's safety. His cabinet members followed, each dropping off as he came to his own office building. Madison and his two aides dismounted at the rear entrance to the Executive Mansion where frantic staff members were closing the doors, ready to abandon the building.

Madison confronted them. "Where is Missus Madison?" he demanded.

The head of staff stepped forward. "She left, sir. More than an hour ago. She ordered us to remove most of her valuables—and yours—into a wagon, and she went with it."

"Where did she go?" Madison was hardly breathing.

"We don't know, sir. She didn't know herself. All she said was that she intended saving the things she took, and she would find you later. She mentioned Virginia, but did not say where."

"What things? What did she take?"

"Valuable government papers. Cabinet meeting records. She removed the great painting of General George Washington from its frame and rolled it up and took it. Dishes. Silverware. Family portraits."

"Did she have an escort? An armed escort?"

"Oh, yes, sir!"

Cannon boomed loud from the north, and the staff all flinched and for a moment involuntarily looked that direction, then back at Madison with pleading in their eyes.

Madison exclaimed, "Leave here. Now. Protect yourselves any way you can. Do not return until you know it is safe."

The entire staff scattered, each in his or her own direction, and within minutes Madison and his two aides stood alone staring at the building, then the grounds with the green grass and the manicured flower beds and trimmed trees, filled with fear of what would remain if the British took the city. With heavy hearts they remounted their horses and left the large, white landmark behind, moving south on Seventeenth Street to Constitution Avenue, toward the bridge that spanned the Potomac River, connecting Washington to the state of Virginia.

The roads and side trails were a quagmire of people and vehicles and livestock moving in every direction, pushing, crowding, women with crying children clinging to their skirts, some with howling infants in their arms, shouting men desperately trying to push through the melee to any place that might offer safety for their families. Uniformed militia, escorting tall, heavy wagons filled with government papers thrown into unsealed crates at random and drawn by wild-eyed horses, shouted and muscled their way through.

It was clear to Madison that the citizens of the nation's capital had disintegrated into a shattered, terrorized, mindless mob. Gathering his cabinet, or even finding them, or Dolley, was impossible. The evacuation plan was ridiculous, abandoned, lost, gone.

With the sun setting, Madison left the main road and picked his way southwest to Salona, the country estate of a longtime friend, John Moffat. Dirty, sweated, exhausted, mind numbed with recognition of the catastrophe he had left behind, Madison and his aides dismounted as Moffat came to the door.

Stunned, Moffatt grasped the bridle of Madison's jaded horse.

"Mister President," he exclaimed. "By the Almighty, what has happened?"

Madison squared his shoulders and declared, "The British are taking Washington."

Moffat pointed. "We heard the guns, and we feared for the city! But we never thought they would succeed."

"They will."

Moffat pulled himself up short. "Missus Madison? Where is Dolley?"

Madison shook his head. "I don't know."

Instantly Moffat's hand shot up to cover his mouth while he held his breath, terrified he was going to hear the worst.

Madison went on. "I came back from Bladensburg and she was gone. Took some valuables from the Executive Mansion and left. Said she was going to somewhere in Virginia. I'll send some officers to find her."

Moffat dropped his hand and shook himself back to his senses. "Here! I'll have my staff take care of your horses. You need to come inside out of this heat. I'll prepare baths for the three of you. Supper. Come in. Come in. You'll stay here for as long as you have need."

The two aides interrupted. "Sir, with your permission, we would both like to go search for Missus Madison. It's important that she is safe. When this is all over, the country will need to know."

Madison looked at the two young men, and they saw the deep gratitude in his eyes. "I would appreciate that. Report back here as soon as you know."

"We will, sir."

Stable boys came running to lead Madison's horse to the shade of a lean-to where they unsaddled it and listened to the suck and the muffled sound of water passing the gullet rings while the mare drank. They rubbed down the sweaty hide and hooked a bag of feed over its head then watched and listened to the grateful mare grinding the rolled oats in her teeth.

Inside the Salona mansion, with the continuous boom of cannon sounding from the east, Madison settled into the comfort of a bath, where he sat for a time, forcing his mind to accept what had happened and beginning the process of creating a plan for the survival of the United States. His host laid out fresh clothes on the bed in one of the bedrooms and waited in the library until Madison came down the long, curved flight of stairs. They walked the long, broad hall to the sumptuous dining room, where John Moffat and his wife shared respectful conversation with their president over roast prime rib of beef with sweet potatoes, fresh corn, condiments, and cider, pausing from time to time to listen to the crescendo of cannon and musket fire in the distant city.

The sun had set and fireflies were darting in the gathering dusk when the headmaster of the house staff appeared in the doorway.

"Sir, it appears there are fires east of us."

Moffat's head swiveled up. "Where? How far?"

"I believe it is Washington, sir. The city."

Both men stood and Moffat exclaimed, "Come with me."

They strode from the room to climb the stairs two at a time to the second floor, down a long hallway, and out onto a huge, sheltered balcony with a white banister. They stopped in their tracks, staring northeast in disbelief.

Stretching for more than two miles, the horizon glowed golden in the gathering twilight, with low yellow flames visible reflecting off the blanket of smoke that hovered over the city and off the bellies of purple clouds that were forming in the heavens, above the smoke. Time was lost while the men peered in disbelief at the sight of their nation's capital in flames, each seeing images in his mind of the British setting the torch to the new, proud buildings—the Capitol, the Executive Mansion, the Treasury Building, the navy yard, the Library of Congress—while they asked themselves the fearful question: *Did our people get the papers out of those buildings, or have we lost it all?*

The two men sat in chairs and remained on the balcony until full darkness, watching the burning of the nation's capital. They were scarcely aware of the quiet gathering of clouds overhead, and both were startled at the rain that came drumming on the balcony roof shortly before midnight to blur the distant fire. They remained on the balcony watching while the steady rain diminished the flames and the bright yellow line dwindled, and then a weary, exhausted, tormented James Madison turned to his host.

"I wonder what history will say about the burning of our nation's capital."

Moffat shrugged. "I expect it will say many things."

"You are probably right. I can only hope I am not condemned by it." Madison stood and started for the large French doors leading into the house.

"It has been a long day. I believe I will retire."

Moffat walked with him to his bedroom and bade him goodnight, and Madison sought his bed.

The rain stopped in the night, and dawn came bright in a cloudless sky. As soon as he awoke, Madison went to the balcony to peer toward Washington, but the rain had quenched the fires and washed the black cover of smoke from the sky. He descended to the dining room to share a breakfast of fried eggs and bacon with a somber John Moffat and was rising from the dining table when a rap came at the front door. Both men rose and quickly passed down the hall where a housekeeper was opening the door. Words were exchanged, and the woman stepped aside to allow Madison's two young aides to enter, unshaven, uniforms damp, hats in their hands, exhausted.

Madison's heart was racing as he reached them and asked, "Missus Madison?"

"She's at Wiley's Tavern, waiting there for you. Missus Madison spent last night less than a mile from here, at the Rokeby estate, owned by Richard and Elizabeth Love. Early this morning she learned James Monroe was at the tavern, where he expected you to be, and she went there hoping to find you."

The wind went out of Madison, and for a moment he stood with slumped shoulders, daring to breathe again.

"James Monroe is there? At the tavern?"

"He is, sir."

"Does he have any word of what happened in Washington last night?"

"No, sir." The young man's eyes dropped for a moment. "Both Missus Madison and Mister Monroe watched from a distance while the city burned. We all did."

Only then did Madison look closely at his two aides. "Have you been up all night?"

"Yes, sir. We had to find Missus Madison."

Madison stepped aside. "Come in." He turned to Moffat. "Could you find it in your heart to give these young men a bedroom? A bath? A hot meal? Some time to sleep? Fresh clothing? Tend to their horses?"

"Absolutely!"

With Moffat leading up the stairs, Madison followed the two young men to their bedrooms, and before they separated Madison spoke.

"I am going to the tavern to find Missus Madison. I will either be there, or I will leave word there of where you can find me. When you've eaten and rested, come find me."

"Yes, sir."

Within ten minutes Madison was in the saddle of his horse, waving goodbye to Moffat as he reined his mount around and tapped spur to raise it to a lope, headed north to Wiley's Tavern, near Difficult Run, not far from Great Falls, Virginia. He rode alone by his own choice, on roads and byways still clogged with vehicles of every description and people showing the strain and exhaustion and the anguish of abandoning the nation's capital and watching it burn through the night.

He reined in at the tavern, swung to the ground, tied the horse to the hitch rack, and pushed through the doors. The clerk at the desk recognized him and pointed up the stairs as he stammered out, "She's up there—Missus Madison is—Lady Madison is up there, room twenty-six. Sir. Mister President. Sir."

Madison raced up the stairs to knock on the door, and in a moment came her voice from within.

"Who is calling?"

"The president of the United States."

The door opened wide and Madison stepped inside to clasp Dolley to his breast, and she wrapped her arms about him. For a moment they stood in their embrace, and then Madison backed up one step.

"Are you all right?"

"Of course," she replied, and then a look of defiance came into her eyes. "But I certainly intend giving those British a piece of my mind!"

Madison closed the door and faced her. "James Monroe?"

"Just down the hall."

"Anyone else? From the cabinet?"

"No, but they're coming. Mister Monroe sent word."

"What did you save from the Executive Mansion?"

"Most of the papers of the cabinet meetings. The painting of President Washington. A few other portraits. Some of our valuables, but not all. You recall the dueling pistols secretary of the treasury George Campbell gave you? I didn't get them. No time. We left with the British right behind."

"But you got the papers?"

"Yes. Safe."

Madison sat down on the bed. "You saw the fires last night?"

Dolley's face fell. "Yes. It broke my heart. Our beautiful new city, burned."

Madison paused for a moment. "We can build a new city. The larger question is can we build a new government?"

Dolley reached to grasp his arm. "Yes. You can. You can!"

Madison stood. "I think I should go visit James Monroe. Will you wait here?"

"Of course."

Within five minutes Madison returned, James Monroe following, and they sat at the small table with Dolley.

"Have you heard anything from any of the rest of the cabinet?" Madison asked.

Monroe shook his head. "Not yet. I have eight officers and aides out scouring the countryside for them. We'll find them."

From downstairs in the tavern, they heard the shout, "They're back! They're burning the city again!"

Both men rose instantly from the table and in two steps were at the window with the curtains drawn back, staring northeast. For a long time they stood transfixed, watching flames leap into the sky while a great cloud of black smoke rose to hover over the city like a pall. Dolley came to look, her hand clasped over her mouth, making tiny sounds as she watched. From the location of the flames and the rising smoke, the three tried to visualize which buildings were burning, but they could not. The only location they could identify with certainty was the navy yards, off to the southeast of the city, on the Anacostia River. The flames were massive, and the black smoke rose over one thousand feet into the clear blue of the sky.

Madison had their midday meal delivered to their room, and they watched the fires and the smoke spread as they ate.

It was midafternoon when they saw flame and black smoke and debris leap three hundred feet into the air, and then felt a tremor in the building, and then heard the heavy thud of a tremendous explosion in the distant city.

Monroe quietly said, "That must have been the powder magazine at the navy yards."

They took their evening meal in the large dining room of the tavern, somber, subdued, each caught up in the images that came and went in their minds of the destruction of the nation's capital. As they finished, they were conscious of the sound of heavy winds outside. They were walking up the stairs when suddenly the sound became a howling, sucking at the fireplace chimney in the dining room, rattling shutters. Madison glanced at Monroe and went to the front door of the tavern to lift the latch. The heavy door was driven inward, wrenched from Madison's hand, while the wind blew window curtains and scattered papers from the tavern desk. Madison seized the door and put his shoulder to it to close and latch it, while Monroe strode to the large front window to stare out.

The trees were doubled over, bent northeast, with limbs and leaves ripped and flying. Debris and shingles and choking dust filled the air. Horses tied to the hitching racks were rearing, fighting the tie ropes, turning their rumps into the wind, while the tops of buggies were ripped free to go flying. The few people in the street were clutching at their hats, heads bent low, seeking shelter wherever they could find it.

Behind the wind came a roaring, and one minute later the rain came in a horizontal sheet that instantly blurred the world and hammered at the windows and the roof. Within seconds everything outside was drenched. The dirt streets were a sea of black mud and water. Those inside the tavern stood at the windows, transfixed at the havoc outside.

Hours passed before the power of the storm slackened and stopped, and an odd silence came stealing. It was one hour short of midnight when Madison rapped on Monroe's door.

"I think we should gather an escort and go looking for the cabinet and heads of departments. We must give the nation every evidence that the government has survived, at earliest opportunity. We should go now. Tonight."

Monroe reflected for a moment. "Missus Madison? Your two aides? The ones you sent to find your cabinet?"

"Missus Madison agrees. She'll meet us later. I'll leave instructions at the desk for the aides."

Monroe bobbed his head and turned to pull on his boots and shrug into his coat.

It was after midnight before they had assembled an escort of mounted dragoons and ridden into the night. They moved northeast, stopping only to rest their horses, and at sunrise to take a hasty breakfast at a tavern. They continued through the day to Conn's Ferry, above Great Falls on the Potomac River, where they paused to loosen the girths on their saddles and feed their tired mounts, then took the ferry to the Maryland side of the river. It was late afternoon when they dismounted before the Montgomery County Courthouse, where Madison hoped to find General Winder.

"No, Mister President," the court clerk said. "General Winder and what little cavalry he had left early yesterday for Bladensburg."

Tired men remounted tired horses and once again the weary presidential entourage rode on. With the setting sun at their backs, Madison guided them to the home of an old friend, and they dismounted, stiff-legged, stiff-backed, at the residence of Caleb Bentley, in Brookville, Maryland.

Their host held back nothing. Beds and bedrooms were made available. Hot water was poured into the white porcelain basins for washing. As if by magic, a huge supper appeared on the dining room table, complete with buttermilk and tarts, and while the hungry men sat at the table, the house staff was in their bedrooms, brushing the road dust from their tunics. Caleb Bentley and his wife and household showed the courtesy of asking few questions.

They were finishing the blueberry tarts when a knock came at the front door. Bentley excused himself and hurried from the room, fearful that the British had somehow learned the president of the United States was inside and had come to complete what would be the master stroke of the entire British campaign—taking the American president captive!

He opened the door and facing him were two young men in the uniform of army officers.

"May I help you, gentlemen?" Caleb asked.

"Sir, we are two personal aides to President Madison. We've been tracking him most of the day. Has he stopped here?"

Bentley said, "Remain here for a moment," and walked quickly back to the dining room.

"Mister President, are you expecting two young aides? In uniform?"

Madison stood, wiping his mouth with his napkin. "Are they here?"

"At the front door."

Madison followed Bentley, who threw the door wide, and Madison faced his two aides, with relief flooding through his system.

"Are you all right?"

"Fine, sir."

Madison turned to Bentley. "These young men have been of tremendous help. Would it be possible for them to—"

He got no further.

Bentley boomed, "Come in, come in! You look like you could use a meal yourselves. And a bath and bed. Follow me."

It was deep into the evening when President Madison gathered his group around the great dining table, tired, weary, needing rest, but determined.

He was brief.

"Gentlemen, I have determined that we are going to return to the city tomorrow." He waited for the shocked murmuring to quiet, then turned to his aides. "Have you been there in the past two days? Seen it?"

"Yes, sir."

"What condition is it in?"

The young men glanced at each other before one answered. "Destroyed. Unbelieveable."

"Did any government buildings survive?"

"Only one that we saw. The patent office."

"The Executive Mansion?"

"Gone."

Madison drew a great breath and slowly exhaled it. "We will return tomorrow. In the morning, as early as you and your horses are fit to travel, would you take half of my escort party into the city and find all the cabinet and government department heads possible? Ask them to assemble at the patent office at one o'clock tomorrow afternoon."

"Yes, sir."

"Thank you. Now I believe we should all get some rest."

A somber, pensive Madison sat for a long time in the yellow lamp-light of his bedroom, pondering, reflecting, searching for a plan to reunite his country, to restore the faith and confidence of the people in their leaders, and he went to his bed and to his sleep with gaps and holes in his thoughts and no conclusions.

He was washed and dressed for breakfast by half past eight o'clock and was greeted at the foot of the stairway by Bentley.

"Good morning, Mister President. I trust you slept well?"

"Good, thank you. Much refreshed."

"Your aides left shortly after four o'clock. They had a good breakfast."

"Excellent."

"Come into the dining room. Breakfast is prepared, and the others are waiting."

It was midmorning when Madison and his escort and the few cabinet and government heads that had arrived at the Bentley estate mounted their horses and turned them southwest, toward the burned-out city. They rode apprehensively, with little talk, as they crossed the Anacostia and came into the streets of the capital. They sat stiff in their saddles, staring at the charred hulks of the government buildings, some still smoldering, with black holes like dead eyes where windows had been, and they felt the eeriness of vacant, silent streets where the clamor and bustle of people and carriages intent on running the United States government had ceased to be.

The party tied their horses before the patent office and followed President Madison inside to the conference room, where they sat at a very long table amidst shelves of the huge ledgers in which the creative genius of a multitude of Americans was recorded. Including his escort and James Monroe, there were more than ten people gathered. Madison drew out his pocket watch—fifteen minutes before one o'clock on the afternoon of August 27, 1814—and sat down at the head of the table.

"We will wait until one o'clock," he announced.

At ten minutes before one o'clock the two aides walked into the room, leather heels clicking in cadence on the hardwood floor.

Madison looked up. "Were you able to find any more cabinet members? Department heads?"

"Yes, sir. Perhaps ten. They should be here shortly."

They came in singly and in small clusters. By five minutes past one o'clock, more than thirty men had gathered around the table or in the room.

Madison took a deep breath and rose and addressed them.

"Thank you for coming. Our purpose today is to make an assessment of two things. First, the condition of the city and the governmental functions, and second, how has this disaster affected the general populace of the country?"

He started around the table, inquiring of each man what he had seen personally, and one by one their dark reports poured out.

The British hit the city at about eight o'clock in the evening on August 24. An infuriated British Admiral George Cockburn demanded burning the entire city—government buildings, residences, memorials—everything—avenge the burning of York, the small capital of Canada on Lake Erie, by the Americans in July of 1813.

British Major General Robert Ross limited the order: burn the government buildings, but spare the residences.

Two lieutenants, George De Lacy Evans of the army, and James Pratt of the navy, were assigned the burning of the Capitol building. With miners and sappers and a company of infantry, they smashed through the front doors and marched into both chambers of Congress, the House and the Senate, searching for records, but found very few; the vital documents had been saved by frantic clerks who had thrown them into wagons and carriages and any wheeled vehicle they could find and whipped terrified horses at stampede gait across the river into Virginia to save them wherever they could find space. The British threw lamp oil onto the draperies and the floors and systematically set each room ablaze, then the great rotunda, and finally the broken doors. The flames leaped high into the night sky while some Americans stood in the streets with tears flowing as the roofs finally gave way and caved in, to throw a mountain of sparks into the sky.

At about ten-thirty PM, Ross and Cockburn led one hundred fifty red-coated regulars from the Capitol building down Pennsylvania Avenue to the Executive Mansion. They battered down the front door and with drawn swords searched every room. On the table in the great dining hall they discovered a sumptuous dinner, still warm, untouched, waiting for the president and his guests. Cockburn and Ross gleefully invited all the officers in their group to take their places at the table where they took devilish pleasure in devouring everything, including that which was in the ovens and on the stoves in the kitchen. Then they set the torches to the Executive Mansion, from the second floor down to the first, and stood surrounding it while it burned. They did not leave until the blazing roof collapsed and sparks leaped upward two hundred feet. The roofless building smoldered until all that remained were the smoke-blackened outside walls, with gaping holes where the windows had been.

It was shortly before midnight when Ross and his men broke their way into the Treasury Building, certain they would find locked vaults holding gold and silver bars. They found the vault doors standing open and all the treasure gone, saved by clerks who had loaded it into army wagons and moved it across the river. Ross gave the orders, and his men emptied lamp oil onto the hardwood floors, backed out of the building, and tossed torches through the open door. The building burned to the ground, a pile of charred timbers and blackened stone.

Cockburn then led his men to the huge navy yards on the Anacostia River, anxious to destroy the single largest naval facility in the United States. Mordecai Booth, a common clerk, had tirelessly worked to load most of the vital records and government properties into wagons bound for Virginia. American Captain Tingey anticipated the arrival of the British and quickly shouted his orders to destroy the stripped-down naval yards altogether. Within minutes the entire place was ablaze, and with it the nearby rope works where hawsers were made. Tied to the docks was a frigate, the *Essex*, and a sloop, the *Argus*, both nearly completed, waiting only for detailing. Cat-footed seamen climbed the ropes into the riggings to set the furled sails ablaze, then retreated into the holds to fire the bowels of the ships. The flames could be seen as far north and east as Charles County, Maryland.

At midnight Cockburn, caught up in his role of conquering hero, discovered the office of the newspaper, *The National Intelligencer*, with its owner, Joseph Gale, standing defiantly on its steps with more than twenty neighbors. Cockburn ordered them to stand down while he burned the building, and Gale, with his neighbors beside him, stood solid, defying Cockburn with their shouts that it would be a travesty to put the entire neighborhood at risk of being burned if fire were set to the newspaper office. Cockburn was caught in a dilemma he could not resolve: how many civilians would he have to shoot before he could burn the newspaper office, and what would become of him if he did it? He relented. Keep your newspaper office but go home. Get off the streets. He posted pickets, and the citizens left.

In the dead of night, with rain steadily falling, both Cockburn and Ross marched their troops back to their camps, only to return the following morning.

Cockburn led his troops to the navy yards and finished the destruction of every building, including the critical rope works.

Ross and his troops sought out the big, square building that housed the State Department, hoping to seize the original drafts of both the

Declaration of Independence and the Constitution of the United States. After all, what greater insult could be heaped on these ridiculous rebels than to seize the documents on which their folly was founded? Ross was angered and frustrated to discover that Chief Clerk John Graham had seized most of the State Department documents, including the Declaration of Independence and the Constitution, loaded them all into linen sacks, and gotten them out of town to Fredericksburg, Maryland. Ross set the building on fire and moved on to the building that housed the War Department, stormed the halls, and set the fires that burned it to the ground.

They came to the patent office and shot the lock off the front door to enter the building. They were met there by Dr. William Thornton, the United States director of patents. White-faced with fury, Thornton shook his finger in their faces and condemned them for even thinking of destroying the patent office. After all, he shouted, it contained only private items belonging to private citizens and records of inventions that would benefit the entire civilized world! How dare they think to destroy it!

Ross backed out of the building and left it intact.

He sent the Twenty-First Infantry to find the fort at Greenleaf's Point and see to it the entire spread of buildings was burned and the huge powder magazine destroyed. The redcoats found the fort partially burned, but the powder magazine intact. They thought they were following their orders when they dropped the hundreds of barrels of gunpowder into a huge well on the grounds, unaware that the water level inside the well was far too low to cover them. The last barrel had just been thrown into the hole when a spark from somewhere—perhaps a cigar—followed it down. Every keg of powder exploded with flame and dirt and wreckage being hurled three hundred feet into the air. The ground tremor reached twenty-five miles, and the resulting crater was monstrous. The explosion was heard twelve miles north of Bladensburg. Forty-two British regulars were knocked rolling, twelve dead, thirty wounded.

Within minutes of the detonation, the heaviest storm in the memory of most descended, sweeping in from the southwest. Winds uprooted trees and tore great limbs from oaks that had been there for one hundred years. Shingles and shutters were ripped away, and some roofs were torn off houses. The streets were filled with flying branches and debris and dirt. A British officer and his horse were knocked off their feet to go rolling over and over in the fury of the howling wind. Close to forty British regulars were thrown down and injured. Then the rains came so thick men had to crouch and cover their faces to breathe. Lightning bolts turned the entire city brighter than noonday while thunder shook the ground.

As the storm raged, Cockburn and Ross shouted orders, and their men retreated from the charred, smoldering wreckage of the United States capital, back north toward Bladensburg.

The destruction of Washington, D.C., was complete.

For a brief time Madison sat in the silence that surrounded the table before he again spoke.

"Does any man present have any evidence of where the British intend striking next? Baltimore? Annapolis?"

There was silence, and Madison moved onto the stand-or-fall question.

"What has all this done to the citizenry? How do they now stand?"

There was a pause, and one man asked, "Are you asking whether the country will continue to support the administration in prosecuting the war?"

"Essentially, yes."

The man took a deep breath, and every eye was on him, waiting.

"May I speak candidly, sir?"

"I expect it."

"Someone has written a message on the burned walls of the Capitol building, sir. It reads 'George Washington founded this city after a seven years' war with England—James Madison lost it after a two years' war.' I apologize, sir. I thought you would prefer to know the truth."

Madison's voice was steady. "No need for apology. I wanted the truth."

The man quickly said, "But, sir, I must add, most people in this city do not blame yourself. They hold Secretary of War John Armstrong responsible. Most feel he is totally incompetent, and there is a rising sentiment among the citizens that if he does return to this city, they'll hang him. The commanders of the local militia have already declared they will not take his orders again."

Madison looked into the man's eyes, and then into the eyes of some of the others, and he saw resolve, and he felt a determination to move past a catastrophic disaster—a feeling that the rank and file of the government and the citizenry were coming together behind his leadership.

The little man rose and squared his shoulders and faced them.

"Gentlemen, it is on our shoulders to step forward and restore the government of our country. Now. Starting today. We will recall the vital records from wherever our workers have taken them, and we will open our government offices in hotels or private residences or wherever necessary, and we will continue with our governmental duties as the United States any way we can. Tell all governors, all generals, to do whatever in their judgment is necessary to start the rebuilding. Tell them to use local resources, and if needed, they have my authority to pledge government credit to pay for necessaries. And at every opportunity, tell the people who took it upon themselves to save our vital papers and our treasure that they have behaved heroically."

He paused, and then concluded. "I will expect a cabinet meeting to be arranged for two o'clock in the afternoon of August twenty-ninth. Two days from now. We will meet in this building. I ask those here to find the absent cabinet members and give them notice."

He stopped for a moment. "If there is nothing else, gentlemen, thank you for your support. This meeting is adjourned."

Notes

On April 11, 1814, Napoleon surrendered to England. By late May, King George III had sent most of the ships and military that had been occupied with fighting the French to America, to end the war it was fighting with the United

States. Almost overnight the British fighting forces in America were more than doubled, with the result that British naval forces came into almost instant control of Chesapeake Bay, Delaware Bay, and New York Harbor, essentially shutting down American commercial shipping and overpowering American military naval and ground forces.

Facing what had every appearance of being the beginning of defeat for the United States, President Madison attempted to rally his politically divided cabinet and generals to determine what course the British would take and where they intended making their heavy attack: Washington, D.C., Annapolis, or Baltimore. Opinions were divided. With secretary of war John Armstrong generally viewed as incompetent, no plan of where to position the American military forces could be made. The result was a disorganized, shifting hodgepodge, with generals ignoring Armstrong and each other and doing what each felt was needed.

The entire episode became a convoluted mess, both for the British and the Americans. Following all the events and all the personalities responsible would require an entire volume. For that reason, this chapter attempts to track only the central core of it. Thus, the names of all persons in this chapter are accurate, as are the events in which they participated. The battle at Bladensburg, reaching outward to at least ten small villages, is as set forth. The subsequent march on Washington, D.C., on the evening of August 24, 1814, is as represented, with the British arriving about eight o'clock PM The destruction of the city and the navy yards were as set forth, with the persons who conducted it accurately identified. British Admiral Cockburn and General Ross took one hundred fifty men to destroy the Executive Mansion, and found a sumptuous meal (as described) still warm and waiting in the great dining room. They promptly sat down and ate the meal, then systematically burned the building. Madison's plan of where to meet in the event of evacuation quickly became impossible, with the result that President Madison fled the city, as did his wife, Dolley, each at different times, to different locations. The estates named Rokeby and Salona, and their owners, are historically accurate, where Dolley and James Madison stayed that night, to be united the next day, August 25, 1814, at Wiley's Tavern.

The systematic continuation of the burning of Washington, D.C., and the navy yards with the two ships and the fort at Greenleaf's Point, with the horrendous blast when the kegs of gunpowder dropped into the well exploded, are accurate. The heroic efforts of clerks in most of the government buildings to save the basic documents necessary to conduct the business of the government, together with the names of those civilians, are accurate. The Declaration of

Independence and original draft of the Constitution were in fact saved by Chief Clerk John Graham. Doctor William Thornton did save the patent office by persuading the British there was nothing of military value there and that the building contained inventions that would benefit all mankind.

On the afternoon of August 25, with the destruction of Washington nearly completed, a furious storm struck the city with winds that actually blew a British officer and his horse off their feet and knocked more than forty British regulars to the ground. Lightning and torrential rain engulfed the city to quell most of the fires. The British concluded that their work was done and marched their troops out of Washington, back toward Bladensburg in Maryland.

On August 27, Madison rallied what he could find of his government leadership to get reports on the damage done, both to the city and to the national mindset. The message written on the wall of the capitol as recited herein, "George Washington founded this city after a seven years' war with England—James Madison lost it after a two years' war" is a verbatim quotation. However, most of the citizenry did not hold Madison accountable; rather, they blamed the bumbling, incompetent secretary of war, John Armstrong. Some did in fact threaten to hang him. Military leaders told Madison outright they refused to follow Armstrong's orders. Almost immediately, James Madison asked for and received John Armstrong's resignation and replaced him with James Monroe.

At the informal August 27 conference, Madison set a cabinet meeting to be held August 29, and the meeting was held.

James Madison and Dolley Madison never again resided in what we now call the White House; Madison's term as president ended before the reconstruction was completed.

See Whitehorne, *The Battle for Baltimore 1814,* pp. 119–43; Hickey, *The War of 1812,* pp. 197–202; Barbuto, *Niagara 1814,* pp. 261–62; Sheads, *Fort McHenry,* pp. 27–31; Stagg, *Mr. Madison's War,* pp. 416–18.

For a discussion of the impact of the war on the economy and the insurance rates, see Hickey, *The War of 1812,* pp. 214–19.

The Dunson family and Billy Weems and Jeremiah Skullings are all fictional characters.

CHAPTER XXIV

*T*he Maryland forests that cradled the craggy, rocky shores of northern Chesapeake Bay were just beginning the magic transformation from the rich emerald green of summer to the indescribable colors of fall. Nights were beginning to lose the heat of the day, and mornings were remaining a little cooler a little longer. Birds of the sea wheeled and glided in proliferation with beady eyes, tracking invisible flying things and searching for offerings washed ashore from the dark blue-green waters of the great bay. Onshore the squirrels and chipmunks and bears, and all furred animals of the forest, were answering the ancient laws of nature that required them to store food for the winter, whether in hollow trees or as fat on their bodies, while their pelts daily grew heavier against the approaching winter.

In the bright sun of midday, with the British Union Jack stirring in the south breeze at the top of her eighty-foot mainmast, the HMS *Tonnant* rocked gently on the outgoing tide. The huge man-of-war, bristling with eighty cannon on two decks, was the flagship of the great fleet of more than sixty British gunboats and schooners and brigs and gondolas that for three months had been gathering on the Chesapeake from the place where the Patapsco River empties into the bay on the north, to the mouth of the Patuxent River, eighty miles south, under orders of the British admiralty to crush the small scatter of American ships that had appeared to make a useless show of resistance.

In command of the British fleet was British vice admiral Sir Alexander Cochrane, aristocratic, taller than average, built well, high forehead, regular features, cleft in his chin. It was Cochrane, together with Rear Admiral George Cockburn and Major General Sir Robert Ross, who had become the instant and spectacular heroes of the British empire when they combined their sea and land forces to overrun the Americans at Bladensburg, and then ravaged and sacked and burned Washington, D.C., less than three weeks later.

The pivotal question that now paralyzed the Americans and teased the British was, where would the British forces strike next? Annapolis? Washington, D.C., again? Baltimore?

Cochrane, Cockburn, and Ross had for days bandied the question back and forth, with their proposals ranging from abandoning the Chesapeake altogether, to relocating at New York, to making sail for the planned assault in the Gulf of Mexico, to crushing Baltimore. The result of it all was their decision to take Baltimore and then get out of the Chesapeake. Their reasons were simple: Baltimore, with its stubborn defiance, had been a thorn in the side of the British for decades. To their thinking, reducing that city of forty thousand to ashes was long overdue. And they all deemed it prudent to be far from the Chesapeake before the malaria season set in.

On board the *Tonnant,* inside the captain's quarters, Cochrane, Ross, and four other officers were gathered around a table, hats hung on pegs and tunics laid on a bunk, shirt sleeves unbuttoned and rolled up, chafing at the confinement and the muggy heat as they pored over a large map of the north sector of the bay, reaching north past the city of Baltimore. The windows were thrown open, and the door from the narrow corridor was half open to allow air to circulate in the small room.

Cochrane tapped the map with a finger and spoke to Ross.

"We're going to have to put your infantry ashore, here, at North Point, on the peninsula, fourteen miles south of the city. They're going to have to march to Baltimore."

Ross looked at him in question, and Cochrane went on.

"At the north end, where you will have to land, both the bay and the

Patapsco River are too shallow for heavy ships. We can get some of the schooners and gondolas closer, up the Patapsco to Baltimore, but none of the heavy men-o'-war. You'll have to make your landing and your march north without support from our heavy guns."

He shifted his finger north, up the Patapsco River to a point near the city of Baltimore, and again tapped the map.

"This is Fort McHenry. Five-sided. Built by a Frenchman named Foncin. Finished about seven years ago. It is very near the water on this small finger of land south of Baltimore and has guns capable of reaching anything within two miles. To get to Baltimore by water, we have to get past this fort. In short, if we mean to move our lighter ships up to Baltimore to give your infantry support from our cannon, we must first destroy Fort McHenry."

Ross scratched at his jaw. "How many heavy guns and how many men in the fort?"

"Forty guns and over one thousand men. Under command of Major George Armistead."

"How many gunboats can you put within range of the fort?"

"Enough to reduce it to kindling in one day."

A look of skepticism crossed Ross's face and was gone. He tapped the map midway between North Point and Fort McHenry, on the east shore of the bay.

"My scouts tell me the Americans have built earthworks right about here and have around three thousand armed militia there."

"That's true," Cochrane acknowledged, "but you will have over four thousand regulars with you. You should have no trouble getting past militia. Many of them—maybe most—are without uniforms and have never been under fire. I expect them to scatter at the first sight of your regulars and the sound of cannon and muskets."

Ross shifted his finger back to Baltimore.

"My infantry can march to Baltimore and attack from the east side, or even from the north side. But any success from our attack will depend on support from your cannon bombarding the city from the south and west."

Cochrane was emphatic. "We'll get our gunboats past Fort McHenry. We'll be there to give you support from the harbor."

Ross raised a hand in caution. "How is Baltimore defended right now? How many men? Cannon? Who's in command?"

Cochrane answered, "Militia. Ten or twelve thousand. At least twenty cannon. Samuel Smith is in command."

Ross's forehead wrinkled for a moment. "General Sam Smith? The United States senator?"

"The same."

Ross's eyes narrowed. "A captured American soldier said Sam Smith's been preparing Baltimore for an attack for the last six months. He has about ten or fifteen thousand men there, and he's been drilling them morning and night. They're armed. They can shoot. They've been digging entrenchments and building breastworks all summer. And Sam Smith is tough. He's put some spirit into that city."

The sound of booted feet descending the short, narrow stairway down to the half-open door brought all six men around to look as a young ensign rapped.

"Yes?" Cochrane said.

The door swung open and the red-haired young man in full naval uniform stood with his hat in his hand, new epaulets gleaming gold on his shoulders. His voice came strong, with a flavor of Irish in it.

"Sir, there's a man here requesting audience with yourself. An American. From Georgetown."

Every officer in the room stared for a moment before Cochrane spoke.

"An American from Georgetown? Military?"

"No, sir. A lawyer. He has a second man with him. He stated he wants to negotiate the release of an American we are holding prisoner."

Cochrane looked at Ross in total puzzlement, then spoke to the young ensign.

"What's his name? His position?"

"Key, sir. F. S. Key. The man with him is named Skinner. Mister Key is not military. Says he represents hundreds of Americans from this area, and about sixty of our soldiers."

Cochrane's head thrust forward. "What? He represents British soldiers?"

"That's what he said, sir."

"Where is he?"

"At the head of the stairs, sir, under armed guard."

Cochrane glanced at the other officers for a moment. "Hold him there. We'll be finished here shortly, and I will talk with him."

"Yes, sir." The ensign turned on his heel and thumped his way back up the stairs. Cochrane turned back to the table and the map and spoke to Ross.

"You say Smith is a hard opponent and has prepared Baltimore for an attack like the one we're planning. You're right. But with your four thousand men attacking from the east side of the city, and my gunboats destroying the west side, it will only be a matter of time before they strike their colors. It is my opinion we can complete the destruction of Baltimore within two days and be well on our way south."

Cochrane straightened, waiting for responses.

Ross drew a deep breath. "The plan appears sound. We may have to make some adjustments as we go, but that's to be expected."

Cochrane turned to the other four officers. "Gentlemen?"

It was plain in their faces. Their desire to sack the city of Baltimore far outweighed their concerns of getting there or the defenses they could expect from the cocky Americans.

With very little comment, they endorsed the plan.

Cochrane concluded. "It is agreed then. We'll have the infantry boarded on the transports by September 10, and we'll move them up the bay for a landing at North Point early on September 12. Any questions?"

There were none.

"Very good. General Ross, would you bring that American who wants a prisoner released back to these quarters? The remainder of you are dismissed."

The four officers gathered their hats and tunics and made their way out through the low, narrow doorway and climbed the stairs to the main deck, relieved to be out in the sunlight and the stirrings of a breeze. Ross followed and stopped at the head of the stairs, where the young ensign stood waiting with two men in civilian clothing.

For a long moment, Ross studied the two Americans. The obvious leader was slightly taller than average, with dark hair, regular features, middle-aged, with dark, intense eyes that were focused, showing no emotion. Beside him was an older man, thin, wiry, hair graying, a prominent nose and thin mouth. Both men carried satchels. Four uniformed British seamen stood beside and behind the two men, with muskets raised and bayonets gleaming in the sun.

Ross spoke to the younger man.

"You have come to secure the release of a prisoner?"

"Yes, sir."

"Follow me."

He led the two Americans and the four armed guards down to the captain's quarters, where Cochrane was waiting.

Ross pointed. "These are the Americans."

Cochrane spoke to the four armed guards. "Go back up on deck and wait there."

"Yes, sir." The four men withdrew, and Cochrane waited until they closed the door before he addressed the two men before him.

"You wish to see me about a prisoner?"

The younger man nodded. "We do, sir."

Suspicion was clear in Cochrane's face. "Who sent you?"

"A group of citizens from—"

Cochrane raised a hand to cut him off. "No. Who in the United States government sent you?"

The man's voice remained firm, steady, unruffled. "No one."

"What is your name?"

"Key. Francis Scott Key." Key turned to his companion. "This is Colonel John Skinner, sir. Colonel Skinner is a regularly appointed American agent for prisoner exchange."

Cochrane studied both men for a moment, then spoke to Key. "You are from where?"

"Georgetown."

"Are you with the Department of War? Department of State? What are you in the United States government?"

"I have nothing to do with the United States government. I am a civilian. I practice law in Georgetown."

"A civilian?

"Yes. I arranged to have Colonel Skinner accompany me to be certain all formalities are abided in our request for a prisoner you are holding."

"Who is the prisoner?"

"His name is William Beanes. Doctor William Beanes. He has served as the community physician in Upper Marlboro for at least the past forty years. Your soldiers took him prisoner for reasons not known. The citizens in Upper Marlboro are fearful he will be hanged. They retained my services to negotiate his release. I requested the assistance of Mister Skinner to be certain such release is full and final."

Cochrane turned to Ross. "A Doctor Beanes? Ever heard of him?"

Ross shook his head but remained silent.

Cochrane turned back to Key. "Unusual. Citizens retained your services? Are paying you?"

"Expenses only, sir. I am charging no fee. You have to understand, Doctor Beanes is one of the most beloved figures for a hundred miles in Upper Marlboro. His entire life has been given to the medical care of anyone needing his services. No one knows how many times he gave of his time and his medical skills to anyone who needed them, without mention of being paid. This man is one of the finest."

"Why was he taken prisoner?"

"He was tending wounded American soldiers when British troops took them all captive."

"Is he an army doctor?"

"No, sir. He is not."

Cochrane summed it up. "You're here to obtain the release of an

American doctor taken in the act of tending battle wounds of American soldiers. That is enough to hold him for giving aid and comfort to our enemy. Unless there is some compelling reason to the contrary, we will continue to hold him until we have a general exchange of prisoners. That could be months."

"There's more, sir," Key exclaimed. He turned to Skinner, who handed him his heavy leather satchel. Key gestured to the small table and Cochrane nodded consent before he realized that the large map on the table and the few scattered papers with rough drawings of North Point and the Patapsco River leading to Baltimore were in plain sight. Quickly he gathered the papers and folded the map to allow Key to set both satchels on the table and open one of them.

"Sir, here are more than one hundred sixty letters from the leading citizens in Upper Marlboro, declaring the invaluable services Doctor Beanes has given in his life. They make it very plain that he has never borne arms against anyone. His life has been a model of selfless service in all seasons, day or night, to anyone who needed him, rich and poor alike. They plead with you to release him."

Key opened the second satchel. "There are more than one hundred twenty letters from British soldiers—enlisted and officers alike—who Doctor Beanes has treated for wounds suffered in battle. Without him, those men would have been dead or crippled for life. Read them, sir. They swear this man has been an agent of mercy. He has been to battle fields while the guns were still firing, to help all wounded. American or British. It made no difference to him. Each of those letters includes a request that Doctor Beanes be released as a prisoner of war and allowed to return to Upper Marlboro. It is not known how many more British soldiers—and American—he will save, if he is allowed to continue with his life. Read them, sir. Read the letters. You cannot read them and remain unmoved."

Key stopped, and for a time Cochrane stared at him before he turned to Ross. The two men did not speak, but a silent communication passed between them. Cochrane turned back to Key.

"You're telling me that you have letters from one hundred twenty

British military who are requesting the release of this man? Doctor Beanes?"

Key leaned forward, eyes alive, focused. "I am, sir. Read them. Every letter includes the signatures of two witnesses. There are more available if you wish to see them."

Cochrane turned back to Ross. "Have you ever heard of anything like this before?"

Ross slowly shook his head. "No, I have not. If this is true, we had better consider it. This comes down to a matter of honor."

Cochrane faced Key. "Leave the letters here. We'll assign you quarters on the ship with an armed guard while we satisfy ourselves one way or the other, and call you back here, likely within the hour."

With Key and Skinner in the first mate's quarters and the four armed seamen standing guard, Ross and Cochrane emptied the satchel containing letters from British wounded onto the tabletop, startled at the number as they spread out, and a few dropped to the floor. For forty minutes they sat at the table in silence, opening the sealed documents, reading them, stacking them. They had finished most of them when Ross leaned forward.

"We can't hold Doctor Beanes. The man has done more for our wounded than most of our own doctors. I've read more than thirty from our wounded enlisted and over twenty from our wounded officers. Nine of those officers swear they would have died without the man's assistance. Day and night. Over sixty years old, and he was there day and night for them. If he had been a British military doctor he'd have received every commendation and medal available."

Cochrane finished the letter he was reading and tossed it onto the table. "I can understand why everyone who knows him—including our own soldiers—swears he must be released." He leaned forward on his forearms. "I'm going to do it. Any question?"

Ross shook his head emphatically. "None."

Cochrane straightened. "Only one problem. When Mister Key was in this room he got a fairly good look at the map and some of the other papers. A clever man could put what he saw together and have a reasonably accurate idea of our plans for taking Baltimore."

He stood. "I'll release Doctor Beanes, but I think we better keep those two Americans in our custody until we have completed our attack on Baltimore. I can't take a chance on their telling the American military what they may have seen on this table."

Ross nodded. "Agreed. Shall I bring them back?"

"Yes."

Minutes later, Key and Skinner were standing in the small room facing Cochrane, with Ross to one side and the armed guards just outside the door. Cochrane gestured to the letters on the table as he spoke.

"We've read most of the letters. We believe they are authentic. I will release Doctor Beanes as you requested. I presume you brought the proper papers."

Skinner stepped forward and drew papers from his inside coat pocket. "Here, sir. The standard acknowledgements and release form. It includes a place for my signature as an authorized agent for the United States to complete the transfer of Doctor Beanes."

Cochrane accepted the papers. "Our agent will inspect them, and I will sign them under his direction." He paused, then went on. "There is one more thing. I must hold you in our custody for the next few days. It is possible you have seen or heard things on this ship that would be helpful to the American military. I cannot risk that. I give you my word that as soon as matters will allow, you will be released."

Key exclaimed, "That is unexpected. Would it be enough if both of us swore to you we would not speak of anything we saw or heard on this ship?"

Cochrane shook his head. "I cannot do that. I believe you are both honorable men, but if I release you now and something goes wrong with our military campaign in this area, I could face an inquiry into my judgment in letting you go. I have no choice. You will have to remain for a few days."

Key took a deep breath. "Then, sir, may I write a brief letter to my wife and children explaining this to them? They will presume the worst if I do not return shortly."

Again Cochrane shook his head. "I cannot allow it for the same reason I cannot let you go. Such a letter could be viewed as a message or even a secret code. That's the end of the question. You will be transferred from this ship to the *Surprise* and then to a sloop where you will remain until we withdraw from the Chesapeake." He gestured to the letters scattered on the desk. "We will return these letters to you at the time of your release."

Standing in the cramped captain's quarters of the *Tonnant*, facing Vice Admiral Cochrane and Major General Ross, with four armed guards within a few steps, it was clear to both Key and Skinner, that Dr. Beanes would be delivered to them, but in the meantime, they would be detained until British operations in Chesapeake Bay were completed.

Cochrane pointed to the door and spoke to Ross. "Would you summon the guards and my first mate?"

In less than one minute the guards were crowded into the small room, followed by the first mate, and Cochrane gave his orders.

"Take these two men on deck and arrange for a longboat to carry them to the *Surprise.* They are not prisoners. For present purposes, they are guests, entitled to every consideration. Then locate a prisoner named Doctor William Beanes. Take him to the *Surprise* to join them. In the event of our moving up the Patapsco River, transfer the three of them to a small sloop that will remain behind. Am I clear?"

He was clear.

Cochrane and Ross waited while the seven men walked out the door and up to the main deck before they gathered the letters and packed them back into the two satchels. Cochrane folded the release papers received from Skinner and tucked them into the inside pocket of his tunic.

"I'll have our agent check these." He paused to look at Ross. "In the meantime, get your men ready to board those ships for the landing at North Point. We're putting them ashore in the early morning of September 12."

Ross nodded. "They'll be ready." He gestured to the two satchels of letters. "Where do you plan to store those?"

Cochrane shrugged. "Likely in my war chest, if there's room. If not, in a chest under lock and key."

Ross started for the door, then paused. "Reports say Sam Smith has had thousands of citizens in Baltimore building defenses."

Cochrane's eyes narrowed. "Slaves and masters, bankers and scoundrels, high and low—all working shoulder to shoulder digging, moving dirt, dragging tree trunks, running wheelbarrows filled with rocks—all as equals. I don't know how he did it. You heard he had a reckoning with Winder? General William Winder?"

"I heard something about it. What exactly happened?"

"Winder was appointed by Madison's administration to command the affairs at Baltimore—a federal appointment. When he got there, he was told very bluntly that the Committee of Safety Vigilance of the state of Maryland had already appointed General Sam Smith to take command of the Baltimore defenses. Winder wrote to secretary of war John Armstrong requesting he—Winder—be commissioned a major general in the Continental Army, to outrank Smith, who was a general in the state militia. Armstrong didn't answer. Winder had to step back and let Smith take command."

Ross chuckled. "I've heard reports that the Madison administration is filled with incompetents. Someone offered to hang Armstrong." Ross sobered, then continued. "Sam Smith is not incompetent. If he's been in command of Baltimore through the summer, we had better be prepared for some strong resistance." He opened the door and turned back for a few moments with a distant look in his eyes. "I wonder where Smith is right now. How much does he know of our preparations to attack his city? How committed are those under his command? Will they stand and fight, or will they scatter and run, like they did at Bladensburg?"

Cochrane did not answer. Ross walked out and closed the door.

To the north, where the Patapsco River touched Baltimore, Maryland militia general Sam Smith stood at the head of a long table in the second floor of the courthouse. Seated on both sides were the military officers and the civilian leaders who had answered his call months earlier to prepare their city for the attack that he had predicted was coming. Sooner or later, he had exclaimed, the British were going to come with enough ships and cannon and infantry and muskets to overrun Baltimore and burn it to the ground. It would be partly in revenge for the fierce, stubborn rebelliousness of the city against Mother England for more than thirty-five years, he declared, and partly because Baltimore was one of the wealthiest, most key seaports in the United States.

It was a grim Sam Smith who had called the leaders of his city together and sworn to them that the British might take Baltimore, but by the Almighty, they would know they had been in a fight! He had laid out a detailed plan of the defenses that would give them the best chance of survival and then made assignments to every organization in town under Maryland State control—military or civil, federal or state, including churches—for each to do its share.

And Baltimore bowed its back and went to work through the summer months of 1814.

Then, as Sam had predicted, on the nights of August twenty-fourth and twenty-fifth, every man at the table had stood in silent shock as they watched the glow in the black night sky far to the south, knowing it was Washington—their national capital—burning in the rain. They had heard the faint rumble of the cannon, and seen the flames leaping into the sky, and felt the ground tremble when the powder magazine at Greenleaf's Point exploded. They had suffered the shameful humiliation of knowing that their President Madison and those in command of the United States government had fled the city—abandoned it—while the United States military had crumbled into a disorganized, panic-driven, useless mob that ran away from the fight at Bladensburg.

With the British armada gathered in the bay, on August 27, Brigadier General John Stricker, Major George A. Armistead, Commodore Oliver Hazard Perry, and Captain Robert T. Spence had persuaded colonels John Eager Howard, Richard Frisby, and Robert Stewart to plead with the governor of Maryland to appoint militia major general Samuel Smith commander of all military forces, state and federal, in defense of Baltimore. The governor did it without hesitating. Overnight, Sam Smith had divided Baltimore into four districts, based on groupings of voting wards, and given the orders necessary to each group for the defense of the city.

Now, in the heat of the second floor of the Baltimore Courthouse, all eyes on both sides of the table were on Sam Smith, waiting to make their reports on how well the city was prepared to defend itself.

"Gentlemen," Smith began, "the assumptions we made months ago have proven correct. With the defenses we planned now near completion, we have forced the British to abandon any hope of a successful assault on Baltimore with infantry coming from the southwest. If they want this city, they are going to have to make an amphibious assault from the east side, on the Patapsco River. The question now before us is simple: Are we prepared to withstand such an assault? I convened this meeting to find the answer."

He paused for a moment while the room became silent, and then started down the table, asking the men one at a time for a succinct answer to a single question: "Did you complete your assignment?"

"Major George Armistead?"

"Yes, sir. I was given command of defenses at Fort McHenry. I have one thousand armed troops that include flotillamen, militia, Captain Joseph H. Nicholson's mercantile volunteers, and six hundred United States infantry. We have thirty-six heavy guns in place in the fort. The entire tip of Whetstone Point is fortified with batteries totaling another thirty-six heavy guns to defend against an amphibious landing. Just over one mile west of the fort, near Winan's Wharf, is another earthwork with six smaller guns and a hotshot furnace. We have sixty men making musket cartridges and casting cannonballs. We are ready, sir."

"Commodore Rodgers?"

"Sir, I have four hundred fifty seamen and fifty United States marines from the *Guerriere,* one hundred seventy marines from Washington under Captain Alfred Grayson, and five hundred flotillamen from Captain Barney. Further, sir, our defenses east of the city include ten thousand troops in trenches, with a total of sixty-two cannon. In addition, we have cannon batteries north and west of the main lines, along with breastworks and trenches. These batteries begin at Harris's Creek with Midshipman William D. Salter in command of one gun with twelve men, and continue northwest, very close to Sparrow's Point Road with five guns and eighty men commanded by Sailing Master James Ramage, and two guns and twenty men fronting Sparrow Point Road. West of the junction of the Sparrow Point and Philadelphia roads, we have one hundred men and seven guns under Lieutenant Thomas Gamble. They can provide a heavy cross fire on the main roads. Lieutenant Joseph Kuhn is in command of marines in trenches extending west from Gamble's battery. The lines now extend west from Philadelphia Road to Belair Road, with seven companies of the Maryland First Artillery Regiment. Each regiment has four guns, and in addition we have stationed sixteen heavier guns in support. There are three cannon in front of the courthouse to warn the city when the attack begins. All told, sir, we have more than ten thousand men in battle position and more than one hundred cannon. I believe we are prepared."

"Brigadier General John Stricker?"

"Sir, I have three thousand one hundred eighty-five men, trained throughout the summer, armed and ready to march out of the city in any direction, to meet any enemy."

"Quartermaster Paul Bentalou?"

"Yes, sir. Citizens from all over Baltimore and even from outside the city were asked to come and bring their own picks and shovels and wheelbarrows to dig the trenches and build the breastworks in and close to the city, according to the plan. They came, sir. Morning and night. We ran out of money at the end of August, but banks made loans and citizens gave contributions, and altogether we got the six hundred sixty thousand dollars we had to have."

Bentalou paused for a moment to pick up a paper. "There's more, sir. We fell short of food and contracted with a bakery to bake bread day and night. They have done well. Farmers began bringing in wheat and potatoes and corn and handing it out free! We have hospitals prepared for wounded, should they be needed. Sir, I can't . . . it's unbelievable! Women all over town are rolling bandages, construction companies are donating lumber and bolts and nails, merchants are bringing shoes and boots. Blacks and whites are out there digging trenches and building breastworks, sweating side by side like brothers. I never saw such a thing in my life! The trenches and breastworks in the city will be finished within forty-eight hours."

"Lieutenant Solomon Rutter?"

"Sir, the boom you ordered constructed south of Fort McHenry is completed. It reaches from shore to shore, four hundred fifty feet in the river south of the fort. It consists of ship masts chained together and timbers laid end to end and secured on piles. I believe the boom will stand against invading ships. If it does not, we have ships in place that can be sunk to seal off the channels."

"Captain Samuel Babcock?"

"Sir, I was ordered to convert the cathedral in the city to a fort and to prepare barricades in the streets around it, in the event the British get that far. I can report that our great cathedral is now fortified, sir. And the street barricades are in place."

"Major William Barney?"

"I was given responsibility to create a system that would keep us informed of British movements by the hour. We now have observation stations on the Chesapeake, from the Patuxent River, eighty miles south of us, to here. We have semaphore signal flags constantly conveying every move the British are making and mounted couriers at the ready to carry written messages should that be necessary. We have been question-ing British prisoners and deserters for every detail we can get. The communication system is in place, sir."

Smith straightened in his chair. "I think we're as prepared as we can get. There will have to be adjustments made once the shooting starts. Stay alert. I will be watching the entire conflict from my base on Hampstead Hill at the edge of the city." He paused to collect his thoughts. "There's one more thing that needs to be said."

He paused and stood. "Most of you know that right now, there are negotiations for a peace treaty with England going on in the city of Ghent, in Belgium. President Madison has sent John Quincy Adams and Henry Clay and three others to represent the United States. The British sent James Lord Gambier and two others to represent England. The strength of our position was damaged—badly—when news arrived over there of the fall of Washington, D.C. If we now lose Baltimore . . . "

He did not finish the sentence.

He looked briefly into the face of each man, and he saw the realization of the pivotal role Baltimore was to play in the future of America. "If the British were to succeed in plundering and burning Baltimore as they did the nation's capital, our delegation in Ghent would suffer a fatal blow. The negotiations for a peace treaty could turn into a total surrender. Everything America had fought for since April 19, 1775, would be gone in the stroke of a pen."

Smith concluded. "Thank you. All of you. Return to your duty posts and stand in a state of readiness, day and night."

The men were gathering their papers when Smith interrupted. "I forgot one thing." He turned to Armistead. "General, would you send someone to fetch the flag I commissioned last month? The one to be made by Mary Young Pickersgill. It's finished. We may need it."

The room silenced as Armistead answered. "Are you talking about the flag I requested?"

Smith's eyes were intense points of light. "Yes. I ordered one big enough to be seen for ten miles. Thirty-two feet by forty-three feet. So big she had to lay it out on the floor of the local malt house brewery. Her daughter Caroline helped her sew it. I got her bill a few days ago. It cost four hundred five dollars and ninety cents."

Surprised murmuring arose around the table, and Smith paused until it stopped before he went on. "To get to Baltimore, the British have to get past Fort McHenry, where you command. When they try, I want that flag mounted and flying where the British can see it for ten miles. They're going to know we're there, and that we intend staying there!"

For a moment there was complete silence, and then Armistead said, "Yes, sir. It will be there, and they'll see it."

Amid exclamations, the officers rose from the table with papers in hand, and Smith followed them down the stairs, out into the sunlight of downtown Baltimore where citizens and uniformed troops mingled, crowded together in the streets, as they sweated and worked on the trenches and breastworks and barricades to complete all defenses for their city.

Night had fallen, and the moon was high when an exhausted rider, dressed in well-worn civilian clothing and riding a winded horse, stopped at the home of Sam Smith and hammered on the door. Smith was in his nightshirt and holding a lantern high when he opened it and faced the man.

"Gen'l, sir, I was sent by Rodgers—beg pardon—Commodore Rodgers—to tell you—we seen British ships—little ones—down by the Patuxent, comin' up the bay. They're headed here for sure."

"How many?"

"Hard to tell in the moonlight, but we counted over twenty-two. They're comin'."

"You need rest? Feed for the horse?"

"No, sir, we're just fine. I got to get back down there with Rodgers. I wouldn't miss this party for nothin', sir. Uh . . . if it's all right with you, sir, can I go?"

"You are dismissed."

Smith remained standing in the doorframe with the lantern high to watch the man swing up onto his horse, spin the animal, and set his spurs. Sparks flew from the iron shoes hitting the granite cobblestones as the horse broke into a weary gallop. Smith watched him out of sight before he closed the door.

The sun rose, a hazy, round, yellow ball in an overcast sky, with criers in the streets shouting the warning—"British ships in the bay! Be prepared!" By midmorning the streets were filled with uniformed soldiers and people leaving their homes and shops to hurry to the trenches or to the cannon batteries, to wait for the messengers that came on the hour with reports of the slow, steady advance of the British fleet. The day wore on with tension mounting. Twilight found people leaving their battle positions while others arrived. Dusk, and then full darkness came, with the rotation of citizens and soldiers ongoing, and the network of observation posts on both banks of the Chesapeake studying everything that moved on the bay, while mounted messengers rode through the night to relay the information to Smith in Baltimore.

The sun was an hour high when two men in an observation tower at Herring Point on bank of the Chesapeake at the mouth of the Patapsco River jerked to a full stop, holding their breath, telescopes extended as they studied vague shapes moving north on the water in the morning fog. Within minutes the fog thinned, and a breeze moved upriver, and suddenly the shapes took form.

"There," one shouted, arm up and pointing. "There they are! See them? Forty—maybe fifty! Big ones! British troop transports and men-o'-war! They're coming!"

He spun and bounded down a flight of stairs to a small, wiry young man lounging near a tall, brown gelding, saddled and waiting. He fairly shouted at the startled boy, "They're here! Fifty of them. British troop transports and gunboats! The invasion has started! Get word to Sam Smith!"

The young man leaped to the saddle and was gone in a clattering of hoof beats. He held his horse to a steady gallop, slowing twice in the twelve-mile run to let the laboring mount blow before he pushed his tired mount through the streets of Baltimore to the house of Sam Smith, to pound on the door.

His voice was high, strained as he pointed south. "They're comin'! Fifty gunboats and troop ships! Right down at the mouth of the river."

Within minutes Smith was at the courthouse, panting from his run, where he stopped short of the twelve men assigned to the three warning cannon.

"Fire those guns!" he shouted. "The British are coming up the Patapsco. The attack has begun."

"Sir," came the reply, "it's Sunday! September 11! It doesn't seem right to—"

Smith bellowed, "The Almighty will understand! Fire those guns!"

Within seconds the three cannon roared in succession, and in the midmorning sun, the defenders of the city came sprinting from their homes and barracks to their duty posts.

Smith quickly ran to the First Methodist Church on Light Street and burst into a Sabbath morning worship service in full session. Every head in the congregation turned to stare at him, and the Reverend John Gruber leaned forward over his raised pulpit, startled, indignant at the unusual interruption.

Smith did not wait for an invitation. He called down the long aisle, "Reverend, the British are in the Patapsco! The attack is started. We need you and these people."

Audible gasps filled the air, and the Reverend Gruber instantly straightened and raised both hands and waited until the church was silent. Then his voice rang from the walls.

"The Lord Bless King George, convert him, and take him to heaven, as we want no more of him! Amen!"

The chapel was filled with amens as the congregation stood and followed Smith out the door into the churchyard where they scattered to return to their homes to retrieve their weapons and change from their Sunday finery into uniforms or clothing suited to their duty stations. Smith worked his way through the people and carriages and wagons jamming the streets to his home, where he quickly changed into the tunic of a major general and buckled his sword onto his left side. Minutes later he was in the saddle of his dappled gray mare, impatiently working his way through the streets to the edge of the city and on to his command post on the high point of Hampstead Hill, where he had a clear view of the harbor and the streets of the city. He was standing on a fortified observation tower with his telescope extended and pressed to his eye, searching the river and Baltimore Bay for British ships, when his aides arrived, followed by a squad of uniformed messengers who tied their horses at the rear of the command post, ready to deliver his orders to any commander or any unit on the Patapsco or in the city.

Smith turned to study the movement of his uniformed militia in the city and watched as they gathered at their assigned rendezvous points to get their ration of one day's food and thirty-six rounds of ammunition for their muskets and rifles. Satisfied they were following the standing orders, he turned back to slowly sweep the bay with his telescope, and in the far distance were the top sails of the British ships moving steadily up the river.

He turned to his nearest aide, and there was a disciplined excitement in his face and his voice. "They intend attacking North Point, just as we expected. Write down the following."

"Yes, sir." The aide produced paper and a lead pencil and wrote rapidly as Smith dictated.

> To General John Stricker. Assemble your city Third Brigade immediately and march them east, to take up positions on Long Log Lane just below Trappe Road. Bread-and-Cheese Creek is to the north, and Bear Creek is to the south. Nearby is a zigzag fence that divides a wooded area from large open fields. Set up your lines in the woods, behind the fence. To get past your line, anyone coming from the east will have to cross those open fields, under your guns. Engage and stop them if possible, or, hinder them and fall back if such be necessary.
>
> Your obed'nt servant,
> Gen. S. Smith.

The aide handed the brief document to Smith for his signature, then folded it and ran for the stairs, down to the messengers waiting in the shade of the rear wall of the command post with their horses at hand. The aide thrust the folded paper into the hands of the nearest uniformed rider and exclaimed, "General John Stricker! As fast as you can."

With the message tucked inside his tunic, the man mounted his horse and reined it around to disappear, moving west at a gallop for the run back to the city. From the observation tower of his command post on Hampstead Hill, Smith watched the messenger disappear into the streets. Within one hour he watched the three thousand soldiers of the Third Brigade assemble in rank and file in the streets of Baltimore, with Revolutionary War veteran General John Stricker, fifty-five years of age and a native of Frederick, Maryland, seated on his black horse at the head of the column. Stricker stood tall in the stirrups to inspect his command, then turned his horse, raised his hand, and shouted the command, and the column followed him through the streets, fifes playing and drums banging, amid the shouts and cheers of the gathered citizens.

Through the heat of the sultry, humid afternoon, Smith watched Stricker's command move steadily west on their seven-mile march, past Cook's Tavern, over the bridge at Bread-and-Cheese Creek, to the Methodist meetinghouse just west of Trappe Road. With twilight coming on, Stricker's entire command was in place in the woods behind the zigzag fence, dug in, tense, waiting, scarcely visible to anyone moving west on Long Log Lane.

In gathering dusk, Smith collapsed his telescope and turned to his aides. "I'm going home for some rest. When your replacements arrive, you do the same. We're going to have moonlight tonight, enough to see much of the Patapsco and any ships that are moving. Keep a sharp watch. Tell your replacements that if they see anything on the water, they're to send for me at once."

He extended his telescope one more time and slowly scanned the river before he descended the stairs to his waiting horse. As he turned his mount toward the darkened town, he glanced to the south, and then the west, as though he could see the river and the roads, with his thoughts and his fears running.

They'll send Ross—he'll land at North Point—they'll march west on Long Log Lane—won't they?—won't they?—how many men?—too many?—too many?

Behind him, in the faint moonlight on the river, the British fleet, led by troop transports and the big gunboats, gathered and came to a halt south of North Point. At the bow of the leading troop ship, Major General Robert Ross turned to the captain.

"This as far as you can go?"

"Yes, sir, it is. The river ahead is too shallow for the men-o'-war and the heavy troop ships. We'll have to land your men here."

Ross turned back to his aide. "Have they all received their rations and ammunition?"

The aide bobbed his head. "A light pack, three-days' cooked rations, eighty rounds of ammunition. Yes, sir, they're ready."

Ross pointed in the dark. "We'll put them ashore there, on the west side of North Point. Send light gun brigs and barges with carronades to escort the landing boats in the event of enemy fire. Start at three o'clock AM."

At three o'clock in the morning, under a waning moon, the British regulars went over the side of the troop ships into waiting landing craft, and oarsmen bent their backs to turn the boats toward shore. Dawn found the British light landing craft steadily moving the red-coated troops ashore, with General Ross and Admiral Cochrane waiting, giving directions to each arriving division. The sun had risen when a scout pulled his horse to a stop before Ross.

"Sir, there's some sort of defenses about four miles west, up Long Log Lane. It looks like the Americans have militia there in a line that could be a mile long."

"How many?"

"I don't know, sir. They're in the woods and across the road. Could be a large number."

"Are they moving?"

"No, sir. Waiting."

Ross turned to Admiral Cockburn. "I think I'm going to scout ahead. Would you care to come?"

The admiral nodded and ordered an aide to bring his horse. Ross turned to Colonel Arthur Brooke, his next in command.

"I'm going on ahead and taking the Light Brigade with me. I'm leaving you in command. When the artillery is ashore, move the remainder of our forces west toward the city, on Long Log Road. I'll be waiting somewhere ahead of you."

The sudden decision caught Brooke by surprise, and for a moment he stared, then spoke.

"Yes, sir. How far ahead?"

Ross shrugged. "That depends on what we find up ahead. You keep coming. I'll find you."

"Yes, sir."

Ross wheeled his horse, and with Admiral Cockburn beside him, led the Light Brigade marching west on Long Log Road toward Baltimore.

Brooke watched them for a time while he adjusted to the shock of finding himself responsible to move more than two thousand men with cannon and horses into what could become a head-on, do-or-die battle with stubborn Americans who had been preparing for months. He took a deep breath and quickly strode to the banks of the river to direct the landing of the heavy guns.

The sun was three hours high when the last of the six heavy cannon and two howitzers, with their carriages and horses, were on land, and the heat of the day was building. There were yet over one thousand men on the ships waiting for their turn to board the barges for the trip to shore. Sweating officers and silent men turned to Brooke for orders.

"I'm taking a company to find General Ross. Continue unloading. I'll either return or send a message back when I know what lies ahead."

With one company of red-coated regulars following, Brooke started west toward the city, sitting tall in the saddle, studying the road ahead and the thick forest cradling the road, missing nothing that moved.

Behind him, Vice Admiral Alexander Cochrane stood on the bow of his flagship on the river, intently watching the tricky business of unloading four thousand troops, with equipment, food, horses, cannon, muskets, and ammunition, without an accident. Noon was approaching when the landing craft delivered the last of the troops and their guns ashore, and Cochrane ran semaphore flags up his mainmast. The message they delivered to his fleet was clear:

"I am transferring to a schooner. All shallow draft vessels bearing guns will follow my schooner up the Patapsco River. We will be visible to all American observation posts and to the city of Baltimore for purposes of distracting and frightening them. We will then take positions to bombard the city when the ground forces of General Ross make their assault."

The light, shallow-draft schooner came alongside the flagship, and the two crews rigged the hawsers between them. Experienced hands tied Cochrane into the wooden chair and swung him out over the rail of the huge gunboat, across the fifteen feet of water separating the two vessels, and down to the deck of the schooner. Minutes later the small ship veered to port and started up the Patapsco River with all other shallow-draft vessels bearing cannon falling into formation to follow.

On the shore, Colonel Brooke turned to his aide.

"How far do you judge we've come?"

"About four miles, sir."

"I expected to meet General Ross before now. Have I—"

The aide's arm shot up to point. "Just ahead, sir. There are some earthworks near that creek and a farmhouse beyond. See them? If I recall the map correctly, sir, that is Back Creek, and a man named Gorsuch owns the farm."

Brooke called a halt while he extended his telescope and carefully scanned the entire area, then handed the telescope to his aide.

"Can you see any Americans—anything—moving in those earthworks?"

The aide raised the telescope for a time, then handed it back to Brooke. "No, sir. Nothing."

"Keep a sharp eye."

Brooke gave the command, and the column moved forward once again, watching the creek bed and the farmhouse. As they reached Back Creek, Brooke called a halt and rode among his troops.

"We'll take one hour here to let the column close up and rest. Eat something. Find some shade if you can."

Grateful, weary, sweating soldiers dropped their packs and reached for their canteens while Brooke rode to the head of his column. He was just dismounting his horse when his aide pointed toward the farmhouse in the distance.

"There, sir. I believe that is General Ross."

Brooke turned to look, surprised to see Ross and Admiral Cockburn sitting on the back steps of the Gorsuch farmhouse, hats in their hands.

Beyond them, in the shade of the farm buildings, were the men of the Light Brigade, at rest. Brooke reined his horse around and rode the dusty road to meet the two as they stood.

Ross settled his hat back on his head. "What's the condition of your column?"

"Good, sir. I stopped them to rest while those behind close."

Ross nodded his agreement. "Admiral Cockburn and I have done some scouting. We're convinced we should move forward to make an early morning attack on Baltimore. I need you to go back to prompt all troops to march here as quickly as possible, with their cannon. We'll be—"

Ross stopped at the sound of an incoming horse at full gallop, and they watched as a messenger reined his mount to a sliding halt.

"Sir," the man exclaimed, "a patrol just captured three American cavalrymen from the First Baltimore Hussars. The patrol's not far behind, bringing them here for interrogation. The lieutenant sent me ahead to tell you."

Minutes later the three grim-faced Americans were standing before Ross, Cockburn, and Brooke, mouths clamped shut, eyes cast down in defiance.

Ross spoke to the sergeant in charge. "You're from the First Baltimore Hussars?"

The man nodded once.

"Who's your commanding officer?"

"Captain James Sterret."

"Where is your regiment located right now?"

"Baltimore."

"Which regiments are between this place and Baltimore? Where are they? How many? Who's in command?"

The sergeant's eyes were steady, unreadable. "There are twenty thousand troops in Baltimore. Armed and ready."

"Militia?"

"Mostly."

Ross tossed a hand up in contempt. "I don't care if it rains militia! How many trained regulars?"

"I do not know."

"Who's in command?"

"General Samuel Smith."

"Smith's at Hampstead Hill?"

"Last I heard."

Ross glanced at Cockburn, then spoke to the lieutenant and his squad. "Take them away. Hold them as prisoners."

None of the British officers saw the quick glance and the silent communication that passed between the three American prisoners. The British officers believed the road to Baltimore was clear of American forces until it reached Hampstead Hill, and the prisoners were not going to tell them otherwise. Not one of the British officers was aware of American brigadier general John Stricker and his command, dug in and waiting in ambush in the forest ahead.

Ross turned back to Brooke and Cockburn as the squad started its prisoners back toward the main road.

"Our scouting patrols have confirmed most of what that sergeant just said. I don't think we're going to meet substantial resistance until we reach Hampstead Hill." He spoke to Brooke. "Colonel, go on back and bring the balance of our forces here as soon as possible. We're moving ahead at once."

"Yes, sir."

Each of them felt the rise of tension as Brooke mounted his horse. It was coming—the long-awaited collision between the stubborn Baltimore defenders and the British who had sworn to punish them.

Ross and Cockburn called for their horses and gave their orders. With an advance scouting platoon moving ahead, they marched their command from the Gorsuch farm to Long Log Lane and turned west, toward Baltimore. They had covered two miles with Ross and Cockburn leading, mounted on their horses, when they heard the distant firing of muskets ahead.

Instantly Ross reined in his horse and turned his head to listen, eyes closed, trying to read the sounds. The shots were sporadic at first, then quickly they were continuous and heavy.

He turned to Cockburn. "The advance scouts are engaged up there! Follow me."

He jammed his spurs home, and his horse reached a full gallop in four jumps with Cockburn straining to catch up. Ross held the reckless pace for more than half a mile through the dense forest that flashed by on both sides of Long Log Road before he burst into the open with flat fields stretching for more than five hundred yards ahead. He saw the crimson coats of his regulars facing the forest, firing and reloading and moving slowly ahead. He saw the gun flashes of American muskets and rifles moving back in the darkness of the woods, and he hunched forward over the neck of his laboring mount as he came in behind his men with but one thought flashing in his mind—*The Americans should not be there—what have we run into?—who are they?*

Then the sure knowledge hit him. *Stricker! We've run into the advance guard of Stricker's command! They were supposed to be back at Hampstead Hill!*

Startled, he pulled his winded mount to a stop near the front of the British line and amid the din of musket and rifle fire and the whining of bullets, shouted to the captain in command.

"How many of them?"

"I don't know, sir. One minute there was nothing, and the next minute those woods came alive with musket and rifle fire."

For what seemed an eternity, Ross peered ahead at the American line. It was only partially visible. The greater part was indistinct shadows and the yellow winking of rifle muzzles in the dark density of the woods. Ross made his estimate of the numbers.

"That has to be some of Stricker's troops," he shouted, "and there are too many of them! We'll need a stronger force! I'm going back to bring up the main column!"

With the captain watching, Ross started to turn his horse when the captain heard the hit and the grunt in the same instant and saw Ross take the shock as the rifle bullet punched into his chest. Ross buckled forward and pitched headfirst from the saddle and hit the ground rolling, and the horse reared and threw its head, pivoted and started to run back, away from the gunfire.

For an instant the captain stood frozen, horrified. Ross was down! Their leader, down! In an instant he was on his knees beside Ross, and he rolled him onto his back. He saw the great red gout spreading on his chest, and he saw the mouth sagged open and the eyes half closed and then other men were clamoring around him, and they seized the limp body and lifted it and started toward the rear of the battle line. Soldiers on all sides stopped to stare as they passed, and those coming forward slowed and gaped in disbelief.

Far to the rear, urging the main body of the command forward, Brooke saw the cluster of men and knew something was violently wrong and started forward on his horse. He had covered thirty yards when he passed Lieutenant George De Lacy Evans standing white-faced, nearly disoriented, and Evans called to him, "It's General Ross, sir! He is fallen!"

Ross! Fallen! Brooke pushed his way to the center of the gathered soldiers and stared down at the lifeless body with his brain numb, unable to accept it. He had no concept of how long he stood thus, staring down, before he raised his head and looked at those around him. The sweating soldiers were staring at him, and suddenly he realized that he was now their commanding officer!

Instinct and British discipline came welling up inside Brooke. He licked at dry lips and heard himself giving orders to his officers as he pointed to them in succession.

"Major, get a detail and move General Ross to the ambulance at the rear!

"Major, go forward and tell the officers to prepare to march. Tell them that is what General Ross would expect of us, and we're going to do it!

"Captain, get my horse and my aides! I'm riding to the head of this command and we're advancing at once!"

With Brooke mounted and leading, the entire force moved forward, across the big open field near the Gorsuch farm, firing, reloading, firing, with the Americans steadily fading back into the woods in an organized withdrawal, returning fire, setting the farm buildings and haystacks ablaze to hinder the British, slowly giving ground while their deadly rifle fire continued knocking British soldiers to the ground.

With the sun setting, Stricker continued the withdrawal to avoid a fight in the night, while purple storm clouds mounted up. In deep dusk a chill, steady rain came pelting, and by midnight the roads and fields were a quagmire of mud. Men in the trenches were standing ankle-deep in water and mud, huddled, watching, protecting as best they could their gunpowder from the rain.

Stricker gave orders, and under cover of rain and the black of night, his force withdrew toward Hampstead Hill, cutting trees and dragging them into the road to slow the British and their caissons of mounted cannon. The rain held, and in the soggy gray of early morning both armies heard the first sound of cannon being fired from British ships anchored in the shallow waters off Fort McHenry.

It was approaching midmorning when Brooke caught his first sight of the battle lines and the gun emplacements and the trenches Samuel Smith had established to defend the city, and Brooke stopped in his tracks. He turned to his aide, pointing.

"I thought Stricker was the main force! He was not! There must be eleven thousand men ahead of us. Over a hundred cannon! Look at those roads and open fields we must traverse—mud! Our troops and cannon would mire down and become sitting targets! A daylight attack is out of the question. We'll send scouts out to probe their lines for the possibility of a night attack."

Brooke gave orders, and his scouts moved off the road, into the woods bordering Philadelphia Road, slipping, slogging through the mud to within one mile of the American lines at the edge of the city. Dead ahead, through the rain, they could see the Americans in the trenches and count their cannon, and they saw the Americans studying their every move through telescopes. The British skirmishers moved to their right, and the Americans followed, then back to their left, and the Americans were there also—waiting.

Without a word, the scouts returned to Brooke and made their report with the boom of the cannon on the British ships to the south sounding in the background.

"Sir, there are thousands of them, and they're watching every move we make. We moved twice, hoping to draw some of them out of their trenches, but they did not move. I believe they mean to make their stand right where they are. A daylight attack would be a serious mistake."

For a time Brooke paced, trying to conceive a plan to attack the American lines, and there was none. In frustration he reached the only conclusion he could.

"We will remain where we are for now. We'll have to wait until the fleet reduces the city's defenses with their cannon. Then we will make our attack. Tell the men to get what rest they can and some food."

Brooke's jaw was set as he peered west, toward the river and Fort McHenry. *Where's Cochrane? When will he take Fort McHenry?*

On board the *Cockchafer,* Cochrane lowered his telescope and turned to his first mate.

"Something's wrong with Ross and his forces. Their guns are silent." For a time he paced and considered before he turned and gave orders.

"Have the fleet take the positions previously described for bombardment of Fort McHenry."

Semaphore flags went up the mainmast, and with the dusk coming on, the British gunboats began to slowly maneuver into battle positions. Through the night, with the rain dwindling, the lighter craft moved ahead of the heavier men-of-war into the shallow waters and avoided the log boom and the hulks of the ships sunk by the Americans to block the British advance. Carefully they came, silently taking their places in the dark of night. The frigates *Seahorse, Surprise,* and *Severn* with their brigs and tenders, remained five miles from Fort McHenry. The bomb ships *Meteor, Aetna, Devastation, Terror,* and *Volcano,* and the rocket ship *Erebus,* escorted by the brig *Cockchafer,* took up positions just over two miles from the fort.

In the early dawn, with the rain thinned, the British vessels were all anchored in place. Cochrane drew his pocket watch and read the time. Exactly five o'clock AM, September 13, 1814. Cochrane turned and nodded to his second in command, and the semaphores went up the mainmast with the message: "Fire for effect!"

The guns of the bomb ship *Volcano* thundered, and the British commanders watched through telescopes while the heavy shot raised geysers forty feet high in the water, short of Fort McHenry. Again Cochrane gave orders, and the British fleet moved half a mile closer to shore, broadside to Fort McHenry, and again dropped anchor.

When they were in place, Cochrane gave the order:

"Commence firing!"

Every gun in the British fleet facing Fort McHenry bucked and roared. The sound and the concussion shook foundations of buildings in Baltimore as the cannonballs and bombs and rockets streaked toward Fort McHenry, and the British seamen heard the distant explosions and saw the orange flames and black smoke erupt into the overcast clouds and the drizzle of rain as the bombardment ripped into the American defenses in and around the fort.

The British were reloading when the guns of Fort McHenry blasted their answer, and the crews on the British gunboats hunched down behind their guns, waiting for the barrage to hit. Geysers leaped thirty feet in the air all through the British fleet, while some cannonballs shattered railings and tore through the riggings. Aboard the *Cockchafer,* Admiral Cochrane peered up at the black, ragged holes in the mainsail and gave orders.

The entire British fleet hoisted anchor and moved back to a range where the American guns could not reach the British ships, but the heavy guns of the British bomb ships could still reach the fort.

The prologue was ended. The time had come. Cochrane turned to his second in command. "Commence firing, and do not stop until Fort McHenry is utterly destroyed."

The semaphores went up the mainmast, and moments later every gun that could be brought to bear on the distant fort fired. Flames and white smoke filled the air, and the constant roar and concussion shook Baltimore in the distance. Rockets streaked through the air. Bombs detonated above the fort to leave ugly black splotches in the sky and blow chunks of white-hot metal onto everything below. Cannonballs tore the ground all around the fort while some dropped inside to smash anything they hit.

Standing on the parapet of the fort, Major Armistead shouted his orders.

"Cease fire! Cease fire! The British are out of range of our guns. Conserve your ammunition."

The American gunners took cover behind and beneath their guns and waited, heads bowed, teeth gritted, hands clapped over their ears to soften the deafening sounds of the heaviest bombardment any American had ever heard. Slowly, as the morning wore on, the skies over the fort filled with clusters of black smoke and the trails of streaking rockets and clouds of gray smoke from the fires, inside and outside the walls of the fort.

In late morning, Admiral Cochrane extended his telescope and for a long time studied the distant view of the battered walls, searching for a white flag, but there was none. He shook his head in disbelief. *What is Armistead doing?—He must know we can bring the entire fort and all his men to the ground—Why is he sacrificing them?*

On board the British bomb ships, the British crews were stripped to the waist, sweat dripping, ears ringing as they continued the loading and firing of the cannon. Gun barrels overheated, and heat waves rose shimmering. Seamen threw buckets of river water on the guns, sizzling, turning to steam instantly, to cool them enough that they would not ignite the next load of powder while it was being loaded. Gun crews were trotting into the hold of the ships to carry barrels of powder and rockets and cannonballs to the gun positions to keep the batteries supplied and firing.

At midday, Cochrane again raised his telescope to study the fort, and again he shook his head. For a time he disappeared into his cabin to write a message, then returned to the deck to find his first mate.

"Have that delivered to General Ross on shore, earliest."

"A message for General Ross, sir?"

"Yes. I doubt we have ever mounted a bombardment as heavy as the one now in progress, and I see no sign of surrender. If we cannot take Fort McHenry, we cannot provide cannon support for General Ross if he attacks Boston. If the Americans in Baltimore are of the same resolve as those at Fort McHenry, taking the city might cost more in British lives than it is worth. I would like an opinion from General Ross."

"Yes, sir." The first mate gave orders, and a longboat was launched. An hour later it returned, and the lieutenant in command reported.

"Sir, General Ross is a casualty. He is dead."

Cochrane's mouth dropped open. "Dead?"

"Some time ago. Colonel Brooke has assumed command of the ground forces."

Admiral Cochrane took his written message, drew a line through the name of General Robert Ross and beneath it wrote, "Colonel Arthur Brooke."

"Deliver it," he said. Less than an hour later the lieutenant again reported and handed a brief written message to Cochrane, signed by Brooke.

"Unless Fort McHenry is taken, committing my command to attack Baltimore would be disastrous."

Cochrane stuffed the note inside his tunic, and the thunder of the cannon and the rockets continued without pause.

On the deck of a sloop not far behind the ship *Cockchafer* where Cochrane stood on the quarterdeck, the Americans Francis Scott Key, John Skinner, and Dr. William Beanes paced the bow, sick in their hearts at the sight to the northeast. The air was filled with white cannon smoke from the British guns and the black trails of countless rockets. On the distant shore, Fort McHenry was lost in a cloud of dirty smoke, and the guns of the fort were silent. The minds of the three American prisoners were filled with their worst fears—*Is the fort destroyed?*—*Are the defenders all dead?*—*or gone?*—*Have we lost Baltimore?*

There were no answers, and they continued to pace, sick with dread, while the British guns continued to roar.

Inside Fort McHenry, Major George Armistead stood outside the door of his headquarters on the edge of the parade ground, where he had been through most of the day. Again and again, he turned to look at the powder magazine, a sizeable red-brick building with a wooden shingle roof, in one corner of the fort. It held three hundred barrels of gunpowder, and only he knew that it was not bomb-proof. If a British cannonball were to ignite the gunpowder inside, the explosion would blow Fort McHenry and everything, everyone inside, into oblivion.

While he stood there, three huge mortar shells landed inside the fort. A woman water carrier, running with water to a waiting gun crew went down and did not move. An officer and the enlisted man next to him were blown ten feet, sprawling, still.

Then, while Armistead watched, a cannonball smashed through the roof of the powder magazine, and for a moment Armistead stood in breathless horror waiting for the blast that would blow the walls of the fort into kindling and kill everyone in sight. A second passed, then another, then another, while Armistead stood staring, waiting, and then he began to breathe again and relief flooded through his entire system.

The British cannonball was a dud! It had not exploded!

Armistead ran toward the magazine, shouting to the nearest soldiers. "Move the gunpowder! Move it! Scatter the barrels in small numbers all over the fort!"

Soldiers broke from cover, battered down the locked door of the magazine, and within minutes the gunpowder supply was stacked under cover at locations along all four walls.

Toward the rear of the fort, a bandy rooster had escaped the partially destroyed regimental hen house, and through the smoke and the terrifying explosions of rockets and bombs, had scurried to an open ditch to take refuge. The disoriented bird was beyond all understanding of what had happened to its dull, repetitive life inside the fort. Gone were the morning reveille, the women gathering the eggs, the grain in the feed troughs, the daily drill of the soldiers on the parade ground— replaced by men and women running in all directions in what appeared to be total chaos, the thunder of rockets and exploding cannonballs, and the strike that had torn down part of the chicken yard, sending hens scattering—the world had gone insane!

The colorful, feisty little bird had had enough! He scrambled out of the ditch and perched himself on top of the dirt bank, threw back his head, and crowed out his anger and his frustration for the world to hear!

A dozen soldiers crouched behind anything that would protect them heard the sound and raised their heads in astonishment. A crowing rooster? In the midst of the worst bombardment in history?

The little bird peered at them with his beady eyes and threw back his head and cut loose again.

A soldier nearby grinned, and the man next to him chuckled, and the laughter spread.

"Little friend," one soldier called, "if we both survive this, you get an extra ration of grain."

It was past midafternoon when Admiral Cochrane again took his place on the quarterdeck of the *Cockchafer* and carefully glassed the fort. He could see little of the structure through the smoke and haze and the light rain that continued to fall. He collapsed his telescope and for a time was lost in thought. Then he raised his head and called orders to his first mate.

"I believe we have crippled them. Order the *Devastation*, the *Volcano*, and the *Erebus* to close on the fort and increase their fire."

"Yes, sir."

Minutes later the huge *Devastation*, followed by her two sister bomb ships, hoisted anchor and began their move toward the fort.

Inside the fort, a gun crew on the parapet peered outward through the smoke and the light rain and shielded their eyes for a moment before they shouted to the nearest officer.

"They're moving in, sir. There!"

Within moments the American gun crews, excited at the chance to fire back, had elevated their gun muzzles and were waiting with smoking linstocks for the order to fire. The officer in charge held up his hand, holding them off, while he gauged the distance, waiting, waiting. And then he dropped his hand as he shouted, "Fire!"

Every American gun blasted, and cannonballs ripped through the rigging of the *Devastation*. The railing of the *Volcano* was smashed, and she was hulled twice. Immediately, the *Erebus* was near totally disabled and survived only because the frigate *Severn* came to tow her out of range. The *Devastation* and the *Volcano* turned about and retreated out of the reach of the American guns.

It was clear to every man in the British fleet that whatever their bombardment had accomplished, it had not yet disabled the American guns, nor had it damaged the spirit and pride of their crews. The British seamen shook their heads in grudging admiration.

Cochrane watched in disbelief. How many tons of rockets and shells and cannonballs had they rained on Fort McHenry? A thousand? How could a wooden fort withstand such an assault?

In frustration, with deep dusk settling and heavy rain now pouring, he ordered landing parties to go ashore, probing, to be certain what Brooke was doing with his land forces and to determine whether or not the American lines defending Baltimore were still entrenched, waiting.

The landing parties returned in the black of night, shot up, bearing their dead and wounded. Their report was clear. Brooke is not going to move without naval support. The American lines are in place, standing in mud up above their ankles, waiting, and full of fight.

Cochrane gave the only order he could to the British fleet: "Continue firing!"

The heavy British guns continued the bombardment. The muzzle blasts of their guns lighted up the night sky, and their rockets made fiery streaks through the rain, while the bombs bursting above the fort showed the gaping, splintered holes where the cannonballs had smashed through. But it was still standing!

On the deck of the sloop behind the *Cockchafer*, soaked to the skin, squinting in the rain, the Americans, Key, Skinner, and Beanes, stood at the rail, transfixed, watching the British warships rain destruction on the fort as never before in history. They saw the yellow fire trails of the rockets and the white bursts of bombs over the fort, and they listened to the continuous roar of the big guns, staring, unable to believe that Armistead had not surrendered rather than face total destruction.

They stood in the rain into the night, watching, hoping, while the

British guns continued—their only evidence that the fort had not fallen. The rain came heavier, and still they paced and watched and listened, not knowing the fate of the fort, only knowing that the British bombardment was unrelenting. Time became meaningless. They were unaware that dawn was approaching until the first hint of the separation of the heavens from the earth came in the east, and then they could see the faint line of the horizon.

Key stood frozen to the rail as the dull light strengthened in the rain, and he could see the dim outline of the fort.

Was it still standing?

Something fluttered above the black outline, and then it took form and shape, and Key gasped when he understood it was the flag! Armistead had raised the largest flag in the United States above the fort! Thirty-two by forty-three feet! Each of the fifteen stars was two feet from point to point, and the red and white stripes were clearly visible as the monstrous flag furled and unfurled in the breeze. Every man on every ship in the British fleet could see it, and to a man they understood Armistead's message:

"We're still here! We've taken close to eighteen hundred rockets and bombs and cannonballs. We've been through the heaviest bombardment in naval history! We've lost men and women, and we've been hurt, but we're still here, beneath the biggest flag in the country!"

Key's heart was pounding in his chest. He wiped at his eyes and then reached inside his coat for an envelope and a pencil, and began to write the thoughts that came flooding from deep within.

> *Oh say, can you see, by the dawn's early light,*
> *What so proudly we hailed at the twilight's last gleaming,*
> *Whose broad stripes and bright stars, through the perilous fight,*
> *O'er the ramparts we watched, were so gallantly streaming?*
> *And the rockets' red glare, the bombs bursting in air,*
> *Gave proof through the night that our flag was still there.*
> *Oh say, does that star-spangled banner yet wave*
> *O'er the land of the free and the home of the brave?*

He paused for a moment, then catching sight again of the great flag waving over the fort, he continued to write, revising as he went, scratching out some words and rearranging lines, as the second stanza took shape:

On the shore, dimly seen thru the mists of the deep,
Where the foe's haughty host in dread silence reposes,
What is that which the breeze, o'er the towering steep,
As it fitfully blows, half conceals, half discloses?
Now it catches the gleam of the morning's first beam,
In full glory reflected now shines on the stream;
'Tis the star-spangled banner! Oh, long may it wave
O'er the land of the free and the home of the brave!

Reflecting on the heroic defenders of Baltimore, Key's breast was filled with patriotic emotion, and he quickly penned:

Oh, thus be it ever, when free men shall stand
Between their loved homes and the war's desolation!
Blest with vic'try and peace, may the heav'n rescued land
Praise the Pow'r that hath made and preserved us a nation!
Then conquer we must, when our cause it is just,
And this be our motto: "In God is our trust!"
And the star-spangled banner in triumph shall wave
O'er the land of the free and the home of the brave!

In the gray of the rainy dawn, a longboat thumped against the hull of the *Cockchafer*, and a dripping lieutenant scaled the rope ladder up to her deck to face Admiral Cochrane and his first mate standing by.

"Sir, a message from Colonel Brooke."

Cochrane unfolded the message, read it, read it again, and nodded to the young man. "You may return to Colonel Brooke. Tell him I understand. I will meet him at the place we landed his troops near North Point. Am I clear?"

"Yes, sir. You are." He turned and disappeared over the rail, back to his longboat.

The first mate, with rain running in a stream from his hat, stopped the admiral.

"Sir, did I understand we are meeting Colonel Brooke and his ground forces?"

Cochrane stared at him for a moment. "You did. He has withdrawn. There will be no attack on Baltimore. He requests that we meet him to pick up his army at the place we put them ashore, far back near North Point. Give the orders by lantern code and by semaphores. All ships are to break off the engagement, weigh anchor, and follow us."

In the overcast and the rain, the lanterns of the *Cockchafer* blinked out the message while the semaphores went up the mainmast, and the British fleet weighed anchor. One by one the ships fell into formation to abandon all thoughts of taking Fort McHenry or Baltimore and followed their flagship back down the Patapsco River to North Point, where they were to load their army back onto the troop transports and leave, a dispirited and unsuccessful army and navy.

True to his word, Admiral Cochrane ordered the release of Francis Scott Key, John Skinner, and Dr. William Beanes, and the three men made their way back to their homes.

At Fort McHenry, when Major Armistead was certain the British retreat was real, the surviving occupants of the fort went into near hysteria with relief. Hats were thrown into the air amid shouts, and a spontaneous celebration lasted through most of the day, despite the rain.

Half a dozen soldiers went to the ditch at the rear of the fort and found the bandy rooster. They returned him to the hen house with the rest of the chickens and very carefully rationed out two-days' worth of wheat and grain, and chuckled as the colorful little fellow strutted about, pecking away at it.

On the parapet, Major Armistead watched with a deep feeling of pride and satisfaction in what his people had done. They had defied the concentrated power of the mighty British army and navy, and with every expectation to be crushed, had by some miracle survived.

His thoughts sobered and deepened—*We turned them, and we hurt them. But they are not defeated. Where will they strike next? And with what force? Have we won the battle of Fort McHenry and Baltimore only to face the loss of the war?*

He straightened and started down the stairs to the shell-pocked parade ground.

Only time will tell.

Notes

The names of all officers appearing in this chapter, both British and American, too numerous to list in detail, and the part each played in this entire episode, are accurate. The geographic locations listed and the names of those locations, also too numerous to list in detail, and the events that took place at those locations, are also accurate. The names of all ships listed, and their participation, are correct.

The participation of Francis Scott Key and John Skinner in obtaining the release of Dr. William Beanes is correctly set forth. The two men were held prisoner during the bombardment of Fort McHenry for the reasons described. The poem written by Key as he saw the huge American flag waving above Fort McHenry the morning of September fourteenth became the American national anthem, "The Star-Spangled Banner."

Mary Young Pickersgill was commissioned by General Armistead to create the huge flag that was flown above Fort McHenry in the stormy dawn hours of September 14, 1814, as proof the fort was still standing and had not surrendered. The flag was in fact thirty-two feet by forty-three feet, with stars two feet between the points. At a cost of $405.90, it was sewn by Mrs. Pickersgill and her thirteen-year-old daughter, Caroline, on the floor of the local malt brewery—the only place in town big enough for the work.

Between fifteen hundred and eighteen hundred rockets, bombs, and cannonballs were fired by the British on Fort McHenry, the heaviest naval bombardment in history to that date.

The rather humorous incident of the Reverend John Gruber of the First Methodist Church on Light Street in Baltimore, wherein he dismissed his congregation to take their places in the defenses of Baltimore on Sunday, September 11, 1814, with his prayer for King George, is accurate. His prayer for the king is a verbatim quotation.

A carronade is a short, light cannon, with less range than the heavier guns.

The comic incident of the little bandy rooster taking exception to the British bombardment, including the fact the little fellow survived and received a double ration of grain, is historically accurate.

The miraculous incident of the British cannonball hitting the powder magazine inside Fort McHenry and failing to explode is also accurate.

The reader is advised that despite its unusual length, this chapter presents only the core events of the British effort to take Baltimore. There were many, many more officers involved, and many more military skirmishes and events; however, including them would have extended and complicated this chapter far too much.

See Whitehorne, *The Battle for Baltimore 1814,* pp. 159–94; Sheads, *Fort McHenry,* pp. 33–43, and see the maps, pp. 36 and 39; Hickey, *The War of 1812,* pp. 202–03; Wills, *James Madison,* p. 140; Stagg, *Mr. Madison's War,* pp. 427–428; Barbuto, *Niagara 1814,* pp. 270–71.

CHAPTER XXV

★ ★ ★

apor trails followed Caleb Dunson as he opened the office door of Dunson & Weems Shipping Company, walked in, and closed it against the light sifting of snow just beginning on the freezing Boston waterfront.

"Gentlemen," he said. He laid a Monday morning newspaper on the counter and shrugged out of his topcoat and hung it on a peg beside the door.

Matthew raised his head, glanced at his brother, said nothing, and continued with the paperwork on his desk. Adam nodded and went on with the papers on his desk. John Dunson muttered, "Good morning," and reached for the next invoice.

"Billy?" Caleb asked.

Matthew answered, "Collecting the mail. Expecting a check from the Hubert Company."

Caleb walked to his desk with the newspaper in hand, laid it down, and stepped to the big black stove. He used a stick of kindling to open the door, thrust half a dozen sticks of wood inside, slammed the door clanging, and returned to his desk. "Seen the morning newspaper?"

His brothers and nephew stopped work and looked up, waiting.

Caleb spread the paper on his desk and tapped the article on the front page. "This business down in Louisiana—New Orleans," Caleb continued, "Andy Jackson's at it again. That war with the Creek Indians wasn't enough. Now he's in New Orleans getting ready for the British."

The other three men said nothing, waiting.

"Seems Jackson got there December 1 on orders from the War Department. Took one look and concluded General Wilkinson had made his usual mess of things and set about getting it all back in order. Declared martial law. Shook the governor—Claiborne-—and irritated the local gentry. He told them they were either with him or against him. No middle ground. Those against him would be treated as enemies. Things got a bit testy, but when he ordered all waterways to the city blockaded and cannon batteries established and a communication system to keep everyone alert to what was going on, they took a better view of him. Things settled."

Caleb stopped to glance at the paper, then went on.

"The British sent a sizeable fleet loaded with troops from Florida to seize New Orleans, and they decided to take up a position on Lake Borgne—close to the city—on the east side—to do it. When they got there, they ran into five American gunboats and a hundred eighty-five men under command of Thomas Jones who had been sent by Jackson to scout out the British. The wind died, and Jones didn't have oars to make a run, so he had to fight the whole British fleet. That lasted about ten minutes. Jones and all his men and ships were casualties or captured."

The other three men were listening intently.

Caleb shrugged. "The shooting's started down there. Jackson's sent out a proclamation, requesting everyone—-military, civilian, regulars—everyone—to help build the defenses. He's determined the big battle he sees coming will not be fought in the city. It will be fought somewhere else, miles away."

Matthew interrupted. "Anyone responding to his proclamation? His request for help?"

Caleb threw up a hand. "*Everybody* down there's responding. Creoles, Cajuns, French, Spanish, blacks, whites, merchants, lawyers, old, young—everybody. The paper says they're building a breastwork along the north side of the big Rodriguez Canal and digging cannon emplacements all along it. Runs about a mile, from the Mississippi to a swamp. That's where Jackson intends making his stand."

Adam asked, "How many?"

"So far, thousands."

Adam continued. "How many are military?"

"The paper says besides those who came with Jackson, he's asked for riflemen from Kentucky and Tennessee. It looks like the governors of those states are going to send them."

Adam asked again. "How many?"

"About fifteen hundred from Kentucky and Tennessee. That will bring Jackson's fighting men to above four thousand."

Matthew broke in. "Who's in command of the British forces?"

Caleb consulted the newspaper. "Pakenham," he said. "General Pakenham. His next in command are generals Keane and Gibbs."

"Where are they right now? How close to New Orleans?"

"Pakenham hasn't arrived yet. He sent a probing party ahead. He's on his way."

"No indication of where the British intend making their attack?"

"It's clear they intend taking New Orleans. Where they mean to attack is not yet known."

Adam said, "Caleb, you met Governor Claiborne. Is he capable of handling all this?"

Caleb shook his head. "No. Not even close. But that problem disappeared when Jackson declared martial law. He now overrides the governor, and Claiborne knows it. I think Claiborne's even relieved about it."

John interrupted. "Is Jackson going to have to contend with Jean and Pierre Lafitte? I know Jackson once called the Lafittes and their whole band of pirates 'infernal banditti.'"

For several seconds Caleb reflected, while all three men stared, not moving, waiting in the silence.

"I've thought about that. I don't know. If Jackson does, he's in trouble. The Lafitte brothers and their bunch are held in high regard by the whole town, or at least they were when I was down there—what, seven years ago? When Governor Claiborne decided to get rid of them he posted a reward for their capture. Five hundred dollars. Jean Lafitte laughed at it and put out his own posters, all over New Orleans. Fifteen hundred dollars for the capture of Governor Claiborne. The town laughed with Lafitte, and the governor backed down. Jackson better be careful. If he provokes the Lafittes, they could do some real damage."

Matthew asked, "How many in the Laffites's crew?"

"About a thousand. A little over. But it's not their numbers. It's what they can do with cannon and rifles and how well they know New Orleans, clear down past Barataria, to the Gulf of Mexico. Those men are the best cannoneers in the country, and they know every creek, every bayou, every alligator within a hundred miles of New Orleans."

"Who are his seconds in command?"

"Beluche and Dominique You. Totally dedicated to Lafitte. Some of the best men in battle in the country."

Adam cut in. "Anyone said how many ships Pakenham has?"

"About sixty."

Adam started. "Sixty! That means he's going to have around ten, maybe twelve thousand regulars, with cannon. That's just a bit lopsided, if Jackson has only four or five thousand."

Caleb shrugged. "That's how it's shaping up."

Matthew leaned forward and broke in. "I think we better be careful here. New Orleans is a long ways away, and there's going to be a heavy battle. I hope none of you are getting any notions about going down there."

Adam stared thoughtfully at Matthew for a moment, while John looked at Caleb.

Caleb stretched. "You mean we can't go down there? It's the only war we got right now. It would be an outright tragedy if we missed—"

The front door to the office swung open, and all four men turned their heads to watch Billy Weems enter. He laid a small stack of mail on the counter then took off his coat and scarf and hung them.

Matthew called, "Did the Hubert check arrive?"

"Yes. It's in the bank."

With the mail in hand, Billy walked down to Caleb's desk and handed him an envelope.

"From President James Madison."

"What?" Caleb exclaimed. "Madison?"

For a moment a sense of foreboding touched all five men. Caleb broke the seal and studied the signature, then silently read the document while the others remained motionless, waiting. Caleb laid the document on his desk and looked at Billy, then his brothers and nephew, and then handed it to Matthew.

"Read it."

The others waited while Matthew read it silently, then handed it back to Caleb. It was Matthew who broke the silence.

"Madison wants Caleb to go to New Orleans. He's concerned that Jackson will offend the Lafitte brothers, and if he does, Madison foresees serious trouble. He went over Caleb's report from seven years ago and is convinced Caleb can be of value in getting the Lafittes to assist Jackson, not fight him. Madison says it is urgent. He wants Caleb to go now."

Matthew sat fixed. Adam rounded his mouth and softly blew air. Billy studied the floor for several moments. John reached to pick up the letter and silently read it.

Caleb spoke to Matthew. "Can you see a choice in this?"

Matthew slowly shook his head. "No, I can't."

"I think I'm going to New Orleans, whether we like it or not."

Matthew drew a deep breath, and his words came soft and measured. "Not to fight. Not to bear arms. Only to head off trouble between Jackson and Lafitte. Your first responsibility is to Barbara and the children, not to take the risk of battle. That's what the letter says."

Caleb studied his brother for a moment. "What do I do if Jackson orders me to get into the fighting?"

Matthew shook his head. "He can't. You're there under orders of the commanding officer of all American military forces—the president. His orders override all others."

Caleb scratched his head and grinned. "I'll be sure to tell Jackson that just before he shoots me for disobeying a direct order." He turned to Adam. "Don't we have a ship going down into the Gulf of Mexico? Soon? Or is it still too dangerous sending ships down there?"

Adam checked the huge wall chart of the schedule for all Dunson & Weems ships.

"Tomorrow morning. On the four o'clock tide. The *Dorian.* Mobile, Alabama. She carries Franklin stoves going down and cotton on the return. Mobile is reasonably safe now. The British left there a while ago. But New Orleans is still bad. The *Dorian* is fast—a schooner—and I think she can get you in during the night, but she'll have to be back out before daylight."

Caleb turned back to Matthew. "Is it worth the risk?"

Matthew ignored the question. "Just remember what you're down there for. And come home as soon as you can. Mother's failing. You need to be here."

Caleb stood. "I think I better go home and tell Barbara and get packed. I'll need to get some money from the bank. If she needs more money while I'm gone, help her. Anything I should do here before I go?"

There was nothing.

He folded the letter back into its envelope, slipped it into his coat pocket, walked to the front door, and put on his heavy overcoat and scarf. He paused at the door to look back at the four men.

"Will you check on Barbara for me while I'm gone? She'll need wood split for the fireplace. Someone to help clear the snow if it gets heavy."

Billy answered, "We'll check. Every day. Stop and say goodbye to your mother. You be careful."

With his thoughts running and vapor trailing from his mouth as he breathed, Caleb worked his way west through the lightly falling snow, past the largely inactive waterfront, into the cobblestone streets lined with white picket fences and skeleton trees, to the home where he had been raised. He pushed through the front gate, walked up the familiar, worn walk to the front door, rapped, and entered without invitation. Inside, his sister Brigitte was just hurrying through the archway from the bedroom hallway, and she stopped short.

"Caleb! Scare a body half to death!" She blanched and raised a hand to her mouth. "What's wrong? Is it Billy?"

"No, no," he answered. "I received a letter from President Madison this morning. It looks like I'm leaving for New Orleans tomorrow morning. I came by to say goodbye to mother. Is she all right?"

The color returned to Brigitte's face. "She's fine. She's in her bedroom—where I was when you walked in."

"Can I talk to her?"

"Yes, but she's had another one of her spells this morning. She's becoming more addled. This morning she thought Father was at his work bench repairing clocks and watches and building muskets."

Caleb studied his sister for a moment—her deep auburn hair, the hazel eyes, the heart-shaped face. The raising of her children—all grown and away—had brought a few lines around her eyes, but she was still a beautiful woman. "You all right?" he asked.

"I'm fine."

"Can I go see her now?"

"Of course."

Quietly Caleb passed down the hall into the large bedroom at the end. He paid no attention to the worn, familiar chest of drawers and the closet and night stands and lamps. He saw only his mother, lying beneath the thick comforter; the gray hair that Brigitte had brushed and pulled back only minutes before framed a face that showed both the joys and sorrows of more than eighty years of life. He did not see the wrinkles, or the hollow of the cheeks. He saw only the eyes, still bright from the fire within.

He went to one knee beside the bed and took the old, gnarled hand between his two strong ones.

"Are you feeling all right, Mother?"

"Of course."

"Is there anything I can do for you?"

"Yes." The pale blue eyes twinkled. "Be good to Barbara and the children."

Caleb grinned and shook his head. "I try. I came by to tell you. This morning I received a letter from President Madison. He wants me to—"

She broke in. "President Madison? What happened to George Washington? Or was it Jefferson? Thomas Jefferson?"

Caleb smiled at her confusion. "They served their term. James Madison is president now. He wants me to go to New Orleans to help with the war."

Her forehead wrinkled in question. "I thought we won the war."

"We did. The British came back. Remember? We're sending them home for good this time. I have to go help."

"When?"

"Tomorrow morning. I came by to see that you are all right and tell you to mind your manners while I'm gone."

The wrinkled face broke into a grin. "Oh, Caleb, you say the most foolish things! Of course I'll mind my manners." She sobered. "You're not going to be in the fighting, are you?"

"No, that's not what the president asked. I'm just going to help General Jackson with a problem. I'll be back soon."

"You be careful. I'll expect a report when you get back."

"I'll be careful. You rest and take care of yourself."

He stood, with the old hand still clinging to his.

"God bless you, son."

"God bless you, Mother."

He laid the hand with the heavy blue veins and the knuckles that were too big back on the comforter and bent to kiss the lined forehead and then straightened and walked out of the room.

Brigitte followed him to the front door. "If you're leaving, Barbara will have to help you get packed. She was coming over here later this afternoon when I go home. Tell her to stay home with you. I'll take care of things here."

"Thank you. I'll tell her."

The walk to his home passed quickly, and as he was taking off his heavy coat, he called out, "It's me."

Barbara appeared from the kitchen, wearing an apron, wiping her hands on a towel, showing surprise at his being home midmorning. She stopped short, and he saw the leap of fear in her brown eyes.

"What's wrong?"

"Nothing. Sit down with me at the dining table."

He took his place at the head of the table with her facing him to his right. He drew the letter from his inside pocket and handed it to her.

"Read this."

She read the neat handwriting on the envelope, and he watched her breathing stop for a moment. She opened the letter and for a time sat unmoving while she read it, then read it again before she raised her head.

She took a deep breath and forced a smile. "Well. It appears you'll be gone for a while."

"I can't see a way around it. Can you?"

"No. When will you leave?"

"We have a ship leaving tomorrow morning at four o'clock. I will be on it."

She drew breath and released a great sigh, then squared her shoulders. "We better get busy. We have a lot to do."

He reached to grasp her hand. "Is it all right with you? The men in the family will see to it you've got kindling. Remove the snow. If you need money, tell them. They'll get it for you. Whatever else you need. They'll check on you."

She nodded. "I'll be all right."

"I'll have to get some money from the bank today before I go. How much will you need?"

"How long will you be gone?"

"I don't know."

"Then I don't know how much I'll need."

"I'll get enough."

She started to rise, and he reached for her hand and held her down. "Barbara, these things are always worse for the woman than the man. I know that. I just don't know what I can do about it."

"It's all right. It started with Mother Eve. You go and don't worry. I'll be fine. Just be careful. I don't know what I'd do if . . ."

He saw the flicker of panic in her eyes, and he saw her rise above it and smile. "We have a lot to do," she said. "We'd better get busy."

The day passed quickly. Together they chose the clothing he would need, and she began packing the big suitcase while he walked to the bank in the snow to draw out the necessary money for both of them.

They finished supper and worked together to clear the table and wash, dry, and put away the supper dishes. Then they opened a large book of maps on the library table, and laboriously located the Mississippi River, New Orleans on the east bank, Lake Pontchartrain to the north, and Lake Borgne to the east. Later that evening, as the clock struck ten times from the fireplace mantel, Barbara and Caleb knelt beside the dining table for their evening prayers. It was Caleb who sought the blessings of the Almighty to be with her while he was gone. Then, as they got into the bed they had shared for so many years, Caleb held Barbara in his arms as they drifted into sleep.

The snow stopped in the night. At half past three, Caleb buttoned his overcoat, wound his scarf, and for a moment held Barbara close. Then he picked up his suitcase and walked out the door into a frozen, white world with a moon and unnumbered stars overhead, and a cold breeze coming from the west. At four o'clock he walked up the gangplank of the *Dorian* and on to his small quarters next to the captain's.

It was breaking dawn when Caleb saw the lighthouse on the great hook of Cape Cod to the east. By midmorning they cleared the cape, and the breeze had strengthened to an icy wind from the northwest that popped the American flag at the top of the mainmast and held the sails full and steady. The schooner was cutting a thirty-foot curl and leaving a seventy-yard wake in the dark, choppy Atlantic waters, on a heading due south. The freezing wind held to form ice on the bow of the ship and in the rigging where the spray hit and held. At dusk the following day they saw the lighthouse of Cape Hatteras to the west, off the shores of North Carolina, and changed their course to south-southwest, angling for the Florida straits. Days and nights blurred together as they contin-ued south by southwest, until they passed the lighthouse on Grand Bahama Island and changed course once again, into a long, curving line around the southern tip of Florida. There they changed course once again, due west, into the Gulf of Mexico, then on to the southern tip of Louisiana, where the Mississippi River reaches the warmer waters of the Gulf.

The captain held the schooner offshore until deep dusk, then made his way up the river in the blackness, past unsuspecting British gunboats, to a place where barges were tied to half a dozen piers on the east bank of the broad river, one mile short of the lights of New Orleans. He put Caleb ashore in a longboat in the dead of night, two hundred yards upstream of the barges, then turned to make his run with the current for the open waters of the Gulf before the British could see him clearly in the light of dawn.

Onshore, with his suitcase in hand, Caleb felt his way east in the darkness, through the undergrowth and reeds and the tall sea grass to a winding dirt road rutted by wagon tracks. For a time he remained hidden, with the wind rustling the brittle sea grass, watching and listening for patrols on the road—British, American, or pirate—and there were none. He picked up his suitcase and walked north toward the lights winking in the distance, alert to the sounds of the night.

He had covered half the distance when the sound of voices ahead reached him, and he left the roadbed to disappear in the shoulder-high grass. The voices came on, and in the dim light of the stars Caleb counted four men walking south, unsteady, speech slurred, arguing in a blend of French and Spanish over a large bottle. He let them pass and waited for a time before he walked back to the road and continued north.

He stopped short of the town to wait for dawn before he entered the outskirts, then continued on into the streets as New Orleans began to wake up. He made his way past the ancient, stately buildings that bespoke a grace and dignity of a time long past, to find the Absinthe House, where he had taken a room seven years earlier. He pushed through the familiar high, black, iron gates, and walked across the vacant cobblestone courtyard into the foyer of the old two-story mansion to the desk, set his suitcase down hard, and waited.

A huge, black, sleepy-eyed woman wearing a faded deep-green gown that fell in straight lines from her throat to her ankles appeared through the door and nodded to him.

"You need a room?"

"Yes."

"Do you have it reserved?"

"No. I just came to town. On a boat."

"How long you need the room?"

"I don't know. Might be three weeks."

"Got one on second floor. Last one on the right. Four dollars a night. Pay in advance."

Caleb queried, "Two weeks in advance be all right?"

"Yes. Need a receipt?"

"Yes."

"What name?"

"Caleb Dunson." He spelled it for her.

Caleb drew his purse from his pocket and counted out fifty-six dollars while the woman laboriously made out a receipt. She counted the money, turned to put it in a small, scarred, iron vault behind the desk, and handed the receipt to Caleb. He glanced at the signature before he put it in his coat pocket. It was a single word, "Matsie."

Her eyes narrowed in question.

"You stay here before?"

"Yes. Seven years ago."

Suddenly her eyes opened wide. "You the one! You had trouble with those two thieves. The constable come. Those two in jail for a long time."

Caleb smiled. "What's my room number? Do you have a key?"

The woman turned and picked a key from a drawer. "I remember. You spent time with a man here before." She laid the key on the table and shook her head. "Sad business. He got in a duel over sellin' slaves and was shot dead. Sad business."

Caleb paused, startled. "You mean Amos Ingersol?"

"I forgot his name. He short, stout, got a big flat nose. Shot dead. Sad business." She pointed. "Up those stairs. Second floor. You been here before, you know where the washroom is."

Caleb picked up the key. "Thank you."

The black woman watched Caleb climb the stairs and disappear down the hallway, still shaking her head about the sad business of men willing to kill each other with pistols to protect their ridiculous male honor.

In his plain room, Caleb hung his heavy coat in the wardrobe, then opened his suitcase and stowed his clothing. He kindled a fire in the stove, removed his suit coat and cravat, draped them on the back of a chair, removed his shoes, and laid down on the bed, weary from his journey.

He did not waken until past noon. He washed, changed into a fresh suit, walked down through the lobby and out to the street, and stopped in astonishment. The streets were filled with carts and wagons and carriages of every description, men wearing the uniform of half a dozen armies, both federal regulars and state militia, and human beings of every description and color, pushing, crowding, shouting, working their way to and from buildings and courtyards. Caleb walked among them, seeking a hack. He found one just leaving a courtyard and hailed the driver.

"Governor Claiborne's mansion."

Twenty minutes later the aged hack stopped before the two-story building in the north section of town that had been a landmark one hundred years earlier. Caleb paid the driver and walked to the high, heavy double doors beneath the six-column portico, and rapped with the huge brass door-knocker. The door was opened by a heavy man in a military uniform that Caleb could not immediately identify. The man had gold epaulets on his shoulders, a receding chin, and an air of smug superiority.

"Sir," he said. His voice was high, officious.

"I am to see the governor."

"That will not be possible at—"

Caleb cut him off. "President Madison sent me."

The man's chin dropped for a moment. "President Madison? James Madison?"

Caleb drew the letter from inside his coat and offered it. "President James Madison."

The man read the document, then spoke. "You will wait here."

He disappeared down a hallway, and five minutes later reappeared. "The governor will see you now. Follow me."

They walked down a broad hall with murals on both walls, to stop before a heavy oak door. The officer rapped, and a voice within called, "Enter." The man opened the door, Caleb entered, and the door closed behind him.

The room was sizeable, with a high ceiling. The furniture and appointments were old, graceful, well-preserved. One wall was covered with bookshelves and books. Opposite was a huge stone fireplace. A huge mural of New Orleans in 1762—the year the French surrendered all their claims to the United States to the British—graced the upper half of the third wall, and a bank of French doors stood behind the huge maple wood desk where Governor William C. C. Claiborne sat with Caleb's letter still in his hand. Claiborne was as Caleb remembered him—sparse, thin face, long aquiline nose.

He rose and came around the desk to offer his hand to Caleb.

"Mister Dunson? Welcome to New Orleans."

Caleb shook the hand. "Mister Governor, it is my honor." The thought flashed in Caleb's mind—*he doesn't remember me.*

Claiborne gestured. "Please take a seat."

Both men sat, facing each other, before the desk. The governor raised the letter and wasted no time.

"President Madison sent you? How may I be of help?" It was clear that Claiborne was suspicious, doubtful, hesitant.

Caleb gestured. "You read the letter. President Madison is concerned about possible conflicts between General Jackson and Jean Lafitte. He wants me to do what I can to be certain the two remain on friendly terms. I need to know what Lafitte is thinking right now. To do that I will have to talk with him. Do you know where I can find him?"

The governor remained still for a moment, studying Caleb. "Yes. I can help you find him. Do you know him?"

"I spent some time with him years ago. At Barataria. Him and his brother, Pierre."

Surprise showed in Claiborne. "Then you know what he is. A pirate, plain and simple. Do you know I was forced to put a price on his head for his arrest? Five hundred dollars?"

"Yes."

"And he posted notices all over town that would pay anyone who would deliver me to him! Fifteen hundred dollars. I thought it complimentary that I was worth more than he!" The governor chuckled, seemingly pleased at the irony of the situation.

Caleb smiled at his wry humor. "I know about it."

"Lafitte's two loyal lieutenants—Dominique You and Beluche—are in our jail right now, on charges of piracy, theft, and selling stolen property."

"Here in New Orleans?"

"Yes."

Caleb paused, with fears rising. "Has Jean done anything to get them out? Made any threats?"

"No. Quite the other way around. Are you aware of the offer the British made to Lafitte several months ago?"

"No. What was it?"

"Last fall the British commenced their campaign to take Louisiana away from the United States. They gave Lafitte a choice: join the British in their plan, for which the British government would pay Lafitte thirty thousand dollars and give him land and make him a captain in the British navy, or suffer the consequences if he refused. The consequences were quite simple. The British would crush Barataria and the Lafittes and all their band of cutthroats. Wipe them from the face of the earth."

Caleb straightened in his chair, his mind running. "What did Lafitte do?"

Claiborne shook his head in grudging admiration. "Told them he would need time to discuss it with his men. It was about then the United States sent a regiment down to destroy Barataria, and they did; but Lafitte and his men scattered into the swamps and bayous where the Americans couldn't follow. Despite all that, Lafitte then sent me a written proposal. If the United States would grant Lafitte and his entire band of outlaws a full pardon for everything they'd ever done to date, he would swear his allegiance to the United States and take up arms against the British."

Caleb's eyes narrowed. "He *what?*"

"He'll join with us if we'll guarantee him a full pardon."

"Anything been done about it?"

"Not yet. This all happened in the past few weeks." Claiborne gestured to a large filing cabinet against one wall. "I have the written documents in those files, if you'd care to see them."

Caleb moved on. "Does General Jackson know about this?"

"I've told him, but he has no patience with it. He told me bluntly that Lafitte and his band are banditti from the infernal pit. He wants nothing to do with them. I think he intends cleaning them out before he leaves New Orleans, whenever that is."

"Do you know where I can find General Jackson?"

"Yes. Either at his living quarters here in town or out at his military headquarters on the Rodriguez Canal, about five miles outside the city." He glanced at the large clock on the fireplace mantel. "It's getting late in the afternoon. I'd guess the general would be at his headquarters on the canal. Let me show you."

Claiborne flattened a map on the desktop and traced with his finger. "Here we are. The Rodriguez Canal is here. His headquarters is just about in the middle, on the far side."

For several moments Caleb studied the map, memorizing roads and swamps and bayous. "Thank you for your time and information. I'll keep you informed as things move along. Can you tell me where to hire a saddle mount? And would it be possible to have one of your uniformed assistants accompany me for the balance of the day?"

"I'll have a mount for you in ten minutes, and a uniformed guide. Armed."

Claiborne walked Caleb into the hall and down to the entrance, where he gave orders to the heavy man with the gold epaulets and the superior attitude. The man hurried out the front door and ten minutes later returned with a brown gelding, saddled and ready, held by a young captain wearing a state militia uniform, mounted on a black mare. There was a pistol in each of his two saddle holsters, and a sword dangled at his side.

The young officer, blond, fair, handsome, handed Caleb the reins to his horse and said, "Captain Robert Doss, Louisiana State militia. At your service, sir."

"Caleb Dunson. Here by order of President James Madison. Can you take me to the military headquarters of General Andrew Jackson by the most convenient route?"

"Yes, sir."

The young officer held to the outskirts of town to avoid the chaos in the downtown streets, working his way north on a rutted dirt road with Caleb following. Forty minutes later he turned east, and they rode for more than half a mile, within yards of the huge Rodriguez Canal. Between them and the canal, hundreds of men of every description were feverishly using picks and shovels to loosen and throw dirt onto a gigantic breastwork. Cannon emplacements were spaced to give a complete field of fire across the canal, into the great open field beyond.

Captain Doss pointed. "That building ahead. That's the general's headquarters."

They reined in their mounts and dismounted near more than ten horses tied to a hitching rail, with officers and enlisted going and coming. Caleb handed Doss his reins. "Would you hold the horses out here? I'd invite you in, but I doubt General Jackson would favor it."

Doss smiled. "I'd rather not offend the general. He takes exception to such things rather harshly from time to time."

Caleb entered the building—plain, square, sparse—with officers glancing at him in question of a man not in uniform. Caleb approached a sergeant at a desk.

"I must see General Jackson. I'm under orders of President James Madison."

The sergeant leaned back in his chair with a look of pained restraint at the interruption.

"President Madison, eh. Who are you?"

"Caleb Dunson." Caleb offered the letter. "This will explain."

The sergeant took the letter and was shaking his head until he opened it and read the signature. He straightened in his chair, his face a study in utter surprise as he read the brief letter. He raised his eyes to Caleb, swallowed, and said, "I'll be right back."

Caleb watched him stride down a hall to his left, pushing his way through officers and enlisted alike, to rap on a door. He disappeared for less than one minute and came back down the hall at a trot.

"The general's right down there, fourth door on the left. He has the letter."

Caleb strode down the hall and knocked on the door. The call came from within, high, forceful. "Come in!"

Caleb pushed into the plain, austere room to face a worn desk of pine. Behind the desk, in a hard-backed chair, sat General Andrew Jackson. Caleb was shocked at the man's appearance. His face was long, hollow-cheeked, with a high forehead and a prominent nose. His eyes were slightly sunken, his skin sallow, sickly. Caleb recognized in an instant that this man was suffering from the ravages of malaria, the result of his unrelenting campaign against the Creek Indians in the hot, humid, tropical climes of Alabama.

Jackson pointed. "Have a seat, Mister Dunson."

Caleb sat down, and Jackson leaned forward, eyes points of light.

"President Madison sent you to do something about Jean Lafitte?"

"He did."

Jackson pushed the letter across the desk. "He's wasted his time. I have no need for that man, nor for his band of cutthroat banditti. Before I leave this area I will have cleaned them all out. My orders were to secure Louisiana and New Orleans as a United States territory, and to do that, Lafitte and his kind must go."

He paused for a moment, then concluded. "Is there anything else?"

Caleb sat unflinching. "Yes. You're dead wrong, General."

Jackson straightened in shock. "What was that again?"

"You're wrong, General. You've misjudged Lafitte. He can make the difference in what's coming between you and the British, one way or the other. You're going to need him."

There was defiance in Jackson's face. "You know him?"

"I spent time with him years ago, enough to know what he and his men can do. I was in Barataria. I met his brother and their two men, Beluche and Dominique. They and their band are the best fighting men on the gulf coast. There are about a thousand of them. Let them pick the time and the place, and they can beat you or the British."

"You have a high opinion of that gang of criminals, sir!" Jackson shook his head. "How is it you can make such a statement? Have you had military experience?"

Caleb's words came spaced, quiet, and his eyes were steadily boring into Jackson. "Camden. Cowpens. King's Mountain. Guilford. Yorktown. With Francis Marion. Pickett. Daviess. Sumter. Washington. Morgan. Greene."

Jackson's mouth sagged open for a moment, and he snapped it shut. For a time he remained silent and motionless, while the full weight of Caleb's words settled in.

"The Revolution, then?" he asked.

"Seventeen-seventy-eight through Yorktown, seventeen-eighty-one."

Jackson cleared his throat. "At Yorktown. Were you there for the surrender?"

"My company was sent across the river to take down Banastre Tarleton. We did it. Yes. I was there for the surrender. So was my brother and my brother-in-law."

Jackson covered his mouth with a large white kerchief to cough, then settled back in his chair to take a hard look at Caleb before he spoke.

"What makes you think Lafitte can be trusted? He's built an empire on crime."

Caleb drew a breath. "To my knowledge, he's never broken his word. If he says he will fight the British, he will fight the British. He and all his men." Caleb paused for a time, then went on. "Have you ever met him?"

Jackson shook his head but said nothing.

"Meet him. Talk with him. You have nothing to lose and everything to gain if he commits to support you."

Jackson remained still, unresponsive.

Caleb continued. "If I arrange it, will you meet him?"

Jackson stood and for a time he paced behind his desk, his long torso hunched forward, hands clasped behind his back, face beginning to flush with a fever. Finally, he returned to his desk and sat down.

"All right. I'll meet with him. Alone. Tomorrow. Second floor of the Exchange Coffee House at Chartres and Saint Louis Streets. Two o'clock in the afternoon."

"If he wants a third party there to witness it?"

Jackson flared. "One of his men? Doesn't he trust me?"

Caleb raised a hand. "It's as much for your protection as his."

Jackson pointed at Caleb. "If he wants a third party, that will be you."

"I'll give him the message. Unless I send word to you to the contrary, he will be there at two o'clock tomorrow afternoon."

Jackson bobbed his head. "Is there anything else?"

"No, sir."

Caleb walked from the room, down the hall, and out the door, where Doss was waiting with the horses. The sun was setting on a chill, late-December day as the two men rode back to town. They reined in at the governor's mansion, and as they dismounted Caleb spoke.

"I've got to talk with Jean Lafitte in the morning. Do you know how I can find him?"

Doss paused for a moment. "I know who to ask."

"I need the answer before nine o'clock. I'll be at the Absinthe House."

Doss led the horses away, and Caleb found a hack for the ride back through the crowded streets to the hotel, where he took his supper in the old dining hall and went to his bed, a tired, aging man.

By half past eight in the morning, he was washed, dressed, and in the dining hall working on a plate of ham and three eggs when Captain Doss walked to his table. Caleb laid his fork down and wiped his mouth with his napkin.

Doss said, "I've located Lafitte." He smiled and shook his head.

"He's just down the way at his old blacksmith shop on the corner of Saint Philips Street. The one Thiac used to run."

"I know the place. I've been there. Did you talk to him?"

"No. I passed by on my horse. I saw him."

Caleb paused to work with his thoughts. "You better go on back to the governor's place. I'll walk down to see him. If I need you later I'll come find you."

Doss looked at him. "You be careful."

Ten minutes later Caleb slowed as he approached the ancient blacksmith shop. The doors of the old corner building were open on both streets, and inside a swarthy, short, blocky man wearing a large, battered leather apron was pumping an aged leather bellows to keep the forge glowing while he heated a huge bolt. Caleb walked in behind the man, waited while his eyes adjusted to the dim light, and slowly studied the room. Seated in one corner, unmoving, was a man six feet tall, built strong, swarthy, solid jaw, dominant nose, handsome. Caleb recognized Jean Lafitte.

Caleb walked directly to him, and Lafitte stood as Caleb spoke.

"I don't have time to waste. I've been sent by President James Madison to find you." He handed Lafitte the letter of introduction. "You'll understand when you read this."

Lafitte unfolded the letter and turned it to better light to read it, then read it again, slowly and carefully. He handed the letter back to Caleb and raised one eyebrow in question.

"Have I met you before?" Lafitte's voice was resonant, strong.

"Seven years ago. I was sent by President Madison to investigate some matters for him. I came under the name of M. E. Hickman and met you with Amos Ingersol. We traveled to Barataria to look at slaves. Twelve of them."

A smile slowly formed on Lafitte's face. "Ah, I remember. We waited for a letter from your company. It did not arrive."

"I never wrote it," Caleb answered.

The man at the forge turned to hold the orange bolt on the anvil with a pair of tongs and began pounding it with a three-pound sledge.

Caleb ignored the rhythmic clanging. He took a breath and came directly to the question. "President Madison sent me to try to reconcile the differences between yourself and General Andrew Jackson. Are you willing to meet with him?"

For a time Lafitte fixed Caleb with a hard stare and then spoke from his heart. "I and my men are accused of crimes we did not commit against the United States. The British offered me position and money and land to join them. I did not do it. Months ago I offered my services to this country, because it is mine. In return I asked only that I and my men receive a full pardon and citizenship."

He paused to order his thoughts. "I received no answer. Instead, the United States burned Barataria to the ground. Still I held to my offer. They have never answered. You come while the British are threatening and have more than twelve thousand soldiers while General Jackson has less than five thousand, and now—only now—does Madison send you to me to get help. I find that to be less than honorable!"

Caleb raised a hand. "That isn't what I asked. Will you meet with General Jackson to reconcile your differences?"

Lafitte's answer came strong. "He has openly called me and my men murderers, criminals, outlaws, banditti. I should consent to meet with him to hear such things?"

Caleb cut him off. "I've talked with him. He's agreed to meet with you today at two o'clock on the second floor of the Exchange Coffee House on the corner of Chartres and Saint Louis Streets. He is an honorable man. Will you come?"

"Alone?"

"Do you prefer a witness?"

"Yes. But not one of his men. I do not trust him."

"Jackson has suggested I be there. Is that agreeable to you?"

Lafitte's answer came slowly. "I will be there."

Caleb turned and walked out of the heat and smoke of the dirt-floored smithy shop into the street and turned toward the Absinthe House, deep in his own thoughts and fears. He scarcely noticed the crowded streets as he made his way back to the aging, crumbling building and walked the stairs up to his room.

For a time he sat on his bed, head bowed as he put his thoughts in order.

Two of the strongest men I ever met—each distrusting the other—both proud— neither one the kind to back down—both masters of battle—both able to see they need each other to get what they want.

He raised his head to stare at the wall.

The fight that's coming will likely determine whether Louisiana will be British or American—whether America continues to grow—what part she will play in the world to come—Madison saw it—that's why I'm here—and it all comes down to what's going to happen between Lafitte and Jackson in about four hours.

He slowly let the foundation thought form in his mind—the one he had known was coming but refused to face.

Why me?

He did not know how long he sat, groping with the awful responsibility that was on his shoulders, feeling his own inadequacies, his own fallibility while his mind took him back to scenes and times locked in memory.

How did we win the Revolution?—we should never have won that war—thirteen little colonies—challenging the mightiest military power of all time—how did we do it?—what did we know that they didn't know?—what did we have that they didn't have?—where did our men come from?—Washington, Greene, Morgan, Wayne, Stark, Marion, Lafayette, Von Steuben, all the others?—and the little men no one ever heard about—the ones who carried the muskets?—how was it they were there, the right man at the right time? How?

He was scarcely aware of the feeling that was rising in his breast.

Those men who met in Philadelphia—1787—fifty-five of them—sat in the heat of that room all summer—fought their own little war—came out with the Constitution—like nothing the world has ever seen—how did they do it?—where did that document come from?—none like it in the history of mankind—how did they do it?

He shifted his weight, and his thoughts ran on with a will of their own.

And somehow it all comes down to two strong men who distrust each other—meeting to see if all we've won stops here—with me in the middle—why me?—I have no political power—no military power—why me?—is this how the Almighty works?—somehow uses nobodies to do his bidding?—is that what's happening today? Is it?

For just one brief moment a feeling surged in his chest like none he had ever felt before. He sat frozen, unmoving, as it dwindled and passed. After a time he rose from the bed to sit at the small desk in the corner, with paper and quill at hand, and began writing brief notes of the events of the past few days to be used later for making his report to President Madison.

At noon he picked at his midday meal in the dining hall, then went back to his room to lie on the bed, trying to clear his mind for what was coming. At half past one he walked into the press of traffic in the streets, hailed a hack, and sat in the old, worn leather seat while the driver worked his way to the Exchange Coffee House. He paid the driver and walked into the small café that occupied one corner in the large office building to wait. Shortly before two o'clock Jean Lafitte walked in, Caleb stood, and Lafitte came to sit beside him. There was no greeting exchanged. Two minutes later the tall, slender Andrew Jackson entered, stopped to survey the room, and came to stand before them.

Lafitte and Caleb stood and Jackson spoke.

"Shall we go to the second floor?"

They followed him up the stairs to a vacant room with nothing but a table and five chairs nearby, all showing a film of dust. Both windows were weather-stained, unwashed. Jackson removed his cape, draped it over one arm, and stood at the table, with Caleb to his right and Lafitte opposite him, both standing. For one instant the stale air was charged with tension, and then Caleb spoke.

"Mister Lafitte, may I present General Andrew Jackson of the United States Army. General, may I present Jean Lafitte, merchant."

Jackson bowed slightly from the hips but did not offer his hand. "It is my honor, sir." His manner was cold, distant.

Lafitte returned the bow. "The honor is mine, sir." His manner was indifferent.

Caleb said, "Shall we be seated?"

They dusted off the table and four chairs. Jackson draped his cape over one, and they drew three others to the table, Jackson and Lafitte opposite, Caleb still to Jackson's right.

Caleb broke the strained silence.

"We are here at the direction of President Madison. You have both seen the letter. I propose we are all practical men with no need for unnecessary formalities. Let me come directly to our purpose."

He paused to select his words.

"The United States and Britain are at war because matters between them must be settled for all time. The outcome of the entire conflict likely depends on what happens here and now, in New Orleans. This entire area will either be British or American in the next few days. You two will decide which it is to be."

Caleb turned to Jackson. "The British have twelve thousand men. You have about four thousand."

He turned to Lafitte. "You have about one thousand men, who I believe are capable of swinging the balance."

He stopped to let each man think for a moment, then went on. "President Madison sees the need for you to join forces."

Again he stopped, then concluded. "I believe I have said enough." He turned to Jackson. "Mister Lafitte offered his services months ago on condition that he and his men receive a full pardon for all charges against them by the United States. The United States has never responded. Do you have a response now?"

For long seconds Jackson stared into the steady, calm eyes of Lafitte. Then he took a deep breath and spoke.

"Sir, you must be aware I have publicly stated my opinion of yourself and your men. Banditti. Murderers. Criminals."

Lafitte nodded, his face an unreadable mask of calm reserve. "I am aware. I am also aware that your army burned my home and village at Barataria and scattered my men."

Jackson continued, hostile, icy. "It is my intention that before I leave this area I complete what was started. Piracy and murders will stop! The criminals will be driven out or hanged! New Orleans will rise above the sin and corruption that have been its hallmark for years. If it requires me to destroy you and your men, then such shall it be."

There it was! Out on the table between the two men. The stand-or-fall challenge upon which the fate of both, and much of the United States, rested. The tension in the dim light was electric.

Lafitte leaned forward, his eyes alive. His voice took on a quietness and a resonance Caleb had never heard. His words came spaced, from a place deep inside the man. Jackson straightened, startled, caught unprepared.

"You do not know this city. You were not here when I came, years ago. When there was no law, no government, no authority. When there were French and Spanish and Africans and Germans. Indians. Seven different languages. Seven different religions. Good and evil. One man's sin was another man's sacrament. That is what I saw when I came with my brother, Pierre."

He paused, and Jackson did not move, and Lafitte went on.

"We lived as they lived. With the good and the bad. The priests and the murderers and the pirates. We survived. And we saw what could be. We saw America growing, moving west. We saw the beginnings of liberty and freedom coming toward us. We saw the British come back to try to cripple the Americans, and we made our choice."

He stopped for a moment.

"We are Americans. This is our country. Because we are part of what New Orleans was—both the good and the bad—the Americans have tried to hurt us, but that does not matter. We are still Americans! The British tried to buy our loyalty with land and money and position, but we refused! We offered our services to our country, if they would excuse our past. We have had no answer. I have come here today with the hope that it will come from you. No one—not you, not the British—knows New Orleans as we do, and my men cannot be equaled in battle. I repeat my offer. You have all that we possess—if you will pardon us and grant us full rights as American citizens."

He laid one hand flat on the table.

"I would be grateful to have your answer."

Caleb looked at Jackson, who was staring at Lafitte in shocked silence. Lafitte was not moving. Caleb waited for a time and then spoke quietly.

"General?"

Jackson moved his head as though coming from a place far away. He licked his thin lips and spoke.

"Do you speak for all your men?"

"All."

"You will lose some of them."

Lafitte did not flinch. "We know that."

"I cannot speak for the United States. Only President Madison has that power."

"I am aware. You can recommend. He will listen."

"How soon can you have your men available?"

"They are ready now. They know I am here. They are waiting."

"Do you want this agreement in writing?"

Lafitte's answer was instant. "It is not necessary. If you give me your word, it is better than a writing."

Caleb saw the change in Jackson. His face, his eyes, his entire demeanor softened.

He leaned forward and his long, thin hand extended across the table. "You have my word, sir."

Lafitte shook the hand and nodded his head.

Caleb quietly exhaled his held breath and settled back in his chair.

Lafitte asked, "What do you want of us?"

Jackson leaned forward, his forearms on the table. "Will you come with me to my headquarters? I have maps. You need to see our battle plan."

"I will come."

Jackson stood, and Lafitte and Caleb also came to their feet. The general was fastening the catch on his cape when he said, "We're short of food and flints and gunpowder. Can you help us find some?"

Lafitte nodded. "I have seventy-five hundred flints hidden in this town. And at least two hundred barrels of gunpowder. Over ten tons of food—dried fish, beef, flour. Would that help?"

Jackson stared. "What price?"

Lafitte shook his head. "You misunderstand. No price. They are yours. I will deliver them on your orders."

Jackson gaped. Caleb looked at him, and Jackson looked at Caleb in near total disbelief, then spoke to Lafitte.

"I have a carriage waiting outside. Will you join me, sir? I think it's time for New Orleans to see us riding in a carriage together." He turned to Caleb. "You are included, if you have the time."

People in the streets stopped to point and stare in disbelief as the carriage made its way north, through the crowds. They continued the five miles to the place where the townspeople and soldiers were working on the breastworks next to the great Rodriguez Canal and there turned east to Jackson's military headquarters. Officers gaped as Jackson led the way into the office and on to his war room.

Caleb lost track of time as Jackson laid maps on the table, one at a time, with markings showing the location of his men, gun batteries, munitions, food, horses, reserves, and the townspeople. Then Jackson laid out the known locations of the British forces and identified them by their officers, their numbers, the terrain where they were, and the terrain they would have to cross to reach the American lines. The names of Pakenham, Keane, McMullen, and Gibbs, among others, were prominent on the British side of the map.

A sergeant rapped on the door and delivered a fire-blackened pot of steaming coffee and three tin cups. Jackson stopped to pour, and the men blew on the smoking, bitter, weak, black drink and sipped gingerly as Jackson continued.

The most detailed map was of the Rodriguez Canal, with the west end on the Mississippi River and the east end in an impassable swamp. On the north side of the huge ditch, Jackson had every gun emplacement, every gun crew, identified, with lines showing the distance the guns could reach to the south, across a great, exposed, open space without a tree or a hill to give cover to anyone. Jackson had centered his entire plan on forcing the British to come across that large expanse of open ground to break his lines. If his plan succeeded, he intended that they never reach the canal.

He laid his last map on the table and pointed to the west bank of the Mississippi River, directly opposite the big canal. A much smaller force would be stationed there, with cannon capable of reaching across the river to give a cross-fire into the big open area where the British were expected to make their attack.

"Ah," said Lafitte. "If the British capture those guns, they can also reach our men on the north side of the canal."

Jackson made a note. "You're right. I'll reinforce that position."

Lafitte ran his finger down the Rodriguez Canal and stopped at a mark near the center, where the fighting was expected to be heaviest.

"May I request that here, at battery number three, you give my men the privilege of running those guns? Beluche and Dominique will pick the men. I give you my word. They will give a good account of themselves."

Lafitte had identified the most critical cannon battery in the entire line. Jackson looked him in the eye. "Done."

Their coffee cups were empty and the last map was being folded when the rap came at the door and a sergeant opened it to thrust his head into the room.

"General, evening mess is ready for the officers."

"Good. Set places for the three of us." He turned to Lafitte and Caleb. "I trust you will not object to dining with me. The food will be terrible, but the company will be excellent."

They ate together, with Jackson's officers trying not to gape and exclaim at the sight of their commander dining openly with a man he had so recently condemned as a pirate and a thief. They finished in the twilight of evening, and Jackson led Lafitte and Caleb down to his private office.

"Mister Lafitte, I would appreciate it if you will accompany me for the next few days, until this is all over."

"It will be my honor."

"Mister Dunson, you are not military, but you are invited to remain with us if you wish. There will be fighting. Danger."

"I will be here, sir."

Lafitte interrupted. "When do you want the flints for your weapons? The food and the gunpowder? And where do you want it delivered?"

"Can you get it here tomorrow?"

"At dawn."

"You will take my carriage to town this evening, and it will be waiting to bring you back in the morning," Jackson said. "I will have saddle mounts here waiting for you for what we must do tomorrow."

The carriage jolted over the dirt roads back into the town, where Caleb stepped down at the Absinthe House and went to his room. With his coat and cravat off and hanging over a chair, he sat down on the bed, and the awful tension of the day began to drain. He was in his nightshirt shortly past nine o'clock, when he blew out the lamp and slipped between white sheets and into a dreamless sleep.

He was washed, shaved, dressed, and finished with breakfast when the carriage stopped in front of the hotel's courtyard in heavy fog rolling up from the river, and with Lafitte seated opposite, they rolled through the streets, out to the headquarters building beside the canal, where Jackson was waiting with saddled horses.

As they mounted, Jackson spoke to Lafitte.

"The flints and gunpowder and food arrived this morning. It's being distributed. You have the thanks of every officer and soldier."

Throwing his leg over the saddle, Lafitte shrugged. "It was nothing."

With the general leading, they rode east in a dank fog that collected on their faces and their clothing, to cannon battery number one, under command of General John Coffee, located at the end of the canal where it stopped at the edge of the great swamp. Jackson conducted an inspection of the breastworks, the equipment, the cannon, the ammunition, the muskets and rifles, and the men, then moved west to battery number two. They dismounted while Jackson talked to the men, soldiers and civilians alike, as though he were their father—stern when he had to be, complimentary when he could be, always leaving them lifted by his indomitable spirit.

He stopped at battery number three to shake hands with Beluche and Dominique and the thirty men they had picked to service and defend the two guns. The short, swarthy, thick-chested Beluche grinned at Jackson when he took the thin hand in his short, powerful one and shook it strongly. "Mon General," he said, and bowed deeply.

With the fog lifting, they shared a scant midday meal with the crew at battery number six, and moved on to batteries numbered seven and eight, nearest the river. Always, Jackson found the time and the expert eye to see the little things that needed his comment, his advice, his admonishment, and never did he leave a crew feeling belittled by his presence. The men stopped to wave at him as he moved on, more confident, more eager, than when he arrived.

The sun had set and the cold of evening was setting in when they returned to headquarters to take their evening mess in the officers' dining hall. They finished in full darkness, and Caleb and Lafitte rode back to the lights of New Orleans in the general's carriage with clouds gathering overhead. Caleb was in his bed before ten o'clock.

A cold drizzle of rain came in the night, and the two men raised their coat collars and wound their scarves high for the ride back out to Jackson's headquarters in the dripping rain and morning fog.

Jackson met them at the door, and both Caleb and Lafitte knew instantly something significant had happened.

"My office," he clipped, and led them down the hall.

"Scouting reports just came in. Pakenham's moving. The rain will slow him, but I expect him to attack the canal line sometime tonight or early tomorrow morning."

He paused and tapped a map on his desktop.

"Our reports say he has scouted the river. If he has, he means to send someone across to the west side. I calculate he wants those gun batteries of ours over there. If he gets them, he can use our own guns to reach the west end of our lines on this side of the river. We could be in trouble."

Lafitte interrupted. "It also means that Pakenham will not attack until he has those guns and the bombardment begins."

Jackson paused, eyes narrowed in thought. "That makes sense."

Lafitte continued. "Do you want my men to keep you informed? They know the river. The British will never know they are there."

"Yes. I'll need those reports hourly."

Lafitte bobbed his head. "It shall be done."

Jackson tapped the map again. "I have riflemen from Tennessee and Kentucky. More than a thousand of them. Battle-hardened. I don't worry about them. But I also have about fourteen hundred state militia. They've never been under fire. I don't know what they'll do in the face of a head-on British assault. If the British overrun them and get behind our lines, our entire defense could collapse. There's little I can do about that except hope they don't break under fire."

He paused for a moment, then went on.

"Mister Lafitte, your command brings our total fighting force on the line to just over thirty-two hundred men."

Again he paused, and his next words were quiet. "The British have more than twelve thousand regulars. A ratio of four to one in their favor."

He looked at Lafitte and then Caleb. "Gentlemen, we are about to find out if one of our men can beat four of theirs." A chuckle rolled out of his chest. "Have you looked at what we've got out there? Blacks, whites, Indians, Creoles, Cajuns, merchants, saints, scoundrels, soldiers, militia—a muddle the like of which I've never seen. I would like to know what Pakenham is thinking about now, moving the best Britain has to offer against a mix like we have."

Nine miles to the south, British major general Sir Edward Pakenham was hunched over a table with his war council in the huge mansion of Villere, which he had commandeered from its owner to serve as his headquarters.

He turned to Colonel William Thornton. Pakenham's finger was moving on a map as he spoke. "Our scouting reports are in. There are no American forces between this command post and the Mississippi. You will march your forces to the river just after evening mess. They will load into the barges and launch at dusk. They will cross the river and be on the west bank not later than midnight. They will move north where they will instantly attack and capture the American gun batteries directly across from the west end of the Rodriguez Canal. They will then turn the guns to bear on the American lines. A rocket will be fired just before dawn, and on that signal you will immediately commence firing. A concurrent attack on the east side of the river will then commence. Are you clear?"

Thornton was clear.

He turned to Colonel Mullens. "Your regiment will be responsible to carry the scaling ladders and fascines to the Rodriguez Canal. Without them, we will not get across the canal and over the top of the American breastworks. They *must* be there when we reach the Rodriguez Canal. Your regiment will be with mine when we make the attack. Do you have any questions?"

Mullens had no questions, and Pakenham went on.

"I will lead the attack. We will move across this open area with all speed, directly into the center of the American lines. Once we breach those lines and are behind the Americans, we can destroy them at will, because all their cannon are pointed the opposite direction."

He straightened and addressed them all. "We have twelve thousand troops facing less than four thousand of theirs. The numbers are in our favor. I have no doubt about the outcome. The more quickly we can move the fewer men we will lose. The weather is not good. It appears certain this will all be done in rain and fog and mud. Rest your men while you can and be ready to complete your duties at the appointed times. That is all. You are dismissed."

The cold drizzle of rain held as the day wore on, turning the roads into muddy ruts and the open fields into quagmires. Jackson rode up and down his lines with Lafitte and Caleb flanking him, talking with his men as they shivered, soaked, unable to build fires to cook, trying to protect their precious gunpowder. It was past noon when he stopped at battery number three to find Beluche and Dominique and their men calmly sitting in the wet with a pot of coffee boiling on a tiny fire beneath a tarp.

"Is that coffee?" Jackson called. "Real coffee?"

Dominique smiled up at him, squinting in the rain. "But of course, Mon General." He poured a cup and handed it up to Jackson, still seated in his wet saddle, then a cup for Lafitte and Caleb. Jackson raised it to sniff, then sipped at it. For a moment he closed his eyes to savor the richness. The three men sipped at it until it was gone, then handed the cups back to Dominique.

Jackson grinned. "Where did you get that? Smuggle it?"

Dominique grinned back at him. "We have our ways."

Dripping wet, soaked to the skin, fevered with the remains of an attack of malaria, Jackson chuckled as he wheeled his horse and continued down the line, talking to his troops, doing all one man could to build their courage in the face of an enemy four times their number.

There was no sunset. The light simply faded beneath the black clouds overhead and through the misty rain and the fog. The tension began to build among the soldiers on both sides of the canal—the British knowing they were soon to attack Americans behind breastworks, and the Americans knowing they were coming, but neither side knowing when the deadly battle would begin.

At dusk, far to the south, Colonel William Thornton took a deep breath, mounted his horse, and called his orders.

"Fall into ranks and follow me to the river."

He led his regiment west, slogging in the mud, wet, shivering, in darkness and swirling mist, until he could make out the broad expanse of the Mississippi River before him and the huge barges waiting to carry his troops across the river. He called a halt and rode on alone to the place where he expected the bank to meet the water, and he felt his horse sink into mud halfway to its knees. The mare stopped, tossing her head, refusing to go farther into the muck.

For a moment Thornton sat still, unable to understand what was happening. Then he swung his leg over to dismount, and his foot sank into the mud eight inches above his ankle. After extracting his foot from the clinging mess, he remounted and turned his mount back, tied her, and walked back to the riverbank. There was only mud. He walked out into the mess, counting steps, judging distance, until he had covered thirty feet. There was no water. He had gone another twelve feet before he felt the splash and saw the water at his feet.

It struck him like a hammer blow, and he thought—*The river has fallen! The water level is down!* He turned in terror to peer back at the invisible bank. *The barges! We will have to drag them fifty feet in mud! We'll never reach the far side by midnight!*

He turned and slogged back through the muck, grabbed the reins of his mount, and galloped back to his command to shout orders.

"The river has fallen! Break ranks! Break ranks! Get to the barges! Throw your backpacks and muskets into them. Drag them to the river. Do it! Now!"

His bewildered regiment broke ranks and trotted to the barges. They threw their backpacks and muskets into the rainwater that had collected in the boats, and then grasped the gunwales to bow their backs and heave with all their strength. The barges began to move slowly, until they hit the mud of the river bottom, and they mired down.

With Thornton shouting orders, the men struggled, slipping, sinking in mud to their knees, straining, moving the barges only inches at a time toward the water.

Nine miles north and across the river, four of Lafitte's scouts moved silently to the place where Jackson and Lafitte and Caleb had settled for the night, huddled beneath a tarp, with their men. The scouts appeared before them from nowhere, and Jackson flinched. Lafitte smiled as he spoke to them.

"You have a report?"

"Oui. The river has fallen. The British are trying to move their barges to the water. The mud holds the barges down. They will not be across the river much before daylight. They will never reach our cannon batteries on the other side of the river by morning. We thought you should know."

Jackson started. "You're certain?"

"Oui. Certain. The mud is deep."

"Well done, well done," Jackson exclaimed.

Lafitte quietly gave his orders. "We are grateful. We will be waiting for your next report."

The men disappeared as silently as they had come. No picket saw or heard them as they moved back to the main road and worked their way south.

Jackson turned to Caleb and Lafitte in the darkness. "If the British don't reach those batteries before Pakenham begins his attack, they could be in trouble."

To the south, Pakenham sat in the kitchen of the Villere mansion, nervous, watching the clock, marking time until the hour before dawn when the rocket would arc into the black heavens to signal the attack. With the advantage of numbers four to one in his favor, he had arranged no scouts, no lines of communication with Thornton, nor had anyone yet come to tell him the Mississippi River had fallen. Thoughts of sleep were gone as he rose and paced, marking time, battling nerves. It was four o'clock when Pakenham fastened his cape about his shoulders, settled his hat on his head, and walked out the door into the blackness to his waiting horse. He mounted and rode to his command, standing in the mud in ranks, waiting for his orders.

He peered to the northwest, with time dragging at a maddening pace. He drew his watch from his pocket and held it close to his face to see the hands in the dark. It was twenty minutes before five o'clock.

Where's Thornton? What's gone wrong? The rocket should have fired half an hour ago!

Across the river, Thornton was in a near panic. He had been three hours late in getting the barges loaded and launched, and then he had miscalculated the swiftness of the Mississippi current. The flowing river had carried the barges one and one-half miles downstream. Dawn was approaching, and his entire force had scarcely reached the place he had intended landing hours ago. Sitting his horse in the rain, his thoughts were nearly paralyzed.

In this rain and mud I will never reach the American guns before midmorning. When Pakenham doesn't see the rocket at dawn, what will he do? What will he do?

At that moment, from a source somewhere in the woods, a rocket arced into the black heavens, high, bright in the rain, far short of the American guns. Thornton's breathing stopped. Pakenham stared, unable to understand why the rocket was fired from the wrong place.

Jackson leaped to his feet and shouted, "Get ready, boys! They're coming!"

Pakenham did nothing, knowing something was badly wrong, but not knowing what it was. Then, according to the plan, with the rocket in the sky, the officers out on his flanks shouted their orders, and four regiments started forward, their drums rattling and their fifes playing. Pakenham jerked as though he had been struck!

It was too late to stop them! Two-thirds of the British command was moving forward—eight thousand men. Pakenham's shouts to halt were lost in the sound of sixteen thousand British boots slogging in the mud, with their regimental bands beating a cadence. The men in his own command heard the regiments on both sides marching in the darkness and started forward with them, not knowing that the entire campaign was on the brink of disaster.

On the red-coated regulars came, twelve thousand of them, rank upon rank, on toward the open fields that lay between them and the Rodriguez Canal, slogging slowly onward through the mud and the river fog, slipping, recovering, moving on with their muskets at the ready. The storm clouds to the east became gray, and then the marching troops could see the skyline, and then the canal and the breastworks were there in the far distance.

Beyond the canal, Jackson sat his horse on a rise where he could see the entire panorama of his own lines, and the open fields stretching into the distance, and the Mississippi River moving south, bordered by fifty feet of muddy river bottom left by the receding waters. Beside Jackson were four of his staff officers, Lafitte, and Caleb, sitting tall, eyes squinted in the rain, straining through the misty fog for the first glimpse of a red line coming from the south.

Suddenly it was there, and then they heard the faint rattle of the regimental drums. From their right, Lafitte's four scouts came trotting, beards and hair wet, muddy to their knees. They stopped before Jackson, and he exclaimed, "What's your report?"

"The British on the west side of the river are yet three miles south of our gun positions over there. Our battery crews are prepared to give support to our lines here."

"Excellent," Jackson said. "Get to your crew and be ready when I give the order to fire."

The four men spun and ran for battery number three, where Beluche and Dominique stood waiting, calmly counting the distant regimental flags of the oncoming British. The fog began to thin as the British came on, and all along the American line gunners were concentrating, calculating the distance. Jackson sat like a statue, eyes locked onto the first rank, waiting, watching.

Three hundred yards! Jackson raised his hand and bellowed, "Ready!"

Twenty-five hundred muskets and long Pennsylvania rifles clicked onto full cock, and men knelt in the mud to steady their weapons while the cannoneers held smoking linstocks above the cannon touchholes.

Jackson's arm dropped, and he shouted, "Fire!"

The heavy guns blasted at the same moment, with every musket and rifle in the line. The ground shook in the deafening roar, and buildings five miles away in New Orleans trembled. Grape shot and canister spread to splatter mud just in front of the first British ranks and rip into the leading British lines like a scythe. The rifle fire from the Tennessee volunteers and Kentucky militia punched into the ranks, and red-coated regulars went down in heaps.

They came on, stepping over their own dead and wounded, breaking into a slippery trot in the mud, following their officers, mounted and riding before them, swords drawn, shouting them on.

The Americans reloaded, and the second ear-splitting report sounded. Again mud leaped in front of the British line as the grapeshot and canister tore into the ranks, and the musket and rifle balls decimated them. The sound of distant cannon reached from across the river, and then cannonballs slammed into the British from the west. Jackson glanced at the white cloud of smoke rising on the far bank of the Mississippi and turned back to the battle that was before him, watching the two positions where the untried, untested militia were gathered. They were slow in reloading, hesitant, unsure. Jackson shouted to Lafitte and Caleb and pointed. "There! See the militia? They need to settle!"

The three men came off the hill at a gallop, in behind the militia, then among them, shouting "Steady, boys, steady! Reload. Reload. You're holding them! Pace yourselves. You can do it." A sense of confidence took root and spread, and the line straightened and held firm.

The sounds of the firing from the American cannon and muskets and rifles settled into a steady, unbroken din. The white gun smoke rose in clouds that hid the British while the Americans reloaded. The rough, long-haired, bearded, tobacco-stained riflemen from Tennessee and Kentucky were loading and firing faster than any other regiment, and they did not miss. The British were falling on top of each other, with those behind stepping over their own dead to charge on toward the canal and the American lines beyond.

The British came on, with the American guns cutting them down by the hundreds. They reached the south edge of the canal, and Pakenham turned to look for the scaling ladders and facines, and they were not in sight!

For a moment he sat his horse in utter disbelief. With near twelve thousand soldiers behind him, his entire army was stopped less than thirty yards from the American guns! Without the ladders, they could not cross the canal nor scale the American breastworks!

He shouted, "Where's Mullens? The ladders?"

One of his officers pointed back, south, and shook his head.

For reasons Pakenham never learned, Mullens was toward the rear, with the scaling ladders!

Instantly Pakenham spun his horse and dug his spurs. The animal leaped to a gallop and the lines opened to let him through, throwing mud thirty feet at every jump, back through the lines, to the rear, where he hauled his horse to a sliding stop before Mullens and demanded, "The ladders! Where are the ladders?"

Colonel Mullens had no answer. He gaped, stammered, then turned to shout to his men, "Forward! With the ladders and the facines!"

Pakenham turned his horse and galloped back through his command toward the front of the lines, shouting as he went, "Hold firm! Hold firm!" with the American guns firing all the way.

He was within fifty yards of the canal when grapeshot came whistling and his horse went down. He hit the mud rolling, came to his feet, commandeered another horse, and leaped into the saddle. He had just taken the far stirrup when grapeshot came singing again, this time through his upper thigh, into his horse, and it went down, dead. Pakenham tried to stand and could not. Paralysis seized him, and he could not move, and he toppled over in the mud. Instantly the soldiers nearest him stopped to protect him from the hail of bullets and grapeshot, picked him up, and started back through the lines with their fallen commander.

He was dead within minutes.

At the front, in the hail of American gunfire, a Tennessee rifle bullet struck Colonel Keane in his left side, and he jerked in his saddle and toppled into the mud, unconscious. One instant later, grapeshot caught Colonel Gibb in the back and knocked him sprawling from his horse, almost dead when he hit the ground.

A few of the British regulars reached the Rodriguez Canal. They leaped down the bank and tried to scale the far side and climb the American breastworks beyond, tearing at the mud with their fingers and boots. At point-blank range, the Americans cut them down. Without the ladders, any attempt to reach the American guns was sheer suicide. The red-coated regulars drew back from the canal, caught in the worst hail of gunfire in their memory.

The British command faltered. Exhausted soldiers hesitated in their forward motion and hunkered down, seeking in vain for any cover from the devastating hail of bullets. Their leader was down, gone, dead. Two of their leading officers had fallen. Thornton had failed to give support from across the river. The scaling ladders—the one piece of equipment on which the entire attack depended—had never reached the canal. The Americans were holding firm, solid, maintaining a steady, deadly fire of grapeshot and canister and bullets that was littering the fields with dead soldiers, in some places two and three deep. The Kentucky and Tennessee riflemen were knocking men down with deadly precision at three hundred yards.

The British had had enough.

Slowly they began to withdraw, stumbling backward over their own fallen dead, moving away from the breastworks that were shrouded in gun smoke, cowering in the face of whistling grapeshot and bullets, away from canal banks now littered with their dead, who had attempted the impossible and failed.

Still riding back and forth behind his lines, shouting encouragement to his men, Jackson pulled his horse to a stop. He stood tall in the stirrups to watch the British falling back, stepping over and around their own dead and fallen wounded, not bothering to fire or reload their muskets. Beside him, Lafitte wiped at his mouth, studying the field, waiting to see what the British would do next. Caleb sat like a statue with one thought foremost in his mind—*Are they beaten or are they gathering for a second try?*

Suddenly Jackson shouted, "Cease fire!" and the American guns went silent. Every man behind the breastworks raised up to watch, wondering, hoping. Minutes passed while the red-coated line continued to fall back, and then suddenly they were in the trees at the distant end of the open field, and then they were gone.

Jackson drew his watch from his pocket. It was twenty minutes past eight o'clock in the morning on January 8, 1815.

He spurred his horse to the top of the breastworks and turned to his men. It had been a long time since Caleb had seen such an expression on a man's face as he spoke to his troops, his voice ringing with pride.

"You did it, boys!"

A shout from thirty-two hundred voices rang across the battlefield and into the woods as the men came to their feet, blacks and whites, regulars and militia, merchants and civilians and mixed-bloods, mindless of their differences, embracing and pounding each other on the back as brothers.

Jackson gave them their time to vent their giddy relief and their growing sense of pride, then raised his hand and they quieted.

He pointed to the battlefield, and they sobered.

"There are many brave men lying wounded out there. I suggest you get your canteens and go among them and do what you can."

Jackson and Lafitte and Caleb sat their horses on the top of the breastworks as the American lines broke, and with canteens in hand, their forces went among the British casualties, doing all they could to help the suffering.

Later in the afternoon, with every wagon and cart and carriage that could be commandeered from New Orleans carrying the wounded back to the city where nearly every home, every building had become a temporary hospital filled with British soldiers, Jackson approached Lafitte and Caleb. There was a strange mix of emotions in his face.

"I just got the count." He looked at both men for a moment. "There are about thirty-two hundred British casualties." He paused. "We lost thirteen men."

For several seconds the three stood facing each other in disbelief. In the history of warfare, none of them had ever heard of such a one-sided victory.

Jackson turned to Lafitte. "I never saw men to equal yours in battle. Battery number three—Beluche and Dominique—fired more ammunition than any other battery on the line, and accounted for more fallen British than any of them. I will be the one in the newspapers, but it should be you, sir. I want you to know that. I will write a letter to President Madison, demanding—*demanding*—that he grant you and your men full pardons for any and all charges, and American citizenship if that is what you want." He thrust out his hand and Lafitte grasped it.

"It is all I ask."

Jackson turned to Caleb. "Madison sent the right man. I'll tell him.

I will never forget you. If there is ever anything I can do for you, you have but to ask."

The two men shook hands.

The battle of New Orleans was over.

Notes

The last great battle of the War of 1812 took place January 8, 1815, five miles from New Orleans, with American lines established on the banks of the Rodriguez Canal. The description of the geography, including Lakes Pontchartrain and Borgne, are accurate. American forces on the battle line numbered about 3,200, with British forces just over 12,000. All officers named in this chapter, British and American, as well as their positions, are accurate, except Captain Robert Doss, who is a fictional character. American General Andrew Jackson was ordered to New Orleans following previous assignments in Alabama and Florida. He had contracted malaria, which left him sick and ailing, as described herein. He arrived in New Orleans December 1, 1814, declared martial law, took a firm hand, cowed Governor William C. Claiborne, sent for reinforcements from Tennessee and Kentucky, and got them. He began assembling every available soldier and civilian he could find, and formed an army of a mix of troops of every color, language, age, and nationality in the area—a strange conglomeration, as described in this chapter. British forces began arriving shortly after. British General Pakenham arrived December 25, 1814.

Jackson regarded Lafitte and his band as murderous cutthroats and had publicly declared so. Lafitte had been offered $30,000 in cash, officer status in the British navy, and land, to join forces with the British, on threat of total destruction if he refused. He played for time and made a written offer to Governor Claiborne to join forces with the Americans if the United States would give him and his men a full pardon of all charges. Claiborne had previously posted a reward of $500 for the capture of Lafitte, to which Lafitte responded by posting throughout New Orleans his own poster offering $1,500 for the capture of Claiborne, much to the amusement of the citizens of that city.

The Americans sent ships that destroyed Barataria. Lafitte still stood by his offer. After Jackson's arrival, Lafitte met with him. Historians differ on the location, some claiming it was at the Exchange Coffee House at the address given in this chapter, others claiming it was at the Cabildo. The result of the meeting was an agreement—Lafitte would ally himself with the Americans, and Jackson would assist him in obtaining his pardon. Lafitte delivered 7,500 musket and pistol flints, with food and flour, to Jackson, who needed both badly. Lafitte frequented an old blacksmith shop that he had used for years as a contact point, formerly run by a giant African named "Thiac."

The entire series of actions that occurred between the two opposing forces is considerably more extensive than set forth herein. There were minor battles fought on December 23 and December 28, 1814, and January 1, 1815, as well as other skirmishes, and a few naval engagements. They are omitted simply because including them in this chapter would at least double it in length. Considering the entire conflict, clearly the core battle was January 8, 1815. The weather during that battle was as described herein. British Colonel Thornton was sent across the Mississippi to capture an American gun battery at night, but failed when the level of the river unexpectedly fell, leaving Thornton's command to try to move barges in mud to their knees, after which the current of the river swept them downstream close to two miles. The battle was to commence before dawn at the firing of a rocket. The rocket was fired, and without the support of Colonel Thornton across the river, British general Pakenham's main force started their march across a huge open field toward the Rodriguez Canal and the Americans entrenched behind it. At dawn the Americans opened fire. The British pressed forward while the American guns cut them down in droves. A few British reached the canal, only to learn that the scaling ladders and fascines needed to cross the canal and scale the American breastworks had never reached the battlefront. They were forced to stand and wait while the American guns decimated them. Pakenham was killed, as were Gibbs and Keane, as described herein. Jackson did in fact ride among his men shouting encouragement.

The incident of Dominique giving Jackson a cup of real coffee is historically accurate. The American lines held. The British realized they could not reach the Americans and retreated. The battled ended shortly after eight o'clock, January 8, 1815. The British suffered over 3,200 casualties. The Americans lost about 13 men. It is noted that historians are not in agreement on the figures of casualties; however, those given herein are representative and probably the most accurate. There were minor skirmishes fought in the following few days while the British retreated and abandoned Louisiana and the Gulf of Mexico, but the battle of New Orleans essentially ended the war.

The Dunson family and Billy Weems are fictional characters.

Latour, *Historical Memoir of the War in West Florida and Louisiana in 1814–15*, pp. 22–126, and see especially the excellent atlases in the pocket part; Saxon,

Lafitte the Pirate, pp. 3–185, and see the sketches of the Absinthe House, the blacksmith shop, and other locations in New Orleans; Wills, *James Madison,* pp. 146–150; Walker, *Andrew Jackson,* pp. 1–366, and note the listing of officers and units and casualties, pp. 362–66; Stagg, *Mr. Madison's War,* pp. 494–500; Hickey, *The War of 1812,* pp. 206–214; Gleig, *A British Chaplain's Account of the Battle of New Orleans (1814–1815),* pp. 422–25.

Boston

February 1815

CHAPTER XXVI

A Chinook wind had moved in from the south to seize and hold Boston for three days, with temperatures ranging up to forty-six degrees in the daylight hours. The sound of snowmelt dripping from the roofs and trees to run in the streets was a low, steady undertone for the ringing of horseshoes and rumble of iron-rimmed wheels of carriages and wagons and carts that clattered on the worn cobblestones, moving people and farm produce and shipping crates among the shops and the offices and the wharves and piers on the waterfront. People had shed their heavy winter coats and scarves in the unexpected thaw, and stepped gratefully around puddles as they hailed each other in the streets, knowing the warm breeze would soon pass to leave them locked once again in the icy grip of a Boston winter, but determined to glory in the lift of soul that was theirs for a brief moment.

On the bay, the wind had drifted chunks of rotting ice north to pile them beneath the docks, wharves, and piers, and along the shore, where the sea birds continued their endless quarrels over the carrion and flotsam that sustained them. With the shocking news of General Andy Jackson leading his collection of thirty-two hundred mismatched rabble to the most lop-sided victory in the history of warfare, ships of foreign flags had begun to appear once again at the docks in Boston Harbor, hesitant at first, then more boldly, as the sea lanes remained clear of the British men-of-war that had for so long sealed off most American ports and strangled the vital trade with all nations. For the first time in more than three years, a cautious spirit of optimism, of hope, was taking root in seaports from Maine to Florida. Was it over at last? The peace treaty had been signed by the American and British negotiators in Ghent, Belgium, but would it be ratified by the United States Congress? Was it really over?

In clear, bright, midmorning sunshine, a train of six, broad-wheeled freight wagons rumbled onto the Boston waterfront, driven by bearded men who had harnessed their teams beneath the stars at four o'clock AM They had drunk strong black coffee and eaten fried sowbelly, mounted the wagon seats, and traveled twenty-two miles east on a muddy dirt road to deliver one hundred twenty barrels of dried Pennsylvania beef to a waterfront warehouse for shipment to a buyer in Charleston, South Carolina. In the confusion of the traffic on the docks and piers, the driver of the lead wagon hauled back on the four long leather lines and bawled his team to a halt long enough for Caleb Dunson to drop coins in his hand, climb down from the driver's seat with his two suitcases and greatcoat, nod his thanks, and walk rapidly toward the office of Dunson & Weems. He set one suitcase down, opened the door, entered, and set both suitcases in front of the counter, with his heavy overcoat on top. He did not expect the rise of emotion that touched him for a moment at being in the familiar office, with Matthew, Billy, and Adam coming from their desks to meet him, warm, eager, smiling, all speaking at once.

Matthew reached him first to thrust out his hand. "We were beginning to worry! Are you all right?"

Caleb grasped the hand of his older brother. "Fine. A little tired."

He shook hands with Adam, then Billy, who asked, "You came home overland?"

"Up the Mississippi, then east. When I left New Orleans there were still too many British ships in the gulf. Too risky."

Adam broke in. "We heard about the battle at New Orleans. Were you there?"

"I was."

"Have you heard about the treaty?"

Caleb shook his head at the unheard-of anomaly. "I heard. Read it in a Philadelphia newspaper. The treaty was signed by both sides in Ghent on Christmas Eve? And we fought that battle two weeks later, on January eighth? Two weeks after the war was over?"

"It's true. The treaty isn't officially binding until it's ratified by our Congress. They're debating it now, but there's no question about it. A matter of formality."

Caleb shook his head again. "We didn't know about it the morning of the fight. Neither did the British. If we had known . . ." his voice trailed off for a moment—"a lot of good men might still be alive."

Billy asked, "Was the fight at the canal as one-sided as the newspaper reported?"

For a moment Caleb was caught up in the memory of the unending, rolling thunder of the American cannon and the rattle of muskets and rifles and the great field covered with crimson-coated British dead and wounded.

"The report I saw in that Philadelphia newspaper came close. The British didn't get their scaling ladders up to the canal and our breastworks in time. They had to stop right there in front of us. It was bad. It cost them about thirty-two hundred men. We lost only thirteen. All within less than ninety minutes."

For a few seconds the four men looked at each other in disbelief and shuddered inside at the thought of the slaughter that had occurred on that distant battlefield.

After a moment, Matthew asked, "You got to see Jackson? And Lafitte?"

"I got them together. They worked things out."

Billy saw that most of the story was missing. "What about Jackson? And Lafitte? What happened?"

Caleb scratched his jaw, and the other three fell silent to hear the story as only Caleb could tell it.

"Well, you know that Governor Claiborne put out a reward for the capture of Lafitte, so Lafitte put out his own reward for the capture of

Claiborne. Problem was, Claiborne only offered five hundred dollars for Lafitte, while Lafitte offered fifteen hundred for Claiborne. The local citizenry couldn't decide which one to capture but were leaning toward delivering Claiborne to Lafitte, mostly because of the price difference." Caleb chuckled, then added, "They argued for a while and then laughed the whole thing off. Nothing ever came of it."

Matthew and Billy and Adam were all grinning as Caleb went on.

"I talked with Lafitte alone. He said all he wanted was a full pardon from President Madison for all crimes and charges, and American citizenship for himself and all his men. In return, he'd help the United States fight the British. And he meant it."

He paused to order his thoughts. "Then I talked with Jackson alone. Now there's one tough, hard-headed, ornery man! He was sick with the fever, and weak, but he just wouldn't quit. He called Lafitte and his men a bunch of bandits and murderers and swore that before he left New Orleans, he was going to clean out the whole lot of them. That's when things got a bit testy between Jackson and me. I saw no other choice but to tell him he was dead wrong. For a minute there I thought he was going to reach for that sword he wears, and I was getting ready to take it away from him. But in addition to being about the stubbornest man I ever met, he's a practical man, and a born leader. He settled down, and I told him that Lafitte and his thousand men were the best cannoneers and fighters in Louisiana and that he was going to need every man he could get. I arranged a meeting between the two of them with me there to prevent a killing, and whatever their differences, something good happened between those two."

Caleb raised a hand in gesture. "At the battle, Lafitte and his men made the difference. I never saw a crew run a cannon battery and handle rifles and muskets as they did. Jackson saw it, too. He's already written to President Madison, telling him we owe Lafitte the pardon he asked for, and American citizenship. I hope Madison listens."

Caleb dropped his hand. "Well, we can talk more about that later. How are things here? I see more ships and dockhands out there than when I left."

Billy answered. "Since the treaty, a steady increase in shipping. I think the worst is past. If business continues to pick up, we'll make it."

"Good. The family? Barbara?"

Matthew's face clouded. "Barbara's fine. You should go home to her. It's mother who has us worried. She's slipping. She's been asking for you lately. You better go see her later this afternoon, after you've been home."

Caleb saw it in Matthew, and then in Billy and Adam. He sobered and spoke to Matthew. "Straight. Are we going to lose her? Is it her time?"

Silence held for a moment. "I think so. Go see her. It'll be a comfort to her."

Caleb stepped back from the counter and drew a leather purse from his coat pocket.

"There's the money that's left."

Billy took it as Caleb drew the letter from his inside coat pocket. "And there's the letter Madison sent. Might want to keep it."

He picked up his suitcases. "I'm going home and then I'll go see mother. Tomorrow I'll be here and write up a report for Madison. Anything else?"

Matthew shook his head. "Good to have you back."

With a suitcase in each hand and his heavy coat over his shoulder, Caleb walked west to the end of the wharves and piers, hailed a hack, gave directions to the elderly driver with the gentle, tired eyes, loaded the luggage, and took his seat with his thoughts running.

Mother slipping—asking for me—why would she be asking for me?

The driver slowed and stopped the hack, gently rocking on its leathers, waited while Caleb set his suitcases on the cobblestones, accepted the coins with a smile and a nod, and gigged the horse to a walk while Caleb opened the gate and walked the stone walkway to the front door of his square, white, two-story brick home. He opened the door, stepped into the parlor, set the luggage and great coat on the hardwood floor, and called, "Barbara? I'm home."

For a moment the words echoed faintly through the house, and there was no answer—only a hollow silence. Caleb had started through the house toward the backyard and the root cellar when a premonition struck.

Mother!

He spun and trotted out of the house into the street and turned east, hurrying back toward Fruit Street. He held the pace for the four blocks to his mother's home, pushed through the gate to the front door, and walked into the parlor.

"Barbara," he called. He heard the hurried footsteps coming up the hall from the bedrooms, and she came through the archway to throw her arms about him and bury her face in his shoulder while he wrapped his arms about her to hold her.

"You're home, you're home, you're home"—she repeated it like a chant.

"I'm here. What's happened? You're trembling."

She drew back her head to peer up at him. "Your mother. She says she's been talking to John. She wants to see you. I think she's going to leave us. She says she needs to go—wants to go."

"Is she awake?"

"Yes. She asked for you again just five minutes ago."

Caleb broke from Barbara to lead her down the hall into the master bedroom shared by his mother and father from his earliest memories and walked softly to her bedside. Her face was turned away from him, with her eyes closed and the gray hair brushed and lying on the pillow. The great feather comforter was drawn up to cover her chest, with both arms lying outside, covered to the wrists with her pale blue nightshirt.

He knelt beside her bed and gently took her aged hand with the large blue veins and the crooked fingers between his. Her eyes opened, clear and direct, and her head turned to face him, smiling warmly.

"Caleb. You came. I need to talk to you." Her voice was strong, her thoughts orderly.

"I'm here, Mother. Listening."

"Do you remember the war? The big one?" she asked.

"I do."

"It came at the wrong time for you. You were no longer a little boy

like Adam, and you weren't yet a grown man like Matthew. When I lost
John, and Matthew went to the sea with our navy, I didn't know what
you needed. I didn't know what to do for you. I watched the anger fester
inside you because they had taken your father away, but I didn't know
what to do."

He gently shushed her. "It's all right. It's all right. It's past."

She went on as though he had not spoken. "Do you remember that
you moved away from the Almighty? Refused to pray? Refused to go to
church?"

"I remember, but it doesn't matter now. That's all in the past."

He felt a tremor in the old, gnarled hand, and he saw her eyes close
and her mouth clench tight as she shuddered. He turned to Barbara and
spoke with a quiet urgency.

"Get the family."

Barbara turned on her heel and left the room, and he turned back to
Margaret.

"Mother, don't worry yourself with those things now. Rest. I'm
here."

Her eyes opened again, and they were clear, focused. "Do you
remember the night you left? Tried to get away in the dark? I stopped you
at the front door?"

"I remember."

"It was almost more than I could stand. But that wasn't the worst of
it. I could face losing you in war, but I could not face you losing your
faith in the Almighty. Can you understand?"

"I didn't then. I do now."

An intensity came into her face that he had never seen before. "I have
talked with John in the past few days. He's in heaven, waiting for me. Our
heaven will not be complete without you. I told John I would not come
until I knew in my heart you had returned to God. I can't go until I know
that. I have to hear it from you."

He saw the excruciating pain in her face and in that instant understood she had lived with it for thirty-eight years, bearing the soul-
destroying torment of believing she had failed him by allowing him to

drift from the anchor of her life—her unshakeable conviction that she could be with her family in the presence of the Almighty forever if they would but remain faithful.

A feeling like none Caleb had ever known rose, choking, filling him. Tears came welling to run down his face. His jaw trembled, and he could not control it, nor could he speak. How could he not have seen what he had done to her? How could he have let her bear the terrible burden of punishing herself for his transgressions?

He looked into her eyes and knew she was seeing into his soul. He tried to speak, but his voice broke. He started again.

"Mother, it is wrong to punish yourself. The transgressions were mine. God in heaven knows what you have done for the family—how you've given everything. A legion of angels could not have done more."

He stopped to swallow hard. "I do not know how to ask your forgiveness. Can you find it in your heart? Forgive me, Mother, for the pain I brought down on you. Forgive me."

He choked, then continued.

"Many times I have been on my knees in the night, seeking forgiveness from on high. God is in His heaven. I believe He has forgiven me."

He saw the tears gathering in her eyes and went on.

"I know He guides the affairs of men. I know He was there during the great war. I can see it now."

He cleared his throat and took control of himself. "I give you my oath, Mother. I will never leave the family. Barbara and I and the children."

He heard the front door open and the sound of many feet crossing the parlor and coming down the hall, and they came into the room behind him to stand quietly—Matthew, Kathleen, Brigitte, Billy, Adam, Laura, John, Barbara. He laid the old hand back on the comforter and rose to let Matthew take his rightful place beside his mother.

Matthew took her hand and knelt beside her, and she peered past him to speak, lucid, clear.

"You all came."

Matthew answered, "We're all here."

"John is so proud of you. So proud. You are our treasure. Forever."

She peered into Matthew's face, and a radiance began to rise in her. "Matthew, John is so grateful to you. You were so young when you had to become the head of the family. I could never have lived through it without you."

"Don't concern yourself about it. Rest. You need to rest."

She smiled. "I need to go. I couldn't until I knew Caleb would be with us. John's waiting."

Matthew felt the hand begin to relax, and he saw her eyes turn away to focus above the foot of the bed. A smile formed on the old, wrinkled face, and the radiance that shone was like nothing any of them had ever seen before.

She said softly, "John? Oh, John! You've come."

Every person in the room peered above the foot of the bed, and they could see nothing.

The old hand went limp, and Matthew felt his mother leave.

He waited until the radiance had dwindled, and then he reached to close her eyes.

Notes

The treaty ending the War of 1812 was signed by representatives from England and the United States on December 24, 1814, in Ghent, Belgium, and is called the Treaty of Ghent. However, it was not ratified by the United States Congress and signed by President Madison until February 16, 1815. Thus the Battle of New Orleans, fought on January 8, 1815, occurred after terms had been reached between the two sovereigns but before they became binding.

See Hickey, *The War of 1812*, pp. 296–98.

Bibliography

Antal, Sandy. *A Wampum Denied.* Ottawa, Canada: Carlton University Press, 1997.

Arthur, Stanley Clisby. *Jean Lafitte, Gentleman Pirate.* New Orleans, La.: Harmanson, 1952.

Barbuto, Richard V. *Niagara 1814.* Lawrence, Kans.: University of Kansas Press, 2000.

Bernstein, Richard B. *Thomas Jefferson.* New York, N.Y.: Oxford University Press, 2003.

Corcoran, Michael. *For Which It Stands.* New York, N.Y.: Simon & Schuster, 2002.

Drake, Benjamin. *Life of Tecumseh and of His Brother the Prophet.* New York, N.Y.: Arno Press & New York Times, 1969.

Gayerre, Charles. *The Story of Jean and Pierre Lafitte.* New York, N.Y.: Historical Publication Company, 1883.

Gleig, Reverend George Robert. *A British Chaplain's Account of the Battle of New Orleans (1812–1815).* Excerpted from *American History Told by Contemporaries, Volume Iii: Building of the Republic.* Edited by Albert Bushness Hart. New York, N.Y.: Macmillan, 1901.

Graymont, Barbara. *The Iroquois.* New York, N.Y.: Chelsea House, 1988.

———. *The Iroquois in the American Revolution.* Syracuse, N.Y.: Syracuse University Press, 1972.

Hale, Horatio. *The Iroquois Book of Rites.* New York, N.Y.: Ams Press, Reprint, 1969.

Hickey, Donald R. *The War of 1812.* Urbana, Ill.: University of Illinois Press, 1990.

Horsman, Reginald. *The Causes of the War of 1812.* New York, N.Y.: A. S. Barnes & Co., 1962.

Latour, Arsene Lacarriere. *Historical Memoir of the War in West Florida and Louisiana in 1814–15.* Gainesville, Fla.: University of Florida Press, 1999.

Leckie, Robert. *George Washington's War.* New York, N.Y.: Harper Perennial, 1992.

Malcomson, Robert. *Lords of the Lake.* Annapolis, Md.: Naval Institute Press, 1998.

Messages and Papers of the Presidents, Volume Ii. Prepared under the direction of the Joint Committee on Printing, of the House and Senate, Pursuant to an Act of the Fifty-Second Congress of the United States. New York: Bureau of National Literature, Inc., 1897.

Morgan, Lewis. *League of the Ho-De-No-Saju-Nee or Iroquois, Volume 1.* New York, N.Y.:

Dodd, Mead & Co; Reprint, New Haven, Conn.: Human Relations Area Files, 1954.

National Geographic Picture Atlas of Our Fifty States. Washington, D.C.: National Geographic Society, 1978.

Parry-Jones, Maria. *The Knitting Stitch Bible.* Iola, Wis.: Krause Publications, 2001.

Peterson, Harold L. *Round Shot and Rammers.* Harrisburg, Pa.: Stackpole Books, 1969.

Roosevelt, Theodore. *The Naval War of 1812.* New York, N.Y.: The Modern Library, 1999.

Saxon, Lyle. *Lafitte the Pirate.* New York, N.Y.: Century Company, 1930.

Sheads, Scott. *Fort McHenry.* Baltimore, Md.: The Nautical and Aviation Publishing Company of America, 1995.

Stagg, J. C. A. *Mr. Madison's War.* Princeton, N.J.: Princeton University Press, 1983.

Walker, Alexander. *The Life of Andrew Jackson.* New York, N.Y.: Derby & Jackson, 1857.

Watts, Steven. *The Republic Reborn.* Baltimore, Md.: Johns Hopkins University Press, 1987.

Whitehorne, James A. *The Battle for Baltimore 1814.* Baltimore, Md.: Nautical and Aviation Publishing Company of America, 1997.

Wills, Garry. *James Madison.* New York, N.Y.: Times Books, Henry Holt & Co., 2002.